The Mafia Saved Me

Jasmin Vizcaya Salgado

AUTHORS NOTICE

The content in this story includes references to topics such as **human trafficking, sexual violence, violence against women, suicide, rape, and torture.** As well as mature content such as **sex, drugs, crime, and mature language.**

As you read, be mindful that although this is a romance story, the heavy topics discussed in the story are a reality for many. With today's media, it's easy to fall into the cycle of wanting to be kidnapped and saved by a sexy Mafioso, but this is a fantasy. I ask that as you read, you're mindful and allow yourself to acknowledge the horror of human trafficking and violence against women, not glorify it. Roughly 25 million victims are trafficked annually across international borders worldwide. The conclusion of this story shouldn't be 'I want to marry a mafia man,' but rather, 'what can I do to help those who suffer at the hands of organized crime groups?' A portion of the proceeds from this book will go toward combating human trafficking and femicide. Together, we can make a difference. For more information, visit my Instagram page @authorjasminvizcayasalgado.

ACKNOWLEDGMENTS

To my family, best friend Erika, and little roses, who have always supported me throughout my writing career, I'm deeply indebted to each of you. To my Papi (dad) and Mami (mom), thank you for giving me the push I needed to find my way back to this story, and for lighting the fire that sparked my creativity after years of dormancy. This final edited and published version of "The Mafia Saved Me" wouldn't have been possible without both of you. This book is as much yours as it is mine.

TRANSLATION OF PHRASES USED

"Ethnic identity is twin skin to linguistic identity—I am my language. Until I can take pride in my language, I cannot take pride in myself... I cannot accept the legitimacy of myself. Until I am free to write bilingually and to switch codes without having always to translate... I will have my voice: Indian, Spanish, White. I will have my serpent's tongue—my woman's voice, my sexual voice, my poet's voice. I will overcome the tradition of silence."

Gloria Anzaldùa, "How to Tame a Wild Tongue" in "Borderlands/La Frontera: The New Mestiza"

- *Don- Boss or leader of a crime family, usually reserved for men of Sicilian descent*
- *Underboss- The second highest position in a Mafia family*
- *Capo- Ranking member of a crime family who heads a crew of soldiers*
- *Papi- Dad/Daddy*
- *Mami- Mom*
- *Mija/Hija- Darling/daughter*
- *Fanculo- Fuck*
- *Idiota- idiot/dumbass*
- *Piccolo fuoco- small fire*
- *Bambina- Baby girl/Babe*
- *Mi amore/Amore- My love/Love*
- *Bastardo- Bastard*
- *Merda- Shit*
- *Regina- Queen*
- *Bellissima- Beautiful, lovely*
- *Uno nunca sabe- You never know (pg. 2)*
- *Cariño- Sweetie (pg. 4)*
- *Vaffanculo- Fuck you (pg. 54)*
- *Chilaquiles, carne ranchera, and huevo ranchero- Fried tortilla chips with Mexican chile coated on it, served with cheese and sour cream, flat steak, and fried tortilla with an egg (pg. 95)*
- *Mi stai uccidendo- You're killing me (pg. 126)*
- *Ti spezzerò le gambe- I'll break your legs (pg. 129)*

- *Sope- A traditional Mexican dish consisting of a fried masa base, topped with fried beans, lettuce, chicken/or steak, cheese, salsa and sour cream (pg. 130)*
- *Dios Mio- My God (pg. 185, 415)*
- *Ragù Alla Bolognese- a traditional Italian dish consisting of tagliatelle pasta and a rich ragù made with beef (and sometimes pork) and tomatoes (pg. 219)*
- *Sitdown- A criminal meeting to settle a "beef" and or a mob peace conference (pg. 225)*
- *Airing- To take someone out and kill him or her (pg. 232)*
- *Va' all'inferno- Go to hell (pg. 235)*
- *Nonno's- Grandfather's (pg. 470)*
- *Ciao- Hello/Goodbye (pg. 254)*
- *È la ragazza del Don, non credo che parli ancora italiano- She's the Don's girlfriend, I don't think she speaks Italian yet (pg. 254)*
- *Tesoro- Treasure (pg. 261)*
- *Todo tuya- All yours (Pg. 262)*
- *Fottuto inferno- Fucking hell (pg. 275)*
- *Noi siamo italiano- We are Italian (pg. 281)*
- *Ti piace davvero suo huh- You really like her huh (pg. 281)*
- *Sì Amore- Yes love (pg. 289, 365)*
- *Così fottutamento bella- So fucking beautiful (pg. 347)*
- *Ay, mira que bonitos se ven Alejandro- Awe, look how cute they look Alejandro (pg. 355)*
- *Gracias- Thank you (pg. 355)*
- *Y entiende Español, que preciosa- And she understands Spanish, how precious (pg. 355)*
- *Puta Madre- Fucking bitch (pg. 387)*
- *Más rápido papi- Faster daddy (pg. 387)*
- *Ven aqui- Come here (pg. 399)*
- *Que te vengas aquí Niña - Come here girl (pg. 400)*
- *Pinche Cabrón- Fucking bastard (pg. 400)*
- *Es una pendeja- She's an idiot (pg. 424)*
- *Desgraciado infeliz no me toques- Wretch don't touch me (pg. 448)*
- *Pinche puto- Fucking manwhore (pg. 437)*
- *Nada- nothing (pg. 470)*

To those who have been left with a gaping wound from abuse and betrayal.
It's not your fault.
You're beautiful, loved, and mighty.

Part 1

PROLOGUE

VICTORIA

My beating heart pulses in my ears.

I can't look away as my mom studies the glossy brochure of the trip to Europe my school is hosting this summer.

Biting my top lip in apprehension, I lean over the kitchen counter. Waiting for her answer.

Was she going to say yes? Or will it be the traditional, maybe?

My mom's bottom lip curves into a slight smile.

So far, so good.

She finds the price of the trip. I hold my breath, and her eyes widen. When the shock passes, her forehead furrows, and a frown appears on her lips. I mentally curse, knowing my dream of going to France isn't happening.

"Victoria, this will cost us a lot of money. But I know how much you want to go to France," she says, a sincere smile covering her tan complexion. "This trip might be a good opportunity for you."

"Are you saying I can go?"

My mom chuckles at my excitement and places her hands on my shoulder.

"It's a wonderful idea Mija, but..."

Great, there's that annoying 'but.'

"But?" I ask, not wanting to hear what comes out of her mouth next.

"You need to ask your Papi. You know how he is with these kinds of things." She gives me an apologetic look.

I groan, remembering how protective my dad is.

Miguel Rodriguez, or who I call Papi, is the family bodyguard on steroids.

He's always behind our backs, making sure we aren't out on the street past curfew because, according to him, "Uno nunca sabe."

"Mami, he's going to say no. What should I do?" The image of me in front of the Eiffel Tower fades away with my words.

"I'll talk to him." She places a hand on my cheek, and I nod in appreciation before heading to my room to call my cousin Sofia to tell her the news. Not even a minute later, her voice fills my ear.

"Hello?"

"Sofia! Remember the trip to France our school is hosting this summer?" My words come out rushed and full of excitement.

"Um, yes?"

"My mom said I might go if my dad agrees!" I beam, and Sofia squeals.

"Victoria, that's amazing. Ahh, hot European guys!" She sighs dreamily, and I laugh at her girlish thoughts.

"Sofia, why don't you come with me?" She stays silent, and I continue, "remember how much we wanted to do this together? This is our chance to see the world."

"I don't know Victoria... I want to go, but you know how my parents are." There's a hint of disappointment behind her words, but after thinking about it for a minute, she caves in, and I'm sure it's from the thought of meeting a *hot European guy.* "I'll let my parents know about it tonight, and maybe your mom can help change their minds if they say no?"

"Of course!" I assure her.

"We're going to France." She sighs.

"Maybe," I correct her.

"Right," comes her sheepish response.

After hanging up the phone, I head to the kitchen when the front door opens, signaling my dad is home.

My eyes fall on the trip brochure, and I bite my bottom lip while my right foot taps below me.

I watch as my dad sets his lunch box on the counter. He offers me a smile, and I give him a nervous one in return. His brows furrow in concern when he notices my nervousness, but he says nothing and washes the dirt from his callous hands.

I warn myself not to say a word about the trip until my mom talks to him, but I don't listen to my conscience, and the next second I'm blurting out my request.

"Can I go to Europe in the summer?" I slap my hands over my mouth and stare in horror as my dad's back tenses through his dark blue work uniform.

He slowly turns to face me.

"What?" His booming voice reflects off the walls, and I grimace when I notice his eyes are wide with shock.

I let out a nervous laugh, avoiding his stare.

"Umm..." I mutter, unable to form any words.

He raises both eyebrows, waiting for my explanation. When no words come from me, he crosses his arms over his chest.

I swallow the tightness in my throat and take a deep breath before telling him about the trip.

"Papi, my school is hosting a trip to France in the summer, and I was hoping I could go." His forehead creases into three lines of disapproval. "Mami said yes!"

My dad exhales a sharp breath and pinches the bridge of his nose in frustration.

"No," he says, and his voice is firm, leaving no room for argument.

The kitchen is silent, and all I can do is look into his eyes, mine becoming blurry from my unshed tears. He didn't even think about it.

"Please, Papi, this is my dream to go to Europe, to Paris. I've been good, and I have good grades." My voice breaks, and his eyes soften when he sees how much I want to go to France. "Can this trip be my graduation present?" I plead, trying to hold in my tears, but it's becoming harder by the second.

There's a moment of silence, which he breaks with a sigh.

He brings me into a hug.

"Cariño, it's too dangerous. I can't let you go to another country all by yourself. I'm sorry." He lets out a breath, and I nod weakly to avoid an argument.

As I make my way out of the kitchen, I place the brochure in his hands, hoping he might reconsider.

A few hours later, I sit in silence as my family has dinner.

When I muster the courage to lift my head, the first person I see is my fifteen-year-old brother, Cristian. Then I glance at my older sister Eloisa and her husband, Mathew. I sigh, watching as they whisper to one another with a smile on both their faces.

A cough from my right brings me out of my daze. I turn toward the noise to see my mom smiling at me. She elbows my dad on his side, prompting me to give them a questioning stare.

"Victoria, I talked to your mom, and she's changed my decision to let you go to France, but—"

I don't let him finish because I jump out of my seat to hug him and my mom.

"Papi, I already know the rules," I say, rolling my eyes, and he grunts. "I need to call you and tell you what I'm doing and where I'm going," I repeat the speech he gives me every time I go out.

"I'm serious, Victoria. I want to know you're safe, and you need to promise me you'll stay close to the adults," he warns, his voice dropping.

"Papi, nothing will happen to me." I smile at him, excited for the next six months to fly by.

1

———

VICTORIA

People rush through the airport in a hurry, trying to get to their flight. Their suitcases roll, swinging from side to side, hitting bystanders. They're caught with a keen determination to get to their 10 a.m. flight before it leaves without them.

A cold sensation cupping my cheek diverts my gaze away from the crowds of rushing people, and I'm met with the earthy brown of my mom's eyes. The corners of my mouth rise to let her know I'm okay, and I lean into her touch.

My eyes soften at the sight of tears resting on the bridge of her eyes.

I offer her a weak smile.

"Mom, everything will be alright. Don't cry," I beg, knowing the moment her tears fall, so will mine.

She gives a weak nod.

From over her shoulder, I catch sight of my aunt hugging Sofia goodbye.

My cousin senses my stare and mouths a silent *'help me.'*

I point a finger at my emotional mom, and Sofia's hazel eyes widen like saucers. A cringe rises on her face.

And she thinks she has it bad.

I ease from my mom's warm embrace and give her one last smile.

She motions with her eyes toward my dad, who stands behind us in uncertainty.

Nodding, I face the rest of my family, and my eyes soften at the sight of my two siblings and tall, unemotional dad.

I'll be back from France before they know it, but because I'm Mexican, this meant we went everywhere together, but not this time. This time, it's only me and Sofia going to France.

I give my dad an assuring smile, expecting one in return, but he stays emotionless.

My dad, like most men, uses a stone-cold front to hide his true feelings from the world.

I wrap him in a tight embrace.

His 6'6-foot frame alongside my 5'7-foot frame means he has to bend to embrace me properly.

My smile widens when his arms wrap around my waist, and he holds me tight, squeezing as I pull away.

"Dad, nothing is going to happen. I'm an adult. I can take care of myself."

He sighs. "I know you're eighteen already." Comes his gravelly voice, and I can hear his Spanish accent leaking through his words.

It's true. I'm eighteen, about to be nineteen in a month. There's no reason for him to be this worried.

"Say your last goodbyes to your family," Mrs. Ross, the teachers taking us abroad, says while looking at her smartwatch. Her eyes widen when she sees the time. "We need to board the plane in forty minutes!"

I release my dad from our embrace when a deep timber from my left catches my attention.

"I can't believe you're going to Europe." My brother grunts.

I laugh and bring him into a hug.

"Don't miss me too much."

"I won't." A grin stretches on his lips. "Remember to bring me something cool," he says, pulling away.

Rolling my eyes, I nudge his shoulder and turn to my sister. Our eyes lock, and she sends me an excited smile.

I let out a breath, giving her a smile of my own.

Her forehead creases when she sees my smile doesn't reach my eyes.

"Come here," Eloisa fusses, her arms opened wide for me. "You're going to have so much fun!" she chirps, and she's right. This is an exciting moment in my life. I'm going to France!

"Make sure to take a picture touching the Eiffel Tower and call us when you can," my sister says, hugging me tightly and then pulling away.

"Alright, everyone, let's head toward TSA," Mrs. Ross says and before I part from my family, I embrace my parents one more time.

"Thank you," I mumble, grateful to have two amazing parents who did everything possible for me to go to France. But now I feel guilty because I'm about to see the world while they stay at home.

My mom caresses the back of my head.

"Have fun Mija," my dad says, nudging my chin.

I take an unsteady breath and detach myself from the familiar warmth of my parents.

The rest of the boarding process was hectic, and now in my seat, I can breathe.

My stomach knots up, and my heart flutters when the lights in the plane turn off.

There's a slight beeping noise, and the lights above our seats flash, telling us to put our seatbelts on.

Everyone becomes silent except for a baby crying in the back.

"Good morning. We'll be leaving Los Angeles International Airport in ten minutes and are expected to land in Paris Charles de Gaulle Airport at 7:30 a.m."

The pilot's words make my stomach churn and my knee bounce.

I glance to my left, where Sofia sits in the window seat. She smiles, showing her perfectly white, straight teeth. I give her a smile of my own, and as the plane takes off, only one thought is on my mind.

Au revoir California, Bonjour France.

2

———————

VICTORIA

France captivates me. Everything about this unfamiliar place has drawn me in, giving me a thrill like no other.

I drone out the noise of my classmates and stare out the bus window. The people riding their bikes, the cute cafés in the streets, and the beautiful architecture all rush by in a blur.

In the distance, the Eiffel Tower is visible for what seems like miles.

I remain transfixed by the Haussmann-style architecture.

"Beautiful," I breathe.

"It is, isn't it?" Mrs. Ross says. I turn to her and notice the bus has stopped moving, and we are the only ones left inside. "You were daydreaming. I had to make sure you got off the bus."

"Sorry," I say, my face turning warm with embarrassment.

"It's okay," she assures me, and we exit the charter bus and head toward the hotel.

"Wow..." I crane my neck to marvel at the thirty stories of classic French architecture.

The pastel blue roof shingles blend in with the sky, and thick green vines drape down the hotel like rain.

When Mrs. Ross opens the glass doors of the hotel, the smell of sandalwood fills my senses.

I admire the Greek-themed interior of the hotel and find my cousin sitting on a couch with our friend Becca.

I sit beside Sofia, waiting for our teacher to give us our room key.

Not long after, Mrs. Ross calls my name, and I walk toward her with Sofia, Becca, and a girl named Elizabeth, who we met on the bus.

I take the dainty gold key, and we make our way toward the elevator with our suitcases rolling close behind us.

"What are we doing first?" Becca asks as we make our way into the room.

Sofia pulls out the itinerary we got on the bus.

"We're going to get some brunch." She purses her lips as she brings the paper closer to her eyes. "Then we're doing a Paris city walk tour to visit Île de la Cité, Notre Dame Cathedral, and the Latin Quarter." Sofia grins when she pronounces the items on the list in a decent French accent.

I make my way toward the window in the room to check out the view, and once again, I'm in awe.

"I never want to leave," I say, while looking at the Eiffel Tower. Sofia and Becca agree.

I notice Elizabeth in the corner of the room, hunched over with her knotted fingers resting on her lap. When she looks up, I send her a friendly smile. Her shoulders relax, and she smiles in return.

"Mrs. Ross wants us to meet her in the lobby," Becca says, putting her phone back in her purse.

I nod, going to my purse to make sure I have everything I need. While rummaging through my bag, I see my passport, and I'm reminded of my mom's warning about pickpockets in certain areas of Paris.

With this in mind, I hide my passport in my suitcase.

"A heads up to take your passport out of your bags and don't bring too much money," I let the girls know, before the three of us make our way downstairs.

While we wait for the rest of our classmates, I text my family to let them know we have made it to France when suddenly a loud voice startles me, and I almost drop my phone.

"Who's ready to go on an adventure?" says a middle-aged man in jeans and a white polo shirt. We all blink at the stranger, and he smiles agreeably. "I'm Nico, your tour guide."

We nod in acknowledgment and wave at the thin man with graying black hair.

He seems nice, and his dark-colored eyes hold a sense of comfort and friendliness.

"Welcome to France, my American friends!" He claps his hands together and motions for us to follow him. Mrs. Ross and Mrs. Jane, the second teacher chaperoning us, talk with him as he leads us to the bus.

"My feet are killing me!" Sofia whines for the tenth time in the last half-hour.

"Sofia, stop complaining. We're about to rest at dinner." I pull her along to keep up with the group.

The last thing we need is to get lost in an unfamiliar city where we don't know how to speak the language.

Nico turns to the group, his everlasting smile still present.

"Why is he so happy? Is he not tired?" Sofia retorts, and some students turn to her in amusement. I elbow Sofia and cast her a warning look.

A tired Sofia is not a Sofia you want to be next to, especially when you add hunger to the equation.

She whines, rubbing her side.

I ignore her and turn my attention back to Nico, who speaks with fondness about the *City of Love*, as he calls it.

After a while of walking, we stop in front of a restaurant, and Sofia lets out a sigh of relief.

"We'll be eating a typical meal here in France called Confit de Canard," Nico says, leading us inside.

"Bonjour," the server by the door greets, as we enter the dimly lit restaurant. The rich aroma of wine, steak, ham, and vegetables wafts around me, making my stomach growl.

From beside me, my cousin and Becca are gawking at something from afar. I can practically see the drool on the corner of their mouths.

Sofia turns toward me and motions with her eyes to a table in the distance where three handsome men sit.

"Check out those hotties." I roll my eyes at her overt dirty thoughts, not the slightest bit taken aback. Sofia's always been a flirt, and she made it clear to me she only came to France for the *'hot European men.'*

My attention falls on the men who have captivated Sofia's attention, and much to my dismay, I find myself entranced by their youthful good looks.

They look to be in their early to mid-twenties and they wear expensive Armani suits. The rich cashmere wool hugs their muscular bodies in all the right places.

The man at the head of the table speaks to the other two in a demanding manner. He has a woman with dark hair on his lap, and she flinches each time he yells.

This man has a glowing tan and black hair which is slick back.

From where I stand, I can tell he has a symmetrical nose to go with his other chiseled features. His five o'clock shadow gives him a rough, sexy look.

A shiver crawls down my spine from his arrogant, ruthless face, and although I know nothing about him, he appears to be rough both on the inside and on the outside. The power surges out of him in strong frequencies.

My gaze trails to the brown-haired man on his left. This man also has a brawny physique, and his hair is in an undercut hairstyle.

He's apathetic as he sits, sipping on his bronze liquor, looking bored out of his mind.

In contrast to the brown-haired man, the last man has dark blond hair, and he listens to every word the raven-haired man says. His pink lips roll into his mouth, and he nods.

As if sensing my gaze, his eyes dart toward me, and the artic blue shade brings tightness to my throat.

I turn away, my face swelling with warmth from being caught staring at them. With hurried steps, I follow close behind my classmates, wanting to get as far away from them as possible.

We take our seats, and I try to focus on my conversation with Sofia, but it's impossible, as I'm too distracted by my thoughts about the three men.

They have sparked my curiosity, and not because of their good looks.

I know I shouldn't, but I can't help myself when I peer over at them one more time.

Their conversation has finished, and they are preparing to leave. The blond man whispers something to the man with black hair, who nods in agreement.

I don't get to see what happens next because there's a hand waving in front of me.

I blink, looking at my cousin.

"Are you okay?" Her right brow rises, and I give her a sheepish smile, pretending I'm listening to her.

A few minutes later, the three men pass our table, and my shoulders become tense.

I let out a small gasp when the woman with them bumps into my chair.

My bag falls to the ground with a loud clatter.

I glance at the woman, who mumbles a silent apology, and I notice her bottom lip is quivering.

Worry rises inside me when I see the bruises on her arms. I'm about to ask her if she's okay when the man with black hair jerks her back and leans in close to her ear to whisper harshly. The girl nods at what he says, while biting her trembling lip. My stomach turns with unease as she gets into the black BMW with him.

The guy with brown hair picks my purse from the ground and hands it to me with a devilish grin. He doesn't break eye contact, and his dark eyes make me feel exposed.

I mumble a silent thank you and grab my bag from his hands. He winks at me and saunters out of the restaurant.

My stare moves to the blond man. The three lines on his forehead suggest he's in deep thought. We lock eyes, and he gives a slight bow to the head before following his friends.

When all three disappear, I exhale. The tension surrounding me diminishes, and my mind continues to run with questions about the three men and the woman.

There's no denying their good looks, but something about the men didn't sit right with me. I can't put my finger on it.

3

VICTORIA

Dark eyes stare into the depths of my soul. A promising grin so sinister it could have been the devil himself staring at me.

I jolt from my sleep before he can get to me.

Fear grips my heart, and the uneasiness from last night returns, bringing a chill and an uncomfortable silence. A mixture of intuition and anxiety seeps into my pores.

The nightmare isn't helping with my anxiety. I already feel like a fool for assuming the worst about men I know nothing about.

I told Sofia about my suspicion during dinner, and she assured me it was all a misunderstanding and I was probably exhausted from traveling. Her words didn't ease my worries. Even after sleeping off the jet lag, I still feel uneasy.

Speak of the devil. I hear her groaning beside me.

Sofia stretches out of bed, smacking me in the face. I groan, shoving her aside, and she laughs, rolling out of bed with a sheepish smile.

Elizabeth and Becca stir awake, and before we know it, we're all getting ready for the day.

Once dressed, I grab my phone from the bedside table and call my sister. Her round face appears on my phone, and her face glows when she sees me.

"Victoria, how's Paris?"

"It's amazing! Check this view out." I show her the streets of Paris and the gorgeous Eiffel Tower.

"Wow, it's beautiful," she breathes.

"How's everybody?" From my question, she smiles, running out of her and Mathew's bedroom. She turns the camera, and I catch sight of my dad sitting on the couch with his tablet in hand while my mom sits beside him, watching a novella.

"Mami, Papi!" They turn toward the sound of my voice, and my mom grabs the phone from my sister's hand.

"Mija, how are you?"

"Hi, mami, I'm good. How's everyone back home?"

"We're good. What are you doing today?" she asks, and I tell her all about the plans for today.

"That sounds nice. Take lots of pictures and send them to me." She pauses and glances to her side. "Mija, I'm going to pass the phone to your papi," she says, and hands him the phone.

"Hi, papi."

"Hola mija, are you enjoying yourself?"

"Yes, I love it here! It's so beautiful, look," I exclaim, showing him the view as I had done for my sister. A smile stretches across his face.

There's a steady knock on the door, and I glance over my shoulder to find Elizabeth talking to Mrs. Ross, who tells her we have to head down to the lobby.

I give my dad an apologetic smile.

"Papi, I have to go." A frown adorns his aging face, and he hands the phone back to my sister.

"I'll call you guys later this evening," I assure my sister, who warns me I better, or I'll be grounded for life.

Breathing slowly, I admire the art village of Montmartre.

I grow eager to get off the bus to continue exploring Paris, but Mrs. Ross wants to go over some ground rules first.

There are some groans until she says this is one of the few times we get to explore Paris on our own.

"You guys are to report back to the bus at 5:30 p.m., and if any of you are one minute late, you will stay in your hotel room with me for the rest of the trip." Her soft feminine features turn serious.

Mrs. Jane rises from her seat. "Please remember not to wander far. We want you all to remain in groups of three to four, and if there are any issues, please call us."

"You guys may go now," Mrs. Ross exclaims, her easygoing persona returning, and we rush out of the bus.

"Come on!" Sofia says, dragging me toward Place du Tertre, where the painters display their art. Becca and Elizabeth follow us with excited smiles.

It's around four p.m., and we've been wandering the streets of Montmartre for an hour.

When I don't hear Sofia beside me anymore, I glance around and realize I'm all alone. I don't worry because they couldn't have gone too far.

I walk through the artist square, and I'm rooted to my spot when I pass by a man drawing the Eiffel Tower with the night sky as the backdrop.

The painting of the Eiffel Tower sparkling like a million fireflies fascinates me. I become excited for tonight when I finally see it light up with my own eyes after dreaming of this moment since I was ten.

Mesmerized by the soft brush strokes, I forget I'm all alone, and any worry I had from earlier fades away.

"Beautiful, isn't it?" says a steady, masculine voice from beside me.

Now transported out of the comforting silence, I turn to the voice, and a set of two dimples greets me. My heart sinks, and the crippling anxiety returns when a familiar set of blue eyes pin me in my place.

"Uh... yeah, I guess." My voice is shaky, and I lean away from him, trying to create some distance between us.

The blond man from the restaurant looks me over. The gesture brings dryness to my throat, and my body grows heavy with dread.

"I'm Andrew, and what's your name?" His blue eyes glisten, and he extends a hand for me to shake. I stare at it and tentatively shake it when I remember how guys sometimes hurt and even kill women who reject them.

"Annabelle," I lie, and the corners of Andrew's mouth tip up.

He brings the top of my hand to his lips, kissing it.

"Beautiful name." He flashes me a smile and returns his attention to the painting before saying, "so what brings you to Paris?"

I'm not sure how to answer his question, and even if I did, I wouldn't have been able to answer because Sofia rushes to me.

"Victoria, we're supposed to stick together." Comes her reproach as she links our arms. Her curious eyes trail to Andrew when he laughs after she reveals my real name. He doesn't mention the false name I gave him and instead introduces himself to Sofia.

"And you are?" Andrew's voice takes on a flirty edge, and he grabs her hand, kissing the top of it as he had done to me a minute ago.

"Sofia," she breathes, her cheeks flushing pink. I mentally groan at my cousin flirting with him, and I tug her arm, deciding this is enough talking to strangers.

"Well, it was nice meeting you, Andrew," I lie, giving a false smile. "But my cousin and I need to go," I tell him, turning us around and whispering to Sofia to keep walking.

Her arm hooked around mine tightens when she sees my worry.

"Why? What's the matter?" she whispers, brows furrowed.

"He's one of the three men from the restaurant," I explain, hoping she'll realize how weird this is. But Sofia doesn't. She's too distracted by his good looks. She always did have a soft spot for blue-eyed blonds.

As she looks at me with sarcastically raised brows, I become aware I might be overly cautious, but I don't care because if my instincts tell me to run, you better believe my ass is running in the other direction.

"But he was cute?" she groans with a pout. When she sees my agitation, she loses her disappointment and places a hand on my shoulder. "Victoria, you're being dramatic. You don't need to be afraid. We're in a public place. We're safe." She motions to the surrounding people.

I sigh. "Sofia, what are the odds of seeing him again when we could have been anywhere in Paris? How come he ran into us?"

"Victoria, I'm sure it's only a coincidence. Come on, let's find Becca and Elizabeth." Sofia pulls on my arm, and I let her drag me toward our friends, who stand in a crowd of people watching two artists having a contest.

When Becca sees me, she smiles in relief and I let out a breath, trying to push my worry aside.

Did Sofia have a point? Am I being dramatic?

Sighing in frustration, I focus on the two artists, and when the tension in my body leaves, I hear Sofia scream from beside me.

Alarmed, I turn to the noise to see Sofia fighting a hooded figure in a ski mask. Their leather-gloved hands grip her purse, tugging. Sofia jolts forward, unwilling to let go of her purse.

Screams ring in the air, and the crowd disperses. The only man willing to help halts in fear at the last second.

I grip Sofia's forearm and catch her when the man takes her purse. In the blink of an eye, he runs in the opposite direction, and Sofia is about to go after him until I grab her arm and pull her back.

She tugs on my grip.

"Victoria, all my money and passport are in my purse," she cries, and my eyes widen. Frustration toward Sofia's stupidity simmers inside me.

"Goddammit, Sofia. I told you not to leave those in your bag!" Her eyes tear up, and her face pales.

"I know I forgot to change bags. I have to go after him!" Sofia shouts, peeling my fingers from around her arm and running in the direction the man went.

"Sofia, come back here!" My heart races as I watch her get further away from me.

I turn to Becca and Elizabeth.

"Find Mrs. Ross and tell her what happened. Hurry."

"Victoria don't go!" Becca grips my arm, and her face has lost its color.

"She's my cousin. I need to make sure she doesn't get herself killed." She sees my urgency and lets me go.

She and Elizabeth run to find our teacher, and I run in the direction Sofia left.

My heart hammers in my ears, and it's as if time has slowed down even though I'm running the fastest I've ever run.

I dodge through the crowds of people, and when I collide with them, they respond by shouting at me, oblivious to the danger lurking in the street.

The silhouette of my cousin appears. I quicken my pace and force my legs to carry me faster through the streets. With the distance, the crowd disappears, and it's only me.

Sofia rounds the corner of an alleyway a few feet ahead. She's close to me now.

"Sofia, stop!" I shout, rounding the corner and almost falling from the sharp turn.

My heartbeat pulses in my ears, and as I near them, the thief lets go of the purse. The strength of her tugging prompts her to fall to the ground with a cry, and she falls into a dirty puddle of water. I run to help her back on her two feet.

"Oh, my god…" Sofia cries, the color on her face draining.

I turn my attention toward the man who has taken off his ski mask, and my heart plummets.

"Andrew?" I whisper, and the chilling blue of his eyes freezes me to the ground.

From behind us, screeching tires shriek, and muscular arms wrap around my waist. I'm lifted off the ground and pressed against a solid chest. The screams that rip out of me and Sofia tear through the air.

A needle assaults my neck. The stab brings a burning sting that spreads like fire, fogging my system. The pain is agonizing, and my fear is crippling.

The man places a black cloth over my head, and the last thing I see before darkness is Andrew waving goodbye to me and Sofia. His sinister smile mocks us.

4

LEO

There's a sharp tension in the air, and I find it difficult to restrain myself from killing the pathetic man in front of me.

"Luigi." The name comes out acidly, and his eyebrows, which are way too big for his eyes, bunch together.

The aging black-haired politician sinks into the chair. His navy blue suit crinkles.

My Giorgio Armani slim black-and-white striped suit remains impeccable, even when my muscles coil with a need to strangle Luigi.

I lift a brow when he straightens his posture, adjusting the black bow tie around his neck.

"It's prime minister Luigi," he says, his fear from earlier no longer in sight.

His arrogance reminds me of why I hate politicians. They're all snobby and think they're better than everyone else when they're all pieces of shit.

I pin him with my gaze, my jaw stiffening, and he swallows when he notices the dark look taking over my face.

"My apologies, prime minister Luigi," I scoff, my left hand resting over my chest.

His lips form into an unpleasant line, letting me know I ticked him off, but it doesn't matter because he's in *my* house, and I'd be damned if anyone ever disrespects me under my own roof.

Having enough of this lousy conversation and the disrespect I draw my gun from my desk.

Luigi trembles in horror as I point the gun between his bulging eyes.

"Leo..." he breaks off, his eyes shifting from the black pistol to me.

The sound of my name coming out of his mouth makes me grip my gun tighter.

I give a sinister smirk.

"It's Don Bandoni to you," I grit out, watching as sweat gathers around his forehead.

Satisfaction pumps in my veins from seeing one of the most powerful men in the Italian government cowering in fear.

No one, especially not this fool, is more powerful than me, the Don of the Sicilian mafia—leader of the Bandoni famiglia and the biggest mafia alliance.

I wait for the moment he begs for his life, a typical reaction from most men who are at the receiving end of my wrath.

"Please, Don Bandoni, I've helped you when you have an issue with the Direzione Investigativa Antimafia. If not for me, you would be rotting in jail for the rest of your life with the number of felonies you have committed."

So not the typical begging for mercy.

It looks like I have to remind him he's replaceable.

I shoot Luigi an unimpressed stare, knowing he's giving himself more credit than what's due.

Sure, he helps get the Italian government out of my business, but I have many politicians lining up, begging me to use them. Their hands eager to be greased up with my money.

The only difference between me and these greedy politicians is I acknowledge my work is illegal. I don't pretend I'm a good man because I'm not. I know that, and I embrace it. That's all I can do. But men like Luigi hide behind a façade of good guys parading in public like saints when under the flashy suits, they are filthy.

I remove the safety of my gun and the click fills the silence in the room.

"Listen carefully, Luigi." He raises his hands, and the color drains from his face. "I'm the one in charge here. Not you. I make the decisions. Not you. And whether you get more money is up to me. Not you. Do I make myself clear?" I say with gentle hostility, and he stays silent, afraid for his life.

My nostrils flare, and my composure snaps. I aim my gun at the ground near his foot and release the trigger. He squeals like a pig, jumping from the chair.

"Do I make myself clear!"

"Yes!" his reply comes frantic.

"Good," I say, retaking my seat, and he releases a long breath when I put my gun away. "Now, how much do you need this time?"

Luigi's eyes follow me, waiting for me to pounce on him and snap his neck. My sudden, calm demeanor has him on edge, and I don't blame him. *I'm a bipolar bastard.*

He doesn't answer me, and I let out an irritated exhale, motioning for my men to get him out of my sight.

When three of my men approach him, he snaps out of his daze.

"Nine million Euros!" he shouts, swallowing hard when he sees my raised brows. "I need nine million Euros," he repeats, voice low this time around.

"Luigi, why do you need so much?" I task, heading toward the black-and-white image of my Familia, my brothers.

I study the picture of us holding automatic rifles with cigars in our mouths. Piles of cash surround our feet.

Although not blood brothers, these men risk everything for me and my family. They all come from a line of mafiosos—men who worked for my father and grandfather.

"You know money in Italy is tight with the recent rise in petroleum prices because of the war." I hum, listening to him explain the crisis of the world. "The government is drowning in debt, and we need help. Banks are under threat of closing. People are freaking out because the government is taking their money," he rants in one breath.

I glance at him over my shoulder before pouring myself a drink.

"So, you need my money to pay the country's debt?" I say in a detached tone, and he nods.

"Yes, it's not long before the people rise in protest. To save the banks, I need the money. I don't kno—"

"Luigi shut the fuck up already," I breathe, chugging the liquor, and it leaves a fiery path down my throat. "Seriously, save the fucking tears for the public."

He looks at me, his cheeks drawn downward in surprise.

His babbling about his crisis is an absolute waste of my time. While he could have simply said, 'I need nine million to pay the banks,' his explanation does well to emphasize the urgency of the situation. Letting me know that if I don't help him, chaos in Italy will ensue, and the last thing I need is for Italy to experience an economic depression. It will affect my business and send the officials snooping up my ass.

"Fine, I'll help you. But the next time I see you, it better be you paying me back, not asking me for more," I warn, and he nods. "Get out," I say and Kaden, one of my capos, takes Luigi outside while I get his money.

After he leaves, I pick up the picture frame I was looking at earlier to reveal a scanner beneath. Placing my hand over it, the bookshelf to the side opens to reveal the metal door to my safe room. I put the code in, and the door opens, revealing a percentage of my wealth.

Grabbing the duffel bags, I have Kaden bring Luigi back to my office. I drop the bags near Luigi's feet, and he flinches.

"I need you to sign this agreement." I push the contract toward him. "You have two years to pay me back, or I'll kill your entire family while I make you watch."

Luigi shudders from my words and accepts the gold pen handed to him.

He signs his name with shaky hands and lets out a breath of relief when he finishes.

He stands under the door and turns back to look at me.

"Thank you, Don Bandoni. Italy is in debt to you." I give him a warning look, reminding him of our deal.

I'm alone for five minutes when the door to my office bursts open. This time my underboss Francisco enters. His dark blond hair sticks to his forehead from the sweat on his temple.

"Leo," Francisco says on edge, and my brows lift from seeing my usually composed friend panting.

Francisco Catalano is one of the most loyal men I have working for me. His loyalty to me, my family, and my mafia made him the obvious pick to be my right-hand man, and because I have no brother, heir, and my father is too busy wallowing in his own sorrow, Francisco will take over my mafia if anything ever happens to me.

"What is it, Francisco?"

He saunters toward me and drops a thick packet of papers on my desk. When it hits the surface, it makes a loud noise.

"What is this?" I ask, furrowing my brows as I scan the papers to see lists of familiar names.

"It's Adriano, your cousin—" he trails, but I cut him off.

"He's no cousin of mine!" My fist clenches tight around the gold pen in my hand. It snaps in half. The black ink bleeds down my right fist, leaving a trail of black streaks.

Francisco rolls his blue eyes.

"Well, whatever the fuck he is, we found him," he says, his hatred for Adriano revealing itself through the hostility in his voice.

From the news of finding Adriano after years of searching, I feel an eagerness to wrap my hands around his throat.

Three years. That's how long we've been looking for the fucker.

If there are two things Adriano is good at doing, it's being a pain in the ass and knowing how to make himself disappear from the face of the earth. He's a coward and a disgrace to this family.

"Where is he?"

"He's in France causing chaos in the city of love."

"What kind of chaos?" I rub my temple with my thumb. The mere mention of Adriano has stirred a headache.

Francisco's shoulders stiffen, and his lips roll into his mouth.

"He's doing business in Paris," he deflects, avoiding my question.

"What business are you referring to? I don't have all day?" I say impatiently. "Is he smuggling liquor, ammunition, drugs? What is it, dammit?" My voice rises, now irritated.

Francisco runs his tongue over his bottom lip and sighs. "He's prostituting women. Particularly young tourists."

I rise from my seat, and my hands itch to throw everything off my desk. I can hear my rage thundering inside me.

Those girls have families and ambitions, and he's robbing them of their future for currency. But not for long, because I'm going to stop this business of his. Not even his little gang can stop my wrath from getting to them.

I straighten my posture, and my fingers fly to my tie, adjusting it. I regulate my breath by inhaling deeply.

"He's sex-trafficking women?" I repeat, making sure I heard him correctly through the ringing in my ears.

He nods, lips pressed into a tight line.

"Get Angelo and tell him to gather men. Tell Luca to find as much information as possible about his affairs." Francisco nods and takes his phone out to make the calls. "Francisco, call my pilot and tell him to prepare the jet. When everything is set, we leave for France."

"On it," he exclaims, his fingers typing rapidly on his phone, as he heads toward the door. "Anything else?"

"Make sure no one tells Cleo what he's doing." Francisco's eyes soften at the mention of my sister, and he assures me he wouldn't tell her anything. He takes his leave, and I sink into my chair. The everlasting tension in my body remains, but now I'm also trembling with rage.

The memories of my childhood resurface, and with it, the pain.

I clench my teeth and allow my anger to burn the grief my past brings.

A few hours have passed since Francisco told me the news of Adriano, and we are ready to leave. The last thing I have to do is tell Cleo I'm leaving.

The second I enter her room, I find her in her usual spot, sitting in the bay window. Her attention is fixed on the gardens outside.

Cleo always found peace in nature. It's the one thing that can comfort her.

When she hears me knock, her chestnut curls fly behind her as she turns, and she smiles at me.

I sit beside her with a sigh.

Her smile fades into a frown when she notices the black ink from the pen I snapped earlier.

Cleo places a comforting hand over my right cheek, her way of getting me to look at her.

The second she has my attention, she signs.

What happened, Leo?

Her hands move delicately, and I see the long, white fading scars running down the length of her soft skin.

My heart sinks from the memory of her dying on the bathroom floor. It's a taunting image forever engraved as a reminder of how I failed her.

It's been three years since she lost her voice, and every day I'm reminded of how Adriano has taken everything from her.

Hell has a special place reserved for him beside his father.

"Nothing," I say, swallowing the lump in my throat.

She sighs, not pleased with my answer.

Leo, tell me what got you so angry you took it out on a pen. Her hands slash angrily, and her expression changes to disapproval.

I sigh, knowing she won't let me leave until I tell her what she wants to hear.

I'm cautious with my words, making sure nothing I say reopens old wounds.

"It's Adriano. He's causing chaos, so I have to go to France for a few days." Her frown deepens when I say his name, and she lets out a shaky breath.

What kind of chaos? She signs.

To prevent her from blaming herself or relapsing, I say nothing.

Cleo frowns at my unwillingness to tell her anything.

Please, tell me. I want to hear about him without being afraid. I need to move on.

Tears rise in her eyes, but they aren't tears of sadness. They're tears of frustration from us tiptoeing around her. But can she blame us?

I sigh, running a hand through my hair before I tell her what she wants to know.

"He's sex-trafficking women." Cleo's eyes fill with tears, and one of her hands goes to her mouth.

You need to save those girls. Make sure they all make it home to their family.

Tears slip from her eyes, and there's a pinch to my chest.

Promise me, Leo.

I'm going to do more than make sure they all get home. I'm going to make sure their attackers lay in a pool of their own blood.

I wipe her tears.

"I'll make sure they all return home to their family where they belong," I assure her, and she exhales deeply, her shoulders dropping.

Cleo points to herself and makes a heart shape before pointing at me.

I smile at the familiar gesture and kiss her forehead before rising.

"I'll be back in three days. Please stay inside. You'll have guards outside your room," I assure her, and she glowers, hating when I treat her like a child when she's nineteen.

Cleo watches me go, giving me a slight wave.

5

VICTORIA

I'm fighting with all my energy, but whatever they injected me with is taking over any strength I have.

The black cloth covering our heads muffles our screams. But not by much. I can still hear them echo throughout the alleyway, hoping someone will come help us. No one comes.

"Victoria!" Sofia screams from my left, and my tears fall when the fear becomes too real.

My feet swing below me, and I kick my attacker. He groans in pain, and his arms loosen, dropping me to the ground.

When I stand, I sway, my head swirling from the drugs given to me.

As I try to remove the cloth from my head, one of my earrings gets stuck, and I desperately pull on the material. In the process, I tear my right earlobe. A fiery pain shoots up my body, sending warm blood trickling down my neck.

I see the man holding Sofia struggling to get her into the van because her arms are flying around, and her legs are kicking below her.

Before I can help Sofia, a hand grabs me from the back of my hair, pulling me into their arms. They put the cloth back over my head, and darkness fills my vision.

I'm thrown into the van, and my head crashes into the side. I groan out in pain, feeling my scalp throbbing. Another loud thud comes from beside me, and Sofia's whimper follows.

My breathing comes out ragged, and fear grips my heart when the door slams shut, the car driving away.

Rough hands grab me by the neck, lifting me.

The stranger caresses my cheek.

"You're a true beauty," he whispers near my ear, and terror consumes me. "My own sex toy."

I cry loudly, and my heart stills with a terror unlike anything I've ever felt.

"What do you guys want?" Sofia says, her voice shaky.

"All we want is you lovely ladies," a deep, raspy voice calls out, followed by throaty laughter.

The car takes a sharp turn, and I roll onto a solid body. The man grabs me, and his hands sink up my legs through the thigh-high black dress I wear.

"Stop!" I scream, thrashing in his arms. "Don't touch me!"

My skin crawls when his bulge pokes my inner thighs, and I try to get out of his grasp, but he keeps me in his arms.

His fingers are going to slip into my shorts, and I scratch him. He shouts, throwing me to the ground. The next second, the air gets kicked out of me when he punches me repeatedly in the stomach.

"Leave her alone!" Sofia cries, and the man stops hitting me for a second.

"Shut up, or I'll cut your tongue out."

Sofia makes a strangled sound when she swallows her cries, and the man pulls me by the neck.

"This will put you down," he whispers, and another sharp pinch to my skin follows, and this time my body grows limp, eyes fluttering shut.

The last thing on my mind is my family, and whether they'll be able to find me while they are on the other side of the world.

The sound of a door opening wakes me, and before I can register what's happening, someone drags me out of the car. Their thick fingers dig into my skin, and my bones ache from how hard they pull me.

My mouth is dry, and my throat burns from screaming and crying.

Aside from the pain in my mouth, my ribs are on fire after being punched, and to top it off, the right side of my face, where I tore my earlobe, is numb.

With every step, the pain increases, and I cry out.

"I'll give you a reason to cry if you don't shut up!" The man holding me shakes me roughly, and I almost fall from how dizzy I am.

I bite my lip, swallowing my sobs despite the scratchy pain it brings to my throat.

The air becomes stuffy, letting me know we're inside. Around me are the sounds of laughter, pleasurable groans, and the soft cries of girls.

"New whores?" a man grunts, running a finger down my neck and chest.

"Don't touch me!" I snap, trembling from fear and anger from being groped.

He laughs. "This one's feisty."

The man holding me pulls me into a room and onto my knees. The metal handcuffs keep my arms behind my back, cutting into the skin around my wrists from how tight they are.

I'm in darkness and rely on my senses to tell me about my surroundings. I pick up the voices of four men; they speak in a language I don't know. It sounds Spanish, but it's not. Perhaps Italian?

The cloth comes off my head, and I close my eyes from the sudden light. I push past the headache and open them again, trying to adjust to the light.

A man enters carrying Sofia over his shoulder. He tosses her onto the ground beside me, and she cries, rolling to her side. When the man removes the cloth from her head, she trembles in fear.

I take in the sight of Sofia to make sure she's okay, and I sigh in relief when I don't see any physical injuries on her. The only thing unusual about her appearance is her disheveled brown hair and the smeared mascara staining her cheeks.

Sofia rises from the ground, and her eyes widen in relief when she sees me. She goes to hug me, but the handcuffs around her wrists halt her movements. She tugs at her restraints, and her face twists as she cries.

The men in the room have their dark eyes fixed on us.

Andrew stands in the corner, and next to him is the brown-haired man from the restaurant.

When the man with brown hair notices me looking at him, he smirks, taking a drag from his blunt. White smoke comes from his grinning lips, and the pungent scent of weed floats in the air.

Sofia and I remain in the room with the men in silence, and after a few minutes, I hear feet shuffling from behind the door.

My breathing quickens when the men in the room fix their posture as they prepare for the person about to enter.

The door opens to reveal the familiar man with black hair.

A lump forms in my throat when I see the leash in his right hand. He tugs on it, and a frail woman with black hair walks behind him.

"Adriano," the men in the room greet.

He walks into the room, ignoring them.

The girl in the short, pastel blue cocktail dress trembles. She looks at Sofia and me, and our eyes lock. Her blue eyes are bright red and glossed with tears. The only color visible on her fair skin is the bruises on her face, thin legs, and arms.

Adriano sits behind the black desk in front of us and draws his bottom lip into his mouth as he watches me and Sofia closely. When this isn't enough, he rises and makes his way toward us.

He motions with two fingers for the men at the back of the room to come forward.

They lift Sofia onto her two feet, and she yells at them to let her go, but Adriano grips her throat, her eyes widening.

"Let her go!" I try to stand, but Andrew shoves me back onto my knees.

Adriano turns to me and backhands me across the face so hard I fall to the ground. The burning sting from his hit spreads across the left side of my face, and my mouth fills with the copper taste of my blood.

The men drop Sofia and lift me onto my feet.

"Name?" Adriano's dark green eyes burn holes into my face as he waits for me to answer. But no words want to come out of my mouth.

I'm both unwilling to give in to his demands and too stunned by everything happening.

I stare at Adriano and then at the girl with a collar around her neck. My disgust toward him rises.

Adriano will do vile things to me regardless of whether I'm submissive. I might as well go down with a fight while I still can.

He repeats his question, and this time I spit on his chest.

"Go to hell," I bite back.

Adriano gives a murderous glance and bends to my level, allowing me to get a breath of his scent of cigarettes and musk.

From behind him, the girl in the room pleads for me to cooperate. But it's too late; he's already angry, and within a second, Adriano wraps his hands around my neck, lifting me from the ground.

Sofia cries as I thrash under his grasp. Little strangled noises come from my mouth. The handcuffs bounding my wrists make clawing at his grip impossible. I'm at his mercy, and I can't do anything but watch as he finds pleasure in hurting me.

"Andrew," Adriano calls, and Andrew straightens, coming toward us.

"Their names are Victoria Rodriguez and Sofia Hernandez." I shudder in disgust when Andrew's filthy finger twirls a strand of my black hair. "They came here on a trip with their school from California. They're eighteen, almost nineteen," he tells Adriano off the top of his head.

Adriano tosses me to the ground, and I burst into a coughing fit, unable to ease the burning in my throat.

"That wasn't so hard," Adriano says, glaring at me. "But the real information I want to know is, are they virgins?"

He stalks toward Sofia and studies her like she's a dog in a pound he's debating on buying.

I watch helplessly as he grips her cheeks, squeezing them together, and turning her face to the side to inspect her.

"Are you a virgin? And don't think about lying. We'll find out if you do, and it won't be pretty," Adriano warns, and when she doesn't answer him fast enough, he becomes angry. "Answer me, bitch!"

"No, I'm not," Sofia says through tears.

Adriano sighs. "Bummer."

He moves his gaze toward me and cups my face doing the same as he had done to Sofia.

"Are you a virgin?" he asks, and I grow fearful of what he will do when I give him my answer.

Adriano's lips form a scowl, and he cups my cheek as he did to Sofia, forcing me to look at him.

"Answer the question!" He squeezes my face, his fingers pinching my skin.

"Yes," I whisper.

Adriano grins, patting my cheek and letting me go.

"You'll make me lots of money." He makes his way to his desk and rummages through a drawer. He pulls out two black leather collars and tosses them in front of Sofia and me.

His men grab the collars and wrap them around our necks. When Sofia and I make a noise, their grip around us becomes rough.

Adriano and the brown-haired man from the restaurant have a heated conversation which I can't hear.

"That's fine, Lorenzo," Adriano says, waving his hand dismissively, and Lorenzo grins.

Adriano's attention shifts to me and Sofia.

"You two belong to me now." Adriano's eyes narrow at us, his lips tipping into a grin when he sees our fear. "And you will obey. If you don't, I won't kill you, but you sure as hell will wish I did." He's looking at me as he says this, and I take in an unsteady breath, biting my tongue to stop the rising sobs which threaten to come out.

"Erika!" Adriano calls and the girl in the room rushes to his side.

"Yes, sir," she whispers in a shaky voice, her head cast down.

"Get the girls cleaned up and into their outfits. I want them ready by eleven, and if you don't do your job correctly, I'll have to punish you."

Erika trembles from his threat.

"Yes, sir," she mumbles.

Two men lift me and Sofia onto our feet, attaching a leash to the collar and tugging us out of the room.

"I'm scared," Sofia whispers, and there's nothing I can do to ease her fears.

I can't hug her because of the handcuffs cutting into my skin. I can't tell her we'll be okay because that's a lie. I can't give her an assuring smile as they drag us out of the room like we're dogs, and I can't ease her fears because I have the same ones.

There's a broken whisper beside us.

"So am I." As Erika says this, she doesn't look at us. Her sunken cheeks are dripping with tears and my heart grows cold with dread.

6

ADRIANO

I review the names of wealthy, influential men attending the auction of women I'm hosting tonight.

They come from all over the world to do business with me. All of them are eager to get their hands on one of my girls. Their wallets are stuffed with millions. They want sex, and I have the perfect girls to do the job.

My gaze falls on the spot where the two recent additions to my property had been. The memory of the little spitfire brings a stirring between my legs, and I make a mental note to have her brought to me after she's no longer a virgin.

Her virginity means a good deal of money, and I know the men will enjoy breaking her.

A knock on the door disrupts my thoughts.

"Come in." The door opens to reveal my underboss, Andrew.

"Boss, you wanted to see me?"

I rub my jaw, thinking about how my plans are playing out nicely and how soon I'll have enough strength to destroy Leo.

The mere thought of my cousin has rage brewing inside my chest.

"Boss?" Andrew's voice is cautious as he observes the fury on my face.

"I need you to go to the police station and tell Moises to call the parents of the two new girls. I don't care what he tells them as long as he makes the girls disappear from society."

Andrew's eyes widen, and he's about to say something when my sharp stare has him swallowing his words.

"Let Moises know he has to make it happen by the end of the week, or we'll kill his family," I instruct, ignoring Andrew's shocked expression.

"But boss, that's a little too early to drop the missing person's case, don't you think?" he persists and says, "people will suspect the cops, and what happens then?"

I let out an agitated breath. "Andrew, do as I tell you, and don't question me. As for the police officers, if people suspect, let them. It won't affect us. Moises made an oath never to speak of us. He knows the consequences if he does."

Andrew nods in understanding, still not convinced this is the right decision, but it doesn't matter because I'm in charge, not him.

"I'll go now. Is that all?"

With a shooing motion, I usher him away, but not before I remind him not to question my abilities again.

"Next time you question my authority, you'll find yourself with a bullet in your head." Andrew's eyes widen when he hears my warning.

He mumbles an apology, closing the door behind him and leaving me to mull over my plans to destroy Leo Bandoni.

7

VICTORIA

*I**t can happen to anyone. It can happen to YOU.*

Those are the words I used to hear on the news after a devastation. My reaction was always the same, a tug to the chest and a shake of the head. The thought *'that can't possibly happen to me'* was silent at the back of my mind each time. Yet here I am.

Sofia and I have become a statistic of human trafficking. We will become a number and a fading memory in society. We are deep in hell.

Around me, the beige wallpaper along the narrow hallway peels to reveal cement, and bullet holes litter the walls.

The deeper we walk, the darker the place becomes, and the smells of cigars, sweat, and weed linger thickly around us.

I glance to my right to see five men snorting coke off a table, their semi-automatic rifles nearby. Behind them, I'm met with the dehumanizing sight of six naked girls chained to the walls, with their legs spread apart. Their faces are pale, lifeless, and smeared with grime and tears.

The bile in my stomach rises, and my tears are uncontrollable. The pain in my chest is overwhelming. I can't take a breath without a sharp pinch.

These girls, including Erika, are sex slaves. They had a life and a family like me and Sofia, but greedy men robbed them of their freedom, and we're next on their list of victims.

My muscles become tense as we continue to walk through the hallway. Each room we pass is horrendous. Behind closed doors comes the sounds of men groaning and beds creaking.

I'm tugged toward a red room, and I remain rooted to the ground, too afraid to enter when I see women giving men blowjobs. The girls are silent, and tears fall from their eyes.

The collar around my neck chokes me when the man dragging me continues to pull me forward.

"Keep moving, or I'll shoot you," the man threatens, his jaw twitching.

Sofia nudges me, her eyes pleading for me to cooperate.

I swallow the lump of fear and step into the room. With every step inside, my freedom disappears into oblivion.

Watching the scenes in the room unfold is painful.

A man has sex with a limp woman. Her eyes are closed, too drugged to fight.

I notice girls around the ages of twelve to thirty huddled in the corner of a caged-off area. Tears run down their cheeks, and their matted hair sticks to their faces.

A small cry comes from my lips when I see five men flocking around a naked woman like vultures. They drink liquor off her body while another man takes her forcefully. Her face is scrunched in pain, and tears seep from her closed eyes.

A concoction of anger, disgust, and fear stirs inside me.

Erika doesn't react to anything we see. Her expression has no emotion, as if what we are seeing isn't even the worst.

From beside me, Sofia spills the contents of her stomach as we pass a room with six men torturing another slimmer-looking man. His screams ring in the air when his attackers mutilate him.

The men ushering us respond with disgust and force Sofia to keep walking.

We are brought to a stop near a beaten-down door, and the men push us inside. They press Sofia and me against the wall and remove the handcuffs from around our wrists. The collar around our neck comes off next.

The two men lock the door from the outside.

Silence fills the room, and Erika hesitantly looks at us. She gives us a sad smile before going to the cupboard in the room.

She pulls out two beige towels, leading us to the bathroom adjoined to the room.

"There's only one shower," Erika explains before asking which of the two wanted to shower first.

Noticing my cousin has bile dripping down her mouth and her clothes are muddy from when she fell earlier, I let her go first.

Sofia goes to shower, and Erika sits on the lumpy mattress in the room. Her hand pats the spot beside her, and I take a seat.

"Erika, what are they going to do to us?" I ask, even if I already have an idea based on what I saw moments ago.

The sight of Erika's eyes glossing over with tears makes my throat tighten, and she doesn't answer my question.

"Please, what are they going to do with me and my cousin, and why do you need to get us ready?"

Erika embraces me.

"Victoria, I'm so sorry you and your cousin got dragged into this," she says sincerely, a hand placed over my left cheek. She then continues to explain in a shaky voice, "I don't know much, only that Adriano is not a good man. He owns a gang and wants to build his empire into a mafia."

"Build his empire?"

Erika nods. "Yes, I also overheard his men talking about a cousin Adriano isn't on good terms with. They didn't say his name, but according to the conversation, this man is ruthless and the leader of other mafias, and I don't mean little gangs. I'm talking about big ones. The top crime organizations of the world."

From the mention of the mafia, my mouth grows dry, unable to believe what I'm hearing.

"Adriano wants to overpower his cousin. But to do so, he needs money, lots of it, and he needs rich men to rely on."

"So, he sells women to do so," I finish her sentence.

Erika nods in confirmation. "He runs the biggest sex trade organization in France. He's going to sell you and your cousin to men who will use and abuse you. The process doesn't stop. The same experience will continue until they break your body, mind, spirit, and soul." Her voice fades at the end as if she's remembering the process of her exploitation.

"But we can escape! You can help us." I interject, placing my hands on her shoulders.

Women have made it out of these situations before. It's rare, but not impossible.

"Oh, Victoria," Erika says, her face revealing pity. "I can't. It's impossible. I tried. Many of the girls have tried."

"No, please don't say that." My voice breaks, and my hands tremble after she confirms Sofia and I are trapped here.

Erika brings me into her chest, letting me cry on her shoulder.

"Victoria," Sofia breathes standing by the bathroom door. She runs toward me, falling on her knees and crying into my lap. "This is all my fault. If only I had listened to you."

I place my hands around her face. "Sofia, stop it. I'm the one who got us to come here in the first place," I remind her, and she's about to say something when Erika cuts us off.

"Stop blaming one another. You both need to prepare yourselves for what's coming." Erika puts a comforting hand over mine and Sofia's shoulders. She then heads to the cupboard again and pulls out a set of lingerie.

The black, white, purple, and red undergarments mock us.

Erika hands me a set of white lingerie, but I don't accept it. If I do, I'm accepting my fate and signing my body away. I'm a person, not cattle to be sold.

My reluctance makes Erika plead with me to take them, and I can see it pains her to do this.

"Please, he'll beat me if I don't get you dressed." Her voice breaks, and I frown, grabbing the white lace thong and matching lace bombshell bra.

Erika places a hand on my arm and gives me an apologetic glance before she hands Sofia a similar lingerie set. The only difference being hers is red.

"Why did we get different colors?" As soon as the words are out of my mouth, Erika stiffens and lets out a sad sigh.

"It tells the men the girls average price. If she wears white, it means she's a virgin, and the men know if they want her, she'll cost more. If she wears red, they know she's not a virgin."

"And the black and purple set?" Sofia asks, the red set of lace trembling in her hands.

"Purple is for transgender women, and the black signifies the woman has had a child. Because she's had a child, her price is much less than the others." Erika explains, and I stare at my set, disgust settling in my stomach.

The lingerie is a price tag for men to gawk and decide if they wanted to buy me. They are going to sell us like cattle to be raped and abused.

It's like Adriano said earlier, my body is no longer mine. It's his.

Sofia and I are going to be separated, and we can't do anything to stop them.

A loud knock on the door makes me jump, and a man shouts we have forty minutes, which makes Erika panic.

"Sofia, I need to get started on your makeup and hair," she says before ushering me toward the bathroom.

After showering and finding the strength to put on the white lingerie set, I find the lace brings an itch to my skin.

Every inch of my body is exposed, and I resent how I look in the white bra and thong.

I stare at my reflection in the mirror and grimace.

My skin is the color of ash, and you can see the imprint of Adriano's fingers forming around my neck. As suspected, I split my earlobe, and fresh blood is oozing out.

I run a finger over my cheek where Adriano slapped me, and the skin pulses under my touch.

Unable to stare at my reflection, I turn away, wrapping the damp towel around my body.

I remove the gold studded diamond heart earring from my left ear. It's the only thing I have from my home and life outside this prison.

My fist tightens around it, and my tears fall again. I use the knuckles of my pointer fingers to wipe my tears. I then secure the earring to the silver heels I wear, making sure it's tight.

The second I enter the room, Sofia turns to me, and she has her makeup done, and her hair is pinned into a bun.

As I near them, Sofia grabs the red lingerie set and makes her way into the bathroom to put them on.

I sit beside Erika, and she does my makeup and hair. When she finishes, she hands me a mirror, and I'm in awe. The smokey eyeshadow and eyeliner enhance the brown of my irises. She has put my long black hair into a slick bun, which helps to highlight my features. My reflection is of seduction, and I want to wipe it all off. I don't want to be attractive because of what it means for my future.

Sofia re-enters the room, holding the towel to her chest to hide her body, and she wears a look of sadness across her face.

As we wait for the men to take us away, I embrace my cousin and bring Erika into our hug, knowing she can also use the support.

"Erika, how did you get here?" I say, and Erika's eyes become misty with tears.

An inexplicable sadness and longing for time to be reversed washes over her as she says, "I also came to Paris…"

8

NARRATOR

A beautiful girl walks into a coffee shop in the early morning.

Her dark, thick curls bounce under her shoulders with every step she takes toward the cashier.

The petite woman looks at the menu above the register, unable to decide what drink she wants.

"Something strong," she tells herself, knowing she has to attend her college classes in a few minutes. Finals are approaching, and the last thing she wants is to fall asleep during class.

As she continues to study the menu above, she's unaware of the dangerous eyes piercing her back.

The man undresses her as he sips from his black coffee with a grin pressed around the rim of the cup.

"What can I get for you?" The nice old lady asks the young woman.

"Good morning. Can I please have a grande espresso?"

The woman nods, placing her order, and the girl hands the old woman her credit card.

"What's your name, sweetheart?" The kind old lady says, grabbing a cup and a pen to write the girl's name.

"Erika," she chirps.

"I'll have your drink made shortly," the older woman responds with a smile.

Erika stands in the corner of the packed coffee shop, waiting for her name to be called.

While she waits for her drink, she pulls out her copy of *A Midsummer Night's Dream* and reads.

When her name is called, she goes to collect her drink, but upon moving, she bumps into a hard chest.

The man she ran into wraps his arms around her waist, securing her.

Erika apologizes, her cheeks warm from embarrassment.

"It's okay," comes the young man's response, his arms slowly coming undone from around her.

Coughing awkwardly, the man with chocolate-brown eyes glances at Erika. His right hand massages the base of his neck, a sign of nervousness.

"My name is Mark." The brown-haired, handsome man introduces himself, giving her a dazzling smile.

"Erika," she replies, face turning warm from the way he looks at her as if she's the most gorgeous girl in the room.

Before the two can exchange another word, her name is called again.

She gives the man a smile before leaving to grab her coffee.

On her way out of the coffee shop, she savors the taste of the rich coffee beans on her tongue. Her mind races with memories of the events which took place moments ago. She can't help but smile.

The bell on the door behind alerts her that someone is coming.

She moves out of the way and bumps into a shoulder.

Erika turns to see who her next victim is, and she lets out a small laugh because beside her stands Mark, who wears an amused expression.

His mouth opens and closes as if he wants to say something, but he stops at the last moment.

"Mark, are you okay?" Erika asks.

"I know we only met a few minutes ago, but I was wondering if you would like to go on a date with me?" he asks, sounding hopeful.

Erika smiles, giving a nod.

He's a nice, good-looking guy. She felt no reason to be afraid.

Mark gives a beaming smile, and they exchange numbers before parting ways. Both promise to see each other soon.

The following weekend, Erika has a smile on her face as she gets ready for her date with Mark.

Throughout the date, Mark and Erika enjoy one another's company.

By the night's end, Erika notices how closed off Mark is. He only gave small amounts of information about himself. She doesn't dwell on this thought and gives him the benefit of the doubt because this is their first date.

Mark's vagueness doesn't stop Erika from falling head over heels for him. He's nothing like the men she dated in the past.

Mark carries himself with confidence and tender gentleness. His eyes on her as she spoke made her giddy. No one has ever looked at her the way he was doing.

The date's success only meant the two agreed to do it again, and again, and again.

Fast forward three months, and the two have grown close, almost inseparable. Mark even bought her tickets to France, which Erika couldn't believe.

She always dreamed of seeing the city of love, but this wasn't possible when her childhood was spent bouncing from one foster home to another. Only to be forced onto the streets when she turned eighteen. Sometimes even affording to attend university was a struggle.

She's never felt an ounce of love and care until Mark came along. Deep down, she knows he's the one she wants to spend the rest of her life with.

On the day of their flight, Erika is excited to be going to Paris, but her mood dampens when she notices Mark has become distant.

She ignores his cold behavior and dismisses it as stress because they are visiting his family upon arrival in France.

Erika assumes Mark never mentioned his parents to her before because he has issues with them.

This is probably why he's so distant. She assures herself.

After landing in Paris, the two make their way to Mark's mansion.

From seeing the enormous house, Erika is stunned, and uneasiness rises because Mark didn't mention his family was wealthy. She second-guesses how much she knows him, and her instincts couldn't be more right.

The moment she enters the house, two men appear from either side. They forcefully grab her arms.

"Hey, let me go!" she shouts, fighting, and their hold around her tightens.

Erika's confused and fearful as the broad-shouldered, tall men with tattoos haul her toward the stairs to the left.

"Mark, help me!" Erika cries out for her boyfriend.

Mark turns around and approaches her with predator-like steps. When he's near, Erika recoils from the sight of his grin, and his eyes have never looked more frightening.

"M—mark?" Erika stutters, her muscles growing heavy with fear.

"Don't cry," Mark taunts with a fake pout, running a finger down her face. She flinches from his touch.

"What's going on, Mark?" Erika says, her voice cracking with anger and fear.

Seeing her distress, Mark laughs. The surrounding men follow suit, bringing a chill to Erika's spine.

Mark grabs hold of her chin, his fingernails digging into the flesh.

"My name isn't Mark... It's Lorenzo," he says, laughing when he sees tears streaming down her cheeks. Her heart breaks from his betrayal.

"How could you?" she whispers brokenly.

"It's not personal. You were simply what we were looking for." His pointer finger runs the length of her jaw and neck.

"Don't touch me!"

"Get her out of my face!" Lorenzo instructs.

The men lead her away, and she screams, fighting as they drag her through the house.

They place her in an office, where she later finds out from Adriano that Mark or Lorenzo, whoever he is, lied to her. Everything they had was a lie. This was the consequence of trusting the first person who gave her kindness.

Love had made her do strange things.

She let her infatuation with Lorenzo lead her to agree to go on a trip across the world with a man she only knew for three months. She felt like a fool.

A year passes and Erika remains trapped, unable to do anything to stop the men from taking every bit of humanity from her.

She saw many girls come and go through the doors of hell, and she couldn't do anything to help them.

They at least have families who are looking for them.

But not her.

Erika is all alone. She's an orphan with no family to cry for her absence.

No one knows she's missing, and no one cares to look for her.

Lorenzo's words come back to haunt her and he's right. She was exactly what they were looking for because forgetting she existed was easy.

9

VICTORIA

Erika's story of imprisonment deflates any of my earlier attempts to escape. Our only hope of getting out of here lies with our family and the police.

The image of my parents' heartbreak after finding out the news of my kidnapping is like a stab to the chest.

I bring Erika into my arms, and she crumbles to pieces.

"You aren't alone, Erika, you have us," I assure her, and my words have incited a sense of relief in her.

"Thank you so much, Victoria. You don't know how much this means to me," she exclaims, looking between Sofia and me. There's a friendly tenderness amidst her unshed tears, and my heart aches for the pain life has given her.

"Erika, what exactly is going to happen to us?" Sofia breaks the silence with her question.

Erika's eyes soften at the sight of our fear.

"Once they drug you both, they will put you in separate cars and drive you to the auction. Wealthy men like politicians, sports directors, judges, doctors, CEOs, and basically anyone with a lot of money will be there." As she explains, Sofia grabs onto me, and a sudden throb of fear clutches my body.

"They bid on the girls they want. Those not bought are brought back here to pleasure Adriano's men unless they're virgins. They save the virgins for the men attending the auction. If the girls get auctioned, the winning bidder gets to spend the night with the girl, and if they like you, they can buy you for an extra cost." Erika wraps her arm around us, and I let out a ragged breath, my eyes blurry. I take in the sight of my equally frightened cousin and look at her hard, knowing this will be the last time I might ever see her.

"Will we see you again?" Sofia asks Erika, wiping her tears with a shaky hand.

"I don't know, but time will tell," Erika says, and I can hear the tears in her voice. "Remember, never give up on hope. Maybe you will have better luck than me, and someone will save you one day. It's only a matter of time."

The door to the room opens, and three men in all-black suits walk toward us, with a syringe in their hands.

Sofia cries out, and she grabs onto me. I hold her as tight as I can, and our embrace is unlike anything before.

"I love you. I'll find you," I whisper, even though I know it might be impossible. But I'm determined not to give up; this can't be our fate. I wasn't born to be a sex slave to these perverts.

Sofia presses our chests together, and her heart beats fast against mine.

Our screams fill the air, echoing and reverberating off the walls.

Their bulky hands grab onto our tiny bodies, and they work to pull us apart.

"No! Stop!" Sofia screams, unwilling to let me go. Her nails dig into my arm.

The man holding her wraps his arms around her midsection, lifting her while the man holding me does the same. Our interlocked fingers pull apart from the growing distance, and it's as if my heart is being stretched as her touch disappears forever.

"Please don't do this!" I beg, dropping myself to the ground. The man holding me struggles to restrain me, his breath labored and hot against my neck.

"No, please, let me go!" I shout, kicking under me when I'm lifted from the ground.

"Don't forget me!" Sofia screams, and the fear in her voice sends me tumbling into a dark pit of sadness and panic.

The man holding her punctures her neck with a needle, and she falls limp in his arms.

I feel intense pressure on my neck, and my world turns upside down.

Within minutes, I lose total control of my body. Before my eyes close, I watch as a man pushes Erika onto the bed, forcing her legs apart.

She turns away, and our eyes lock. Tears stream down her pale cheeks, and she gives me an assuring smile even though she's in pain.

Her eyes screw shut right as the door to the room closes.

The man's moans resonating from behind are the last thing I hear before I succumb to profound darkness.

10

LEO

The laughter of my men fills the private jet. They drink whiskey, enjoying themselves in a game of poker.

I divert my gaze back to the file with the names of the men Adriano has been doing business with.

The information wasn't easy to get, but not impossible when you have the best hacker on the market. Unfortunately, Adriano isn't all that stupid, and getting the location of the auction is more complicated than expected.

As of now, we are heading in blind, and I'm not sure we'll be able to find the bastard.

I skim through the long list of names, and my finger stops on the name Luigi Vitale.

The name of my good old friend, the prime minister of Italy, stares back at me.

I scoff, feeling my anger rise.

"This motherfucker." My teeth clench together, and my fingers curl into my palms.

My men notice my anger, and their laughter subsides

"Where's Luca?" I ask Francisco, who is reassembling his pistol in the seat in front of me.

His gaze falls behind me, and he motions toward the bathroom where the door is opening to reveal a whistling Luca drying his hands.

When Luca notices our eyes trained on him, his whistling stops, and he takes slow steps toward us.

"What's up?" he says, taking the window seat beside Francisco.

I flip the file, and he lifts a brow. "Find me the name of the hotel he's staying at. If he has money to spend on sex, then he doesn't need my money after all," I grit out, and Luca nods, taking the file to his original seat to find the information I want.

I watch as the youngest member of my mafia leaves to get to work.

Luca is unlike any of my men. He's less uptight and serious. But despite his lack of a backbone, he's earned my trust and respect for his exceptional hacking and computer skills. He's the complete opposite of his bastard brother.

"What's the plan?" Francisco's voice brings me out of my daze.

"I need to get into the auction. But knowing Adriano, he'll have tight security. Only those invited can enter. As of now, we have the advantage. He doesn't expect us, and I want to keep it this way. Which means we need an invitation."

"Which we don't have?" Francisco points out, rubbing the base of his chin.

"Oh, but we do."

Realization dawns upon Francisco, and he lets out an airy laugh.

"Ah, you want to kill two birds with one stone." He grins. "And that's why you're the Boss."

I shrug at his compliment and explain every detail of my plan. It's not until an hour later that Luca finally makes his way toward us with his laptop in hand.

"I reserved a room on the same floor as him."

"Perfect, thank you, Luca." He nods, and a strand of his dyed ash-white hair falls in front of his blue eyes, which glint with mischievousness.

When we land in France, I pull Kaden aside.

"Take the rest of our men back to my estate in Paris to wait for my instructions on where to go." He nods. I turn toward Francisco, Luca, and Angelo. "You three come with me. We're going to show Luigi what happens to men who rape women." Their faces morph into grins, and they follow me to the car.

Once checked into the hotel, the woman behind the counter hands me the electric room key.

She keeps her cold boney hand over mine. Her long lashes flutter.

"Enjoy your stay with us, Mr. Bandoni. If you need anything, *anything* at all, ring me up at the front desk."

I draw back my hand with disgust, my eyes hardening into a glare.

"No, thanks." My voice is flat, and her mouth drops in disbelief as I turn around and leave.

I don't need a woman. Not when I have everything I want. The responsibilities of my job means love hasn't once crossed my mind since taking over at eighteen, almost six years ago.

The idea of 'love' brings a sourness to my mouth. It's dangerous and a weakness my enemies can use against me.

Love and the mafia *can't* coexist without pain. I've seen how it consumes men. When not careful, this love can lead to a man's downfall.

If I don't want to end up like my father, I have to avoid it at all costs. I've done so for the past few years; there's no reason I'll stop now.

Hearing my blunt disinterest in the woman, Francisco and Angelo throw their heads back in laughter.

The woman huffs in annoyance, and Luca, being the flirt he is, gives the woman a cheeky wave with a grin.

I hear Luca's attempts to flirt from where I stand, waiting for the elevator to open.

"So, what time should we meet?" he asks her, and right after comes the sharp sound of her hand slapping his cheek.

I roll my lips to stop laughing and enter the elevator.

Francisco and Angelo snicker as an angry Luca grumbles under his breath.

Luca angrily scans the hotel key I give him and presses the button to take us to the thirtieth floor.

Angelo pats our friend on the back of the neck, and his grin says everything he wants to say.

"Shut the fuck up," Luca grumbles, even though we aren't saying anything. His whining is enough for us to laugh at him, and his cheeks turn red.

My knuckles smash into Luigi's solid jaw. His head swings to the side, and he spits a thick chunk of blood.

"So, you need money to save the Italian banks?" I bend to his level. "Yet here I find you going to buy sex instead?" My voice is full of anger, and I clutch the back of his head, my fingers digging into his scalp.

His stare pleads for a mercy he won't be getting.

"I do need your money!"

"Then what the fuck is this?" I show him the list with his name on it, and his eyes widen from fear after being caught in a lie.

"Where did you get this?"

"I'm the one asking the questions here," I remind him, and he stays quiet. "Now I need to know some information, and you know exactly what I want to hear," I say, and he tugs at the restraints, keeping him tied to the chair.

"What information?" he says with clear agitation.

I lift an annoyed brow and draw my fist back, landing a blow to his cheek.

"Where's Adriano hosting his auction tonight, and what time?"

"Vaffanculo!" he spits, sending me a menacing glare.

I exhale a sharp breath and bring my fist back down, hitting him until his face splits and swells. His sudden boost of confidence and stubbornness is infuriating.

"I'll ask again, where is the auction being held?"

"I'm not telling you shit!" He spits blood on my face, and my fists tighten at my side.

I pull a handkerchief from my pocket, wiping his blood-coated saliva, and Luigi smirks like he's won a prize.

I stare at him, grinding my teeth together, suppressing the urge to snap his neck.

With a snap of my fingers, I motion for Luca and Angelo to haul him toward the bathroom, where the bathtub is filled with ice-cold water.

They place him on his knees in front of the tub.

"Where's the auction going to be held? We can do this all day," I say, my words laced with boredom.

Luigi laughs.

"You don't have all day. You have until midnight," he says with a stupid grin.

A literal fucking idiot.

His response elicits a grin from me and a laugh from my men.

Luigi's eyes widen when he realizes his mistake.

"Now, that wasn't so hard," I taunt, his lips forming a scowl. "Now tell me, where is this meeting happening?"

"Do your worst." He glares at me.

I shrug my shoulders and instruct Luca and Angelo to dunk Luigi's head into the water. When they bring him to the surface, he gasps for air, coughing forcefully.

"Where are the girls being auctioned?" I ask again, getting irritated with the little fucker.

"Why do you care?"

I don't answer him.

"Where?" I repeat, and although my words threaten pain, he stays quiet.

Luca and Angelo prepare to dunk him again, but this won't get him to talk. He needs more convincing.

I stop them with a raise of my hand.

"Last chance." I flip open my pocket knife. He swallows, responding with silence. I grab his ear, and he screams as I cut it off. His hot blood douses my fist.

Francisco hands me my pliers while Luca and Angelo hold Luigi down. I position his pointer finger between the blades of the pliers, and I press down with all my force, tugging on the flesh until his finger comes off.

His screams continue filling the bathroom, and when he doesn't give me the information I want, I grab the blade and move it to his groin. As soon as I do, he crumbles in defeat.

"Wait, I'll talk!" He pleads with me not to castrate him. "The auction is taking place in La Reina hotel!"

Hearing his response I pat his bloody cheek.

"Thanks for cooperating, prime minister. But I'm afraid it's still not enough to get you off the hook." The color drains from his face.

"Here's some advice." Luigi stiffens. "Get to know those you plan on pissing off. We wouldn't want to overstep any boundaries." My words are venomous, and he trembles. "For instance, I don't like sick fucks who rape women." I grab the plugged iron and drop it into the bathtub.

"Drop him in," I instruct, and Luigi screams, begging me not to kill him, but I ignore his pleas. When he's tied back to the chair, Luca and Angelo drop him into the tub.

The moment his body hits the water, he's electrocuted and thrashes around. The water from the tub spills out, getting my Dior Timeless Derby shoes soaked.

I feel no remorse when his body stops thrashing. Not for men like him, who thought they had the right to abuse women because of their wealth and gender.

As they say, a dead man can't rape a woman.

Francisco gives me a towel to wipe the blood off my hands.

"Call Kaden. Tell him to send some men to clean this mess up," I tell him before turning to face Luca and Angelo. "You two help me find the invitation to enter the auction." They nod, and we get to work.

Not long after searching Luigi's bags, Luca makes an *aha* sound.

"Found it!" he shouts, holding up a white envelope.

Luca hands it to me, and I pull out the heavy matte black card with the red silhouette of a woman.

I place the card in my pocket, and we make our way out of the hotel to get ready for tonight's main event, and I don't mean the auction.

11

—————

LEO

The fake mustache and black wig have transformed me into Luigi, or as close to him as possible.

There's an irritation forming around my mouth from the synthetic fibers of the mustache. My patience thins by the second, but I force down my annoyance and continue my strides through the hotel.

Adriano's men are at every turn.

From beside me, Luca is grooming his fake beard and joking around, saying he looks like Abraham Lincoln. Which doesn't make sense because Abraham Lincoln wasn't as white as his pale ass, and he didn't have blue eyes.

Luca's ridiculous comparison receives an eye roll from me, and from beside him, Kaden punches him on the shoulder, telling him to shut up. I stiffen when Adriano's men give us questioning looks.

I glance at the two idiots beside me, warning them to knock it off. They separate without another word.

Kaden looks visibly annoyed as he runs his fingers through his black hair. The constant scowl remains on his lips while his steel eyes scan the area for any threats.

Although a black suit covers his body, you can still see the tattoos crawling at the base of his neck and peeking through the sleeves of his suit. He's removed the piercings on his bottom lip, right eyebrow, and nose to conceal his identity.

To add to his unapproachableness, Kaden looks like an athlete with broad shoulders and a height about as tall as my six-seven-foot self. He's an image of a man you don't want to cross.

My and Kaden's height, next to Luca's six-three-foot self, makes our friend look like a child.

Luca doesn't fit the image of a capo for a mafia. He resembled more of a college student trying to figure out his life, who took to dying his hair in weird colors to cope with an existential crisis. Which works perfectly in keeping him on the down low from the law.

We disperse, and I take a right toward the elevators, which are only available to those with VIP cards.

Luca and Kaden are to cover me while I'm inside scouting the auction, and much to my displeasure, I need to place a bet to get the location of where they take the girls.

By the elevator stands a man in an all-black tuxedo. He stiffens at seeing me until I hand him the VIP card.

The identification photo on the back is grainy and faded.

"Luigi Vitale?" he asks, moving his gaze from me to the picture, his eyes squinting, unable to make out Luigi's features.

"Yes." This is enough confirmation for him to scan the card over the panel near the elevator.

"This way." He ushers me into the elevator, following behind me.

"Any good girls today?" I ask, when he looks at me suspiciously, and the words are bitter in my mouth.

He grins, no longer wary of my presence.

"Yeah, lots of good ones, and we also have one with a nasty attitude any man would love to break," he says, licking his lips, and the bastard even adjusts his pants.

His response fuels my anger, and I clench my fists as I try not to shoot him between the legs.

The elevator doors open, and a good thing too because I was so close to snapping his thin neck.

He leads me down the hall and opens a door to reveal a red room. I look around and notice a window in front, but I can't see anything. It's pitch black on the other side.

He hands me a tablet.

"If you want to bid, you press the button on the screen," he says, as I sit on the red leather chair. "Happy bidding."

The door closes behind him, and I pull my phone out to let the guys know I made it inside. A voice from the speaker above fills the silence, and a man walks out onto the stage.

Adriano.

All the pent-up anger inside me flares when I see him after years.

"Welcome, gentlemen. Today, we have thirty beautiful girls for you. So don't waste all your money at once." The idiot is grinning sinisterly.

He won't be grinning for long, that's for sure.

"As usual, we save the best for the end."

My fingernails dig into the leather of the chair as I listen to him objectify these women.

Adriano is the prime example of what happens when two incompetent, greedy assholes have a child.

"Let's begin!" He walks off, and the first girl in red lingerie sways as she strides across the stage, barely able to stand upright.

The tablet in my hand shows her bidding. It starts at three million and stops at thirty million euros.

One after the other, girls of all ages come out, and when the first girl in white appears, the men perk up; the numbers rising at lightning speed.

As the process continues, I'm on edge. My hands have grown numb from how hard I'm clenching them.

I try to see where they take the girls, but I can't see anything amidst the darkness of the room.

Adriano's voice cuts through the silence once more, and my ears ring from his words.

"We have two more girls, both virgins. The next one is an American, a true spitfire. Let the bidding for her start at twenty million."

The lights turn on, and my damn heart leaps out of my chest from the girl staring at me.

Before I understand what's happening, I rise from my seat, and on their own accord, my feet take me to the window.

Her brown eyes pierce into me, and my body trembles. My throat closes with a dread I've only ever experienced twice.

Around me, time slows, and I stand still, fully aware of the fear she's displaying. Her eyes are pleading for help, and she doesn't know I'm centimeters away from her, hearing her silent cry.

Her eyes are hypnotic, and the way she's staring at me makes my heart race and my hands grow clammy.

What's happening to me?

An uncontrollable restlessness is brewing inside me from our distance. I want to break down the glass and pull her into my arms. I want to protect her from the hungry eyes looking at her.

My fisted hands are clenching and unclenching in anticipation. I don't believe in love at first sight. But this girl is making me question my morals.

Something I haven't seen in years burns in her eyes, which I didn't know I was missing until now. From the sight of it, a wave of indescribable protectiveness, unlike before, overwhelms my entire being.

I draw in a sharp breath when the loud rings of men placing bids fill the room. My anger and anxiety rise.

The number moves from twenty to thirty to forty until it's at fifty million within seconds.

I blink out of my daze and completely forget about my earlier hesitation to touch the tablet because of the urgency to protect her.

My consciousness becomes tormented by the terror in her eyes.

She's aware of her surroundings, as if the drugs given to her have faded. She has tears cascading down her bruised cheeks, and from the sight of the handprint around her neck and the bruise under her rib cage, my heart sinks to my stomach.

Even though buying her disgusts me, and I realize how wrong it is, I can't help myself from putting in my bid. I'm in an irrational state of mind; all I can think about is making sure she's safe.

There's no way in hell I can lose her, not when there's still uncertainty about where they might take her. I have to get her out of there. I wouldn't forgive myself if they hurt her more than they already have.

But it's impossible to keep up with the others, and her bidding grows within milliseconds, going up to eighty million euros.

The light over her turns red, and my finger presses onto the screen of the tablet, unsure of what's happening.

Then on the screen appears the word sold, and I watch them drag her off the stage. She disappears into the darkness, and from her absence comes a heaviness to my chest.

A fit of rage takes over, and I throw the tablet at the wall with a curse.

Frustrated, I press the palms of my hands onto my temple.

Fuck Leo, get a hold of yourself!

Unable to stay in the room longer, I put the silencer on my gun and walk out of the room. The man who escorted me into the room furrows his brows when he sees me leaving.

I shoot him in the head before he can even blink. The only sound in the hallway is the whizzing of the bullet and the sound of his body falling with a thud.

I drag his body inside the room I left, and leave the area.

"So? Did you get the location?" Luca asks when I meet up with him and Kaden.

A muscle in my jaw twitches, and I shake my head. Luca and Kaden turn to one another with furrowed brows.

"Why not?" Kaden asks, and I can't tell them why. I'm too consumed with trying to ease my racing heart and the powerful dread.

"I just didn't," comes my simple reply.

"Just didn't? or just couldn't?" Luca says, and the corner of his mouth tips up as he holds his amusement from seeing me space out.

By his response, I'm grateful I didn't tell them what happened because they would never stop ridiculing me if I did. The last thing I need is Luca teasing me when I'm already on edge after what I've seen.

"What are we going to do?" As Kaden says this, the men attending the auction trickle through the lobby. They all have smiles painted across their faces, and fiery anger crawls up my spine from their excitement.

"Let's get out of here." Luca and Kaden follow me to the SUV waiting for us out front.

When I'm inside the car, I rip off the stupid disguise. My stare darts out the window to face the sparkling Eiffel Tower, and I try to decipher why those brown eyes affected me the way they have.

Angelo, who sits behind the wheel, turns to us, his eyebrows raised.

"Where are we going?" he asks, and Luca cuts me off before I can speak.

"He couldn't do it," he says, with a hint of humor, and I send him a warning glare.

Francisco scrunches his brows in confusion. "So, what do we do?"

"Hang on," Luca says, pulling out his phone, his lower lip drawn between his teeth in concentration. A beaming smile tugs at the corners of Luca's mouth. "I placed a tracker on one of the men on my way out."

"Luca, you're amazing!" Angelo exclaims, prompting Luca to flick his wrist. I say nothing, too engrossed in my emotions.

The guys notice my deflated mood and look at one another with an intense curiosity to know what's stirred my distress.

I'm relieved when they don't question me.

Angelo follows Luca's directions, and I can only hope they take all the girls to the same location. If not, then I've lost her forever.

Francisco turns his head toward me, his forehead bunched together, silently asking me to tell him what's bothering me. I ignore him because I'm not entirely sure what's happening to me.

One glance into those brown eyes and the confidence to swear off a woman has dissipated into oblivion.

Francisco notices my resistance and turns back around without another question asked.

12

VICTORIA

When you're in darkness, and only silence surrounds you, the only thing you can do is think. Which is what I do when I wake up.

I'm disoriented, and everything moves at a slow pace. My ears ring, and I'm in and out of consciousness, but this doesn't stop the dark thoughts from clouding my already foggy mind.

The silence is vicious to my thoughts. I can't stop thinking about how I'll never see Sofia or my family again. How I'll never get an education or a life of my own or have any human rights. All of it gone, stripped away.

I also think of Erika, and the hopelessness in her eyes. She wants us to have hope, but she doesn't have any. She's reached the point of defeat. They broke her physically, mentally, and spiritually.

The car stops, and the door opens. A rough hand grabs me and drags me out. My heels make it hard to catch my footing, and I almost fall.

As the sound of people in the distance becomes clearer, a glimmer of hope flickers within me. But before I can open my mouth to scream for help, my captor shoves me into a room, causing me to fall hard onto the cold floor. A cry of pain escapes my lips as I scrape my knees on the rough surface.

The cloth comes off my head, and when I glance at the door, the man who brought me here looks at me with lust. His tall height looms over my hunched body. There's a scar running down his face, and his black hair is thick with grease. His stench of alcohol and sweat reaches me, bringing bile to my mouth.

He licks his cracked lips and moves toward me. I shrink back, and a raw fear spikes through my chest when he shoves his hand into his pants and jerks himself. His lips are between his teeth, and his eyes stare at me.

I'm crying, the sobs slipping from my lips. My body shuffles back until I'm against the wall, and my hands cover my ears to drone out the sound of his groans.

I'm about to squeeze my eyes close when he prepares to pull down his pants, but the door to the room opens.

A man with dark hair looks at us, his lips set into a hard line.

"Don't even think about it, Richard. This one is pure, and if the boss finds out she's not the same when she leaves this room, you're dead," he warns.

The creep named Richard backs away and huffs, taking a seat in the chair. The two men don't remove their eyes from my hunched body.

I lift my knees, trying to hide my chest and lower half. A flood of emotions rush out of me in the form of hot tears.

I'm sick to my stomach as Richard continues to ogle me. The bulge between his legs grows, and I want the floor to open and swallow me whole, but it doesn't.

Sofia comes to mind, and I grow worried for her. The only reason I'm not being raped right now is because of the white lace on my body, but what about Sofia? Oh God, my poor cousin. I don't know where she is or what they're doing to her now.

The silence in the room is frightening, and any time they shuffle in their seat, I flinch, my heart squeezing in my chest.

When they rise and grab my arms, I can't control the loud screams coming from my mouth as they drag me through the hall.

Richard turns to me and backhands me across the face.

"Shut the fuck up or I'll shove my dick down your throat and make you shut up!" he says with a grin. The man beside him laughs.

From his threat, I bite my bottom lip to silence my cries.

At the end of the hall, we reach a royal blue velvet door, and when they open it, I'm met with a circular platform in the center of the room.

I'm pushed onto the stage, and Richard bends to my ear, his hot breath fans my cheek. "Be a good girl and smile." He slaps me on the butt and gives a biting laugh, leaving me in total darkness.

"We have two more girls, both virgins. The next one is an American, a true spitfire. Let the bidding for her start at twenty million."

I jolt when Adriano's voice booms loudly through a speaker.

The lights turn on, and I stumble when I see blacked-out windows surrounding me. It's like I'm an animal in a zoo, an object of entertainment for those watching behind the glass.

What's most frightening is I can't see who's on the other side, but they can see me.

My reflection stares back at me through the window, and amidst the dark glass, I look for mercy.

As I take in my almost naked body, I notice the bruises on my skin are getting darker, and I don't look like myself.

The lights turn red, and I'm in darkness again.

Richard grips my arm and drags me out of the room. He pushes me down a hall and out of the building.

The cold air nips at my exposed skin, and I see the Eiffel Tower glittering. Tears fall from my eyes because this isn't how I was supposed to see the Eiffel Tower sparkling at night.

Darkness fills my sight once more when Richard puts the cloth over my head. He shoves me into a car. The door slams behind us.

I'm still not sure if someone has bought me or if I'm safe for now. The uncertainty of my situation makes my knee bounce with nervousness, but my movements stand still when a heavy hand falls on my thigh.

Richard's voice comes from my left, and I stiffen.

"Whoever bought you is one lucky bastard." His grip on my thigh becomes rough and his fingers trail upward.

I try to fight him off, but he restrains my cuffed hands.

Everything after happens fast, and I can't do anything but cry when his fingers roughly slip inside me.

Richard's barbaric laugh fills the silence in the car, and he removes his fingers. The hairs on the back of my neck rise, and my heart is racing in my chest.

I want my parents. I want to be at home with my family. I want the pain and fear to end. It feels like an eternity until Richard pulls me out of the car.

There are three steady knocks, prompting a door to open. The hot air from inside meets my skin, and goosebumps rise on my arms.

As we make it deeper into the fog of perspiration, I shudder from the familiar sounds of men's pleasure and girls begging for it to end.

There's a rotten stench in the air, almost like death, and it makes me gag.

I'm pushed a second time, and fall on a lumpy mattress.

"Make your owner proud bitch," Richard sneers, slamming the door behind him.

I'm left on the bed, head covered, waiting for the unavoidable. A few moments of the uneasy silence and the door opens. Heavy footsteps head toward me. My body trembles as the bed creaks, and a hand presses me down onto the bed.

They hover above me, their lower half keeping my legs restrained. They grope my left breast, and with their free hand, they run it down my body.

"I told you, you'd be my sex toy." The familiar voice knocks the breath out of my lungs, and I fight under him.

"Please don't do this," I beg, but he ignores me and grinds into me.

Although he still wears his pants, I'm repulsed when his bulge presses against my lower half.

No amount of clothing could stop me from feeling his desire.

I try to fight him off, but my body is no match for his heavyweight.

"No. No. Stop!" I scream as he kisses down my neck. He doesn't give me mercy. My pleads go in one ear and out the other.

When I don't stop kicking, he ties my legs to the bedpost and lifts my cuffed hands over my head.

"Stop it! Let me go!" I continue to shout, fighting as much as I can.

"Shut up. I paid a lot for you, and you better enjoy it. I want to hear you moan when I'm inside you."

I cry out when I hear his zipper come undone, and I knee him between the legs. He groans and wraps his hands around my neck.

"You fucking bitch!" He's about to pull off the cover from my head, but he doesn't get to because the sound of three gunshots rings in the air.

"Shit!" He gets off me right as I hear the door swing open.

"We're under attack!" a man shouts.

The man assaulting me curses again and shuffles to pull his pants up.

"I'll be back. This isn't over," he whispers, and the door slams shut.

More gunshots and screams follow. I flinch each time, unsure of what's happening.

Did the police find us?

The door to the room opens, and I cry out when a sharp needle pierces into my arm. A heavy body falls on me, and they press their hand against my underwear.

"Get off me!" My screams mingle with my tears.

"Shut up!" they shout, pulling off the black cloth. I stiffen, my face growing heavy with terror, when I see Richard staring at me with a satisfied grin.

He grinds into me, and I continue to fight under him. But he ignores my resistance and kisses down my neck. He's about to remove my underwear when the doorknob rattles. He doesn't acknowledge the noise and continues to assault me.

He slaps me when I don't stop fighting. I ignore the stinging pain and thrash under him, wanting his vile lips off my body. But fighting is useless.

When Richard takes his pants off, I close my eyes, and the next second there's a loud crash from the side. The moment I open my eyes, I see Richard flying across the room and into the wall.

I make a startled sound, and the man who threw Richard turns to face me; his eyes widen when they land on me.

Richard groans and something inside my hero's eyes snap.

With a hardened jaw, the stranger looks down at Richard and

delivers a kick to his ribs, causing him to double over in pain. He then lifts Richard from the ground and punches him. The sickening sound of breaking bones comes from each strike.

The man doesn't stop punching Richard until he hears me let out a small cry when I see the gruesome sight of Richard's mangled face.

He looks at me and drops Richard's lifeless body to the floor.

As he nears me, I grow dizzy, and black spots cover most of my vision. I can barely make out the face of the man who has saved me.

I only know he's tall and wears an expensive Armani suit, like the ones I've seen men in luxurious magazines wear.

He takes the needle out of my arm and hastily unties my body from its restraints. He wraps his suit jacket over my shoulders, and his warmth encases me.

The stranger cups my cheek, and his touch is delicate. I'm still not sure who he is or if he's a threat to me. But from how he's being gentle, I don't feel threatened by him.

"Thank you," I mumble.

My body is growing heavy by the second, and my lips tremble with an icy chill, even though the room is hot and thick with sweat.

The stranger lifts my body from the bed, and when I'm in his arms, the smell of his rich musky cologne masks the stench in the air. He runs out of the room with me in his arms.

His voice is foggy to my senses.

"Don't—"

That's all I hear before I succumb to blackness and collapse into the arms of my savior. My hero in Armani.

13

LEO

The GPS takes us to a three-story abandoned building.

The house hasn't been maintained, and it looks ready to collapse. My men stare at the building in disgust, their jaws clenched. We all glare at the men snorting powdered cocaine off a table by the door.

After scouting the perimeter, we found the house has an entrance on all four sides, and now my men wait for my command. But we can't do anything because SUVs are still arriving. Luca counted fifteen cars before stopping when he got tired. His expression reveals disbelief at the number of cars arriving without a sign of it ever ending.

I'm discussing the plan with Francisco, Kaden, and Angelo when Luca announces the last car has arrived. We make our way to see, and my adrenaline kicks in when I see the girl from earlier being dragged out of the car.

A wave of protectiveness consuming me from the inside out, and it takes every morsel in my body to restrain myself from killing the man with his filthy hands around her.

I'm naturally protective of my men and family, but never of a random woman, at least until today.

It's those damn brown eyes of hers. They keep flashing in my mind, and my heart rate quickens.

Francisco and Luca notice my body has become rigid, and my breathing has become hard. Their gaze bounces from one another to me with a brow raised.

I clear my throat, trying to compose myself because Leo Bandoni isn't soft-hearted.

I usher my men to surround me, and they gather around with their heads held high and a thirst for violence lingers on their faces.

"I need five of you to follow Angelo." I divide the men and usher them to the left, where my capo Angelo stands static in his position. "Angelo, you'll take the back of the building. No one attacks until I give the signal," I instruct, and he nods in understanding.

"You five will follow Luca and take the left side of the house. Kaden, you take these five men. You will take out the right side of the house. And Francisco, you and I will take the remaining men, and we'll attack from the front of the house."

Once everyone is in their respective sections, I give my men a pointed stare. They stiffen under my gaze.

"Kill them all and save every girl. If I find out any of you laid an inappropriate finger on *any* of the girls"—I say in a harsh voice, giving them a warning look— "I'll cut off your fingers and your dick, feeding them to you before I kill you with my bare hands. Do I make myself clear?" My men nod in understanding, muttering, "yes, boss."

I dismiss them to get to their positions, and they all scatter to wait for my signal. I head toward Francisco at the edge of the tree line. He has his sniper aimed at one of the five men sitting by the front door on the porch.

Kaden, Angelo, and Luca all confirm they are in position, and I give the signal.

Bullets fly, hitting their targets in the head, and no one suspects the threat.

Our breathing and shuffling feet are the only noise as we make our way across the field.

As we inch closer to the building, the sounds of groans and crying become louder. The sounds freeze the blood in my veins, and without another second to waste, I kick the door, and it falls from its hinges. My ears pick up the sound of the other three doors breaking down, and my men run inside.

"None of these bastards live!" I shout to Francisco, who nods before running inside, shouting orders to the other men.

The sound of screams and gunshots surrounds me, and when the smell of weed, alcohol, and sex fills my nose, I grimace.

I lift my gun and release the trigger, shooting three warning bullets into the roof.

After hearing the gunshots, men walk out of the rooms, and their eyes widen in fear at the sight of us.

I shoot a man who comes out of a room to my left. The bullet hits him between the eyes, and his blood splatters on the door behind him.

Stepping over his body, I walk into the room to find a girl tied to the bed with nothing but a thin white sheet.

When she sees me, she cowers back.

"I won't hurt you," I say, my hands lifted in front of me. She gives a hesitant nod, wrapping the sheet around her body.

I untie her legs from the bedpost.

"Can you walk?" I ask, and she nods without saying a word.

Her brows bunch together, trying to figure out my motives as I lead her toward the door, where we run into Luca, who has three girls following him.

I stop him. "Take her to the bus with the others."

He gives the girl a friendly smile. She hesitates, not trusting us, and I don't blame her after what she's been through.

"He'll take you with the other girls to safety." She shakes her head in defiance. Her lips quiver in fear, and she clutches the dirty bed sheet closer to her body as she backs away.

"What if you guys are tricking us so you can sell us yourself?" When she says this, the other girls back away from Luca.

I roll my eyes in annoyance because I don't have time for this. I still have to find the girl from earlier.

"You have my word that nothing will happen to you all. We want to take you girls back to your family." She's still uncertain, and I grow agitated. "If you don't want our help, then go," I exclaim, pointing at the door, my voice harsher than intended.

The loud gunshots make her jump, and she goes with Luca without another complaint.

They disappear out of the building, and I look at the surrounding mess, content with the sound of us killing Adriano's men and *"business"* partners.

"Let's burn these fuckers," I mumble as I run through the dark hall and up the stairs.

After a few minutes of looking through rooms, I grow frustrated when I haven't found the girl who has me on edge.

I continue making my way through the hall, opening many doors only to find them empty, with a few bodies lying in a pool of blood.

I exit a room and see Francisco carrying a girl I recognize from the auction.

He stumbles toward the stairs. The girl in his arms thrashes around, hitting him, and he makes a frustrated sound when she punches his jaw.

"No, please, I can't leave her!" she shouts, and Francisco assures her he'll have someone go back and check, but she doesn't want to leave unless her friend is with her. She kicks her legs in the air, almost making Francisco fall.

She looks at me pleadingly as I make my way toward them.

"I can't go without her," she repeats.

"I'll go check, but are you sure she's still here?" I ask, knowing there's a good chance her friend is already outside with the other.

"Yes, I heard her scream, but this asshole wouldn't listen to me and kept walking away." The girl glares at Francisco, who rolls his eyes. "Please hurry. She's wearing white and has black hair." The girl grabs onto my arm in a desperate grip.

"I promise I'll bring your friend back to you, but you need to go with Francisco."

"She's my cousin. I won't be able to live with myself if I survive this, and she doesn't." Her voice breaks, and her cheeks are wet with tears. "Please bring her back to me."

"I'll find her," I assure her again, and she stops struggling in Francisco's arms. They head in the opposite direction, and I find myself alone in the hallway.

I continue through the rooms, and as suspected, they're empty. I'm about to leave, assuming the girl's cousin is already outside, but there's a nagging feeling in my stomach telling me to keep searching.

The promise I made to the girl comes to mind, and I continue looking through the rooms when a scream comes from down the hall.

I run toward the noise to find a secret door inside a room I already checked. I curse myself for not checking better and try to open the door, but it's locked.

The door muffles her cries, but I can still hear her begging the man to let her go.

I bang my shoulder against the door, putting all my weight into breaking it down. After the third try, the door comes crumbling to the ground. As soon as it does, I'm met with the sight of a man on top of a girl. His body covers her, and she's trying to get him off, but she can't because the rope around her ankles restrains her movements.

Without batting an eyelid, I grip the back of the man's neck, launching him across the room. A gasp from behind draws me to turn to the girl he was harassing. The second I turn, my eyes lock with those beautiful brown eyes which captivated me two hours ago, and my heart stops for a second.

A sense of relief washes over me, and my heart beats fast from having found her. But my relief turns to anger when her assaulter groans, and the sound pulls me out of her hypnotizing gaze. The blood in my veins boils when I see he has his pants lowered.

He reaches for his gun, but I grab his hand, twisting it. The bone cracks in my powerful grip and his groans turn into cries.

I lift the man by the throat, choking him against the wall with one hand, and with the other, I punch him in the face until he's unrecognizable.

He's stopped breathing from my tight grip around his neck, but I can't stop. A wave of burning anger consumes every ounce of my being, and it takes over my movements.

A soft cry comes from behind, and it halts my punches. When I turn to her again, I notice her eyes flutter with sleep, and she's as pale as death. From the sight of her losing consciousness, my chest tightens with worry, and it increases when I see the needle stuck in her arm.

I drop the dead man and run to her, removing the needle and cupping her face. She's so cold and fragile.

"Thank you," she mumbles, her eyes open and close as fatigue consumes her.

Panic overtakes me, and the promise I made to my sister and her cousin comes to mind. I don't intend to break any more promises.

I lift her into my arms and run out of the room.

"Don't close your eyes." My words have a sense of urgency, and my legs run fast down the stairs, trying not to drop her as I go.

My heartbeat quickens when I see her eyes are closed. Her breathing is shallow, almost nonexistent.

"Shit!" I clutch her to my chest, afraid she'll slip from my hands.

She's overdosing in my arms, and I can't do anything but run as fast as I can to get her to a doctor before it's too late.

"We're almost there. Hold on a little longer for me," I plead, hoping she can hear me.

As soon as I step out of the building, I hear her cousin's panic.

"Victoria! Let me go!" The girl thrashes in the tight embrace Francisco has around her waist, and when he doesn't release her, she knees him between his legs and stomps on his foot. Francisco lets her go and falls to the floor, groaning, while holding his junk.

The men surrounding him laugh but clear their throats when he sends them a menacing glare.

She runs toward her unconscious cousin and me. With one hand, she clutches the towel around her, and with the other, she caresses her cousin's temple.

"Oh, Victoria, I'm so sorry." Her cries turn to hiccups, and she cringes when she sees the red handprint on her cousin's swollen cheek.

I look at Victoria, and her name produces a warm sensation. My desire to be with her intensifies as I hold her. It's so powerful I have to remind myself that what we want isn't always what we should want. No matter how pleasurable the tingles are, I can't let them control me.

Francisco limps toward us and glares at Victoria's cousin.

"Not nice piccolo fuoco," he grumbles, and the girl's head abruptly turns toward him. She sends him a menacing glare, shouting at him in Spanish.

My brows lift when Francisco's amusement increases at the sight of her rage.

"Fuck off!" she retorts in English, seizing Francisco in a challenge with her arms crossed over her chest.

My men laugh, which makes her even more mad.

"What are you assholes looking at? Get my cousin some help!" As soon as she says this, Victoria whimpers, nuzzling into my chest. The gesture causes a traitor smile to stretch onto my face, but I quickly conceal it when I realize what I'm doing.

"Follow me," I mutter, ignoring Francisco's questioning stare after he saw my fleeting smile.

Although he's curious, he doesn't press me for answers, at least not yet. He follows us into the car, and Victoria's cousin scoffs, her eyes narrowing at him.

Francisco rolls his eyes and pulls out his gun, caressing it teasingly to frighten her.

His silent threat has her cowering away, and her eyes fill with tears.

I give him a warning glance, to which he responds with a huff and puts his gun away.

"Take us to my house. Step on it," I order, and my driver does as I say.

I focus on the girl in my arms, and my worry intensifies from seeing her unconscious.

The unexplainable force from before returns, and with her now in my arms, I find pushing her away more challenging. It's as if my morals and judgments are no longer relevant.

I can't take my eyes off her. I'm afraid if I blink, she'll disappear or stop breathing.

I bring her closer, trying to warm her ice-cold skin, and I feel Francisco and Victoria's cousin's piercing stares. They say nothing, and my throat tightens because of the strange emotions swirling inside me.

My driver stops the car in front of my estate, and I run to get her help. I don't bother checking if the other two are following me. All I can think about is making sure Victoria is okay.

I enter my bedroom and place her on my bed right as the doctor I had Francisco call enters the room.

He places a hand over her forehead and frowns.

From his expression, I feel a surge of panic.

"What's wrong?"

"She's overdosing," he says, checking her heartbeat and pulse. His response annoys me because I already know this, and I'm more interested in knowing if I'm too late.

"Will she be okay?" My words come out rushed, revealing my impatience.

The doctor looks at the door.

"Is she okay?" Victoria's cousin asks while Francisco stands beside her.

The doctor nods, and we both sigh in relief.

"I told you she'll be fine. Come on, Sofia, let's get you cleaned up," Francisco says, ushering her out of the room.

Sofia hesitates, but when I promise to take care of Victoria, she leaves with Francisco. Who, much to my surprise, is being nice to her when he notices her distress.

I return my attention to the doctor to see him piercing Victoria's arm with an unknown liquid.

As the needle digs into her arm, she whimpers and moves away from him. She only relaxes when I hold her down.

"This should flush the drugs from her system," the doctor assures me, and I let out a deep exhale.

He takes his leave, and I sit on the edge of the bed, swallowing the lump in my throat as I process everything that has happened in the last few hours.

I'm relieved I found her and that she's out of danger, but I can't help but feel like now I'm the one in danger.

I have no doubt in my mind that this woman will be the downfall of the mighty Leo Bandoni.

There's an internal conflict inside me, and for the first time in my life, my heart and brain disagree. My brain tells me to run away from her, but my heart tells me to keep her close, and I agree with both.

Not knowing what to do with these new feelings, I run my fingers through my hair, and my gaze falls to her motionless body. The tension inside me eases with one look at her.

I take my time admiring her delicate feminine features.

My gaze moves from the long thick black eyelashes to her diamond-shaped face adorned with a cute button nose. Then my stare falls on her slightly chapped pouted lips, which are the shape of a heart. My breathing grows heavy from seeing her.

What are you doing to me, Victoria?

There's a knock on the door, but before I open it, I walk to my closet and grab one of my shirts. Carefully, I remove my suit jacket from over her shoulders. As I glimpse at her nearly naked body, I fill with rage at what Adriano did to her. I avoid looking at her for too long, not wanting to see the bruises they inflicted on her delicate skin.

I put the shirt on her and place her under the covers. Before I go, I put the back of my hand over her forehead and relax after noticing she isn't as cold as before.

I open the door to see Francisco

"Leo, what's going on with you?" he says, demanding answers, and he's right, I am a mess. With this realization, I remind myself how love can immobilize you.

One glance at Victoria is enough for me to understand the gravity of these words. The warmth in my chest, which she brings, would be my weakness.

"In my office." That's all I say before shutting the door in his face.

I sigh, leaning against the door, trying to compose myself, and when my stare falls on her, the tough exterior I've worked hard to keep up crumbles beneath me.

Victoria nuzzles into my bed, and my heart skips a beat. The lightness she produces in my chest is addicting, and it dawns on me that pushing her away is going to be difficult.

14

VICTORIA

Pain shoots through my head when I open my eyes. The pounding in my temple is like a hammer smashing against my skull.

Silence surrounds me, and the memory of what happened before I lost consciousness comes rushing back.

Somebody rescued me, but I don't know who, and this worries me.

I scan the room. The masculine scent in the air is familiar. I inhale it once more and recognize it as the scent of the man who saved me.

A shiver runs down my spine when I remember everything that happened to me.

I'm thankful for the man who saved me, but now my concern is finding out who he is and what his plans are for me. Sofia also comes to mind, and I panic, wondering where she is.

My breathing continues to become frantic, and my hands tremble.

I have to get out of here and find her.

I'm about to rise from the bed when the door to the room opens, and in steps a tall man with a powerful physique.

Our eyes lock and I stiffen. The familiar green eyes stare at me in surprise before they fill with relief. I cower back from the sight of him, and he senses my uneasiness.

He stills under the doorway, his towering height filling every inch of the space.

My forehead scrunches when his upturned eyes soften. He doesn't seem like the type of man who's easily worried. So, when a frown draws upon his lips and worry lines appear on his forehead, I'm surprised.

Still looking at me, the stranger rolls his lips into his mouth as if he's unsure of what to say. He pauses before saying the first thing that comes to mind.

"I won't hurt you." His voice is deep and strong. But gentle and velvety all at once. I say nothing, too intimidated to speak.

The throbbing pain in my temple returns, and I wince, clutching my aching head.

From the sound of my pain, the stranger rushes to my side, placing the palm of his hand on my forehead, and his frown deepens.

He's so close to me, and I can't look away. Everything about him is alluring and dangerous. His hair is the darkest chocolate brown I've ever seen. From afar, I noticed his strong jawline and defined cheekbones. But with him now centimeters away, I realize just how chiseled his features are. It's as if Michelangelo carved him with his own mallet and chisel. He's beautiful.

I've never found men with facial hair attractive until today. The perfectly trimmed five-o'clock shadow surrounding his full lips makes him look handsome and rugged.

My eyes freeze over the spot, his tongue delicately runs over as he looks me over for any injuries. When I glance up at him, he's already looking at me. There's a weightless turnover beneath my rib cage from his intense gaze.

I stare down at my knotted fingers, and he exhales, drawing my attention back to him. When I look at him this time, I notice the white scar on the right side of his face. It starts on his temple and ends near the tail of his brow bone. The scar is a slight imperfection, but it makes him more attractive.

He stares at me, and another flutter erupts in my stomach. It's a reaction I don't understand. He's a stranger, and it's not right for me to let his good looks or the fact that he rescued me tempt me. But my body is acting like I've never seen a man before. I was almost raped for crying out loud! Why am I feeling this way toward him? I have better things to worry about, like my cousin and where she is.

As if sensing my worry, he answers my concerns.

"Your cousin is here. I'll bring her to you," he says, and I pick up on the slight Italian accent in his dialect. It reminds me of Adriano and his men. A terror pulses through my veins.

He hears my breathing turn frantic, and a line appears between his brows. He says nothing and rises from the bed, heading toward the door.

Many questions are going through my head, but there is one I'm dying to know the answer to.

"Who are you?" My voice is timid, even to my ears.

His strong back stiffens, and he turns to the side.

"Leo," he says, hesitating for a second before leaving the room.

Alone again, his name comes from my parted lips in a whisper. It rolls pleasantly off my tongue.

A few minutes pass, and he still hasn't returned.

When the stabbing pain in my head becomes unbearable, I lay down and close my eyes. I'm about to welcome the darkness when the silence in the room end.

"You told me she was awake?" Sofia remarks with accusation.

"She was awake when I left," Leo says condescendingly.

"Sofia," I whisper, and she whirls around to look at me. Her brown hair flies behind her.

When she sees me awake, she sighs and crouches beside me, wrapping me in her arms.

"Oh, thank god, Victoria, you scared me." She looks me over, and her eyes stop on the black shirt I'm wearing.

I glance at the shirt and then at Leo, who wears a similar one. He's already looking at me, and his intense stare brings heat to my face. Trying to avoid his penetrating gaze, I quickly turn to my cousin.

"Did they touch you? Are you hurt?" I ask in a panic, and now it's my turn to look her over for any injuries.

"No, I'm fine. It's you I was worried about." Her hands are now around my face. "Victoria, you overdosed on heroin! I was so scared." Her eyes glisten with tears, and her hands around my cheeks tremble.

From this information, I grimace, and my body shudders. Disgust settles inside my stomach, assuring me I haven't grown addicted to the drug.

"How long was I out?"

"Two days!" Sofia says, and I don't believe her until I turn toward the window in the room to see the sun setting, which tells me I woke up late in the evening.

Leo remains in the middle of the room, deep in thought. His full lips are pressed into a thin line.

"Thank you for saving us," I say, and a slight smile tugs on his lips.

Sofia glances from me to Leo. Her eyes shimmer with a look I know all too well.

"Where are we?" I ask, looking around the ebony walls and modern gray furniture adorning the room.

"My house in France," Leo says.

"What do you plan on doing with us?" Sofia asks him.

"Nothing," comes his simple reply as he looks at his ringing phone, which demands his attention.

"Nothing?" Sofia remarks, flaring her arms in the air. "When can we go home?" she shouts incredulously after Leo. He glares at her and leaves the room to answer the call.

"Asshole," Sofia grumbles when the door closes after him.

I haven't had time to process what has happened to me until now, and I find myself panicking when my family comes to mind. I gasp, realizing they must be in a panic right now.

"What is it? Are you okay?" Sofia asks, when she sees my worry.

"Our parents don't know where we are. They must be worried sick." Sofia's eyes widen in realization, and she runs her fingers through her hair, releasing a deep sigh.

"You're right. We need to call them to let them know we're fine, or at least I think we're safe here," she says as the door opens.

Leo saunters into the room, his tall height towering over us.

"Are you hungry?" he asks me, and I open my mouth to decline, but my stomach growls loudly before a word can come from me.

When he hears the noise, a corner of his mouth quirks up.

"I'll take that as a yes. Come," he instructs, his large hand outstretched for me to take.

I stare at his hand. My heart is racing so loud I can hear it in my ears.

He makes me nervous, both from his good looks and because part of me acknowledges he looks like my kidnappers, and I'm not sure if I can trust him. But seeing him act differently than those monsters is throwing me off.

The silence ticks between us, and when I become nauseous from hunger, I decide to take his hand.

Our fingers interlock, and my throat tightens. I slowly rise from the bed, and my legs wobble under me. Dark spots cover my vision as a wave of warmth consumes me, and my legs buckle.

I'm about to fall to the ground when Sofia, who's right behind me, places a hand on the small of my back. Leo encircles an arm around my waist, keeping me upright.

I mumble a silent thank you, and he leads us out of the room.

As we approach the railing, I see two elegant staircases, one on either side leading to the first floor.

My gaze stills on the center of the foyer, where a round gold-encrusted design of a crown and a lion is embedded into the white marble flooring.

At the sight of the mansion, my mouth falls open, and Sofia, who's to my right, nods, agreeing with my awestruck expression.

Leo doesn't notice my shock and continues leading me down the stairs, and I ponder what he does for work to afford such a beautiful house.

My focus moves to the enormous living room to the right, where men sit on the couch with their guns on the coffee table. From the sight of the weapons, I panic as the memory of what I saw in the red room resurfaces.

Leo senses my panic and shuts the door to the room.

When he returns, he brings me plush against his chest. I'm trembling, and he whispers comforting words. I close my eyes, trying to push the horrific images to the deepest corners of my mind, and when I open my eyes, I exhale.

Leo's still holding me, and I stiffen.

"I'm okay," I assure him, pulling from his arms, and an air of awkwardness rises between us.

Sofia grins, and the twinkle in her eyes burns even brighter.

I give her a stern look, telling her to knock it off. We know nothing about him. She shouldn't encourage this behavior, and I shouldn't let myself feel this way about him.

Leo says nothing, and I can tell he's battling something himself because his fists clench as if restless.

He clears his throat and ushers us into a beautiful kitchen where two guys sit on a stool eating a piece of chocolate cake.

I chew the inside of my mouth and take in the sight of the guy close to the door.

He has dirty blond hair and looks to be in his early twenties.

My stare falls on the other slightly younger looking guy. His dyed ash-white hair looks silky, and the color compliments his baby blue eyes and fair skin.

When he sees us walking in, he rises from his seat, and his electric blue eyes now stare at me in curiosity.

His stare makes me uneasy. I can't help but feel a sense of familiarity as he looks at me, but I can't put my finger on it.

Leo senses my discomfort, and his sharp gaze lands on the guy.

"What is it, Luca?" Leo's voice is dangerous, and I jump from the harshness. Leo notices I'm trembling, and he sends me an apologetic glance. He repeats his question, and this time his voice is softer.

Luca shakes his head dismissively.

"I thought the girls we rescued were at the hotel, so we can send them home?" Luca says, scratching the back of his neck when Leo glares at him.

Luca's eyes move from Leo to mine, giving me a toothy smile. I give him a tight-lipped smile in return.

Leo doesn't answer Luca. Instead, he looks at me and asks, "what do you want to eat?"

I shrug, ignoring his hesitation to answer Luca. I'd ask him about it later.

Sofia takes a seat beside the other guy in the room. She takes the chocolate cake he's eating, and he looks at her in annoyance before pulling the plate back in front of him with a grin.

"Hey, give it back, Francisco!" she says, going for the cake again, and I watch the pair with amusement.

Leo places a plate of food in front of me, and the smell of rice, chicken, and vegetables makes my stomach growl.

"Thanks," I mumble, giving a gentle smile before taking the fork from his hand.

Leo stares at me in amusement as I dig into the food, shoving in big bites.

I swallow the food and glance down at my plate to conceal the flush sure to be on my cheeks. I eat the rest of the food in silene, and after a while of being in the kitchen, I learn Luca and Francisco are good company. Leo, on the other hand, is quiet the entire time. It's like he's walking on eggshells, and I'm not sure what to make of it.

After talking with Luca, I find he's both smart and flirty, and he's also a total prankster who isn't very smart with his words.

Luca looks at me. "So, Shortcake—" my forehead furrows at the name, and he smiles. "Can I call you that?"

"Sure," I say, raising a brow when Luca glances from me to Leo.

"I have to say you're very curvy and beautiful." Luca's mischievous eyes dart to a rising Leo, and within seconds Luca is pressed against the fridge. Francisco groans and stands between them as two other guys enter the room. All three of them work on pulling Leo off a laughing Luca, who he's choking.

Sofia and I stare at them with wide eyes, wondering what made Leo react with such anger when Luca was joking around.

"What the hell is going on?" One of the new men grits out, and the tattoos on his arms and neck tighten when his body grows rigid. His sharp gray eyes look at us, and his voice is laced with annoyance.

I cower back at the sight of the hard-core biker-looking man with a scowl. This man looks like he kills for fun.

"Kaden, I think Luca's being a pain in the ass again." The other tall guy with black hair sighs before he directs his blue eyes toward me—confusion and curiosity taking over his expression. His stare moves from me to a fuming Leo.

All the men turn to look at me and Sofia. Before anyone can say anything, Leo drags me out of the room.

As he pulls me, I try to stop him, not wanting to be separated from my cousin. But Leo is too strong for me to stop on my own. From his grip around my wrist, my anger spikes.

I've had enough of men moving me around like a chess piece. Being good-looking isn't an excuse for him to pull me around like a doll.

I fist my hands, and my feet dig into the ground. When Leo sees me putting up a fight, his jaw clenches, and his eyes narrow into a warning, which startles me.

I back away from him, and he freezes, his anger morphing into regret.

"Please," Leo says, and I raise a questioning brow because the word from his mouth sounds odd, almost as if he's never had to say it.

My arms cross over my chest, and the oversized shirt rises. Looking at my bare legs, I panic, my face blazing with warmth. I tug at the shirt's hem to cover my legs.

Leo sees my discomfort, and his expression softens. He extends his hand for me, and I don't take it until I hear the door to the living room opening, letting me know the men with guns are coming out.

Fear takes over, and I forget my anger. I grab Leo's forearm, using his body as a shield, and my fingers tremble against his black dress shirt.

Leo's muscles tense briefly at my touch, but then he relaxes. He turns around slowly and takes my trembling hands, guiding us back to the room I woke up in.

As soon as he opens the door to the room, I bolt inside, and he follows close behind. I'm frozen in place, watching him run his fingers through his hair in frustration.

"Leo?" I ask. He hums, eyes now staring at me. "When can Sofia and I go home?"

Although he's scaring me with his erratic behavior, I have to ask. But his reaction tells me I probably shouldn't have, and my fear rises when he stares at me stoically, his jaw clenching.

I cower back, and in his green eyes grow dark. His expression shifts from gentle to aggressive. It's a look that resembles the one Adriano gave me while choking me.

"What?" His voice is deep and icy, daring me to repeat myself.

I hesitate. "Isn't that why we're here?" I ask, my arms hugging my chest, afraid of what he'll do to me.

"If you want, I can take you back to where I found you!" He towers over me, and I flinch.

The harshness of his voice and his intoxicating musky scent make me want to cower back in fear and curl my toes.

I've only known him for two hours, yet in those minutes, I have learned he's gentle, scary, and unpredictable. A mix of characteristics that confuses me.

His words sink in, and I snap out of my trance. My eyes fog with tears because he's exactly like Adriano. He didn't save me at all. I'm still a prisoner, only without handcuffs and a leash.

Leo sees my tears, and his hand extends toward me. I shrink away from his touch, afraid he'll hit me for crying. His hand drops to his side, and he swallows hard. I think I even see regret flash in his eyes. But I'm not sure because he storms out of the room.

The door slams shut with a thud, and I jump from the sound.

As I stare at the door, I feel neither safe nor in danger. Two emotions I didn't know I could feel at once.

When the gravity of his threat comes to mind, my heart drops to my stomach because I won't be going home. This is enough for me to fall to the floor, where I pull my knees up to my chest. I can't control the tears and the sobs which rack my body.

Never in a million years did I think someone would ever kidnap me. But here I am, weeping, on the floor of a stranger's house. A stranger who saved me but who is now threatening to take me back to hell, where I was almost raped.

When I asked to go to Europe, this wasn't what I had expected.

15

LEO

The door slams behind me, and the noise reverberates throughout the house.

There's a quick rise and fall in my chest, and my blood is boiling.

As I come down from my rage, the warm blood in my veins freezes when I realize what I've done.

Behind me, I've left a crushed Victoria, and regret toward how I handled the situation seeps in, but it's too late. I've already said the harsh words.

I realize my outbursts confuse her, and why wouldn't they? She doesn't know I'm a bipolar asshole who doesn't know the first thing about being gentle.

The need to go back inside and beg her to forgive me increases, but I stop myself because I know if I go inside, I'll frighten her more than I already do.

Victoria's afraid of me, and to admit this hurts more than it should.

I saw her fear downstairs, and I saw it again ten seconds ago. She thinks I'm like Adriano, but I'm nothing like that bastard!

To see her flinch from my touch brings an inexplicable amount of grief. I never want to see the look of fear on her face again. However, I'm not doing a very good job. In fact, I'm giving her more reasons to be afraid.

I close my eyes for a second and sigh. When I open them, Angelo stands in the corner with a stupid grin.

A stiffness rises in my shoulders, and I glare at him. He rolls his grinning lips into his mouth, stifling his laughter as I walk past him to get to my office.

Once there, I try to focus on the documents I brought to France, but I quickly realize I won't be getting any work done because the guilt is eating me alive.

All Victoria wanted to know was when she could go home to her family, but I neglected her request. She needs to know my intentions toward her are not to harm her. I simply want to make sure she's okay to travel after what her body has experienced. Or at least I tell myself this. But who am I fooling? This isn't close to the truth. I don't want to let her go because the mere mention of her leaving fills me with rage.

Victoria is making me question my sanity.

A frustrated sigh escapes me when I'm consumed with selfishness to keep her with me for a little longer. It's not like I haven't done worse. Yet, I'm aware I can't keep her with me. She doesn't belong to me. She doesn't belong to anyone but herself, and I will let her go. But I first want to get to know her, even if it might make letting her go more painful. She's worth it.

I'm also not comfortable letting her go home while Adriano is still on the loose. The risk of her getting kidnapped again is high, so long as Adriano is alive and knows she exists.

The comment from Sofia about how they didn't see much of France enters my thoughts. With this in mind, I'm determined to make sure they both get the experience they came here for, and it's a perfect opportunity to get to know Victoria. Maybe then I can figure out why she has such a hold on me.

I can't help myself from wanting to get to know her. She's enticing, a closed book I want to read.

The problem now is getting her to trust me after I threatened her.

I groan in frustration. The consequences of my actions weigh heavily on my shoulders.

There's no way she'll trust me after the way I spoke to her.

My thoughts halt when I notice her picture under the stack of papers I'm supposed to be looking over.

The documents have information about the girls we rescued. I haven't been able to look at them until now. Victoria was on my mind the entire time, and I couldn't focus on anything other than her.

She had been out from the drugs for almost two days, and I worried something was wrong when she didn't wake up this morning. But this evening, when I entered my room to check on her and our eyes locked, I was both relieved and frozen in my spot.

I waited hours for her to wake up, and now that she has, I'm not sure how to talk to or approach her. She disorients me, and my men have noticed.

My curiosity gets the best of me, and I open the file. Allowing myself to read the brief note under her picture. The words on the page are like a peek into her life.

I sigh in relief when I read she isn't much younger than me, and I push the thought aside because her age shouldn't matter to me. Her life is miles away from my own. She lives a life different from the violence I'm used to. Soon everything will return to normal with her in America and me in Italy.

I scan over the words on the pages, and the back-and-forth tugging between my brain and my heart gives me whiplash. One moment I want her to be a part of my life, and the next I want her away from me to protect her.

I let out a nervous breath and rise from my chair. I need to apologize and make things right.

The entire walk toward Victoria I contemplate what I want to say, and my heart races when I'm at the door.

A slight pause comes over me, and my hand rests on the doorknob.

As I stand nervously in front of the door, I'm again reminded of how weak I'm becoming. Nothing scares me, and certainly nobody. Two facts which were true until today because now I'm afraid to face Victoria.

I take a deep breath and knock on the door before pushing it open.

The first thing I hear is her soft cries. Her distress makes my spine lock up.

I open the door further to find her at the foot of the bed, hugging her knees to her chest. Her head is tucked tightly between her knees.

The cold, numbing sensation of guilt shoots through my body, and I pick her up in a flash. When I do, she makes a frightened sound.

"No, don't touch me!" She's hitting my chest, and I hold her fists, pressing them against my fast-beating heart.

"Please don't take me back there." Her voice rises with terror, and her distrust toward me brings a painful clench to my chest.

I place her on the bed, kneeling in front of her, and she's shaking. Her hands, which I hold, continue to fight me. I let her go. Uncertainty marks her features, and I swallow the lump in my throat.

"I'm sorry." There's a raw sincerity in my words that throws her off. "I would never take you back there. I shouldn't have said what I did." She's silent, staring at me, and her breathing comes out hard.

When she relaxes, I sit beside her, and she looks at me for a minute before giving a hesitant nod.

With slow hands, I reach toward her, and she flinches when I wipe the tears running down her high cheeks.

Victoria blinks, staring at me, her body slightly drawing back. She's afraid of me, and it's killing me inside. But I did this to myself.

We sit in silence until her soft voice breaks it, and from the sound of her talking to me, I relax.

"Why did you say it if you didn't mean it?" Her question is unexpected, and I don't know what to say because there's no excuse for how I talked to her.

"Because I'm a bipolar asshole," I say, and there's a slight tug on her lips when she hears my blunt response.

Victoria yawns, worn out from all the emotions of the past few days, and I rise from the bed. She watches me, and I don't know what she's thinking, which makes me anxious.

My stare falls on the dark bruise on her cheek and the fingerprints over her neck where they choked her. The muscles in my hands tense when I clench them.

She almost died in my arms, and if I didn't save her when I did, she would have died on that filthy bed.

When Victoria senses my anger at seeing her bruises, she hesitantly places a shaky hand over my right fist. Little tingles shoot up my arm.

She's swallows hard, and her eyes avoid mine. I'm not sure if she's nervous, scared or both.

I sigh, and before I know what I'm doing, I kiss her on the top of the head, and she stiffens under my touch.

Fuck!

I panic, not sure what to do.

What is wrong with me?

"Good night, Victoria." My voice is hesitant and shaky after what I've done. She remains quiet, and I feel her eyes pierce into my retreating figure.

When I'm outside, there's a peacefulness taking over my body, and it feels so good I never want it to end. I make my way to the room next door, relieved to have made some progress after I fucked up earlier.

Tomorrow will be a new day, and for the time being, I'm no longer Leo Bandoni, the Italian Don. To her, I'll only ever be Leo. But when my time with her ends, I will return to being the most feared mafia Don I'm known for.

A few days with her is all I need to show her France.

16

VICTORIA

It's the next day, and I'm lying in bed, unwilling to get up.

The memories from last night remain with me. Particularly how Leo apologized to me with intense sincerity, and looked at me as if seeing me in pain hurt him. The mere thought of these things causes a turnover in my stomach.

I know the constant fluttering and nervousness I feel toward him isn't normal. The events of my kidnapping have left me vulnerable, and I can only assume the little flutters toward Leo are because he saved me. But as worrisome as these warm feelings are, I like them and don't want them to stop, which tells me I have lost my mind.

I drag a hand down my face and turn over on my side, pressing my face into the cold pillow.

When I rise, I notice a pile of clothes on the nightstand. There's a little paper on top, and I grab the note. My heart rate increases with an eagerness to read it, and I find myself smiling as I trace the black ink of Leo's elegant handwriting.

> *I thought you might want some real clothes.*
> *PS Everything is new.*
> *Leo*

I put the note aside and lift the simple knitted long-sleeve black dress. When I do, a set of matching undergarments falls out. The sight of the undergarments reminds me of what I'm wearing under the t-shirt. Disgust settles in my stomach, and my skin crawls with an irritation.

I approach the bathroom adjoined to the bedroom. My mouth drops at the enormity of it.

To the left, I notice a walk-in closet. Inside is an array of expensive suits. Leo's scent is thick in the air.

This is his room.

There's a pang in my chest, and I can't help but feel like a burden.

I suck in an unsteady breath, exit the closet, and see my reflection in the mirror. I gasp at the sight of the dark bruises littering my face and neck. They look worse than when I last saw them.

My fingertips are gentle on the bruised skin, but I still feel a sharp pain when I touch them. Tears cloud my vision, and they don't stop falling when I see myself in the white lace. All I see is a price tag instead of undergarments. Crying uncontrollably, I take off the lingerie, rip them into shreds, and toss them into the trash.

While showering, I try to wash away the unwanted memories of my kidnapping. But no matter how hard I scrub, I can still feel my abusers' burning lips on my body and their filthy hands slithering up my thighs.

The memories are too painful, and every time I close my eyes, it's as if I'm back in that room.

There's a hatred toward my body growing inside me, and I can do nothing to make the pain disappear.

As I sit at the bottom of the shower, I bury my head in my knees, and my shoulders shake from the intense sobs coming from inside me.

I can feel Richard's fingers, and panic rises in my chest. Biting my lip hard, a penny-like taste fills my mouth. Then there's silence, and my cries turn into hard breathing.

The scorching hot water from the shower turns my brown skin red and the blood in my veins fizzles up. My hands ball into tight fists, and I'm filled with anger toward Adriano and his men for what they did to me and what they are doing to others. Then a wave of irritation washes over me as I try to understand Leo's confusing behavior. I'm not sure if he's my savior or if he's also kidnapped me. He's nice one second and a total ass the next, and despite this, I can't help but want to be near him, which makes me angry at myself.

Maybe I'm also bipolar?

Showering didn't get rid of the itch on my skin. There's no forgetting what they did to me. Especially not while I still have the giant bruises and busted lip.

My battered body reminds me of the violence I've been subjected to, and all because I didn't submit to Adriano and his men. They hit me because I retaliated and didn't bite my tongue when a man disrespected me. These bruises are proof of my rebellion. A marker to tell the world I didn't go down without a fight.

Unable to look at the bruises any longer, I return to the room and contemplate what to do. At this moment, I don't know what I can do. I'm not sure if I'm free to go where I want or if I'm bound to this room. Leo never told me what he wanted with me and Sofia.

After debating my next actions, I give in and decide to go outside. I can't stay in here forever.

I approach the door and hesitate to open it, afraid of who will be outside. There are men in this house who carry guns that can kill ten people in a minute.

The only thing pushing me to open the door is knowing Sofia is somewhere alone in the house.

I continue through the mansion, intending to find her.

While making my way through the hallway, the sound of men speaking makes me stop. I have the urge to run back to the room, but I force myself to keep walking, determined to find Sofia.

As I pass the group of tall men, I stiffen.

When they notice me, curiosity reveals itself in their expressions.

They don't stop to question me, which I'm thankful for because I won't know what to tell them if they ask me anything about why I'm here.

If what Luca said last night is true about the other girls rescued being sent to a hotel, then why are Sofia and I here and not there?

I dismiss these thoughts and enter the kitchen to find Sofia preparing food. Luca hovers behind her, and I notice him lick his lips, visibly excited to eat.

When they hear me come in, they turn in my direction. Sofia's face glows when she sees me.

"Morning," I say, helping Sofia with breakfast, since I have nothing better to do than think about the uncertainty surrounding our predicament. Thinking about the past few days will only upset me more than I already am, and the smells of home wafting from the stove do well to ease the grief in my chest.

When we finish cooking, men pile into the kitchen with hunger. I turn to Sofia, and we exchange a knowing look, both amused by the men salivating from the delicious aroma in the room.

"What is that?" Luca asks, swallowing, and his eyes widen with hunger.

I slide a plate in front of him, and he mumbles a "thank you" before digging into the dish without a utensil. I laugh at his excitement and hand him a fork. He gladly takes it and continues to stuff his face, moaning as he chews.

"No, seriously, what is this?" he says through a mouth full of food.

Hearing his appreciation, Sofia and I glance at one another, satisfied with our work.

"It's chilaquiles, carne ranchera, and huevo ranchero. Or at least close to what we could make with what you guys had in the fridge," I tell him in my mother tongue before placing a plate in front of the guy with blue eyes I met yesterday.

Blue eyes nods in gratitude, and he elegantly places a napkin on his lap. I lift a brow at his sophistication.

"I don't understand half the things you said, but it's good," Luca praises, taking another bite of the chilaquiles. I laugh before explaining to him in English what the food is.

"Where is this dish from? And what language do you speak?" Blue eyes asks after swallowing a bite of food and wiping the corners of his mouth.

He notices my curious stare and gives me his name. "I'm Angelo," he introduces himself with his right hand outstretched for me to shake. There's a gentle smile stretching on his full lips.

I shake his hand, and his grip is firm.

"Victoria," I say before answering his question as I serve myself a plate. "And it's a Mexican dish. Our family is from Mexico." Angelo nods, and his eyes trail to something behind me.

My forehead furrows from the gesture, and I turn, only to bump into a broad chest covered in a perfectly pressed black button-down shirt. My lungs constrict from the familiar scent. A strange mix of uneasiness and excitement washes over me. The excitement I could do without, considering he's a stranger.

I have to keep reminding myself of this, but even then, the stupid flutters won't go away.

A pair of intense forest-green eyes pin me in place. I give a nervous smile, and Leo's eyes flicker with an unknown emotion.

I don't know what takes over me, but I lift the plate in my hand, ready to give it to him, and Leo looks at the plate hesitantly.

"It's not poisoned." My voice comes out with a hint of offense, and his eyes widen in panic.

"I know it isn't." He pauses and rubs the back of his neck. "This is your plate."

When he says this, my stomach flutters and I curse myself.

"Just take it. I can serve myself another plate," I assure him, this time forcing it into his hands.

Although he has us trapped here, he's a somewhat better host than Adriano. Making them breakfast is the least Sofia and I can do, and who knows, maybe he'll let us go if we befriend them. My mom always did say the way to one's heart is through their stomach.

Leo hesitates at first, but when he sees how serious I am, he takes the plate from my hand. When he grabs it, our fingers touch, and electricity passes through us, shocking me.

My body warms, and Leo's intense gaze has me looking behind him. I'm desperate to find anything to distract myself from the warm, tingly feelings his touch brings me.

The kitchen is silent, and everyone looks at us, making me more nervous.

I lick my lips, willing the dryness away, and turn around to serve myself a plate to hide from everyone's intense gaze.

As I grab a plate, Leo places a hand on mine, stopping me.

My brows draw together in confusion when he grabs the plate from my hand, and I watch as he puts food on it before handing it back to me. This gesture makes everyone in the room drop their mouths.

I try my best to ignore them and sit beside Sofia, who's equally shocked.

What are you doing to me, Leo?

Heat rushes to my cheeks when I notice him looking at me whenever he lifts his eyes to put food into his mouth.

LEO

I couldn't sleep at all last night.

All I could think about was what I was going to do about my situation with Victoria. I know I have to let her go, but I'm not ready to lose her. I just found her.

Aside from my reluctance to part with her, I also couldn't stop thinking about what Adriano and his men did to her. If I had known her before they kidnapped her, I would have protected her, and she wouldn't be suffering.

Since she woke up, I noticed she's terrified of men, including me. Luckily, after apologizing to her, she's becoming more comfortable with me. If I could even call it that.

"Why didn't you answer?" Francisco says, appearing in front of me, face scrunched in annoyance.

I lift a questioning brow.

"I was knocking for five minutes!" he says, crossing his arms over his chest.

"What do you need, Francisco?" He rolls his eyes at my exasperated tone.

"The girls we saved are asking our men when they can go home. They think we're planning on selling them," Francisco explains, and his expression tells me to get my shit together, and I know he's right.

He follows close behind me as we approach my office. On the way there, I stop near Victoria's door, and Francisco gives me a knowing look. He swallows his snarky comment when he sees my silent warning.

"Didn't I tell you to send them home already?" I exclaim, my pointer finger under my jaw. "I must have forgotten."

"I wonder why," Francisco grumbles low enough for me to hear.

"Shut up and follow me. I need to make a few calls," I say, irritated by his cockiness.

Once in my office, I call the hotel where the girls we rescued are staying, so I can let them know I want the girls to be gathered for a quick announcement.

After hanging up, I motion for Francisco to follow me.

"Let's go. I want to make this fast," I say, walking out of my office, only for him to stop me by placing a hand on my left shoulder.

I turn and narrow my eyes at him, noticing his amusement as he tries to hand me a comb.

"Unless you want bedhead, then don't take it. But a word of advice from your trusty underboss..." Francisco's face is aligned with humor, and my annoyance rises. "...you need the groom."

He makes his way toward the door, but before he opens it, he turns around. A glint in his eyes.

"Oh, and here." He tosses me a packet of gum. "In case you run into Victoria." He winks with the corners of his lips lifted.

My eyes harden, and he laughs at my newfound restlessness.

"Idiota," I mutter grudgingly, and when he's not looking, I comb through my hair and chew on the gum.

The moment we walk into the kitchen, Francisco's nostrils flare, taking in the aroma of freshly cooked food. His mouth salivates from the new smells, and I do the same.

My gaze lands on the girl who has stirred unfamiliar emotions in me. Warmth spreads across my body as I near her.

Victoria turns around, crashing into my chest, and she lets out a barely audible gasp. I wrap an around her waist, keeping her steady. Our eyes lock, and her cheeks flush a dark color.

She offers me her plate of food, and I push it toward her, but she takes offense to this.

Her serving me didn't sit well with me. This isn't how we did things in Italy, at least not how I want to do things. I don't want her lifting a finger.

Victoria's lips press together, and her perfect eyebrows scrunch.

She forces the plate into my hands, and her stubbornness in taking no for an answer is a pleasant surprise.

When she gives me no other choice, I take the plate, and our fingers graze. There's a zap of electricity. The sound of her surprise lifts the corner of my lips. Her eyes avoid mine, and she bites the inside of her mouth. My heart races from how she responds to my touch.

Victoria grabs another plate, and I take it from her hands. When I hand her back the plate filled with food, she stares at me, taken aback.

Through our exchange, I don't miss the nosey stares which belong to Sofia, Francisco, Kaden, Luca, and Angelo. Who have their mouths wide open at the sight of me serving a plate.

I shrug off their look of surprise and sit across from Victoria, who's quiet. Her hair covers her face from sight.

After breakfast, I instruct Luca to give Victoria and Sofia a house tour. This way, they don't get lost.

Before heading out, I pull Victoria aside.

"I'll be back. I have something to take care of. You have my word that you and your cousin are safe. When I get back, I will explain everything to you." I place a fallen strand of hair behind her ear, and she shudders when the pad of my thumb touches the edge of her ear.

I don't get to tell her anything else because Sofia pulls her toward Luca. I watch her disappear with a sigh before heading out to the Black Mercedes waiting for me.

Before I know it, we make it to one of the many hotels I own in France.

I fix my black suit jacket, grumbling in annoyance, wanting to be somewhere else, or rather, with someone else.

Francisco and a few of my men follow me into the hotel, taking their positions behind me.

The second my men and I enter the multi-purpose room, the girls share a look of fear. I can feel the tension in the air. It's thick with uncertainty as I make my way across the stage.

"I hear many of you are asking when you can leave. Which will happen as soon as I finish here," I assure them, and they relax from the news of going home. "But before you can leave, we need to go over some rules."

The girls panic, and the noise level rises. I'm quick to reassure them.

"You guys are not allowed to speak of this place or me to the officials or your family. If you do, I will find out, and you don't want to know what I'll do to you." There's a warning in my voice.

A woman with auburn hair raises her hand, and I let her speak.

"Does this mean we have to lie about where we've been all this time?" she asks, and many others nod, having the same question.

"You can tell them you were kidnapped. But when they ask how you escaped, tell them whatever you want. As long as you don't mention my men or me." The girl nods in understanding.

"Anything else?" I ask, and another girl raises her hand.

"It's not a question. I just want to say thank you for all you guys have done for us." As she says this, her eyes gloss over with tears.

I nod and walk off the stage to speak to the woman I put in charge of the girls.

"Have some of your staff help you categorize each girl by their location." I hand her a big envelope with one-way tickets to any location and some extra cash for transportation. "Also, please make sure they all sign one of these forms before leaving." I hand her another envelope with non-disclosure agreements. "Give them to Kaden when you have them all signed." She nods again before hurrying away to do what I've asked.

I head out of the building and back to the car.

"Now what?" Francisco says, and I keep my face straight as I look forward.

"How do you feel about staying in France for a few days?"

He shakes his head.

"This is because of *her*, isn't it?" I don't answer because he's right. Victoria is the exact reason I'm not on a plane heading back to Italy.

Taking my silence as an answer, Francisco sighs.

"You know she has a home where her family is probably freaking out looking for her, for both of them," he says, his expression dulling.

"I know. I want a little more time with her, that's all," I say, and Francisco looks stunned by my defeated tone. "She'll go home soon."

Unfortunately.

We make our way back to my estate in silence, and when I step into the living room, I see Victoria and Sofia laughing at a sleeping Luca.

The two have gotten comfortable and are no longer afraid of us. Luca's tour and charm have made them feel welcomed.

Their soft laughter fills the living room as they draw on Luca's face with a Sharpie marker. Which I may or may not have given them.

In my defense, declining Victoria's requests is hard—even impossible.

Luca snores, moving his head to the side, giving them better access to draw on his left cheek.

I laugh, noticing they drew a mustache, unibrow, and a dick smack dab on his forehead.

From the sound of my chuckle, Victoria looks at me with her infatuating smile. My breathing stills, and my cold heart warms from the sight.

If beauty is a person, she is it.

Francisco, Angelo, and Kaden walk into the room. They all burst out in obnoxious laughter when they see Luca on the couch, sleeping with his face tattooed by a Sharpie.

Kaden's lips, which never tip up, curve into a slight grin, and I'm surprised to see these two girls have made grouchy Kaden smile in a short amount of time.

Luca shuffles from his sleep and groans, scratching the top of his head.

"Can you all shut up? Some people are trying to sleep!" he grits in annoyance, unaware of the disaster on his face.

His sleep-filled eyes land on the two girls hovering near him, each holding a Sharpie marker.

Victoria and Sofia look at one another in a panic and chuck the markers into my hands. The smell of Sharpie is quick to drift to my nose.

"He did it!" they shout in unison, and the guys laugh again.

Luca's eyes widen, and he jumps from the couch, running to the mirror hanging on the wall on the other side of the room.

He gasps when he looks at his reflection and slowly turns to face the culprits.

"You two better run for the hills!" Luca says, prompting Sofia and Victoria to turn to each other in worry.

"You're both dead," he grits, trying to suppress his smile.

The next second, the two girls run out of the room.

"Catch us if you can!" they taunt, their heads peeking from behind the door. Luca groans in annoyance and runs after them.

I watch them go, certain that having them around will be a breath of fresh air for us all.

17

VICTORIA

Luca's charging after me and Sofia throughout the house.

We've been running for a while now, and I'm slowing down. But not Luca. He's still hot on our tails, approaching us at full speed.

His fingers graze my left shoulder blade, and I shriek, willing myself to run faster.

Sofia takes a sharp turn, disappearing to my left and leaving Luca to chase after me. I huff in annoyance because drawing on his face was her idea.

Up ahead, I see Leo coming out of a room. I run toward him, knowing Luca won't hurt me if he's nearby.

Noticing us, Leo raises a brow in surprise before his eyes widen when he sees how fast I'm running toward him.

I crash into his solid chest, and he doesn't stumble back from the force. He catches me as if I weigh nothing.

Luca approaches us, huffing, and Leo's hold loosens around my waist, allowing me to hide behind him.

A smile tugs at my lips when Luca groans in defeat. He then makes a beeline in the other direction and grumbles incoherent sentences under his breath.

Sofia appears from the corner with a grin.

"Nice mustache." Comes her snarky reply.

"Shut it!" Luca grunts, and she laughs.

My attention shift to Leo, who has a dazed, faraway expression.

"Is everything okay?" I ask.

He nods and grabs my right hand, giving it a gentle squeeze. His warmth brings a sense of comfort and protection.

I'm not sure what to think about his constant gestures of affection toward me. I know I should find them creepy, but for some weird reason, I don't.

My brain keeps telling me to stop falling for his charm. But my heart keeps skipping a beat anytime he treats me as if I'm his.

It's his stupid, handsome face that's making me go crazy!

Leo's voice breaks through my thoughts.

"I need to speak to you both." His expression and tone are unreadable, and this makes me nervous.

His comment from this morning comes to mind, and I realize he's going to tell us what he's going to do with us. A shiver runs through the length of my body. Afraid of what he has to say.

We nod, and he ushers us inside the room he was leaving earlier.

Sofia and I take a seat in front of Leo's desk. There's a tension in my body, and Sofia looks at me with a nervous expression.

"You asked me when you could go home..." Leo draws out.

"Yes," I mumble.

"Adriano and his men know I had something to do with your rescue." My eyes shoot up to stare at him, and I'm sure he can see the terror in my eyes.

Leo continues, his voice steady, "we're still not sure if he'll track down the girls he lost. Which is why you both need to stay here until we're certain he won't go after you both." As he says this, he shuffles the many papers on his desk, avoiding our stare.

His words have produced a hollowness inside me because I won't be going home, and now there's a possibility I'm still in danger.

Sofia's chair makes a harsh sound when she stands.

"Are you kidding me!" she shouts, her arms flinging around her in anger. I extend a hand to calm her, and she pushes me away, too consumed with distress.

Leo's face hardens, and he rises from his seat.

"Sit down." There's a warning in his voice, and Sofia shrinks back into her chair.

I bite my bottom lip, unsure of what to say because this Leo is a force I'm afraid of.

He wasn't kidding when he said he was bipolar.

Leo sits down with a sigh.

"Would you much rather go home and risk being taken again?" he asks Sofia in a calmer voice. She shakes her head and looks down at her hands resting on her lap.

"It's not fair! Why can't he leave us alone? I want to go home and forget this ever happened." She swipes at her fallen tears, and I place a hand on her forearm.

The grief of not seeing my family after what happened has also upset me, but I don't cry because crying won't help us escape the mess we've been thrown into. We need to be grateful Leo is willing to protect us and has given us a place to stay until it's safe to leave.

"Sofia, I understand you miss your family. But if we need to stay here a little longer to make sure we're safe. Then we need to be thankful we're here together." Her teary eyes meet my stare, and she sighs before nodding in understanding.

"How long do we have to stay here?" she asks.

"Maybe two weeks, or at least until we're sure it's safe for you both to return home." When he says this, he's watching us, waiting for our rejection. We give none and instead nod in understanding.

Sofia rises from her seat, saying she's tired when she's really missing her family.

As she leaves, she casts her head down, and I feel hopeless when I can't do anything to ease her grief.

Leo and I are the only ones in the room now, and I can feel his intense eyes holding me in place, making me nervous.

"Thank you for everything, Leo. I don't even want to think about what would have happened to us if you all didn't save us when you did." I say, my voice trembling. Memories of the girls still trapped with Adriano flood my mind, and tears well up in my eyes. Erika comes to mind, and my chest becomes heavy from the last memory I have of her.

My words have upset Leo, and he makes his way over to me and crouches beside me.

"I will always protect you," he says, his eyes looking right into mine, and it's as if time has slowed. My heart is beating fast with him close to me, and I can see there's a question he wants to ask me, but he's afraid to say it.

"You're probably wondering how Sofia and I got trafficked." My tone is a little off and the words come out, and I'm also aware my hands are shaking in my lap.

He notices the fear rising inside me, and his big, warm hands seize mine into a tender embrace. With his comfort, I explain pieces of what happened during my kidnapping.

He's quiet, and his jaw hardens as I tell him what I saw and what they did to us.

Throughout our conversation, I find myself with the urge to ask if he can rescue the others, but I'm not sure how to tell him, or if asking him for this favor is even possible. But I still can't forget about the other girls. Especially Erika, who has no one looking for her other than me.

"What's wrong?" Leo asks when he notices my turmoil.

I sigh. "Everything's been so crazy, and I feel bad because I got saved, but others like Erika didn't." My face is warm from my tears, and the pain I harbor inside me leaves with each droplet. "I can't go on knowing he's still hurting her and many others. To top it all off, I ruined the trip for the rest of my classmates by getting kidnapped." I scoff, angry at how messed up this trip turned out.

Leo grabs my chin, and his touch is soft. I stare into his jade eyes and almost lose myself in the green hues.

"It's normal to experience survivor's guilt after everything you've been through," he says, voice velvety. His thumb rubs the skin near my fading bruise, and he stares at my busted lip, anger washing over his expression for a second.

"I can't promise to make the pain disappear, but I can try my best to help in any way possible." He's now cupping my face between his hands, and I'm sure he can hear me breathing hard from how close he is. "I'll see if Luca can track where Adriano has Erika, so we can rescue her and the rest of the girls."

"You would do that?"

Leo flashes me a smile when he notices my wide-eyed expression.

"I'll do whatever it takes to make you happy."

I'm silent as I stare at him. My heart beats vigorously from his words.

I'm not sure how to read his comment. Whether he's simply a decent human being who wants to help another person in need, or if there's another reason why my happiness is important to him. Regardless, his words have sent a wave of warmth through me, and there's no controlling the tumbling in my stomach.

"But I won't be able to get her out within a few days because things have become complicated." He sighs. "Adriano won't be as careless as before."

I nod in understanding and wrap my arms around him. His musky scent sticks to my skin.

"Thank you so much, Leo."

His arms wrap around me, and his chin grazes the top of my head. When I pull back, I feel intense happiness from his promise to save the others. I'm not sure what takes over me, but I kiss him on the cheek, and heat rises to my face when I pull away.

Way to be embarrassing, Victoria! I groan and mentally facepalm myself.

Leo says nothing about what I've done and instead lets out a soft laugh, the corners of his mouth lifting into a slight smile.

I put a strand of hair behind my right ear to distract myself from the tension between us, and Leo's eyes fall onto my torn earlobe. His face hardens.

"Which of the bastards did this to you?" His voice is deep, and a nerve ticks in his jaw.

"I—I—" I stutter, completely losing my train of thought from this dominating yet comforting side of him.

I draw in a deep sigh.

"I forgot to tell you, but when they kidnapped me, they put a bag over my head. When I got one of them to release me, I tore the bag off, and my earring got caught with it," I mutter, watching his eyes simmer with an unknown emotion. "So I guess I'm the said bastard," I say, trying to make light of the situation.

Leo's face contorts into disapproval at my comment.

"I'm sorry I wasn't there to help you sooner. But I'm here now, and no one will ever hurt you again. If anyone even tries to hurt you, I'll cut their hand off myself," he grits out, and I'm not sure if he's only saying this to make me feel better or if he's being serious.

Leo's eyes waver to a stack of papers on his desk, and then back to me.

"Victoria, since you and Sofia never got to see much of France, how would you feel about having us show you two around Paris?"

I shuffle in my seat at his words.

"You don't have to do that. You've already done so much for me. I wouldn't want to be a burden."

"You're not a burden, Victoria." The corner of his mouth tugs into a frown. "Let me show you around France. You deserve it after everything they put you through."

I let out a heavy breath and give a hesitant nod. Leo smiles, pleased with my answer.

"But you have to promise to stay by my side." This time he speaks in a deep, firm tone, like my dad. I laugh at his overprotectiveness, and he looks at me with curiosity.

"What's so funny?"

"You sound like my dad." When I say this, Leo's forehead scrunches, and his eyes widen. My words have brought an obvious grimace to his expression.

"Your dad?" he says in disbelief.

LEO

When Victoria kissed my cheek, her lips against my skin brought tingles to my body. This unfamiliar sensation that I once called a weakness brings pleasure, and I want more of it. Her touch makes me feel good.

I can't stop myself from growing attached to her. She smells nice, she's beautiful, and her long hair swooshes behind her like the finest drapes from Egypt. Being around her makes my heart race. I'm falling faster than I thought, and this scares me.

"Your dad?" My voice comes out slightly off from her comment.

Did she dad-zone me? Is that even a thing?

Victoria's laughing, and the back of my neck turns warm. My mind is going crazy after being compared to her dad. I'm not that much older than her.

"You should see your face!" She places a hand on her chest, her cheeks are stretched from how wide she's smiling, and her smile, God, her smile is so gorgeous it's like I'm looking at an angel.

I send her a teasing glare.

Normally, when anyone makes fun of me, they find themselves with my fist in their face, but not Victoria. Hell, she could slap me with a whipped cream pie, and I won't care as long as it means I can hear her beautiful laugh and see her smiling like she is right now.

"Your dad though?" I say with a slight grimace, and she bites her top lip to stop from grinning. "Do you think I'm that old?"

She shakes her head, and I let out a breath.

"I said you sound like my dad, not you look like my dad." Her voice still holds a level of tease.

"Oh." I scratch the back of my neck, and her face glows with amusement.

I rise from my crouched position near her, and she cranes her neck to look at me.

When I extend my hand, she only takes a second before placing her delicate hand in mine, allowing me to help her out of her seat. I guide us out of my office, not ready to let her go. Not when I've been waiting to spend time with her since she woke up yesterday.

"Where are we going?" she breathes, trying to keep up with my long strides. I slow my steps when I remember her legs are much shorter than mine.

"What do you like doing for fun?" I ask, wanting to get to know the woman who has my heart beating in my ears and my hands turning clammy.

She thinks for a second before her beautiful smile graces my sight.

"I like to read." She pauses, biting the inside of her mouth. "I also like to take pictures of nature and architecture."

"Do you trust me?" I ask when an idea comes to mind.

Victoria's cheeks flush with color.

"Although we just met, I do trust you," she says in a whisper, and my heart skips a beat from her answer. With her words, I'm certain that if I died right now, I'd die a happy man.

My heart races as I take us to the backyard toward the mini-Versailles Gardens. When we're outside, she gasps and releases herself from my hand. She runs toward a rose bush, looking at the surrounding greenery in awe. The pad of her finger brushes along the soft velvet red petals, and I soak in the sight of her.

Victoria's eyes sparkle in excitement, and she's more vibrant than the red roses she's touching.

I send a quick message to Francisco asking him to do me a favor, and his reply comes within a second. It wouldn't be Francisco if he didn't tease me about Victoria. But I can't help it. I want to do something special for her. If it was that easy, I would give her the world in a heartbeat.

"Where I come from, we don't have many gardens or architecture like this," she says, looking at me and motioning to the mansion behind us.

I approach her with slow steps, asking her to elaborate, wanting to learn as much as I can about her before our time together ends.

"Sofia and I are from Southern California, where everything is as dry as this rose." She plucks a dead rose from the bush and crumbles it between her fingers.

I let out a breathless laugh at her little joke.

"Tell me more about you," I edge, and she smiles, sitting on the grass.

"What do you want to know?" She looks at me and lifts her right hand to block the sun from beaming into her eyes.

"Everything," I reply, sitting beside her and using my body to shield her from the sun.

Her lips curve into a slight smile.

"I'm about to be nineteen. I'm a middle child...What else...? Oh yeah, I want to study business."

From the mention of her wanting to study business, I have to contain my laughter at how ironic our situations are. She's literally perfect. I just know we would make a powerful team if there's any chance of us ever being together.

I nod and listen to her words with interest, finding myself more mesmerized by her.

"What about you? I want to know who Leo—" She pauses in thought, looking curious, and a frown appears on her face. "See, I don't even know your last name."

"Bandoni," I answer, looking at the rose bushes ahead.

"What?" she says, her face scrunched in confusion.

"My last name is Bandoni, I'm twenty-four, and I live in Italy," I tell her the basics of who I am without mentioning my work. She doesn't need to know she's sitting beside the Don of the Italian mafia. This information is enough to send a grown man running, and she's barely warming up to me.

"What do you do for a living? You seem to be loaded. Are you some famous actor or something?" she asks, and I catch the teasing note in her words.

I laugh at her comment.

"Sorry to disappoint, but I'm not an actor," I say with humor. "I'm a businessperson. Let's leave it at that," I tell her, and she nods in understanding, but I can tell my answer hasn't convinced her.

She nibbles on her bottom lip, and my heart rate speeds up from the gesture. She doesn't notice how her little nervous habit frustrates me because her eyes are busy looking around the garden.

I push aside the desire to kiss her and focus on the receding sunset. We continue to talk like I have wanted to do since I first laid my eyes on her, and by the end of the night, a newfound sense of comfort forms between us.

It's as if the last few hours we spent together have created a bridge I can use to cross over to where she is. Talking to her came easily, and that's saying a lot since I'm a man of little words.

The loud ringing from my phone disrupts the comfortable silence between us.

Despite the noise, Victoria's eyes don't waver. They continue to stare ahead in deep solitude. I can't take my eyes off the side of her face, which is glowing from the fiery orange hues of the sunset.

The sound of my phone going off continues, and this time Victoria emerges from her trance.

She looks at me, and my face becomes warm when she catches me staring at her. Her brows lift as if asking me whether I'm going to answer the call or not.

I inwardly groan and pull out my phone to check the caller ID. I panic when the name of Cleo's guard flashes on the screen.

Victoria's forehead creases, having sensed my agitation.

"Good evening, boss. Sorry to interrupt. But your sister was worried when you never returned when you promised." Cleo's guard's voice fills my ear.

"Put me on speaker," I tell him, and I talk to my sister. "Cleo, I'm sorry I forgot to tell you. I'm going to stay in France longer than I thought." I glance at Victoria, who's staring at the water fountain ahead. "Something came up..."

Her guard tells me what she signs.

"Boss, she's annoyed, but she wishes you the best. She says—" He pauses, and I hear his conversation with Cleo. "Do I have to say it?" he grumbles at what she signs. "Fine, she says she loves you." There's a hint of discomfort in his words, and I laugh.

"I love you too, Cleo." From beside me, Victoria briefly turns tense. I turn to see what's wrong and sigh in relief when I find her safely watching the Eiffel Tower. "Cleo, I have to go, but I'll see you in a few weeks," I assure her before getting held up talking to her guard, who tells me everything that has happened since I left Italy.

By the time I end the call, the sun has disappeared, and Victoria has fallen asleep.

Her head rests on my shoulder, and her soft breathing comforts me.

I smile, caressing the top of her head, and I'm gentle as I lift her and carry her back inside.

Like the first time I held her in my arms, she molds perfectly into my body.

18

VICTORIA

"Why do I have a blindfold on again?" I ask Leo, and his right arm wrapped around me tightens as he leads me through the house.

This is the third time I've asked him this question, and this time he responds by sighing in annoyance.

"I told you already. I have a surprise for you," comes his reply, and I can imagine him shaking his head in disbelief.

I nudge him on the side.

"That's not what I meant," I explain, tilting my head toward his voice.

"And you don't know what a surprise means." His tone is sarcastic and if I didn't have a blindfold on, he'd see me rolling my eyes.

The new teasing tone and light air to Leo remind me of how he's a different person today. He's more excited and less tense than before. It's as if he's changed overnight.

He has this rough exterior around him. His shoulders are always rigid and hostile. He also carries himself with a dominating force, which is so strong it chokes you with fear and intimidation. But now, the rough edges he carries himself with are barely there. Nevertheless, the little voice in my head still warns me that something is wrong.

Leo has secrets, but what are they? Who is he really? I'm not sure, and he won't tell me.

I don't know if he's the Leo from a few days ago, who pulled me by the wrist as if possessed with anger or if he's the Leo who woke me up this morning with a charming smile.

I don't have the answers to these questions, and it's the only thing I can focus on as he guides me through the house.

The vague response he gave me yesterday didn't sit comfortably with me.

"I'm a businessperson; let's leave it at that," is what he told me, but what did the *"let's leave it at that,"* even mean?

"Victoria?" Leo calls out, and he has a perfect eyebrow arched in concern.

I no longer have the blindfold, and I'm standing unfazed.

"Sorry," I reply sheepishly. Leo smiles, stepping aside to reveal the enormous buffet behind him. At the sight of the terrace overlooking the beautiful gardens, my mouth widens. A silent "wow" is all I can muster.

An array of pastries, fruits, jams, and much more is spread across the vintage white rectangular bistro table.

"Leo, this is amazing!" A hand rests over my chest as I take in the sight of the French breakfast.

"I have another surprise," he tells me, pulling out a white bag from behind him. At the sight of the familiar Chanel shopping bag, my eyes widen.

"Leo, I can't take that," I say, pushing the bag toward him, knowing whatever is inside is expensive.

"You don't know what it is," he complains.

"It doesn't matter." I cross my arms over my chest, and Leo grins at my reaction. "I'm serious. I can't accept it."

"Why not?" Three little lines appear on his forehead as he says this.

"Because you've done so much for me already. It would be wrong of me to take advantage of your money like this."

Leo grabs my hand and leads me to the table. As soon as I sit down, he places the bag on my lap.

"At least open it," he begs, sitting beside me.

I give a hesitant glance before slowly removing the tissue paper.

My fingers touch a soft material, and I pull out a white tweed Chanel jacket with a matching white skirt that has black stitching. At the bottom of the bag is a box with a pair of beautiful black booties with chunky heels.

I stare at the gift in surprise, and before I can say anything about how expensive it is, his eyes narrow into a warning.

"You will accept it and wear it today because I can't have you roaming around Paris wearing my t-shirt. Even if you look good in it." His eyes trail from my face to the black t-shirt I'm wearing, and the temperature in my body rises, despite my attempts to stop it. It's wrong for me to feel the little flutters when he's nearby. He has Cleo waiting for him in Italy.

His conversation with her yesterday told me where things will always stand between us.

Before I even knew it, I found myself hiding behind a dark curtain, and the imaginary veil was keeping me from seeing the truth behind Leo's intentions. I now know he's only been friendly. But I mistook his affection for what I secretly craved.

The little flutters I get when he's near have blinded me. He already loves someone else, and I'm setting myself up for heartache if I don't create some distance between us, and fast.

I say nothing and glance at the table. Too afraid to speak because my voice might break and reveal how much he makes me nervous.

Leo serves me a plate of food, and I stare at him, wondering how I will survive the next few days without growing more attached to him than I already am.

Our time together the previous evening was dangerous. Before I was able to use the excuse that it was his good looks that made me weak to the knees, and it still is, but after speaking with him and learning certain things about him, I can't help but feel like I know a little more of him, and I like what he's shown me. It doesn't help that he's always taking care of me, whether that be checking in on how I'm feeling, serving me food, or just being there for me.

My stare remains on him, and he looks handsome in his all-black fitted suit, which outlines his muscles perfectly. I feel as my heart sinks because he's the right amount of captivating, alluring, gentle, and mysterious.

How couldn't I fall for him?

The sound of feet and an angry shout makes us turn to the door where a soaking wet Sofia marches after Francisco, who has a satisfied grin on his lips.

When she reaches Francisco, she stops in front of him and stomps her foot over his right one with a huff.

Francisco curses in Italian and jumps on a foot, massaging where Sofia has crushed his toes with her weight.

"Never pour water on me when I'm sleeping." She glares at him and crosses her arms over her wet-clad shirt.

Leo clears his throat, catching their attention.

Sofia turns toward us and sends a sweet smile my way. Her eyes widen when she sees the food, and her mouth falls open.

She pushes Francisco aside, and when he almost falls, he glares at her.

"Food!" she squeals, running to the table and sitting across from me. Her anger and drenched body are forgotten as she serves herself a plate.

Francisco grumpily sits beside Sofia, and she sends him a disapproving glance. She huffs and childishly turns her head toward me. Her wet hair splashes Francisco, and he wipes under his eye with a flick of his finger.

Leo and I glance at the two trying to suppress our comments.

After breakfast, Leo and Francisco leave to do some last-minute work. With them gone, Sofia and I have time to talk and get dressed for our day trip around Paris.

Sofia and I plan to get ready together, but she disappears without a trace.

I smooth out the material of the Chanel outfit when arms wrap around me from behind. A smile falls into place, but it dampens when I see Sofia. The reaction is one I'm not proud of.

She sees the frown and her lips tip up.

"What was that?" comes her teasing remark, and her fingers pinch my left cheek.

I slap her hands off me.

"It's nothing. Now, where have you been?" I rush out before she can tease me.

Sofia blushes and her response is one only produced by oxytocin, which I am also suffering from, as much as I want to deny it.

"Oh, you know, *around*," she says, waving a dismissive hand.

"Is that code for *with Francisco*?" I tease, receiving a flustered scowl from Sofia.

"Oh, you want to start?" Hearing the threat in her words, I shake my head swiftly, and we laugh, only to silence when we hear a steady knock from behind.

We turn around to find Leo and Francisco waiting by the door. They lead us to the car waiting outside and thankfully don't question our previous laughter.

As we make our way to the city, I'm once more excited to explore Paris. But this time, I'm not afraid because Leo is with me.

From the corner of my eye, I notice Leo glances at Francisco, who nods. It's as if they're having a telepathic conversation.

I ignore them and stare out the front of the car when I feel a heavy weight on my lap. With furrowed brows, I look at the source of the weight to find a baby blue box.

I glance at Leo, and he's already looking at me. Disbelief once again rises inside of me from receiving yet another gift from him.

Sofia, to my left, nudges me to open it, and I can practically hear her beaming in excitement.

"Seriously, Leo?"

He gives me a boyish grin. "Let me spoil you."

The words *'spoil Cleo'* are at the tip of my tongue, but I don't say them because I'm a coward around him. Instead, I push the gift back into his hands, rougher than I intended, which makes the contents inside shuffle.

Leo frowns but masks it when he places the box back onto my lap.

"Open it, and I'll take it back if you still don't want it," he says, and I suck in a breath from his dejected tone.

I look once more from the box to him.

"Fine, but I'm not happy with you wasting your money on me. You're already taking us around Paris after saving our lives. I'm the one who owes you, not the other way around," I mumble, and he places a hand on mine.

"You owe me nothing." His voice is firm, and I don't say anything because I'm too busy trying to contain my beating heart.

"Can you promise me no more presents if I open it?" I beg with my hands pressed together in front of me.

"I'll think about it." His grin stretches when he notices my unimpressed expression.

Sighing, I unwrap the white ribbon and open the lid. When I see what's inside, my eyes widen in shock.

"Leo," I breathe, looking at him and then at the Nikon camera with wide eyes. "This is too expensive." I hand him the box.

Why does he keep buying me expensive stuff?

He pushes it back into my hands.

"You said you owe me for saving you..." he draws out, and I nod. "Well, I want you to take the camera, and we can call it even."

I jerk my head back.

"That's not how it works," I say incredulously.

"It is if I say so," he replies smugly, and my gaze shoots up at him, ready to argue, when Sofia cuts me off.

"Victoria, if you don't take the camera, I will." The corners of her mouth are lifted into a smile. I look from my cousin to Leo, who's waiting to see what I'll do.

I groan when I realize I won't be winning this battle. My mouth shuts and I swallow my reproach, giving a defeated nod.

Leo's face lightens with a smile, and I again struggle to fight off the butterflies he stirs in my stomach.

Leo

Victoria smiles in awe as she looks at the famous art around her. Her smile brings a lightness to my chest, and a smile rises to my stiff lips.

An impatient sigh comes from her.

"Leo, come on, you're walking so slow," she whines, grabbing my hand and dragging me through the Louvre. Behind us, Sofia and Francisco are arguing as per usual.

"I want to see the Mona Lisa," Victoria breaks off before rising on her tippy toes, trying to see past the mob of people surrounding the famous da Vinci painting.

As we reach the portrait, she whispers her disbelief and I let out a small laugh at her obvious disappointment.

"It's so small."

"It is, isn't it?" I mumble, standing behind her, using my body to shield her from being pushed by the surrounding people. She looks up at me through her thick lashes. She's so close I can see every perfect edge of her face, and my heart does a little skip at how beautiful she is.

Victoria fidgets nervously and clears her throat, her eyes looking anywhere but at me.

I let out a breath and grab her hand, leading her through the rest of the museum. Afterward we go to Tuileries Garden, and I find myself grinning at her excitement at the simplest things.

Victoria hands her camera to Sofia, and she surprises me by grabbing my hand and pulling me to stand to her right.

"Smile!" Sofia chirps, snapping a picture of us. I don't turn to the camera because I'm too busy looking at Victoria and her gorgeous smile. Her almond-shaped eyes glow like amber when the sunlight hits the irises.

With Victoria near, my heart races, and I lose all my senses. She's the only person who has this effect on me, and I don't know what to do to control myself around her.

"Leo, you weren't looking at the camera." As the words leave Victoria, Sofia whispers something to her, and her cheeks burn a deep red, making Sofia's grin widen.

I take the camera from Victoria and stare at the image, trying to engrave it into my mind. Not wanting to forget how perfect she looks standing beside me.

This morning I promised myself I would push the thought of

having to part from her aside, and it's like a switch has turned on inside me.

While I have her near, I'm determined to live in the present and not think about the future. For once, I want to experience something other than being angry and cold.

Today is for her.

I hand her the camera.

"We have two more places to go to," I tell her, and she nods, allowing me to take her to the car.

When the car stops in front of the Opera house, Victoria and Sofia run out and stare at the building in awe.

As Francisco appears behind Sofia, Victoria takes a picture of the two who are, to my surprise, getting along.

When she nears me, she shows me the picture of them. Right away, I notice how Francisco has his arm around Sofia's shoulder while her face is attentive, listening to what he tells her.

I shake my head, a smile on my face, knowing what Victoria is inferring from the little twinkle in her eyes.

The sun is now setting, and we make our way toward the last destination, the Eiffel Tower.

When we arrive, Victoria and Sofia crane their necks to stare at the Eiffel Tower looming over us.

Awe shimmers in both their eyes, which makes Francisco and I send one another a satisfied grin.

"It's more beautiful up close," Victoria whispers in awe, and I lead her toward the elevator, which will take us to the top of the Eiffel Tower. Everything after is a blur, as I'm too infatuated by the happiness visible on Victoria's face.

Even when we ascend to the top I'm only interested in looking at her, not the city.

Victoria's engrossed looking out the glass window. Her eyes light up like the city lights below, and her wide smile is permanent.

Our hands are side by side, and I can feel her warmth.

I rub the pad of my thumb and forefinger together. The imaginable force between us returns, and the temptation is too much to fight. I lace our fingers together like I want.

Victoria shifts her attention from the window to our hands. Tears gather in her eyes, and I panic, afraid I've upset her.

"What's wrong?" I use the pad of my thumb to wipe her tear.

"Thank you for today. I don't know how I can ever repay you." Victoria's voice breaks, and she wraps her arms around my torso, pressing her cheek against my chest.

I hold her tight and lace my fingers through her soft hair. She looks up at me, and I want to lift her chin and press my lips to hers. But I don't because if I kiss her, I'll grow more attached than I already am.

Kissing her will be like divulging in a rich red wine. There's no such thing as one sip because one taste is all it ever takes for you to want more.

Victoria has captivated me from the moment I laid my eyes on her. But now that I know a little about who she is, she has bewitched me with every single part of who she is. Victoria has me in her grip, and she's somehow turned me into someone I didn't know I could become. I can't help but feel like she's the other half I've been missing.

She's as gentle as a red rose and as fiery as its bright red pedals.

A lively rose in a bundle of pansies I don't dare pluck.

"Being here with you is enough," I whisper, and her cheeks burn bright.

The lift stops moving, and the doors open. I take Victoria's hand, savoring her touch before it disappears for good. She leads us toward one of the Eiffel Tower's legs, and I watch as she touches the wrought iron with her free hand.

I place my hand beside hers, and she looks at me with a smile and takes a picture of our hands.

She shows me the picture, and my heart beats hard at seeing her tiny hand beside mine.

Her being here is enough, but for how long is the real question.

With each passing day, we are closer to separating, and it reminds me of how nothing lasts forever. Not when you run a mafia.

My father lost the love of his life because of the violence in our world, and I promised myself when I held my mother's lifeless body that I would never fall in love.

I can't let history repeat itself.

19

VICTORIA

I wouldn't have believed it if someone told me my summer would end with me kidnapped and rescued by a handsome Italian man who's now made it his mission to protect me. Yet here I am, side by side with the said man, walking through his own Versailles Garden.

I take a quick peek at Leo, and marvel at how his all-black suit doesn't have a single wrinkle in sight. He's the image of a million dollars.

A lump forms in my throat as I glance down at the pair of jeans and the black T-shirt I'm wearing. The contrast in our styles creates a distance between us, and there's no denying Leo and I are different.

I try not to dwell on this thought for long because it will only make me feel worse.

The tips of my fingers caress the bright pink tulips, and the trees dance with the chilly breeze in the air. Another gust of wind comes and I shiver, wrapping my arms around myself.

Leo shuffles, removing his suit jacket. My heart races as he wraps it over my shoulders. His warmth and musky scent quickly seep into my skin.

A lone strand of his hair falls from its slick back tousled style. I stare at it, and my fingers itch to reach out and put it back in its place. But I restrain myself. Instead, I admire his handsome face.

Leo is one of the most handsome men I have ever seen. A step up from the pubescent high schoolers I graduated with.

He isn't your typical looking twenty-four-year-old. He has the maturity you expect from a thirty-year-old man.

Our eyes lock, and my face gets hot beneath his gaze.

I find myself trapped by his stare. The seconds tick, and there's an all too familiar stirring in my stomach. My nervous habit of biting my bottom lip returns, and I try to ignore the tingly feelings spreading across my body.

Leo lifts his left hand and moves a strand of my hair behind my ear. The pad of his finger grazes the side of my face, and a shaky breath leaves my mouth.

I watch his Adam's Apple move up and down when he swallows, and my stare falls on his full pink lips, which have never looked plumper and more kissable.

I roll my dry lips into my mouth, wetting them. Leo's gaze drops to my mouth, and his eyes darken with a deep, emerald hue.

The tension between us fizzles with temptation. To ease my nerves, I look anywhere but at his hypnotic eyes, and my stare lands behind him at the round, pillared gazebo. I'm in awe at the sight of it.

Leo notices my reaction and grabs my hand. Our fingers interlock, and I can't help but stare down at them with a smile.

Things between us have changed since he took me around Paris three days ago. He's always with me, and we're always talking, and it's nice until I remember Cleo.

Although we always talk, he never mentions her, which is confusing. The way he spoke to her last time on the phone sounded like he really loves her, but he never expresses his love for her to me. I know there's still a possibility she can be someone other than a lover, but even if isn't with her romantically, I can never be with him. Eventually we'll have to part ways, and what will happen then? Heartbreak, that's what.

Leo leads us across the bridge over the small river. Now in front of the gazebo, I notice the dozens of daisies that grow around it like a veil of nature raining over the white marble platform.

Around us, nature's soft tune is playing, and when I enter the dome, my eyes shoot up to the ceiling. The sunlight shines through the glass panels, and a little rainbow is born. I lift my hand, allowing the rainbow streak to graze my palm.

I wish I could freeze time and stay like this with him forever. But it's not possible. Life goes on, and people come and go from your life.

He's going to forget about me when I go home.

This thought brings a pinch to my chest.

Through the corner of my eye, I peek at him, leaning on the railing. His eyes are busy looking out at his property.

Sensing my stare, he turns to me and gives me a gentle smile. The little grin has my knees turning to jello. I curse my heart for making me feel this way. But no matter how hard I push my crush for him aside, I can't do it. The feelings he brings to me are no longer sprouting but blooming like a rose bush in spring.

It's impossible not to fall for him when he's gentle, caring, and protective. Men like him are hard to find.

Leo's gaze falls on a bush of daisies to the side of the dome, and I see a hint of grief washing over his expression.

"My mom and I planted those together," he confesses, a sad smile playing on his lips as he plucks a daisy and puts it behind my ear.

"They're beautiful," I reply, admiring the bright white flowers.

I want to ask him about his mother after I noticed the hint of sadness talking about her has brought him, but I don't dare ask because I don't want to overstep any boundaries. I also don't expect him to tell me anything of sentimental value.

The sun is disappearing, and it's getting cold.

Leo and I make our way back inside. His long legs mean his strides are wider and faster than mine. He's a few feet ahead of me, and I don't mind as I can admire his wide back, thick with muscles.

My spine locks up, and my shoulders stiffen when I notice something sticking out near his waist.

I stop walking at the sight of the gun, and the color drains from my face. The weightless sensation in my stomach disappears and turns into heavy fear.

Leo notices I've stopped walking and turns around to look at me with furrowed brows. As he stares at me with worry, the fantasies I created about him become overpowered with uncertainty.

His comment about being a businessperson has to be a lie. The gun is proof enough.

I surrender to the nagging suspicion I pushed at the back of my mind, and I reflect on everything that has happened since he saved me.

Leo must be someone powerful to break into Adriano's sex house. The way he killed Richard with his fist, turning my attacker's face into smashed flesh. No regular person can do that, and no ordinary businessperson would ever go out of their way to save a few girls. Unless he's some undercover agent or bodyguard. I'm not sure what to think.

I take slow steps toward him, keeping a safe distance between us. The gun tucked behind him reminds me of how he isn't who he says he is, and my heart twists at this thought.

His face morphs into concern when he senses my hesitation to get closer to him.

I tuck my hands into the pockets of his jacket, and I'm not sure if I should ask why he has a gun or if I should pretend like I never saw it.

"Victoria," Leo says, closing the distance between us, and when he tries to place a hand on my arm, I move aside. His face deepens with worry. "What's wrong?"

"Nothing." I stare at the ground, and my words are steady despite the apprehension coursing through my veins.

He sighs in frustration, and his thumb and forefinger clutch my chin, lifting my face.

"Nothing, really?" He lifts a brow, and his tone is sarcastic.

I let out a shaky breath, trying to find the courage to tell him what's been bothering me. The words are at the tip of my tongue.

"Leo, who are you?"

My question surprises him, and his posture goes rigid.

"What do you mean?" he asks with a hint of panic.

"Are you really a businessperson?"

"Of course I am," he says indignantly.

My lips roll into my mouth, and I tilt my head to meet his eyes. I can smell his aftershave when I step closer and wrap my arms around his waist. He holds his breath.

"Then why do you have a gun?" As the words flow from my lips, I pull the weapon from behind him and place it against his chest.

His eyes widen.

"Victoria..." He glances from my face to my shaky hands, and he peels my fingers off the gun, taking it away from me.

"Well?" I wait for his response, holding my ground.

Leo puts the gun away. He sets his lips into a thin line, and he doesn't know what to say.

"I have a gun to protect you from Adriano." Leo's words hold a sense of confidence, and his disregard for my question is making my blood boil. He's making me feel like I'm overthinking everything.

Is he gaslighting me?

"See, that's the thing. I don't understand why *you* are protecting me from Adriano," I blurt, frustrated, and he stills under my gaze.

"Why are you protecting me from Adriano?" I whisper, voice rough as I try to hold back the tears of frustration that want to fall from being lied to by him, of all people.

After another long pause, a noisy exhale leaves him.

"Mi stai uccidendo." he says, voice thick and rough with emotions.

I blink. His words, which I don't understand, echo in my mind. I gasp when he pulls me into him, pressing our chests together. He cups my face, and his touch is warm against my cold cheeks.

"Do you really want to know?" he asks, staring at me.

Yes! I want to shout, but all I can muster is a weak nod, too captivated by our proximity.

His eyes fall to my mouth when I bite my bottom lip.

"Damn it, Victoria, because I want to!" Frustration clouds his expression, and I'm stunned by his agitation. "You drive me insane," he mutters, cupping my chin.

I can hear my heart thumping in my ears. Fear, desire, and confusion combine, fogging my brain.

Leo leans forward, and his nose caresses mine. He's going to close the distance between us, and my lips tingle with anticipation.

"Leo, I have the—Oh shit!" Luca's voice lifts the fog from inside my mind, and my senses rush back. I push away from Leo, no longer captivated by his stare. Those green eyes of his are both comforting and deceiving.

I look toward a grinning Luca, whose blond brows rise. His amusement increases as he looks between my flustered self and an angry Leo.

Luca opens his mouth, but I don't hear what he says because I run away.

I ignore the strange looks the men inside give me as rush to the room I've been staying in. Once inside, I lean against the door, trying to ease my racing heart.

"This is not good," I whisper, the pad of my fingers touching my lips. Leo's scent is in the air, and my stomach knots in pleasure. The constant flutters he brings me are worrisome.

Leo Bandoni is driving me insane, and I don't know how to protect my poor heart from the unavoidable heartbreak sure to come.

2 0

LEO

I glare at a grinning Luca, but a grimace quickly replaces my anger when I remember how fast Victoria ran away.

I can still feel her warmth, and it causes a stirring in my stomach.

Despite my best efforts, I can't seem to push her away. It's impossible for me not to fall for her when she has the rosiest cheeks, radiant brown eyes, plump lips, gorgeous warm brown skin, and long black hair, which I want to run my fingers through. And her smile... *fuck*, it's the most beautiful thing I've ever seen.

A few seconds ago, I was ready to swoop her in my arms and take her to Italy. The more she questions me and becomes frustrated, the more I want to tell her who I am and make her mine. It sounds easy, but it isn't. Nothing is ever easy. Not when you run a network of crime organizations. Bringing her into my life is equivalent to putting a gun against her head.

I'm brought out of my daze when Luca pinches my right cheek. I push his hand away, and he laughs.

"Well, if I do say so myself, it looks like you're infatuated with Victoria." His eyebrows lift suggestively.

"What do you want?" I ask, tone flat.

Luca's arrogant smile falters when I don't confirm or deny his accusations.

"You're no fun," he says, handing me a large envelope.

I mutter unpleasant things to him as I make my way inside. The document he handed me reveals Adriano hasn't tried kidnapping the girls we rescued. We still don't know where he's hiding. But I know one thing: Adriano will be back for vengeance, and Victoria can't be anywhere near when it comes.

My time in France with her is ending. I can feel it. The longer she's with me, the more she suspects my identity. Soon I won't be able to keep her in the dark.

The half-lie I fed her fills me with guilt, but in my defense, I didn't lie to her. I am a businessperson. She simply didn't ask what kind of business I did.

I let out a breath remembering how she shivered from my touch and how her eyes darkened.

If Luca hadn't come when he did, I would have thrown all my restraints out of the window and kissed her, and she was ready to let me.

Luca, to my left, is looking at me, and he finds humor in my distress.

The left side of his mouth tips up, and he makes kissy faces.

Heat rushes up my body, reaching my face.

When he's going to say something stupid, I cut him off.

"Ti spezzerò le gambe." There's an edge to my voice, and he dodges my fist. All I hear is his obnoxious laughter as he rushes away from me.

21

VICTORIA

Loud music blasts throughout the kitchen and Spanish words come from Sofia's mouth as she sings while cutting meat for today's dinner.

I find myself humming the cumbia song while shredding some mozzarella cheese.

Luca kept asking if we could cook some more Mexican food, and because Sofia and I are thankful for all they have done for us, regardless of how secretive they are, we gave in to Luca's persistence. After all, they saved our lives and treated us like visitors, not prisoners. But this doesn't mean I'm not angry about the lies I know are being thrown at me.

Leo keeps lying to me and tiptoeing around my questions. It's aggravating, but at the same time I want to kiss him for how he speaks to me as if he wants me. It's hard to stay angry at him when my nerves coil whenever he holds me close.

To forget about these mixed feelings, I turned to making the traditional Mexican Sopes dish with Sofia and Luca, who tried to help us cook. However, we quickly realized he was only making a mess and decided it was best if he stayed as far away as possible.

The music is so loud we don't hear when Leo and Francisco enter the kitchen. I only know they are here when Francisco scares Sofia, who responds by throwing a piece of raw meat at his face. It lands on his lips, and he grimaces.

I don't turn to face Leo, whose sharp stare I feel burning into my back. With him close, the tingly sensations inside me stir and I try to push them down, but it's no use. The attraction is there and strong, even if I feel uneasy about him. I have somehow formed an attachment toward my savior.

Sofia tilts her head quizzically when she notices my distant behavior toward him.

I haven't told her what happened last night. Not about the gun, my suspicion of him, or how we almost kissed. I'm hesitant to tell her because the last time I told her about my intuition, she waved it off as nothing and we got kidnapped. She wouldn't understand if I told her.

Heat gathers at the base of my neck when I remember how close Leo's lips were to mine. When the temptation of the memory becomes too good, I close my eyes and squish the butterflies.

I place the full dinner plates on the counter, and Leo and I lock eyes when I turn. My heart picks up speed, and I hand him a plate with shaky hands while trying to contain the fluttering in my stomach.

Disapproval reveals itself on his face when he sees us cooking.

"I thought I told you two not to make food. That's why I pay for a cook to come."

"Too bad," I retort, forcing the plate into his hands. "We like to cook." As I say this, I avoid his eyes and continue handing out the plates of food to the other men, who have quickly piled into the kitchen after they smelled the handmade tortillas.

Leo releases an exasperated breath and says nothing else. But he does shock me when he bends down and presses a chaste kiss on my temple.

I become tense as his lips rest over the area, and I'm left feeling cold when he removes his touch. My eyes follow his retreating figure as he approaches the dining room.

When it's only me and Sofia, she pokes my side.

"What was that?" she says in a teasing tone.

"Nothing," I say avoiding her stare.

She hums, unconvinced. Then her hands rise to her chest, to form a heart with her fingers.

"We don't know each other like that."

"Whatever you say, dear cousin," she says, her voice still teasing.

I glare at her as she hands me a plate before encouraging me to follow her to the dining area, where everyone is already enjoying their food.

When I enter the room, a wave of testosterone hits me in the face. From seeing the thirty strong and intimidating men, my hands around the plate become clammy.

They also notice our presence, and their talking fades away as they all look at me and Sofia.

My throat tightens, and I scan the room, looking for a corner away from them all, but the only seats available are the ones beside Francisco and Leo. My breath gets caught at the idea of sitting next to the man I'm avoiding.

I make my way toward the seat beside Francisco, away from Leo, and when I'm about to sit, Luca takes the seat, giving me a grin.

I send him a glare before making a beeline toward the seat on the other side of Francisco, but Sofia sits down when I get there. She gives me a cheeky smile and pats the top of the table next to her. I swallow my nervousness because this is the only available seat left, and it's the one right beside Leo.

My gaze drifts to Leo, and there's a surge of guilt inside me when I see his forehead bunched up and his lips slightly pursed into a frown.

With shaky hands, I pull the chair out. When I do, it makes a loud, screeching noise. Everyone's eyes turn to me.

As I go to scoot my seat forward, I silently gasp when an invisible force pushes my chair in.

Swiping my head around, I find Leo hovering behind me. He gives a curt nod before returning to his seat, leaving me in a state of shock.

Sofia nudges me from under the table and she's grinning.

I ignore her and glance around the table, only to be met with similar expressions of shock on the men's faces. Their eyes move from me to Leo, who takes a lazy sip from his glass of red wine.

Luca, across from me, opens his mouth in disbelief. The unchewed food is visible in his gaping mouth.

There's a slight tremble in my body from their eyes on me, and when Leo senses my agitation, he places a comforting hand on my thigh. The warmth from his hand eases my worries.

"Go back to eating your food," he demands, voice stern. The men's eyes widen, and they all turn away. The room is quick to grow loud as they talk to each other.

Leo removes his hand from my thigh, and coldness fills the spot.

My attention is once again drawn to Luca, who has beans smeared all over his face. I laugh out loud, and Sofia turns to see and laughs at the mess around his face.

Luca rolls his eyes, and his cheeks turn red. He wipes his face with a napkin, completely missing the food on his nose, and we laugh at him again.

Leo shakes his head at the sight of a messy Luca and lifts his Sope, trying to eat it without getting dirty.

The moment he lifts the round tortilla toward his mouth, the Sope falls apart and drops onto his plate in a messy mountain.

Everyone at the table laughs out loud, but the men turn quiet when Leo glares at them, muttering words in Italian, no doubt curses.

Noticing the sudden mood change in the room, I lower my laughter to silent giggles, and Leo gives me a teasing glare.

Narrowing my eyes in a challenge, still annoyed with him, I give a small huff before skillfully lifting my Sope and eating it without getting dirty or spilling the contents.

The men all watch, amazed when I lift the round tortilla. They glance down at their plates, where their Sope is a pile of mush from when they failed at picking it up.

A grin stretches on my lips when the men try to mimic my movements but fail and end up having to use a spoon to scoop the contents.

When everyone finishes eating, the men leave their plates littered around the table, and they are ready to leave until I raise my brows in disapproval.

I clear my throat to get their attention. I say nothing, simply point to their mess, and they nod in understanding. Shame fills their faces as they pick up their plate and take it to the sink to wash.

Leo chuckles and takes my plate from me. As he does this, a small ounce of my anger evaporates. He made being mad at him impossible, a thought which fills me with annoyance because of the lack of restraint I have when it comes to him.

When he disappears into the kitchen, the door to the dining room swings open. The sound of sharp heels clicking on the marble tiles has my brows furrowing in confusion.

I turn around and I'm met by a glamorous blond woman wearing a gorgeous tight black dress.

She gives a spiteful scowl. But as fast as it's there, it disappears into a fake toothy smile when the door to the kitchen swings open, and Leo enters the room.

She squeals in excitement and runs toward him, wrapping her long arms around his neck and forcing his head down. The woman kisses him, and I stare at them. My chest clenches with a sudden, intense feeling of jealousy.

This must be Cleo.

Leo throws her off him and wipes his mouth with the back of his hand.

My brows rise from his rejection.

Okay, so maybe not Cleo.

From the sight of his anger, a wave of relief washes over me, and I'm curious to know who this woman is, if not Cleo.

Leo's eyes launch knives at the woman, and she gives an innocent smile, which makes him clench his fists at his side.

"What the fuck!" Leo retorts in a voice so cold it brings a chill down my spine.

The beautiful woman pouts from his rejection, and Leo's eyes flash with hatred.

Her pouty lips turn into a wicked smile when she notices me still in the room.

I look between the two, feeling uncomfortable, and I'm about to take my leave with Sofia, but before I go, I lock eyes with the unnamed woman. There's a challenge sparkling inside her brown eyes.

"Oh babe, you got a new maid. What a tiny little thing she is." Her sickly sweet voice coos as she gives me judgmental elevator eyes.

Her comment hits a nerve, and I want to punch her for stereotyping me.

Racist bitch.

Leo, beside her, is still wiping his mouth in disgust, but after hearing her words, he sends me an apologetic glance.

I give a tight-lipped smile, which comes out more like a grimace.

"Umm, I'm going to go," I say, making my way toward the door, and when I'm about to exit, Leo's hand stops me, his fingers wrap around my wrist.

"Don't. If anyone needs to leave, it's her," Leo says with an obvious distaste for the woman now glaring at me.

Her voice is whiny, and I have to restrain myself from rolling my eyes.

"What! I'm not going anywhere!" She stomps her foot like a toddler, and her red heel scrapes under her.

Leo strides toward her with a dark look over his face. His intentions are to cause pain by the way his fists are set into a tight clench.

My eyes widen in horror when his hands clasp around her neck, lifting her off the ground.

As I watch the scene unfold, a wave of Déjà vu sweeps over me, and I remember when Adriano choked me. Clearing my mind of the memory, I rush toward them and try to get him to release her.

"Leo, let her go!" I pound my fisted hands on his solid back. He doesn't budge. "Please stop!" I beg, trying to pry him off her. My throat tightens as I remember the way my throat burned and the panic I felt when I was in her position.

Leo turns rigid, and releases his tight grip, dropping her to the ground.

She coughs on the edge of hysteria, trying to catch her breath, and despite not liking her, I know the right thing to do is to help her up.

I extend my hand for her to take, but she slaps it away.

In disbelief, I pull my now stinging hand away from her reach, and Leo brings me behind him in a protective stance.

"How did you find out I was in France, Rebecca?" he grits, revealing her name to me.

Sensing his rage, I grasp Leo's forearm to ease his anger, and the tension in his body relaxes, but he's still on edge, especially when Rebecca rises from the ground.

A smirk lifts her face. "Someone told me."

Her response doesn't please Leo, whose jaw ticks in frustration, and he goes to grab her neck again when she steps back, afraid of him.

Now trembling with fear, she gives him the answer he wants.

"I overheard some men outside my hotel say you were in the city!" she shouts, her voice breaking.

"Leave Rebecca." Leo's voice is dark and deadly, but Rebecca holds her ground, challenging him.

"It's because of *her*, isn't it?" She points an accusing finger at me, and I scoff. My blood bubbles from her accusatory tone and her distaste for me. I don't let her disrespect me any longer. I had a limit, and she crossed it when she slapped me. If Leo wouldn't pacify her, then I would.

Standing in front of her, I give a stony stare, and Leo's arms wrap around my waist, tugging me back. I become angry and try to pry him off, but he won't budge.

Sensing my frustration, Leo bends, whispering in my ear, and the hairs on the back of my neck rise from his husky voice.

"I got this," he insists, the pad of his thumb rubbing soothing circles around my hip.

Sighing, I back away when his voice and closeness work to wash away my anger.

"Rebecca, I won't repeat myself." He directs his response to her this time, and his words carry a threat, but she still doesn't seem to care.

I fix my eyes on an unmoving Rebecca, wondering why she wouldn't go. With her still glaring at me, I know if Leo doesn't get her out in the next minute, I won't be able to hold back.

"I think you should go," I say calmly, only to receive an icy glare from her.

She makes her way toward me, and the strong chemical floral scent of her perfume chokes me.

"I think *you* need to go," she says, mocking me, and my hands ball into fists at my side. A sting follows when my nails dig into the palms of my hands.

Leo, who is between us, looks at us in shock, and before anyone can say anything, we hear shoes squeaking on the marble floor. The next second, Sofia pushes Rebecca.

My cousin now stands in a defensive stance in front of me, making sure Rebecca can't touch me.

"Don't talk to her like that!" Sofia warns, inching closer to Rebecca.

"Or what, little girl?" Rebecca threatens, escalating Sofia's anger.

Francisco enters the room after hearing the noise, and his eyes widen at the sight of the fight bound to break out.

"I'll kick your ass, bitch," Sofia snaps, kicking Rebecca in the shin, and her screams fill the room. Leo and Francisco laugh in amusement until I narrow my eyes at them. They swallow down their laughter and clear their throats.

The last string of my composure snaps when Rebecca lifts her hand to smack Sofia.

I'm quick to shove my cousin aside, and before Rebecca's boney hand can reach my cheek, I grab her wrist, twisting it, making her shriek in pain.

"I told you to leave nicely once, and I won't ask you again," I warn, and when she remains defiant, I tighten my hold on her wrist, making her whimper.

Rebecca nods in understanding, and I let her go. When I do, she strikes me across the cheek. The blow is hard and unexpected, causing my entire face to turn to the side. The sound of the slap resonates throughout the room, along with Sofia's gasp.

Within a second, Leo grabs me. His eyes look over the spot she slapped, and from over his shoulder, I see Rebecca approaching me again. My instinct, or anger, whatever it is, drives me to push Leo off me with a force I didn't know I had.

I grab her by the hair while my other hand swings at her, hitting wherever I can land a punch. My fist keeps slamming into her.

Her screams are loud, and I don't let her go when she tries to pry my grip off her.

The more she fights me, I yank her down, my fingers curling around her blond hair.

Strong arms wrap around me, trying to pull me off Rebecca, but I don't let go. Then a stronger force tries to get me off her again, and this time they separate us.

My chest is heaving in anger, and when I calm down, I notice it took Leo and Luca to separate me from Rebecca.

I focus my angry eyes on Kaden and Angelo, who are busy securing a disheveled Rebecca in their arms. My stomach twists with anger at the sight of her, and the burning pain on my barely healing cheek pulses with heat.

"Get her out of here," Leo instructs, receiving a nod from the two, and they drag Rebecca through the door. "Don't fucking come back to my house, or I'll have my men shoot your ass the moment your face shows up again." Leo's voice goes an octave deeper when he threatens her.

"You'll regret this!" Rebecca shouts, and Leo scoffs, which makes her more furious. "Mock my words, but you will all pay." she sneers, glaring at us.

"No, you'll regret ever coming to my house, harassing me, and hurting Victoria!" Leo interrupts, voice deep and full of anger.

She fights in Angelo and Kaden's grip as they take her away.

When she's out of sight, a huff escapes my lips.

Good riddance.

22

LEO

Victoria launching herself on Rebecca and standing her ground was the most alluring thing I've ever seen.

The way her delicate fingers curled around Rebecca's hair filled me with pride. It's nice to know she has a fire to herself.

Victoria huffs, removing blond strands of hair from between her fingers. The sight makes me laugh, and her angry eyes land on me. She raises her chin defiantly and sets her lips in an angry pout, which ignites a familiar desire within me.

"Let me go, Francisco!" Sofia complains, trying to get his arms off so she can go after Rebecca. He doesn't budge and instead rolls his eyes. The grin on his lips tells me he's anything but annoyed.

I ignore the two and focus on Victoria, who Luca is teasing.

The corners of my mouth twitch when she gives him a warning glare. Her right fist rises in a warning, and Luca lifts his hands in front of him, declaring surrender. He laughs as he walks back toward the exit.

I grab her tiny fist, and she relaxes from my touch. A reaction that fills me with ease to know I'm not the only one affected by the powerful force between us.

Victoria looks at our hands, and for a second, I think I see uncertainty flash in her brown eyes. But if it's there, it's gone within a second, and the corners of her mouth tip up the slightest bit.

When she smiles, her lips stretch, and my attention falls on the blood seeping out of the torn skin on the corner of her lower lip. My anger rises at the sight of her injury, and I have to contain the urge to tell Kaden and Angelo to lock up Rebecca so I can deal with her later.

Victoria sees me glaring at her lips and runs her tongue over the cut. When the taste of blood fills her mouth, she cringes.

I pull her toward the kitchen.

"Where are we going?"

"To get your cut cleaned up. I don't like seeing you hurt," I say, cupping her chin between my fingers, and looking over her injuries. Her throat moves with a visible swallow, and her eyes smolder me with warmth.

I can't help myself when a grin rises to my lips from the memory of a jealous Victoria.

Although I didn't appreciate Rebecca's attack on me, her arrival made me realize Victoria doesn't like seeing me with another woman. Something about seeing her jealous makes my heart beat hard. But she has nothing to worry about because Rebecca is nothing to me but a mistake of my reckless youth, way before I ever took over as Don. A fling who didn't understand what *fuck off* meant.

Victoria's face contorts into curiosity from seeing my grin.

"Come on, my little fighter," I tease, and she presses her lips together, cheeks turning crimson.

I lead her into the kitchen and grab her waist. She lets out a small gasp, and her body shudders under my touch. With her now sitting on the counter, she's at my height, and our eyes connect.

I wish I could stare at her all day, but when my gaze falls on the bright red cut on her lip and her slowly irritating cheek, a deep sigh escapes me.

None of this would have happened if I had gotten rid of Rebecca. I know I could have used more force to kick her out. But because Victoria was beside me, I didn't want to scare her by showing her how cruel I could be. I already scared her when I choked Rebecca.

I head to the freezer to grab an ice pack, followed by finding the first aid kit. As I approach Victoria, her fingers go for the ice pack, but I ease them back on her lap. I'm gentle as I rest the ice pack over her jaw.

The once fading bruise is now turning red again. My blood runs hot, and the tension in my jaw only melts away when Victoria's tiny hand lands on my cheek. Her touch brings a thousand little tingles to the skin, and her hand is soft against the bristle of my stubble.

I stare at her and notice how close we are. I'm standing between her legs, and her thighs caress the sides of mine, bringing warmth down south.

Our faces are mere inches apart, and the proximity allows me to get a hint of her scent. I'm pleased when I realize my smell is now stuck to her skin because she's been sleeping in my room and wearing my shirts.

As I press the ice pack against Victoria's cheek, she lets out a hiss, and my hand draws back involuntarily.

I give her an apologetic glance before my pointer finger softly runs over the curve of her face. Her lips look plump and soft, and I feel a powerful urge to feel them pressed against mine. I restrain myself and turn my attention to the first aid kit to distract myself from the sweet temptation.

I'm gentle as I dab ointment over her cut, and the fire burning inside me intensifies. There's no escaping the desire between us. In fact, it has increased over the last few days.

Victoria's eyes dilate, and my last restraint snaps like a rubber band when the brown in her eyes turns almost black.

I lift her face gently and bring her lips near mine, ready to seize them. The alarms in my head are shouting at me to stop being reckless, but I can't hold back anymore. I need to know what it feels like to kiss her before it drives me insane.

Our breaths mingle, and I lean in to close the small distance between us, but the door to the kitchen slams open with a sharp bang, making Victoria jump back in surprise.

I sigh, unsure if it's a sigh of annoyance or relief because, once again, I've been stopped from making a beautiful mistake.

The sharp glare I send Luca tells me my sigh was from annoyance.

My glare falters when I notice he's panting and is as white as a ghost.

His blue eyes immediately go to Victoria, and I sense a hint of pity in their depths.

From his worry, a line appears on Victoria's forehead, and before we can ask him what's wrong, Sofia and Francisco enter from the dining room. The two stop in their tracks when they notice a rigid Luca.

"What's wrong?" I ask, and his eyes glance between Victoria and Sofia. There's a grimace on his lips.

"You guys need to see this." Luca sounds panicked as he motions with his head for us to follow him.

I help Victoria down from the countertop, and she's flustered, mumbling a silent "thank you."

With her head lowered, she follows Luca, and I walk right beside her into the living room. Kaden and Angelo are already there, their arms crossed over their chests, and their faces hold a hint of worry—an expression they rarely show. Seeing their uneasiness, my body grows tense, and worry consumes me.

I sit on the couch with Victoria beside me, and Sofia sits to Victoria's left, with Francisco behind her. We all share looks of perplexity.

My hand seeks Victoria's, sensing her distress, and I gently squeeze her hand. She looks at me with a sincere smile, and we turn our attention to the paused news channel on the television screen.

"Luca, I don't care about the weather forecast," I tell him, lifting a brow in disbelief. My sarcastic reply has him glaring at me in annoyance.

He scowls and points his finger at the television.

"Shut up and listen."

I roll my eyes, ready to yell at him for talking back to me, when Victoria squeezes my hand, telling me to let it go. Her eyes are stuck on the screen in front of her.

With a sigh, I turn my attention to the television when the news reporter's voice fills the silence in the room.

"We have news about the recent disappearance of girls in France. Unfortunately, this news comes at a price that has left two families heartbroken. About a week ago, two American girls who visited Paris on a school trip were filed missing by their teacher." As the reporter's voice echoes in the living room, Victoria stiffens in my arms. "Witnesses have footage of the two girls being attacked in Montmartre by a hooded figure whose identity remains unknown. Here is the video sent to us by a witness."

The video plays on the screen, and my heart drops from seeing Victoria struggling to hold back Sofia. I watch the events she told me about earlier this week unfold, and it knocks the breath out of me to see the fear in her eyes as no one helps them.

Victoria rises from her seat in agitation, biting her nails.

"Victoria..." I call out in a soft voice, rising from my seat. She stops pacing and looks at me. From the sight of her rising tears, a weight lands on my chest.

"I don't understand why they didn't help us, but still had the audacity to record on their phones like it was some sick joke. We could have died!"

She's distressed, and I bring her plush against me, unable to do anything to help take her pain away. Victoria wraps her arms around me and buries her face in my chest.

I run my fingers through her hair and listen to the news reporter.

"After this video, the girls disappeared, and the only remaining evidence left behind was the stolen purse and a diamond earring. Officials tried to find the two girls, and we now have news of their whereabouts. But it's not the news their family wants to hear. Take a listen to Commissioner Moises, in charge of the case." The television shows an aging officer with black hair, and I can't help but feel a rising panic inside me as chaos ensues in the background with flashing lights and yellow tape.

"It's unfortunate, but earlier this week, there was a report of two female bodies found decapitated on the side of the highway. A DNA test on both bodies has returned, and they match the two girls."

"Oh god," Victoria breathes. Her hands cover her mouth, and she has turned pale after hearing the officials declare her and Sofia dead.

"It's a tragedy in which two families now mourn the loss of their loved ones. We have Grace from DBC News in California, who is with the family now."

Victoria's eyes widen, and I can see the grief in them. Her pain fills me with regret for not contacting her family to tell them she's safe. Just like I forgot to tell Cleo I was staying longer in France, I failed to call Victoria's family. All because I lost track of time while in her presence.

"Yes, a tragedy indeed...I'm here with Maria Rodriguez, mother of one of the victims."

The camera pans out to reveal a middle-aged woman crying in the arms of a man. From seeing her, Victoria falls to pieces in my arms, and I realize how selfish I've been for keeping her with me this entire time.

"It's not fair," Victoria's mother says, and I can hear the tears in her voice. There's another woman with her who looks like Sofia, and she's clutching onto Victoria's mother. "All they wanted was to see the world, but they robbed them of this opportunity. They took them from us, and it hurts so much," she says, pressing a fist to her chest. "Today, our family didn't lose one person. We lost two, and we're shattered. A mother shouldn't have to bury her child."

"What have the police told you about your daughter and niece's case?" the reporter asks Sofia's mother.

"Nothing. They only tell us they found their bodies beaten beyond recognition, and now they won't send them back home to us for a proper burial. We want the police to bring our daughters back to us, even if it's in a coffin. We also want whoever did this to our daughters to pay."

The anger and grief from Victoria's family confirms that my time with her has ended. I press Victoria tighter to my chest, and her arms tighten around me as if she realizes the same thing I have.

From the corner of my eye, I see Francisco comforting an upset Sofia. He looks at me, and his expression tells me what I already know I have to do.

I give him a simple nod before focusing on comforting a crying Victoria.

"I know it hurts, but everything will be okay. I'll take you and Sofia to your teacher tomorrow morning."

"But what about Adriano?" she asks, and there's a powerful fear behind her words.

"I'll handle him, but it's time you go home," I tell her, wiping her tears with my thumbs. "Your family needs you both,"

Victoria gives an unsure nod, and I fill with dread from knowing she'll no longer be by my side.

VICTORIA

Seeing my parents grieve on television after being told I'm dead brings unbearable pain.

There's a wave of emotions washing over me. They're so strong my chest tightens with intense pressure.

I can't stop the guilt and homesickness from taking over my body after seeing my parents' heart torn apart, and I'm responsible for their pain.

If I hadn't begged to come to France, Sofia and I wouldn't have been kidnapped and assaulted. But then I wouldn't have met Leo, and I realize there's no changing the past.

Although I'm frustrated with Leo's lies, I realize I'm screwed as I clutch onto him for what may be the last time. My grip tightens around him, not wanting to say goodbye. But he's right; my parents need me. A phone call wouldn't be enough, not when they were told I was dead. I need to be in their arms for them to be at ease.

"Leo," I whisper, and he looks at me with a strange mixture of emotions. Sadness? Pain? Longing? I'm not sure what it is, but it's consuming him. "Are you sure it's safe for us to return to our family?"

Leo says nothing for a few seconds before he lets out a deep sigh.

"I don't know," he breathes, and I grow rigid.

Having sensed my distress, he cups my face between his hands.

"But I will make sure nothing happens to you, Sofia, or your family," he says in a level tone, and I know he'll keep his promise by the way his eyes stare hard into mine.

I nod and kiss his cheek, no longer holding back because it doesn't matter what happens between us. I won't be seeing him again after tonight.

My attention falls on the four other men in the room. Although I only met them a few days ago, they have all been kind to me and Sofia.

They welcomed us into their home and made us feel safe after what we experienced.

To my right, I see my cousin breaking down in Francisco's arms. His face reflects deep concern as he holds her.

Then I notice Luca sitting on the couch on the other side of the room, his elbows resting on his knees and his head is between his hands in frustration.

Kaden has a faraway, dazed expression. While Angelo sits on the couch, staring at the television with furrowed brows and a slight frown.

I'm going to miss them.

The silence in the room is heavy, and it's now late in the night.

Leo notices my eyes drooping from exhaustion, but I can't bring myself to sleep, not when I have to say goodbye in a few hours. He doesn't notice my resistance in fighting off the sleep because he leads me to the room I've been staying in.

I sit on the bed, and Leo kneels in front of me. He looks at me for a second, deep in thought, and grabs hold of my face. His touch brings forth a jolt of electricity.

We stare at one another, and the blood in my veins rushes with warmth when he leans in. His lips land on my temple, leaving them there for a few seconds. He then rises and leaves me in the room, dazed and unsatisfied.

I watch with a heavy heart as the door closes behind him, and reality catches up to me, making me feel cold inside.

I try to sleep, and although my eyes are heavy, my mind won't let me rest. The tears keep falling because I not only have to heal from the trauma left after my assault. But I also have to heal from the disappointment of letting Leo go. Tomorrow I say goodbye to the weightless flutters, the warmth, and the safety he has somehow brought to me.

Leo saved me from Adriano, but he can't save me from my broken heart. This is something I have to heal on my own because I'm the one who delved deeply into these feelings. This is the consequence of seeking comfort from someone who can never be mine. All of this is my fault for letting myself fall for my savior.

23

VICTORIA

I don't sleep all last night; it's now around ten a.m., and getting out of bed is difficult when I know it means I'll leave a particular person behind. So, I don't get up. Instead, I stare at the space ahead and reminisce over the last few days. Only to realize I've never had so much fun or felt so happy in my entire life.

I don't understand how I can feel this much grief from having to leave a place and people I hardly know anything about. But the pain is there, and questioning why it's there won't do anything to alter it.

I'm curled to my side when the door to the room opens. I freeze as heavy footsteps sound from behind me. Leo's strong, musky scent fills my nose, and I pretend to be asleep.

The left side of the bed drops as he takes a seat. The familiar gentle touch of his hand strokes my cheek, bringing little tingles to the skin.

His deep voice fills the silence, and he thinks I'm sleeping.

"Victoria, the first time I saw you, you stole the breath right out of me. The fear you had across your face had my blood rushing and my eyes seeing red." I hear the loud, rhythmic beating of my heart in my ears, and I have to take slow breaths to steady the pulsing.

Why is he telling me this? What about Cleo?

"After I lost you, I was a mess, and when I found you tied to that bed with a man on top of you, something inside me snapped. I didn't understand these feelings, but I do now after spending time with you." His voice has an edge, and my heart tugs as I listen to him. "I want to be selfish and take you with me to Italy. But I can't. You have a life back in California where your family waits for you."

His face lowers, his lips are near my mouth, and my heart races violently inside my chest.

"Bambina, you have a bright future, and I can't take that away from you. Which is why I'm letting you go. Even if it'll make me miserable." He kisses the corner of my mouth, and the heat from his lips radiates throughout my body, sending sparks.

The bed shuffles and his retreating footsteps slowly fade away.

I want to tell him I don't want to go back home, but I can't do it. It's an absurd idea. It's like he said, my life is in California.

My heart hurts from going back and forth between wanting to be with my family and my savior.

Frustrated, I rise from bed and run my fingers through my hair. Leo's words race around in my mind like a carousel, and my stomach churns when Cleo comes to mind.

I can't throw myself at a man who's likely already taken, and I won't settle for being the other woman. No matter how much it hurts to turn the other cheek.

A sigh escapes my lips, and I wipe the single tear from my cheek. Stretching the inevitable is no use, and I have to get ready.

The white blouse with a sweetheart neckline lays next to Leo's black T-shirt. The one I wore the first night I woke up in this room.

When I extend my hand to grab the white blouse, my fingers detour, and I find myself in Leo's shirt instead. His scent clings to the fabric, and his cologne comforts me.

When I'm dressed, I slowly make my way downstairs, and my legs shake with every step.

I enter the kitchen, and I'm met with a quiet Sofia pulling apart a chocolate croissant. Francisco sits beside her, not a word uttered between the two.

When she sees me, she gives me a sad smile. I return the gesture with one of my own before pouring myself a cup of coffee, since I have no appetite.

When I sit on a stool, Luca, Kaden, and Angelo enter the room.

Kaden and Angelo's expressions are emotionless and guarded. But not Luca. I can see a hint of sadness in his eyes.

The door opens again, and this time Leo enters in all his handsome glory. He's wearing a beautiful black three-piece suit with the first few buttons of his black dress shirt undone, exposing his structured chest. His hair is pushed back, giving him a handsome, rugged appearance.

I glance at him and notice the warmth from his eyes is gone. He doesn't look at me; his attention is on his friends.

"Ready?" His voice is marked with a coarse edge. It's as if a switch has been flipped inside him. His friends don't react to his cold personality. They answer him by rising from their seats.

Leo doesn't acknowledge me. It's as if I'm a ghost, and I don't know what happened to make him distant toward me.

Luca places a soft hand at the base of my shoulder, and when our eyes meet, he's sympathetic.

I smile, assuring him I'm fine, but he sees right through me. And he's right; I'm not fine. How can I be when Leo confessed what I thought were his feelings for me a few minutes ago, but now he can barely look at me. Did he realize he has Cleo back in Italy waiting for him? Did he not mean what he said to me?

The sudden change in Leo's demeanor leaves me with a knot in my stomach. His coldness is confusing, and I don't know if I want to cry or scream in anger.

I stare at my knotted hands, engrossed by my thoughts that I don't see the person in front of me, until I bump into their hard chest, making me stumble back.

"Sorry," I mumble, and I lock eyes with Kaden, who gives me a genuine smile.

"It's fine," he assures, looking at my shocked expression with a frown. "Victoria, I know we didn't get to know much of each other, but our few instances were memorable. Just know that we're all going to miss you and Sofia." Kaden shocks me when he brings me into his hard chest for a brotherly embrace.

"I'm going to miss you all. Thank you for everything." Kaden hears my defeated tone and squeezes me gently before letting me go.

His eyes avert to something behind me. When I turn to see what it is, my breath gets stuck in my throat at the sight of Leo staring at us.

His eyes melt my insides, but I grow cold when he looks at the silver wristwatch and leaves the room.

My teeth clench, and my anger rises from him being an asshole after he's been a sweetheart for the past few days.

I'm livid as I watch him go, and hot tears of frustration are brewing, but I don't let them spill.

Two can play that game.

My back straightens, and I make my way outside.

Kaden gives a quizzical brow and says nothing as he follows me.

Once outside, Leo waits near the door of a black Mercedes SUV, his fingers typing angrily into the phone in his hands.

I make a beeline toward the other car, and his eyes follow me.

When I'm inside, I mutter a string of curses in Spanish, and Luca, who's sitting in the passenger seat, turns to face me. He lifts a brow in amusement.

I grit my teeth and stare out the tinted window to see Leo closing the car door. He's shaking his head in disbelief, which fuels my anger.

So now he wants to be chivalrous.

The door beside me swings open to reveal Leo's towering form looking at me. His face is void of any emotion.

When I don't move, his brows tip up. His attention falls onto an amused Luca, who's suppressing a smile from our silent banter.

Leo sends him a glare, making Luca's eyes widen, and he hastily turns around, his cheeks inflated with air.

A frustrated sigh comes from Leo before he closes the door and makes his way to the other side of the car.

He takes the seat across from me, and although the space between us is a few inches, in its place is a thick imaginary brick wall rooted firmly. Unwilling to tumble from our matching stubborn temperaments.

Neither one of us looks at the other, and it's so silent you can hear the car breaks.

The only time the silence is disturbed is when Leo tells the driver the directions to the hotel where my classmates and teachers wait—unsuspecting of me and Sofia's arrival from the so-called grave.

Before I know it, the car parks across from the hotel, and I stare at the building.

There's a cramp in my chest, and my hand goes to the area where the pain is coming from. I take deep breaths, trying to regulate the pain, but it's as if I'm drowning with every intake.

I'm terrified Adriano will kidnap Sofia and me when we're out of Leo's protection. I'm also nervous about confronting my classmates and teachers.

Sensing my anxiety, Leo takes the space between us and brings me into his arms. There's a lightness in my chest from his touch. But then I remember I'm mad at him and I push him away.

"Goodbye," I mutter, looking at my hands lying on my lap. He says nothing, and I don't stay long when the tears rise.

As I stretch my arm to open the door, it swings open, and Luca smiles at me. He has his right hand outstretched, and I take it, allowing him to pull me out of the car.

The second my feet hit the pavement below, Luca presses me to his chest. His arms bound tightly around my waist, allowing me to smell his fresh pine scent.

"I'll miss you, Snow White," I mumble, calling him the nickname I had given him because of the color of his hair, which is as white as snow.

His shoulders rise when he laughs.

"Take care, Shortcake," he says, squeezing me before letting go.

I glance behind him where Angelo, Kaden, Francisco, and Sofia all stand, exchanging farewells.

Luca and I approach them, and Angelo opens his arms for me to hug him.

"Bye, blue eyes," I mumble, wrapping my arms around his torso.

"Bye V," he whispers, pulling away with a sad sigh. "Try not to get kidnapped again, yeah."

I laugh. "I'll try, but that's up to my cousin." Angelo shakes his head.

My stare falls on Francisco, who looks torn. I pull him into my arms, and the tears I have been working so hard to hold back are now on the brink of falling down my cheeks.

"Thank you for saving my cousin and for everything after." My voice cracks, and his expression softens. "Francisco, can I ask you for a favor?"

He nods, and I let out a breath, which reveals how upset I am.

"Take care of him." As I say this, I can't help but look toward the SUV with Leo inside.

Francisco doesn't need me to say his name to know who I'm talking about, and he gives me a firm nod.

Worry lines resurface on his forehead when Sofia appears from behind me. Their eyes lock, and I can tell Sofia is as emotional as I am. I grab her hand and look at the four handsome, broad-shouldered Italian men who saved our lives.

My eyes soften at the sight of them, and I give them one last smile, knowing this is goodbye for good.

The empty spot beside Francisco reminds me that one of them is missing. My stomach twists, tearing apart because this is how Leo and I will part ways after everything we've been through.

As Sofia and I approach the edge of the sidewalk, my breathing becomes shaky, and my heart feels heavy when I look ahead.

I go to step off the sidewalk when a hand around my waist stops me, and I'm pulled into a muscular chest.

The familiar warmth and scent make me sigh in relief.

LEO

The silence in the car is loud, and I've never felt more alone. Whiteness surrounds my knuckles as I clutch the phone in my hand.

I want to press Victoria against my chest one last time. But I can't do it. Not when it physically hurts me to think about how she'll no longer be a part of my life.

I thought confessing my feelings for her would help make it easier for me to let her go. But I was wrong, and when the weight of my confession remained strong, I resorted to my usual defense mechanism—pushing her away by being a dick. And it worked a little too well.

Her anger was oozing out of her the entire car ride, and now I sit here feeling worse than before.

Groaning in frustration, I look out the window to see Victoria embracing my friends as if she has known them her entire life.

Her eyes glance into the car, and my heart skips a beat. The cold exterior I put up tumbles, and the door to the car opens, revealing Kaden. He looks at me with judgment in his angry eyes.

"Don't do this to yourself," he grumbles in disbelief.

I stare at him, my lips in a thin, hard line.

"I'm not doing anything," I say, devoid of emotion.

Kaden's jaw twitches, and he lets out a huff.

"Fine, whatever, but I hope you realize she'll hate you for the rest of her life and wish she never met you." His words pierce my chest like a bullet, and when I say nothing, he sighs in exasperation.

"Do you want Victoria to feel this way after you led her on? Tell me, Leo, was it your plan to woo her with sweet gestures, hugs, and smiles, only to dump her on the side of the road when it's all over?"

I still say nothing. My lips remain in a tight line, and my heart clenches with regret as his words sink in.

My resistance to give into my feelings angers Kaden, and his fist clenches at his side as he continues to try to get through to me.

"Not only are you hurting yourself, but you're hurting her. So, stop being an asshole and drop the tough act for once." Kaden slams the car door, and I watch as he walks away to stand beside Angelo, who looks at me with disappointment.

Kaden's words ring in my mind, bringing some sense into me, and I let out a curse when I realize he's right. I'm being stupid and selfish. By protecting my feelings, I've hurt Victoria, and she's going to leave France angry with me. I didn't want her last memory of me to be filled with resentment.

There's a sense of urgency within me as I open the door and run toward her.

I reach her right when she's about to cross the street, and before she can take another step, I grab her from behind and pull her into my chest.

She sighs in relief. "Leo, thank you for everything."

My name coming out of her mouth sends a tremble through my body, and I hold her tight.

"I'm sorry." My voice comes out strained, and she nods, accepting my apology. Our eyes remain firmly on one another. No one else matters right now.

I kiss her temple, leaving my lips resting on the spot for a few seconds, not wanting to let her go. But I have to.

"Goodbye Bambina," I breathe, and she swallows the lump in her throat.

I stare at Victoria, trying to stamp her image into my memory, when I notice she's wearing my shirt.

Victoria's cheeks flush red and there's another sharp pinch in my chest because this is the last time I'll ever see those red cheeks and deep brown eyes.

"You look better in it than I do," I assure her, and her cheeks turn even darker.

Victoria bites on her bottom lip, and her face lightens for a second. She pulls something from her back pocket, grabs my right hand, and puts whatever she has taken out from behind her into my palm. My forehead bunches in confusion, and she quickly closes my fist before I can see what she's given me.

"A token of my appreciation," she exclaims with a bittersweet smile, and my fist tightens around the object.

From beside her, Sofia speaks.

"Thank you for everything," she says, giving me a watery smile. I nod, and my body grows heavy when she grabs Victoria's hand. They look at me one last time before crossing the street.

An emptiness grows from the distance between Victoria and me, and as it stretches, I become cold and the heaviness of what I've lost crushes me.

To distract myself from the grief of letting go the only woman I'll ever go soft for, I open my fist to see an earring.

The heart-shaped gold band embedded with tiny diamonds knocks the breath out of me, and my fist clutches it, afraid of losing it.

Although the weight in my chest draws me downward, I square my shoulders and return to the car.

I have to force myself not to turn around, and when I'm inside the car, Luca looks back at me. He wants to say something, but he doesn't when he senses my distress.

"Where to, boss?" the driver asks, looking at me from the rearview mirror.

"The airport," I tell him, looking at the earring. The only thing I have to remember her by.

She's gone, and I won't see her again. But at least she's safe and away from the danger and chaos I bring.

It's time for her to return to her life, and it's time I return to mine.

I have a mafia and people counting on me to protect them.

It's time to be the man I was before her.

The heartless Leo Bandoni.

The Italian Mafia Don.

24

VICTORIA

Uncertainty paralyzes me. Every step forward is frightening. The world has never felt this big or eerie.

I press my teeth together, and my neck twitches with a need to turn around to get a glimpse of Leo. But I know if I turn around, I'll break to pieces.

Don't do it.

Remember Cleo.

He isn't mine.

As we near the hotel, I see our teacher, Mrs. Ross, sitting outside with her face buried in her hands. Her cries are loud, and they blur out the sound of the cars humming behind us as they pass.

She's a complete mess. Her dark hair is dull and tousled, and her gray yoga pants have coffee stains.

My heart squeezes from seeing her grief.

I'm about to place a hand on her shoulder when my curiosity gets the best of me, and I glance toward the spot the two black Mercedes were parked, but they're no longer there.

I see the cars turning the corner, disappearing forever, and I blink away my tears.

There's a loud gasp from beside us, and I'm met with the sight of a colorless Becca. The cup of coffee in her hand falls to the ground. Its contents splash on the pavement below her.

"Victoria? Sofia?" Our names come out of her mouth in a broken whisper.

When Mrs. Ross hears our names, she lifts her face from her hands. Our eyes lock, and she jumps from her position with a gasp.

Her arms are tight around Sofia and me.

"Oh my, you guys are alive"—she stutters—"but the police said you were dead."

"They got it wrong," Sofia explains, tears falling down her cheeks.

"What happened to you guys?" This time it's Becca who speaks.

"We got kidnapped by human traffickers." My voice is silent. I'm not sure they heard me until Mrs. Ross gasps. Her face pales in horror at my words.

"I'm so sorry. Please forgive me," Mrs. Ross says, her grip around me and Sofia tightening.

"It wasn't your fault." My voice is firm, but she's still upset. "They didn't get to touch us. We were rescued before they could do worse," I say, rubbing her back.

But they did touch me.

I push back the memory of my assault when the anxiety returns.

Mrs. Ross and Becca share a look of confusion.

"Saved by the police?" Mrs. Ross asks, and I shake my head.

"Then who saved you?" Becca's forehead bunches in confusion. Her question makes my mouth dry because I'm not sure who saved me. A businessperson?

"It doesn't matter... what matters is that we're here now." My attention falls on my teacher, who sniffles and nods.

"Your family thinks you two are dead. We need to call them and get you two home. Everyone is still here." As Mrs. Ross says this, I feel a sharp stab in my chest at the mention of going home. I'm not sure if it's because I'm about to confront my family after what happened or because I know once I get on a plane, I'll never see Leo again. Who knows, maybe it's from both.

We make our way inside the hotel, and Mrs. Ross speaks to herself, but the comment she makes is one which hasn't left my mind.

"I don't understand how the police found both your DNA on the bodies?" she mumbles. "I was talking to the police commissioner, and he was certain it was you two. Yet he wouldn't let me see the bodies, and now, with you two alive, I'm not sure what's going on."

Realization draws upon her, and her thin brows snap together.

"Did Moises lie to us?" There's an air of disbelief in her words, and her nose scrunches. "I never trusted that man when he came into the crime scene with a snotty attitude and lack of sympathy. I wouldn't be surprised if he knew where you two were this entire time."

Her steps are fast as she approaches a group of police officers. When they see me and Sofia, their heads jerk forward, eyes blinking with their mouths parted in shock.

"Where's officer Moises?" Mrs. Ross asks them, and a man with ginger hair shakes his head, coming out of his shocked state. He points his finger toward the couch across the room where his boss Moises sits.

Mrs. Ross storms toward the man on the phone. She rips the phone from his grasp and smashes it on the floor.

The man rises, towering over Mrs. Ross. His lips set into a sneer, and he shouts at her.

"Mrs. Ross, I can arrest you for harassing an officer!" he says, voice harsh, and his handcuffs clink as he pulls them out.

He grabs her shoulder, and my blood burns when he tries to restrain her.

Mrs. Ross pushes him, and her eyes narrow into a glare.

"And I can take you to jail for lying!" She motions toward Sofia and me. "You knew where they were at, didn't you? There's no other explanation, and don't give me none of this flawed DNA test bullshit because it's two bodies we're talking about, not one!" she says coldly, gaining the attention of everyone in the room.

Moises looks at Sofia and me, and we wave with sarcastic smiles plastered on our faces. His eyes widen, and his eyebrows rise with his expression of shock.

"Why did you lie? Who are you protecting?" Mrs. Ross questions him, pointing an accusing finger at his chest.

His face shows fear for a split second before a hard look replaces it.

"I don't have to answer you," he sneers, backing toward the exit, and some of his officers look at him in disbelief.

He's about to run when I stick my foot out, and he tumbles to the ground, cursing me in French as I hover above him. Fear washes over his rugged features when his men surround him.

"What are you guys doing?" He fights in their grasp as they handcuff him.

"Moises, you are now a suspect in the abduction of Sofia Hernandez and Victoria Rodriguez."

"Let go of me!" Moises demands, voice sharp. "I swear I'll fire you, all of you!"

His fighting and air of superiority tell me he's guilty of the accusations made against him, and my blood boils.

Mrs. Ross comes to stand beside me and Sofia.

"We're going to get to the bottom of this. But you two need to tell the detective about your kidnapping." Sympathy marks her face as the detective approaches us.

I clutch the bottom of Leo's shirt, twirling the fabric around my fingers. The dread of having to relive my kidnapping brings anxiety. But we need to do this to help Erika and the other girls Adriano still has kidnapped. Their missing faces need to be recognized. Light needs to shine on their files again, and we are their only hope in making sure this happens.

As expected, retelling the events of my kidnapping brings a heavy weight to my body. The most difficult part of the process was having to strip in front of an officer so they could take pictures of the bruises left behind by my kidnappers.

I've never felt more humiliated in my entire life as the female officer examined me. Although she was only trying to document my injuries, I couldn't help but compare it to how Adriano looked me over like I was cattle.

I found that as I told the events of the most traumatic experience of my life, the buried memories Leo helped me forget resurfaced.

I was fortunate enough not to get raped, but I was sexually assaulted and physically abused. They stripped a part of my humanity when they wrapped a collar around my neck and sold me like a dog.

The fear which consumed me that day was unlike anything I had ever felt. It's a fear of knowing you will lose yourself and die inside. But being helpless because you know your heart will still beat after the abuse.

Sofia and I have been to hell, and we came out alive because of Leo.

My kidnappers tried to break me, and they did. They left me with a cut which my time with Leo has healed. But reliving these memories has reopened the wound.

After hearing our statement, the detective shows us photos of the missing girls they have been trying to find, and sure enough, most of the pictures are of the girls I saw in chains.

The only photo not in the stack is Erika's, and when I realized she wasn't lying when she said she felt like a ghost to society, the tears wouldn't stop falling.

The detective apologizes for what happened to us, but his words mean nothing without action. They have to stop Adriano from doing more harm to other women. What he's getting away with doing isn't right.

As I exit the room with Sofia, I let out a breath. My tired gaze falls on our two teachers, who are approaching us with a phone in their hands.

Tears prick my eyes, knowing who's on the other end of the phone.

I meet Mrs. Ross halfway, with Sofia trailing behind me.

Our teachers wrap their arms around us, but they bring no comfort. The only person whose touch I want right now I can't have.

Mrs. Ross gives me her phone while Mrs. Jane hands hers to Sofia.

As I bring the phone to my ear, it shakes in my cold hands.

"Mami..."

A string pulls from my spine the further Europe becomes.

With the distance increasing, I realize there's nothing worth staying in France for. Leo has gone back to Italy.

A low, soft beeping sound cuts through the stuffy air.

"We'll be landing at Los Angeles International Airport shortly. Please fasten your seat belts."

The mention of landing back home produces a churning in my stomach. My mom mentioned how crazy the media has gone after hearing about the scandal in France. Everyone wants to know what happened to me and Sofia. They want the inside scoop on what it's like to be trafficked. They don't stop to consider the pain reliving the events might bring us. Or the fear we have of our captors returning for us if we say anything.

Beside me, Sofia is playing with the bracelet around her wrist. Her fingers fidget with the dainty Eiffel Tower charm Francisco bought her. A bittersweet smile rises when the memories of Leo showing me around Paris resurface.

I miss him.

I stifle a sigh and direct my attention out the window. The bright orange and yellow lights of Los Angeles glow like sapphires.

I'm home.

Since returning from the dead the previous morning, few words have come from Sofia and me. And although our classmates want to know who rescued us, we don't talk about the five mysterious men whose absence has brought us grief. I know the moment I talk about Leo, the tears will rise, as will the fear of possibly being kidnapped again.

Leo's absence has filled me with a sense of vulnerability. Gone is his protection, and I hate feeling like I need to rely on a man to feel safe. I don't want to conform to gender stereotypes, but the fear of Adriano coming back for me is so intense it drives me to a corner. I can't do anything when the trauma of what I saw and how they hurt me comes crashing into me like an angry tide. The fear follows me like a shadow, and it's there when I hear a loud noise or when someone's body heat seeps from behind me. Every man scares me, and I don't know who to trust. The fear is suffocating, clawing at my insides.

I pull my suitcase from the overhead compartment, trying to bring it down, when a deep masculine voice comes from behind me, startling me.

Green eyes peer down at me with a smile, but they aren't the eyes I've grown to find comfort in.

"Do you need help?" The man asks, and when his eyes remind me of Leo, the vise around my heart tightens until it crushes the organ. The pain serves as a reminder of who I left behind.

My lower lip trembles, and when the man sees this, he furrows his forehead. His lips press together, unsure of what to make of my reaction.

I nod hesitantly, and he smiles, bringing down my suitcase.

"Thank you," I mumble, grabbing the handle and hauling it toward the exit of the airplane.

My steps through the airport are slow, and my mind is a whirlpool of thoughts and emotions. Sadness, fear, anxiety, and relief become one, bringing a cold sweat to the back of my neck.

As the exit nears, my vision tunnels and I'm brought out of the hazy fog when the sounds of cameras clicking and people clamoring increases. The noises become more vibrant as we round the corner.

I scan the area, trying to figure out if there's a celebrity in the airport, but I see no one other than my classmates.

Mrs. Ross hears the noise and frowns. She comes to a stop and pulls her bag in front of her, rummaging inside it.

"I'm sure you two saw the news," she trails off as she looks through her bag. "You guys are popular, *the girls who came back from the dead.*" Mrs. Ross puts air quotes on what the media is calling us, and she hands Sofia and me each a pair of sunglasses. My stare falls toward the bright flashes, and I step back, realizing they're waiting for us and not a celebrity.

The pressure in my chest rises, and Sofia huddles near me. Fear of Adriano seeing us on the news stirs in her hazel eyes, and I'm sure she sees a similar look in mine.

Breathe Victoria.

"We're here with you guys," Becca assures, coming from behind and placing a hand on my rising shoulder. The rest of our classmates gather around us in a protective stance, and my panic attack simmers down.

Sofia and I say nothing. Too afraid to say a word.

I pull the hood of my sweater over my head and place the sunglasses over my eyes. Sofia does the same.

Our classmates walk beside us, and I clutch onto Sofia as the noise becomes louder. My vision hazes with tears, which I blink away, but I have to blink repeatedly when the tears don't stop rising.

"I'm scared." My voice cracks, and the lump in my throat chokes me. Even swallowing won't get rid of the tightness lodged inside.

Mrs. Ross brings me into her arms.

"I know, honey. But your family is waiting for you both," she adds lightly. "Ignore the reporters. You don't need to speak to them."

I want to tell her I'm not scared of the reporters, but I don't have the courage to tell her.

Sofia squeezes my hand, assuring me I'm not alone in this.

I inhale deeply through my nose and release my breath.

Fingers locked with Sofia's and with my classmates near, I exit the airport, and we are immediately met with a swarm of reporters.

A man points in our direction, and I stare at my shoes as I walk through the crowd. My body grows warm from the many bright flashes.

As we make our way through the crowd, my classmates push the reporters, shouting for them to back up, but they persist. Two security guards nearby try to help, but the reporters don't stop trying to advance toward us.

Their questions echo in my head, and I become dizzy.

"Sofia, Victoria!"

"Is it true you guys ran away?"

"Why do you think the cops lied about the DNA tests?"

"Sofia!"

"Victoria!"

Make it stop! Go away!! Leave me alone!!!

The reporters' questions overrun me as they become louder and more periodic the deeper we walk into the crowd. The flashes from their cameras disorient my steps, and I'm almost certain I'm going to pass out from the intense emotions coursing through me.

A man jumps in front of me, and I almost fall back.

"Who kidnapped you guys?" he asks, sticking his microphone in my face. The sunglasses slip down my nose, allowing him to see the pain he has brought me. He stiffens and swallows thickly when he sees my tears.

"The girls are not saying anything right now!" Mrs. Ross says, guiding us through the crowd with the help of airport security, and slowly they spread out, giving us room.

We reach the end of the mob, and I take off the sunglasses, letting out a breath of relief. Sofia's warmth disappears when she lets my hand go. Her screams and cries fill the surrounding space as she runs toward her family.

My own tears fall fast when I see my family. Their eyes shimmer with unshed tears, and they look exhausted. Dark circles surround my dad's eyes, and my mom's face looks red and puffy from all her crying.

Like a bursting pipe, the lump in my throat cracks, and I'm calling for my parents, relieved to see them.

"Mami! Papi!" I'm running toward them, and my parents run toward me.

"Victoria!" My dad's voice cracks, and I fling myself into his arms. He catches me, and his hands go to the back of my head.

As soon as he has me in his grasp, he sighs in relief and falls to his knees with me clutched securely in his arms like a baby. I feel his warm tears fall on my cheek, and he's shaking feverishly from his heart-wrenching sobs.

My mom wraps her arms from behind me, and I'm now nestled between my parents. Her words are a jumble, but they reveal her relief at having me in her arms. She places kisses all over my face, and her misty eyes soak in the sight of me alive, unable to believe I'm in her arms.

"Mi Hija," she cries, kissing my forehead. I lean into her touch and close my eyes, savoring the warmth of being in their arms.

"I'm so sorry," I whisper through my tears, and my dad shakes his head, caressing my face.

"This is not your fault," he croaks out.

My siblings come around us, and they embrace me. neither one of them wants to let me go. They're afraid this is a dream, and they'll wake up to find I'm dead.

With my family in my arms, I'm still empty inside, and I can't do anything about it. I know I have to move on and try to live my life, but both the good and the bad that happened in France have taken a toll on me physically and mentally. I can only hope that with time, I'll find the strength to forget what happened to my body and for the emptiness inside me to be whole again.

My tears continue falling when I realize nothing will ever be the same again.

I want to be the girl I was before being assaulted. The girl who didn't look over her shoulder or who didn't feel exposed while wearing sweats and an oversized sweatshirt. But I'm afraid the lingering effects of my assault are permanent.

In my chest is a cavity where my innocence used to be, and right now, I feel helpless, like I'll never be able to fill it again.

I don't want to live in fear for the rest of my life, but there's no way around it as it grapples with my broken heart, leaving me cold and afraid.

25

VICTORIA

Home doesn't feel the same. It doesn't feel safe anymore.

Two months later, and the effects of being kidnapped loom over me like an oppressive dark cloud. Added to the painful memories is the weight of the survivor's guilt, which has become a part of me.

Sleeping is the worst. It's when I find all my emotions become heightened to one hundred percent.

When I close my eyes, I see pain and my attackers. The darkness sucks me into the past through a series of nightmares. The dreams are always the same. Five men are on top of me, and I'm chained to a table. Their filthy hands and dirty mouths dominate my body. My eyes are Erika's, and I yearn for death.

This isn't my reality, but it is for others. My dreams are the day and night of Erika and those who have yet to be rescued. They can't escape their abusers, and I can't escape the nightmares.

In my dreams, Leo never comes, and his name is always the last thing I shout out into the abyss.

My parents have been with me through every step of my healing journey. Whenever I wake up screaming, they are beside me. They want me to tell them what exactly happened in France, but I can't tell them.

The shame of my assault makes talking to them about it painful. I don't want them to see me differently.

To tell the police what happened to me is one thing, but to tell my parents how my body was violated is another story. It would kill them to hear how they touched me.

Time hasn't erased the touch of Richard and my other attacker. No amount of showers can wash away their touch. I'd scrub until my skin peeled and was blistering red, but nothing would get rid of the irritation.

My parents hope therapy will help me cope with the trauma. It doesn't. The memories of my kidnapping remain engraved in my mind.

I can tell it pains them not being able to shelter me from the past. But I'm more worried they won't be able to shelter me from the present.

Whether Leo will keep his promise and protect me, I'm not sure. There hasn't been a single word from him, and his silence hurts more than I imagined. I'm not sure he even knows where I am.

Regardless of how little I know of him, I still miss him, secrets and all.

He's my savior, and I grew up watching fairy tales where a damsel in distress marries her knight. But this isn't a fairytale. This is reality, and I'm dealing with the effects of human trafficking. Which means I don't feel safe unless I'm with Leo. The man who saved me from it all.

I don't doubt that I'm suffering from some weird form of Stockholm syndrome. But I'm not sure what this feeling is because Leo didn't kidnap me. He saved me.

I haven't told my family about Leo because there's no point in telling them about someone they'll never meet.

My silence worries my family, but no matter how much they prodded for answers, they wouldn't get any. My hesitation in speaking and the tears the mention of France brought me drove them to stop trying to get me to open up.

I'm thankful they are respecting my wishes not to speak about it. At least not right now, not when the wound is still fresh. Maybe I'll be ready to talk about it in a few more months or a year… maybe never… I'm not sure.

Since coming home, it's like the days drag on, and I'm numb inside despite having my freedom back.

It's hard to go to university and live my life while knowing girls are being sold like property and raped every minute of every day.

This information and seeing the abuse firsthand means I can't live how I used to. There's a beauty to the unknown, which I have previously taken for granted. Once you see the filthy darkness this world offers, there's no wiping the smudge from your eyes. It's there in sight forever, making it difficult to find beauty in other parts of the world.

My thoughts are broken when I hear a throat clearing. I look up to see my therapist, and I say nothing to her. I never do, even if the silence is torturous.

Like most times, we stare at each other, with her trying to get me to talk when she asks me one of her questions. It never works. I don't want to be here.

To talk about the past and how I'm feeling doesn't help. It makes me remember, and I don't want to remember, especially when I'm already reminded of what happened to me every single night.

I'm tired of the pain.

Her voice cuts through the awkward silence, and she says something I haven't considered before.

She wonders if my fear of Adriano coming back to get me is pushing me into a corner of silence. It's an idea I can't stop thinking about.

Is this what's happening to me? Does Adriano still have power over me?

This thought angers me, and something inside clicks—a pettiness to overcome this fear. To prove to myself Adriano didn't win because I'm strong and didn't need Leo to feel safe.

After months of trying, my therapist has somehow broken into me, and I realize the past is the past. I can't change what happened to me. What I can do is lift my head and march into my present and future, scars and all.

This information has sparked my determination to use my vulnerability to channel my strength and not let my past affect my future. I won't let a man push me into silence.

The question now is whether I'm strong enough to move on and forget. Or if I'm speaking out of my ass in hopes of convincing myself I'm okay.

After my therapy session, I go straight to my room and pull out the camera Leo bought me. I'm giving myself this one last time to reminisce on the pictures before I move on.

To be stuck in the past isn't healthy.

There's a knock on my door, but I don't turn to see who it is because I'm engrossed with the image of mine and Leo's hands side by side. His fingers graze the top of my hand, and the image brings a flutter to my stomach. The first one in many days.

My sister's warm almond-shaped eyes stare at me with pity. I have to turn away because I don't want people to see me as broken glass.

She draws her bottom lip between her teeth and looks at me, silently asking if she can see.

I let out a deep sigh and hand her the camera.

She's quiet for a minute.

"Whose hand is this? I know it's not Sofia's," she asks with a teasing smile resting on her pink lips, trying to lighten the mood.

I'm aware of what she's doing when I see the glint in her eyes. Eloisa is trying to butter me up into telling her what's bothering me. She's my big sister and can read me like the back of her hand.

What my therapist told me comes to mind, and I decide I'm tired of being silenced by my fear. If I have to choose one person to open up to, it's her, and now is my chance.

I smile after months of frowning, and my sister doesn't expect it. Her eyes widen in shock, and relief swirls in her eyes.

I take the camera from her hands and scroll to the picture of me and Leo. You can't see his handsome face because he's not looking at the camera, but you can still see he has a little smile on the corner of his lips.

"His name is Leo." Realization draws upon Eloisa as the name she's heard me scream at night comes from my lips. But this time around, no tears are falling from my eyes.

"I owe him my life. I wouldn't be here if it weren't for him." My voice is soft and the grief of missing him numbs me.

Eloisa frowns. "What do you mean?"

Her question is enough for me to tell her what happened in France, and she's pale by the end.

In a flash, I'm pressed tight to her warm chest.

"You love him, don't you?" she asks me, and her question makes me nervous.

I'm not sure how to answer her because I'm not sure what love is, and as I ponder her question, I realize I've never felt like this for anyone.

Love seems like such a powerful force, and I thought you could only love someone when you know them well. This isn't the case between me and Leo. So where does this leave my feelings for him?

There's no formula to tell me why I'm still missing him after this long. The only thing I can think about is what I've learned in my philosophy class.

I wonder if *Diotima* was correct in her thoughts of love in *Symposium*? Is love eros? The desire to look for what is beautiful in the world.

Did Leo's inner and outer beauty captivate me after my traumatic experience? Have I looked at him to show me that all men aren't as evil as my kidnappers? I can't help but feel like this is one of the reasons why Leo has the effect he does on my heart in such a short time.

I've climbed the *ladder of love*. Going from lust to morality in a blink of an eye. It's as if I've now ascended to the beautiful ideas and values of love, all of which revolve around him. It's left me flustered; with emotions I don't understand.

If this is love, then it's painful.

Where's the beauty in love when you can't have the person your heart is calling for?

"What's wrong?" Eloisa asks with furrowed brows.

"Why do I feel this way toward him?" My voice cracks, and the tears rise. "It's not fair that I won't ever see him again, and I'm pretty sure he already has someone in his life."

"What makes you think he already has someone?"

"He told some girl named Cleo he loved her over the phone right next to me! And yet the entire time we were together, he would treat me like he wanted me. He would buy me clothes, and a camera, kiss my head, and declare to protect me—confusing me." I sigh, resting my head on my sister's shoulder.

Her laughter bursts out of her, and I send her a glare.

She flicks a finger over the center of my forehead, and I whine.

"Victoria, have you ever considered Cleo being, I don't know... his sister, mom, or aunt? Come on, Victoria, we tell each other I love you all the time," she says with a hint of amusement.

I roll my lips and digest her words.

She places a hand on my forearm.

"Honey, love has blinded you."

"I don't love him." The lie slips out of me, and my face turns warm.

"Whatever you say," Eloisa mumbles, patting my shoulder. I watch as she rises from the bed and walks toward my closet. She throws articles of clothing onto the ground behind her.

"What are you doing?" My annoyance grows when the clothes she throws pile before my feet.

"We're going out. But first, you need to shower and change. You're still young. Don't waste yourself over a guy you met for a week." She throws a dress my way, and it hits me in the face. "There's plenty of fish in the sea for you to catch." My sister wiggles her eyebrows and sends me a wink.

"You're one to speak. You married your first love and only boyfriend," I mutter, watching as she flicks her right hand, rolling her eyes.

"Oh whatever, now go shower," she orders, and I groan, doing as instructed, when she sends me a pointed stare.

Although hesitant to go out, I'm glad I did because talking with my sister and having a night of fun showed me what I've been missing—a world full of life and hope, which isn't all bad and scary. I only have to change my mindset to move past the darkness. It's easier said than done, but it's not impossible. I know I can do it with time.

As my sister said, I have my whole life ahead of me, and I'm wasting it away.

The girls Adriano has kidnapped are fresh in my mind. But what can I do? I did what I could and told the police everything I knew. They promised me they would do their part to find them, and now it's time I put my trust in them and Leo, who told me he would try to rescue them as well.

By the end of the night, I accepted that Leo wasn't someone I get to keep. Rather, he's someone who entered my life to give me a second chance.

Our memories together will remain with me, but it's time I move on from the past.

I'm ready to find peace.

You can only live in darkness for so long before it kills you.

26

LEO

It feels like a lifetime without Victoria when it's only been three months.

Inside me is a surge of anger and resentment toward anything and everything.

I'm a bitter bastard.

My sister instantly noticed how my cruel personality doubled with my return from France. She wasn't happy with my new attitude and demanded answers, even if it meant tapping my shoulder for an entire day.

I eventually caved in, and Cleo's excitement grew when she found out it was a girl who was making me this restless. She made me tell her everything that happened between me and Victoria.

As expected, Cleo wanted to meet the girl who captivated the heartless Leo Bandoni. But I told her it wasn't possible. She was disappointed, but she understood my hesitation.

If anyone knows about the pain that comes with being affiliated with the mafia, it's Cleo.

I want nothing more than to bring Victoria into my life, or at least check up on her. But it would be wrong of me to do that.

She's moving on with her life, and I don't want my arrival to bring back any past trauma she has worked hard to overcome. She deserves peace and a long life full of happiness, both of which she can't have if I bring her into my life.

I'm not the only one suffering. Francisco is also experiencing his own form of silent grief.

A particular spitfire named Sofia has Francisco wrapped around her pinky despite all the headaches she gave him.

The fucker fell for her.

My phone rings loudly, bringing me out of my meditative state.

As the shrilling continues, I push aside the thoughts of how much I miss Victoria.

I ignore the call and draw my attention to the stacks of papers set before me. One look at them and the thought of Victoria strike me as more intriguing than looking over new business deals with notorious mafia families or hunting down those who owe me money.

She's a beautiful distraction, even when she isn't a part of my life.

The second I let her go, I knew my heart belonged only to her. She's my hardest goodbye, alongside my mother.

A sigh drags out of me, and I close my eyes, trying to ease the intense feelings coursing through my veins.

I have to stop being this way. I have an empire to run, which needs stability. But Victoria is making it damn difficult to even move on.

I miss her.

Cupid's love dart has lodged itself straight into my cold heart, and it's stuck in there. My constant efforts to push love away have been for nothing. I can't fight the intense pull tugging me toward Victoria.

I'm drunk in love and I can't focus on anything other than her. She has taken over my *mind*, my *dreams*, and my *heart*. It's an instant affection that is irreversible.

Sometimes at night, I can't sleep when I think about her falling in love with someone who isn't me. The mere thought of another man holding her in his arms sparks a fit of anger. It makes me want to fly to California to scare any of those pathetic boys away because she's mine to love.

She's not yours.

I have to remind myself of this frustrating truth.

Glancing down at the document I'm signing, I find I wrote her name instead of mine.

This is getting out of hand. I'm not in the right state of mind when she isn't near me. I need her as much, if not more, than I need air.

How can I have order amongst many other ruthless mafiosos worldwide when I'm lovesick?

I rub my temple, pondering over what my mafioso friends would say if they only knew about my internal struggles as of late.

Would they question my power and ability to keep our family alliance strong?

Notorious mafia families from China, Russia, America, and Cuba depend on me to ensure our mafias continue thriving. I can't allow our hard work to fall apart because I'm not in the right state of mind.

If another Bandoni goes off the rails because of love, they might challenge my leadership, and I can't let that happen.

I'd be damned if they tried to question my authority and ability.

My family worked hard to be where we are today, and they are nothing without us. They owe us their respect and loyalty after everything my grandpa did for them after the huge war that broke out and nearly destroyed all our mafias.

The Bandonis are the reason they still have the influence they have today. If not for the alliance my grandfather created, they'd be nothing but mediocre gangsters on the streets.

The mafia alliance keeps a sort of balance between the five biggest mafia families. It's a pact made to ensure we don't kill one another over money and power.

Given my family's influence in creating the alliance, we became the peacekeepers, and over the course of a few years, we have somehow become the leaders they often look to.

My phone rings again, demanding my attention, and this time the person calling me has fueled my short temper.

"Who is this?" The irritation is clear in my voice.

"Hey, cousin."

From the sound of Adriano, my grip on the phone becomes tight.

"You have some nerve calling me!" I grit out, remembering what he and his men did to Victoria and Sofia.

His breathing is harsh over the line.

"I'm still mad about what you did to my men and business partners, but I might consider forgiving you if you give me back my property," he says in frustration, prompting me to raise a brow.

What is he talking about?

"Adriano, I don't have time for your bullshit, so why don't you stop hiding and come face me like a real man."

"Fuck you!" he says violently over the phone. "I won't ask again. Remove your security from the girl, the one with the attitude. I'm sure you know which one." His words hint at a sinister mockery. Almost as if he's telling me he knows about my affection toward Victoria. From his words, my heart sinks to my stomach, and my body grows heavy.

How did he find out?

He continues his threat, "she belongs to one of my men. He paid good money for her. I made him a promise, and I keep my promises." He pauses, and my neck stiffens with his next words. "It would do you well to remember this."

"You will never touch a hair on her head!"

"Fine, if you don't remove the men around her, I will grab her myself. As a matter of fact, I have men down there with strict orders to kill her pathetic bodyguards. Should I send you their heads when they're done?"

"You fucker! When I find you, I'm slitting your fucking throat!"

"Did I hit a nerve, Leo?" He laughs, and I'm going to curse him when he cuts me off. "Look, I have to go. My plane is about to leave for California. I'll tell her you miss her."

"I'm going to fucking kill—" I'm cut off by the sharp sound of the call being ended. His laughter is the last thing I hear.

"Mother Fucker!" I throw the phone across the room, and it shatters into pieces upon impact with the wall. A powerful desire to kill Adriano crawls up my spine, and my hands tremble from rage and fear as unpleasant possibilities rise in my mind.

I spring out of my seat with a force so strong I kick the chair behind me.

As I thunder out of my office, some of my men watch me with wide, curious eyes.

"Where's Francisco?" I ask one of them, and he swallows, visibly afraid.

"In the training room." He watches me warily, and I say nothing else.

My steps toward the training room are fast, and I make my way toward Francisco, who's getting ready to lift weights.

He drops what he's doing when he sees me, and his thick blond eyebrows rise.

"Leo—"

He never finishes because I grab him by the back of his white muscle shirt. It tears under my grip.

"What the fuck? Let me go!" he retorts as I drag him out of the training room, away from anyone listening. It was impossible for Adriano to find out about Victoria's importance to me. Someone close had to have told him.

We arrive at my office, and I let him go.

"What the hell is wrong with you?" he shouts, adjusting his shirt. "I understand you miss Victoria. I also miss Sofia, but I don't make people miserable because I'm miserable," Francisco snaps. "So, stop being a little bitch!"

"Are you done now?" I say, voice thick with anger.

Francisco huffs, dropping himself onto the couch in my office. He crosses his arms over his chest, and a line appears between his brows.

"Why are you angry this time?"

I pour myself a glass of bourbon to ease my nerves before I explain to him the call I received.

"Adriano plans on kidnapping Victoria."

As soon as the words are in the air, his eyes widen.

"Shit!"

I nod, chugging the liquor. The alcohol burns my throat, but nothing compares to the burning flames of rage Adriano's threat on Victoria's life has brought to me.

"We need to go get her before it's too late," I say urgently, and he rises from his seat.

"I'll call the pilot to get the jet ready. How many men do you want to take?" he asks, pulling his phone out.

"Five should be fine." I pause and suppress my grin when a thought comes to mind. "I'm guessing you're going to want to come?" I ask, knowing there's no way he'd pass on the opportunity to see Sofia.

Francisco becomes tense and slowly looks up from his phone. His cheeks are a deep red. I lift a brow when he says nothing and decide to provoke him some more.

"I'm taking your silence as a no..." The second I say this, his eyes widen. "You can stay here and cover for me while I'm gone."

"What the fuck do you mean? I'm going with you," he reproaches. "Tell Kaden to cover for your ass."

As soon as he loses his composure, his face turns even more red, making me laugh. Francisco curses me before leaving my office to prepare for our departure.

When he's gone, I let out a breath and make my way toward Cleo's room to tell her I'm going to California.

It looks like she'll meet Victoria after all.

Immense excitement surges within me at the thought of seeing Victoria again, but it falters from the gravity of the situation.

I've once again failed at keeping my promise.

The violence of my work has somehow found its way into her life, and now she's in danger while I'm miles away.

I hurry out of my office so I can get the hell out of here and get to Victoria before I lose her.

VICTORIA

A month has passed since I told my sister what happened to me, and everything seems to have returned to normal. Leo still comes to mind, but whenever I think about him, it brings me happiness, not sadness.

Unfortunately, the survivor's guilt continues to weigh down on me, and I know it will always be there.

I fix my stare on the yellow, orange leaves of the oak trees on either side of me. The branches sway side to side as I make my way across my college campus.

The sun is setting, and night is approaching. Yet the campus is still full of life. It's midterm season, and everyone is busy trying to cram last-minute studying before the first round of exams in the quarter.

A cool breeze licks my skin, bringing goosebumps. I wrap my arms around my midsection as I make my across campus to reach the parking lot.

After walking for twenty minutes, I sigh in relief when I see my car ahead.

I go to grab my phone from my backpack so I can let my parents know I'm heading home, but my spine locks up from fear when I hear heavy footsteps approaching from behind me. I try to fight the rising panic when I don't remember seeing students heading toward the parking lot.

The steps nearing behind me are heavy, urgent, and angry. Different from the soft, tired steps of a college student leaving after a long day of classes.

I hurry my steps. The traffic zooming nearby match the hurried sound of my footfalls. The person behind me increases their speed, and dread twists in my heart.

The contents in my backpack rattle when I move it in front of me so I can pull out my keys with my taser and pepper spray.

My heart jumps, and a scream bolts out of me when someone comes rushing from behind. Their strong arms wrap tight around my midsection.

"I told you I'd be back for you."

I stagger from the sound of the familiar rough voice of the man who called me his sex toy. His voice brings back the memories of him almost raping me, and I become paralyzed with fear.

This can't be happening.

He inhales my scent and buries his head in the crook of my neck.

"Leave me alone," I plead, the tears rising. They chuckle and it vibrates against the back of my neck. Their breath brings an unpleasant chill.

"You belong to me, remember?"

"I don't belong to anyone, dickhead!" My arms continue to fight under his grasp, but the more I fight, the tighter his grip becomes.

When I shout for help, he moves his calloused hand to cover my mouth.

"Shut up and stop fighting!"

I don't listen to him, and my fighting instincts kick in. I press my taser to his neck with no remorse. His screams fill the night air, and he pushes me to the ground as the electric currents shock the veins of his jugular.

"Fucking bitch!" His voice is loud and deadly as he withers in pain, holding his neck.

I lift myself from the ground and look at my attacker. When I do, I'm met with dark eyes, and my heart drops to my stomach because glaring at me is none other than Lorenzo. The same man from the restaurant in France who handed me my purse.

He leaps toward me at the same time I prepare to run to my car. But before I can leave the area, the sound of a car screeching to a halt comes from behind me. The air fills with the smell of burned tires, and the door to the car opens.

Muscular arms wrap around my waist and pull me inside. My screams echo throughout the parking lot.

It's happening again. I'm being kidnapped, and Leo can't save me this time because he's on the other side of the world.

The car lurches forward at lightning speed and screams of terror keep coming from me. I'm fighting in my attacker's arms, and my elbow hits them in the face.

They grunt in pain, and their hold around me releases.

It's dark, but I can still see the silhouette of a man beside me. I pepper spray him, and his screams fill the car.

I get whiplash when I'm turned around, and my heart stops for a second.

"Miss me," my attacker says with a devilish smirk, and I fall faint in their arms, allowing darkness to take me under.

Part 2

27

LEO

My heart beats heavily as I run out of the plane, rushing to get to Victoria.

I have to get to her first. If not, Adriano will do the unimaginable. He's been waiting for this opportunity since we were boys.

Adriano is a replica of his father, Marquez. He has the same power hunger and doesn't know the first thing about respect.

Marquez and my father, Estephano, were twins, and despite their similar faces, the two were *very* different.

My father's fault had always been giving his brother the benefit of the doubt, and it led to his downfall.

This feud between me and Adriano is more complex than two cousins at odds. This is a war between brothers that has been passed down to their sons. A war in which the women in our lives pay the price, and I have now thrown Victoria into this family feud.

Arriving in her neighborhood with armed men isn't how I would have wanted to meet her parents. But I'm not a regular man, and this isn't a regular visit. This is a rescue mission.

"Are you fucking serious?" My hand clenches to my side as I glare out the window. "Can these assholes drive any slower?"

For a freeway, they don't drive fast, and I'm already impatient as it is.

Angelo, who's behind the wheel, presses on the gas, and we zig-zag through the Los Angeles traffic, earning some angry honks.

Luca, who's clutching the car's grab handle as if his life depended on it, laughs at my frustration.

I send him a glare, and my knee bounces with anticipation. It's like the first time I found her all over again. The fear of not knowing if she's okay makes me a nervous wreck.

"I swear I'm going to blow Adriano's brains out if he touches a single hair on her perfect head."

Francisco turns to me with lifted brows.

I'm about to tell him to wipe the stupid grin off his face when Angelo finally tells me the words I've been waiting to hear.

"We're here!"

"Fucking finally!" I sigh and throw open the door. I position my gun in front of me and I scan the area for any sign of Adriano. Francisco follows closely behind.

Where is he?

My uneasiness rises from the quietness of the neighborhood.

I pound my fist on the front door, and a petite older woman with black shoulder length hair and brown eyes stares at me with a warm smile. The color drains from her face, and her smile falls when she sees my gun pointed at her.

She makes a startled cry and moves to close the door, but I put my foot in the way, forcing it back open.

She cries even louder, and her hands rise in front of her.

"Please don't hurt me! I don't have much, but you can take whatever you want. Just don't kill me. My family needs me." She's shaking under the door, and tears quickly rise to her eyes.

I give a gentle smile at the similarities between Victoria and her mother, and I lower my gun.

"Maria?" A deep, masculine voice comes from behind her, and a large man with broad shoulders and brown skin appears. His eyes widen in shock at the sight of me, and his expression hardens into a glare.

He brings his wife behind him in a protective stance, and I grimace at how bad this entire meeting is going.

I'm not making a good impression, that's for sure.

The older couple watches me and Francisco wearily.

"Where's Victoria?" I ask, and there's a panic in my voice which startles them.

"She's not here," Victoria's dad says, his voice holding a challenge.

She can be dead, and he's being vague now!

I turn to the short woman peering from the side of her husband.

"Where is she?" I ask softly, not wanting to frighten her more than she already is.

"You won't find her." Her voice holds a hint of sass, but I can still hear the slight tremble behind her words.

From their reluctance to answer me, there's a tic in my jaw, and I glance at Francisco for help. His blue eyes widen, and he lifts his hands, taking a step back. His attention flickers from me to Victoria's parents, watching our interaction with a grin.

Fucking asshole.

"I'm trying to save her. Tell me where she is before it's too late."

"Bullshit!" her dad shouts, coming near me, his fists raised.

Another voice comes from inside the house, and a young woman with lighter hair and olive skin appears from behind them.

"Mami? Papi? What's going on?" Her eyes travel from her parents to me, and they widen. "It's you!" she beams with a glowing face.

"Do I know you?" I ask, and she shakes her head with a smile on her thin lips.

She opens the door wide, ushering me inside, which makes her parents shout their disapproval. She ignores them and pulls me and Francisco into the house.

"No, you don't know me, but my sister showed me pictures of you guys in Paris... It's Leo, right?"

"The one and only," I respond with a grin.

She extends a hand. "I'm Eloisa, Victoria's older sister." I shake her hand, and her mother speaks from beside us.

"Eloisa, how do you know this kidnapper?" At the sound of her mother's condescending tone, Eloisa rolls her eyes.

She turns to me with an apologetic look.

"Mami, don't judge people before you get to know them. Trust me. He's no kidnapper." She laughs, glancing at me.

I want to laugh at her comment because I've done worse than kidnap people. But she doesn't need to know I run one of the biggest crime organizations in the world.

"How do you know he isn't?" This time it's her father who speaks. His stare falls on me before landing back on his daughter. "Eloisa, look at him." He points at my gun.

She sighs. "Dad, he saved Victoria and Sofia. If it weren't for him, I wouldn't have my little sister, and you wouldn't have your daughter, so be nice."

Victoria's mom gasps and wraps her thin arms around me.

From the sudden embrace of a mother, buried memories resurface, bringing a tightness to my throat.

Maria detaches herself from me.

"I'm so sorry for being rude. Victoria wouldn't tell us what happened to her in France. She would wake up screaming your name at night, so I assumed you were the one who kidnapped her."

My body grows heavy from this news, and Eloisa notices, and her lips lift into a slight smile.

"What are you doing here?" she asks.

Finally someone who will tell me where Victoria is!

"Your sister's in danger. Adriano, the man who kidnapped her, wants her back."

"Dios mio no!" Victoria's mom gasps, and the color drains from their faces.

"I need to know where she is before it's too late."

"She's supposed to be in class right now. I can take you to her school," Eloisa says, ready to grab her car keys.

"No, it's fine. I know where she goes to school," I say, making my way to the door, and when I'm about to leave, a small hand around my arm stops me.

Victoria's mom stares at me. Her eyes misting with tears.

"Please bring her back to me." I nod, giving her an assuring smile, before rushing to the car and starting the forty-minute drive to Victoria's school.

When we arrive, it's dark, and the school is huge, which makes finding her difficult. To make matters worse, I haven't heard from the bodyguards I assigned to her.

My heart beats hard in my chest, and the fear increases every second.

"Take a right," I order, and Angelo does a sharp turn.

I scan the area, and my stare falls on Victoria, struggling in the arms of a man.

A raw fear spikes through me when I notice a black van speeding toward them.

"Over there, hurry!" Angelo steps on the gas, trying to beat the van rushing to pull up behind her.

When Adriano's men notice us heading straight toward them, the van swirls to the side, almost tipping over.

My eyes zero in on Lorenzo, the dick who embezzled money from me a few years ago and who ran away like a coward.

I want to jump out of the car and strangle him for touching Victoria, but I don't have time. I need to focus on getting her out of danger first.

Luca swings open the door, and I grab Victoria from behind. I pull her into the car, and Angelo swerves sharply to avoid the van now chasing us.

Victoria's screaming and flailing around in my arms, unaware that it's me.

Her elbow connects with my nose, and my hold around her loosens. As soon as she's free, she pepper sprays Luca in the eyes.

"Ah, fucking shit!" he screams, his hands rising to his eyes.

I turn her in my arms, relieved to see her face in the flesh and not in my dreams.

"Miss me?" I say, feeling complete with her in my arms. But my relief is short-lived when her eyes roll to the back of her head, and she falls limp in my arms.

"Fuck!"

VICTORIA

"What happened to her?" I hear my mom say as I'm placed on a soft surface.

The bed dips beside me when someone sits down.

"She fainted when she saw me," Leo says, and my eyes flash open, unable to believe what I'm hearing.

"Leo?" I call out in a tired voice. He turns to me, his eyes bright with relief.

I pull him into a tight embrace. The sudden motion makes black dots cloud my vision, and my upper body sways.

Leo notices and steadies me by cupping my face. There's a frown locked between his eyebrows.

"You're here," I breathe, unable to believe it.

"I'm here," he whispers, his thumb grazing my cheeks.

"But why?"

"Remember what I promised you?"

My lips draw into a frown at what he's implying.

"I'm in danger," I whisper, and he sighs, giving a defeated nod.

I study his olive skin and notice it looks ashen, and his eyes are droopy, filled with tiredness and worry.

He must have rushed to get here.

"I'm sorry," I mumble, feeling guilty for causing him trouble.

"This isn't your fault." Leo's voice is firm, and he doesn't break eye contact with me.

"What does Adriano want?"

Leo grabs my hand.

"I promise I won't let him or Lorenzo hurt you."

The mention of Lorenzo brings a tremor, and along with it comes worry for my cousin's safety.

"What's wrong?" Leo asks when he sees the panic on my face.

"What about Sofia? Is she in danger?"

"She's okay." He places a hand on my forearm. "Adriano threatened me about taking you back for one of his men." Leo's face darkens, and his jaw twitches as he says this.

"It's Lorenzo. He's adamant about having me as his sex toy," I whisper, and it kills me inside to say the words.

"Bambina, I won't let him hurt you again," Leo says with an air of determination.

I lift a brow at the nickname he's given me.

"Bambina?" I ask, and the corner of Leo's mouth tips into a half smile.

Heavy breathing by my bedroom door has us all turning to my dad, who's glaring at Leo.

"How are you going to protect me from Italy?" I say, trying to break the tension in the room.

Leo's lips roll into his mouth, and he rubs the back of his neck.

"About that...to make sure you're safe, I need you to come back with me to Italy."

My dad, who's been silent this entire time, speaks up.

"Absolutely not!" His voice has an icy edge, and Leo tenses beside me.

"Victoria is in danger," Leo interrupts in disbelief, and my dad crosses his arms over his chest with a raised brow.

"Would you let your daughter go across the world with a man who had a gun pointed at you two hours ago?"

Leo sighs. "I see your point, but if I have to take her by force to make sure she's safe, then I will." He rises from my bed. "And even *you* won't be able to stop me."

My dad and Leo approach each other. My eyes widen, and I rush toward them. Both their jaws are tight, and their fists are clenched, ready to strike at one another.

"The answer is still no, and I'd like to see you try to take her without my permission." As my dad says this, I move to stand between the two angry men, and my mom holds my dad back.

"Leo, sit down," I demand, before turning to my dad. "Apa, stop challenging him."

My dad huffs in annoyance but steps back when he hears me call him Apa, a term reserved for when I'm angry at him.

"Leo..." I warn when he doesn't stop glaring at my dad. I place a hand on his arm, and he relaxes.

"Leo, what about school? or my family? Will Adriano not hurt them if they stay?"

A thoughtful expression crosses his face.

"See if you can do your schoolwork online for the time being," Leo says, making it sound easy. But it's not possible to do online classes this far into the quarter. I have exams next week, and I'll fail if I can't make it. The only choice I have is to take a leave of absence.

"That's not possible this far into the quarter." Understanding washes over his face. But I realize my life is more important than a degree. "School can wait," I say in defeat, and his shoulders relax. "But what about my family?"

"I'll have guards stationed around your house to protect them. Your family will be safe. I promise you nothing will happen to them," Leo says, having everything planned out.

"Okay, then I guess I need to pack."

"Victoria, you're not leaving!" my dad warns, saying my name with a Spanish accent.

"Apa..." I make my way toward him, and there's a tug in my chest when I see the pain in his eyes.

"No, Victoria. The last time you left for another country, we got a call in the middle of the night saying you were dead."

"Dad, this time it's different," I assure him, placing a comforting hand on his stubbled cheek. "Nothing is going to happen to me. Leo is going to protect me."

"Miguel, Victoria's right. She's better protected with Leo than she is here with us. Leo will bring her back when everything is safe again," my mom assures my dad as she runs a comforting hand down his back.

My dad looks from my mom to me in contemplation. His stare then falls on Leo, and a skeptical frown pulls at his mouth.

"Papi, I'm not safe here, and as long as I'm here, neither are you guys." My dad's frown deepens, and after a few seconds, he nods in understanding.

"Okay, you can go. But for how long?" he asks Leo.

"I'm not sure, but she'll be under my protection for as long as it takes..." Leo states, glancing at me for a second. "It can be days, weeks, or months."

"Months! Maria, are you hearing this?" my dad says in disbelief.

My mom gives a simple nod, her lips set into a grimace.

"Anything for our daughter's safety." She struggles to keep her voice steady as tears well up in her eyes, and she and my sister leave my room.

"Maria, where are you going?" my dad shouts, chasing after her.

"To get the suitcase, she needs to pack!" As soon as she says this, I hear his disapproval and I laugh at their bickering.

"Victoria, did you see the three big ass dudes outside our—" My brother Cristian rushes into my room, and when he looks up to see Leo, his eyes widen in shock. A thousand questions loom in his eyes. "There's another one?" he mutters, craning his neck to stare at Leo, who lets out a breathy laugh.

My brother's eyes are weary as he stares at Leo, but it disappears, and his face glows with excitement.

"No way!" he blurts. "You have a gun?"

"Um, yeah. Do you want to hold it?" Leo stupidly offers, and my brother eagerly nods, grabbing the gun from Leo's outstretched hand.

I send Leo a glare, and he rolls his lips into his mouth when he sees my anger.

"Awesome! Dad would freak out if he saw me holding one of these bad boys," Cristian exclaims before shouting for our brother-in-law. "Matthew, come here! This dude has a gun!"

Matthew is quick to run into the room, and he stumbles back when he sees Leo. Apprehension is visible in his hazel eyes.

"What type is it?" Mathew asks.

"It's a Desert Eagle." Cristian takes the safety off and Leo takes the gun from his hands. "Woah, I don't want your dad to kill me if you shoot someone's toes off." Leo laughs, putting his gun away.

"Right, sorry." A sheepish twitch curls around the corner of his mouth. "My name's Cristian," my brother says, shaking Leo's hand and puffing his chest out.

I let out a not-so-ladylike laugh at the sight of his frail chest, and Cristian glares at me when I take a jab at his masculinity.

"Nice to meet you... I'm Leo."

"Why do you carry a gun?" my brother asks, and my brows rise, wanting to hear what Leo will say.

Leo turns to me with a slightly nervous expression, but it's only there for a second.

"To protect your sister." Leo's reply is once again vague.

"Are you a bodyguard?" Cristian edges for more information.

"Yeah, I'm a bodyguard of some sort... your sister's bodyguard, to be exact." Leo turns to me and winks, a grin covering his full lips.

My mom enters carrying my suitcase, and she lets out a breath.

"Cristian, leave them alone and go do your homework," she warns, and my brother groans, taking his leave. Matthew follows after him.

My mom turns to me and Leo.

"Here you are. Do you need any help, Mija?" My mom smiles, but it doesn't quite reach her eyes. It's clear that having to let me go abroad after what happened last time is taking a toll on her.

"I think we've got it, right?" I ask Leo, who nods and takes the suitcase from my mom.

My mom leaves, and when she's gone, Leo flashes me a cheeky grin. I lift a brow, watching as he places my suitcase on the bed.

"So, Bambina, where are your panties? We can pack those first."

My eyes widen, not believing what I just heard him say. The amusement on his face assures me I did hear him correctly.

"Shut up!" I say, crossing my arms over my chest, trying to cool down the warmth rushing to my face. "You can start by helping me get the clothes I need out of my closet."

"Fine, we'll pack the panties last," he mumbles, opening my closet.

Huffing in annoyance, I grab a pillow off my bed and throw it at the back of Leo's head. Upon impact, his back straightens, and he stops dead in his track. He turns to face me with false disbelief.

"Did you just throw a pillow at me?"

"Maybe," I exclaim with raised brows. "What are you going to do about it, *bodyguard*?" My words are challenging, and Leo pauses in thought. His face glows when he's struck with an idea, and he prowls toward me with a mischievous grin.

I backtrack until the side of my bed stops me, and I have to crane my neck to stare at him, but as I do, I find myself falling back.

Leo wraps me in his arms, trying to keep me up, but he gets caught between my legs and comes tumbling onto the bed with me under him.

I close my eyes, waiting for the moment we butt heads, but we never do.

My forehead creases, and I open my eyes, only to find Leo centimeters away from me.

His gaze trails over every inch of my face, and with him this close to me, I get a whiff of the familiar, comforting scent of his musky cologne. It brings a chill to my body.

Leo's eyes linger on mine, his expression passionate.

I can't help it when my stare falls on the familiar scar running down the right side of his temple. The pad of my pointer finger runs the length of the mark.

His eyes fall on my lips, and my heart is beating so fast I can feel it in my throat.

A loud cough from the door has me abruptly looking away from him.

Leo sighs, also turning to the door where Luca, Angelo, Francisco, and my siblings stand.

They all gawk at us with mixed emotions—amusement from Leo's friends, disgust from my brother, and my sister is grinning.

I remove my hand from Leo's face, and my insides flush with embarrassment.

2 8

ADRIANO

There's no way Lorenzo can fail such a simple task. Or so I thought.

My eyes narrow into slits as I glare at the idiot.

Sweat beads his forehead, and my own skin is sticky from the humidity in the room.

The fan churns above us, but instead of cooling the room, it only makes it hotter. Nothing can cool the moisture of the green hell we've taken shelter in.

I fucking hated this shit.

Having to hide from Leo and the fucking police while still trying to run a business in the dark sucks.

"It was a simple task." My words are harsh, and I rub my temple in frustration.

Lorenzo gulps harshly. "Boss—"

I lean over my desk, grabbing him by the collar of his shirt.

"You useless fuck!" I snap, trying to restrain myself from killing him. I thrust him back with a frustrated sigh.

"Bring me the girl. That's all I asked of you."

His eyes calculate my next move. He's afraid. *Good.*

"I had her! But your bastard cousin came from behind and swooped her up," he defends.

"You had her?" My tone is sarcastic, and Lorenzo tenses under my glare. "Then where is she? You dipshit!"

This time I don't hold back, and I wrap my hands around his thin neck. He struggles under my deadly grasp, eyes open wide in fear.

What a useless piece of shit.

"Get out of my sight." I release him, and he rushes out of the room, rubbing his neck.

Idiota.

My jaw cracks from how tight I'm clenching my teeth, and I can't believe I let the one missing piece I needed slip from my grasp. Victoria is Leo's weakness. The Stephanie to Estephano.

Victoria better hope Leo can protect her because I'm coming for her, and I have a sinister plan set for the two of them.

They say not to let history repeat itself, but if I have anything to do with it, I will make sure Victoria is ten feet under.

Her death means Leo's heart crumbles under my grasp, giving me total power over not only the Italian mafia but the mafia alliance.

The door to my office opens, and my annoyance increases at the sight of yet another idiot.

I glare at Moises. "And to what do I owe the displeasure of seeing you?" I mock, my attention moving to the door when my favorite toy finally arrives.

"Come here bitch." Erika trembles and takes slow steps toward me. She lets out a small cry when I pull her onto my lap. I trail my finger up her thigh, and she stiffens, her teeth chattering from fear.

Moise's eyes darken with desire for the woman in my arms.

I lift an annoyed brow. Moises coughs, rubbing the back of his neck when he notices my patience is thinning.

"Adriano..." he sighs, his face pale and haggard. Dark circles adorn his eyes like half-moons. "Help me, please."

Scoffing, I shake my head in disbelief.

He did this to himself.

"I lost my job, and my lawyer says it isn't looking good for me."

I remain unfazed, and he lets out a frustrated breath when I show no ounce of remorse.

"This is your fault!" he accuses, and the anger boils inside me. My fingers dig into Erika's boney waist, and she whimpers but says nothing. She's learned to be a good girl.

"Watch your mouth." My words come out deadly. "First, this is your fault for being messy, and second, I sent you a notice about the girls being rescued."

His eyebrows furrow in confusion.

"I didn't get anything."

"Check your emails, dumb ass," I grumble, and he stiffens. "Because of your mistake, I have a burden to deal with myself." I remind him of the snooping police looking for me. "How should I punish you?" I rub my chin in thought.

"Let's not be so rash, Adriano," he rasps, his eyes shadowed with fear when two of my men enter the room. "You want the girl. Let me get her for you!"

I lift my hand and motion for my men to halt. "What do you know about her?"

"Victoria?" Moises asks, and Erika stiffens on my lap. A smile stretches on her chapped lips, and it falters when I send her a warning glare.

"How are *you* going to get her for me?" I ask, and his body straightens, relief clear in his pathetic eyes.

"I'll do whatever I have to!"

"You didn't answer my question!" I grumble. "What do you have that my men don't?"

His lips form a thin line, and when he can't find anything to say, I motion for my men to grab him.

"Wait! wait! I'm a trained police officer, and I know how to manipulate!" he shouts whatever he can come up with. "I have skills you criminals don't have!"

"I'll think about it," I reply, shooing him away.

When he hears my willingness to consider his offer, he sighs in relief and rushes out of the room.

I wrap my hands around Erika's neck. She struggles under my grip, clawing at my hands.

"Smile like that again, and I'll kill you and have my men fuck your corpse!"

She gasps, struggling against me.

I throw her to the side, and she hits the floor with a thud.

"Don't get too confident about your little friend..." She glares at me, and my grin has her swallowing thickly. "She'll be back," I assure her.

"Get the fuck out of here!" I yell, and she runs out of the room, wiping her tears.

Fuck Lorenzo, Fuck Leo, Fuck Victoria, Fuck Erika, Fuck Moises. Fuck them all.

I wouldn't let my father's death be in vain.

Leo will pay the debt he owes me, and he will do so with the life of Victoria.

A life for a life

29

LEO

Victoria purses her lips, a hand under her chin, as she thinks about what else she needs to pack. When she can't think of anything, she turns to me.

"Did you see me not pack anything?"

A grin stretches onto my lips, and she lifts a questioning brow.

"Yeah, your panties," I say, biting back my laughter when her mouth falls open. The shock on her face only lasts a second before it disappears.

"I'm not even going to say anything to you because you have a point," she grumbles, heading toward a drawer near her bed. I peer over at her, and she tenses under my stare.

Victoria turns over her shoulder, and our eyes lock. I gulp, my neck prickling with heat from being caught trying to see.

"Leo, if you don't turn around, I'm not going to Italy with you." She grins, satisfied when she sees the panic on my face.

"Alright, alright," I mutter, turning around and looking at the interior of her room when my stare falls on the framed pictures on her black vanity.

My heart melts at the sight of five-year-old Victoria. Beside her is Sofia, and the two are smiling from ear to ear in ballerina flats and pastel pink tutus.

My gaze moves to the second image of a younger version of Victoria's dad. He has Victoria and her brother, Cristian, hanging upside down by one of their legs, and they're all smiling.

A little yellow sticky note on her mirror catches my attention. Curious, I pick it up, and when I read it, my heart grows heavy from the message she scribbled on it.

It's not my fault. I'm not broken.

I glance from the note to Victoria, and an indescribable pain consumes me. One glance at her, and you wouldn't be able to tell she's suffering inside.

Pain is no stranger to me. I've experienced almost all forms of it. The pain of grief, the pain of a bullet, the pain of being stabbed. I've taken it all with a grain of salt, but for some reason, her pain hits the worse. Knowing she's suffering inside and I can't do anything to help take away her sadness hurts more than being shot three times in the chest.

I pull out a pen from inside my suit and write a message under it.

You're beautiful and loved.

Swallowing the tightness in my throat, I stick the note back where I found it.

From behind me, Victoria huffs in frustration.

My right brow rises in both confusion and amusement when I see her standing on top of the suitcase.

"What are you doing?" I make my way toward her and extend a hand. She places her hand in mine, and I help her off the suitcase.

"The stupid thing won't close," she grumbles and gets on her knees, determined to close the overfilled suitcase.

"You don't need to take all those clothes."

"That's easy for you to say. You aren't the one having to pack your entire life in a few hours." Her face scrunches, and worry lines appear on her forehead.

I sigh, realizing she has a point.

Here I am, beaming with joy because she's coming home with me, but at the cost of separating her from her family and putting a hold on her education. Victoria is giving up everything in her life to come with me.

The mafia has once again stolen from the innocent.

I can see the uncertainty on her beautiful face as she looks around her room with sadness. And as much as I hate taking her away from everything she knows, I can't risk having her miles away from me. Not when she's in danger. She has to come with me, and I will not be leaving this house without her.

"Victoria, I will provide you with anything you need." I help her back onto her feet and place a hand over her cheek. "You need clothes, done. If you want a new laptop, I'll buy it for you. And if you want a million books, I'll buy you the biggest library in the world. Hell, I can buy your university and force them to let you take online classes." I list items receiving a beautiful laugh from her in return, but I'm not joking. I'd go to hell and back for her.

"Leo…" she breathes and I don't let her finish.

"I'm serious. As a matter of fact, let me make some calls," I say, pulling out my phone, ready to figure out who I need to call to buy her school.

Her eyes widen, and she takes my phone away, ending the call.

"Are you crazy!"

Yes, crazy for you.

"Leo, are you trying to buy me off?"

"Is it working?" I ask with a grin.

She frowns.

"Are you telling me you think I'm a gold digger?"

"Wait, what? No!" There's panic in my voice from the sound of her rising anger.

"Good, because I'm not, and you don't need to spend your money on me. I won't have it," she warns with a pointed finger.

I lift my hands in front of me, trying to bite back my grin because I already know I can't stop myself from giving her whatever she wants.

Victoria's attention wavers back to the toppling suitcase. Her face scrunches into a grimace.

I lead her to the suitcase, and when I sit her on top of it, her forehead bunches with confusion.

She stares at me as I kneel in front of her, and I extend a hand to the zipper while my other hand presses down on the suitcase between her thighs.

Victoria freezes.

I look at her to find her lips pressed into her mouth, and she takes unsteady breaths. My stare remains on her, and I fiddle with the zipper, wanting to stay like this for a little longer.

Killing my enemies has always satisfied me, but right now, making Victoria flustered is at the top of the list of my favorite things to do.

"Dinners ready—" Eloisa stops under the door and says, "Oh my..." Her mouth forming into a grin.

"Eloisa!" Victoria stands, almost tripping over the suitcase.

I watch her run after her laughing sister.

Does no one knock in this house?

I zip the suitcase with ease and roll it out of her room.

Luca moans as he tastes Maria's cooking, and I follow the noise.

"Are you okay?" I ask Victoria.

She looks away from her family and peers up at me. Her sparkling eyes are dull with sadness, and I want to wrap my arm around her waist, but I don't when I see the sharp glare her dad is sending my way.

Victoria nods with a little sigh before she makes her way toward her dad, whose eyes soften upon seeing her.

Victoria's mom approaches me with a sad smile.

"Please keep my daughter safe."

"You have my word." I place a hand on her shoulder. "She's in good hands," I assure her when I notice her fighting back her tears.

My stare lands on Victoria's dad, who surprises me when he gives me a nod of acknowledgment. I give him one of my own, assuring him the same promise I made to his wife, but with my eyes.

Victoria stands beside me again, and she lets out a tired breath.

"I have someone I want you to meet when we get to Italy. I know you'll love her," I say and she gives a tight-lipped smile and goes to the trunk of the car to give Francisco her suitcase.

Eloisa approaches me.

"You care a lot about my sister, don't you?" she says, getting straight to the point.

I clear my throat, warmth rushing to my cheeks.

"I guess you can say that," I confess.

Eloisa smiles, but it falls, and her face turns serious. "Leo, can you promise me you'll protect my sister and never let her get hurt by either you or Adriano?"

My answer comes within a heartbeat. "I won't let him hurt her, and I will never dream of hurting your sister," I say, receiving a smile of approval from Eloisa.

As my promise sinks in, the tightness in my chest becomes heavy. I basically assured her that nothing could ever happen between me and her sister.

If I don't want to hurt Victoria, I have to make sure our relationship remains professional. Her parents are counting on me to return her to them when Adriano is dead.

Victoria wraps her arms around Eloisa one last time before letting go and making her way toward me.

I open the car door for her when a familiar voice halts our movements as we prepare to leave.

"Wait! Don't go!" Sofia shouts, running like a crazy person through the street in the middle of the night. She drags her suitcase behind her.

Victoria's head swipes around to face her cousin.

"Sofia, what are you doing here?"

Sofia gasps, trying to catch her breath.

"I'm going with you," she breathes out, wrapping her arm around Victoria. She turns to glare at me. "I don't care what you say. You won't separate us."

I nod, not in the mood to fight with her request. Plus, I'm sure Francisco will appreciate having her come along with us.

Right on cue, Francisco appears from behind the car when he hears her voice.

"Piccolo fuoco?" he says, sounding hopeful.

Sofia turns around, smiling at him.

"The one and only." She grins before running into his awaiting arms.

We all watch as he wraps her in a tight embrace, and she laughs when he lifts her off the pavement.

Victoria looks at me, unsure if this is a good idea.

"I think she should come to keep you company and also as a precaution," I say, and she nods, agreeing when she remembers how easy it is for Sofia to get herself kidnapped.

"Sofia, what about school and your parents? Do they know?" Victoria asks, and Sofia points to the four-door Honda pulling up to the house.

"They said I can go. My dad, not so much, but mom worked her charm. As for school, most of my classes are online."

Victoria bites her bottom lip, unconvinced, but says nothing because we all know Sofia is coming no matter what anyone says.

"Alright then," Victoria says, and her face takes on a questioning stance. "Wait, how did you find out about them being here in the first place? And why did you run here?"

Sofia looks at her family with annoyance.

"They were taking too long to get into the car, so I ran to get here before you guys left."

Victoria nods and gives her cousin a teasing smile.

"I'm sorry, but I didn't hear you answer my first question?"

Sofia's cheeks turn bright red.

"Francisco texted me," she mutters.

My brows rise from this news and when I turn to Francisco, he gives me a sheepish smile, scratching the back of his head. I shake my head in disbelief.

The lucky bastard had communication with Sofia the entire time. No wonder he wasn't as miserable as I was these past few months.

"You can come, but I'm only letting you go because I can't part from you," Victoria tells Sofia, who responds by laughing and blowing Victoria a kiss.

Victoria and Sofia say their last goodbyes, and we get into the car.

When I turn to my side, I find Victoria staring out the window, watching her house fade away. I want to wrap her in my arms to assure her that everything will be okay. But I stop myself when I remember the promise I made to her sister.

"Have you ever been to Italy?" I ask Victoria, trying to distract her from her grief.

She looks away from the window.

"No, but I always wanted to." She fidgets with her fingers and draws her bottom lip between her teeth.

My eyes fall on the gesture, and I groan inwardly, realizing how damn hard it'll be to restrain myself.

I'm going to have to keep my distance to protect her heart. From this point forward, I will be her bodyguard. Nothing more. She will leave me for good when the threat to her life is gone.

"Then I'm glad I get to make another one of your dreams come true," I tell her, receiving a beautiful smile in return. The sight of it has my heart beating hard in my chest.

Only her bodyguard.

I repeat this to myself and take a deep breath, feeling both content and miserable because, although she's with me, I know I can never call her mine.

She deserves a life of peace, not violence.

A flower can't survive in a storm.

30

VICTORIA

My hometown disappears, and there's a loneliness filling my heart.

The warmth radiating from Leo is comforting. But it isn't enough to stop the numbness from encompassing me whole.

I'm a homebody. My culture values family and togetherness. Being ripped apart from everything I value brings a discomforting emptiness.

This time the situation is different from when I left for France. Italy isn't going to be a three-week vacation. I can be gone for half a year or more.

My life is now on pause. Everything I envisioned for myself since I was twelve is now like a distant allusion.

Adriano now stands between me and my old life and aspirations. And sure, I felt a sense of comfort and excitement about being with Leo once again. But despite the force pulling me toward him, I know he's still a stranger to me.

I inhale a shaky breath and stare at Leo for a moment. The palpable energy between us is so intense that it continues to pull me toward him.

He gives me whiplash whenever he's close. There's no controlling my fast-paced heart rate or the sweaty hands he incites.

These emotions lead me to question my sanity.

Since France, it's as if my entire being is at a constant tug between wanting two things: Leo and my family.

I'm not whole, no matter who I'm with.

If I'm with Leo, I want my family. But if I'm with my family, I'd want Leo. I'm locked in an internal battle.

I hate myself for being extremely unbalanced and emotional. I want the fog inside my brain to clear so I can understand these feelings.

The car stops, and a nervous flutter inside my stomach overpowers my earlier thoughts.

The emotions now blooming inside me are the ones you get when you are both excited and afraid of what's coming.

Leo turns to look at me, tenderness glowing in his eyes as he extends a hand. The second our hands join, I'm enveloped in his warmth. Everything about Leo is a fusion of opposites, including his touch. His hand is rough and calloused, but still soft.

He helps me out of the car, and my eyes widen in bewilderment at the sight of the beautiful, matte, sleek, black private jet.

"Wow," I mutter, unable to stray my eyes from the jet. Leo laughs at my reaction, and warmth rushes to my cheeks.

Never in my wildest dreams did I think I'd fly on a private jet. Hell, I'd never even think I'd get to fly business class.

When I enter the plane, I see Luca and Sofia playing a game of cards. Francisco sits beside my cousin with his eyes closed in a deep sleep. There's a glint in Sofia's eyes as she points to a sleeping Francisco, asking me to get her a Sharpie marker.

I mouth a 'no' to Sofia, who pouts, wanting to stir trouble for a poor jet lag Francisco.

My body melts into the gray cushions, and I glance at Leo, who's talking with a man in the cot pit.

After not seeing him for three months, I take this opportunity to study him, and my mouth waters at what I see.

He's lost his black suit jacket, and his black button-down shirt is crisp. You can see the tight outline of his biceps around the fabric.

Unable to help myself, I stare at his muscular arms.

He's rolled his shirt sleeves up to his elbows, so I get to see how strong he is under the rich fabric. The silver watch on his left wrist and the rings on his fingers give the impression of a flashy busi-nessman.

Leo leaves the pilot and makes his way toward me.

He takes the space to my left, and notices I haven't put on my seat belt. He frowns and extends his arm to fasten the safety belt. As he reaches over, his arm grazes my lower half, and I stiffen, trying to keep myself collected.

Leo notices the position of his hand and hesitates briefly before clicking the seatbelt into place. I don't miss how he tries to contain his grin when he finds my agitation amusing.

To distract myself from the rising desire, I grab the nearest thing, which happens to be the flight safety pamphlet.

Leo looks at me, and he lifts a brow. His eyes move from me to the pamphlet in my hand.

I groan inwardly, my desire now replaced with embarrassment.

"Victoria, we're here. Come on, wake up," says a resonant timbre to my left, and when I don't move, they sigh. "If you don't want me to carry you, you better wake up," Leo warns with a hint of a tease.

Humming, I crack open an eye. I groan from the uncomfortable ache in my back, and my eyes close again, too tired to move.

"Carry you it is," he says, his arms going under my knees, and I wake with a jolt.

"I'm up. I'm up," I blurt in a panic. "No need to carry me."

Leo nods in approval, and my face grows hot when I hear his soft laugh.

"That was easy," he mutters as I follow close behind him.

I step out of the jet, and the Italian breeze nips at my skin. The air is filled with the salty smell of the ocean, and my eyes feast on the setting sun, which leaves behind a glowing yoke of red and orange.

Leo places a hand on the small of my back and helps me down the steps.

I notice three black-tinted Porsche SUVs surrounding the plane.

At the end of the carpet is a beautiful black sports car with blood-red rims.

Men in black suits surround the cars with unemotional expressions. They are stone cold and stand like statues. These men look like soldiers waiting for their sergeant to give an order. And from how they bow their heads toward Leo, I can only assume he is their sergeant.

What is going on?

The scary men in all black and the expensive cars overwhelm me with questions.

A tall man with broad shoulders and curly hair nears us.

"Mr. Bandoni," he says, and his eyes glance at me. He gives a tender smile. "Madam."

"It's Victoria," I correct him with a smile.

The man smiles, showing a dimple, but it vanishes, and his lips press into a tight line when Leo roughly clears his throat.

I look at Leo and notice he wears an expression void of all emotions.

His tough exterior makes me uneasy.

Before I can ask if he's okay, he opens the passenger door of the car for me. I hesitate, but find myself sliding into the car when he gives me an encouraging smile.

"Welcome back, boss," the man from before says, and when he peeks into the car to look at me, Leo sends him a menacing glare.

The man cowers back in fear.

"Luciano, can you please have Kaden call me? Also, did the shipment from China make it?" Leo glances at me before closing the door to the car.

The last thing I hear him say is if a man named Lei sent him the correct amount of *things*.

For some reason, the code language between the two doesn't sit well with me.

I try to decipher what *things* they are talking about, but I come to no possible conclusions. Although he told me he was a businessperson, I can't help but wonder what kind of business he runs. "Things" doesn't really tell me much.

He's not a drug dealer, is he?

I look at Leo and shake my head at the ridiculous thought.

Sitting in the car I try to listen to their conversation, but the car muffles their voices, and my nosy ass becomes agitated.

Nothing frustrates me more than being left in the dark, particularly when it concerns my and Sofia's safety.

After sitting in the car for a few minutes, Leo finally makes his way to the driver's side. The car turns on with a roar, and the vibration of the car's engine travels from the bottom of my feet to my chest, bringing a tightness to the area.

Leo reaches over the counsel, and his hand rests on mine. The pad of his thumb runs over the area. His touch generates tingles throughout my body, and I'm not sure if I'm trembling because of the car or his touch.

Then something inside him switches, and he pulls his hand back.

There's tension between us, and I'm confused by the mixed signals he keeps sending me.

I swallow the thick lump in my throat, now on edge from his two personas. Although I stare ahead of me, I notice from the corner of my eyes as Leo pulls out his phone. His attention is now focused on the screen.

We sit in the car for a few minutes, and I can't take the awkward silence any longer.

"Where's my cousin?" I ask, and Leo continues to type on his phone. I feel my anger rising.

"Leo?" My voice is firmer this time around.

He doesn't take his eyes off his phone.

"Francisco and Sofia are behind us in one of the other three cars," comes his simple reply.

I say nothing and gaze outside the window in boredom. A few seconds later I hear him sigh, but I don't turn to face him. I'm too busy thinking about everything that didn't sit right with me.

"Bambina?" he breathes.

The familiar nickname makes my stomach flutter, and I scold myself for giving in to him so easily.

Turning to face him, I try to hide my annoyance. Once again, I remember where we left off in France. I still don't know who he is or what secrets he holds. I've disregarded these thoughts because I missed him, but now the questions have returned full force.

"Yeah?" I say, my fingers playing with the gold heart pendant around my neck.

Leo looks at my fingers, toiling with the necklace, and he frowns.

"I'm sorry." He places a hand on my thigh again, and I wait for it to be drawn back like earlier, but he doesn't move it.

I bite my bottom lip and look at him, really look at him, and I can see he's stressed.

"Leo, it's fine. You're busy, I get it," I assure him, and my earlier anger diminishes at the sight of the worry lines present on his rough, handsome face.

He sighs.

"I'm going to be busy trying to find Adriano and doing my other work. I won't always be with you." As he says this, frustration and something else clouds his expression.

After hearing about all the work he has to do, I feel guilty because I can't help him. But what I can do is get out of his way and let him do what he needs to without the added weight of having to be a host.

"I understand. I'll have Sofia to keep me company," I say, trying to ease his worries.

He once again mentions the name of the woman who produces a pinch in my chest.

"And you'll have Cleo to keep you company. She's been wanting to meet you." I can hear his smile through his words when he talks about her, and I have to control my voice to hide my disappointment.

"Cleo?" I ask, giving him a tight, closed-lipped smile.

The suspense of their relationship is killing me.

"She's my sister. She's about your age."

"You have a sister?" My voice reveals my surprise, and Leo nods.

It turns out Eloisa was right after all.

His hand moves to the car's gear, and he drives out of the airport and through a cliff side overlooking the ocean.

The entire drive, I take in the colorful yellow and orange houses lining the mountains. After a while, we pull into a closed-off area with an enormous black gate.

I'm instantly drawn to the familiar lion and the crown seal in the middle.

The gate opens, and I stare ahead at the long, cobbled road with trees on either side.

Leo looks at me for a second and then drives forward.

Seconds of waiting turn into minutes, and finally, I see the beautiful creme-colored Greek-style mansion.

I take in the sight of the enormous four-pillar columns, and my mouth opens in shock at the luxury of Leo's estate.

My attention flickers to the center of the roundabout, where I see white rosebushes encircling a white marble fountain with a lion statue spurting water.

I look at the entrance, and my heart drops because standing in front of the house are five enormous men with assault rifles.

"Welcome to your new home." Leo's voice makes me jolt.

Home?

He gets out of the car, and I continue looking at the men, stuck in a trance of fear. I try to assure myself that these men are here to protect me. But despite telling myself this, I can't help but get Déjà vu when I remember Erika's story.

The door swings open, and I lock eyes with Leo. He leads me into the house, and my hand trembles in his. Leo looks at me; his expression is one of assurance.

We pass the men with rifles, and I hold my breath. The tension remains in my body until the men put their guns behind their backs, smiling at me.

The tiny smiles catch me off guard, but I have little time to process the surprise because when we enter the house, my mind becomes over-powered with awe by the extravagant interior fit for royalty.

The inside of the house is a beautiful contrast of sparkling gold and pristine white. A thousand diamonds sparkle and glimmer from the crystal chandelier suspended above us.

I knew Leo was rich, but I didn't think he was this rich.

Embedded into the milky-white marble floor is the prominent crescent that follows Leo everywhere.

"I'll have Luca give you and Sofia a tour of the house." I look at Leo, and his intense green eyes make me nervous.

I give a quiet nod when the sound of quick steps echoing down one of the two flights of stairs fills the stillness of the foyer.

Leo and I glance to the right, where the noise is coming from. My stare lands on a gorgeous-looking girl with light brown wavy locks that reach under her breastbone.

She has a perfectly symmetrical nose and an agreeable figure. As well as other goddess-like features. But most striking is the gentle air floating around her.

There's a nervous smile painted on her full, pink lips.

The beautiful woman shares similar features to Leo, and I instantly know this is Cleo.

To add to the siblings' similarities, Cleo is also tall. If I have to guess, she stands at about five-nine inches. About two inches taller than me.

Cleo's eyes flicker between mine and Leo's intertwined hands. There's a glisten in her eyes, and her smile widens when she sees Leo. A pair of straight white teeth reveal themselves.

She hurriedly descends the staircase, and Leo brings my fidgeting figure toward her. When the sun shines on her peachy skin and the light hits her hazel eyes, I see the vibrant green centers of her irises sparkle.

"Cleo, this is Victoria... Victoria, this is my sister Cleo," Leo introduces us, with a smile permanently resting on his lips.

Her doe eyes don't leave mine, and I nervously smile at her.

"Hi, Cleo. It's nice to meet you." My voice is soft, and I extend my right hand for her to shake.

She looks at my hand, grasps it, and pulls me close to her chest, her embrace so strong it almost takes my breath away.

A sweet rose scent encases me, and I wrap my free hand around her. Leo's chuckle echoes behind us.

"She likes you," he says, and Cleo's face brightens as she shakes her head in agreement.

Her quietness draws my attention.

"She's mute," Leo explains. His voice is low and measured as he speaks, and his right fist balls up at his side.

Cleo's left hand rubs over her covered wrist. The white long-sleeve shirt she wears rises, revealing long, fading scars.

Seeing them, a wave of sadness washes over me, and there's no doubt in my mind that Cleo has experienced something truly traumatic.

I turn to Cleo and wonder if she understands English ASL. I highly doubted she did, since she lived in Italy, but it's worth a shot.

Hello, Cleo. Do you understand English ASL?

Cleo beams in excitement. Her smile reaches her eyes, and her hands clap excitedly in front of her when she sees me signing. She then responds, confirming she does understand.

"You can sign?" Leo says with a shocked expression marked across his face.

"Yes, I took ASL classes as my elective in high school," I confess, shrugging my shoulders.

Leo's amazement from beside me grows, and he's about to say something when Kaden walks into the room, a phone in hand.

Kaden smiles at me, and I give him a smile in return, having missed him.

"Boss, Lei Shein is on the phone for you," Kaden tells Leo, handing him the phone.

Leo's smile disappears and turns into a look of irritation.

"I have to go. Maybe you two can get to know each other?" he asks, glancing at Cleo and then back at me. We both nod.

He kisses the crown of Cleo's head and surprises me when he gives me a quick peck on the cheek.

Flutters rush through my core, but the feeling falters when I see Cleo beaming. Her grin brings an explosion of heat to my skin.

We watch as Leo walks up the right staircase with the phone clutched to his ear, and Kaden follows close behind him.

"Victoria, are you seeing this place? It's like a freaking castle!" Sofia's voice hints at her awe, and Francisco follows her.

Sofia stops when she sees Cleo.

"Oh, hello, I'm Sofia," she says, smiling at Cleo, who responds by giving my cousin a wave.

Cleo's everlasting smile remains marked on her face.

"Cleo, this is my annoying cousin Sofia," I introduce the two, and a familiar voice sounds from behind.

"Alright, ladies, let's get this show on the road."

There's a grin on my face, and I whirl my head toward Luca's voice.

When he reaches us, he kisses Cleo's cheek, and he wraps his arms around mine and Sofia's shoulders.

"Where did you disappear to, Snow White?" I tease, nudging his side.

"Hiding from you!"

I lift a brow.

"Why?"

"Why?" he repeats in disbelief, tilting his head. "You pepper sprayed me!" he says matter of fact, and his response makes me grimace.

"In my defense, I thought you were one of Adriano's men."

"Well, I wasn't, but I'll forgive you only because you're my favorite." Luca sends me a teasing wink before extending his arms wide. "Now, who's ready for a tour?" he asks with mock excitement.

Luca begins to guide us toward the opposite side of the house when Francisco's phone pings.

"I have to go," he says, putting his phone in his back pocket. He then heads in the direction Leo and Kaden have disappeared.

Sofia shrugs, watching him go, and she wraps her left arm around Cleo, following close behind Luca.

"Are you coming?" Sofia asks with a lifted brow when she notices I'm rooted to my spot, looking in the direction all three men have gone.

I sigh and force a false smile onto my face before facing my cousin.

"Coming," I say, trying to shake off the unknown emotions swirling inside my mind.

Everything from the past hour settles, and the red flags rise.

Welcome to Italy.

31

VICTORIA

Two weeks in Italy have stretched by, and true to his words, Leo has locked himself away to do his work.

The only time I ever see him is during breakfast. But even then, he's on his phone.

I can say the same about the other guys, who all disappear and don't return until late at night.

As time passes, it becomes more lonely, and I begin to wonder how Cleo has remained sane from being alone.

The only thing keeping me from going crazy is having Sofia and Cleo with me.

Speaking of Cleo, she's incredible! She made it easy for me and Sofia to adjust to the big house and its secrets. She's gentle and witty all at once, and she drew Sofia and me right toward her.

I sigh, closing my eyes as I soak in the sun. There's a soft tap on my left shoulder, and when I look into Cleo's vibrant green eyes, I'm reminded of the tall, handsome Italian man I haven't seen in two days.

She signs.

Do you want to see the gardens?

I glance around the backyard, where the lush green grass stretches for what seems like miles.

"Sure, I can use the escape in nature." When I say this, her dimples deepen, and her smile grows wider.

Do you also find comfort in nature?

Her eyes are shimmering with anticipation as she waits for my answer.

"Of course! Who wouldn't?"

My response excites Cleo, and she jumps from the lawn chair, pulling me toward the gardens.

I follow her through the labyrinth of shrubs until we reach the center, where a magnificent fountain sparkles under the hot sun.

We take a seat around the fountain, and I look around me in awe, the sound of trickling water filling the air.

Beside me, Cleo is in the sublime of nature.

She has her eyes closed and a smile on her face.

"Cleo, do you like nature too?"

She says nothing for a second, but the smile on her face is enough to give me an answer.

She opens her eyes and signs.

I always enjoyed being outside, but it wasn't until a few years ago that I fell in love with it.

She confesses, and it's as if a painful memory has awakened inside her.

She continues.

When you go through tough times and find yourself alone, you try to find light in the darkness of your thoughts. The sun helps me feel less alone and less cold. When I'm outside, it's a temporary light shining into the dark box that is my life.

As she expresses her isolation, my heart becomes heavy.

This constant loneliness she's used to isn't good for her mental health. I'm surprised she hasn't started to see the wallpaper of the house move or even fallen into deep insanity.

One week, and I'm already getting antsy from being locked up in this house, and I have Cleo and Sofia to keep me company. But she didn't have anyone until we arrived.

"Cleo, I'm sorry you were all alone." I place a comforting hand on her shoulder. "I'm happy Sofia and I are here now to fill the void of your isolation."

Her eyes glisten with unshed tears, and I want to hug her, hoping I can take some of her pain away.

Thank you. Before you two, my only real companions were my thoughts.

Her lips quiver as she thinks of her past for the second time. I don't dare ask what happened to her because, although I'm curious, it isn't my place to ask these questions.

The short time I've been here has been enough for me to realize the Bandoni family has a lot of secrets, such as the mystery around Leo's parents and the constant code messages spoken in front of me.

Every day it becomes more obvious, Leo and his friends aren't your typical nine-to-five guys. They dress differently and carry themselves with an overpowering dominance. The less time I spend around them, the more their gentle front drops. I'm starting to see them for who they are—dangerous and unapproachable.

Sensing my weariness, Cleo touches my cheek, drawing my attention to her.

She looks at me with concern, her feminine features softening.

What's wrong, Victoria?

I sigh, debating whether to tell her how confused I've been about being shoved into this new world—her world.

When I don't respond, Cleo raises disapproving eyebrows as if telling me to lay all my deepest, darkest secrets on her because she will catch them.

The expression she gives is one you can't ignore.

I let out a breath and explain what's been bothering me, hoping she might say something to ease my worries.

"I'm now realizing I moved miles away from my family to live with strangers." My gaze falls on the crystal blue water of the fountain, afraid to see Cleo's reaction to my words. The last thing I want is for Cleo to think I'm ungrateful for everything Leo has done for me, because this isn't the case. I'm simply feeling uneasy about my safety being in the hands of people I know nothing about.

"Don't get me wrong, I'm happy to be here because I wouldn't have met you or your family, but I can't help but feel like everyone is hiding something from me"—she frowns—"this, of course, excludes you."

As I say this, I glance at Cleo, expecting to find her smiling at my stupid thoughts, but she instead looks on edge, almost as if she's guilty of something.

I lift a questioning brow. "What is it, Cleo?"

Her eyes waver, and she gives me a forced smile.

My brother wouldn't dream of hurting you.

She insists, but that's not what's bothering me.

I give her a meek nod, knowing she's right, but her answer doesn't change the fact that I still feel like an outsider. Her vague response tells me she's also keeping secrets from me, a realization that makes my stomach drop.

You know he likes you.

Cleo signs, and a smile overpowers her frown.

My lips roll into my mouth.

"He doesn't like me," I say, my face growing hot as the words leave my mouth.

Leo couldn't possibly like me. If he did, he wouldn't be keeping secrets from me. You don't do that to someone you care about.

My response causes three little worry lines to appear on Cleo's forehead.

I know my brother, and he likes you. Why else would you be here under his protection? Family is everything to us Italians, and we protect one another.

Cleo's eyes pin me in place, and I'm consumed with those damn flutters after she called me family.

Victoria, you've somehow made it into our family, and you still don't see it. Trust me when I say he likes you. He never introduced a woman to me until you, and he never smiled as much as he does now at the mere sight of your presence.

She finishes signing, and her hands fall tiredly onto her lap, but she isn't done. There's still more she wants to tell me.

Victoria, don't let your insecurities and fears build a wall between you two. I've lived this way for too long, and I know what it can do to a person.

Cleo confesses, looking into the darkening sky as she soaks in her words.

She turns back to me, and her eyes are pleading.

Let him in. Let us in. Trust us.

Cleo grabs my shoulders and shakes me, hoping the gesture will knock some sense into me. But I can't shake off the uneasiness.

Let me in! I want to shout.

"Thank you for trying to make me feel better, but we wouldn't work out. I know nothing about Leo besides his name, age, and that he's somehow super rich. He won't tell me anything else, and neither will anyone in this damn house!" I flare my arms, and she looks shocked by my sudden burst of frustration.

"He's a closed-off person, and so am I. There would be no communication," I say in a defeated tone, but Cleo is still adamant that Leo and I are soulmates.

Leo's reserved and cold. But this is who he is and who he's been forced to become.

Forced to become? What does she mean?

Victoria, he knows no other way, and if you say you're also reserved, then you understand him better than anyone. You understand why he might close himself off. You both need to take a step toward one another to meet at the halfway point. I know you're the one, and I believe one day soon he will cave in and tell you everything. He doesn't know it yet. He's too stubborn. I ask that you only be patient.

She reasons with me before standing and extending a delicate hand for me to take.

"The one?" I mumble, and my stomach lurches with excitement.

Cleo wraps her left arm around my waist. We make our way into the mansion to meet up with Sofia, who's been working on some assignments from school.

By the time we make it inside, dinner is ready. To my disappointment, today is no different from the previous days.

Cleo, Sofia, and I once again sit alone at the long dinner table full of the finest china.

We're all quiet, absorbed in our own thoughts.

I twirl my fork over the Ragù alla Bolognese, and I seem to have no appetite after my conversation with Cleo.

Did she mean it when she said I was the one?

I debated whether I should take her advice and meet Leo halfway or if I should keep my distance like before.

Sighing, I push the plate away, not hungry.

The plate I pushed moves back toward me, and I lift a brow. Cleo gives me a smile, which assures me everything will fall into place. She hands me a piece of bread, and I take it, giving her a grateful smile.

I stare at my food, realizing Leo probably hasn't eaten all day. He's always working in his office. I don't think he ever leaves the room.

After finishing my dinner, I prepare Leo a plate. Taking him food will give me a reason to see him, and who knows, I might grow the nerve to follow Cleo's advice and meet him halfway. And if what she told me is right, then Leo will do the rest.

With this newfound determination and confidence, I approach Leo's office with a plate of food in my shaky hands.

But as I near his office, it's as if I'm about to enter a dragon's pit.

This entire situation is intimidating.

I'm not good at expressing my emotions to others, and I'm not a go-getter. It was easier for me to wait for things to fall into place, and if they didn't fall onto my path, then it wasn't meant to be. Yet here I am doing the opposite of what I'm used to, and all for a guy.

The door to his office seems to loom over me, and I can hear my fast heart beat as I stand in front of it, unable to find the courage to open the door.

A thick force of dominance seeps through the door.

You can do this, Victoria. It's only Leo.

I take a deep breath, and right as I lift my hand to knock on the door, I hear a loud and angry voice from the other side.

My curiosity gets the best of me, and I listen to what's happening.

"What's the damage?" Leo demands, his voice harsh, sending a chill down my spine.

This isn't the Leo I'm used to hearing. This voice sounds like it belongs to a man capable of murder.

"Fucking bastard!"

I close my eyes when I hear splintering wood and the crunch of shattering glass ringing from behind the door.

"Who was in charge of the area?"

I'm filled with apprehension as I listen to him speak on the phone.

My hands shake and my stomach twists, yet despite my fear, I want to make sure he's okay.

I chew down any hesitation and remember Cleo's words about how her brother would never hurt me. This thought alone gives me the courage to push open the door, and I'm met with his looming figure. His strong back faces me.

I shift my gaze away from his well-built frame, and my breath gets caught when I see the mess in the room.

The contents of his desk are all on the floor, and there are shards of glass, along with papers littering the ground. In the air is the odor of alcohol from the broken bottles he launched across the room.

I avert my attention to Leo. He has his left hand set into a painful clutch while the other hand runs down his face in frustration.

I'm hesitant, as I slowly tap him on the shoulder.

His body stiffens under my touch. Within a second, he's crushing my wrist, and I let out a small cry. A fiery pain spreads throughout my arm, and the plate of food in my left hand slips from my grip, crashing to the ground and shattering into a million pieces.

A look of horror overtakes Leo's angry expression, and he releases me as if I burned him.

His face pales.

"Victoria, I'm so sorry." There's a raw panic in his voice.

I pull my sore wrist to my chest, trying to suppress the tears.

So much for meeting him halfway.

"I thought you might be hungry since you didn't come to dinner," I whisper, looking at the ground to see the mess I've created. I grimace and fall to the ground to pick up the pieces of glass with my one good hand, but I end up cutting myself.

A slight hiss comes from my trembling lips, and I draw back my hand. I watch as the blood seeps from the cut on my pointer finger.

I ignore it and continue to pick up the mess I made.

"Victoria, stop!" Leo demands, lifting me onto my two feet.

He guides me to sit on the black vintage leather couch and then rushes to his desk. When he returns, he has a first aid kit in hand, and he kneels in front of me, grabbing my bleeding hand.

"You don't have to do that," I say in a cautious whisper, going to take the box from him, but he pushes my hand aside.

"Leo, I can do it myself," I insist, but he won't release my hand.

A long, shuddering sigh escapes Leo, and regret lingers in his eyes.

"Victoria, you shouldn't have come in here. I hurt you, goddamn it." There's a harsh sound at the back of his throat, and his jaw tightens.

The pain in my wrist increases as the depths of his eyes absorb me.

With him in front of me, the loneliness from before melts. I know the normal thing would be for me to be afraid of him, but the pain flickering in his eyes and the regret in his voice tell me he didn't mean to hurt me. This is enough to push any fear out of my mind.

"It's my fault. I shouldn't have sneaked up on you like that. I'm sorry," I say, watching as he tenderly cleans my cut. There's a frown between his eyebrows as he wraps my bleeding finger with a band-aid.

"I appreciate you worrying about my health, Victoria, but don't come in here when I'm working." He casts an agonizing glance at my wrist, where the skin is turning red. His face hardens. "What if I had done something worse to you?"

"I'm fine," I assure him, but the pain in my wrist tells me otherwise. "You won't hurt me."

I'm spewing random words, unsure of what to say to fix the mess I've created by coming here. Everything is going wrong. It's as if we have taken two steps back instead of two steps forward.

"And what do you call what happened?" he says, and the anger in his voice does well to make me stare at my knotted hands like a child being scolded.

"You didn't mean it." He lets out a bitter laugh.

"It doesn't matter whether I did it intentionally. I still hurt you." I look at him, and I can see he's convinced I'm delicate. And maybe he's right, but it doesn't matter to me because I'm already falling for him, and I can't do anything about it.

Leo closes his eyes, and I can see him lifting his walls higher than before.

"You should go to bed. It's getting late," he breathes.

I bite the inside of my mouth and notice how his hand is about to rise to touch me, but he pulls away at the last second.

I say nothing, rise from the couch, and walk toward the door. Before leaving, I turn over my shoulder and find him looking at my retreating figure. His eyes show traces of guilt.

I feel my heart sink as I slowly turn around and walk out of the office. When I'm outside, I lean against the door and release the breath I'm holding in. The throbbing pain in my wrist intensifies, and I wince, cradling my bruising hand to my chest.

His constant mood swings irritate me beyond belief, and I question whether I can handle being with a man of such temperament.

"What kind of business does he run that makes him angry and busy all the damn time?" I say under my breath as I enter my room to get ready for bed.

When I'm in bed, I rub lotion on my aching wrist, trying to keep my tears at bay. The skin around my swollen wrist is turning purple, and the dark blotches form in the shape of Leo's fingers, a sight that makes me cringe.

How am I going to face him now?

When the thoughts become too much, I try to find some rest, and I eventually fall asleep. Only to wake up a few hours later from thirst.

I grab the glass cup from the nightstand and groan when I find it empty.

I crawl out of bed, taking the cup with me. My steps are quick as I make my way through the dimly lit hallway, hoping no one is awake.

The kitchen is dark, but I find the fridge and pull out the glass water jug.

I yawn, my eyes drooping with exhaustion. The pantry creeks, and I freeze at the sight of a tall figure appearing from behind the darkness. The fridge light aluminates their face, and my lungs construct.

The water jug falls from my hands, and a wave of fear crashes over me, making my skin crawl.

The sound of glass shattering in the dead of night fills my ears, and I jump back. The cold water spills all over my feet, and I tremble, not because of the coldness of the water soaking my legs, but because of the grotesque sight standing in front of me.

In horror, I stare at Leo's body, caked in blood. I try to hold back the bile, which wants to rise from the smell.

His entire hands are stained red, and his once crisp white dress shirt has blood splatters all over it. Even his neck and jaw have dried droplets of blood covering the exposed skin.

I know the blood isn't his because he isn't in pain and has no injuries other than the torn skin around his knuckles.

Leo freezes in place, and his eyes are wide, as if I'm the one covered in blood.

He advances toward me, and I want to scream and run. But my body doesn't react until the copper stench of death becomes prominent when he's four feet away from me.

I lift my hands in front of me.

"Don't—" I plead, but he keeps taking steps toward me. Frightening me even more.

He's at a loss for words, and his face is marked with a deep frown.

Leo's bloodied hand extends to touch my face, but I scream, flinching away from him.

"Stop it, Leo," I beg, but he doesn't listen. "I said stop it, goddammit!"

My words get through to Leo, and he stops. His body stiffens, and he watches me with surprise.

I take slow steps toward the door, and our eyes don't break contact.

Tears blur my vision when his eyes, which once filled me with comfort, are no longer reassuring. Not while he's covered in blood.

The door to the kitchen shuts, and I run to Sofia's room, almost tripping over the last few steps of the stairs.

I reach her room and lock the door behind me. I quickly move the nightstand in front of the door as an extra precaution.

The noise of the furniture being moved doesn't wake up my cousin, as she's still asleep when I look at her.

I'm shaking uncontrollably as I make my way to her bed, and I take deep breaths to steady my pounding heart. But nothing can console the fear and heartbreak that is taking over.

Every creak and noise from outside makes me want to bury myself under the covers.

A dizzying array of questions and fearful thoughts race through my mind, bringing panic to my chest.

Leo killed someone, and he had no remorse. His only regret was that I had seen him.

The tears fall because the Leo I've fallen in love with is an illusion—a fairytale version I've created of the man who saved me. I put him on a beautiful pedestal because he saved my life, and these fantasies have blinded me. I can no longer hold back my tears. They come rushing out when I realize I've fallen in love with a criminal.

Today's events come to mind, and I think about the violent tone of his once soothing voice, his deadly grip, and then the residue of his murder. It's all too much, and the more I think about it, the more I'm sure the warmth of his eyes is gone for good.

"Who are you, Leo Bandoni?"

My heart shatters as the perfect image I created of him smashes into a million pieces.

32

———

LEO

"Leo, my good ol' pal, how are things shaking in Italy?"

I stare at Lei Shein, the man behind the mafia in China and one of the four families of the mafia alliance.

His face appears on the screen of my laptop, and he looks relaxed, as if he hasn't stolen from me.

His cheerfulness and the stupid grin on his thin lips fuels my anger.

I didn't call him so we can gossip. This is a fucking *sitdown*.

Francisco enters my office with curiosity painted on his face. Kaden explains the situation, and Francisco makes a grimace.

"Hello, Lei," I greet lowly, and my jaw tics from the coolness in his tone. Lei senses my anger, and his thick, dark brows pinch together.

He's about to say something about my angry tone when I cut him off.

"We received the delivery of cocaine, but the heroin never arrived."

I narrow my eyes, demanding answers.

Lei is one of my most trusted business partners. We've never had shipment issues in the last two decades of doing business with the Shein family. So, when half our cargo arrives missing, it's cause for concern. I don't want to use force on him.

Lei sits up from his chair and tilts his head to the side. He purses his lips, and his thumb and forefinger rub his pointed chin as he soaks in my words.

A sense of relief courses through me when he shakes his head of black hair, denying the accusations.

I wait for his proof, and if I find he's lying, there will be repercussions.

"Leo, I made sure 300 kilograms of heroin were in those cargos," he assures me as he rummages through some documents on his desk.

Lei's eyes move across the words on the paper in his hands.

"Yes, it should have all been there. I have everything that goes in and out of my ports noted," he exclaims, scanning the documents in the printer behind him. "See for yourself."

After he says this, my printer runs, letting me know he has faxed me the documents.

Kaden brings them to me, and I look for myself, and he's telling the truth.

"You know what this means," I tell him, and his lips form a thin line.

"Either I have a traitor, or you do." His words ring with frustration, and his jaw flexes into a clench from the thought of a rat in one of our mafias.

A traitor is the last thing I need right now.

"Lei, a shipment of explosives is heading to you now. It may take about a week or two to get to China, but once it lands in your port, use this as a trap," I suggest, and he nods. "I'll do the same with Alexander's shipment from America. This should let us know where the traitor stands."

"Got it!" he exclaims, leaning into his brown leather desk chair.

His tattooed hand rises, and he runs his long fingers through his straight black hair, while letting out a frustrated breath.

"Lei, is everything good?" I ask when his body grows rigid.

He opens his dark eyes.

"Yeah, it's the government. They're up my ass these days." His voice is laced with exhaustion. I lift a brow. "It's nothing serious. I have it handled." He assures me when he sees my concern.

I say nothing else because if he says he has it handled; he has it handled.

"What about you? How are things with Adriano?"

"He's being the nuisance he's always been," I grumble.

"Do you think this missing shipment is his doing?" Lei's words register, and I exhale an irritated breath, knowing this isn't a far stretch.

"I wouldn't doubt it."

"Leo, if you need anything, I'm here, and so are the other mafia families. Adriano isn't like any of our other rivals. He was once one of us." The corners of his mouth turn down in an apologetic smile. "As much as you hate it, he's your blood. There's a reason you Bandoni's run this system."

Lei's right. Adriano is a Bandoni, which means he's discreet, strong, and determined. He knows how to get what he wants, no matter how dirty he has to get. I know this because I'm the same, minus the thirst for power, and I'm also not a rapist.

"Thank you, Lei," I say before cutting the call and turning to Kaden and Francisco. "I need you both to be on alert for any suspicious behavior. Tell Luca and Angelo." They nod in understanding. "We have a traitor. I can feel it."

Both of their faces harden from this suspicion.

We don't take it lightly when one of our own betrays us. Especially after our men take an oath of secrecy, brotherhood, and loyalty. Betraying your mafia is like stabbing your brothers in the back.

I'm not sure if I'm more angry with the traitor or myself for allowing this to happen under my nose.

As the Don, my job is to make the major decisions about what we do and how we do it. I make sure the money keeps flowing into our business by shouting orders, reading through documents, meeting with business partners, making connections with powerful men, and staying out of the eyes of the law. I make sure order is kept, but a traitor among us means I have failed at my job.

Francisco and Kaden leave my office, and my stare falls on the skyscraper of papers waiting for me.

A harsh sound comes from my throat, and I begin my work.

My mind often drifts to Victoria, who I've had to leave the second we arrived. But the distance is what's best for us. When I'm around her, I'm more likely to fuck up and give into the desires burning inside me.

Like a few minutes ago, I kissed her cheek after promising myself not to give into these affections.

I'm trying hard to keep my distance from her, but it's difficult.

Am I making the right decision by pushing her away?

I keep asking myself this question, and each time I know the answer, and it hurts. Although I hate the answer, I know I can't let the darkness of the mafia taint her delicate soul as it has done to my mother and sister.

I don't want to lose her.

Two weeks have passed, and the tension that impeded me has evaporated.

The quick glimpses of Victoria gave me a sense of comfort during the long work hours.

I miss hearing her call my name. Especially how her tongue rolls when she pronounces the "L." I also miss the way her beautiful chocolate-brown eyes stare at me.

With her warm vanilla scent lingering in the air, I find I crave her more with every passing day.

Frustration claws at my heart from having her close to me but being unable to have her in my arms.

Her body pressed tight against mine is all I want to feel.

I toss the document I'm reading aside.

The pulsing heat coursing through my body tells me how much I want her. Every single part of her. It doesn't help when my mind tortures me by reminding me of what I saw yesterday.

I throw my head back in a groan, and the tightness between my legs becomes unbearable.

Fuck.

My thoughts fill with images of how her curvy waist swayed to the beat of the Mexican Cumbia.

Victoria has awakened the raging libido I have contained for six years. And all it took was one glance at her, rocking her hips to the rhythm of the music.

The way each curve and dip were right on the beat with the drums, maracas, and accordion made me fucking hard. But the actual killer, and what got me painfully hard, was the way her tight, round ass would rise and fall with each step she took.

I was a goner, and it took every morsel in my body not to strangle Luca, who was dancing with her.

The dumbass gave me a knowing grin when he noticed my deadly grip over the doorframe—the wood splintering under my grasp.

Cleo, who was studying them, smirked when she noticed me drooling.

I ignored them and fixed my dark eyes on Victoria. I found her more attractive when she shouted at Luca about what a terrible dancer he was. She was saying something along the lines of Cleo not being able to learn how to dance because he keeps messing up the steps.

She never noticed me in the room because the moment Luca was going to twirl her, I left sexually frustrated.

I knew the moment our eyes met, I'd lose all my restraint.

"Fucking hell!" My dick is now solid hard.

I lick my parched lips and pour myself a glass of liquor, hoping the burning alcohol can contain the lust now dominating me.

I chug the glass of whiskey like a thirsty man. The robust and rich spicy taste of the alcohol takes my mind off the tightness springing between my thighs.

I fix my gaze out the window and notice Victoria and my sister heading toward the hedge maze.

To see them together and getting along is a relief.

My sister looks happier than before, and all because of the two fresh faces now in her life.

I tried my best to find time to keep Cleo company, but it's hard when I'm busy running our family's mafia and making sure the families of the alliance keep their end of the deal.

As the head of the alliance, or as they called me, the mafia king, I have a duty to my men and the mafia princes. This often translated to never having time to spend with my family.

Victoria and Cleo disappear into the maze of greenery, and I head back to my desk. I'm glad to see I only have a small stack of papers left to review.

It doesn't take me long to finish reviewing this month's financial statements, and I'm content when I notice everything is correct.

There isn't a single flaw in our system. The money made via smuggling drugs, operating sex houses, and gambling all looked like it came from legal business deals.

Laundering money is easy when my family's name is on almost every building on the east side of Sicily.

My influence means I can buy police and political power. I have them all in my pocket.

I learned everything about running my family business from my father and his capo, Luca's father. My training started when I was ten. The same night I took my first life. My mother was no longer alive to shelter me from the mafia, and my father needed me to grow up.

Estephano Bandoni lost himself to grief, and his pain sparked my hatred of love.

I lost more than my mother that night. I also lost my father, who had given his absolute power to the imaginary force known as love. When his love took to flame, he became lost to himself forever.

I didn't want to become like him, so I pushed love out of my life. But I have failed and let myself become enchanted by Victoria. And now I'm caught between choosing what my heart wants and what my brain tells me to choose.

Love is viciously beautiful.

It made no sense to me how, to give in to love, I had to be selfish, which I am. It's how I've kept my mafia running, but I can't find it in me to be selfish when it comes to Victoria.

Love is a strange concept in the mafia, in which choosing love means choosing to be with the one you love, but at the expense of their safety.

Giving Victoria up or giving in to my feelings and risking her life are the two prices I have to choose to pay for my crimes.

My phone ringing pulls me from my turmoil, and I answer the call.

The door to my office opens, and a rigid Francisco enters.

He sits on the Valmonte chair in front of my desk and waits for me to finish the call.

"Hello, old friend." A familiar, deep Brooklyn accent rings through the phone.

"Alexander," I greet the mafia boss of the biggest mafia in America. "What do I owe the displeasure of hearing your annoying voice?" I say, knowing he won't take offense at my comment.

Alexander has been my friend since childhood. My parents raised him when his family had gone to war with rival gangs in New York. His parents sent him to us after they lost his sister in a shooting, and he didn't leave us until he was eleven.

Alexander was with me through the loss of my mother, and he understood best what the pain of losing someone you love to the violence in our world can do to us.

His thick laughter fills my ear.

"It's nice to hear your voice as well." There's a pause, and he lets out a tired breath. "I call with important information."

"What is it?" I ask, and there's an edge to my voice.

"It's Adriano," he announces, and my heart rate rises and my anger boils when I hear that asshole's name.

I fucking hated that bastard, and lately, it's as if I can't escape the madness he's creating.

"What about him?"

"Some of my men have found him communicating with the vipers, the rival group I'm currently at war with."

I sigh, and Alexander continues, "Leo, that's not all. Arthuro also mentioned to me that his men spotted him in Russia. He's doing business with the Bloods."

At the sound of my cousin being all over the fucking planet, my fingers curl into my palms.

This situation with Adriano is becoming more serious by the day. He's building an army of those who disagree with our powerful alliance.

This only left one more mafia family, Alejandro—the man behind the mafia in Cuba.

Turning to Francisco, I ask him if Alejandro has been dealing with any suspicious behavior.

Francisco inhales sharply, and his lips draw into a thin line.

"That's why I'm here," he says thickly. "Alejandro called a few minutes ago to tell me his tobacco farm was ambushed. They caught one of the men and tortured him." He flashes me a look I know all too well. "Leo, he was one of Adriano's guys."

My jaw locks, and my already blazing anger rises.

"Leo, is everything alright? Is there something I should know?" Alexander inquires.

"I think it's time," I tell Alexander.

He lets out a tired breath.

"I figured."

Our fathers warned us that our system wasn't perfect. We had it engraved into us that we would always have enemies trying to tear us down. What our fathers cautioned us about was here. War has arrived, and Adriano is the enemy. But he will fail, and we will be ready for his attacks.

"Earth to Leo?" Alexander whistles as if I'm a dog.

"What?" I snap.

"Why haven't you dealt with your cousin yet?" His tone is accusing, and I grow irritated at being talked down upon, but he's right. Adriano has caused my family many problems. The issue is that killing him has been difficult because he's good at disappearing. He's always one step ahead of me, and it fucking pissed me off.

"Leo, I know you feel some guilt for what happened between you and Adriano, but enough is enough. He needs an airing."

"Alexander, I don't feel any remorse about what I did. Not anymore."

Alexander makes a deep, snorting sound.

"Ha! Sure, and I'm a girl," he counters, and I can imagine him grinning. "Seriously, Leo, that's a load of horseshit."

"Go fuck yourself, Alexander," I say in annoyance. "Marquez got what he deserved."

When Francisco notices Alexander is being a nuisance, he grins. I pin him with a furious gaze and flip him off. Francisco throws his head back in laughter.

These assholes are getting on my last nerve.

"First off, that's Emma's job"—Alexander laughs—"and second, why haven't you killed him? Leo, it's clear he's planning something, so why are you waiting?"

"I'm trying to find him. But it's been hard to do when I'm busy protecting Victoria—" Her name flows from my mouth before I can stop myself, and I press my teeth together when I realize my mistake.

Oh no, I fucked up.

Alexander, being the good listener he is, won't let this little slip-up go.

His obnoxious laughter comes from the phone.

Here we go...

I glare at Francisco, who makes kissy faces at me.

"Ah, I see. So, someone finally broke down the mighty Leo Bandoni's walls." He teases. "Doesn't your last name mean a sheet of iron? What happened?"

"Shut up, Alexander. She's someone I'm protecting, nothing more." My voice is firm, leaving no room for argument. But Alexander, being the pain in the ass that he is, continues to mock me.

"Right, and I'm secretly a girl." He snorts. "Leo, I know you, and you wouldn't protect anyone, especially a woman who isn't Cleo," he says, his laughter now gone. "So tell me, who is she?"

Flying to New York and slapping the grin off his face has never sounded so tempting.

He asks me to tell him who she is one more time.

"Fine!" I exclaim in irritation. "Fuck, you and Francisco are a real pain in the ass," I grumble.

Francisco places his hands over his chest, faking hurt with a pout before his lips spread into a grin.

'Shit head,' I mouth, and he rolls his eyes.

"I rescued her from Adriano," I explain to Alexander, and the words are bitter on my tongue.

Alexander lets out a breath. "So Adriano knows about her?"

"Yes, I had to take her from her family to protect her when he threatened to use her life against me."

"Oh, so you really like this Victoria chick?" He jokes, and my face becomes warm. "Is she—"

He's about to ask something crude when he's interrupted by a familiar female voice. Over the phone, I hear Emma shouting at him. What follows is the sound of a slap. Alexander's groans of pain make me grin.

Serves the dickhead right.

"Ow, woman. I already told you not to hit me. I hate when you do that shit," he protests, only to be hit again.

"Who the fuck is Victoria?" Emma shouts in accusation.

"Leo, I have to go. Do you remember my darling princess, Emma? Well, she's abusing me again," he says over the line, annoyance leaking through every word.

I snicker, remembering the first time I met her a few months before I met Victoria.

Emma is a girl like Victoria who has a lot of fire inside her. The only difference is that she uses her wrath on poor Alexander, who she initially disliked, because of the circumstances under which they met.

The first time I met her, she was still angry with him. But the attraction brewing between them was as clear as day.

"How can I forget her? She beat the shit out of Luca," I say in amusement from the memory of Luca learning the hard way that you don't comment on a woman's figure, especially when she's a model.

"And don't you forget it, Bandoni." Her smooth voice takes on a warning tone, with a hint of amusement present.

"She's driving me insane," Alexander mumbles.

"Then let me go home!" she shouts in annoyance.

"No, you're mine," comes his reproach. "Look, Leo, I have to go, but we'll talk more about what we'll do about Adriano later," Alexander assures me between breaths. Emma giggles and scolds him for something he did.

The sound of their whispers and laughter makes me cringe.

"Yeah, yeah. Bye," I rush out, ending the call, disgusted by what I heard.

Those two might want to kill one another, but this didn't stop them from being rabbits.

I shudder in disgust and avert my attention ahead of me, where an amused Francisco sits like an idiot.

My gaze burns him with a glare, and he rises from his seat. Now that the show is over, he leaves me, his laughter ringing behind him.

"Idiota," I mutter as he leaves.

When I finished my work, I hoped to check on Victoria, but I'm again disappointed because I now have to prepare for a war.

One trouble after another follows as my phone rings.

This time, it's Angelo who's calling me.

"What is it, Angelo?"

In the background rings the familiar sound of guns being fired and shouting. The sounds are enough for my blood to run warm.

"Boss, Adriano's men attacked one of our gun warehouses," he says out of breath, and I rise from my seat. "We're killing the ones still here, and I have the traitor in front of me ready for you to deal with." A scream of agony follows, and he places the phone near the traitor.

"Tell him who you are!" Angelo orders.

"Va' all'inferno!" The traitor says violently. The sound of flesh meeting flesh comes from over the phone.

"His name is Antonio Lopez," Angelo tells me. "He's one of our own."

"What's the damage?" I say through clenched teeth.

"Ten of our men are dead, five injured, and they stole most of the ammo in the warehouse."

The sound of ringing in my ears is loud, and my fists are clenched so tight that my nails dig into the flesh of my palms.

"Also, the men on board the ship heading to China haven't arrived yet. And we haven't been able to reach them either," Angelo reveals, and he waits for my burst of anger.

"Fucking bastard!" My anger gets the best of me, and I throw everything off my desk.

"Who was in charge of the area?" I demand, knowing they wouldn't have gotten away with so much of our inventory if our men were doing their job.

"I'm not sure. I only checked if everything was okay when the alarms went off. When I arrived, bullets were already flying."

I let out a frustrated breath, and it leaves behind a trail of fog.

Before hanging up the call, I let him know I'm on my way there.

The molten anger inside me is suffocating. I kick the liquor trolley across the room. The bottles break when they hit the wall.

I run my hands down my face in frustration when someone touches me from behind, and I snap, grabbing their wrist, crushing it until the bone cracks.

The familiar scent of warm vanilla and the sound of a whimper bring a rush of coldness to my body. When I turn around, my nerves coil at the sight of the tears in Victoria's eyes. I immediately release her wrist from my deadly grip.

She presses her limp hand to her chest, and her bottom lip is drawn tight between her teeth to stop her from crying.

I look at her now bruising wrist, and a numbing coldness encompasses my insides from the damage I have done.

I could have pulled my gun out and killed her. This thought is enough for me to push her as far away from me as possible.

My eyes soften from seeing the food she has brought me, which is all over the floor. My nerves run with panic when she scrambles to the ground. Her body trembles as she picks up the broken pieces of the plate. When she cuts her finger on the broken shards of glass, I pick her up, not wanting her to hurt herself further.

The sight of her bleeding finger, swollen wrist, and trembling body is like being hit by a truck.

I'm gentle as I try to fix my mistake, and the entire time I clean her cut, she's adamant that it's her fault and that she's fine, but I can tell she's lying. I hurt her, and she's afraid of me; she just doesn't realize it yet.

Victoria wears a deep frown, and I want to cup her face in my hands. I want to tell her how sorry I am and that it won't happen again. But I'm afraid she'll reject my touch.

"You should go to bed. It's getting late," I say, my voice raw with emotions. Self-loathing is taking over every part of me, including my voice.

Victoria says nothing and makes her way toward the door. I swallow the thickness stuck in my throat and watch as she walks away.

My stomach clenches when I see her shoulders slumped. She tilts her head to the side, and our eyes lock.

The look of disappointment on her face pains me, and the tears in her eyes let me know I've broken my promise to her sister. I've hurt her.

My breath gets caught when the door clicks shut. Silence follows, and my thoughts of regret pound in my head.

"How could I have been so stupid?" I grumble, looking at my hands with disgust.

After a few minutes of wallowing in my guilt, I find the energy to leave.

Even when my thoughts are elsewhere, I still have work to do. And right now, I have a traitor to deal with.

I pass Victoria's room, and I want to check on her.

My fingers curl into a fist, ready to knock on the door. But at the last second, I withdraw my hand because I'm afraid of seeing the hurt and pain I've caused her.

With a heavy heart, I leave the house and drive to where Francisco and the rest of my capos wait for me with the traitor.

As I speed through the winding road, I leave behind tire marks. My thoughts swirl over what I did to Victoria.

I push my guilt aside and press on the gas, allowing my anger to numb my regret because now is not the time to wallow in pity.

I have to be a ruthless Don.

The sound of my men clamoring loudly drifts around as I enter the warehouse.

When I pass, they stiffen, bowing their heads, and they scurry away after seeing my anger.

In the air is the smell of gunpowder and blood. My jaw hardens as rage rips through my veins.

There's a need to kill inside me.

To my left and right, I notice my men working on lifting their dead brothers' corpses from the ground.

Angelo, Francisco, Luca, and Kaden appear standing near a bloodied and beaten Antonio.

Kaden has his fist ready to launch another blow when all their eyes shift to me. Kaden withdraws his fist and runs his hand over his slick, black hair.

Antonio stares stoically at me as I pull back the material of my white dress shirt until it rests below my elbow. When I'm in front of him, I launch a punch to the side of his bloodied head. Then another punch, and another, and another.

Rage takes over my body, and I feel nothing other than the ripples of a thousand tingles shooting up from my knuckle to my shoulder blade.

Blood pours out of Antonio's nostrils when my fist connects with the bottom of his nose.

I'm unstoppable now that I have him in front of me, and my fist attacks him until his face becomes mangled.

The only reason I stop hitting him is because Francisco and Angelo pull me off him after they see he's on the brink of death. We still have to interrogate him.

Antonio looks at me through the slit of his eyes. The small opening reveals the blood coating the white part of his eyeball.

A grin stretches across my face when I see his split skin from where my rings tore into the flesh.

His face has swollen and turned lumpy, almost as if a thousand wasps have attacked him.

My grin falters, and I press my lips tightly together when he smiles sinisterly.

The nerve of this asshole!

"Bastardo!" I snarl, my arms going to his neck. "Where's Adriano hiding?" I demand, my voice deadly.

"I'm not telling. I'm better off dead." His voice is thick with the blood he's swallowing.

I breathe through my nose and punch him in the face. The force is so strong, he falls back, still tied to the chair.

He groans when he hits the floor, and my men's laughter follows.

I snap my fingers over my shoulder, and two of my men lift the chair back up.

When I bend to Antonio's level, he coughs, getting blood on my chest and neck.

Francisco hands me a metal bat.

"Let this be a lesson to you all about what happens to traitors." When I say this, the surrounding men stiffen, their throats contract as they swallow.

I swing the bat, striking Antonio in the knees. The sound of a loud crack and his screams ripple through the silence.

"Let's try this again." My words are dangerous. "Where. Is. Adriano?"

Antonio doesn't respond, and his unwillingness to cooperate has me swinging the bat into his stomach. He doubles over, shouting in pain when his ribs crack.

I throw the bat on the ground, and it makes a sharp ping sound.

Drawing a hand behind me, I don't take my eyes off Antonio.

Kaden hands me the pliers, already knowing what this gesture of mine means.

This is my favorite part of torturing my victims.

My signature move.

Such a tiny little tool has incited fear among many men when they see me with the pliers in my hands.

When they say I'm ruthless, they aren't bluffing.

Nothing is more satisfying than cutting off your enemy's fingers and forcing the chopped meat into their mouth.

It's a vile act that ensures no one would ever want to find themselves at the receiving end of my wrath. But Antonio didn't heed the warnings. So here we are.

"Words better come out of that pathetic hole of a mouth, or I swear you'll regret ever fucking with me." Antonio cowers back into the metal chair, but still doesn't say a word.

To my side, Luca and Kaden turn to one another with a grin because the show is about to begin.

Without remorse, I position the blades of the pliers over the base of where his pinky finger bone begins. He winces, even though I haven't even pressed down.

I ignore his thrashing, and my hands tug at the finger. With each painful pull, he throws his head back.

His screams of pain flicker throughout the room, launching off the walls. The sound is like a sweet melody.

Amidst his screams is the sound of the pliers slicing through his finger. Blood trails from my hands to my elbows, soaking my shirt.

I stare at the torn flesh and white bone.

Antonio quivers in his seat. His eyes pinched closed.

The pliers move to his middle finger, and he fights my grasp, but his restraints keep his hands tied. I take no time to chop off a second finger.

Satisfied, I pick up the fingers and grab his face.

Antonio vigorously shifts his head, trying to stop me, but my grasp around his mouth tightens. I pinch his cheeks, forcing his mouth open. When there's a gap, I shove his now severed fingers inside.

From the corner of my eye, I notice one of our recently recruited younger soldiers has turned pale. He's about to look away when Kaden forces him to watch.

A lesson to be engraved into his brain about what would happen if he ever fucked with me.

"Start chewing or talking, asshole." My hands are around Antonio's jaw to keep his mouth shut.

Antonio shakes his head, tears flowing from the slits he calls eyes.

Behind me, the younger boy spews the contents of his stomach. Luca grumbles in disgust when chunks land on his shoes.

The air lingers with the stench of copper, gunpowder, sweat, and vomit.

These are the smells of the dark side of the mafia.

I release Antonio, and he spits out his fingers. They hit me on the chest.

"You bastard!" he cries.

"That's not what I want to hear."

"Vaffanculo!" he curses me, and I realize he won't be talking. I can tear him apart limb by limb, and he still won't say a word.

"Don't worry. I'll make sure I send your family what's left of your body." I grab the bat from the ground and swing with all the force in my upper chest.

The end of the bat hits the side of his face. Antonio's right eye bulges out, and blood sprays us. His blood continues to squirt out of him in little droplets.

I swing the bat once more, hitting him on the top of the head. I close my eyes when blood and tissue splatter all over my face.

The smell of rust surrounds me, and he mumbles something inaudible.

I hand the bat back to Angelo, and he grimaces at the sight of a barely breathing Antonio convulsing behind me.

I give Francisco a side glance.

"Kill him."

Francisco waves a hand, motioning for the surrounding men to finish Antonio off.

The sound of five men jumping Antonio rings behind me.

Francisco is beside me, waiting for my next order.

"Throw the bodies of the traitors into the ocean and make sure they take those of our men to the morgue. I'll let their families know."

He nods, and the loud bang of a gun echoes throughout the warehouse, followed by silence.

Without another word, I make my way into the office in the warehouse. I spent the next few hours looking at the footage we caught of the men who got away. I hoped I could find a lead or even a license plate we could use to trace back to Adriano. But there was nothing useful in the footage.

It's frustrating not knowing where Adriano is hiding. From what Alexander told me earlier, he has his men on every fucking continent. I'm not sure if he's in America, China, Cuba, Italy, France, or Russia. He's left a trail in all the places our mafias run, and we can't track him down.

He's out there, and he's laughing at us.

Adriano is a problem I can't handle alone. Which means that for the first time in our mafia, it's time for a reunion among the five powerful mafia families. The last reunion was on the day the alliance was formed.

If I'm going to kill Adriano, it's going to be through the combined forces of the Mafia Alliance.

When I step out of the warehouse, darkness surrounds me, and I look at the time to see it's about to be three in the morning.

By now, Antonio's blood has dried on my clothes and stained my arms red even after washing them.

When I arrive at my estate, I walk through the back to avoid bumping into anyone, particularly the girls. They didn't need to see the violet residue of my actions.

As I'm about to leave the kitchen, my stomach grumbles in the dead of night.

Victoria bringing me food comes to mind, and the guilt takes over as I remember what happened a few hours ago.

I head toward the pantry to grab something to take with me to my room. But when I open the pantry door, I hear soft feet pattering from behind.

My body grows rigid, and that's when I see Victoria pulling out a jug of water from the fridge. Before I can hide, she turns around and lets out a strangled scream.

The jug of water falls from her hands, shattering and spilling all around us.

I jump to grab Victoria, so she doesn't hurt herself with the shards of glass. But when I approach her, she retreats away from me, and her eyes flash with fear.

The disgust and betrayal on her beautiful face pierce my chest, and my stomach is heavy with regret.

I want nothing more than to hold Victoria. But every time I get closer, she takes two steps back.

Seeing Victoria slip away from me reveals the gravity of my affection for her. I can no longer hide who I am from her, and I can't keep myself away either. It physically hurts.

The distance I have stupidly put between us over the past few months is pointless. All it took to realize this was watching her fall through my fingertips.

The trust she once held for me is no longer there. In its place are now disgust and betrayal.

The terror on her face makes me speechless, and I make my way toward her, hoping her touch will help me find the words I want to say.

"Don't—" she pleads, her lips quivering.

She slowly backs away from me until she reaches the door. I can't stop myself from going after her. I want to assure her I'm not the monster she thinks I am, at least not to her.

"Stop it, Leo." She has her arms in front of her, and her voice breaks. "I said stop it, goddammit!" Her voice is loud, almost harsh.

My eyes widen from the roar she has produced. The sound is something unheard of from her, and I feel small even when I tower over her.

Victoria lets out a breath of relief when I halt, and she rushes out of the kitchen. Our eyes never disconnect.

The sound of her fast feet running up the stairs has my heart racing.

As she runs away from me, I realize I haven't only lost the love of my life. She's also terrified of me.

Today has not been my day.

"Merda!" I curse as I make my way upstairs.

My hunger is long gone, and in its place is regret for not telling Victoria the truth about who I am sooner. Now I've lost her because of my lies.

Before, I wanted to push her away to protect her from the mafia life. But now that I have pushed her to the edge, I want to take it all back. I can't bear the thought of not having her beside me.

My father's pain after losing my mother to death was something I never wanted to experience. Yet I can feel an ounce of his pain coursing through me now.

There's no escaping my love for Victoria. No matter how hard I try.

A stab to my chest knocks the breath out of me when I see the door to her room is opened and her bed is empty.

She was so scared that she ran to Sofia's room.

Tomorrow, I have to tell her the truth. There are many reasons I'm done holding back, but the main one is that I care about her so much that it's impossible not to want to call her mine.

I can now see that there's no difference between the mafia world and the real world.

If there was a difference between the two, I wouldn't have found Victoria where I did.

At least with her by my side, I know she's safe because I can protect her.

33

VICTORIA

Even though my eyes are heavy, sleep refuses to come.

It's impossible to fall asleep after finding out the man I not only care about but who I put my wholehearted trust in, isn't who I thought he was.

The memory of Leo covered in blood makes me shudder.

Most concerning is that I'm still drawn to him, even if I'm slightly afraid of him.

Fear and uncertainty are waging war on my feelings of attraction toward Leo.

It's always this way with him. He makes my mind and body react in ways I don't understand. Like right now, the tiny voice in my head is telling me to run, but another part of me doesn't want to.

The feelings I have for Leo aren't only physical. They are deeper than that. He makes me feel beautiful and protected; I don't want these feelings to end.

Have I lost my mind? Did my kidnapping leave me more unhinged than my therapist, and I thought?

I close my eyes and bury my face in a pillow, wanting to scream in frustration, but no noise comes out.

The night and morning seemed to last forever, and I was grateful when the sun's rays filled the room, waking Sofia.

She looks over at me, and her forehead wrinkles in concern.

"Victoria, what's wrong?"

With her staring at me, the dam inside me breaks. I press her to my chest, needing something to anchor me from the overwhelming feelings of deception and confusion.

"Everything is messed up," I say through tears.

"What's messed up?" There's a hint of panic in her words.

"He lied to me. They lied to us, Sofia!" As I say this, all the red flags from the past few weeks come to mind. Leo's vague response to who he is, his relationship with Adriano, the guns, and tall scary men roaming the halls. He's a gangster. He has to be. I'm an idiot for not seeing it sooner, and I'm more of an idiot for thinking he was some undercover agent.

"Who lied, Victoria? You aren't making any sense right now."

"They aren't who they say they are, Sofia. They're criminals! I saw Leo covered in blood. He killed someone." My voice is unsteady, and my hands shake from fear of what this information now means for me and Sofia's safety.

Sofia exhales a soft breath, pressing me to her chest in a tight embrace.

"What did he say?" she asks.

"He didn't get to say anything because I ran straight to your room."

"Victoria, I'm sure it's all a misunderstanding. Leo would never hurt you." She tries to ease my worries, but it doesn't work.

Why does everyone keep saying this!

"Sofia, are you listening to me?" My words are harsh, and her eyes widen in surprise.

"Victoria, please calm down." She clutches my shoulders, and I try to steady my racing heart, and when it slows, I find the willingness to speak again.

"Why are you so calm?" I ask, and she gives a sad smile.

"I was awake when they rescued us, remember?" Her response piques my interest, and she grabs my hands, squeezing them. "Luca, Angelo,

Francisco, Kaden, and Leo killed to save us," she explains, and I blink, my breathing coming out hard from this information. "But Victoria, they aren't bad people, not to us. Have they given us reason to fear them?"

I sigh and cast my eyes on my lap because Sofia's right. Leo's been nothing but good to me. The least I owe him is the opportunity to explain himself.

"Victoria, we might not know everything about them, but maybe they have a reason for keeping us in the dark."

I nod. "How am I going to face him now?"

"Stop overthinking," she says in exasperation. "It's Leo we're talking about! He's the same man who was holding onto your unconscious body for dear life. Afraid you would slip from his grasp."

Her words bring warmth to my face, and she moves a strand of hair behind my ear.

"Talk to him. Let him explain and listen."

"Okay." The word leaves my mouth effortlessly.

Sofia smiles and gets out of bed, extending a hand for me to take, and together we head toward the door, but before she can open it, I become nervous from the fear of hearing the truth.

Sofia notices my hesitation and turns to me.

"You can do it," she encourages, but she's wrong. I can't do it.

I'm not ready to face the truth. I first need time to sort out my feelings for Leo. The truth is something I have wanted to know since France, but now that it's here, I'm afraid of what the truth will mean for my feeling toward him. I don't want his words to change how I feel about him. I've become addicted to the butterflies he brings me.

"I'll bring you something to eat," Sofia says.

I nod, and she leaves the room.

By noon, I was going insane. The entire morning, I thought about Leo and how much I still care about him. But then the smell of blood came with his memory, leaving me more turbulent.

I won't be able to make sense of my feelings for him until we talk.

Slowly, my hesitation from earlier disappears, and my legs carry me to the door.

When I open it, Cleo is in front of me.

She has her hand raised, ready to knock on the door, but she lowers it when she sees me.

Her hazel eyes stare at me, softening when they notice my distress. Her bow-shaped lips tug into an apologetic smile when she sees she has frightened me.

I bite the inside of my mouth, feeling nervous with her in front of me. Leo wasn't the only one who lied to me.

She sees my hesitation and gives me a friendly smile. She extends a hand for me to take.

I don't take it at first, but when a frown draws onto her face, my heart tugs, and I give her my hand.

I'm uneasy as she leads me through the hall.

She looks nervous, and that's when I realize Cleo is innocent, and her only crime is being related to Leo.

We walk through the house for a few minutes until we enter a massive library. At the sight of the Gothic library, my mouth drops.

Cleo stops in front of a bookshelf. Her eyes run along the shelf, looking for a specific book. Her gaze falls on a royal blue book, and she pulls it like a lever.

The silence of the room is filled with a faint cranking noise. The bookshelf opens to reveal a secret room, and a rush of cold air hits my face. I try to make out what's inside the dark, eerie room where the smell of dust is strong.

Cleo tugs me inside, and she flicks the switch to reveal a round room with a swing in the center and books stationed all around the walls.

I'm intrigued by a large portrait encased in gold. It hangs on the wall like a distant memory. There's a heaviness in my chest when I see the image collecting dust.

As I make my way to it, Cleo stands close behind me, her eyes glistening with tears.

The pad of my fingers swipes at the dust, and the breath leaves my lungs when I see Leo as a child. The picture in front of me is the first family portrait I've seen in the entire house. I can't take my eyes off it.

There's a flutter of warmth as I soak in the sight of Leo standing proudly with a smile, revealing two little dimples.

He stands beside Cleo, who couldn't have been older than five. Behind them are a man and a woman, their parents. Leo's mom's eyes draw me to her.

Her hazel eyes, which Cleo inherited, are like a portal that lets you read her like an open book, and the smile on her lips reveals how much she loves her family. You can see it in how she looks at Leo and Cleo with deep affection instead of looking into the camera.

It's as if her universe revolves entirely around her children and the man holding her close to him.

In contrast, Leo's dad has his eyes solely on Leo's mom, and you can see a powerful love written all over his face, like a script of their perfect life.

My breath gets caught by how alike Leo and his dad look.

Like Leo, this man stands by his family with pride written all over his face. He's tall and determined to protect his family from harm.

I flicker my gaze to the words engraved on the wall, and a tightness consumes my throat after I see what is carved into the wood.

Stephanie and Estephano
  forever and always

My gaze falls on Cleo, who sits on the couch in the center of the room. She's engrossed in the darkness of her mind. Her grief is so intense it seeps into me.

I take the space beside Cleo and notice she swallows hard many times. It's as if she has something clogged inside her throat. Her right hand rises to her neck, caressing the spot, letting me know something is wrong.

I place a hand on her shoulder.

"Cleo, are you okay?" She opens her mouth, trying to speak, but when no sound follows, she purses her lips in frustration.

"You can do it," I encourage.

Cleo takes a deep breath, glancing at the picture before swallowing. Then I hear the faintest whisper coming from her lips.

My eyes soften, and my heart warms at the sound of her voice.

The consequences of not speaking in years means her voice is rough and broken. Yet this doesn't stop her from trying to speak.

"That's my mama," she whispers, and a single tear falls from her eye. Her eyes are on the picture of her family—more notably, the woman with golden brown locks of hair.

In Cleo's eyes, I see the longing of a daughter wanting nothing more than to make her mom proud. The pain in Cleo's eyes tells me something terrible happened to her mom. She expresses the same grief Leo had in France.

"She's beautiful," I say as I stare at the woman, who looks of gentle manner and kindness like no other.

"She was, and her personality was as beautiful," Cleo whispers, her voice cracking.

"Cleo, does your brother know you're talking again, or at least trying to?" As soon as I ask this, her head drops. I grab her hands. "Why not? He should be here right now with you," I say, knowing I don't deserve to be the first to hear her voice.

"He's busy trying to find Adriano." I notice her arms erupt with goosebumps when she says Adriano's name, and my forehead bunches. "Don't tell him I'm talking again, not yet." Her voice hints at her panic at the thought of me telling everyone she's talking again.

"Your secret is safe with me," I assure her, and she lets out a sigh of relief before swallowing as if she's in pain.

"Cleo, if it hurts to speak, then sign to me." Cleo declines this idea and continues to speak, regardless of the pain.

"I know you're scared of Leo. But I can assure you he won't hurt you." Her eyes pin me in place. "I think he loves you."

I blink, her words echoing inside me.

Do I love Leo?

The thought of loving a murderer sends a chill down my spine.

"I can't love a killer," I tell her, and Cleo pinches my arm. The skin erupts with a fiery numbness.

"Cleo, what was that for?" I complain, rubbing my arm where she pinched me.

She raises her eyebrows.

"Victoria, don't be stupid, and stop denying your feelings for my brother. Leo is a killer, but he has his reasons. He will tell you, but you need to give him a chance to explain himself."

A tiny choking sound rasps at the back of my throat when she confirms Leo is a killer.

She notices my disappointment and presses me against her chest. Her warmth and rose scent cover me like a heavy blanket.

"Please don't run away from us," she pleads, and her warm tears fall on my shoulder. "Don't abandon us too."

I hold her tight as she folds in my arms. Her words have brought a gut-wrenching tug to my insides.

Don't abandon us too. What did this mean?

"Cleo, I don't know what to tell you."

"At least give him the chance to tell you the truth," she bargains.

"I'm scared of him, Cleo. But I'm also not scared." I confess, and she smiles, already knowing this.

"My mamma was a lot like you."

"How so?"

"She was the daughter of the police commissioner here in Sicily. She was the golden girl. My parents fell in love, but they would always be star-crossed lovers."

"Star-crossed lovers?" I whisper, and she responds with a slow, sad nod. Her attention flickers back to her family's portrait.

"It was hard for them to be together. Forces were pulling them apart from every angle. My Nonno's and Marquez made it hard for them to be together," she says the name Marquez with distaste, and I become curious about who this man is. "But none of them could stop my parents from being together. At least for a few short years." Cleo looks away from the picture, wiping her eyes.

"The thing about love is that it creeps on you without your knowledge or consent. It happens naturally. Like breathing."

I absorb her words, and my heart races as the darkness in my brain lifts.

Cleo's words have opened my heart to what I've been telling myself isn't possible. Her words assure me I'm not crazy. My feelings for Leo are justifiable. They crept up on me before I could realize it, and they escalated until they became a natural part of my existence. The answer I've been looking for has been in front of me this entire time. I just didn't want to accept it.

All this time I've been fighting the natural urge to be with Leo. The constant resistance and questioning of everything has been keeping me from the one thing I wanted. I'm the sole reason behind my distress and the key to ending it. All I have to do is let go of the control I clung to and let the feelings consume me.

"Why are you telling me this?"

"I can tell you're afraid of my brother because he kills, but you shouldn't be afraid of him. He cares about you more than anyone, including myself," she says with a hint of a smile.

"Victoria, you should have seen him this morning. He was a mess during breakfast. His eyes kept looking at the door, waiting for you to come in. It was very cute, if you ask me. You have him smitten." She laughs, bumping her shoulder with mine.

"Smitten, huh?" I tease, finding humor in knowing a tall, handsome Italian man who made those around him cower in fear found me attractive.

"Yes, now go to him!" she says, lightly pushing me to stand.

"Victoria, Leo will never hurt you, and if he does, he has to deal with me afterwards."

Cleo lifts her hands into fists, and I wrap my arms around her shoulders.

"You're the best, Cleo." Her shoulders shake with laughter, and her arms tighten around me.

"I know, I know! Now find my brother and end his misery! It's your turn to rescue him."

"I'm going," I say, and a wave of confidence takes over the fear I had this morning. "Thank you for opening my eyes." She gives a gentle smile.

"Victoria, some words of advice." She places a hand on mine. "Don't run from your problems like me and my mamma. Because then you'll be in darkness, and you don't want to be there." Her eyes flash with shame for a second before she gives a false smile.

From the pain in her eyes, I want to hold her, but she gives me a warning look to go to Leo.

I make my way to the door, but before leaving, I take one last look at her, and my heart breaks at what I see.

Cleo stands in front of the picture of her family, and what she says has the tears slipping from my eyes.

"I did it, mamma. I opened her eyes, and now Leo will get the happy ending he deserves."

A lump of grief forms in my throat as the door to the hidden room closes behind me. And with an open mind and heart, I make my way toward Leo, ready to listen to what he has to say.

34

VICTORIA

I make my way through the hallway. My chest swells with a newfound lightness and confidence.

With every step, I throw away the rational part of my brain—the one telling me to run in the other direction.

The conversation I had with Cleo has opened my eyes.

She's right. Running from my problems won't solve anything. I have to head toward my fears with a steady chin.

The toxicity of my thoughts has poisoned me long enough. I may not know Leo's secret, but I'm ready to listen to him.

To say it surprised me how fast I changed my mind would be an understatement.

I'm certain Leo's bipolarity is starting to rub off on me.

The corners of my mouth tip up at this thought.

It only takes a few minutes to reach the familiar office, and when I'm near, I take a deep breath. The sound of men speaking in thick Italian accents comes from down the hall, and I stiffen.

The three rugged men pass by, and they all have cigars in their right hands. They mumble in Italian, and I understand a phrase or two from the similarities between the Spanish and Italian languages.

They are talking about their families from the word famiglia, which appears twice in their conversation.

When they notice me, they smile before bobbing their heads in acknowledgment. The breath I'm holding releases, and I give them a thin-lipped smile as they disappear down the corner of the hall.

Once they are out of sight, I take the few steps left to reach Leo's office. A stiffness rises in my throat, and my hands become clammy when I'm in front of the powerful door.

"You got this, Victoria," I murmur, and I open the door, not sure what I'm going to say. All I know is I'm not leaving his office without getting the answers I want. Leo's time is up. If he doesn't want to lose me, he needs to stop lying to me. There can't be secrets between us. Not if he wants me to give him a chance. I need to know who I'm getting myself involved with.

My confidence turns to disappointment when Leo is nowhere in sight.

Outside the door, I hear men talking, and I stick my head out, hoping it's him. But I'm disappointed for a second time when I see two unfamiliar men and no sign of Leo.

Determined to find him, I clear my throat and call after the two men passing by.

"Umm, excuse me?" My voice comes out in a nervous whisper.

The two men jerk their heads back in surprise because this is the first time I've talked to any of the men I've seen around the house.

"Ciao," the older of the two men replies, and his dark eyes are anything but frightening.

I stare at them, unsure of how to communicate with them or if they understand English.

They stare at me as if I have grown two heads, and my body temperature rises when they blink, waiting for my response.

The man beside the one who talked to me notices my insecurity and nudges his friend.

"È la ragazza del Don, non credo che parli ancora italiano," he tells the man.

The two men stare at one another before looking back at me, and the man who first spoke, nods in understanding. He clears his throat and tips his head back, eyes locked on the roof as he considers his next words.

"Is everything okay?" he asks me, and there's a sharp sound behind his accent.

"Hi, do you know where Leo is?" I ask, and he turns to his friend, who shakes his head with his lips pursed.

"Sorry, mi regina, but we haven't seen him."

From his response, I suppress my frown and put on a fake smile.

"Thank you anyway." They nod, disappearing down the stairs.

I enter Leo's office, deciding to wait for him inside.

My eyes sweep across the room, taking in the space where Leo spends most of his time.

Unlike the previous night, the room is clean, and the stench of the liquor he shattered is gone. In its place is the rich, musky smell of his cologne, and my stomach churns. A reaction that relieves me to know I still find comfort in his scent after last night.

I greedily take in the sight of the beautiful wine-red Persian rug and the enormous Gothic library.

The room is bigger than I remembered.

I sit on the black leather couch in front of the fireplace when, from the corner of my eye, a black-and-white portrait on the wall catches my attention.

Curiosity gets the best of me, and the force emitting from the picture draws me to it.

As I take in the picture, my heart thumps at the sight of Leo surrounded by men who all look as strong as him.

Leo wears a black fedora hat. His left arm is crossed over his chest, revealing his muscles. With his other hand, he carries an automatic rifle, and a cigar rests between his lips.

In the back are unfamiliar faces, but in the front, beside Leo, are the faces of Francisco, Luca, Angelo, and Kaden. They also have a gun in their hands and cigarettes in their mouths.

My heart races in my chest from the intense energy radiating from the picture.

Typically, guns of this style scare me, like they did the day I arrived here, but this time they don't. Not when Sofia's words from this morning remind me how these men are harmless to me.

Where fear once used to be, there is now a sense of pride in seeing them dominate the space they occupy. There's a weightless turnover occurring inside me because these gruff men trusted me and Sofia enough to show us a softer side of them.

I fix my stare on Leo, and his robust and handsome physique steals the breath out of my lungs.

The men surrounding him both respected and feared him. It's noticeable in a single moment captured in time.

My pointer finger caresses the image, and it's smooth and cold to my touch. When I draw back, the door to the room opens, and the air rushes out of my lungs. My knees weaken at the sight of Leo.

His eyes, which are adorned with dark circles, are wide in surprise.

The silence between us is thick with anxiety. With his eyes pinning me in place, I forget why I'm here.

I say the first thing that comes to mind.

"I'm sorry; I shouldn't be in here." My words come out with a slight tremble, and I avoid his stare.

"Victoria..." My name melts into a breathy sigh of relief, and the corners of my mouth want to rise into a smile. But then I remember why I'm here, and I try my best to be firm.

"I want answers, Leo." My arms cross over my chest, and I'm proud of myself when my voice doesn't come out shaky.

There's a twinkle in his eyes as he approaches me, and I watch with weary eyes as he gets closer until he stands a foot away.

With him now hovering over me, I stand self-consciously before his tall height.

"Where should I start?" His right hand rises to the back of his neck.

"From the beginning."

Leo sighs deeply.

"Bambina, promise me you won't run away. I need you to hear everything I have to say." His right hand rises to hold me, but he stops himself and drops it back to his side.

"Leo," I say, knowing I can't promise him I won't run away.

He senses my hesitation toward his request, and his eyes fall to the floor in thought. He drags his bottom lip between his teeth, and when our gazes lock again, I see the fear and uneasiness in his eyes.

He's afraid of losing me, and I'm afraid of losing my feelings for him.

"I'll tell you everything, but I want to clarify that I won't ever hurt you." He glances at my bruised wrist with a grimace. "At least not again."

I swallow, willing the dryness away, and my left hand covers the bruise from his eyes. His attention drifts back to my face, our tired eyes lock. In one breath, he tells me his secret.

"Victoria, I'm the Don of the Italian Mafia." He watches me wearily, and I find that although he speaks low, it's as if he's shouted his secret.

Leo's secret echoes in my thoughts, bringing a hollowness to my insides. I'm too stunned. I don't say anything.

"I'm not only the Don of the Italian mafia. I'm also in charge of the biggest mafia alliance." His eyes don't leave mine, and I remain frozen without uttering a word.

The word mafia is circling in my mind, making me dizzy, and I'm sure I look ridiculous with my mouth parted and eyes bulging, unwilling to blink.

What am I supposed to say to this news? I've just been told the man I'm falling in love with isn't a mediocre criminal. He's *the* criminal—the boss of many other dangerous men.

I look at Leo and notice how he doesn't fit the image I have in my mind of what a mafia boss looks like.

Weren't they supposed to be old, crusty weirdos? Where's the beer belly, the long, prickly beard around his chin, or the tacky tattoos?

"Victoria, you're scaring me. Say something." There's panic in his voice.

"You're scared?" I snap, and Leo looks taken aback by my tone.

He's scared? And what the hell am I?

I try to absorb this news when I'm reminded of the time Erika mentioned to me how Adriano belonged to a powerful mafia family.

Is it possible that Leo is the powerful cousin Adriano doesn't like?

I take a good look at Leo and notice his green eyes and chiseled features are like those of Adriano. I've never quite noticed the resemblance between my kidnapper and my hero until now.

"Is Adriano your cousin?" The question slips out of me, and Leo's jaw goes slack for a second. When the shock passes, his face hardens.

"Yes." His response is flat, and it's mixed with hostility. My heart drops, and the color must have drained from my face from the panic washing over Leo.

"Do you also…" I'm unable to say it, afraid to find out if he takes part in human trafficking.

"Traffic people and sell them." As he says this, he has a slightly cocked brow. "No, of course not." The words come out acidic, as if the thought of him doing this type of business repulses him.

I sigh in relief, and Leo stands in front of me, shoulders sagging, mouth twitching as he bites the inside of his bottom lip. In the rich green of his eyes, I see the same look Cleo gave me earlier. He's afraid I'll abandon him. But I now realize I can never leave him. There will always be a force pulling us together. No matter how hard I fought it and no matter how crazy I sounded, Leo is the one I want to be with, secrets and all.

He may be a criminal in the eyes of the law, but to me, he's always going to be my knight in shining Armani, who saved me when the law let me down.

Unable to hold back, I wrap my arms around his waist, pressing my cheek against his solid chest.

His steady heartbeat becomes frantic against my cheek, and his arms wrap around my waist, holding me tight.

I don't let the fact that Leo is in the mafia get to me because this information surprisingly doesn't change who he is to me. All this news did was close the holes in our relationship that he created between us, which reminds me of how easy it was for him to lie to me.

The constant lies he fed me make my blood simmer, and I detach myself from him.

His dishonesty and lack of communication caused me pain and confusion. Everything between us would have been easier if he had told me the truth from the beginning.

Leo's lips twist into a deep frown when I pull away from him.

I narrow my eyes, and he looks at me with worry. He opens his mouth to say something, but my hand slaps him across the cheek before he can say a word.

Leo's eyes enlarge in shock, and his mouth twists into a grin.

"I deserved that," he says, and I roll my eyes, crossing my arms over my chest.

"Lie to me again, and I'll hit you on the back of the head with my shoe," I warn, and he responds by lifting two fingers and placing them near the right side of his temple, saluting me. I laugh, and he steals a gasp from me when he draws me into his chest.

His eyes study me, and I can sense my heart racing from how his eyes soak in every inch of my face.

A fierce heat burns in his eyes, and my tongue peeks through the seams of my lips to wet the dry skin. The moment I do this, he makes a rough sound of frustration from the back of his throat. His next words are exhilarating, and they incite a fever.

"Fuck, you're so beautiful." His voice has a rich, husky tenor, and his eyes are dark.

My hand on his chest tightens into a fist, and I try to stay upright. The thundering rings of my heart pulse in my ears, and he bends his head.

"Leo," I breathe. He lets out a silent hum, and my heart flutters when the arm he has encircled around my waist pulls me tight against him. His other hand finds its home on my right cheek, and his touch is as velvety as the petals of a red rose. When the pad of his thumb caresses my bottom lip, I shudder.

Kiss me already!

My breathing becomes hard, and my lips tingle to feel his. His warm breath is intoxicating, and he stares into my eyes. There's a silent question behind them, and I realize he's asking if he can kiss me.

I wrap my arms around his neck and lift my chin. He doesn't need more convincing, and he cups my jaw. His lips fall onto mine in a tender caress.

The second the warm, soft flesh of his lips fills my mouth, everything around me becomes fuzzy. All that matters to me is Leo and how his lips land over mine with a gentleness I didn't know existed.

As he kisses me, I melt into his touch, seeing sparks. There's a sigh stuck in my throat now that this moment has finally arrived after waiting for months.

His lips continue to move over mine in a slow, loving kiss. The sparks exploding inside my abdomen force my knees to shake.

Leo brings me closer to him, allowing me to feel every inch of his body, and I gasp into his mouth.

I cup his stubbled cheeks between my hands, and his perfectly trimmed five o'clock shadow tickles my palms.

Leo's tongue swipes at my bottom lip before jutting into my mouth. I welcome him, allowing his tongue to dominate every inch of my mouth.

Our lips move in sync, and an intense passion and need burns inside me.

Leo pulls away from my mouth; his lips travel down my jaw to my neck, and my eyes close in pleasure. As soon as I'm in the darkness, unwanted memories resurface.

The warmth of Leo's mouth turns into the touch of Richard and Lorenzo. I tremble from the terrorizing memories of them on top of me.

I'm breathing loudly, and the tears start to fall.

Leo becomes rigid and removes his lips, having sensed something is wrong. When his touch disappears, so do the memories.

The sight of his panic punctures my gut, and I'm not sure what to tell him.

I try to blink the tears away, and Leo frowns when he sees me breaking apart in front of him.

He takes my shaky hands, puts them over his beating heart, and holds them there. His eyes never leave mine, and he holds me until the fear passes.

"I'm so sorry, Bambina." He wipes my tears, and all I can do is stare into his eyes regretfully.

I hate how, even months after what happened to me, I still feel my attacker's lips on my body. And now, my past trauma is interfering with my relationship with Leo.

I don't want Leo's touch to feel like theirs. I thought I had healed, but the past is unerasable. It will always be a part of me, and the memories will creep back into my mind as they did moments ago. There's no true escape from the past.

I sniffle and cup his face. He nuzzles into my warmth.

"I'm sorry. I don't know what happened." The lie comes easily, but he sees through me, and sadness sweeps over him.

He sighs, bringing me into his arms, and his warmth eases my nerves. With him holding me, I know everything will be okay.

"Tesoro, I don't want to hear you apologize for something out of your control," he says, his voice soft but firm. "You are strong, and I admire you for your strength." I stare into his compassionate eyes and fall deeper in love with him.

A comforting silence passes by, and we both stare at one another in bliss when the richness of his voice breaks through the silence.

"Victoria, be mine," he says softly, and his words have left me breathless. I respond with silence from the overwhelming amount of love, happiness, and self-doubt raging through me. "Be my amore," he says again, caressing our noses together.

"I don't know what to say," I whisper, unsure if I can meet his expectations.

"Say you'll have me." He draws back, and I suck in a small breath at his eagerness to make me his.

My chest becomes heavy because I want this, but now that I know he's a mafia Don, I'm not sure if I have what it takes to be a part of his world, and this makes my heart twist.

"Bambina, what's wrong?" he says, cupping my face, and his green eyes settle on me with concern.

"I don't know if I can," I confess, but quickly clarify when his face drops. "I want to."

"Then what's the problem?"

"I don't think I can meet your expectations. Or your men's," I say, chewing on my bottom lip.

Leo's face relaxes, and he throws his head back, letting out an airy laugh. My face warms from embarrassment and annoyance.

Noticing my rising anger, the corners of his lips tip up into a grin.

"Unable to meet my expectations?" he says in disbelief, cocking a brow. "Bambina, you are everything to me. You are enough, and you have what it takes. Just five minutes ago, you slapped me and threatened to hit me with a shoe, remember?"

My lips roll into my mouth, and my heart pounds in my ears from how much he means to me.

"Bambina, you fit the role, and if anyone says otherwise, I'll kill them." His face tightens at the thought of anyone second-guessing me.

I restrain myself from rolling my eyes at his overprotectiveness.

"No, you won't," I warn him. "If they second guess me, let me prove them wrong," I tell him, and a smile appears on my face.

"Wait, is that a yes?" he asks, his face glowing like a million stars.

Laughing, I nod, and Leo lets out a breath of relief. His stare falls to my mouth before landing back on my face. His dark brows lift the slightest, asking me for permission. I say nothing and do a better one by grabbing him by the collar of his shirt and pressing our mouths together.

Inhaling his scent, I savor how he holds me as if I mean the world to him. As we kiss for a second time, I allow his touch to help me forget how Lorenzo and Richard touched me. This time I remind myself that it's only Leo. His touch is not theirs. He holds me close with gentleness and doesn't grip me like an object. He holds me with the intention of loving me, not dominating me.

This is enough to help push the haunting memories of my assault aside.

Leo pulls away from my lips, leaving behind a lingering sensation of tingles.

"Mi amore," he breathes, love glowing in his eyes.

I give a smile and position my mouth near his ear.

"Todo tuya," I mumble, breathless, and he smashes his lips onto mine in another powerful kiss.

35

VICTORIA

My body ignites with the fires of pleasure. The tingles spread from the tips of my toes to my cheeks.

"Leo..." His name is a breathless whisper, and the surrounding skin of my collarbone vibrates when he hums. His lips graze over the area behind my neck, and they continue their gentle caress.

After my panic attack earlier, I was sure I wouldn't be able to have Leo kiss me in other places that weren't my lips, but I was wrong. His gentleness and slow pace made it so that the memories of my past remained at bay. I found his touch to be enjoyable.

"Leo!" This time I say his name in annoyance when he nibbles on my earlobe, unwilling to let me go.

"Yes, amore," he murmurs against my neck.

"I still have questions." I push on his chest, creating some distance between us, and he grumbles.

"What do you want to know?" The pad of his thumb brushes against my bottom lip, which tingles after having been ravaged for the past half hour.

His admiration creates a tightness in my stomach, and my tongue runs over my bottom lip. In the process, I end up licking his finger, which is placed against my lip.

His eyes dilate, and his head dips to kiss me again. But when his lips are near my mouth, I swipe my head, and he's met with my hair.

"Not so fast." Leo lets out an annoyed breath, and my right brow lifts higher. "And you tell me you're a mafia Don?" I tease, pinching his right cheek.

Leo responds by sending me a glare, but it turns into a grin at the last second.

"I am, and the best at that," he urges, which receives a laugh from me.

"Mm-hm," I mumble condescendingly.

"You don't believe me?" he says, faking hurt.

I shrug my shoulders.

"I don't know. You haven't told me much about what it is you do." My voice is serious now, and a small sigh comes from his lips.

Leo takes my hand and leads me toward the couch in his office. He takes the space to my left, his hand not leaving mine. Warmth flutters through my insides from seeing his long fingers wrap around my small ones. A sight that reminds me of the time we were under the Eiffel Tower all those months ago.

Leo lifts our hands to his mouth and kisses the top of my hand. His eyes watch me the entire time, and they flash with adoration. A smile stretches across my face.

"You already know I don't work the same way as Adriano." When he speaks, he's gentle, and he makes sure nothing he says triggers the memories of my kidnapping. His delicate care of my wellbeing has my heart leaping out of my chest.

For a mafia man, Leo is a sweetheart. He respects women and isn't greedy like Adriano and his men, who tear into women's bodies like bandits.

My Leo is different, and although his actions are the bare minimum, the truth is that even these insignificant gestures from a man are hard to find.

For centuries, some men have let women down because all they ever want is in their best interest and never ours. For many men, their conception was that our bodies were for their taking.

Their excuse is that Eve was a product of Adam's rib, which meant we were theirs, and by nature, they had every right to our bodies. But we weren't theirs for the taking, and they forgot one key detail. The story of Adam and Eve is a *myth*, a tale passed down through history and written to accommodate the agenda of powerful people and institutions, who are more than likely always men.

It's easy for misogynistic men to remember this story of Adam and Eve because it serves their interests. But it's also easy for them to forget that the one who gave birth to them was a woman.

This lack of acknowledgment meant that throughout history, women have been mistreated and seen as mere spectacles for other men to gawk at—the pearls every man wants to stash in their tight pockets, only to pull them out and show the world when it's most convenient for them.

A quiet woman is the wine of their choice, and the loud woman becomes the image of the unattainable, the undesired—a woman who, in the eyes of their bigotry, needs to be fixed and conditioned to obey.

Leo has proven to me that he doesn't think this way. He's one of the few men who sees the pain and struggles women go through. He works hard to protect me, Cleo, and Sofia from the darkness brought on by his gender.

My thoughts on how amazing he is burst when he reminds me of how greed will always have a prominent role in our capitalistic society.

"But this doesn't mean my mafia doesn't make money from sex work," he says, and my heart falls to my stomach.

There's a ringing in my ears, and a tide of disappointment hits me.

I'm disgusted by what he has told me, and I don't want to hear anything he says after this. But then I remember what Cleo and Sofia told me. They said to listen to what he has to say.

"I don't understand?" I confess.

"I don't expect you to," he assures me with a tenderness unheard of. "There's no denying that a sexual need drives our society." Little lines appear on his forehead as he says this.

"Many of those in this field of work are struggling financially, and this career is all they have to support themselves and their families. The issue is that sex work is a tricky career, and it's easy for workers to get exploited or misunderstood. Which is why, when my father and I took over the family business, we stopped forced prostitution." He pauses for a moment to check if I have questions, and when I give no inclination to have any, he goes on, "the women who work for us do it out of their free will. Consent is important to me. If they don't want to be in the job any longer, they don't need to stay."

The more he explains, the tightness in my chest lifts. Everything he says makes sense.

"My men all understand what needs to be done if any of the workers mention an incident in which they feel uncomfortable. I don't take these things lightly. Those who do business with me in this area understand this and don't cross me. Not after they saw what happens to those who ignore my warnings."

"What else do you do?"

"I mainly give orders and keep track of the money. I only get involved when I need to, which is rare."

"Last night was one of those nights?" I exclaim, my nose scrunching, and Leo grimaces.

"Yes, it was." He gently grabs hold of my face. "Amore, I'm sorry you had to see me like that."

"Did you kill them?" I ask, already knowing the answer. Leo stiffens and says nothing for a second before confirming my suspicion with a simple nod.

"Did they deserve it?"

"Yes, he was a traitor. One of Adriano's men who killed some of our own," he explains, and I can see the anger and grief in his eyes.

"I'm sorry." My hands mold around his chiseled jaw. "Does this mean the issue with Adriano is bigger than I first assumed?"

"I won't lie to you," he says, and I roll my lips into my mouth, now worried to hear the gravity of the situation with Adriano. "Victoria, things are not looking good. But I have it under control." He quickly assures me when the worry on my face alarms him.

"What does he want?" My voice is shakier than I would have liked. No one else terrifies me as much as Adriano and his men.

"He wants a war so he can get his revenge and my title. He plans to use you to do so." As he says this, his eyes flash with guilt, and all I can think about is his safety. Adriano not only wants me dead; he also wants

Leo's head, and I know Leo will do everything possible to make sure I'm safe, even if it means dying while protecting me. I can't bear this thought.

"Amore, I won't let anything happen to you," Leo assures me, his pointer finger caressing the skin near my jaw. I bite my tongue to stop the rising tears from falling because Leo has proven me right. He'd die trying to protect me if he has to, and I don't want this to be our fate.

"I'm not afraid of him hurting me." His frown deepens at my words. "I know you wouldn't let him touch me. Leo, I don't want to lose you because you are too determined to protect me."

"Victoria, I'll be fine. This isn't my first time dealing with him," he says, pressing a chaste kiss to my temple.

His words don't ease the fear in my stomach. Nothing can.

"So, what are we going to do?" Leo's face turns to disapproval as soon as I say this.

"You will not be involved." He says voice firm. "I can't have you getting hurt. You don't even know how to punch," he says with humor, but the seriousness of his decision is still present.

I glower at his insult and cross my arms over my chest.

"If I remember correctly, I pepper sprayed Luca and punched you in the face the other day at my school parking lot," I remind him with a huff.

"You got lucky," he says, waving a dismissive hand, and I let out an annoyed breath.

"Fine, then teach me how to fight," I edge, and Leo smiles, shaking his head in disbelief.

"You want to learn how to fight when yesterday you freaked out at the sight of me covered in blood?"

"That's not fair. I thought you were going to kill me, but now I realize how stupid that is." Leo's face falls, and I can tell my words have hurt him.

"I'm sorry for doubting you," I whisper, and he sighs.

"Amore, I will never hurt you. But if you want to learn how to *defend* yourself, then I will teach you," he says, emphasizing that he will teach me how to defend myself but not how to fight.

I give a simple nod, and he smiles, bending lower, and pressing our lips together. My arms wrap themselves around the back of his head as the kiss turns heated.

Our lips move hungrily, and the force pushes me back until I rest on the side of the couch. He hovers above me, one knee on either side of my thighs. His mouth feels like velvet, and a little sigh rests at the base of my chest when he clutches the back of my head.

The door to the room bursts open, and with it comes the sound of familiar voices.

"Leo the mafia—"

"What the fuck?"

"Ahh! gross, man!"

I pull away from Leo, who groans in annoyance.

The condescending stares of a shocked Francisco, a grinning Angelo, a grossed-out Luca, and an unfazed Kaden all greet me.

My face becomes hot under their intense stares.

"Shortcake, are you okay?" Luca's voice is one of mock concern as he gets near. He places his icy hand on my forehead, checking if I have a fever.

I lift a brow, and he grins.

"Blink twice if you need help," he whispers loudly, glancing from an unimpressed Leo to me.

"Snow White, I'm fine," I breathe, feeling a wave of heat spreading over my body.

Francisco coughs to get our attention, and he has a boyish grin.

"Did we miss a few chapters?" he inquires, a hint of laughter in his voice.

Mortified, I want the ground to cave under me and take me out of this situation. Thankfully, Leo's voice cuts through the awkward silence.

"What do you guys want?" he grumbles, glaring at the four grinning men in the room. He helps me up from the couch and wraps an arm around my waist. The gesture prompts the grins on his friends' faces to widen.

"I'm going to go," I say, pointing to the door.

Leo grumbles a protest but lets me go when he notices my discomfort.

As I pull from his arms, he brings me back, and the air escapes my lips in surprise.

He kisses my temple and leans against the side of my face. His mouth grazes the side of my ear as he whispers.

"I'll find you after."

I swallow and nod. I make my way to the door and try to control the emotions of happiness and embarrassment racing through me.

When I'm outside, I sigh in relief. My eyes shut; thankful I escaped their questioning.

A throat clears to my left, and I jump, my eyes widening.

My breath gets caught in my lungs when I'm met with the grinning faces of Cleo and my cousin.

Great...

36

LEO

The scowl on my face makes it clear to the four nitwits that their presence is unwanted.

"Was there a reason all four of you barged into my office?" I look from one to the other. They're all smirking.

"Yeah, we actually came in for the free porn show," Luca says coolly, taking one of the empty seats in front of my desk. The other three idiots laugh and nod in agreement.

Fucking dumbass.

My glare deepens.

"Luca..." I say in a voice that would make grown men run for the hills, except for Luca, who has a death wish. He smiles, showing his teeth.

To say I'm irritated is an understatement. Not only have they ruined my first intimate moment with Victoria, but now they're mocking me.

I haven't even been able to process what happened, and now that Victoria is out of my sight, I miss her, even if she left two minutes ago.

A grin threatens to rise when the sweet, chocolaty flavor of her lip balm fills my senses.

My thoughts stray from the four idiots surrounding me, and a weightless feeling takes over my body because Victoria has accepted who I am.

All last night I was pacing at the foot of my bed, trying to force myself not to go to Sofia's room to explain myself. If I showed up at Sofia's door at four a.m., Victoria would be more terrified than she already was. So, when morning came, I was out of my room, wandering around the house, hoping to bump into Victoria, but she wasn't anywhere. My disappointment only increased when Sofia walked into the dining room without Victoria.

Cleo, being the excellent observer she is, sensed my restlessness, and when I explained what Victoria had seen, there was a glimmer of alarm washing over her expression. She disappeared afterward, and when I returned to my office to find Victoria waiting for me, I knew this was Cleo's doing.

Now that I don't have to hide my true identity from Victoria, I feel much lighter.

"Guys, we officially lost him," Angelo says, his blue eyes shining with humor.

"I don't believe it..." Francisco's mouth falls open in astonishment. "...the one and only Leo Bandoni is whipped!"

I make a gruff sound at the back of my throat, and they burst into deep laughter.

"You guys are enjoying this, aren't you?" Annoyance seeps from my words.

"Very much," Kaden exclaims, handing me a black folder.

Francisco clears his throat. "All jokes aside," he says, and his voice has now lost its humor. "The shipment heading toward China arrived..." I sigh, relieved to hear our missing shipment has been found. But before I can ask why they took longer than usual, Francisco cuts me off. "With their throats cut," he says, motioning for me to open the folder Kaden gave me. His words ring in my ears, and the folder in my hand trembles when I see what's inside.

My anger turns to rage as I flip through the pictures Lei and his men had taken of the disaster that had arrived at their port.

The images of my men's decapitated bodies fill my sight. Their blood paints the entire floor of the cargo ship. With each photo, my body trembles, and rage burns through my veins.

"That's not all... Adriano's men nearly kidnapped Emma in Times Square the other day."

"Shit, is she alright?"

"She's fine, only a bruise to the head, but Alexander is livid," Francisco says. "The rest of the mafia families are also concerned and want to know what we plan on doing about Adriano."

I let out a breath, placing a finger over my top lip in thought.

"If Adriano wants war, then let's give him one. But we need all four mafia families to cooperate with us. It's their duty as members of this alliance."

I glance at my three capos and under-boss, their faces screwed with anger.

"It's time for a reunion." They nod in understanding.

"Do you want me to call the members of the alliance?" Francisco asks, preparing to pull his phone out, when I motion him to stop.

"No, it's okay. I'll do it."

I couldn't have Francisco do my job for me. Not only will it be inconsiderate of me not to reach out to apologize for the trouble Adriano has been causing them, but it would show them my inability to do a simple task, such as calling them to tell them the plans for a war that is partially mine.

My capos and underboss make their way out of my office, leaving me behind to process the news.

Not only has Adriano highjacked a million euros' worth of supplies, but he has also taken the lives of thirty of my men, and now he's also after our women.

Taking our supplies is one thing, but trying to take our women is on a whole other level you don't want to cross. I'd rather lose my entire mafia and be dirt poor, so long as Victoria is by my side.

I pull out my phone to call the mob bosses. All except for Alexander because of the time difference. I'd have to call him later tonight.

I first call Lei.

"Leo," he greets. "I'm guessing Francisco told you about the present your cousin left for us."

"Yes, and I'm sorry you and your men had to clean up the mess. I'll have Angelo reimburse you what we owe you. But I won't be able to have a new shipment sent out until I know Adriano won't hijack me again."

"It's no problem, and this isn't your fault," he assures me.

"As you can tell from recent events, the issue with Adriano has worsened—"

"No shit," he replies, cutting me off.

"If you let me finish, I can make this call quick."

Lei laughs at the sound of my annoyance.

"I forgot how impatient you are."

"I need you to come to Italy as soon as possible," I say, ignoring his comment on my inability to be patient.

"Things are that bad, huh?"

"Yes, this issue is no longer about me. It involves us all. We can't risk having Adriano breach any of our emails, which is why we need to meet in person to discuss how we want to handle this situation." My words are firm, and he assures me he understands and will plan for the journey to Italy.

The rest of the hour I spent having similar conversations with Alejandro and Arthuro.

When I finish, I lean in my chair and breathe in, only to get a whiff of Victoria's scent. The warm, sweet fragrance lingers around me. There's a stirring inside my stomach when I remember how her delicate fingers threaded through my hair.

As predicted, her kisses are sweeter than the finest red wine, and one taste of her mouth has left me drunk.

The urge to see her becomes irresistible, and I rise, leaving my office when I give myself in to the force, pulling me toward the woman who has captivated me from the first second I saw her.

37

VICTORIA

"Victoria, tell us all the details!" Cleo's soft voice fills the silence of my room.

I hold in my laughter when Sofia's mouth drops wide when she hears Cleo talking.

"Cleo, you talked?" Sofia says, dumbfounded.

"I did…" Cleo grins and turns to me. "Now, where are those details?"

Sofia looks shocked by Cleo's ability to sweep over something of this importance. She has questions but doesn't get to ask them when Cleo presses me for the information she wants to hear.

With little choice, I dive into the events of the hour, much to my embarrassment.

"No way! He called you his amore!" Sofia bursts, and my body grows warm.

"Sofia, I told you Leo is the Don of a Mafia, and all you got from my explanation is him calling me his amore?"

Sofia's expression is one of, *'can you blame me?'*

Exasperated, I sigh and take hold of their hands, dragging them toward the door. They groan the entire time.

"Now that you both know everything, can you guys leave me alone?"

Sofia pouts.

"Fine, but we haven't finished here," she complains, allowing Cleo to pull her out of the room.

When they leave, I head to the shower, hoping the water will cool the fire blazing within me.

In the shower, I can't help but smile at the memory of Leo kissing me.

His taste invades my senses, and my hand falls toward my neck, where he had ravished. The tingles spread throughout my body, and my hand descends to my left breast. I don't stop until my fingers skim over my pelvic bone.

The temptation is overwhelming. I close my eyes and pull back my hand with a frustrated sigh. The pulsing between my legs twitches with a need for relief.

There's a quickening to my breath, and the water droplets fall over my sizzling skin.

Even after my shower, I ache to be touched by Leo. The feeling rages like a flickering flame on the verge of exploding.

I take a look at my reflection, and my breath quickens when I see the love marks across the base of my neck.

The dark blotches make my stomach churn pleasantly, and I run the tip of my pointer finger over the sensitive area.

What's happening to me?

This new carnal desire is shocking. I don't know what to make of the feelings Leo has stirred inside me. He makes me think sinfully.

I take steady breaths to calm my racing heart, and I make my way out of the bathroom. I open the bathroom door, and the door to the room swings open to reveal Leo.

His eyes draw up from his phone to look at me, and when he sees me in nothing but a towel, his eyes flare with lust. The water droplets running down my legs turn hot when his eyes pin me to the ground.

Leo's throat moves when he swallows hard. The hunger across his face incites a twitch within me.

"Fottuto inferno," he says thickly as he stalks toward me in powerful strides.

I don't have time to react before he presses me against his solid chest with an undeniable hunger. One of his hands fists the back of my wet hair, and the other hand positions itself at the base of my jaw, tipping my head back.

My fingers dig into the towel for dear life as heat lashes across my moist skin.

All I want is for him to kiss me. To put the fire inside of me out.

Leo senses my need and gives me the relief I crave when he captures my lips. He's intoxicating, and I'm becoming greedy for his touch.

Gone are our restraints, and we can no longer hold off on our desires.

His tongue strokes the inside of my mouth, while my hands move from the towel to wrap themselves around his neck.

Although Leo is bent to my level, I still need to lift myself on my toes to reach him, and after a while, my legs start to tremble.

A deep groan comes from the back of his throat, and the vibration of the sound against my mouth makes me whimper.

Leo grips my thighs, lifting me in his arms. His touch ignites little fires, which burst with wetness when his bulge presses into my inner thighs, allowing me to feel how hard he is.

My stomach clenches, and I choke from the thickness rubbing against me.

Leo continues to dominate my mouth before trailing kisses down my neck. His touch, like earlier, sends ripples of pleasure throughout my body.

The throbbing desire raging havoc in my lower half is a sensation I've never experienced. With the twitching comes a heightened understanding of my racing heart and twirling stomach.

A need for friction to ease the pulsing between my thighs moves me to rub myself against him, and he lets out a pained groan.

Between his skilled mouth kissing my neck and his bulge pressed between my thighs, I lose control over my body. To ground myself from the overwhelming lust pumping through my blood, I grab the back of his head and run my fingers through the silky brown locks.

Leo's leaving me breathless, and all he's doing is kissing me with a deep hunger and passion. His touch alone is enough to awaken the sexual viper within me.

I want to feel the warm, twitching sensations he ignites within me every second of every day. It's addicting and euphoric. All that matters is him and me and the explosive chemistry between us.

The legs I have wrapped around him tighten, and I press myself as close to him as possible, completely forgetting I'm naked under the towel.

Leo responds by squeezing my waist and letting out a deep grunt. He captures my mouth, and his lips overlap with mine in a slow, sensual kiss, unlike the ferocity of our strokes seconds ago.

I'm sure he can hear my hard breathing and little cries of pleasure, but I don't care. I'm overcome with the way our tongues are a tangled mess. The temptation to have him fuck me hard against the wall sounds nice. But the little voice in my head tells me I'm crazy and not ready for any of that, and the voice is right. I don't want Leo to fuck me hard, not when we barely had our first kiss. I want him to take me slowly, sweetly, and passionately. But above all, I want him to fuck me with *love*, not lust.

Then there's the fact that I'm not sure if I'm ready for him to touch me in that way. Deep down, I'm afraid I'll panic like I did earlier.

I'm still getting used to the idea of letting him kiss me. I can't let myself freak out like I did earlier, not when I saw how much it hurt him to see me trembling from the past because of his touch. But I also know that soon we both won't be able to resist the growing desire between us.

I shudder when the cool air pinches my breasts.

My brows furrow, no longer feeling the warmth of the towel, and I stop kissing Leo. He moves his attention to my neck, and I lean to the side to give him ample space.

Amidst my desire, I glance down, only to be horrified by the sight of the top of the towel now lying around my stomach.

I press my erect breasts against Leo's white button-down shirt and black vest. I'm relieved to see Leo hasn't noticed, as he's too busy devouring the skin of my neck.

His lips stop their sweet torture, and he's about to pull back when I panic and grab the back of his head, keeping him in place.

"What's wrong, amore?"

"Don't look." A quaver creeps into my voice, and Leo runs his fingers through my wet hair.

"I won't look," he says, burying his head into my neck.

With my right hand around his neck, my left hand grabs the towel, clutching it to my front.

I unwrap my legs from around his waist and fall back onto my two feet. Leo winces when I rub against his bulge.

"Sorry," I say, my tone a little off. With shaky hands, I secure the towel around my body.

My stomach flutters when I see his eyes pressed tightly together to give me privacy.

I rise on my tippy toes, pressing a chaste kiss to his lips, and he smiles against my mouth. When I pull back, we lock eyes. The beautiful jade green hues break into my soul. There's a prominent heat flaring within his eyes, and his stare is solely on my face.

"Bellissima," he breathes, his index finger running down the right side of my face. He tilts my chin and gives me a soft, quick kiss on my lips.

For the first time in my life, I feel beautiful despite not wearing makeup and my hair being unruly from where he fisted it.

Leo's hand rests around my waist as he leads us through the house, and I have to contain my happiness.

The few men loitering in the foyer notice us and bend their heads in acknowledgment.

A smile tugs across their mouths when they see Leo's arm around me. Their grins and knowing looks make me fidget.

Leo ignores them and continues leading us into the dining room. I glance at him in awe, unable to believe he's going to sit down and have dinner with me after being locked in his office for the past few weeks.

We enter the dining room, and a warmth spreads through my veins when I see all my new friends gathered around the long rectangular table.

The two beautiful crystal chandeliers cast a shimmering light on the elegant table. The warm, inviting scent of pasta, sauce, and freshly baked bread hangs heavily in the air.

Leo guides me toward the far end of the room and pulls out my chair. Once seated, he pushes the chair in for me and takes the seat at the foot of the table.

To my right, Sofia sways with excitement when she sees Leo's affection for me. Across from her sits Francisco, who shakes his head in disbelief at my cousin. Sofia responds by flipping him off, and Francisco lets out a noisy exhale.

Leo covers my lap with a white cloth napkin before resting his hand over my thigh. The gesture makes the surrounding men press their lips together to suppress their laughter.

"Thank you," I mumble, and when Leo hands me a plate filled with Fettuccine Alfredo, the door to the dining room opens. Everyone glances at the tall man with graying brown hair, and Leo stiffens. With this man's presence, the room becomes tense.

The familiar-looking man notices the change in the air and clears his throat.

Everyone stares at him without saying a word as he confidently enters, his eyes scanning the table.

Kaden rises from his seat and allows the older man to sit beside Cleo. Her eyes gloss over with unshed tears when she sees him.

My curious eyes remain on Estephano Bandoni.

A man who I thought was dead.

I'm not the only one staring at the elder Bandoni. Beside me, Leo follows his dad's figure. An unknown expression stamps his face.

I place a gentle hand on Leo's forearm. His attention moves toward me, and he smiles in appreciation.

As I turn to Estephano, my breath gets lodged in my lungs because he's staring at Leo and me.

Estephano is a handsome, rugged man, probably in his early fifties, and he has dark green, almond-shaped eyes like Leo. The only difference between father and son is Estephano's faint under-eye wrinkles.

Estephano's bow-shaped lips, surrounded by a medium stubble beard, lift into a friendly smile as he looks at me. The curve of my bottom lip forms a slight smile, returning the gesture.

No one utters a word to him, and it's as if they are all looking at a ghost. Estephano pays no attention to their stares as he's busy looking at his daughter, whose face is glowing with happiness to have everyone she cares about sitting together for a meal.

Leo's face darkens, not from anger but from sadness and confusion. I grab his hand to comfort him, and it works because the stiffness in his body slowly leaves him.

The rest of dinner is quiet, and the stifling tension in the air is suffocating.

I don't understand why everyone is on edge when Estephano doesn't seem like a terrible man. The hostility toward him raises a series of questions. And when everyone has finished eating, no one dares leave the room. It's as if the air suffocating us has made moving impossible.

Leo and his dad are staring at one another, and not a minute later, the muscles on Leo's right arm ripple as he adjusts the collar of his dress shirt. He rises from his seat and grabs my hand. Everyone slowly starts to rise.

He secures an arm around my waist and leads us toward Estephano, who's talking to Cleo. Noticing us approaching them, Cleo gives me and Leo a warm smile before she kisses her dad's cheek.

Cleo leaves the room, and I wish she had stayed to help ease my nervousness at the thought of meeting her dad.

Estephano smiles when he notices us, and he rises from his seat. The closer we get to him, my hands dampen, and my heart quickens with anticipation.

Leo presses me flush to his side to ease my rising nerves.

"Papà, this is *my girlfriend*, Victoria." Leo's voice has a hint of pride, and his eyes land on me.

The phrase "my girlfriend" coming from his mouth has me swooning and the hairs on the back of my neck rise.

I nervously offer my hand for Estephano to shake, and his large, warm hand captures mine. His handshake is firm and soft.

"It's a pleasure to meet you, sir."

"The pleasure is all mine. Victoria, please call me Estephano." He squeezes my hand, and from the corner of my eye, I notice Leo looking at our exchange with an indecipherable look on his face.

"It's great to see you, Papà." Leo hesitantly pats Estephano on his left shoulder.

His dad responds with a grin and shakes his head in disapproval.

"Leo, my boy, what kind of greeting is that?" Estephano laughs and places a hand on Leo's shoulder. "Noi siamo italiano," he remarks before kissing Leo on the cheek.

When Estephano lets him go, Leo looks mortified and glances at me. His cheeks turn scarlet, and I have to bite down on the grin that threatens to spread across my face.

"Papà," Leo says like a little boy, and I laugh, causing the two Bandoni men to turn to me, both sporting smiles.

"I'm sorry for not coming down sooner." Estephano wears a look of regret as he looks from Leo to me.

The two are looking at one another in silent conversation. I take this time to consider for a moment what could have prompted the two to have a tenuous relationship.

The way Leo looks at his dad is a look you give someone you haven't seen in years. Which makes no sense, considering they live in the same house.

"Why today?" Leo asks his dad with his forehead scrunched in curiosity.

Estephano sighs and glances at Cleo, who's grinning at a bickering Sofia and Francisco.

"I had someone talk some reason into me." His words bring me a burst of pride to see Cleo finding her strength again. But amidst this pride, I'm hit with a pang of guilt because Leo still doesn't know she's talking again.

Estephano's response is good enough for Leo, who doesn't question him further.

"So how is everything with—" Estephano pauses and looks at me, unsure if he can discuss their family business with me beside them.

Leo lets out a small laugh.

"She knows," he assures his dad, whose eyes widen in shock.

"Ti piace davvero suo huh," Estephano tells Leo, whose eyes remain fixed on me.

Leo nods, and I'm curious to know why he's now staring at me with what I can best describe as admiration.

"And you didn't run away?" Estephano asks, looking in my direction. With his and Leo's eyes on me, I feel embarrassment wash over my face because I did run.

Leo lets out a soft laugh, nudging my side.

"Not entirely," I confess, and Estephano looks amused.

I'm quiet as I listen to the two discuss their family business. When the conversation moves to the topic of Adriano, Estephano grows rigid. His fist clenches at his side with every detail told to him.

I excuse myself to give them privacy and because the talk of Adriano brings back haunting memories and guilt.

I approach Cleo and Sofia, and a few moments later, I watch Leo and his father make their way up the stairs to his office.

LEO

To see my father sitting in my office smiling as if he hadn't locked himself in a pit of depression for the past year has left me shocked. This behavior shouldn't surprise me. I already know his sudden burst of energy is temporary. He's bound to have another episode, and grief will drown him again. When this happens, the cycle will resume all over again. He'll spend one year locked away, returning to society for a few months before he draws himself back to his darkness.

My attention remains on my father, and I try to understand what drew him out of his room. The pain written across his face proves he isn't mentally stable. Grief has a chokehold on him, and he hasn't found his way back, as most people do after a few years of grieving.

While growing up, it hurt to know Cleo, and I hadn't been enough to patch the massive hole in his chest. All we could do was watch as his grief turned from one year to five, then ten, and so forth.

My sister and I grew up without a mother and a father who abandoned us because of his grief.

Physically, he's alive, but mentally, he's dead. He's lost in the darkness of his sadness, with no way to find his way out. The light of his love had been blown out, and he can do nothing to get that spark back.

Love had killed him.

His lack of stability meant that I had to carry the responsibilities of my family and our mafia at a young age.

At first, it was me pushing my father to do his work, but when I was ready, I took to the streets.

By fifteen, I had killed twenty men and was deeply involved in the mafia scenes.

I may have been the youngest, but I was the most ruthless—an angry child with family problems.

The circumstances of my mother's death and my father's grief filled my early childhood with resentment toward him, the world, and love.

It wasn't until meeting Victoria that I understood the gravity of his pain. To lose someone you care for on such a deep level—someone who is your other half—is sure to be a pain strong enough to drive any man to insanity.

There's a chill in my veins at the thought of losing Victoria, and the mere image of her blood on my hands haunts my heart.

"Leo?" my father calls out, and he sounds concerned. I glance at him, and he raises his eyebrows before speaking, "you never told me how you plan on handling Adriano?"

"I'm working on the details," I assure him, but he's not content with my response.

"Do you know where he's hiding?"

"We're working on it," I tell him again, but this time my voice hints at an end to the conversation.

My short answers have everything to do with the fact that I'm tired of hearing the bastard's name. I want one hour where his name doesn't come up. Is that so much to ask for?

He sighs. "Leo, what's all this about 'we're working on it' or 'I'm working on the details'?" There's an edge of disapproval behind his words, and a muscle in my jaw twitches.

"You're in no position to criticize my ability to run *my* mafia," I retort, my voice colder than intended.

A frown stiffens his expression, and I sigh, feeling guilty when my words have hurt him, as they remind him of his inability to be present in both his roles as Don and Papà.

"Adriano hasn't made finding him easy." I rub my temple in frustration. Annoyance creeps into me because we have to wait for him to fuck up, which means that as of now, he has the upper hand, and this infuriates me.

"He's untraceable. Even Luca hasn't been able to find anything. He's in America one day, and the next, he's in Russia. It wouldn't surprise me if the fucker is on the moon as we speak."

"You'll think of something," he assures me.

There's a steady knock on the door.

"Come in." Francisco appears with perplexity written over his features. "What is it, Francisco?"

"Did you order anything?" he asks, and I give him a blank stare.

"What are you talking about?" My brows knit together, and he glances out the door.

"A package arrived for you."

I rise from my seat to see what he's talking about, and when I reach the top of the stairs, I see my three capos, my sister, Sofia, Victoria, and a few other men of mine. They surround an enormous, sealed wooden crate.

My steps down the stairs are heavy, and I make my way toward the crate. I rip open the note nailed to the wood and find someone has written my name in red ink.

I stare at the crate in confusion, and motion for my men to open it.

As they work on opening the box, Victoria comes from behind me. Her arms wrap around mine.

I quickly grab Victoria and move us back when the crate spreads open from all angles with a loud crash.

The stench of death and flies swarm the area. Behind me, Sofia and Cleo gasp while Victoria's arm tightens around me.

"Oh god," Victoria says, pressing her face to my forearm, and all I can do is stare with fury at the gruesome sight of a mutilated lion.

I crumple the paper in my hand and tremble with silent rage.

"Get this shit out of here!" No one moves, and I'm filled with more anger. "Now!" I shout, outraged, and from the sound of my anger, my men come out of their trance and rush to remove the dead animal.

Someone threatened me, and I know of only one person stupid enough to do so.

Victoria's phone rings. The shrill sound cuts through the silence, and she pulls it out of her back pocket.

"No caller ID," she says, and her forehead creases. She's about to silence the call when I stop her.

"Luca, get your laptop and hook the phone to it," I say, and he runs to the living room to get his laptop.

Victoria hands me her phone, and I give it to Luca to see if we can track where the person is calling from.

I put the call on speaker.

"Who is this?"

"Ahh, just the man I wanted to talk to." The patronizing sound of Adriano's voice provokes my breathing to quicken. My fingers curl inward. "Did you get my little gift?" he asks.

I grind my teeth, trying to restrain myself from crushing Victoria's phone in my grasp.

"You're going to regret threatening me."

Adriano's menacing laugh fills the room.

"I take it you didn't like my present?" he exclaims, followed by the laughter of his men.

The sound of them taunting me furthers my already boiling rage. Victoria rubs my chest, clearing a little of the fury clouding my sight.

"This is only the beginning, cousin. Right, boys?" he says in sinister amusement, and his men cheering behind him ring from the phone. My men's faces scrunch in anger as they listen to Adriano and his men threaten us.

"You haven't even seen my big surprise for you." Adriano taunts.

"I'm going to find you, and when I do, you're going to wish death when I make you choke on your limbs," I threaten through clenched teeth. From beside me, Victoria grimaces but says nothing.

"Oh, no, cousin, when you find me, it will be too late because I'll already have you, your men, and the mafia bosses in my grasp. And when we have you all tied, I'm going to fuck Victoria and my men, the mafia women, in front of you all."

"Over my dead body!" My arm instinctively tightens around a trembling Victoria.

"That can be arranged," he asserts. "I'll see you soon, cousin." There's a pause in which I can imagine him grinning. "Oh, and tell Cleo I miss her." His deep laughter follows his sinister remark.

My attention flickers to my sister, who's in Kaden's arms, her face buried in his chest. She's crying silently. Before I can say anything to him, my father grabs the phone from my hands.

"Listen here, you piece of shit!" My father yells into the phone. "You threaten my family, my *daughters*, and I'll look under every fucking rock on this fucking planet until I find you. And when I do, I'm going to rip your molding heart right out of your chest with my own bare hands." My father is shaking, and his nose is flaring. There's a fit of anger in him that matches mine.

"Old man, your threats don't scare me, and neither does your bastard son!" Adriano's words are poised with venom, and they are followed by the sound of the call being cut.

My father curses and throws the phone across the room. Within seconds, Victoria loses her phone, and she doesn't mind because she's too consumed with fear after hearing Adriano's threat.

"Victoria," I whisper, cupping her chin, and she says nothing. Her eyes gloss over, and she's trapped by her thoughts. "I won't let him touch you. He won't hurt you," I promise her. My words upset her, and tears are shimmering in her eyes.

She wraps her arms around me and presses us into a tight embrace. My chest becomes heavy as I hold her shaking body in my arms.

The room is silent, and we all try to process the emotions coursing through us after Adriano's threat.

I lift Victoria, bridal style, and she leans into my touch. I hold her tight, not wanting to let her go after hearing Adriano's plans for us all.

Before heading upstairs, my father and I make our way to my sister.

"Cleo, he won't hurt you again." I kiss the top of her head, and she looks at her feet in shame without uttering a word. My eyes soften when she clutches onto my father, who now has her in his arms, promising he wouldn't abandon her.

I take Victoria upstairs when I'm sure my sister is safe with my father and Kaden. From the corner of my eye, I catch Francisco comforting a trembling Sofia. His arms are around her, and her head is pressed against his forearm.

I send him a look he knows all too well, and he nods, assuring me he will increase the security around the house.

"Leo..." The sound of Luca behind me halts my steps.

"The call was a dead end," he reveals, his blue eyes softening when they glance at a dazed Victoria.

My jaw ticks as my blood pumps with anger, fear, and frustration.

"Thank you, Luca. Keep trying to breach any of his accounts. We need to find him."

He nods and takes his leave.

I glance at Victoria and realize Adriano is more insane than we first assumed. His threat, fresh in my mind, makes me queasy. I lead us toward my bedroom, right beside her room, and I don't miss how her face morphs into confusion as I pass her door.

Tonight, I can't sleep without her beside me, not after Adriano's threat.

We enter my room, and her eyes glance around us, taking in the interior. I place her on the bed, and she bites the inside of her bottom lip, nervousness painting her beautiful face.

To see her in my room and on my bed brings me comfort, easing the tension in my stiff shoulders. I bend to her level, and she looks at me through her thick lashes. Her lips part, and they are calling for me to take them between my own, which I plan on doing, but I first kiss her right cheek before moving to the left side.

Victoria closes her eyes, and they don't open until I place a sweet kiss on the corner of her mouth. She looks unsatisfied, and I bite back my grin before I give in and capture her pink, heart-shaped lips against my mouth.

I release her and make my way to my closet to change and get her clothes to sleep in. When I return, a smile stretches across my face at the sight of Victoria looking at her surroundings in awe.

She looks at me, and when she sees me in my gray sweatpants, she wets her lips. I lift her chin, unable to resist kissing her.

I could kiss her forever if not for the need to breathe.

Her soft breathing is equivalent to a lullaby, and her waist-length black hair is silky and thick around my fingers. We pull away, and her chest rises and falls softly.

"Stay with me tonight," I plead, and she fights back a smile but nods. "Stay with me forever?" My voice is hopeful, and Victoria's brows lift, a breathtaking smile gracing my sight.

"Okay," she breathes before placing her lips right at the base of my jaw, leaving behind tingles.

She grabs the black t-shirt from my hands, and now it's my turn to watch her retreating figure. When she returns, I breathe deeply at the sight of her. Memories of our time in France come to mind, bringing warmth and lightness to my body.

Victoria fidgets under the bathroom threshold. Her face no longer has the soft makeup she wears daily. The sight of her natural beauty steals my breath away.

I extend a hand for her to take, and she makes her way toward me on the bed.

My heart leaps with love when I see the little dark freckles, beauty marks, and minimal blemishes. They're all on full display, and she's gorgeous.

With her soft hand in mine, I pull her to me, and she stumbles, falling onto my chest with a small gasp. I let out a soft laugh as I carefully set her down on the bed beside me. My left arm wraps around her waist, and she scoots closer, relaxing her head on my chest.

I twirl a loose strand of her hair, and the silence between us is comforting. The sounds of our soft breathing harmonize beautifully.

Victoria breaks the silence.

"Leo, you're going to find him, and when you do"—she lets out a yawn—"make him choke on his dick," she mumbles, letting sleep consume her.

My laugh is soft, and when her head falls on my chest, sleep wins over her body.

"Sì amore," I mumble, kissing her temple and turning off the lights.

3 8

___

VICTORIA

Leo's head is buried into the crook of my neck, and his soft breath fans the skin, sending a shiver down my spine.

I turn in his arms, and he gives a low groan, his eyes still closed with sleep. My stare falls on his lips, which are set in a thin line with a slight pout. His ever-lasting rugged exterior is nowhere in sight.

Leo's eyes flutter open, and his mouth tugs into a sleep-filled smile when he sees me.

I go to draw my hand back, but he grabs it and presses it against his heart. His bare skin is soft under my touch, and my breath gets caught at the sight of his Greek-sculpted chest.

Leo notices my appreciation of his body, and he lets out an airy laugh. My cheeks tingle with warmth, but the embarrassment turns to surprise when I see the dark ink covering the area where my hand was.

"You have a tattoo?" Leo gives a simple hum. "Why a crown? And why here?" I ask as I trace the intricate lines etched into his soft skin.

Leo grabs my hand and presses a chaste kiss on my palm before placing it flat over the tattoo. I feel the soft thumping of his heart.

"My dad has the same tattoo, and my mom had a crown on her wrist." He lifts my right hand and traces the backside where my veins are. "It symbolizes our leadership. So long as the veins pump blood, we promise to be good to those who work for us. It's a promise forever written on our bodies."

"That's beautiful." As I say this, we hear a loud knock coming from the door, and it's followed by two familiar voices.

"I told you to wait, Piccolo fuoco," Francisco grumbles.

"And I told you not to call me that!" Sofia snaps. There's another knock on the door. "Is Victoria in there?" she shouts, with a hint of panic behind her words.

"Coming!" I call out, ready to make my way toward the door, when Leo grabs me from behind, trapping me. Before I can complain, he nuzzles his head into my shoulder, making it impossible to want to leave his arms.

Another knock follows.

"Leo," I breathe, trying to peel him off me. Sofia won't leave until she gets what she wants, and right now, she wants to see me.

He grumbles against my neck.

"Maybe if we wait long enough, they'll go away," he mumbles, closing his eyes.

"Leo, you let my cousin go! You hear me?" Sofia remarks from behind the door, and Leo makes an unsatisfied sound deep in his throat.

"Sorry boss," Francisco interjects, followed by Sofia telling him to let her go. He doesn't listen, and a thud follows.

"Fanculo!" Francisco curses.

"Don't do that again!" comes Sofia's warning, and Leo groans something inaudible as he releases me. I kiss his cheek and go find out what Sofia wants.

I open the door, and my attention is directed to a red-faced Francisco massaging his foot and my cousin, who's glaring at him.

"Yes?" I say with a lifted brow.

Sofia smiles. "I wanted to make sure you were okay. I got scared when I didn't find you in your room this morning."

"Leo didn't want me sleeping alone after what happened last night," I explain, and a flush creeps up my neck when Sofia and Francisco look at each other with a grin.

"Oh, okay, so it was only sleeping, huh?" she teases, cocking a brow.

"Yes, Sofia, now I'm going to go change," I tell her, preparing to close the door, when her next comment has me freezing in place.

"Have fun and be safe," she teases, leaving with Francisco.

Their laughter bounces off the walls, and I groan, wanting to strangle my cousin.

The moment I reenter the room, Leo walks out of the bathroom, now dressed in a perfectly tailored three-piece black suit. Two buttons on his shirt are open, revealing his smooth chest.

Leo notices me eyeing him and raises a perfect brow. He takes long strides toward me, and his intoxicating musk scent and warmth chokes me with lust.

He leans down to my ear.

"If you keep looking at me like that, I won't be able to let you leave this room." I shudder at his words, and Leo flashes me a grin.

His laughter at my flustered state makes me cross my arms over my chest. When I do this, the T-shirt I wear rises dangerously high.

Leo's eyes fall to my bare legs, and his stare lashes me with the heat of his appreciation. He's about to pull me into his grasp, but I slide out of the door before he can reach me.

This is payback for him teasing me.

"Victoria!" He groans from behind the door. I don't acknowledge him, and I definitely don't go back inside because if I do, he'll keep his word and not let me out of the room.

The door starts to open, and I run next door, which is where I've been staying for the past few days.

I'm busy adjusting my white corset top that I don't notice the intruder who has materialized in my room.

"I got you," Leo whispers, and his heavy arms embrace me from behind.

"What are you doing?" I breathe out when he places a gentle kiss behind my ear.

"You didn't think I would let you get away from me so easily, did you?"

I turn to face him, wrapping my arms around his torso.

"Well, now that you have me, what are you going to do?" I say, holding his stare.

A mischievous grin appears on Leo's lips.

"I would love to toss you onto that bed—" he motions to the side, and my heart beats fast. "—and do many despicable things to you, but we don't have time for that." He sighs and tilts my chin. "So, for now, kissing you will have to suffice."

Without wasting a second, he presses our lips together. A surge of warmth spreads from his touch, and my hands freely go to the back of his hair. I tug on the thick, soft strands, and Leo lets out a soft murmur of pleasure against my mouth. The sound makes my stomach twist into knots.

He breaks our kiss and cups my face with one hand, while the other keeps me flush against him.

"Amore, I have a few things to do today, so I won't have much time to spend with you. But I'll see you tonight," he apologizes, and the tip of his finger runs over my face tenderly.

With this news comes disappointment, but I don't show it and instead give a weak nod.

With everything that happened yesterday, I forgot Leo's work often keeps him busy. I know nothing about what it takes to run a mafia, but from how much he's spent in his office the last week, I can only assume it's a lot of work.

As I casually acknowledge he's in the mafia, I laugh at what my life has become.

"What's so funny?" he asks, and his forehead creases, revealing a deep line.

"I never thought I would find myself in the arms of a mafia man."

"Does my work bother you?" His voice takes on a serious tenor, and he looks for any signs of discomfort coming from me.

"No, it doesn't."

It's true, it doesn't bother me that he runs a mafia. As long as his work doesn't change who he is when he's with me, he will always be the Leo I fell in love with.

"You don't know how much I love hearing you say that," he

confesses, hugging me. I wrap my arms around him and soak in his warmth, knowing I won't be seeing much of him today.

"I'm not going anywhere," I assure him, and he presses small kisses on my lips.

"If you need anything, you know where my office is." His eyes lock on me, and his stare produces a surge of electric warmth that brings a feeling of comfort and pure joy.

"I'll be fine," I assure him, and he kisses my temple before making his way to the door. He turns back to look at me, and it's obvious he doesn't want to go. I give him a warm smile, and he reluctantly leaves my room, and shortly after, I also make my way out.

When I enter the kitchen, I see a familiar person sitting on a kitchen stool with their back to me. An idea comes to mind, and I glance at Cleo, who's leaning against the fridge.

I position my pointer finger to my mouth, and she raises her cup of coffee, her lips tug into a smile around the rim.

Luca is still unaware of my presence, and he continues eating his cereal.

"Boo!" I shout in his left ear, my fingers grabbing his sides.

Luca jumps, nearly hitting me in the face. His scream is similar to those of a little girl.

As the shock passes, he turns to face me, and his face is flushed crimson.

"Shortcake!" he grumbles.

"Snow White, you have some lungs," I tease, cupping my right ear for emphasis.

"You're evil," he grumbles, wiping the milk dripping down his chin.

I laugh, wrapping him in a hug, and he rolls his eyes. His smile tells me he's anything but angry.

I take a seat beside him and notice the cereal chunks spilled over the counter. Luca's eyes move to where I'm staring, and he shrugs his shoulders before picking up the soggy bits of cereal and eating them with a grin. He laughs when he sees my and Cleo's disgust.

After cleaning up his mess, or rather, eating his mess, Luca tells us he has to work on finding Adriano.

When he's gone, Cleo sits beside me and hands me a piece of cornetto bread with a gentle smile.

"Thank you," I say, giving her a smile, and taking the pastry from her hands.

A heavy silence surrounds us, and I wonder when Cleo is going to tell Leo she's talking again. It felt wrong to keep this news from him, and I'm not sure how much longer I can keep the weight of this secret.

As if sensing something is bothering me, Cleo nudges my side.

She glances around the kitchen before she whispers to me.

"What's wrong?"

I let out a breath and set my mug on the table.

"Cleo, I know this is none of my business, but when are you planning on telling Leo you're talking again?"

She frowns, but is quick to mask it with a smile. As I take in her appearance, I notice her eyes are red and puffy, as if she's been crying the entire night. The sight of her sadness pierces my chest, and my mouth dips into a frown.

"I'll tell him soon," she whispers, and I place a hand on her arm.

"Your brother only wants the best for you, and if you aren't ready to tell him, I understand," I assure her.

"Thank you, Victoria." Tears glisten in her eyes, reminding me of the previous night and how Adriano taunted her.

His sinister words have been enough to tell me he was the reason for her pain, and whatever he did to her was so horrific it led to her traumatic mutism.

Cleo's deep in her thoughts, and a lone tear trickles from her eye. She swipes it, hoping I didn't see, but it's too late. I can see the pain stabbing her.

I bring her into my arms.

"Why don't we go out to the gardens," I offer, and she sniffles, letting me take her outside.

We walk along the luscious gardens in silence when Cleo's gentle voice echoes to my left.

"Victoria?"

I lock eyes with Cleo, who places a strand of her hair behind her ear, and I see the self-inflicted scars on her wrist.

The bright white horizontal marks bring a heavy weight to my chest. Among the many scars, one stands out the most. It's the scar that runs up the entire length of her left arm.

Cleo's shoulders drop, and she runs a finger along the scars.

"I was sixteen."

My throat becomes dry, and the vise around my chest tightens because she's prepared to tell me her story.

"Cleo, you don't have to tell me if you aren't ready."

"I want to tell you. I trust you so much, Victoria. You and Sofia are the only people I may ever trust besides my brother and Papà."

I'm terrified to hear the truth about her past, but I can tell she needs to talk about it.

Cleo's silence will always give Adriano power over her, and she needs a release so she can find peace.

After all, a woman's silence is both powerful and frightening. You can never tell if the silence in a woman is burning her with anger or if it's freezing her with pain.

For Cleo, her silence has frozen her in time, and now she's melting away the pain and taking back her fire.

"I was sixteen when the problem between Adriano and my family got out of hand for a second time. He wanted to avenge his father's death, but at the time we didn't know because Adriano came to our doorstep pleading for forgiveness and a second chance. No one believed him, but I did. I was the only one who gave him the benefit of the doubt because I wanted to believe he wasn't as awful as everyone had told me. I realize now how stupid I was for believing he wasn't as evil as his father," she says coldly, and her fingers dig into the palms of her hands.

"Cleo, you're not stupid, and it's not your fault." I grab her shoulders, and Cleo gives a meek nod. But a small part of me feels like she will always blame herself for what happened to her. How do I know this? Because deep down, I still blame myself for what happened to me in Paris. Our minds can be vicious to us. We may acknowledge our assault wasn't our fault, but our consciousness will never fully allow us to accept this truth.

Intrusive negative thoughts will sometimes pierce their poisonous daggers into our psyche. Meanwhile, the villains of our wounds remain unbothered. This is what it's like to be a victim of abuse, and often, this pain registers most with women.

"Leo was ready to kill Adriano, but I convinced him to give our cousin a second chance. I told him Adriano was also a victim of his father's greed, but I was wrong. Adriano was as bad as his father." Cleo takes a few seconds before she continues. "Leo had gone on a mission, and I was in my room when Adriano came stumbling inside, intoxicated."

A prickle of uneasiness takes over the blood rushing in my veins. It intensifies as I listen to the details of the violence Cleo's body had to endure. As she speaks, Cleo looks like a little girl who has lost her entire world, and I hold her tight as she breaks in my arms.

"For the first time, I saw his hate and lust for power. But it was too late. I will always remember how his hands touched me in places he shouldn't have. After he raped me, I was afraid to tell anyone what happened because he threatened to kill my Papà and Leo. I didn't want to lose the only family I had left. Things got worse when I got sick."

I gasp, and she nods, confirming my suspicion.

"I was pregnant, and to make matters worse, I forgot to close the door to my room, and Leo walked in and saw the tests. He flipped out, and I had no choice but to tell him everything."

"What did he do?"

"He tortured Adriano and kept him locked away. But Adriano had been gathering men from our mafia to betray my brother. They got him out from under our noses," Cleo says, her voice thick with anger from the betrayal. "My Papà found out what happened to me, and because he was still grieving our mother's death, the news broke his already shattered heart. He blamed himself for what happened to me, and so did Leo."

The more she tells me, the more my heart aches for the Bandoni family. Her words have shed light on her family's history and given me a better understanding of what I noticed when I met her dad.

Last night, after meeting Estephano, I couldn't help but acknowledge the haunted look carved into his expression. Behind his confidence and smile, it was as if there was an invisible weight on his shoulders, and I now know that the weight I saw on him was that of grief.

"My Papà couldn't look at me because he thought I resented him for not protecting me. But this wasn't true. The lies he fed himself made him shut me out when I needed him the most."

Cleo cries uncontrollably as she talks about how her dad abandoned her, and I can't do anything to ease the sobs coming from her.

Though choked with tears, she perseveres through the hurt ripping at her insides.

"After finding out I was pregnant, I fell into a deeper depression. The pain was too much. I wanted it to end, and death seemed like the only way to escape the thoughts that tormented me every second of every day. I started cutting my wrist, and when it wasn't enough to numb the pain, I turned to pills. I took it too far, and the pills killed the baby, and I almost killed myself when I cut too deep," she explains in a soft voice, and she traces the scar running from her wrist to her elbow. Tears prick at my eyelids from how long the scar is. This is the cut that would have killed her.

"You know what the worst part of failing to kill myself was?" she asks me, and I'm speechless, unsure how to respond. All I can muster is a weak shake of the head.

"The guilt..." she whispers in a broken voice. "To see the pain your actions have caused those close to you is a whole other level of guilt no one understands unless they are living it themselves. Since cutting and pills didn't kill me, I resorted to the only other method I could think of." Shame takes over every inch of her face, and her hand, which I'm holding, shakes. "I wanted to kill myself slowly, to punish myself for what I did. So, I stopped talking and eating. I allowed myself to fall into the abyss of depression, waiting to hit the ground."

"Leo got me help, and it didn't work at first, but after a few years, it did. But it was too late. I had forgotten how to talk. When I met you and Sofia, you both didn't let your past haunt you, and I wanted to be as strong as you two. I wanted to find my voice again, so I practiced in front of a mirror, trying to find the words stuck in my throat. After many attempts, it worked. But by then you had seen the truth, and I couldn't let you run away from the good standing in front of you. Victoria, I just want to say thank you for helping me find my strength again."

She launches me into a tight embrace, and I squeeze her back, trying to regain my composure after everything she's told me.

"Cleo, thank you for trusting me with your story. You have been through a lot, and I'm proud of you for not letting Adriano affect your life more than he already has," I say, wiping the tears streaming down my cheeks. "I understand it's hard to accept, but being raped isn't your fault, even if you misunderstood the asshole's character."

"I know this now," she assures me with confidence, unlike herself, and the power of this confession coming from her mouth is strong enough to make the earth tremble. It's as if she has stepped out of the darkness, never to turn back again.

Cleo has taken back her power.

"We should make some tacos!" Sofia suggests, her mouth watering.

Cleo nods, her face glowing with excitement to try some Mexican food.

Sofia and I are missing a taste of home, and this has prompted our sudden craving for tacos. But we're disappointed when we find no ingredients to make them.

"How is there no food in this mansion?" Sofia complains, putting back the packet of pasta she grabbed.

"It's because of all the men who live here," Cleo says, shaking her head in disbelief.

"Maybe we can go to the grocery store?" Sofia offers, sounding hopeful.

"Leo won't allow that," I say, knowing her request is out of line, especially after Adriano's threat last night.

Sofia groans, and not a minute later, her eyes widen when she gets an idea, which is never a good thing when it's coming from her.

"You can convince him!" she says, as if it's easy, and my rejection of this ridiculous proposition comes quick.

"No Sofia."

"Come on, Victoria, don't you want tacos?" She pouts, her hands set in front of her pleadingly. "If not for me, then for Cleo, who's dying to try Mexican food."

My attention falls on Cleo to see what she thinks of Sofia's bad idea, and much to my surprise, she's not opposed to it.

"It's worth a shot." Cleo shrugs her shoulders, and she gives a subtle nod.

"He's working right now. I don't want to bother him." I try to end the discussion, but Sofia wants those damn tacos.

"O come on, Victoria, he won't mind if it's you," she laments. "Please, we've been stuck in this house forever."

I let out a breath, knowing she has a point, and I start to feel myself become antsy.

"Fine, but I won't promise he'll say yes," I warn with a pointed finger.

"You can do it. I have faith in you!" she encourages, tugging me up the stairs.

"Sofia, I can walk there myself."

She gives me a sheepish smile and lets me go.

"Sorry, I need to get out of this house before I go crazy!"

"You're unbelievable," I exclaim when she trembles, running her hands down her forearms for emphasis.

"Unbelievably awesome!" she responds with a smirk. "Now get in there and convince him! Even if it means getting on your knees," Sofia says with a wink.

My mouth falls open, and I slap her shoulder. Cleo stands to the side with a grin.

"Sofia!" I reply in disbelief, and she motions for me to go inside.

I grumble under my breath and knock on the door.

"Come in," Leo calls out from inside, and from the sound of his voice, my stomach erupts with little weightless flutters.

I take slow steps into the room and find Leo sitting behind his grand mahogany desk with a pile of documents in front of him.

Leo looks away from the paper he's reading, and his face lights up at the sight of me.

As soon as he's in front of me, he wraps me in his arms.

"Amore, what are you doing here? Is everything okay?" He scans me over for any injuries. The gesture has me breaking into a slight smile.

"I'm okay," I assure him, placing a hand on his cheek.

He's silent for a second, his eyes calculating as he looks at me. Then he lifts a brow.

"You're up to no good. I can feel it."

"Mr. Bandoni, I'm hurt you think that." I fake being hurt, placing my right hand over my chest.

Leo makes an *aha* noise, not believing a word I say.

"Fine," I huff, and the corners of his mouth lift into a smile. "The girls and I want to make tacos, but we don't have any ingredients."

His thumb runs over the seams of my lips, which I've set into a pout.

"Mmm... I see," Leo draws out, his eyes focused on my mouth, and it sounds as if he's not against the idea. "I'll send someone to get what you guys need."

My forehead immediately bunches, and I let out an annoyed breath.

"Wait, what? They won't know what to get."

"Victoria, you're not going out by yourself." His voice drops three notes.

"Can't you have some of your men go with us?"

"That doesn't sound like a good idea."

His continuous rejection of the idea reminds me of Sofia's words, and she had a point. Although I won't get on my knees, as she suggested, I'll do other things.

I lift a defiant chin and hold Leo's stare, drawing my bottom lip between my teeth, knowing it drives him crazy when I do this.

Leo's eyes fall on the gesture, and a look of intense passion and hunger reflects in his eyes. I'm not done tormenting him, and I trail my fingers to trace the exposed skin of his chest. Curling my pointer finger around the gold chain he wears, I pull him to my level. My lips are a breath away from his.

"Are you sure about that?" I whisper against his mouth, and he lets out a choking sound, his hands gripping my hips.

He prepares to kiss me, but I pull back.

"Not so fast," I tsk, grabbing his chin.

"Victoria," he warns, and his voice is heavy with desire. I give a simple hum, kissing the spot under his jawline. My lips trail down to his neck, and he groans when I suck on the skin.

"I know what you're doing," he breathes, pressing me closer, allowing me to feel his desire.

The air is electric with our lust, and the pulsing between my legs intensifies.

"It's working, isn't it?" I breathe, and he says nothing, only stares at me hard. He's holding onto his restraint, and I realize I have to step it up if I want to convince him to reconsider.

I remove my hand from around his neck and boldly place it on his erection. He's hard against my palm, and from my touch, the last of his restraint snaps. I stare at him through my lashes, watching as he tumbles into my palm.

"Can we please go to the grocery store?" I whisper, rubbing my palm against him.

"Fuck." Leo lets out a little breath, and his dark hooded eyes smolder me. After a few seconds, he nods, and his face goes hard with seriousness. "Fine, you guys can go, but you need to take Luca and some of his men."

Beaming in excitement, I give him a kiss. Leo's more than willing to accept my touch, and his lips move with a desperate hunger over mine.

When I pull away too soon for his liking, he groans in disapproval.

"Victoria, you guys are not to leave their protection," he says firmly as he places a strand of hair behind my ear.

"I promise!" I assure him and hurry toward the door before he changes his mind.

"Victoria..." Leo's voice halts my movements, and I turn to look over at him, and my heart jumps from my chest when he flashes me the sexiest, most arrogant smile to exist.

I lift a brow, feeling my throat tighten from the look he's giving me, which promises trouble.

"I hope you realize you played with fire." There's a challenge flashing in his eyes, and I swallow hard, feeling suddenly hot. "I'll see you later tonight, amore."

His sexual threat drives my thighs to clench as warmth pools between them.

Leo's eyes fall to my lower half, and he rolls his lips into his mouth, moistening his pink lips. I tremble under his stare, and I'm not sure what to say.

As I leave his office, I try to ease the excitement and nervousness now raging through my body like a fire that only he can put out.

39

VICTORIA

"What did he say?" Sofia asks the moment I step outside.

"He said it's fine, but there's a catch." My words come out breathless, and I try to steady my racing heart.

"What's the catch?" she asks, and one of her thin brows lift.

"We need to take Luca and his guards with us."

"I guess that's fair," she says, shrugging.

"Why did you take long to come out if he said yes?" This time it's Cleo who speaks, and her question makes me choke.

"What did you do?" Cleo says, even though she and Sofia know why I took long.

I don't say a word as Sofia answers for me.

"Oh, a little of this..." she teases, making kissy faces. "... and some of this." She runs her hands up and down my forearm.

I push her hands off me.

"Haha, hilarious. If you guys are done making fun of me, can we go find Luca," I say, trying to cool the warmth in my body. The two follow close behind me, their laughter ringing in my ears.

We enter Luca's room and find him doing his nerdy stuff.

"What brings you ladies to my humble abode?" he asks, his arms behind his head as he leans back in his gaming chair.

"We want to go to the grocery store, and Leo said you have to come and protect us." Sofia narrows her eyes on him as he takes a lazy sip of his soda.

"Great...Babysitting duties," he grumbles, leaning further into his seat and closing his eyes.

His comment prompts us to cross our arms over our chests, and we stare at his unmoving figure. A minute passes, and I clear my throat to get his attention.

He cracks an eye open.

"Fine, come on, let's go," he says, standing from his seat with a teasing smile after noticing all three of us glaring at him.

Luca leads us outside, where two black SUVs are waiting for us. Near the two cars are six men.

The drive to the store is short, and before we go inside to get what we need, Luca stops us. The carefree persona he carries most days is nowhere to be found.

"You guys can't wander off, and two men are to be with you at all times." His words are firm, and I want to laugh at the sight of him being serious for a change.

We nod in unison, and make our way inside to get the ingredients to make carne asada tacos.

"You guys are making dinner tonight?" Luca asks with delight.

I nod and hand him some tomatoes to put in the cart. Luca wrinkles his brows, unsure of what to do with them. I laugh at how clueless he looks. If I didn't know better, I'd say he's never been grocery shopping before.

His phone rings, and he groans from the clattering sound coming from his pocket. He puts the tomatoes back in the pile I got them from.

Is he serious? I glare at him, and re grab the tomatoes.

"It's Leo," he says, glancing up from his phone. "I have to take this. Will you be alright if I leave for a second?" he asks, and I pay little attention, not taking my eyes off the ingredients in the cart.

"Yeah, I'll be here." I wave him away.

"I'll be like ten feet away." He points a few feet from me, and I hum. The other guard is also looming over this section. Nothing can happen when they're near. Plus, it's mid-afternoon, and nothing dangerous ever happens inside a grocery store.

Luca's shoes squeak on the floor as he walks away, and a minute later, I feel his presence behind me.

"That was fast. What did Leo want?" I inquire, while looking at the limes. He says nothing, and I glance behind me to find nobody.

My forehead creases from uneasiness, and I turn to where the other guard is standing, but he's missing. A chill sweeps the back of my neck, and worry creeps up on me. I swallow the dryness in my throat, and a rough hand grabs my forearm.

"Hello again." A familiar voice whispers by the side of my face.

A wave of déjà vu hits me. The pressure in my chest rises, and my heart drops when I come face-to-face with Andrew. The sound of his voice and his violent grip remind me of the pain he has caused me, my cousin, and many other girls.

"Let me go!" I say through clenched teeth, trying to peel his fingers off me. My fighting angers him, and he places his gun against my side, jabbing it into my rib cage.

"No can do. I have strict orders to bring you back with me to Adriano." He tugs on my arm. "Lorenzo misses you," Andrew mocks, and I want to slap the sinister grin from his face, but I'm afraid he'll press the trigger.

I'm not prepared for a situation like this, and in a grocery store, of all places. I'm starting to regret letting Sofia convince me that going to the store was a good idea.

The people around us see the gun pointed at my side, and they whisper, fear etched onto their faces. They watch helplessly as Andrew leads me toward the exit.

I scan the store, trying to find Luca, and when I see him, I'm filled with panic when I notice he has his back turned to me.

Really Luca!

He isn't doing a good job of being a bodyguard.

My heart goes still, and my knees grow heavy when I realize I'm screwed. There's nothing I can do to save myself while at gunpoint.

The store's exit is now ten feet away, and a man waits for me near a van with a grin.

I stop walking, and my resistance makes Andrew angry. He clicks his gun, and my heart caves in as I gasp from pure terror.

"Keep walking, or I swear I will blow your guts right in the middle of this store for Leo to mop up." Andrew clicks the gun again.

By now, tears have risen in my eyes, and I do as he says, knowing that the third time he clicks his gun, a bullet is likely to follow.

"Good girl." Andrew pats the back of my head with his free hand.

I shudder in disgust and try to move from his grasp, but he grabs me by the back of my neck. He roughly pushes me forward, and I almost fall.

"Let her go!" Luca's voice booms from behind, and Andrew makes a sound of irritation, forcing us to turn around. He places me in front of him as a shield.

"Hello *baby brother*, how's mom?"

I'm sorry, what? Brother?

My eyes widen, and I'm sure the color has drained from my face after processing Andrew's words.

As I look at Luca, I finally understand why there was a sense of familiarity the first time I met him. He and Andrew have the same blue eyes. The only difference between them is Luca's dyed white hair, which makes his skin lighter and his eyes clearer.

"Mother hates you. Now give me Victoria," he says, and a muscle in his jaw twitches. Sensing my gaze, Luca's eyes fall on me, and they soften upon seeing the tears resting in the corner of my eyes. His gaze flickers to his brother, and he sends Andrew a glare, which promises a fight.

Luca points his gun at Andrew, who responds by removing the gun from my head and pointing it at Luca.

"Luca, I don't want to hurt you, so stop pretending to be a hero," Andrew breathes in exasperation.

Within seconds, the store erupts with panic, and people scramble to hide.

In the corner, I see Sofia and Cleo fighting to get to me, but Leo's guards don't budge. They have strict orders to protect them at all costs. When they don't stop struggling, I give them a warning glare, and the two cower back, allowing the two guards to take them to a room at the back of the store.

"Tell your men to put their guns down. We wouldn't want this little princess to get injured," Andrew threatens, pressing the gun to my temple.

Luca glares at his brother, and worry reveals itself as Luca tries to figure out his next move.

When Luca takes too long to follow his orders, Andrew sighs in annoyance and goes to pull the trigger.

Luca panics and flicks two fingers, signaling the two men with him to do as Andrew says.

"Good. Now, if you don't mind, we must be going." Andrew pulls me backward toward the exit, and my heart rate increases.

As the distance between me and Luca stretches, I notice he's pale with worry. I smile, assuring him I'll be fine, but I know this is a lie.

"Walk faster!" Andrew warns, and my teeth clench together.

"I can't when you have a gun pressed against my head and are making me walk backward!"

"Watch your tone, or I'll cut your tongue off." I bite back my reproach, and he looks back to see where we're walking. As he becomes distracted, the gun on my temple moves.

With the gun no longer pressed against me, I jerk my head forward and then throw it back as hard as possible. Upon impact with Andrew's face, my world spins, and pain shoots through my skull. I push past the burning sensation and throw my elbow back, hitting his throat. I finish by thrusting my fist into his nose, like my dad taught me.

My attack is unexpected, and Andrew shoots his gun at the roof. His hands go to his bleeding nose, and I run toward Luca, who's already approaching me.

Luca's hand extends for me to grab, and our fingers graze right when I hear Andrew behind me.

"You bitch!"

Luca's eyes widen in panic.

"Duck!" Luca shouts, and I throw myself to the ground with a scream.

I wrap my arms over my head, and my screams keep coming as the loud popping sound of firing gunshots surrounds me. My tears soak the dirty floor, and all around me I hear the sounds of screams, guns firing, and the loud crash of glass breaking. The sounds ring like a chorus of war and then silence.

Two strong arms pick me up from the floor, and a scream of horror emits from inside me. I fight in the person's arms.

"Shhh, it's me," Luca's soothing voice whispers, and I sigh in relief, wrapping my arms around his waist. I press my face to his chest and he hisses. I jolt back, gasping at the sight of the blood flowing out in a steady pour from his shoulder.

"Luca, you got shot!" I cry out. "We need to take you to the hospital."

"This is nothing, Shortcake. Did you forget I'm in the mafia?" he teases, and I glare at him.

"Where's Andrew?" I ask, looking around, glad to see no one else got hurt.

"The asshole started shooting like a madman and got inside a getaway car before running like the little bitch he is." Luca's voice goes an octave lower. I place a comforting hand on his shoulder, and he gives a thin-lipped smile.

Andrew and Luca are brothers. Who would have thought?

With this news and learning Leo and Adriano are also related, I realize that those in the mafia have severe family issues.

It wouldn't surprise me if Kaden and Angelo also have relatives on Adriano's side.

Two pairs of arms wrap around me, and the force is so strong I almost fall to the ground.

"Victoria, thank God you're safe. I was so worried," Sofia cries, and Cleo places a trembling hand on my cheek. I give them an assuring smile, relieved to see they're okay.

"Let's go. Leo is freaking out as we speak... he's going to kill us all." Luca's lips curl into a grimace, and I groan, knowing Leo is going to put me under house arrest indefinitely.

Despite our urgency to leave, Luca lets us pay for our groceries. But if we're being honest, he lets us get the ingredients only because he wants to postpone getting back to Leo for as long as possible and because he wants to eat tacos for dinner.

He was so nonchalant as he waited for us to pay for the groceries, even if his blood dripped all over the floor.

We eventually do leave the store, and I sit beside Luca, who's putting pressure on his bleeding shoulder. He sticks his finger into his wound, trying to find the bullet. I have to look away, trying to hold back my gag. He notices, and his laughter fills the silence of the car. Luca points his bloody fingers near my face, and I almost throw up.

"Luca!" I give him a warning glare, telling him to stop being a pain in the ass. He gives a sheepish smile before resuming his activities.

I sigh and face the front. My heart beats in my ears as the mansion comes into view. From here, I can see Leo shouting into his phone, and I can hear what he's saying because Luca now has his phone pressed to his ear. He cringes at each word Leo yells at him, and I fill with shame as Luca gets scolded for my and the girls' poor decision to go grocery shopping.

The car pulls to a stop next to Leo, and the moment my feet touch the ground, he pulls me into his arms.

I sigh in relief, glad to be home.

Leo

After I take a cold shower, thanks to Victoria, I head back to my office to review the arrival information for the mafia families.

Now that I'm back in my office, I'm anxious, knowing Victoria isn't here.

She successfully seduced me into letting her go to the grocery store. I'm not proud of it, but I couldn't help it. She was a temptress with a mission who knew perfectly well what to do to get what she wanted.

When my anxiety becomes too overwhelming, I call Luca to make sure they are alright and to ask him for the information on Moises I told him to get for me.

"Hey, boss, how can I be of service?" he asks the moment he answers my call.

"First, how are Victoria and the girls?"

He laughs. "They're fine. Now, what else do you need?"

"Do you remember the police officer I asked you to find me information on?" He isn't sure what I'm talking about, so I explain. "The one in charge of Victoria and Sofia's missing case in France."

"Oh yeah. What about him?"

"I need the file. Do you have it in your—"

"Fuck!" he curses, and my shoulders go tense at the sound of his panic.

"What is it, Luca?"

"Andrew has Victoria!"

"Why is no one watching her?" My chest constricts, and a cold panic rises inside me, freezing every organ with dread.

"I was with her, but left to answer your phone call. There's another guard... shit." The sound of his worry and not knowing what's happening has fear galloping in my chest.

"What's going on, Luca?" I grab my gun and rush out of my office.

"The other guard is dead. Leo, I have to go; he has a gun to her," he says, preparing to hang up on me, and I warn him not to fucking do it, but the shithead ignores me and cuts the call.

"Fucking Luca!" I mutter, running to get in my car before Victoria gets hurt.

When I make it to the steps outside the house, my father places a hand on my arm and steps in front of me.

"Move." I try to pass him, but he remains motionless, blocking my way.

"No, you look ready to do something stupid."

My jaw tics, and my anger rises.

"I know what I'm doing."

"And what's that?" He crosses his arms over his chest.

I don't have time for this.

When I try to push him aside, his eyes continue to glare at me, and he doesn't budge.

"Victoria is in danger because the guards I assigned to protect her don't know how to do their fucking job." My father responds to my frustration with laughter.

"You're like me. Never trusting others with the ones we love." His face becomes gloomy when his words remind him of my mother.

"Papà, please move."

He shakes his head like a stubborn mule.

"No. Leo, trust your men. They are more than capable of bringing her back. If you go, it will only put her and you in more danger." He places a hand on my stiff shoulder.

Trust your men. Trust Luca.

The words repeat themselves in my mind.

"Fine, but if they don't come back, or at least call me in the next ten minutes, I'm leaving. And no one, not even you, can stop me," I warn, taking a seat on the last step of the stairs.

He chuckles and sits beside me, patting my back.

"You sure are a Bandoni," he mumbles, and a sigh passes his lips.

A few minutes later, my phone rings. I answer it on the first beat, and sigh in relief when Luca tells me they are here. As soon as he says this, the cars appear.

"Luca, what the fuck happened, and why were you not with her?" I shout through the phone, listening to his excuses, knowing damn well he could have answered the call beside her. His actions were plain idiocy and almost cost Victoria her life.

Apparently, everyone is making stupid choices today.

I hang up the call when the car pulls up next to me, and Victoria walks out with her head lowered. The sight of her eases the stiffness in my upper body, and I pull her into my arms.

"Are you okay?" I ask, cupping her face and checking her for any injuries. "You're not going anywhere without me from now on." My voice is firm, leaving no room for argument. But it's Victoria we're talking about. She doesn't like to be told what to do.

"Awe, come on, please don't get all overprotective of me. I kicked his ass. Ask the guards,"

My decision stays the same, and I only give a slight head shake. I try to fight back my smile after hearing her say she kicked his ass.

"Is that so?" I say, and she nods right as Luca appears behind her. His head is cast down in shame.

I'm annoyed with him, but when I notice his bleeding shoulder, I'm thankful he protected Victoria when I wasn't there.

"Are you alright Luca?" I ask him.

"Yeah, it's only a slight cut," he says, waving a hand. "You should have seen her boss. She got Andrew good," he says, ruffling the top of Victoria's head, and she glares at him, muttering words in Spanish. "Where did you learn to do that, Shortcake?"

Victoria blushes and nuzzles into my side.

"My dad taught me some moves when I returned from France," she says, massaging the back of her head with a pained expression. When she lowers her hand, it's painted red with blood.

"Fucking shit, amore!" Panic courses through my veins, and I pull her in front of me to look at the back of her head. Her scalp has gone murky from the blood seeping out of a cut. "What the fuck happened to your head?"

She bites her lip and stares at her bloody hand with a crinkle to her nose.

"I might have butt-headed Andrew in the face, punched him in the throat, and maybe broke his nose."

"It was amazing!" Luca beams, still standing beside us with his arm bleeding.

"Luca, go get your arm stitched up," I say in disbelief.

"I'm going; damn, you guys need to relax. It's not that serious," he groans, and leaves to get the bullet out of his shoulder.

To my left, I see my sister, and I'm glad she's safe.

Cleo smiles at Victoria and me before she and Sofia go inside with my father. My forehead furrows when I see the shopping bags, which tells me they finished grocery shopping after being attacked.

Victoria notices my disbelief and smiles at me. Her expression changes to a grimace when she sees how upset I am.

"You come with me. We need to get you checked out," I say, lifting her bridal style and ignoring her complaints as I walk us up to our room to tend to her cut.

"Leo, I'm fine!" she groans, and although her stubbornness brings me turmoil, I find I love it and need it in my life.

Victoria is like a rare diamond that money can't buy. One which my enemies would want to steal, as today has proven.

Although Victoria can somewhat defend herself, she doesn't know how to do so without getting hurt. She needs to be trained, and I have the perfect trainer for her.

Angelo is one of our best-skilled fighters in hand combat. If I know one person who can teach her the art of kicking ass, it's him.

Of course, I can always teach her myself, but I don't want to hurt her, and this thought alone will make it impossible for me to give her the proper training she needs. Angelo is our best bet at making sure Victoria gets the best training.

I finish cleaning her wound, and Victoria tries to get out of my grasp, but I wrap an arm around her waist, bringing her back to my chest.

"Where do you think you're going?" I ask, and she lets out an exasperated breath.

"To go help make dinner," she replies without hesitation.

"O no you don't," I object, lifting her in my arms and carrying her to our bed. "You might have a concussion and pass out." Victoria's face scrunches in annoyance.

"Leo—" she's about to complain when I raise my brows in a warning, silencing her reproach.

Victoria crosses her arms over her chest and sends me a sideways glare, and I just know she's going to be the death of me.

40

VICTORIA

Overbearing. That's the one word I can use best to explain Leo's behavior after yesterday's incident.

Even after I told him I was fine, he wouldn't let me move or lift a finger because of the possibility of having a concussion.

His paranoia meant he spent all of yesterday watching over me. Of course, I wouldn't have minded spending time with him. But when someone asks you how you feel every ten minutes, you quickly become annoyed with them.

When morning arrives, I know that if I want to avoid a repeat of yesterday evening; I need to get out of his arms before he wakes up.

Leo's soft breathing tells me he's deep asleep, and I unravel his arms from around me. He makes a soft grunt noise, and I tense for a second. When he remains asleep, I grab the pillow under me and place it between us. Leo pulls it against him, assuming it's me, and I have to press my lips together to stop from laughing at how adorable he looks.

I bend down to kiss his cheek, and when I pull back, my stomach flutters when he smiles in his sleep.

The gray carpet against the pad of my feet is like silk as I make my way toward the walk-in closet.

Leo had all my clothes moved into what he now calls *'our room.'*

He wasn't bluffing the other night when he asked me to stay with him forever. I didn't mind since I slept better in his arms anyway.

I enter the closet and gasp at how big it is. The sleek black interior and the dozen rows of clothes reveal Leo's wealth.

The pads of my fingers trace the soft fabric of his suits hanging on the rack along the wall to my left. My hand stops on the designer heels and extravagant dresses Leo bought for me.

"Ay, Leo." There's a hint of a Spanish accent in my words as I push the fine silk gowns aside so I can find my clothes.

No matter how many times I tell him, Leo doesn't seem to understand what "stop buying me unnecessary things" means.

I pick an outfit and head toward the cabinet in the middle of the closet, intending to find my undergarments.

The first drawer I open has an extensive assortment of Leo's silk ties and bows. The next has sunglasses, and the third has his boxers. Heat rushes to my face, and I close the drawer. It springs back, and I panic, afraid Leo might find me like this.

He'll think I'm a creep for going through his boxers.

The thought mortifies me, and I jiggle the drawer, trying to get it to close.

"Come on, stupid thing." When it still doesn't want to close, I stick a hand inside and pull out a smashed box that was stuck at the back of the drawer.

"Oh, my—" I feel a knot forming in my throat from the sight of the extra-large, unopened condoms. The box shakes in my hands, and my heart races as I place the condoms inside the drawer.

I take steady breaths to calm my nerves, and with trembling hands, I open the fourth drawer, glad to find my undergarments.

Once dressed and ready for the day, I make my way back out to the bedroom, and I'm greeted by a confused Leo who's glaring at the pillow he was cuddling.

When he sees me, he relaxes and rushes toward me. He's warm from sleep, and I sigh, pressing my cheek against his bare chest. His heart is beating fast, but it slows now that I'm in his arms.

"You're up early," Leo breathes, kissing me on the forehead,

"I wanted to shower after yesterday." Leo nods and is about to ask me how I'm doing when I cut him off. "Leo, I swear if you ask me that damn question one more time, I'm going to lose my mind."

"Well then, if you're so fine now, you can start your training today." My eyes widen in surprise at this news.

"Really?" I beam, and Leo laughs.

"Yes, after what happened yesterday, I need to make sure you know how to defend yourself without getting hurt." Leo frowns, looking at my head.

"Are you training me?"

"Angelo's training you. But I'll be there to watch."

"Okay," I say, trying to push aside the disappointment, and Leo smiles, kissing my forehead.

He gives a teasing grin and breaks the silence between us.

"Are you sure you're—" I glare at him when he's about to ask me that damn question again, and he laughs, enjoying pressing my buttons.

"I'm going to help make breakfast." My words come out rushed, and I pull from his arms. "I'll see you downstairs."

I swear it hasn't been twenty minutes since being apart from Leo when his arms snake from behind me.

"You smell good," he mumbles, pressing soft kisses along the base of my neck.

"Leo, stop being so touchy." I try to sound firm, but my words come out breathless.

"I'm hungry," he murmurs, dipping his finger in the strawberry jam beside us and spreading it along my neck. My eyes close as his mouth cleans off the jam from where he smeared it.

My heart rate quickens when he slips a hand inside my ivory silk cami, and his touch ignites goosebumps on my arms. The grip I have around the spatula tightens when he presses me to his front.

I arch into him, and he has me at his mercy.

Leo stops kissing me and slides his hand out of my shirt. A cold chill runs through my body when his warmth disappears.

I stare at him, my eyes fogged with lust, and my chest heaves.

Leo grins when he sees me flustered, but it drops, and his eyes widen at something behind me. The smell of burnt pancakes wafts around us.

Leo quickly grabs the pan, tosses it in the sink, and turns off the stove.

"Leo, look at what you made me do," I whine, motioning to the burned pancake and the thick smoke floating around us.

"I can't help it if I'm good-looking, baby." He gives me a wink, and my entire body tingles.

I roll my eyes. "Whatever you say, hot stuff."

Leo's smile widens, and he grabs my hand, leading me to the dining room.

The moment we enter the room, Estephano looks up from the newspaper he's reading, and there's concern written all over his face.

"Son, Victoria's all over the newspaper." Estephano hands the newspaper to Leo.

I become tense when I read the charges against Moises were dropped. They are saying the DNA tests mistaking me and Sophia as dead was an error by the pathologist in the laboratory. Something I know is a lie.

"That asshole is working with Adriano." Leo's anger is visible, and his grip on the newspaper tightens until he wrinkles the pages.

Estephano snatches the newspaper from Leo's hands and rolls it tightly. He then hits Leo on the head with it.

"Idiota," Estephano murmurs, and Cleo grins while I stifle my laughter.

I grab his cheeks, pinching the skin.

"Awe, did Leo get in trouble?"

"No," he grumbles, lifting his cup of coffee to his lips.

Estephano huffs in disagreement.

I laugh and stretch to grab a plate when Leo stops me. I lift a brow.

"What did I say about you lifting a finger?"

"Leo..." I groan in annoyance, only to be left speechless when he piles food onto a plate. He sets it in front of me, and I'm about to pick up the fork when he takes it and cuts the pancake for me. He brings the fork to my mouth, and heat races to my cheeks when everyone stares at us.

"Are you being serious?" I whisper.

"Just open your mouth Victoria." He narrows his eyes, and I slowly open my mouth. Leo grins, putting the fork in my mouth and feeding me the pancake.

Before my training, I wanted to check up on Luca.

When he sees me at his door, he smiles.

"Shortcake, come on in." He opens the door for me, and I see the white bandage on his shoulder has blood seeping out of it. My forehead bunches, and I embrace Luca.

"Thank you for saving me."

"Shortcake, I didn't save you. You saved yourself."

"That's not true. You were the one who told me to duck!" I remind him, and he gives a thin-lipped smile. His body language is oozing with sadness.

"Are you okay?" I place a hand on his uninjured arm, and Luca draws in a deep breath.

"I'm assuming you're here because you have questions," he says, referring to him and Andrew being brothers.

"I have questions, but I came to make sure you were okay, not to interrogate you."

Luca smiles and flexes his muscles.

"Well, in that case, I'm as healthy as a horse."

"Whatever you say, Snow White," I tease, punching his uninjured shoulder. He groans in pain, and I lift my right brow. "Healthy as a horse, huh?"

"Victoria, I'm fine. It'll heal in no time," he assures me, and I give a weak nod.

Luca's teasing tone disappears, and a dark, sad look takes over his expression.

"Andrew never cared about me." Luca takes a seat on his bed, and I sit beside him. "I looked up to him, but he despised me. But I still tried to break through to him, and each time he told me to fuck off. Victoria, my brother hated me from the moment I learned how to walk, and I don't even know why or how to fix my relationship with him."

As he explains his situation with Andrew, it's as if the pain he feels isn't from the bullet, but from the fact that it was his brother who shot him.

Luca's an open book at this moment, and I can tell he's hopeful his brother still has some good in him.

From the way Luca speaks with hope, I can tell he's one of those people who will forgive those who have harmed him. Even if the person is more rotten than a four-week-old moldy sandwich.

"Luca, I know you still love Andrew. But this love is only going to hurt you." The blue in his eyes turns murky from his rising tears.

"I know, Shortcake." He gives a sad smile. "I only wish things didn't end the way they did between us." I place a hand on his cheek, wiping the lone tear that slipped from his eye.

"Luca, you're amazing, and Andrew is losing out on the best little brother." Luca laughs, bumping my shoulder.

"A funny one, too," he adds with a boyish grin.

"Yes, a funny-looking one." Luca sends me a playful glare, making me laugh.

"Shortcake, aren't you supposed to be in training?" There's a hint of amusement in his words.

I slap my forehead, realizing I'm late for my training.

Groaning, I pull Luca up with me.

"What are you doing?" he asks as I drag him through the house.

"I need cheerleaders if I'm going to be learning how to fight."

Luca grins and lifts his hands into fists, shaking them like pom-poms.

"Go, Victoria!" he cheers, and I laugh at the goofball, who, although hurting inside, still tries to bring a smile to my face.

"Tap out," Angelo teases.

I grind my teeth, growing frustrated at having him toss me around the boxing ring.

There's no way in hell I'm going to give up, even if I'm turning blue from losing air because of his choke hold. I can't give up, not when it's important for me to learn how to fight.

Adriano's men won't let me tap out. But even if I try my best, I'm no match for Angelo's strength. The only fighting skills I have are the few lessons my dad gave me, and the lesson Angelo gave me before jumping into the ring.

For the twentieth time in the past hour, I find myself pinned to the ground with my front half pressed between the black mat and Angelo's broad chest.

My attempts to free myself are futile.

I glance to the side where Leo grimaces, pleading with me to tap out, but I ignore him and continue to fight Angelo.

"Come on, tap out," Angelo repeats, lifting his free hand to his mouth as he fake yawns.

"Fuck no!" I bite back, trying to free my hands from under me.

Angelo laughs and looks toward Leo to see what he should do. His grip around me loosens, and my right hand slips from under my body. With my arm free, I punch Angelo's throat, and he releases me so he can clutch his neck, gasping for air.

"Sorry, blue eyes." I dust imaginary dirt from my hands, and Leo's laughter sounds around me. Our eyes lock from across the ring, and he gives me a wink.

"Nice one baby," Leo compliments, and I grin, turning my attention to a red-faced Angelo who's regaining his senses after the little stunt I pulled.

"Come on, I want to go again," I say as Angelo straightens his posture.

"Fine, last time," he grumbles, getting into position in front of me. His knees are bent, his fists are lifted, and leveled with his face. And his eyes follow my every move.

I got lucky this one time because I preyed on the element of surprise. But this doesn't mean my win is any less satisfying. But if I'm being honest, seeing Angelo lose his composure is more satisfying than beating him.

"Awe, don't cry," I say, jabbing at his masculinity.

Men are irrational, and when someone takes a stab at their egos, they lose their composure like Angelo here. This is how I can win against him.

"I know what you're doing, V." Angelo eyes me with suspicion. I bite down on my rising smile when I notice him still getting mad despite knowing my intentions.

And they say girls are emotional.

"Oh, yeah?" I retort. "What am I doing, sore loser?"

"You're trying to make me angry." Angelo wipes the sweat from his forehead. His eyes pin me in place, and I scrunch my face in bewilderment as I fake innocence.

"What? No way! It's not my fault a girl blew the air out of you." He grunts in disapproval, and everyone around us watches our banter with amusement. "Maybe you should apply for the role of a nanny, since training doesn't seem to work for you anymore," I say, biting my lip to keep my laughter at bay.

Angelo turns red as the surrounding men laugh at him.

Of course, my comment about him being a nanny is a joke, but I have to tick him off somehow, and it works because his composure snaps and he runs toward me. His punches are fast and sloppy.

I gasp and launch myself aside to avoid his hits, but my feet get caught between his, and we both tumble to the mat.

Angelo grabs my ankle, and I go to kick his shoulder, but I accidentally kick him in the chin. His hand flies to his jaw.

"Ah fuck, I bit my tongue," he complains as I rise from the mat.

I swiftly wrap my arms around his neck in a chokehold.

"Tap out," I say, and the men in the training room laugh. Leo's laughter being the loudest.

Angelo flips me over his shoulder, slamming me onto the mat below us with a loud thud.

I groan when a sharp pain shoots from the cut on my head, and I don't miss the way Leo's fists clench against his side. He looks about ready to come get me, and he would have if not for Francisco telling him something, which eases Leo's anger.

"Look at who's down now," Angelo taunts, pressing me into the mat. Black dots cover my vision, and I'm about to accept defeat when I hear a cheer of encouragement coming from the one and only Cleo Bandoni.

"Come on, Victoria, kick his ass!" she shouts, and the room grows silent. Leo, Francisco, Luca, Kaden, Angelo, and the other few men in the room all stare at her in shock. Sofia beams at Cleo, her eyes gleaming with pride.

Angelo's hold on me falls after hearing Cleo talk, and I elbow him in the rib, taking him to the mat below. He lets me win and rushes to Cleo like everyone else.

I smile at the sight of Cleo embracing her brother, and after a while of the two talking, Leo glances at me, motioning for me to come over.

When I'm near, I place my hand on the lower part of Leo's back, and he turns to me.

"You knew?" he asks, and I grimace, afraid he's angry because I didn't tell him.

"Yes, she was the one who convinced me to speak to you after I saw you covered in blood," I confess, cringing at the memory.

Leo's face softens, and he smiles before he brings Cleo and me into his arms.

"Leo, stop being touchy-feely," Cleo whines, detaching herself from his arms and walking toward the surrounding men, who all have questions for her.

Leo turns to me and puts a loose strand of my hair behind my ear. His touch is cool on my flustered skin.

"You did great, amore," he says, about to kiss my sweaty forehead, but I pull away, and he groans. "Come back here." He tries to grab my waist, but I dodge his attempts.

"I don't think so," I retort with a grin. "If you want me, you need to fight for me," I tease, getting into the ring, and he follows after me.

"Fine, but I always win," he says, sounding confident. My attention falls on his toned arms when they flex as he puts on the boxing gloves.

Not this time.

I grin mischievously, knowing I can use our attraction for one another against him.

"Whatever you say," comes my sarcastic remark.

Leo ignores it and pulls his black t-shirt off, exposing his toned chest.

"Ewe!" Luca grumbles in distaste, followed by the others' complaints.

"Get the fuck out of here then!" Leo glares at them, and they wave him off. I say nothing, too stunned by his abs.

Leo's lips tip into a smirk when he sees my appreciation for his toned body. I scoff and remove my tank top to reveal my black sports bra. His grin turns into a scowl when the surrounding men whistle at me. He sends them all a warning glare.

"Victoria, put your shirt back on," Leo warns, brows bunched together.

"You put your shirt back on," I retort, and his eyes widen in shock.

"What am I going to do with you?" Leo shakes his head, his voice a whisper.

"Fight me." He laughs and takes slow, calculated steps toward me. He bends to my ear, and my blood stills from his words.

"I'm more than happy to fight with you, but I think we have different meanings of what kind of fighting we're talking about." I look at him with my eyes wide, and he flashes me an arrogant smile as he backs away.

I push past the dirty thoughts, but the condoms I found earlier don't make it easy. It's almost impossible for my eyes not to wander down to see if he's really that big.

Leo tips his chin, edging me to hit him first.

"Chicken," I mumble, and I launch myself at him. He dodges all my punches and grabs my wrists between his hands, bringing me plush against his chest.

I thrash in his hold, and his eyes pierce into me.

I'm sucked into his stare until I realize he's taking advantage of my attraction to him. With this in mind, I lift my knee, hitting him in the stomach.

"Sorry, pretty boy," I tease, watching him clutch his stomach with a groan.

"Victoria, I think you broke something," he says through staggered breaths, and panic courses through me, unable to believe I hit him that hard.

"No, I—"

Mid-sentence, Leo grabs me and drops me on the mat. He hovers over me with his hands on either side of my head.

"False alarm," he whispers, his eyes falling to my mouth.

He goes to kiss me, but freezes when I wrap my legs around his waist. I press myself against him, and he takes an unsteady breath when I swiftly roll us over, so now I pin him down.

"Now, this is a position I like," he mumbles, and I kiss his cheek, feeling the same way.

Our audience groans in disgust. But I ignore them because Leo told them to leave, and if they stayed, then it's their fault.

"Gross!" Luca shouts, walking out of the room. I roll my eyes, knowing he isn't a saint himself, as three days ago I almost walked in on him getting it on with a girl.

"Tap out," I whisper, my lips caressing Leo's earlobe, and his hands tighten around my waist. He swallows, and his eyes dim when I wet my chapped lips to moisten them.

"Alright, you win," he groans in defeat, and I release him. When we are both back on our two feet, Leo lifts me off the ground, swinging me over his shoulder.

"Put me down, you big brute!" I shout, pounding my fist into his back. Leo laughs, and his hold around me tightens.

"Nope, this is payback for all the times you leave me hot and bothered," he says, making his way toward the exit.

The sound of the men cheering him on from behind us makes me groan in embarrassment. I spot Cleo looking our way with a smile.

"Help me, Cleo! Your brother's crazy!"

Cleo laughs, putting her hand by her ear.

"Sorry, what did you say? I can't hear you with how far away you are!" Her voice takes on a sweet, innocent tone, and my mouth falls open in shock as she waves goodbye.

"Leo!"

"Yes, amore?"

"Put me down!"

"No, I think I'm okay like this." He places a hand on my butt and pats the area.

"Hands off the merchandise, buddy."

"What do you mean?" he says, faking innocence, and I can already picture his grin.

He takes fast steps through the hall, and I stiffen when his index finger travels the length of my spine. His hand slips through the back of my sports bra, and my breath gets caught in my lungs.

"Leo…" I caution, lifting my torso.

"Well, what do we have here?" he says, placing me back on my two feet.

I glare at him.

"What are you talking about?" I say, and he turns me around to see Sofia and Francisco kissing up against the wall.

At the sight of them, tongue deep into one another, my mouth falls open.

"Well, aren't we all full of surprises today?" I say as they pull apart.

"We can explain!" They shout and look at each other wide-eyed.

Leo and I glance at one another, and we're both holding in our laughter.

"Enlighten us then," Leo edges, wrapping an arm around my waist.

Francisco groans and brings Sofia close to him.

"I like her, and she likes me, so we gave it a shot." Francisco shrugs and kisses Sofia on the top of her head.

I run to embrace my cousin, and I give Francisco a warning look.

"If you hurt her physically or mentally, I will sneak into your room when you're sleeping…" I pause, and he gulps. "… and I will shave your head bald and put a bullet through your dick," I say lowly. "Capiche?"

He nods, his gaze moving from me to a grinning Leo.

I wrap Francisco in my arms.

"Make her happy," I tell him, and he hugs me back.

"Alright, that's enough hugging. Come amore," Leo says, dragging me to our room.

Once inside, I head toward the bathroom to shower.

"Where are you going?" Leo asks, and I turn around with a crooked brow.

"To shower."

"Can I join? I'm all up for saving money on the water bill," Leo says, heading my way with a grin.

"You're funny. But no. If you have enough money to own twenty sports cars, then I'm sure you have enough money to pay the water bill," I say and close the door, locking it behind me.

"Victoria!" Leo's fist pounds against the door.

I didn't expect Leo to be this flirty. To be honest, I'm not sure if I'll be able to resist him if he keeps looking at me the way he does, and don't get me started on the way he's suggestive with both his words and actions.

41

LEO

Victoria's asleep in my arms. Yesterday's training left her drained.

It's now noon, and I don't have it in me to wake her up. I enjoy having her next to me. When she's near, I'm whole. Victoria has given me another purpose in life other than my mafia. This new purpose to make sure she's loved, protected, and happy is now my number one priority. Nothing else matters to me.

The pad of my index finger traces Victoria's high cheekbones, and her skin is velvety. Her heart-shaped lips roll into her mouth, and mine tug into a smile when her lips form a slight pout.

I press a chaste kiss on her cheek. My conversation with Cleo the previous day comes to mind.

After years, Cleo is finding her way back to herself, and the reason for this is my Victoria. Her strength seeped into my sister.

Victoria's the missing piece in our lives. The calmness amidst the violence, the softness I needed in my rough heart.

I kiss the corner of her mouth, and she groans, scrunching her nose.

Victoria doesn't like to be woken up, and the crinkle of her nose tells me she's not happy with me, but I don't care. I'm going to savor this moment while I still can.

My arms around her tighten, knowing the next few days will be chaotic once the mafia families arrive.

Everything is ready for their arrival. I only need to tell Victoria they're coming. The thought had slipped my mind. But now I have to tell her before she gets angry with me for keeping her in the dark again. I only hope she doesn't hit me in the head with a shoe for not telling her sooner.

I laugh at the thought.

Like my mother, Victoria is gentle and fierce when she needs to be—a perfect combination of the two.

There's a sharp jab to my chest because the two won't get to meet.

"Leo, what's wrong?" Victoria says, now awake. Her eyes flash with worry as she grabs my face between her hands.

"It's nothing. I was thinking, that's all."

Victoria frowns.

"Leo, you can tell me if anything is bothering you, and I'll always listen." She offers me a gentle smile, and my heart skips a beat at how beautiful she is, both on the inside and on the outside. It's always the little things she does that make me fall in love with her even more.

I bring her to my chest.

"Thank you for everything. I don't know what I did to deserve you." I draw back and tilt her chin, kissing her lips softly.

She sighs as our lips dance in sync, moving in a perfect symphony of passion. When her lips aren't enough, my mouth runs down her neck, pressing open-mouth kisses over the skin. Her little pants bring a rush of heat down my spine.

"Victoria—oh shit, sorry!" Sofia shrieks, and Victoria draws back in surprise.

I groan in annoyance at having Sofia interrupt us *again*, and my eyes remain focused on a flustered Victoria. Her swollen lips tempt me into taking them against my mouth one last time. There's another rapid knock coming from the door.

"Leo, I need my cousin," Sofia shouts. "Now!"

"This better not become a regular thing," I grumble, climbing out of bed and pulling Victoria with me.

She arches a brow and tilts her head to the side.

"What?" There's confusion in her voice, and I bite back my smile at how innocent she is.

"This whole thing," I say, pointing between us and the door where Sofia is knocking. "These people interrupting us better not become a regular thing, or I'll kick them all out of this house."

Victoria laughs, and I can't help but stare in awe at how perfect she is.

Her cheeks flush red when she notices my heated gaze, and she bites her bottom lip. I draw it out from between her teeth with my thumb.

"If you keep doing that, I won't be able to keep myself away from you," I say, and her eyes widen in surprise at the sound of my desire. Before she can say anything, there's another knock on the door.

"You have got to be kidding me." I sigh, frustrated.

"I'll be right back," she says, making her way to the door. The second she opens it, Sofia pulls her outside, and she gasps from the sudden tug. I can hear their conversation because Sofia doesn't know how to talk low.

"Ou girl, you're in trouble," Sofia scolds.

"What do you mean?"

"Your parents are mad because you haven't called them in almost a week!"

"Oh no, I'm dead," Victoria groans, and I grimace, feeling guilty for not reaching out to her parents personally. As the two continue to talk, I get ready for the day and make a mental note to call her parents.

When I enter the bedroom again, I find Victoria on the phone, and she looks stressed. I approach her and kiss her temple before peeling the phone from her hands.

"Victoria, I warned you to call me once in a while, and what do you do?" Her mother scolds me, assuming I'm Victoria.

"Hello, Mrs. Rodríguez," I greet, and she stops her rant.

"Oh, Leo honey, hello." Her voice has taken on a softer tenor, and I want to laugh at the complete change in demeanor. "How have you been?" she asks sweetly.

"I'm doing good," I respond. "I want to apologize for having Victoria go MIA for some time, but we had a good reason for it."

Victoria looks at me with her forehead bunched in confusion. I smooth out the worry lines that have risen on her forehead.

"We wanted to make sure Adriano wasn't listening in on your conversations with Victoria." When I say this, a mixture of disbelief and gratitude takes over Victoria's features.

Maria's quiet for a second.

"That makes sense, I guess." There's a gasp over the line. "I hope I didn't put anyone in danger by calling!"

"No, it's fine now. You can call whenever," I add, trying to ease her panic. "I'll pass the phone back to Victoria. Goodbye, Mrs. Rodríguez." I'm about to hand Victoria the phone when her mom calls my name.

"Leo, you can call me Maria," she insists before continuing in a melancholic voice. "How is she adjusting?"

"She's doing fine. Anytime you and your family are missing her, please use my private jet to visit. I'll send you the number of my pilot."

"Thank you Leo. We might take that offer soon."

I bid her goodbye once more and hand Victoria her phone.

"You are a lifesaver," Victoria says, pressing a kiss to my cheek, and I smile, taking a seat on the couch in the room.

I wait for Victoria to finish her call to tell her about our upcoming guests. But while waiting, I fall asleep, and I only wake up when Victoria places a hand on my cheek. I pull her onto my lap, and a small shiver moves through her body.

"How do you feel about having guests over next week?"

"What do you mean?" she says, her right brow lifted, and her eyes look at me suspiciously.

"Amore, it's time you meet the mafia princes and princesses."

VICTORIA

"I'm sorry, who?" I blink through my apprehension.

"Did I not tell you they call me the mafia king?" Leo places a finger under his chin.

"No, you didn't." Hearing my accusing tone, Leo grimaces.

"I swear I thought I did?" he says under his breath, giving me a sheepish smile when he sees my glare.

"Leo, what are you talking about? What is all this fairytale nonsense?" I say, my voice dripping with exasperation.

"This will take some time to explain, so get comfortable."

I heave a breath and move to sit beside him on the couch, but he pulls me back onto his lap.

"Leo, you told me to get comfortable."

"Yes, on my lap. Now sit and listen."

"Fine." I sigh, giving up and wiggling on his lap to get comfortable. When I do this, his grip around my waist tightens, and he stiffens under me.

I let out another annoyed breath.

"Now what?" I grumble, turning to see his lips pressed into a tight line and his face screwed with pain.

"You drive *us* insane," he breathes, his eyes glancing down. I follow the gesture, and my eyes widen in surprise when something hard pokes between my thighs.

"Leo, stop being such a tease," I breathe, and he gives a sly grin. "Wipe that grin off your face and explain why they call you the mafia king." My voice is firm, letting him know he's going to explain everything to me and we won't be getting distracted this time.

"It's stupid, but Alexander and Lei insisted on the titles, and I agreed with them because who doesn't want to be called the mafia king?" Amusement enters his eyes briefly before it disappears, and he turns serious again. "What do you know about the mafia?" he asks me, and a smile creeps across my face.

"Only that it's filled with irritating alpha males who have a lot of *family issues*." My mouth splits into a wide grin when I see his displeased expression at my comment. But I'm not lying. This is the truth.

"Fair enough," he says, shrugging his shoulders in defeat.

"Well, because of these family issues..." He pokes at my side, and I stifle my laugh. "In the past, my great-grandfather joined the top five mafias in an alliance to ensure peace."

"An alliance?" I whisper to myself, and Leo nods.

"It's an alliance that makes sure none of us becomes greedy."

"I see..." I hum, soaking in his words.

"My family created this structure after war broke out between the families. To make a long story short, their feuds with one another destroyed their mafias. Fortunately, my family helped get them back to the top. That's why we hold the leading position as mafia king and queen. Our role in creating the successful alliance and our impeccable trust and wealth made it an obvious pick for us to be in charge."

"Wait, did you say there's a mafia king and a queen?"

"You heard correctly, my mafia queen." Leo grins, and I don't know what to say to such a title. He studies my reaction as I try to process what he's told me, but I can't quite wrap my mind around what he's saying. It's as if my life has taken a turn toward fairytale land, and I'm not sure what to think.

"As mafia king, does this mean you control their mafias?" I ask, trying to understand how powerful he is.

His features soften when he notices how overwhelmed I am.

"I don't control their mafias. I only make sure they follow the protocols stated in the alliance. Over the years, they grew to look to us as an example."

"Which mafia families are part of the alliance?" I ask, eager to learn more.

"There are a few small mafias worldwide. But none are as powerful as the families that make up the alliance. The families include Alejandro Martinez. He runs the mafia in Cuba. Alexander Knight runs the mafia in America. Lei Shein runs his family's mafia in China, and Arthuro Petrovo runs the biggest mafia in Russia."

"And the princesses?"

"They are their partners, except for Chloe. She's Lei's twin sister." Leo places a strand of my hair behind my ear, his eyes not wavering from mine. "Any more questions?"

"I have so many," I breathe.

"It's okay, amore. Ask away."

Shoot, he doesn't have to ask me twice! Very quickly, one question after another arises until I find myself asking them with the intent of understanding everything that Leo does.

"Do the mafia princesses need to be married to their partners for the title?" I ask, nervous about finding out the answer because I'm not married to Leo, yet he called me his queen.

"No, only Alejandro is married. He and his wife Layla are also the oldest."

I nod in understanding, feeling much better, knowing the girls are less likely to call me a hypocrite.

"What about the Italian mafia structure? How does that work?"

"It's a complex structure, but I'll try to give you the basics. I don't want to overwhelm you more than you already are," Leo adds lightly. "You already know what I do. But I don't do it alone. Some other more important roles in our mafia include my underboss. I also have three capos who oversee a section of soldiers who are the ones who do the dirty work for us."

I give a simple hum, assuring him I'm still following.

"Francisco is my underboss. He takes over for me in case something happens to me. Luca, Kaden, and Angelo are my capos."

From hearing Leo has a replacement, a chill spans through my bones.

He places a hand on my right cheek and is about to ask me what's wrong when I cut him off with another question. I don't want to talk about the possibility of him dying or going to jail. It will only upset me more.

"Leo, why are the mafia families coming?"

He sighs deeply, and his forehead carves with faint worry lines. I run my hand down his jaw to ease the tension building inside him.

"You know Adriano wants war. He wants to take over, and he has been recruiting some of our rival gangs to his side. We need to gather to create a plan to stop him."

"Why does he hate you so much?" There's a delicate waver behind my words, and it reveals fear and frustration in knowing my life and the life of the man I love are in danger.

"It's a long story...Do you want to hear it?" Leo says in a level tone. His face looks haunted as he says this.

"Yes, but only if you want to tell me. I can sense your anger and distress," I say, cupping his face in my hands, and his eyes gloss with an unknown emotion so raw that my stomach flutters when his over-whelming stare full of devotion, warmth, and care kisses my face.

"I want to tell you, and it's only fair, considering my family problems have now put you in danger."

I swallow hard and watch as Leo's vulnerability reveals itself to me as he tells me about his past.

42

NARRATOR

Leonardo Bandoni stares at his twin sons.

They are way past the age of knowing who will take over the family business. He's waited as long as possible to avoid the conflict his decision will bring. But he can no longer hold off on naming his heir.

The elder Italian Don leans into his chair. His eyes move from one son to the next.

The oldest twin, Marquez, grins, confident his father will choose him.

Anyone can see he craves the power and respect that comes with being Don.

Marquez's eyes flicker like greedy flames as he looks around the room. He notes what he wants to change when it becomes his.

He's so close to getting what he worked hard for. The power is seeping out of his father like a diffuser, flowing straight into him.

Beside Marquez, Estephano Bandoni sits tense.

Estephano knows Marquez is more cruel, stronger, and bolder than him. His brother also gave their father less trouble. There's no denying that, as of late, he's been careless. But Leonardo understands Estephano's recklessness was the fault of the sweet drunkenness of love.

The Bandoni men love hard, and Estephano is no exception. Marquez, on the other hand, didn't love anyone.

Estephano waits for his father's decision. He wants to get this over with so he can return to his wife. He didn't care about the title, but he also wasn't an idiot and knew that if Marquez became Don, he would ruin the peace amidst the mafia alliance. His father is also aware of this, which is why it's been difficult for him to figure out which of his two sons he will make his heir.

Everyone is counting on Leonardo to make the best decision for their mafia.

Who will it be? The drunken in love fool Estephano or the drunken with power lust Marquez. The options are not in their favor.

Leonardo clears his throat. His forehead wrinkles as his eyes dart between his two sons.

"As you both know, only one of you may become Don." His voice takes on a firmer tone. "I don't want this decision to cause a split in your relationship with one another." Leonardo's stare falls on Marquez, who's notorious for getting into fights over the littlest things.

"Yes, sir," the young Bandoni men say in unison.

"Marquez, you have shown excellent fighting skills and have every-thing a mafia leader needs to have—"

Marquez straightens in his seat, and a wide grin rises on his stiff lips. But as quickly as it's there, it falls, and his anger surges, ready to erupt with its hostile venom.

"But you lack the charisma and honesty of a genuine leader. Which will not work as a peacekeeper for the alliance." Marquez's hands tremble with rage, and a muscle clenches in his jaw as he sits stunned.

Leonardo turns to Estephano, who, despite the trouble he's caused, has shown ambition like a genuine leader.

"Estephano, my boy, you're kindhearted. But you also know when to be tough, but not tough enough." Leonardo sighs deeply, looking at a raging Marquez from the corner of his eye.

"Estephano, you hold the attributes of a leader and have shown me you will fight for what you want." After many years of struggling to say the words, he lets them out. "Estephano, I am naming you my heir and future Don of the Bandoni famiglia." Leonardo hands his son the gold ring with the dark red ruby, which he wore next to his wedding ring.

Wide-eyed, Estephano looks at the red gem glistening under the bright lights of the room. He swallows down his shock and slowly takes the ring from his father.

Like daggers, a sharp sound comes from Marquez.

"This is bullshit!" He rises, and the chair almost falls to the floor. "Father, I'm the oldest," argues Marquez.

Leonardo rises from his seat.

"Marquez, sit down!" Leonardo's words come out deadly, and even Marquez can't disregard the warning in his father's voice.

"You have proven to me you are unfit to hold any position of power." As soon as Leonardo says this, Marquez combusts in a fit of fiery rage. He throws a right hook toward his father's face, but before his fist can land its blow, Estephano rises, grabs Marquez's hand, and twists it.

A left hook from Estephano lands on Marquez's jaw. His punch is answered with one of Marquez's own forceful hits.

The twins throw repeated punches at each other. Their bodies slam into walls and create dents.

Leonardo's men run into the room when they hear the resounding clash of fists hitting flesh. The twins mother, Melanie, who has been listening from behind the door with her daughters-in-law, rushes in to see the conflict.

She cries, begging her sons to stop fighting. Meanwhile, Marquez's fiancé, Emily, stands by the door. Her eyes flash green with jealousy as she looks at Stephanie, who comforts Melanie.

Stephanie's soft hazel eyes glance between the twins, and although the men are identical in every physical essence, they are different inside.

Estephano's black eye and bleeding nose bring a weight to Stephanie's chest, and her fingers itch to hold him, but she restrains herself, knowing this isn't the right time to be affectionate.

The twins are separated, and Leonardo looks at Marquez with disappointment.

"Marquez, I want you to respect my decision, and if you refuse..."

Leonardo turns to his wife, knowing his next words will break her heart. But they have to be said. "I want you out of my house!"

Melanie weeps loudly, and Stephanie holds onto the brokenhearted mother.

Estephano looks at his brother, waiting to hear what he has to say. He doesn't want their relationship to be ruined over a title, but this decision wasn't his to make.

"I'm leaving, fuck you all!" Marquez shouts, storming out of the room. He grabs Emily, and the power duo made to destroy disappear.

Estephano stares in disbelief at his brother's retreating figure. The clamor of men in the room and his father's loud remark brings him out of his daze.

"Everyone welcome the new Don of the Italian Mafia!" Leonardo boasts amidst the awkward tension.

The mood in the room changes, and everyone celebrates, ready to spread the word to the rest of the members and mafia families worldwide.

Leonardo glances at his wife, who's weeping. Inside her is a fierce determination to mend the broken pieces of her family.

With Stephanie in his arms, Estephano promises to fix his relationship with his brother. He's going to do so by allowing Marquez to be his underboss. Deep down, he hopes the good in his brother still exists. He'd help his brother prove their father wrong. That Marquez *can* hold a position of power.

Like his mother, Estephano is determined to mend the scar marked by the conflict of their father's decision because family meant everything to him.

Estephano throws his head back in laughter after a joke Marquez makes.

Ten years after their big fight, their relationship couldn't have been better.

The two already have their own families.

Estephano and his wife, Stephanie, have two children and one on the way.

Their first child is a son, the destined heir to the Bandoni mafia. Ten-year-old Leo Bandoni, named after his late grandfather, is a force not to be reckoned with.

A smile stretches across Estephano's mouth as he recalls his ten-year-old son's determination to rule like him.

Cleo comes to mind, and his heart softens at the thought of his principessa. The five-year-old has him wrapped around her tiny finger.

As for his wife, she has aged beautifully.

Stephanie Bandoni is a woman of grace—a ray of sunshine in a world of darkness.

Estephano's eyes fall on his laughing brother, and he wonders how he tolerated his wife. The woman made Estephano's blood boil anytime she spoke a single word.

Emily is a gold digger and a total joke around the house. She'd jump on anything with a pulse and a dick so long as she got diamonds in return. Meanwhile, her nine-year-old son, Adriano, wonders where his parents are all day.

The door to Estephano's office opens, and a beautiful nine-month pregnant Stephanie reveals herself. Her golden brown locks hang around her oval-shaped face like a fine, silky drape.

"Amore," Estephano greets, grabbing her soft hand in his. "How is he behaving?" Estephano asks, rubbing her swollen belly.

Stephanie places her hand over his.

"He's been kicking all day," she confesses, blowing a tired breath. Her gaze momentarily falls on Marquez. She trembles when he gives her a sinister smirk.

Marquez is a manipulator. He has convinced Estephano that he is no longer angry about their father's decision. But she knows this is all a bunch of lies. Marquez is still bitter from the past. But it's been difficult for her to reveal Marquez's ill intentions.

Annoyed at the sight of the lovers, Marquez slides out of his chair with a slight sneer, and the two lovebirds don't notice.

"I'm going to go. Emily wants me to take her out for dinner," he exclaims, making his way toward the exit, all while trying to hold in his distaste.

The door closes behind Marquez, and Stephanie reveals her discomfort with him living under the same roof as her children.

"Estephano, do you not see the anger your brother holds against you?" says Stephanie, hoping her husband will hear her silent cries for help. "When will you stop turning your cheek when he challenges your leadership?"

Estephano sighs, hearing the frustration in his wife's voice.

"Open your eyes before he hurts you or the kids. I can't lose any of you," she cries, almost telling him everything she's been harboring in her heart.

Estephano frowns, wiping his wife's tears. He's never seen her this scared.

"Amore, nothing will—"

The door to the study opens, and their two children come into sight.

When Leo sees his mother's tears, he runs to her and wraps his arms around her waist. He buries his head into her blue dress.

"Mamma, what's the matter?" Leo's face scrunches into worry, and his tiny fists ball together, ready to hurt whoever has made his mother cry.

Stephanie places a kiss on top of her son's head and smiles at him in adoration.

"Nothing, bambino," she assures, tapping a finger on his nose, making him scrunch it in annoyance.

"Father and I won't let anyone hurt you or Cleo," Leo says, wrapping a protective arm around his sister.

Estephano chuckles at Leo's determination, and he can feel the power of a leader emitting from his tiny body.

He's going to be a great leader one day. Estephano thinks with a sense of pride.

Leo's smile falters into a frown when he remembers why he came to his parents.

"Papà, Adriano has been acting differently."

Estephano's forehead furrows.

"What do you mean, son?"

"He keeps saying how his Papà should be Don and how he will beat me up."

Stephanie lifts her brows with a tilt of the head toward her husband, who begins to see reason in her previous concerns.

"What else, son?" Estephano edges Leo to continue after sensing there's more to the story when he sees Cleo's teary eyes.

"He tried to hit Cleo a few minutes ago. But I pushed him away," Leo says, clutching his little sister's hand. Cleo's bottom lip quivers, and she has tears once more brimming her eyes.

Estephano exhales deeply, realizing he and his brother have to talk later tonight. His wife is right. He has to confront Marquez. What kind of leader would he be if he tolerated disrespect from his own brother? No one gets special treatment in the mafia. Either you respect the boss and family, or you're out.

Later that night, Estephano gets ready to talk with his brother when he's stopped by one of his capos. There's been confusion with a shipment about to head to Russia, which needs his immediate attention.

Estephano sighs in frustration and heads toward his car to go to the port to settle the issue. His conversation with his brother will have to wait.

When he returns home, it's already two in the morning, and Estephano heads toward his room, deciding he will confront his brother tomorrow.

When he enters his bedroom, he sees his children sitting in a pool of blood. A hollowness drowns him when he sees Leo clutching Stephanie's lifeless body for dear life.

Her blood trickles across the floorboards, and it reaches his feet.

Estephano is used to the smell of death. It never bothered him, but right now, the smell of his wife's blood brings a chill down his spine.

His knees buckle under him, and he has to hold on to the door. The sinking of his heart has stabbed him with cold, cold grief.

Fast, desperate steps carry him to what remains of the love of his life. The floor boards cry when he falls to his knees, cradling her limp body. Her skin is ghostly white, and she's as cold as ice. The baby in her stomach no longer moves. Blood is oozing out of her stomach, and a massive hole has torn through her delicate skin. Her sweet smell of roses has become masked by the smell of death.

"No! No! No! Don't do this to me. Amore." His wails are soaked with anguish, and his pain dunks him in coldness. "You can't leave me."

He rocks her in his arms and closes his eyes, unable to stand the sight of her lifeless body.

"Come back to me," Estephano says in a broken whisper as he runs his fingers through her hair. When he realizes he has failed at protecting her, the broken pieces of his heart turn to dust.

He looks at his two children, and his eyes soften at the sight of Cleo with her knees to her chest. Slow tears trickle down her chubby cheeks.

His eyes land on his colorless son.

"What happened?"

Leo is stuck in a trance of grief, and doesn't hear his father.

"Leo!" Sadness and anger mingle in Estephano's voice.

Leo swipes at the blood running down the right side of his face from the gash he got when the butt of his uncle's gun lashed at his temple. With heavy eyes, Leo looks at his father with sadness and guilt.

He blames himself for not protecting his mother as he promised he would. The tears rush down his cheeks like an angry waterfall during a storm. There's a thundering pain inside his head, and it won't stop crashing inside him.

The memory of a few minutes ago returns to torment him.

Leo explains to his father what happened through sobs.

He details how he woke up to his mother's screams and ran into the room to see his uncle choking her against the wall.

As soon as he saw this, Leo ran to his uncle and kicked him between the legs.

Upon seeing him, Marquez hit Leo on the temple with his gun and picked the boy by the throat, throwing him into the wall across the room.

Marquez had smiled maliciously at Leo, and he was ready to shoot him when Stephanie jumped in front of the bullet, and *it happened again. A mother took a bullet for her child. The past repeated itself, and fate sat back and laughed at its doings.*

The sound of Stephanie's scream and the gunshot rang in the dead of night, waking everyone up.

Leo presses his hands against the wound, but it's too big for his hands to cover. Her blood paints his fingers and palms crimson, staining them red for the rest of his life. The stench of an overdue death lingers thick in the air.

"Awe, poor Stephanie, always wanting to be selfish," Marquez mocks, leaving the room. On his way out, he pats Cleo's head with the barrel of his gun.

She recoils from the monster she calls her uncle.

"Say bye to mommy Cleo." Marquez pushes her, and she falls onto her knees, burning the soft flesh on the hardwood floor. She whimpers. Her small doe eyes glance from her mother to the blood painting her trembling hands.

Stephanie caresses her children's teary faces, and her tears fall when she realizes she won't get to say goodbye to Estephano.

"Don't cry." Her words are a whisper, but her children hear her loud and clear. "I love you both, but our time together has ended." She winces in pain when the bullet burns her insides. The baby inside her stomach is motionless after taking the bullet.

Leo shakes his head, unwilling to accept his mother's words.

"No, Mamma." His voice trembles. "You can't leave us." Cleo nods, unable to form any words.

"I will always be with you in here," Stephanie says, placing her bloody hand on Leo's heart. "And here," she says, tapping Cleo's temple.

"I don't want you to leave," Leo chokes out. "Mamma, please stay." He clutches onto his mother's body, afraid of letting her go. He knows if he does, she will take her last breath, and he will lose her forever. But even with him holding her, she closes her eyes, and the last thing on her mind is her husband and children.

Stephanie takes her last breath, and her body falls limp in Leo's arms.

The children let out broken cries, and a deep hole forms in Leo's chest. It fills him with anger, hatred, and grief.

Estephano weeps as he listens to his son explain what happened, and rage consumes him until it becomes him.

His wife warned him, but he was too late, and now his brother has taken his world and crushed it without remorse.

He places one last kiss on Stephanie's cold cheek. His lips tremble, and his tears land on her face.

People have now gathered by the door after hearing the deadly gunshot.

Estephano rises, and approaches his motionless mother, whose face has gone white from horror.

Mother and son exchange no words. Their eyes do all the talking, and all sympathy for Marquez has disappeared from inside Melanie.

Marquez has committed a sin no mother can forgive.

Estephano walks toward his brother's room, ready to take revenge. He enters the room to find Emily packing her bags with a smile.

At the sound of the door opening behind her, she looks at him. Her face reveals fear, as she didn't expect him so soon. They were supposed to be distracting him back at the port.

Estephano pulls his gun out, pointing it at her, his eyes full of hatred.

"Where's Marquez?" he shouts, and she cowers in fear, only for her coral-red lips to turn up when a gun clicks from behind Estephano.

"Turn around, brother."

Hearing his voice, Estephano turns in anger, and both twins are now pointing their guns at one another.

Marquez grins when he sees Estephano's teary eyes.

Emily continues to pack her bags while her son Adriano stands by the corner, filled with curiosity and worry at the sight of his father and uncle at gunpoint.

"Why?" Estephano's voice breaks.

Marquez scoffs.

"You know why... I was supposed to be Don, not you!" Marquez pushes the barrel of his gun into his brother's chest.

Estephano throws a swift blow to Marquez's face. The two break out into a fight.

Emily ignores them and continues to pack while Adriano looks at the two, afraid his father will get hurt.

The sound of a gun going off and the smell of burned metal makes Emily stop to see who received the blow. She sighs in relief when she sees Estephano's bleeding arm.

Marquez kicks Estephano's gun and shoots him in the leg, forcing Estephano onto his knees in front of him.

Estephano's tears fall as he only ever kneeled before one other person, and now she's gone.

"Say hello to Stephanie for me," Marquez mocks, ready to pull the trigger, and Estephano says nothing. He willingly gives himself to death when the grief of losing his wife dominates him. The pain of living without Stephanie is worse than the bullets in his body.

Estephano hears the rushing feet of his men. He ignores them and looks into his brother's eyes with a mixture of hatred and betrayal.

The blast of a gun cracks through the air, and Estephano's eyes widen in shock as his brother's head jerks forward—blood and tissue splattering his face.

Emily screams in horror, watching her husband's body fall to the ground, revealing young Leo with a gun.

Leo's face is void of any emotion, his eyes are cold, and his docile innocence has morphed into bitter anger. This is the beginning of a long list of the many deaths Leo Bandoni, the future Italian mafia Don, will take.

Adriano runs to his father, cradling his dead body. When he looks at his cousin, he fills with hatred, and prepares to launch himself at Leo, but his uncle grabs him from behind and throws him toward his grief-stricken mother.

"I want you both out of my fucking house in the next five minutes, and if you're not gone by then, I will shoot you both in the head!" Estephano shouts, wanting them to live with the grief he and his family now have to endure. They are now even.

Emily grabs her and Adriano's bags, rushing out of the room and down the stairs. When the two reach the front door, Adriano looks up to see Estephano and Leo embracing. His eyes harden, and he promises to avenge his father's death.

Marquez's darkness seeps into every crevice of Adriano's being.

Adriano is leaving for now, but he will be back, and when he returns, he will rain hell over Leo Bandoni. Marquez was gone, but this doesn't mean they are safe.

Leo Bandoni will crumble at Adriano's feet.

43

VICTORIA

The memory of Leo's mother's death flashes behind his eyes like a shadow of grief. His eyes are unfocused as the past takes over his thoughts. Even more heartbreaking is how they flicker with tears, which he's unwilling to let fall.

When I cradle him in my hands, he melts into my touch—the tough exterior surrounding him begins to crumble.

Leo takes a shallow breath, and we don't talk. The silence is one of grief, and my heart twists at the expression of self-loathing on his face.

"Leo, what happened to your mom isn't your fault."

A muscle in his jaw twitches, and he refuses to look at me.

"It is. I promised her I would protect her, and she's dead."

"You didn't pull the trigger," I say, and no words come from him. The only sign I get that he's still with me is his throat tightening as he swallows the pain.

"Please stop blaming yourself for the sins of others." My voice breaks, and the sound is enough to bring him back to me.

"I can't," he says in a broken whisper, and I know he means it.

Leo will always blame himself. In his heart, he sees himself as a failure. A man incapable of protecting his family has somehow translated itself into being weak. But what he needs to understand is that these weaknesses have the potential to strengthen us.

We are the ones who give our weaknesses power. Leo is allowing his weaknesses to torment him, and in doing so, he's blocking any possibility of healing from his past.

"Don't let your self-loathing become your weakness," I plead, and Leo frowns.

"Victoria, you are my weakness," he admits, caressing my cheek. "I love you so much. It hurts to think about losing you like I lost my mother." His grip on me tightens, and I let him hold me as I absorb his words. His confession echoes in my ears like a sweet melody.

"Leo, I love you too, you hot-tempered fool."

His mouth forms the slightest smile, and he takes my hand and puts it over his heart. I place his over mine, and his gaze doesn't waver from my face, and his stare is of the tenderest caress.

"You're both my weakness and my strength." Leo's lips fall onto my forehead, where he presses a feathery kiss. His lips trail to my left cheek, and he kisses me there before doing the same to my right cheek, and then my chin.

My eyes flutter, and I'm filled with pure bliss from his lips caressing my face. His heart beating against my palm is gentle.

"Everything I do is for you," he whispers, sealing his confession with a kiss on my lips.

His lips move perfectly against mine. Passion flickers inside me, sprouting like flowers in spring.

A harsh breath comes from me when he kisses the base of my neck. He gives a small bite to the skin, and a wave of pleasure spreads throughout my body. I feel a twitch of excitement in my lower half when he rises from the couch with me in his arms.

Leo lays me on the bed, and cages me between the mattress and his chest. His hand slides up my shirt, and his mouth presses kisses over the exposed skin of my chest.

His thick fingers toil with the clasp of my bra before switching courses and removing my shirt. He tosses the blouse to the side, leaving me in my jeans and black lace bra.

"Così fottutamento bella," he mutters. His touch is feathery as he trails a finger between the valley of my breasts and down my stomach.

I shiver, my skin exploding with the prickles of love.

Noticing he still has his shirt, I pull him by his tie. He stares wide-eyed at my aggressiveness as I work to remove the tie around his neck. He helps me unbutton his black dress shirt. His muscular chest is as smooth as oil against my touch.

I've seen him shirtless before, but now that it's only us, I can look at him, and my god, is he strong and chiseled. It should be a crime for him to hide his eight-pack and firm pecks under his wool dress shirts.

I'm stuck in a trance, and my feral desire cracks. I grab Leo's belt buckle and press our chests together. His hard abs press deliciously against my belly.

My mouth latches onto the base of his neck, and my tongue twirls over the sweet, salty skin.

Leo's groans flow out of his lips sinfully as I kiss over his chest and up his neck until I have his mouth against mine. His warm tongue plunges into my mouth, and his erection rubs against me. The friction brings a rhythmic pulsing in my clit.

The extra-large condoms I found the other day come to mind, and I let out a little moan, grinding myself into him. He responds with his own sounds of pleasure.

The throbbing heat of desire rises and rises and rises, but it's not enough; I want to go higher until I explode from a sweet, sensual bliss.

Leo senses my distress, and his fingers go to the clasp of my bra, ready to remove it. My hips rock against him, and he unclasps the first hook. The second comes undone, and when the third hook is about to burst, a knock sounds, followed by the door opening.

"Leo—"

My eyes flash open, and Leo tenses. Our grinding seizes.

"Oh shit!" Francisco curses in horror. The door slams behind him. "Sorry!"

Leo makes a low, frustrated sound as he pulls away from me, running a hand through his hair. He's looking at me hard, and his stare burns me with the flames of his desire.

His dark green eyes trail down to my chest, and they enlarge when they fall on my breasts.

I glance down at my heaving chest to see my right nipple peeking from the edge of the cup.

Leo groans and bends to cup my chin, ready to kiss me, and I know if he does, we won't be able to stop.

"Leo, what about Francisco?"

He sighs through his nose.

"Cock blocker," he grumbles, looking at the door and back at me. "Fine, but this isn't over," he says, kissing my lips one last time and heading toward the door.

"Aren't you forgetting something?" I say, lifting his shirt in my right hand.

Realization dawns upon Leo, and he heads toward me, grabbing his shirt from my hand and putting it on.

He kisses my forehead before leaving, and I hear him curse Francisco.

"Do that shit again, and I'll kick you out of my damn house. You and Sofia both."

Francisco laughs at Leo's threat, and I listen as their heavy footsteps fade with the distance.

It's the next day, and I'm still burning for Leo.

Whatever Francisco told him made him stay in his office, and he didn't return until late at night, when I was already asleep.

Today the mafia families are arriving, which makes me a nervous wreck.

They were mobsters and bound to be intimidating people.

Leo places butterfly kisses on the base of my neck.

"Leo, stop," I whine in a breathless whisper.

"Nope, you're too tempting." His mouth against my neck muffles his words, and he continues to kiss me. I surrender to his sweet touch and lean to the side to give him ample access.

Before our kiss gets more heated, I pull away from his touch.

"We need to get ready," I remind him, disappointment dripping from my words.

Leo buries his head into the nook of my shoulder and grumbles. Then he pulls away, gets out of bed, and lifts me over his shoulder. My black silk nightgown rises to expose the curve of my ass, and I try to cover myself with my right hand.

Leo laughs and pulls down the nightgown for me.

"Leo Bandoni, put me down!" I grumble, pounding my fist into his bare back.

We enter the closet, and he sets me back on my two feet.

"Happy?" he says, and a grin broadens his expression.

"Very," I respond, heading toward my clothes to pick an outfit.

When I finish getting ready, Leo makes his way out of the closet wearing a fitted black suit. The collar of his white dress shirt is undone, and he has his black tie in his right hand.

"You look beautiful. As always," he says, his eyes roaming my exposed legs before trailing up to see me in a tight black skirt and white silk top.

Turning in his arms, I grab the tie from his fingers and wrap it around his neck, bringing him to my level.

"You look handsome. As always," I breathe while adjusting the collar of his dress shirt. Leo looks at me as I fiddle with his tie, and when he sees me struggling, he guides me through the task. I admire the way his forehead creases when he concentrates while looping the tie.

Leo looks at me and sees me staring at him. The corner of his mouth tips up, and a tiny dimple reveals itself.

Rising to my tippy toes, I press our lips together, and he is more than happy to accept my touch. We're forced to pull apart when there's a soft knock coming from the bedroom door.

Leo sighs.

"I'll get it. You finish getting ready," I tell him, running my fingers through his ruffled hair. As I walk away, I can feel him staring at my backside.

I open the door, and I'm greeted by Francisco. He wears a navy suit, and his dark blond hair is gelled to the side.

"Good morning," I chirp, and he smiles.

"The guest should be here in the next few minutes." As he says this, he glances behind me toward Leo.

"Alright, we'll be down in a minute," Leo says, wrapping an arm around my waist, and Francisco walks away.

"Let's go, amore." Leo interlocks our fingers, and we follow Francisco.

As we reach the top of the stairs, my heart hammers in my chest, and I stop in my tracks, feeling intimidated.

"What's wrong?" Leo asks in a soft voice. My breath turns shallow when I peek at the front door. Leo tilts my chin, and his eyes are aligned with worry.

"I'm nervous," I say, and Leo's arm around me tightens, and he brings me into his chest.

"They will love you, and if any of them gives you a hard time, you tell me, and I'll deal with them personally." In his voice is the presence of an unyielding rage brought forth by the thought of anyone hurting me.

"Leo, I can fight my own battles."

The last thing I wanted was for them to say I'm a crybaby who has her boyfriend kill her bullies.

"I know you can. But it doesn't matter because I will always protect you, no matter how strong you are."

The sound of cars pulling up in the driveway has my heart jumping. Leo squeezes my hand, and we descend the stairs until we stand in the middle of the foyer.

To distract myself from the nervousness brewing inside, I focus on the design of the lion with the crown. A cold sweat gathers from the memory of the mutilated lion Adriano sent a few nights ago.

As if sensing my distress, Leo presses me close to his side.

"I'm right here, amore." I take my eyes off the design and nod absently, eyes glued to the front door now opening, revealing the first couple.

My throat tightens at the sight of them.

When I inhale Leo's musk scent, a speck of my worry eases, and my spine shoots straight. I muster some courage and put on a smile to conceal how terrified I am on the inside.

Upon seeing me, the olive-skinned woman's face lights up. Her cheeks curve into a beaming smile, and her shoulders rise from her excitement.

The woman rushing toward me is gorgeous and easily six feet tall. Her shoulder-length brown hair is in voluminous curls. They bounce with each step.

She pulls her partner forward, and he almost trips over his brown leather point shoes from how fast she's walking. And although she walks fast across the foyer, she walks with grace. She carries herself with her shoulders held high, and her legs cross over one another as if she's walking along a runway.

My eyes travel to the muscular arm wrapped around her waist. The man's black eyes look from me to Leo, with a grin adorning his five o'clock shadow. His already chiseled jaw becomes more defined when the muscles around his mouth stretch from his teasing expression.

As I take in the perfect pair, I find there's a strikingness to their features. It's almost as if they walked out of a magazine.

The pretty woman embraces me in a tight hug, and I'm taken aback by her friendliness.

"Oh, aren't you gorgeous!" she compliments, her face and dark, ocean-blue eyes glow with excitement.

"Hello, I'm Victoria," I say, my cheeks turning warm from her staring at me with intense admiration.

"Hi, I'm Emma," she says in a thick Brooklyn accent before pulling her partner aside and introducing him to me.

"This is my boyfriend, Alexander." The man shaking Leo's hand turns to me, and a strand of his chestnut brown hair falls out of its slick back hairstyle.

He gives me a friendly smile and grabs my hand, pressing a kiss to the top.

"Pleasure to meet you," he says, looking at Leo, and his head tips in approval. Leo rolls his eyes.

Strong footfalls come from the entrance to announce the power couple now heading our way. Their expressions are tight, and they carry themselves with an aura that screams, *don't mess with us.*

The two are as stoic as machines and align with what I imagined a mafia couple to look like. *Powerful.*

Emma places a gentle hand on my arm. She gives me an assuring smile, sensing my uneasiness.

As the new couple approaches, Emma and Alexander greet them before entering the living room.

I stare at the woman with dark blond, almost silver hair, and I feel like a child in front of her, even though she can't be more than two years older than me.

The woman with chiseled features is almost as tall as her partner, and I have to crane my neck to look into her eyes. The moment our eyes lock, her electric blue eyes soften, and her thin lips tip up into a smile. The man with her remains stoic.

He seems like a man of few words.

I take in his towering height, and like Leo and Alexander, he has dark brown hair, but his is cut short. This man also has high cheek-bones, a well-trimmed stubble, muscular arms, and broad shoulders.

His dark eyes pierce my own, and there's curiosity behind his gaze.

Leo notices my discomfort from the man's intense stare, and his hand on my left hip caresses the area. His touch brings me comfort.

"Arthuro, Nora," Leo greets, shaking the couple's hands.

"Nice to see you, Leo," Arthuro greets, and Nora smiles. The two then look at me.

"This is my girlfriend, Victoria," Leo says with pride. "Victoria, this is Arthuro and Nora. They run the mafia in Russia," Leo explains, and I give a tentative smile at the couple. I shake Arthuro's hand, and he stuns me when he smiles.

Nora brings me into a bone-crushing hug.

"It's so nice to meet you, Victoria," she says with a bite of a smile on her lips. Her attention lands on Leo before falling back on me. "Your beauty explains how you could tame the heartless Leo here."

"I don't only love her for her looks, Nora," Leo says, his eyes not wavering from mine, and his words ignite a spark of warmth that radiates from the back of my neck.

Nora grins at Leo's response. His words have satisfied her, judging by the curt nod she gives.

"Come find me after meeting the others. I can tell we're going to be great friends." She squeezes my shoulders in a hug, and I assure her I will see her in a little. The two make their way into the living room, where Alexander and Emma are conversing with Francisco and Sofia.

"She's nice." Leo nods, pleased to see my fear from earlier has evaporated.

A voice filled with excitement and warmth beams at us.

"Hay, mira que bonitos se ven Alejandro!" A woman squeals, her nude heels on the marble floor click as she tries to reach us in fast strides.

I smile at the pretty older woman, and the corners of her full lips tug up while her brown eyes glow like flecks of gold.

"Gracias," I say, and the woman with golden-brown hair squeals and pinches my cheeks.

"Y entiende Español, que preciosa," she coos and kisses my cheeks. She then embraces Leo and is gently pulled into the arms of a rugged-looking older man.

"Sorry, she gets excited when meeting new people, don't you, mi amor?" The muscular man says, his dark brown eyes gleaming with love for the woman in his arms. She pouts in annoyance and slaps him on the chest, which prompts the man to let out a rumble of laughter.

"Alejandro, Layla, welcome," Leo greets the couple, who look no older than thirty-five. "This is my girlfriend, Victoria."

"Hola, mija!" Layla's brown eyes beam with warmth. "Are you from Latin America too?" she asks after my accent and brown skin have piqued her curiosity.

"I was born and raised in the United States, but my parents are from Mexico," I explain, and Layla nods as she looks between Leo and me.

"Alejandro, isn't she perfect for Leo!"

The man nods.

"I might even say she's too good for little Leo here," Alejandro ridicules, patting a scowling Leo on the shoulder.

"There's nothing little about me, old man," retorts Leo, and I press my lips together to hold in my laughter.

"The best of the best is here!" says an unfamiliar voice behind Layla and Alejandro.

We all turn to see a towering, built with muscles Asian man walking through the door. His thin lips are set into a smirk, and a pretty Asian girl walks close behind him. Her eyes are sending daggers at the man's back.

"Shut up, Lei!" she hisses, punching his right forearm, which is littered with tattoos. "No one thinks that," she says, striding past him and coming toward us with a smile on her red-tinted, heart-shaped lips.

"I'm sorry about his cockiness," she apologizes, putting a strand of her shoulder-length black hair behind her ear.

Layla greets the two before she and Alejandro leave for the living room.

Her small hand stretches out in front of me.

"Hi, I'm Chloe, and the dumbass behind me is, unfortunately, my twin brother Lei."

"Nice to meet you. I'm Victoria," I greet, grabbing her hand, and she pulls me into a tight hug.

"Woah, Leo, is this your girl?" Lei whistles lowly, giving me elevator eyes. "She's a real hottie," he says with a smirk. Lei grabs my hand and presses a slow kiss to the top.

"Yes, and she's mine, so back the fuck off." Leo warns, pulling me into his arms and away from Lei.

"Leo, be nice to our guests," I tease, and he huffs in disapproval.

"Welcome, Chloe," Leo says, ignoring a laughing Lei. "I don't know how you can handle him."

"I ignore him," Chloe replies, and Lei's mouth falls open in disbelief as if saying, *'I'm right here.'*

There's a roar of laughter from the side, and Leo glances toward the noise.

"Shall we?" He offers me his hand, and I let him take me to where the rest of our guests are waiting.

Chloe and Lei follow us, the two arguing. I have to stifle my laughter when I hear a slap followed by Lei's cries of pain.

Emma approaches me and links an arm around mine.

"This gathering is going to be a memorable one," she whispers, and I can't help but agree with her.

I feel both excited and nervous when the girls make their way toward me with the biggest smiles.

Yes, it will be.

44

VICTORIA

I sit nervously with the girls. They all stare at me with warm eyes and a smile. They are holding back their excitement, waiting for me to speak first.

I try to talk, but no words want to come out.

I was never good at making friends, unlike my extrovert cousin Sofia. She isn't here now. She's preparing for her date with Francisco. Cleo is with her for support, and the men left an hour ago to discuss the situation with Adriano. Which means it's only me and the girls.

Emma senses my uneasiness and turns to me, her smile not once wavering.

"Tell us about yourself," she inquires.

"Well, I'm from Southern California, and I'm nineteen," I say, growing nervous when a mischievous grin spreads across Nora's face.

"Since you're old enough, have you and Leo..." Nora lifts her hands to her mouth and makes sexual gestures.

My mouth falls open, and heat rushes to my cheeks. The girls laugh at my reaction.

"Nora, I don't think they have, by the look of horror on her face." This time, it's Layla who speaks, and she sends me a warm smile, assuring me there's nothing I need to be embarrassed about.

"No way you guys haven't had sex yet!" Chloe blurts in disbelief.

I hold my breath, my ears turning hot from having such an intimate conversation with people I met four hours ago. But, if I'm being honest, I don't mind. I've needed to vent to someone about my feelings.

Sure, I have Cleo and Sofia, but I can't talk to Cleo about her brother, at least not about certain topics. And Sofia, I can't tell her anything, or she'll make the rest of my life a living hell with her teasing remarks.

"It's true," I confess, and they all stare at me with wide mouths.

"Shut up!" Emma exclaims in disbelief. "How long have you two known each other?"

Her question prompts my lips to line into a smile as I remember my time spent with Leo in France.

"About three, maybe four months." I pause, debating whether to tell them how we met. When I see their excitement in wanting to get to know me, I'm unable to control myself from telling them. Talking to them is easy once our conversation has started.

"He saved me from Adriano." Fear rises from the memory of my kidnapping, but I don't show it. I keep my voice flat and my face void of the pain I feel from what I saw and what they did to me.

The room grows silent; the girls become stiff, and a sense of melancholy is in the air.

"I'm okay. It's all in the past now," I assure them when a frown takes over their beaming smiles.

"I could tell you were strong when I first met you a few moments ago," Emma says, grabbing my hand. "I'm glad Leo found you, Victoria. You two are perfect for each other. Everyone knows Leo needed someone like you to brighten the darkness in his life." She sighs, her eyebrows bunching together.

"From what I have seen, being in charge of a mafia isn't easy," she says, and her comment has hit close to home from the look of defeat marking all their faces.

As I take in the girls, I marvel at how different we all look, from facial features to the sound of our English accents. The color of our skin varies from shades of white to peach to brown. We were different on the outside, but the same on the inside. They understand what it's like to worry if our partners will return home alive. Or if, one day, the law will come busting down the door to take them and even us away. Both scenarios send a prickle of uneasiness through me.

"Thank you. That means a lot, especially coming from you all. I guess we're all trying to navigate this mafia lifestyle," I say, and they all nod with wide eyes.

"So, what about you guys? All I know are your names," I remind, curious to learn more about them.

Emma's eyes shine with excitement.

"I'm from New York, and I met Alexander about half a year ago while on set at a photo shoot. Then everything after was quite chaotic," she says, grimacing. "But I wouldn't change anything about it," she admits, her voice wavering, which reveals how talking about her past brings back painful memories. We don't ask her for more information because we can tell her past is a sour topic.

Nora stands across from me.

"I met Arthuro when he came to collect a debt from my father. It took a lot of time to get to where we are today, especially when you add being sold off by your father into the mix. But it's been worth it." She extends her hand in front of us to reveal the enormous diamond ring on her finger.

Our eyes widen, and the girls gasp before asking her questions about her upcoming wedding.

"Congratulations!" I say, and she embraces me.

Nora continues to surprise me as I spend more time with her. She carries herself with an unbreakable toughness. But it's all a front. She's actually a quirky girl who is anything but serious; all it takes to see this is talking to her.

"I expect to see you all at the wedding," Nora says, pointing a finger at us. We all laugh at her change in demeanor, and she breaks out into a cheeky grin. "I'm serious. You all better come, or I'll hunt you down," she warns one last time before taking her seat.

Chloe goes next, and she has a smile on her porcelain face.

"I'm, unfortunately, Lei's twin." Chloe sticks her tongue out and points her finger near her mouth to mimic a throwing-up expression. "The idiot is older than me by ten minutes, and I'm twenty-two."

Chloe sits back down, and Layla speaks.

"I'm the oldest of you all, at thirty." Layla smiles, and her sun-kissed skin glows, radiating youth. She looks nothing like her age. If anything, she looks closer to being twenty-five instead of thirty. "I've been married to mi amor, Alejandro, for three years, and it took many years of fighting and crying considering it was an arranged marriage, but I'm happy to say we're expecting a baby in the next five months." She places a hand on her stomach, and we all congratulate her on her growing family.

There's a bump on my shoulder, and I turn to see Emma grinning.

"I'm sorry. I realize we just met, but I have to ask." I give her a quizzical brow, feeling nervous to know what she wants to ask me.

"Are you a virgin, Victoria?" Her question has me choking on air. "You don't have to answer," she assures me. "I only wanted to ask because I can sense the sexual tension between you and Leo."

Is it that obvious?

"I'm curious because you mentioned how you two have done nothing, but it's crystal clear you both want one another. I wanted to see if this was because you were nervous about having sex," she says.

"If I'm being honest, I'm overwhelmed," I confess, no longer afraid to tell them my deepest, darkest secrets. I couldn't explain it, but these girls didn't feel like strangers. The mafia connected us. Our fates have brought us together, and we instantly clicked. I can tell this is the beginning of a beautiful, long friendship.

"Awe, Leo's going to be your first! That's so cute!" Nora smiles dreamily.

I fidget, not knowing what to say, when Chloe cuts the awkwardness in the room.

"Have you two at least kissed?"

I nod, and my body tingles from the memory of his lips trailing down my neck and collarbone.

"Yes, we have kissed," I say, biting my lower lip as I remember how good it feels to have him hold me.

"Oh, my gosh, look!" Emma squeals, tipping my head to the side, exposing my neck to them.

"What is it?" I ask, a hand over the base of my neck.

"You won't be pure for much longer," Nora exclaims in a teasing tone.

My right brow shoots up in confusion.

"The big hickey on your neck says you two have been very busy," she reveals.

My blood stills, and I touch the sore spot on the crease of my neck.

"I can assure you we won't be doing any of what you may think," I say, knowing it will be weird if we have sex while they're here.

I'm still terrified about the entire concept. My body wants Leo, but my mind warns me to think about whether this is my body speaking out of lust or my heart speaking out of love. It's easy to get caught in the heat of the moment when his lips are pressed against mine. Sometimes I forget to think, and I'm not sure if this is a good or bad thing.

"Why the frown?" Layla asks, when she sees my nervousness.

"It's nothing," I tell Layla, not realizing my face twisted at the thought of having sex with Leo.

She sighs and grabs my hands. She wants answers, and she's set on getting them. Layla is soon to be a mom, and her instincts to care for others, are kicking in.

"No, don't give me that. I'm a woman and can tell when something upsets one of us. Now come on, spill." Her voice is serious, and she sets her right brow into a perfect arch, daring me to lie to her.

Letting out a defeated breath, I tell her what's on my mind.

"I don't know how to tell if I'm ready to have sex, especially with what happened to me a few months ago."

"Do you love him?" Emma asks me.

"Yes, a lot." I can feel my cheeks stretching into a smile when I remember our love confessions from the previous evening. "I want to be with him in every sense, but I'm scared we're moving too fast. How did you guys find out you were ready for sex?" I mumble, not sure they heard me until Layla answers my question.

"Mija, I don't know what happened to you in your past. But I can tell it affected you, and now you're afraid and insecure when you shouldn't be. If Leo loves you as he shows with his entire being, then all your worries are for nothing." She places a hand on the side of my face.

"Victoria, no matter how small, big, wide, or thin your body is, or if you're scarred from your past, I'm certain Leo will love you and wait until you're ready."

"Victoria, love is pure. It turns any imperfection into perfection in the lover's eyes. Whether you are ready for sex is something only you and your heart can decide. Neither I nor any of us girls can tell you when you're ready for sex because we're not you. But we can help ease your worries and educate you on the topic." Layla's eyes tear up as she speaks, and she huffs, fanning her cheeks. "Stupid hormones."

Layla's words comfort me, and I find she's right.

I have once again let my thoughts consume my actions. This flaw has stopped me from getting what I wanted time after time, and I almost ran away from Leo the first time because of it.

As Layla said, love can turn any imperfection into perfection.

If I let my guard down and stop worrying about my morals and what other people's relationships look like, then the love I have for Leo can consume me.

It didn't matter if I only knew Leo for a few months. I love him with every beat of my heart. Our love is not measurable, and our age gap doesn't matter either.

"I'm ready," I mumble, intending the thought to be said between myself, but I'm so into my feelings that I say the words out loud.

"What was that?" Layla asks with a knowing smile.

"I'm ready," I mumble, feeling light all over.

"Do you have sexy lingerie?" Emma asks, and I nod.

"Good," she exclaims in pleasure, with a finger tapping her chin. "Now, are you familiar with the art of being sexy?"

My face becomes hot from embarrassment because I'm not sure how to be sexy.

They sense my hesitation to answer and pull me out of the living room.

"Where's your room?" Emma asks me as she glances around the foyer, looking lost.

There's a glint of excitement on all four girls' faces, and I lead the way to mine and Leo's room.

About two hours later, we decide to check on the men, and when we reach the door, we find them in deep conversation.

Our judgment gets the best of us, and we all hover behind the door, trying to listen to what they're saying.

LEO

Around me are the most feared and powerful men in the world, and they wait for me to speak.

We spent the entire evening catching up on business. It took longer than expected because Adriano has been attacking us left and right, adding more to our already busy work schedules.

I sit with my thumb tapping against my lip as I stare at the ice cubes floating in my bourbon. A deep, noisy exhale comes from me, and I avert my gaze toward the four men with serious expressions cast upon their faces.

These men are all counting on me to help keep the peace, and I sure as hell don't intend to fail.

"As you are all aware by now, Adriano has threatened our mafias."

When I say his name, the letters are doused with rage.

"We need to act fast and protect what is ours. Which is why I'm asking you all to join forces with one another to fight alongside me as one family." I pause, making sure neither one of them is showing signs of disapproval. When I get no inclination toward such feelings, I continue, "we may be of different ethnicities and families, but we're all bonded by the oath our fathers made many years ago." I remind them of our alliance, and my hard tone does well to let them know there will be consequences if they decline.

"I'll fight alongside you, Leo." Alexander is the first to speak up.

I nod in appreciation for his quick response before looking toward the others.

"That's some serious shit." Lei groans before chugging the rest of his bourbon. His face morphs into a cringe from the alcohol. "I never liked the dick," he says in distaste. "You can count on my family to stand behind you, and not only because of the alliance, but because we're all family, and family has each other's back."

"Thank you, Lei. Your father would be proud if he heard you speak right now." He gives a thin-lipped smile at the mention of the retired mafia boss, who has given him a tough time while growing up.

"I know you're new to this role, and it's hard to keep up, but you're doing one hell of a job." I praise him, and Lei winks, a lopsided grin rising.

A deep voice diverts my attention toward Arthuro.

"Let's rip the fucker to shreds," he says, and his lip curls in disgust at Adriano. I give my serious friend a curt nod.

We all turn to stare at Alejandro, who's looking at the surface of the glass table in front of him. He removes the thick cigar from his lips and blows a puff of tobacco before saying, "I'll be fighting with you as well. That asshole won't steal what our families have worked hard for. My mafia is for my child to inherit," Alejandro says, extinguishing his cigar on the ashtray.

"Then it's settled. Let's prepare our men to go to war with Adriano and end what his father started many years ago."

As I say this, I hear the sound of familiar female voices, and shuffling from behind the door. The men and I all let out a collective chuckle, and their faces depict amusement.

"You guys can come in," I say, and they silence. I bite my tongue to stop myself from cracking a smile.

The door opens to reveal Victoria. The first thing I notice is how her cheeks are a rose red, and she has her lips set into an embarrassed smile from being caught eavesdropping.

I let out a breath at the sight of her beauty and rise from my seat, extending a hand for her to grab.

The men do the same when they see their partners, except for Lei, who groans in annoyance.

When Victoria is near, I lace our fingers and pull her to my chest.

"Amore mio," I whisper, inhaling her intoxicating scent. I expect the familiar vanilla fragrance I've grown to love, but this time, I get a fruity aroma from her. My mouth waters even more.

"Cherry?" I question, sniffing the new scent coming off her. My body reacts to the smell with a fierce lust.

She nods and kisses the spot under my jaw, leaving her lips there for a second before whispering her response so only I can hear.

"Sì amore," she says, and her eyes trap me in place. She smirks when she sees me lick the corner of my mouth.

There's a groan stuck deep in my throat, and my body ignites into a pleasurable fire. The magnetic pull between us has me pushing her tight against me, and I feel myself getting hard from her scent and the way the Spanish accent rolls off her tongue.

"Get a room!" Lei groans, and the men all agree with him. A round of slaps follows when the girls hit the back of their heads, telling them to shut up.

"What do you say we do that?" I ask, lifting a suggestive brow. My voice hints at my excitement, and Victoria laughs. The sound is enough to make my heart go crazy inside my chest. It takes every inch of restraint not to bend her over the table and plunge deep inside her.

45

ADRIANO

The dark blond strands of my whore's hair are rough against my palms. My fingers dig into her scalp as I hustle the back of her head to my pulsing cock.

She bobs fiercely in and out as she sucks me.

Drool gathers around the corner of her mouth and it glistens.

She looks at me with hooded eyes filled with lust, and my cock jerks against her twirling tongue.

Women craved my touch until they met the real me. Then their smell of arousal turns into pure fear. Except for Rebecca. She isn't afraid of me, and it's infuriating, but some days it's nice to have a woman suck my cock with dark eyes and not tears streaming down their cheeks. Today is one of those days.

My groans and her gargling rebound against the walls of the room. Sweat forms at the base of my forehead. The cool wetness runs down my neck.

When my hot release is ready to bust into her mouth, my balls spasm. The tension in my body rises, letting me know I'm coming, and I would have if Rebecca hadn't slowed down.

I let out a deep sound of anger, and she gives a teasing smile.

Her grin infuriates me. She wants me to beg her for more, but I don't beg… I take.

"Faster." There's a warning in my voice, and I push her head deeper into me. My cock hits the back of her mouth, and she gags. The look of desire and pride on her face angers me.

Without warning, I pull my cock out of her mouth and grab her by the back of the neck. She gasps when I press her front side over the surface of my desk.

"You think you have control over me?" I say near her ear, and my voice is low and deep.

Rebecca whimpers, not from fear but from pleasure. Her legs spread open.

"This should teach you a lesson on who's in charge," I sneer, my hands going inside her white skirt. I pull her lacy thong until it lies pooled around her ankles. She moans when the hot air of the room kisses her wet pussy.

I thrust my erect cock into Rebecca. My hands squeeze her fat ass as I breach her walls. With each jerk, my desk scrapes across the floorboards. I dig my teeth into my bottom lip, grunting as I focus on thrusting into her, intending to break her until she can't walk.

My cock throbs, ready to explode, when a knock on the door cuts through the sound of her ass slapping against my thighs.

"Don't stop. Ignore them." Her French-tip nails puncture the skin of my hand.

I remove her grip from around me and push her aside. I put my erect cock back inside my briefs, zipping my pants.

"Get the fuck out, Rebecca!"

She's only a good fuck who wouldn't cry. Nothing more, and I have to remind her of that.

I avert my attention to the letter my mother found. Its contents are equal to winning the lottery.

My mother hoped the letter had information about some secret savings account left by my father. But the words written by my father didn't state a fortune, much to my mother's gold-digging dismay. Instead, the letter held a truth never known—a family secret.

Even when ten feet under, my father has a way of causing chaos for Estephano Bandoni.

I look away from the letter to find Rebecca hasn't left. I pull out my gun faster than she can blink. The barrel of my gun is aimed at her pussy.

"I said get out!"

She jumps from fear, and I grin when I see the tears in her eyes, but she sucks them back up and lifts a pointed chin in defiance.

I'm amused, as she adjusts her skirt and walks out the door, bumping into Andrew, who raises a brow in disbelief at her insolence.

My attention falls on the red lacy thong near my desk. I grab the material, placing it inside my pocket, knowing she'll be back. She always is.

"Boss," Andrew greets, standing in front of my desk.

I sneer at the sight of the second idiot who doesn't know how to follow simple instructions.

Get the girl. That's all he and Lorenzo had to do. But they failed me miserably.

I gave them an opportunity for a second chance after getting out of Leo's good grace, and this is how they repay me. I'm furious.

Andrew senses my anger. His eyes waver from my sharp stare.

"What is it, Andrew?" I say in annoyance as I light the blunt between my lips.

"The last of the recruits have arrived," he says with a grin. "Our men also tell us the members of the mafia alliance have gathered in Sicily. All four men have taken their significant others."

I inhale deeply and blow smoke from my lips. Weed consumes my senses, and pleasure settles in my stomach from this news.

"All are in one spot, as you have predicted." Andrew's laugh fills the room, and I stifle my chuckle.

Leo thinks he's one step ahead of me, but he isn't. By being cautious, he's making it easier for me to take away their lovers all at once.

We only need one little slip-up to swipe one or all of the mafia women from under them. The mobsters will tumble like dominos once we have their lovers.

Their first mistake was falling in love, when we all know there's no room for love in the mafia.

Before his death, my father drilled it into my brain that women would lead to weakness. They are only good for fucking, he had said to me.

Victoria comes to mind. A curl to my lips reveals how content I am with the woman who has claimed Leo's heart.

I spent my entire early years trying to break the mighty Leo Bandoni, and when I fucked his sister, it wasn't enough to break him. But Victoria is the missing piece of my plan. She's his weakness, the key to destroying the Italian Mafia Don.

"Send men straight to Sicily. I want eyes on them at all times." My words are firm. "As soon as an opportunity opens, we get the girls."

"On it," Andrew says, about to take his leave, when my voice stops him.

"And Andrew—"

He stiffens and turns to look at me.

"If you fail me again, I will kill you this time." He swallows, his face paling. A second passes before he nods in understanding.

The door closes behind him, and I marvel at my accomplishments.

I'm one step closer to getting my revenge. The best part of it all is Leo doesn't know where I am, and he won't be able to find me because I'm deep in the Amazon in no-man's-land.

The image of killing Leo makes my hands tingle, but I won't kill him the first chance I get. Oh no... first, I will make him watch as I torture the love of his life, and before she stops breathing, I'll fuck his whore in front of him. I'll fuck her until she dies with my cock buried deep inside her, and Leo won't be able to do anything but watch as I strip his entire world right in front of him.

I unfasten my pants. My hand goes to my hard cock, and I pump, and pump to the sound of Victoria screaming for me to stop.

Her cries and Leo's pain bring me pleasure until I explode all over my hand. The hot liquid trails over my knuckles.

All I can think about is how sweet revenge is near.

46

VICTORIA

Emma is a detailed person when it comes to explaining stories.

Unfortunately, the story she's telling us now is a detailed recount of her first time having sex with Alexander. And I'm talking about sounds, smells, and tastes. The whole nine yards! How she remembers all this, I don't know.

I cringe for the fifth time as she now explains how Alexander railed her during their flight to Italy. Which I sincerely did not need to know.

The girls notice my red face and tease me, saying I'll be getting railed soon. I know they aren't far off from the look Leo gave me an hour ago.

He was ready to toss me over his shoulder and take me to our room. He would have done so, and I would have let him if the girls hadn't pulled me out of the room.

So here we are in my and Leo's bedroom. The girls are preparing me for what to expect when I have sex with Leo.

They warned me that because he's a mafia boss, he'll be possessive and have an intense sexual drive.

What followed were the stories of their first time with their significant others, who are mafiosos. All apart from Chloe, who hadn't found interest in the dominating nature of mafia men.

My thoughts are disrupted when Emma presses play on the video of a woman and a man getting it on.

I'm thankful when Sofia and Cleo enter the room.

The two stop dead in their tracks, and Sofia's lips roll into her mouth. Her eyes widen at the sound of moaning coming from the phone in Emma's hands.

I jump to greet the two.

"Are you ready for your date?" I ask, and her cheeks turn red from my question.

Sofia shakes her head.

"That's why I'm here. Can I borrow something from your closet?"

"Of course!" I drag her to my closet, and the girls follow us.

Before we know it, we're all on a mission to prepare Sofia for her date.

When we're done, she's dressed in a beautiful tight pink cream-colored dress and black heels picked by me and Chloe.

Sofia's makeup is soft and elegant, thanks to the work of Emma and Nora. Meanwhile, Layla and Cleo had taken it upon themselves to style her brown hair into voluminous curls.

"You look gorgeous," I tell her, placing a strand of hair behind her ear. "Francisco is one lucky man."

"Thank you for helping me get ready! It means a lot to me." Right after she says this, there's a knock on the door.

"Come in," I call, giving my cousin a grin when I notice her release a nervous breath.

Francisco peeks through the door and smiles when his eyes land on Sofia.

"You look beautiful," he breathes, kissing her.

We awe at the two, and they pull apart as if remembering they aren't alone.

"Ladies," Francisco greets with a tip of his head.

I level a firm stare his way, and he stiffens.

"Francisco, you better bring her back before eleven," I say, my voice firm, and Sofia rolls her eyes.

"Yes, ma'am," he replies, wrapping an arm around her waist. We watch them disappear, and we girls talk for a few minutes when the door to the room opens again, and this time Leo enters.

His head jerks back when he sees all the girls in our room.

The girls glance at me with knowing looks.

"It's getting late. We're going to head out," Emma exclaims through laughter. "Have a *ravishing* night, Victoria," she says, and the others all nod, rising from the ground.

Leo cocks a brow, picking up on her suggestive tone, and I'm mortified.

It's only us in the room, and he smiles at me. I give him a smile of my own before my attention draws to the mess on the floor. Groaning, I pick up the makeup and hair tools left behind.

I'm on all fours, and when my fingers stretch to grab the curling iron, a pair of polished black wingtip shoes appear in front of me.

Taking in a sharp breath, my gaze trails up Leo's body, and he's already staring at me with dark eyes.

I sit on my knees in front of him and wet my lips. Leo's eyes flicker toward my mouth, and his hands bunch into tight fists.

With shaky fingers, I grab the curling iron from between his legs and rise from the ground. I turn around to head toward the bathroom and smile to myself when I hear Leo hot on my heels.

Nora told me to make him work for it, and I intend on doing just that.

With him still following me, I walk toward the closet and pull out a nude lace lingerie set.

Leo stands leaning against the door. His hard, dark eyes stare at the material in my hands, and his left hand is gripping the edge of the door with his fingers digging into the wood.

Giving him an innocent smile, I extend a hand, and he readily takes it, allowing me to lead him back to our room.

We stop under the door, my fingers gripping the front of his dress shirt. I pull him down to my lips. He swallows; his gaze doesn't stray from mine, and I kiss him before pulling away.

"I'm going to shower," I mumble, and before he can respond, I push him back, close the door, and lock it behind me. My chest rises and falls, and I hear Leo muttering something in an Italian accent—frustration and desire are clear in his voice.

I thought making him work for it would be easy, but I was wrong. My choice to tease him is making us both flustered.

When the cold water cascading down my body isn't enough to cool down the heat coursing through my veins, I lean my forehead on the shower wall, trying to keep my composure. But I can't because my body craves Leo even more after being deprived yesterday.

Sighing in frustration, I finish my shower and put on the nude sheer lace bralette, which is more for show than actual support. I slip the thong up my legs, knowing it will come off soon. Also to come off will be the black satin nightgown I slip into before heading back to the room.

My heart races when I notice Leo standing in front of the window with the sleeves of his white button-down shirt pushed below his elbows. His muscular forearms are visible to my hungry eyes.

He senses me and turns around. His eyes move from my face to the nightgown, and he lets out a strangled breath. His hands loosen the tie around his neck as if the material is choking him.

I stalk toward him and cup his face when he's a foot away. His lips curl into a breathtaking smile.

"How was your day?" I wrap my arms around him, and he pushes me tight against his body.

"Good. How was your evening with the girls?"

"It was fine." My fingers go to the collar of his shirt, unfastening the tie. "They're amazing." I start to unbutton his dress shirt. When I get the first four buttons undone, the side of my hand touches the exposed skin of his smooth chest, and I love how my finger glides across the skin.

I undo all the buttons except for one, and the pad of my finger grazes the skin near his toned abdomen. Leo shudders, and his hand stops me.

He lifts my chin with his pointer finger, forcing our dark eyes to meet.

"If you continue teasing me, I won't be able to keep my restraint any longer," he says through clenched teeth.

My heart beats with a force that leaves me breathless. It's obvious I want him, yet he doesn't assume my advances mean my consent. That's what I love about Leo. He always put my needs and comfort before his.

A boldness seeps into me, and I rise on my tippy toes to meet his towering height. My lips skim his earlobe as I whisper my desire for him.

"I didn't say I wanted you to hold back."

When he hears my confirmation, he grunts low and presses our chests together.

"I love you," he whispers, our breaths mingling.

"I love you too. Now kiss me."

He lets out a breathless laugh.

"Your wish is my command," he says, closing the gap between us. The moment his lips capture mine, I can taste the bourbon he drank, and his strong scent fills my senses. Everything about him makes my head spin.

I grip onto the back of his head and press our mouths closer together, our tongues exploring with vigor.

I groan into the toe-curling French kiss, and I want Leo so much that my knees buckle under me. Before I can fall to the ground like a puddle, he grabs me, keeping me steady.

"Jump," he grunts against my mouth. His warm breath brings a chill to my spine, and I do as he says.

Now secured in Leo's arms, his stubbled chin tickles my breasts, and his eyes peer inside the robe. He lets out a deep sound of pleasure and places kisses all over my chest and collarbone.

Leo leads us toward the bed, his mouth not leaving mine.

I expect a soft mattress, but my back hits the hard bedpost from the canopy bed instead. I press myself into it with a whimper when his thick finger runs the length of my thong. The wetness between my folds makes the pad of his finger roll over my clit, and I get a whiff of my desire.

His touch adds the right amount of pressure, and I double over from the tension rising in my stomach. The unfamiliar sensation is so intense I cling to Leo. I want nothing more than for him to take away the itch deep inside me where I can't reach.

"Leo, please..." My words come out desperate, and he lets out a low, strangled groan. The hard wood of the bedpost no longer supports me, and I sink into the soft mattress.

I take in the sight of his flustered cheeks, plump red lips, and tousled brown hair, which I was pulling seconds ago. My eyes dart to the large print between his legs, and my pulse quickens.

"It's all yours, amore." Leo's voice is strangled, and I unconsciously spread my legs.

His eyes bulge, and the green shade is almost nonexistent when he peeks between my legs.

My stomach knots up when he closes his eyes, and I listen as he takes steady, deep breaths.

Leo reopens his eyes and walks to the door. My heart races when he turns the lock.

"No interruptions this time," he says with a grin as he stalks back toward me. I swallow the dryness in my throat, and Leo's eyes burn me with his intense stare.

He grabs my ankles, bringing me to sit on the edge of the bed. I'm now looking straight at his erection, and I'm breathless.

"Look at me," he whispers, and I tip my chin up to face him.

He dips to my level, and his lips caress mine in a quick kiss.

"Are you sure you want this?" he asks, still wanting to make sure I'm comfortable.

I smile in reassurance before grabbing his belt buckle and pulling him closer. He staggers and would have tumbled on top of me if he hadn't grabbed the bedpost to keep himself steady.

"I've never been so sure in my entire life." My words are laced with sincerity, and Leo responds with a slow kiss, which turns fiery the moment his tongue dominates my mouth.

I crawl back on the bed, and he follows after me, not once stopping our kiss.

His elbows keep him up, and my eyes flutter shut with bliss when he trails one of his hands to the end of the nightgown. He peels it off my body, leaving me in nothing but the soaking-wet thong and matching bralette. His attention is on my now visible dark brown nipples, calling for his attention.

Leo's eyes glow like two shiny diamonds. His hands stretch out to touch me, and my thighs quiver when his thumb lazily caresses my sensitive nipples. A gasp comes from me as he continues to rub the fabric over them. He smiles at my reaction before grabbing my round breasts in his palms and squeezing them.

He grips the middle of the bralette, and I close my eyes. The next second, the material shreds in half as he rips it off my body.

My eyes flash open in surprise, and my breasts come tumbling out.

"I'll buy you more," comes his husky response to the look of shock on my face. I respond by throwing my head back when he cups my breasts. His thumbs circle over the peddled nipples, flesh against flesh. The hairs at the back of my neck rise when he lightly kisses each nipple before pulling back and looking at me.

"You're fucking beautiful."

I'm exposed to him, and I look away when shame consumes me. He isn't happy with my reaction.

"Look at me." His words are gentle, and he cups my jaw as if I'm the most delicate thing in the world.

When I stare into his eyes, I can see his pain from seeing me upset.

"Why are you being shy?"

I remain silent when the knotted ball in my throat stops any words from coming out. "You're beautiful, and you should be proud of your body."

His arms caress my sides lovingly, and my heart wants to come tumbling out of my rib cage from his words.

"I was scared you'd be disappointed," I confess, and my words don't stop flowing. "I thought you'd be disgusted after what Adriano's men did to me." My tears burn in the corners of my eyes, and I look away, not being able to face the hurt my words have brought him.

Richard and Lorenzo may not have raped me, but they touched me, and I've felt dirty since that night.

As much as I want to pretend it isn't true, I can't hide the fact that my body disgusts me to the point where I sometimes can't look at myself.

"Victoria, I would never laugh at you or your body, and it doesn't disgust me," he says with raw tenderness. "I love you because of who you are as a person. Not for your ass or boobs."

I can't hold on to my tears, and they come flooding out because of his words.

"Amore, what they did to you hasn't tarnished your body." His voice is deep with sadness, and the tears don't stop falling. They keep coming with every word he says, and he wipes every tear away. "You are still as perfect as the day you were born. No amount of darkness or greed could ever taint your goodness. Do you hear me?"

By now, my sight has blurred from my tears, but I can still see him, and it's as if he's removed my pain with every word, every touch, and every look he gives me.

"I hear you, and I believe you," I say, pressing my lips to his.

He's gentle with me, afraid I'll break again, but I won't. Not anymore, as long as he's with me.

My fingers find their way back to the last button of his shirt, and I rip it.

Leo presses our naked chests together, and my hard nipples glide across his hard abs.

My sensitive buds tingle with ecstasy, and with him holding me, I feel alive, never wanting to part ways with him.

His lips suck on the base of my neck and trail down to my breasts.

I quiver when the pad of his thumb brushes over my right nipple, and there's a turnover occurring in my stomach when he lowers his mouth to the hardened bud.

He moves his mouth to ravish the left one, and his free hand kneads the other breast like dough. He adds just the right amount of pressure, which has me panting his name.

He's been the one pleasuring me this entire time, and I want to show him how much I love him.

I grab his shoulders and force him to release my breast.

"What is it, amore?" Leo's face reveals panic, and I shut him up by smashing my lips against his.

I flip us over, and he lets out a ragged breath when I sit behind his hard shaft. With him nuzzled against the lace fabric of my thong, I tremble with anticipation.

His hard nipples press against my soft palms, and I quiver as I rotate my hips over his clothed midsection.

Leo makes a strangled noise at the back of his throat, and my stomach bubbles when his eyes flutter shut from the pleasure.

I stop grinding into him and slowly kiss down the base of his jaw and neck, sucking on the skin until I know I've left a hickey.

He trembles under my touch, and when I reach above the waistband of his pants, I run my tongue across his hips. The sound of his groans has my stomach clenching with warmth.

I remove my mouth from his body, and he grunts in frustration, flipping us again. My heart jumps when I see his sexy grin, which promises sweet sexual torture.

"Oh, you want to play, huh?"

I squirm under him as he trails kisses down my body. His mouth glides down my lower half until his teeth graze the edge of the lace material of my thong. My heart thumps in my ears as he tugs the material down with his mouth.

His nose caresses the curve of my pussy, and I bend, my knees rising when his breath fans my throbbing sex.

When the thong glides down my legs, it leaves behind the warm, wet substance of my desire.

I kick off the thong with the help of my toes, and Leo's warm breath disappears when he falls on his knees at the edge of the bed.

His tongue runs over his lips like a man deprived of food, and he grabs my ankles, pulling me toward him until my exposed pussy is a few centimeters from his hungry mouth.

He places soft kisses all up my left leg, stopping when he reaches my inner thigh. Then he does the same to the other leg.

"Tell me what you want me to do to you," he rasps, his eyes penetrating my soul.

Silence weighs heavily on my lips as I'm unable to find the words or the courage to tell him what he wants to hear.

"Come on, amore."

I still can't form the words, and his fingers run up my inner thigh painfully slow.

"I want you to tell me exactly what you want me to do to you." His palm cups my sex, and I bow into his touch, telling him what he wants to hear.

"I want you to devour my pussy and your tongue to lick every inch of my body," I say, sounding breathless.

"Whatever my amore wants, my amore gets." Leo grunts, grabbing my legs and placing them over his shoulders.

I steady myself on my elbows, watching as he lowers his head between my legs. He strokes the skin of my inner thighs with such delicacy that my body ignites in little fires.

Leo stares at me as his lips latch onto my inner thigh. When his tongue runs over the skin, my belly convulses with a need for him to flick his skillful tongue on my clit. But he instead teases my folds with his fingertips, and my head sways to the side.

"Leo," I moan, pleading for him to stop teasing me.

"Patience, my love."

Not a second later, his finger sinks deep into my entrance, and my eyes shut, as I fall back from the pleasure that comes with him finger-fucking me.

"You're fucking tight, baby," he groans. "Open your eyes, beautiful," Leo orders, and I do as he says. My blood pressure rises when he brings the finger he used to fuck me to his mouth. He sucks on it, and his eyes shine with excitement before falling shut in pleasure.

"You taste so fucking sweet," he groans, putting two fingers in his mouth and wetting them. He pulls them out of his mouth and slips them deep inside me. His fingers stretch me and curl around the hot flesh of my throbbing pussy.

He bends, disappearing between my legs, and his tongue laps at my throbbing clit.

Leo's tongue twirls around the pulsing nerve, and my fingers grip the bed sheets under me. My feet curl, trying to find some sanity, but I find none. The pleasure is too much.

The feral pleasure in me returns, and I lift my hips off the bed, pressing his mouth into my sex. His rumble of pleasure sends a wave of thrilling vibrations through me. My heart lurches in my chest when he grabs me by the waist, pulling me closer to him. The only thing keeping me on the mattress is his mouth fucking me and my legs, which I have crossed over the back of his head.

I'm spasming against his taste buds as he delicately flicks his tongue across my clit, and I see stars when his tongue slides between the folds where my juices have gathered.

His lips nibble on the swollen clit, and I bite my tongue to stop from screaming in ecstasy. But it's impossible, and I groan louder and louder. Even muffling my cries with the palm of my hand or biting into the skin won't soften the sounds coming from my mouth.

The twitching sensation inside me rises, and I'm about to combust. My stomach clenches, my body stiffens, and I feel like I'm about to pee.

Leo speaks against my hot folds, and I squirm from the pleasure.

"Relax," he coos, rubbing my thighs before continuing my sweet torture and his sweet satisfaction. I do as he says, and with every stroke of his tongue, the tension in my stomach intensifies.

I moan his name loudly, and the release bubbling inside me explodes, coating Leo's tongue with the warm liquid.

He groans, and his fingers dig into my ass as he plunges his tongue deeper into my pussy until he sucks me dry.

Even after I have released myself all over his mouth, I find the tightness inside me remains alive.

Around us are the sounds of my heavy breathing and the slurping sound of him eating me out.

Satisfied, he lifts his face from between my legs and crawls over me, bringing my lips to his in a slow, sensual kiss, and my mouth fills with the taste of my sweet release.

I groan against his mouth, curious to know what he tastes like.

Leo's right hand grabs my thigh, and I wrap it around his waist. He pinches my clit, and a little moan comes from me when he shoves his finger deep inside me, pumping.

I grind myself into his fingers, and when I'm about to find my release for the second time, he stops.

"Not yet. I want you to cum when I'm inside of you." Leo's reply comes out choked with lust, and he kisses me quickly before getting out of bed.

I study how his back muscles flex when he strolls into the closet.

The tightness in my lower stomach is still raging, and the pulsing between my thighs matches my rapid heartbeat.

I cross my legs and clench them together, hoping it will ease the painful desire. It doesn't, and I groan in frustration.

Leo returns, and when our eyes lock, I fall apart. My eyes draw to his lower half to see he's only wearing black briefs. His bulge stands tall and proud. I whither from the sight of it.

Leo smirks, enjoying the sight of me wilting and spreading my legs open for him.

"I need you," I stagger, getting on my knees.

Leo's throat moves when he swallows, and his eyes stare at my breasts as they sway. His fingers wrap around the fabric of his briefs, pulling them down to reveal his large and girthy shaft. My eyes widen because he's easily six inches, maybe more.

He's so big and thick.

I bite my lip, fear taking over my pleasure.

"Will it hurt?" The words come out fearful, and my chest tightens.

"I promise I'll go slow." Leo caresses my face, and I close my eyes, letting out a breath I didn't know I was holding. "If it hurts, you tell me, and I'll stop."

I give him an assuring smile, and he opens his palm, revealing the shiny gold square wrapper of a condom. He tears it open, about to put it on, when I stop him.

Confusion is visible in his expression. I smile in assurance and boldly grab his thick, hot length, loving how soft and heavy he feels in my tiny hands.

"Victoria," he groans, trembling from my touch.

I grab the clear rubber from his shaky hands and slip it over his thick, pulsing cock. When the rubber covers his length, he pushes me back on the bed and crawls over me.

Leo spreads my thighs apart and aligns our hips. His eyes swirl with love and desire, and my stomach explodes like a million fireworks when I see the gorgeous smile he only ever gives me.

He caresses the spot near my sex, and I shiver when his tip nudges my entrance.

"I love you, Leo." The words come out hoarse but full of love and devotion. My confession makes him smile.

"And I love you, Victoria," he whispers breathlessly before pressing our mouths together.

As our mouths become one, he gently sinks inside me, and I whimper against his mouth when the intrusion brings a burning pain between my thighs.

My fingers dig into his back, sure to leave behind crescent moons on his soft skin.

He continues slipping his entire length inside me, and I hiss as the burning sensation spreads throughout my body.

As Leo's enormous cock sinks deeper and deeper inside me, I stretch for him.

The pain is too much. I whimper against his shoulder and press our naked, sweaty chests together. I want the pain to end and transform into the pleasure I was told I would feel.

"I'm sorry, baby." He slides into me slowly to ease my pain, but it doesn't help, and a choked sob comes from my mouth.

"Shit," he curses, stopping his movements and wiping my tears.

He's about to pull out, but I don't let him. I need him, even if it hurts at first. He has to fit. There's no way he wouldn't. I'm determined to make room for him, even if it tears me apart.

"No, keep going," I beg, my hands around his cock, which is half buried inside me.

"Are you sure?" he croaks, gripping the headboard with his left hand.

I don't answer and instead wrap my right leg around his waist. The heel of my foot digs into his backside, and my other hand grips his ass, pushing him into me.

His cock disappears inside me, and I hear a pop mingle with my cry.

"Fanculo Victoria," he moans, his breath fanning my already scalding face.

As fast as the pain arrives, it diminishes, and I adjust to his cock. Our hips rotate in a steady motion, and when this isn't enough, he spears into me. My hard nipples glide up and down over his sweaty chest with each powerful thrust.

The sounds of the bed jerking and squeaking fill the dead of night, and I don't care if the entire house hears us, because the girls already know what we're doing tonight.

We don't hold back, and our groans harmonize beautifully.

I open my eyes to see Leo biting his bottom lip. The sight of him deep in concentration while fucking me makes me buckle into him.

"Fucking hell Victoria." He buries his head into my shoulder blade and gives a tender bite to the skin.

"Faster!" I cry out, rolling my hips.

My plea has him convulsing above me, and a nerve in his jaw twitches.

His thrusts grow rough, almost feral, and my muscles tighten when his stiff cock twitches inside me.

My release is culminating inside me, and I'm so desperate to reach the top that I meet his thrusts halfway.

Heat spreads under my prickling skin, and my eyes roll to the back of my head from the pleasure.

One earth-shattering thrust from him is all it takes for my juices to coat his hot, covered length, and a few thrusts later, Leo's hard cock thickens deep inside me.

"Victoria..." comes his throaty groan against my neck as he releases into the condom.

When he pulls away, he pants, trying to catch his breath. As we slow our movements, I'm aware of two things: his heart racing against mine and the warm substance of my orgasm trailing down my legs as he slowly pumps into me. He's unwilling to stop.

My hands around his back move to cup his face, and his eyes flutter open. When he sees my smile, he stops his grinding and holds me tight.

Leo kisses me and pulls out so he can dispose of the full condom.

I watch his backside as he disappears into the bathroom, and through the ringing in my ears, I pick up the sound of the bath running.

I'm motionless on our bed, and when he appears again, he lifts me in his arms, taking me to the bathroom. He places me on the toilet.

"I need you to pee, amore," Leo says, and my face becomes hot.

"Can you step outside?"

Leo lets out a soft laugh.

"Amore, I fucked the living hell out of you, and now you're too shy to pee in front of me." Two little dimples stare at me, and I grow warmer in response to his teasing remarks.

I say nothing, and he dips to my level and kisses my lips before giving me privacy. When I'm done, I climb into the warm bath water.

Closing my eyes, I sigh when I inhale the rose-scented oils he's poured into the water.

The water splashes when Leo gets into the tub, and he nuzzles behind me.

I lean into his touch as he scrubs my body with gentle hands, taking me to pure bliss.

Leo's left hand holds my right breast, and the other hand drags down to my stomach.

I press myself tight against him when his finger trails along my folds, and a moan rips from me when he cups my pussy, bringing me tight to his chest.

Panting, I grip his inner thighs, making him grunt, and I huff, satisfied.

Serves the tease damn right.

47

LEO

Victoria is pressed against my body, evoking feelings of warmth and passion in me. Her taut nipples brush painfully slow against my skin with every breath she takes.

I kiss her forehead and down the side of her face until I rest my mouth on her collarbone.

"Leo, let me sleep," she complains, turning in my arms and burying her head into the pillow beside her.

I gape at her bare back, and an idea comes to mind.

She sighs when I unwrap my arms from around her waist, and she falls back to sleep.

My lips tug into a grin, knowing she'll be craving my touch when I'm done with her.

I dip under the sheets and turn her on her back. She groans in annoyance, but I pay no mind to it as I'm too distracted by the sight of her pussy, which is soft and wet with her arousal.

Like a starved man, I spread her legs, and my mouth dives into the moist folds. The second my mouth latches onto the warm skin, her long legs draw up, and her fingers grip my hair.

She's whimpering my name, and her tugging on my hair only encourages me to mouth fuck her some more.

I flick my tongue on her clit like I know she likes it. She responds by lifting her hips and spreading her legs for me.

I'm euphoric when her delicate hands push me deeper into her, guiding my mouth where she wants me.

I groan as I continue to eat her out, savoring the sweet, tangy taste her body produces.

"Oh god," comes her staggered moan, and I detach my mouth for a second.

"I'm not God, amore," I rasp, and her thighs twitch under my palms. "I'm Leo."

Her skin erupts with goosebumps as I drag my hands up her body, and I sigh when my hand cups her full breast, squeezing.

"Fuck Leo!" she screams. Her voice is husky and sensual, and my cock aches from the sound of her moans.

As predicted, she's enjoying being woken up by my tongue deep inside her, and I'm more than happy to provide her with more mornings like this.

I toy with her hard nipple, pinching and squeezing the round breast. The hunger to suck on them increases, and I remove my mouth from her wet folds, substituting my mouth with two fingers.

I love hearing how my fingers pump in and out of her, but not as much as the sound of my cock ramming deep inside her.

The bed sheets covering me are suffocating, and my breathing comes out staggered.

I peel the sheets off, and when I peek from under the covers, I notice Victoria is as breathless and sweaty as I am.

Her eyes roll to the back of her head when I curl my fingers deep inside her.

My cock is stiff, and I know I won't be able to hold off longer. I ignore the fire blazing between my legs and focus on ravishing her breasts.

I groan against the hard, milky-brown nipples.

Victoria wraps her legs around me and is on the brink of her release. She only needs a little push to find it.

I put another finger inside her, and my pumping increases. She lets out a tiny scream, and my jaw clenches when her juices trail the length of my fingers. With her now wet, I know she's ready for me.

I extend my arm, looking for a condom, but I stop when my cock rubs against her pussy. My body quivers with need, and I shut my eyes, trying to find the willpower to hold on a second more.

When I'm collected, I grab the damn condom from the nightstand and tear it open.

The second it's secured, I plummet deep into her, and her jaw ticks as she grinds her hips.

"Fanculo Victoria!" Her eyes flash open when she hears me speak her name in Italian. She grips my ass, her nails dig into the skin, and she forcefully pushes me to tear her until I hit a wall.

My balls tighten, and hotness races down my spine from the fierce heat burning in her eyes.

Her reaction to my accent tells me it's a kink of hers, and I make a mental note to speak Italian to her more often.

"You like that baby." I grunt, my hips plunging faster, deeper, and *harder*. She bounces with each thrust, letting out strangled noises of pleasure.

I'm clutching the headboard so tight that my knuckles are white, and my cock throbs, ready to find my release.

"Puta Madre!" Victoria cries in Spanish, and my cock pulses as the accent rolls off her tongue.

"Talk Spanish to me, baby." I groan, letting go of the headboard, digging my head into the crook of her neck and shoulder, where I suck on the skin.

"Más rápido Papi."

The desire intertwined in her words pushes me to the edge, and I become blinded when her walls flutter around my cock.

A trail of fire springs from my balls and up to my spine. I'm about to burst deep inside her when a loud knock cuts through the sounds of our bodies slapping and our mouths moaning with our pleasure.

Victoria freezes, and I groan in annoyance, ready to kill whoever is disturbing us mid-climax.

At this rate, I'll have to put a *fuck off* sign on the door.

Instead of acknowledging the knock, I keep pounding into her, and she grinds into me. We're forced to break apart when another loud knock follows.

She curses the person and tries to pull away, but I keep her in place.

"Fuck them," I say, kissing down her neck, and her eyes close in bliss. There's another knock, this one much more urgent. I hear the gnashing sound of her teeth grinding together in aggravation. My own temper rises, and I pull out of Victoria.

"I'm going to kill them," I grumble, rising from the bed, grabbing my gun, and heading toward the bathroom to discard the condom and put on a pair of briefs.

When I return to the room, I kiss Victoria's warm temple and take in the sight of her beautiful naked body before I cover her with the bed sheets.

"Leo, what's with the gun?" she says, the corner of her mouth lifted in amusement as she stares at the gun in my hand.

"I'm not going to kill them. Just give them a scare," I say, my tone a little off from the restlessness weighing down on me. Her soft laugh rings behind me as I approach the door, ready to kick whoever it is out of my house.

"What the fuck, Francisco!" I grit through clenched teeth.

He looks at my gun, and his eyebrows shoot up in humor.

As if remembering why he's here, his face turns pale.

"We have a problem," he says, his eyes pointing downward, and I lift an annoyed brow.

Yeah, I have a massive boner, and you won't stop cockblocking me. The words rest at the tip of my tongue, but I don't say them. Instead, I say, "what kind of problem?"

"A family problem," he explains, and he lets out an exasperated sigh when I don't piece together what he's talking about. "Victoria's family has joined us this weekend."

My shoulders stiffen, and the bastard finds humor in the situation.

"You might want to hurry before they come up here and see you deep inside their daughter. I don't think her *Papi* would be too happy," he muses, turning around to leave when he stops and turns again. "And next time, be quiet. Some people are trying to sleep; please and thank you."

I stare at his retreating figure, now dumbfounded and nervous.

Victoria gasps from behind, and a thump follows. She stares at me with the bedsheets tangled around her.

My eyes soften at her panic, and I lift her in my arms and head toward the bathroom.

"By your reaction, I'm guessing you know who's here."

She nods, dropping the bed sheet covering her when I set her back on the ground.

Victoria stretches to turn on the water from the shower, and I can see the wetness from her orgasm running down her inner thighs.

I take a staggered breath, and my cock stiffens even more.

I sigh, glancing at my erection.

Cockblocked once again.

She gets into the shower, and I'm hot on her trail, pressing her back-side to my front.

My cock presses into her lower back, and she groans.

"Leo," she whines, her voice pained, knowing we can't continue, not when her family is waiting for us.

I let out an annoyed breath and massage shampoo into her head. When I'm done, she turns around in my arms and motions for me to bend.

She rises on her tippy toes, her fingers scrubbing the shampoo into my hair. Her breasts are dangling centimeters from my mouth, calling for my attention.

I can't help myself when I clutch onto her hips, keeping her steady. My greedy mouth takes her left breast, and I groan when the dark tip pebbles under my tongue.

Victoria stops rubbing my hair and grips the strands.

"You're unbelievable," she breathes, looking at me with hooded eyes.

I peer up at her, my mouth forms into a cheeky grin, and I release her nipple.

"Fine, let's hurry and say hello so we can disappear midway through their visit," I grumble, her chest vibrating against mine when she laughs.

We didn't fuck in the shower, and I still have a raging boner, which is becoming more painful as I watch her get dressed.

Thoughts of how fucking beautiful she is cloud my brain as my eyes travel the length of her long legs.

My stare lands on her round, perky ass, being hugged by the cheeky, high navy blue panties.

She notices me gawking at her, and her cheeks flush red.

I lean off the door frame and purse my hand, bringing it to my mouth in the familiar Italian al bacio gesture.

Victoria clenches her thighs, and I grin at her reaction.

I'm weary when the look of lust on her face turns into one of trouble.

The corners of her mouth lift into a grin, which makes my throat go dry with nervousness.

She drops the bra in her hands, and my eyes practically fall out of their sockets when she bends to pick it up from the floor.

At the sight of her ass spreading open, heat flares from my stiff cock, and the waves ride up my spine.

Oh, so she wants to be a tease.

I tug at the towel around my midsection and expose my erection. Her mouth falls into a silent 'o,' and a gleam of seduction shines like a full moon in her eyes.

My steps toward her are slow and meticulous. When she's in front of me, she's barely breathing, and the sight has my heart swelling with pure bliss.

I bend to her level and capture her mouth in a sweet tongue kiss.

Everything about this little rose of mine is perfect. Even the way her mouth tastes makes me fall in love with her all over again.

Her arms lace around my back, and I almost forget I'm teasing her. She moans, melting into my touch.

I pull away with a smirk, leaving her flustered.

She sets her lips into a pout and says nothing, her chest rising and falling unsteadily as she tries to control herself.

The entire time we get dressed, it's constant eye fucking. I wasn't sure we would make it downstairs, but we somehow managed to get dressed.

"You look beautiful," I whisper as I marvel at the sight of her in the baby blue dress. Her brown skin glistens like the finest bronze sculpture ever to exist.

"Thank you," she says, her eyes roaming the light blue suit and Gurkha pants I wear. "You look handsome," she says in admiration while adjusting my suit jacket.

I stare at the hickeys covering her neck, and I stiffen.

If her dad sees them, I'm confident he will try to take her away from me. A flick of anger takes over my body, and my grip around her tightens.

"Leo?" Her soft voice calling after me brings me out of my anger. I suspend a deep sigh, my pointer finger skimming over the bruised skin.

"We need to get those marks covered."

Victoria shudders under my touch and nods in understanding.

"You go downstairs and tell them I was sleeping when you woke me up." She kisses me and ushers me out of the bathroom.

As I leave our bedroom and head toward the noise of people, my stomach knots with anticipation.

Hopefully, her father has forgotten all about our last encounter.

VICTORIA

It took some time and lots of foundation, but I covered the bruises littering my neck and collarbone.

My legs tremble with every step closer to the living room. I'm trembling from fear and soreness.

It's been a month since I saw my family, and so much has happened since then. I feel weary of having them in Italy. With them here, there's a possibility of them becoming suspicious of Leo's wealth.

I'm not sure if I can tell them he runs a mafia. I assume this information is top secret, and I hate to keep secrets from my parents, but I also don't want the entire world to know my boyfriend runs a mafia. Not because I'm ashamed, but because the more people who know, the more at risk it puts us all in.

I clutch the railing when the ache in my lower half pierces my insides like sharp glass.

I'm thankful when I make it to the door of the living room. From where I stand, I hear Leo talking to my family, and his voice stirs the flutters in my stomach.

"Let me go see what's taking her so long," he says, and the door in front of me opens. He jolts, not expecting to see me.

I crane my neck to meet his gaze, and he smiles, offering me a hand.

When my mom sees me, her eyes widen in delight.

"Mi Niña!" She hurls toward me, and her arms wrap around my body. I ease into her touch, glad to be in her arms again.

"Hi Mami, how have you been?"

"Ay mija, we've been great," she says with a beaming smile, her hand on my left cheek. "We've all missed you and Sofia. Right?" she says, glancing over her shoulder to look at my sister and dad.

My dad nods in agreement, his eyes not straying from Leo, who hasn't taken his eyes off me.

I take nervous steps toward my dad, bringing him into a hug.

His arms circle my waist, and he squeezes me. A wave of pain takes me under, and I bite my tongue to stop myself from hissing.

"Hola, Mija, how have you been?" he says, letting me go.

"Good Papi, I missed you."

Leo stiffens beside me, and my face warms when I remember what I called him earlier.

I make a mental note to either call my dad Papá or not call Leo Papi.

My dad notices the tension between me and Leo. He purses his lips, and a line forms between his brows. He's going to say something when two slender arms wound themselves from behind me.

"Eloisa, I've missed you so much!" I exclaim, turning in her arms.

"I missed you too!" she says, and I notice my brother and her husband are missing.

"Where are Matthew and Cristian?"

"They're with Francisco and Sofia's family, taking a tour of the house. Which is beautiful, and not to mention HUGE."

I nod in agreement, and from the corner of my eye, I see Leo and my parents in deep conversation. My mom is doing most of the talking, and Leo gives an occasional comment or nod.

"Wow... sis, you're glowing," Eloisa whispers lowly with a knowing smile.

"No, I'm not," I retort, trying to ease the rising temperature in my body.

"Don't lie to me. You have the after-sex glow. You look different, and dad noticed too, so spill! How was it?"

"I look the same. You probably see me differently because it's been a month since you last saw me," I insist, and she lifts her brows in a challenge.

"Are you going to make me force it out of you?"

I raise my eyebrow at her, and she huffs, blowing out air from her mouth.

"How was the sex Victoria?"

My eyes widen, and I elbow her.

"Shh, any louder, and the whole world will hear you."

"So?" She leans forward, waiting for me to tell her the juicy details.

"Later," I whisper, and she pouts.

"Fine, but at least tell me if you and Leo are official?" she asks with a beaming smile, and I give her a simple nod. From the gesture, her face glows.

"Awe, I'm so happy for you both." She brings me into her arms. "And to think me and mom were afraid you would be a single cat lady," she teases, and my mouth falls open in disbelief.

"How long are you guys staying in Italy?" I ask, trying to change the topic.

"Only the weekend. Matthew and Dad have work. We only came to make sure you were adjusting, and we missed having you around. But now that you two"—her eyes travel between me and Leo—"are together, I assume he won't let you go home when this whole Adriano thing blows over. Am I right?"

"Most likely," I say, and a cough comes from behind us.

When I whirl around, Leo is there.

"How do you feel about taking a tour of Sicily?" Leo looks from me to my parents and sister. "All of you."

My sister and mom respond with an excited squeal, and my father nods with a grunt.

"Leo, what about our friends? We can't leave them."

"They can come with us," he assures me, as he presses me against his chest.

A rough cough from behind has us pulling apart, and we're met with the sight of my angry dad, grinning sister, and smiling mom.

The sounds of laughter and multiple voices cut through the awkward tension.

Our friends and the rest of my and Sofia's family enter the room.

Cleo makes her way toward us and introduces herself to my family. I'm filled with ease after seeing my mom, sister, and Cleo click like magnets.

After her talk with my mom and sister, Cleo comes to stand beside me. I pull her into a hug.

"It got crowded, didn't it?" The smile on Cleo's face from having many people in her once desolate home tells me she's happy.

She nods, squeezing my hand before going toward her dad and pulling him out the door despite his attempts to go to his room.

Leo wraps an arm around my waist, ignoring my dad's glare. He kisses my temple, but I don't savor the feeling as the fear of Adriano lingers in my thoughts.

"Leo, what about Adriano?"

"I have it covered, amore," he assures, and I furrow my brows in perplexity when I think back to the incident at the grocery store.

Leo senses my uneasiness hasn't gone away and holds my face between his hands.

"I'm taking your family to areas closed off to tourists. Adriano and his men won't be able to get near you or your family. I will also have men patrolling the area."

"I don't know..." I say, watching as everyone disappears outside.

"You are safe with me." He looks around the foyer, and when he notices my dad is gone, he kisses me.

"I will let nothing happen to you or those you love."

Another kiss from him follows, and I clutch his white dress shirt.

"Do you trust me?" he asks, and the air leaves my lungs from the tender look he's giving me.

"More than myself," I admit, and he smiles, caressing my cheek.

"Then let me show you a piece of my hometown."

Leo traps me in his stare, and when I nod, he smiles, taking my hand and leading me outside.

48

VICTORIA

Taormina, Sicily, is beautiful and filled with overpowering views.
The rocky mountains are illuminated with vibrant colors of orange, salmon pink, and yellow houses.

It's a beauty I never knew existed, and it reminds me of why I always loved the idea of traveling. There's so much out in the world to see.

Even though the last time I traveled I was kidnapped, I don't want this fear to stop me from being able to see the world.

The cool, crisp wind caresses my cheeks, and tiny droplets of water land on my face when the waves crash into the rocks below.

The sound of familiar heavy steps approaches from behind, and Leo's arms wrap around me.

"Did I tell you how beautiful you look today?" he whispers, staring at the side of my face. My mouth tugs into a smile, and I turn in his arms.

"Only every minute in the last hour."

"Good, and that's how it'll be for the rest of our lives." He stares at me passionately, and my heart warms at his promise of a future together, but the feeling turns to dread when I see my dad approaching us.

In the past thirty minutes alone, I've counted five instances where my dad has challenged or said something rude to Leo. Each time, I'd see

Leo swallow down his anger. He's been holding himself back, but soon he won't be able to.

I can sense the tension between the two is more than ready to snap, which tells me I need to pull my dad aside to talk to him.

I smile at my dad and pull Leo toward the small shops on the street before the tension turns into a full-blown fight.

My dad is about to follow us when my mom stops him. I let out a breath of relief, and she sends me a cunning wink while tugging my dad in the opposite direction.

Free from my dad's judgmental eyes, Leo and I walk through the streets. We listen to the soft Italian music floating in the air from one of the open windows above.

"Are you still sore?" Leo asks, and I fight the rising smile at how concerned he sounds.

"I'm okay," I say, trying to hide the fact that my insides ache every time I walk on the cobbled streets.

My response doesn't convince Leo, and his brows knit together with concern. He isn't able to say anything because my mom makes her way toward us.

She smiles, and her eyes land on me, a sign that she wants to talk to me alone. Her brown eyes fall onto mine and Leo's interlocked fingers, causing my insides to churn with uneasiness.

Leo squeezes my hand, sensing my panic.

"I'll give you two some space." He kisses my temple and heads toward his father and Francisco.

"Is everything okay?" I ask my mom, and my voice hints at my nervousness. She nods and gives a simple smile before getting straight to the point.

"You realize Leo doesn't stop staring at you? And he also can't keep his hands off of you," she teases, wrapping her arm around my left one.

If only she knew how we were last night.

"Mami, if it isn't obvious, I love him," I confess with a smile, but it falls when I remember my dad doesn't like Leo.

"What's wrong Mija?" She places a hand on my shoulder after seeing my face twist with frustration.

"It's dad; he doesn't like Leo," I say, and I grow angry because of how easy it is for my dad not to be ashamed to show Leo how much he hates him, even after everything Leo's done for our family. For starters, he wouldn't be here right now if it weren't for Leo offering them his private jet. I also wouldn't be here if it weren't for Leo saving me from Adriano.

My mom's soft voice breaks through my inner thoughts.

"Everything will be fine, Mija. You'll see. Come on, let's get back to the rest of the group," she says, guiding us toward the docks where everyone has gathered.

As soon as we arrive, I hear Sofia and Francisco fighting, and on any normal occasion, I'd find humor in their banter; but my mood has been dampened because of my dad's spoiled attitude.

I'm jolted out of my trance when Leo whispers behind me. His voice is velvety against my ear.

"Amore, we're going on a boat ride," he says, grabbing my hand, and his long, thick fingers wrap around mine like vines, keeping me close to him.

We make it to the wooden rowing boats, and most of our friends and family are being taken deeper into the crystal blue water.

"How many?" The fisherman asks.

Both Leo and my dad answer in unison:

"Two."

"Three." My dad gives Leo a sideways glance.

The fisherman looks between them, unsure what to make of their different responses.

"Dad, Leo can't go on a boat by himself. That's weird." My dad remains void of any emotion, and I sigh. "You don't want to go alone with mom?"

"No, no, come with us," he insists, ushering me into the boat, and Leo grips my hand, breathing hard as he tries to level his anger.

Leo's glaring eyes drift from my dad to me, and when he sees me growing upset from the two silently fighting with their eyes, he frowns, letting out a breath. His anger washes away for the time being.

I ignore my dad's complaints and usher Leo and me into the boat with my parents.

I'm going to make them get along, whether they like it or not.

Leo and I sit on the other end of the boat, across from my parents. I'm on edge as the engine attached to the boat comes to life, and we leave the docks.

"Your dad hates me," Leo whispers, glancing at my dad, who looks unsatisfied with Leo being in the boat.

"I'm sorry," I say, my voice hinting at my frustration.

Leo kisses the side of my head.

"It's okay. We'll figure it out." He gives me a reassuring smile, and I clutch his hand with a fierce grip while my other hand grabs the side of the boat as we crash against the waves.

Leo notices my fear and pulls me close to his chest.

"I got you," he whispers. I release a ragged breath and lean into his touch. My dad's heated stare burns holes at us.

His angry voice cuts through the motor.

"Hands off!" My dad's voice is as sharp as broken shards of glass, and everyone stiffens.

"Papá..." I warn and my mom grips my dad's forearm, but he shrugs her hands off. She becomes angry and crosses her arms over her chest while muttering unpleasant phrases under her breath.

"Don't touch my daughter or look at her!" my dad demands, and Leo scoffs, bringing me to his chest possessively.

"She's old enough to make her own decisions. If she wants me to remove my hands from her, then she'll tell me herself." As he says this, he holds me tightly, and his response fuels the flames in my dad's eyes.

The man driving the boat stops the motor, looking intrigued by their conversation.

"Victoria ven aquí," my dad says in a warning tone as if I'm a child, and I stop breathing for a second.

I don't know what takes over me, but I boldly reject his warning.

"No," I say, and my voice holds a reproach. Leo draws me closer to him when he senses my uneasiness after talking back.

"Victoria..." My dad says my name in a Spanish accent, letting me know I'm in big trouble.

I recoil into Leo's comforting embrace, trying to hide from my dad's eyes, which blaze with anger.

Leo kisses the side of my head when I tremble, and my dad snaps.

"Que te vengas aquí Niña!" I still don't budge, and the ringing of my heartbeat crawls up my throat and into my ears.

My dad rises from his seat, and my eyes widen, watching him wobble as he tries to find his footing. The man driving the boat panics and tells him to sit. My mom also shouts at my dad, tugging at his blue shirt. He doesn't listen, and angrily heads toward me and Leo, who sets me aside and rises. His composure has snapped.

The power emanating from both men crashes against one another, and they are ready to tear at each other's throats.

I know Leo isn't used to being disrespected, and if he ever is, he'd put them in their place. And my dad is protective of my sister and me to the point that he would climb out of hell itself if it meant saving us. Their determination to do what's best for me is frightening, and I don't want either of them to get hurt by the other.

When neither men listen to the poor fisherman or my mom, I sigh in aggravation and rise. My legs tremble as I make my way toward them.

"Both of you, stop it and sit down!" I stand between the two, trying to ease the tension between them.

My dad grunts and pulls me toward him. Leo doesn't like this, and he pulls me into his chest. I'm now being tugged like a piece of rope, and I realize what a big mistake it was to bring them both into a tiny boat.

"I'm not a fucking toy!" I shout, and they tense from the anger in my voice. My mom's mouth falls open in surprise, and my dad lets out a noisy exhale and lets my arm go.

A wave crashes against the boat, and I stumble to find my footing. I'm about to fall out of the boat, but Leo catches me. The top of my dress lowers and reveals the big hickey on my chest.

Leo's eyes draw to the love bite, and panic washes over his face.

I'm going to hide the hickey before my dad sees it, but it's too late.

"Pinche cabrón!" My dad launches himself onto Leo, and I fall back, as the two break out into a fight.

The boat rocks back and forth with a powerful force, and my mom and I shout at them to stop. They continue to throw punches at one another.

Leo rises from the bottom of the boat and wipes the blood from his mouth. As he does, my dad throws himself onto Leo with a shout, and this time, the impact is so strong the boat flips over, taking us all into the water with a splash.

My mom and I let out a yelp, and the cold water swallows me.

I gasp, returning to the surface, my hair sticking to my cheeks.

Leo's eyes flash with worry as he looks for me in the ocean. When he sees me, he fills with relief, and swims toward me.

"Are you okay?" He clutches onto me, his hair flat on his head from the water drenching him.

"Yeah," I say through chattering teeth.

I wrap my legs around Leo's waist, and he presses me to his chest. My gaze falls on his bottom lip, where he has a slight cut, and his jaw is bruising. The pad of my thumb runs over his cut, and my eyes burn with tears. I love Leo, and it hurts to know he and my dad aren't getting along.

"I want to go home," I mumble, shivering from the cold water soaking me. Leo nods in understanding and puts a strand of wet hair behind my ear.

"I'm sorry about my dad," I whisper, and my voice breaks.

"Amore, please don't cry. I hate seeing you upset. The one who should be sorry is me. I shouldn't have let my anger get the best of me. I'm sorry."

His apology only makes me feel worse because he's such a sweetheart and didn't deserve to be treated like dirt by my dad.

From over his shoulder, I'm satisfied to see my mom shouting in Spanish at my dad. He grimaces with each word as he helps the angry fisherman flip the boat back over.

Leo swims toward the boat and lifts me, placing me inside before climbing in after me. We're all quiet. No one said a word the entire boat ride back, and when we reach the dock, I rush out of the boat. Leo follows me and pulls me into his arms. I press myself into him, trying to find warmth.

"Victoria—" I hear my dad plead, but I shake my head. I'm too upset and cold to think about what I want to say to him.

When he sees my unwillingness to hear him out, he frowns and says nothing. I make my way toward the rest of the group. All their eyes are on us, and they have shock written across their faces.

"Victoria, what happened?" My sister rushes toward me, placing her warm hands on my cheeks. I say nothing and look at my dad, who's getting an earful from our angry mom. From the looks of it, she isn't going easy on him. Her arms are flaring, and my dad's eyes are cast to the ground in shame.

A blanket is wrapped around my shoulders, and Leo's strong arms wrap around my side.

"Where did you get the blanket?" I say, looking at the way droplets of water trickle from his wet, disheveled hair.

"I bought it. I can't have you getting sick."

Nora approaches with an amused Arthuro trailing a few steps behind.

"Wipe that damn smirk off your face, Arthuro," Leo grumbles, and Arthuro's grin widens.

"We saw what happened. Are you alright?" Nora asks.

"Yeah, it's only water," I assure her, and I tremble when a gust of wind passes.

"Come on," Leo says, leading me to the car.

"Whipped!" Alexander calls out as we pass.

Lei and Francisco nod in agreement.

"Fuck off!" Leo tells them, and they all throw their heads back in deep laughter.

49

VICTORIA

Leo and I sit in his office with my parents, and in the room hangs a heavy tension. No one says anything for a few minutes until I can no longer stand the awkward silence.

"Papi, why are you rude to Leo?"

My dad presses his lips in disapproval, and when he says nothing, I let out an annoyed breath.

"Leo's been nothing but good to me. Can you at least respect him when you're in his house?"

"I won't respect him when he keeps eye fucking you around me," he snaps. His left hand forms a fist, and his other hand points an accusing finger at Leo.

"Sir, I love your daughter, and I can see how us not getting along hurts her." He turns to look at me and then back at my dad. "For your daughter, I would like to start fresh."

My dad says nothing, and my mom elbows him in the ribs.

He looks at me with watery eyes. When I see his unshed tears, I go to him and place my hands in his.

"Why are you crying?" I say in a soft voice.

"Victoria, you're my little girl." His voice breaks, and he caresses my cheek as if he can't believe how fast I've grown up. "I can see how much you two love each other. And I know I should be happy for you, but when I see you with him, I don't see my little girl anymore. You'll forget about your mom and I and no longer need us."

"I'll always be your little girl," I say, knowing there will never be a day I won't need them. I found it weird how he worried about me not being a part of their lives when I worry every day about them and what I'll do when they aren't here anymore.

"I guess I wasn't ready to lose another daughter so quickly," he mumbles, and my mom wraps an arm around his side.

"Papi, I love Leo and want you both to get along. Can you do that for me?"

"For you, I'll do anything," he says, making his way toward Leo.

That was surprisingly easy, and I find his words have lifted the weight from my chest.

"I want to apologize for my rude behavior. Leo, you look like a good man, and I know you wouldn't hurt my daughter." My dad extends a hand for Leo to shake, and Leo takes it in his.

"Thank you for trusting me with her, sir—"

"Leo, you can call me Miguel," my dad corrects him.

"Thank you, Miguel. I promise to keep her safe and happy," Leo assures my dad, his eyes looking nowhere else but at me.

"You better, or I'll be your worst nightmare."

Leo laughs.

"Deal, but I'll never dream of hurting her." He wraps his arm around my midsection.

"You two remind me of us when we were young, right, Miguel?" my mom says, looking at my dad passionately, and he kisses her temple.

"Yes, Amor," he mumbles, and I grin at the two.

"Well, we better get to our room. We have a long day tomorrow," my mom says, her voice filled with sadness at having to go back to California. Her words bring a sharp pinch to my chest because I don't know when I'll see them again.

The door shuts behind them, and Leo leads me toward his desk. He sits me on top, and I lift a brow when he goes toward the door.

He turns the lock, and a suggestive flicker of seduction shines in his eyes.

Leo slowly stalks back toward me, and my breath gets stuck in my throat when he spreads my legs and presses himself between my thighs. The pad of his finger trails up my chest to my neck until he cups the curve of my jaw.

He bends his head, and my lips part, welcoming his soft and warm mouth. The pulsing between my legs increases when he slips a hand under my shirt. His fingers run along the edge of my bra.

"Leo, what are you doing?" I ask, sounding breathless.

He grins against my neck when he hears the desire in my voice.

"Finishing what we started this morning," he mumbles, undoing the zipper of my jeans, while his other hand fumbles with my breast.

"But my family," I breathe, my stomach tightening when his cock presses into my inner thighs. He's becoming harder by the second.

"We'll have to be quiet then," he says lowly as he pulls me closer and grinds into me. My head falls back, and I let out a breathless pant.

"I guess so," I mumble, no longer able to resist him.

Leo hums and peels off my shirt and bra. His shirt comes off right after.

His eyes roam my naked upper half, and his heated stare is enough to make me wet.

I try to catch my breath and control my lust, but I can't when my body remembers how good it felt to have him pumping in and out of me. The need to feel him increases, and I grab his belt. He makes a deep noise behind his throat as I unfasten it, shoving my hand inside his briefs and grabbing his hard cock, pulling it out.

"Fucking shit!" He sounds on the edge of falling into ecstasy when my hand slides up the length of his shaft.

The sound of his pleasure encourages me to keep going, and I trace the letter V on his wet tip. He shudders, gripping the edge of the desk on either side of me.

Leo watches with hooded eyes as I suck the tip of my finger where his glistening pre-cum has gathered. I let out a moan, and something inside him snaps. The forceful sweep of his hand pushes the contents of his desk to the ground with a loud clatter. A gasp rips from inside me when he presses my chest down on the cold, bare surface, and my hard nipples are sore against the mahogany wood.

My jeans come down forcefully, and cold air fills my hot pussy, but it turns to heat when he inserts a finger into me and then two—pumping three times before adding another finger and pumping again.

My mouth parts open against the desk, and Leo groans from the wet sounds my body makes.

I'm a mess and have to bite the inside of my mouth to stop screaming. My pleasure comes out as little noises trapped inside my mouth.

Leo curls his long fingers deep inside me, and I can't hang on. I need to feel his cock impeding deep into me.

"I need you," I beg, and he grunts. The sound of him dropping his pants mingles with the sounds of my little sighs.

My body spreads with waves of pleasure when the warm tip of his erection kisses my entrance. The absence of rubber is amazing, and I want him deep inside me.

Leo slips into me with ease, and I gasp at how good it feels when his soft skin glides against my pussy lips.

He pounds into me ferociously, taking me from behind, and with every plunge, he takes a piece of my sanity.

I brace myself over the sides of the desk, hoping it will keep me from sliding across. But it's impossible. Each jerk has my body edging across the desk until I'm on my toes.

Leo lifts me slightly from the desk, his right palm over my stomach, and he takes me hard and fast until my vision clouds with black spots.

The sound of our bodies slapping against one another is louder than our groans.

A whimper comes from me when he pinches my clit.

"So fucking sexy," he breathes, nibbling on my ear and sending a prickle of pleasure.

With my back still pressed against his chest, I lift my right hand and wrap it around his neck. He bends and captures my mouth in a tongue kiss. At the same time, he gropes my left breast, pinching at the nipple, and the other hand grabs his cock as he rams into me.

Cold air fills my hot pussy when he pulls out, but warmth fills me again when he drives his solid cock back into me, and I let out a heavy moan.

"Amore, shhh," he rasps, but I can't control the sounds pouring from me.

My stomach spasms, and my clit throbs in sync with my heartbeat. I feel myself coming, and I know when I do, I'll scream so loud all of Italy will hear. Leo senses my struggle to remain quiet and pulls out, lifting me in his arms.

I wrap my arms around his neck and my legs around his lower half. He heads across the room, and I rub myself against him as we go.

Leo lets out a rumble from deep in his chest, and he grips the wall beside him, when his knees buckle.

Behind us is the mess we've left behind. Our clothes are scattered all over the room. Pens and sheets of paper are on the ground. Warmth rushes up my spine when I see his desk moved five feet and was about to hit the wall.

Leo approaches the picture of him and his men. He removes it and presses the wall to reveal a scanner.

My mouth falls open when the bookshelf in the room opens to reveal a metal door. Leo smiles at me and puts in the code 0620.

"Is that your birthday?" I ask, my voice laced with curiosity.

Leo laughs.

"No, it's the date I found you." My breath hitches, and I feel like I'm flying on a cloud of love and ecstasy.

"I love you so much," I whisper, crashing my lips onto his. He brings us through the door, and when I pull away, my mouth drops at the sight of the secret room.

Leo places me on my feet and shuts the door. I admire the room filled with racks of money, and the shiniest diamonds I've ever seen.

I gasp when he grabs me by the hips, pressing my chest against the cool metal door, and caging me in.

His sweet mouth trails kisses along my neck, leaving behind warmth. I bend into him when his thick, long fingers play with my clit, pinching and flicking at the pulsing nerve.

"I want to hear you scream my name as I fuck you from behind," he rasps out, thrusting into me like a savage. He isn't holding back this time, and with every thrust, my ass cheeks graze his balls.

"What happened to being quiet?" I breathe, my voice quivering at the end.

"This room is soundproof," he whispers, sucking on my earlobe, and my skin turns hot from head to toe from the word *'soundproof'* coming from his lips.

The carnal desire dormant within us reveals itself as he fucks me mercifully against the door, and we don't hold back.

Leo grabs a fist full of my hair, gripping the strands as he fills me with the sweet pleasure his cock brings me.

Desperate to grab onto something, I reach behind me and find his balls. He fits in my palms, and he's heavy. I moan from how soft he is and squeeze. A deep sound comes tumbling out from the back of his throat.

"You like that," I say, my voice deep with lust, and his moans tickle my ear, bringing goosebumps to my hot skin.

He pulls out and turns me around.

"Keep it up, and I won't be able to pull out of you on time."

I grin, grab his shoulders, and press his back against the door. He watches me fall to my knees, and his Adam's apple moves when he swallows.

"Victoria..." As he whispers my name, his eyes smolder me, and my stomach twitches.

I lick my lips, wrapping my fingers over his girthy cock. My eyes stay fixed on him, and he closes his eyes when I kiss his wet, circumcised tip.

I blow on the moist tip, and he convulses when my lips curl around him. His right hand goes to the back of my head, twirling my hair as I suck him.

His hooded eyes open with a flutter, and they are watery. A shiver passes through his body when he sees me looking at him through my lashes.

I keep bobbing my head, trying to fit as much of him as possible into my mouth. The tip of his cock hits the back of my throat, producing a gag, and the noise makes his knees tremble.

I'm mesmerized as his toned stomach flexes, and he bucks his hips into my mouth when I suction his cock.

Leo lets out a loud groan, throwing his head of dark hair back against the door. He jerks inside me, filling me with the taste of his sweet and tart orgasm.

I swallow him, licking the base of his tip clean, and he falls out of my warm mouth with a pop.

Leo falls to his knees in front of me, and he grabs me by my waist, pulling me onto his lap. My legs hook around his midsection, and I grind myself against him, wanting my release. The itch deep inside me is back, and it's fierce.

When I grind into him, his hard cock brushes my throbbing clit, and I don't know when or how, but he somehow finds his way back inside me.

I press myself to his chest, wrapping my arms behind his head, and when he thrusts inside me, I bounce on his thighs.

He fucks me hard on the black carpet, and my breasts hit his chin, smothering him.

My stomach clenches, and the pressure inside increases. The quivering between my legs tells me I'm close.

Soft cries of pleasure flow out of me like a waterfall as he pierces my G-spot. I explode all over his cock, and he continues to pump inside me as I come undone.

A cold sweat races down my spine, and midway through my orgasm, he lets out a deep, throaty moan. Right as he's about to find his release, he pulls out. His passionate desire pours over the skin of my abdomen.

I gasp, arching at the sight of him exploding.

"Merda Victoria!" Leo groans out, and I get goosebumps all over my body from the sound of his pleasure.

We stare at the white substance trailing down my lower half. There's nothing to clean me with, so he grabs a five hundred euro note and wipes the area where he emptied his release. His movements are gentle, and he's careful not to touch my lower half.

He notices my heated gaze on him and smirks.

"It looks like you were the one screaming my name," I tease, cupping his face, and his glassy, lustful eyes blink at my words.

He's a captivating sight with his tousled brown locks, rosy cheeks, and Italian tan shining with sweat.

Leo notices me admiring his body and groans.

"Round two?" he asks, his voice thick with lust, and my thighs clench from his words.

He sees the gesture and licks his lips.

Lust pumps through my veins as I get on all fours in front of him, and he grabs my ass, taking me repeatedly on the ground.

50

LEO

"I say we use one of the girls as bait," Lei suggests, and we all stare at him incredulously.

"Lei, we aren't doing that," I blurt. Outraged, he would even consider such a stupid idea.

He heaves an annoyed breath.

"Then how else are we going to find satan's spawn?" he says patronizingly.

We all stiffen, realizing he has a point. Regardless, using one of the girls to lure Adriano is a stupid and reckless idea.

I rub my thumb across the stubble on my chin and survey the room.

"Anyone have any other ideas?" My question is met with silence and pursed lips.

"Boss?" From the sound of Luca's voice, I lift a brow and crane my neck to where my friend stands.

"What is it, Luca?"

"Why don't we question the police officer accused of tampering with evidence in Victoria and Sofia's case?" he says, running a hand through his tousled ash-white hair.

The men become intrigued by what Luca is saying.

"You said he was most likely involved with Adriano. Which means there's a chance he might know something." Luca hands me a black envelope as he finishes his explanation, and I pull out a packet of papers with Moises's information.

"That's a great idea, Luca." I look at the men surrounding me. "How about a visit to France?"

"Boss, what about the girls?" Francisco says with a sarcastic inflection in his voice. I repress my groan because he's right. We can't take the girls with us or leave them here alone.

"Kaden, Angelo, I have a mission for you both." Excitement is clear in their eyes as they make their way toward me. "Take some of your men to France and bring Moises to us."

"Where do you want us to take him?" Kaden asks.

"Not here. I don't want the girls to run in on us torturing him," I say when I remember Victoria's reaction to seeing me covered in blood. "Take him to one of the warehouses. We'll interrogate him there."

Shortly after, they make their way out of the room to prepare for their mission.

"So, no chick bait?" Lei asks, his hands resting behind his head, and he leans back in his seat.

We all glare at him, and his lopsided grin widens.

"Kidding!" he says with a deep bay of laughter.

"Now that we have a plan, we can call it a day," I say, ignoring Lei's comment, and they all disperse until it's only me left in the conference room.

I lean into the black leather chair, closing my eyes, when two familiar hands run down my chest.

Victoria's signature scent fills my senses, and I relax under her touch. I let out a ragged breath when her hands reach for my abdomen.

Swiveling my chair, I place her on my lap, cradling her.

"Is everything okay?" she asks, staring at the side of my face and caressing my growing stubble.

"Yes, we finally have a lead." She glows from the news.

"Really?" she says. I hum and press my face against the crook of her neck, inhaling her sweet scent. Her hands run through my hair, and I sigh.

"Kaden and Angelo are going to France to bring Moises for us to question him." She stills for a second as she absorbs my words.

"I suspected he was working with Adriano," she says, and her confession has visibly lifted the tension in her shoulders.

I kiss her cheek and take in her delicate feminine features. Her beauty is out of this world, and my love for her grows every minute I'm with her.

"Are you done working?" she asks, her voice hopeful. My gaze falls on her fingers, playing with the tie around my neck. There's a tightness in my throat, and heat rushes between my legs where an uncomfortable thickness is forming.

Victoria's breaths are quick and shallow when she feels the large print between my legs.

My erection springs up, pressing on the zipper of my trousers, and it feels like it's going to come busting out through the seams.

I curl my fingers around her chin and press her lips against mine.

"What did you have in mind?" My brows rise suggestively, and my voice is low.

"Whatever you want, as long as it's with you, I'm happy," she says, giving me a breathtaking smile.

"I have a few ideas," I hum, rising from the chair with her wrapped around me. I exit the room, and my lips skim the shell of her ear as I whisper what I have in store for her. "And all of them end with me deep inside you."

She shudders, and her eyes shut when I suck on her earlobe.

The rapid beat of my steps reveals an urgency to get to our room. The tightness in my pants intensifies, and my cock aches to plunge into her.

When our room appears, my skin erupts with tingles.

"I have a present for you," I say as I push open the bedroom door. Her face screws into confusion.

"A present?" I nod and place her on our bed. Her eyes follow me as I head toward the closet.

When I return to the room, I find Victoria reading a book. She's engrossed with the words on the page and doesn't see me until I take the book from her hands.

Victoria looks at me. Her eyes land on the red box in my hand.

She raises a questioning brow, watching me loosen the tie around my neck.

"Come here, amore." Her throat moves when she swallows, and she looks at the black tie in my hands. She slowly does as I say, and her skirt rises when she crawls toward me.

I wrap the tie around her head, covering her eyes.

"Leo, what's with the blindfold?" she asks, almost choking on her words.

"Shhh, lie down." I push her shoulders, and her cheeks flush from the rising heat between us. My eyes remain on her, lying blindfolded on our bed, and I unbutton my shirt and unzip my trousers. I sigh when the thick, burning friction from my cock rubbing against my zipper eases.

Although I'm soaked and ready for her, I don't ram into her. Even if I'm going crazy to feel her tight pussy fluttering around me.

I grab the box and hover above her.

Her brown plaid mini skirt rises when I spread open her thighs, and she trembles under my touch.

"Leo?" she calls out in uncertainty.

"Relax, baby," I whisper, and pull out the black vibrator from the box. She lets out a small whimper when my fingers tug down her purple thong, and my thumb rolls over her soft clit.

My breath becomes heavy from how soaking wet she already is. I twirl the wet fabric around my finger. The smell of her sweet arousal overwhelms my mind, and I have to take deep breaths to contain myself.

She spreads open for me, and her glistening pussy greets me. I want to mouth fuck her so good that all she'll feel is the ghost of my tongue plunging into her for the next few months.

"That's right, baby, open up for me," I groan, and her legs widen even more. Her delicious clit glistens from her wetness. I grind my teeth together and bend down, tempted to give in, but I stop myself. Her pleasure comes first.

I grab the bottle of lube from the box and lather the tip of the vibrator. My fingers run over her pussy, lathering her before we play.

She twitches under my touch when my finger drifts against her walls.

I drag the tip of the vibrator along her left leg and through her inner thigh. She quivers, and goosebumps rise on her legs and arms. Her delicate fingers grip the bedsheets beside her, and she arches when I press the vibrator against her entrance.

Fucking hell, she's already turned on, and the vibrator isn't even on.

Sensing her distress from not getting the pleasure she craves, I turn on the vibrator, and her mouth falls open. Her knees rise, and she arches into the toy.

I drag the vibrator across her moist pussy, and she clenches her legs together to suppress her pleasure. When she does this, she presses the vibrator further into her, and she's hit with a fresh wave of pleasure.

"Dios Mio," she squeaks out, her head rolling. My lower half becomes tight, and I'm dripping from the sounds she's making.

I grab her hands and place them around the vibrator. She grips the rubber, gliding it where she wants it. Now that my hands are free, I lift her and remove her shirt and bra. Her breasts spill out, and I cup them. Her nipples stand erect, and I take those chocolate Hershey kisses into my warm mouth.

Giving one last twirl around her right nipple, I detach my mouth from it and lick the skin between her chest until my tongue flicks over the left one.

I nip at the bud, my teeth teasing her. Victoria's back bends, forcing her breast further into my mouth.

"Fuck, you are so precious," I breathe before latching onto her neck and sucking the skin. The vibrator between us presses into my cock, sending a thrill of pleasure through my veins.

Her hips roll around the rubber, and seeing her eagerness for the toy to fuck her makes my stomach tighten.

I grab the vibrator from her hands and push it deeper into her. Victoria's toes curl, and a hand covers her mouth to muffle her pleasurable groans. She shoves her other hand inside my pants, and she jerks my hard cock.

Burning flames of pleasure crawl up my skin like needles. We are breathing hard, and our mouths open as we let out strangled moans.

"Leo," she cries, and I press my mouth to hers, pumping the toy inside her.

"Tell me which is better," I pant, biting my lip when she jerks me faster. "My cock or this piece of rubber," I grunt, and she moans when I increase the speed of the toy to the highest level.

"You!" she screams and doubles over, orgasming all over the toy, and when I see her release dribbling down the rubber, I'm no longer able to hold off.

"Then show me," I say, removing my pants and briefs. "I want to feel you wrap that tight pussy around me."

I turn the toy off, toss it aside, and pull the skirt down her legs. I remove the blindfold, and her eyes flash open, but they screw shut again when I plunge deep into her.

My gut clenches when she tightens her pussy around my cock, as I told her to do.

"Good girl," I praise, taking her mouth in a kiss.

"Ahhh!" she screams, her nails digging into my shoulder blade. I grunt, continuing my merciless, rhythmic thrusts. Her pussy tightens and flutters around me with each press of my hips.

"Nnngh fuck..." I stutter when my cock hits her G-spot, and she releases herself, my name coming from her lips.

Her pussy lips suction my shaft as she spasms, and the pressure mixed with the hotness of her juices takes me to the edge. I spill myself inside her, unable to pull out.

"Fuck!" I groan, and it's impossible to stop myself from creaming her now that I've started. Victoria trembles under me as I pull out, still squirting. I reach for a condom for the next orgasms to come, when Victoria grabs my cock, and pushes me back inside her.

I stagger, and my vision hazes.

I fucking love it when she does that shit.

Her unwillingness to let me go tells me she wants more, and I'm not about to stop her from getting the pleasure she and I both cling to.

I roll us over, and she presses her lips onto mine, rocking those sexy hips of hers around and around.

My fingers dig into her ass, and I watch as she rides me like she hasn't had me in decades. Wisps of her black hair hang over her hot face, and she bounces high in the air.

The hands I have holding her waist guide her up and down. When she comes down on me, her ass presses into my balls, making them pull tight.

Victoria moans, throwing her head back when the V shape between my index finger and middle finger pinches her nipples.

I lift my lower half, rutting deep into her. The muscles of her thighs spasm as she once again finds her release, and I follow right after.

She falls out of breath on my chest, and I move a strand of her hair from her sweaty forehead.

As we work on steadying our breaths, I run my fingers through her soft hair.

My cock twitches inside her, and she groans against my chest.

I glance at my cock buried between her thighs and see our milky juices seeping out of her. I remind myself to have someone go to the store and get her the day-after pill, and while they're at it, they can bring us about ten more because I don't see us stopping.

Two days later

"Where the fuck is Adriano?"

"I don't know!" Moises cries out in pain.

"Wrong answer," Alexander says from behind. He gives me my pliers, and Moises's eyes widen in fear.

I wrap my hands around his thick neck and squeeze. His mouth falls open, and tiny gasps come from him. I press the blade of the pliers near his fingers, ready to mangle them.

"Wait!" I remove my hand from around his neck, the pliers still near his finger, in case he gives us bullshit. "He's somewhere in Latin America!"

"Where in Latin America?" I question putting pressure on the pliers, and they break the skin, drawing blood.

His split lip trembles.

"I don't know where because he never said."

I glance at my watch and back at him with a sneer, not content with his response. He senses my impatience and stiffens, tears falling from his pathetic, bloodshot eyes.

I dig the pliers into his finger, and he screams in agony.

"Try again, or I'm going to tear apart every single fucking finger on your hands, until all that's left is the bone."

His body trembles uncontrollably, and I move the pliers to the next finger.

"Fuck okay! I'll talk... just no more, please no more..."

At the sight of the officer crumbling, I feel my lips curl into a grin.

"They blindfolded me when I last saw him, so I'm not entirely sure where he is exactly, but I remember hearing some of his men say something about the Amazon rainforest."

"Well, that doesn't help us now, does it?"

"Wait, please, there's more!"

"Go on," I say, and he relaxes when the blade of the pliers stops cutting into his finger.

"Adriano's having a masquerade in two, maybe three, months. It's supposed to be an opportunity for him to gather with the higher-ups of gangs he wants to join forces with."

I glance at the men behind me with a grin. This is the opportunity we've been looking for.

"Where is this event happening?" My tone is deadly, and he cowers back.

"I don't know," he cries, closing his eyes and shaking his head. "Please don't kill me."

His cries for mercy remind me of how he let Adriano get away with kidnapping and trafficking women.

He doesn't deserve any mercy. Not for what he's done. What I'm doing to him doesn't even come close to the pain the women he failed to save had to endure.

I clamp the pliers down on his stubby finger, and he screams, squirming in the metal chair. Every tug drives him to unbearable pain until the lump of skin comes off.

Lei grabs the chopped finger and hands it to me. I'm going to shove it down his mouth, but stop when he gives me the answer I want.

"He's going to Paris to host the event. But I swear he didn't tell me the location!"

Satisfied, I step away from Moises.

"How do you want to kill him?" Arthuro asks, his eyes glancing at Moises.

"Concrete shoes?" Alexander offers with a glint in his eyes.

"Why not?" I shrug indifferently. Lei's eyes widen in excitement, and he goes to get a bucket.

"Wait, what are you guys doing?" Moises's voice cracks when Lei brings the bucket with wet concrete toward his feet.

"No, please don't kill me. I told you everything I know!" Moises shouts, fighting in Arthuro and Alejandro's arms. "Don't do this, please. Have some mercy!"

"Shut the fuck up!" I sneer, and he recoils back from the harshness in my voice.

This greased up cop only cares about his money and not the lives of Victoria, Sofia, and the others.

A raw fear sweeps through me at the thought of what would have happened to my Victoria if I hadn't saved her. The mere thought of her body littered with bruises and being assaulted brings my blood to a boil.

I grip his face between my hands, and his jaw pops.

"Did you show any mercy to the girls you let Adriano kidnap?" He remains silent, and two tears trickle down his bloody cheeks.

"Thought so... Put him in," I order, and Lei grabs Moises's feet and shoves them into the wet cement.

"No, stop, you fucking assholes!" Moises kicks Lei in the mouth.

"Mother fucker!" Lei grunts and punches Moises in his broken ribs.

"That's enough!" I shout, not wanting to be here longer than I need to be. "Let's get this shit over with."

I grab Moises' left foot while Lei grabs the other. We chain his feet and force them into the cement-filled bucket. I drop the lock of the chain into the wet cement, and the sharp ring of a phone shrills through the room. I pull my phone out to see Francisco calling me.

When Moises continues to curse us, I give Alexander a look, and he and Alejandro place a rag into his mouth, sealing it with duct tape.

"Francisco, what's wrong?" I ask, my attention drawn to the chaos ensuing over the line. He shouts orders, and I pick up on the familiar popping sounds of bullets going off like crazy. My body stiffens.

"Leo, we're under attack!" he says into the phone. "Kaden! Angelo! Where are the girls?" he shouts, and my body goes cold, the adrenaline in my veins pumping.

"They're in the backyard!" my father says over the line, followed by more guns going off.

From hearing the house is being attacked, I succumb to a vortex of molting anger. It rolls through me like sound waves. Then the fiery rage dulls when a pinch in my chest brings a prickle of fear at the thought of losing Victoria or my sister.

"Do whatever you have to, but get the girls to safety! We're on our way."

The look of concern on the guys' faces greets me, and they stand on edge.

"Adriano's men are attacking my estate!" The moment the words are out, fear and anger take over their expressions.

"Fuck, let's go!" Alexander says on the brink of despair.

"What about dickhead here?" Lei points his chin at Moises.

I turn to my two men guarding the door.

"When the cement hardens, dump his ass into the ocean," I order, and the two nod in understanding.

Without another word, we race toward the house, and Alejandro breaks every traffic law to get there.

The pinching pain in my chest intensifies, and I crack my knuckles. My hands tremble as I'm tormented by the memory of my mother's body lying on the ground with her blood on my hands.

I run my fingers through my hair, and dread runs through my body.

Not again.

Not my Victoria.

51

VICTORIA

All around me are the sounds of the girls talking amongst themselves. The smell of warm bread, coffee, and other pastries mingles with the fresh air.

I take a sip of the fresh homemade lemonade. My lips around the glass rim spread into a smile as I remember how Leo cleaned me last night.

"What's with the grin, Victoria?" Emma asks, her mouth spreading into a toothy smile. My cheeks warm when all the girls study me with curiosity.

"It's nothing."

Emma laughs as she rests a delicate hand on my forearm. She leans into me and whispers in my ear.

"It's got nothing to do with Leo taking you *another* Plan B the other day?"

My eyes widen, and my face is burning at this point.

"Emma!" I say in shock, and her smile widens.

"I'm happy for you, Victoria," she says, squeezing me to her side. I'm about to thank her when I hear a loud crash coming from the front of the house.

My stomach knots with uneasiness.

I try to make out what the noise was, but all my ears pick up is the sound of the girl's talking and the wind rustling the trees.

"Did you guys hear that?" I ask.

"No," Nora says with furrowed brows, and the others agree.

Emma looks at me with knitted brows.

"I think I did, but I wasn't paying much attention," she says with a frown. "I'm sure it was nothing but a bad driver," she tries to assure me, and I decide she's right when I hear nothing else.

I extend a hand to grab a strawberry when the sound of loud bullets ringing in the air has me jumping in my seat. The sounds are coming from the front of the house, and as the familiar clicking sounds continue to go off, the girls scream. Their faces lose all color.

"We're being attacked!" Nora says, rising from her seat and grabbing Cleo.

"What do we do?" Sofia asks, her eyes welling with tears.

I panic, frozen from fear.

Emma shakes my shoulders.

"Victoria, we have to go!" The panic in her voice pulls me from my trance.

A staggered breath comes from me, and I look at Cleo, who's biting her bottom lip, looking dazed.

"Cleo, is there somewhere we can hide?" I ask, and she jolts at the sound of my voice.

"Yes, but it's inside the house," she whispers, looking fearful. "I don't know if it's safe to go inside."

"Is there anywhere in the backyard you think we might be safe?"

"There's this little house my dad built for my mom when she wanted a place to escape from the mansion. But it's about a ten-minute walk." She points to the huge backyard. "If we run, we might make it in six minutes."

"Take us," I tell her, and all seven of us run after her.

Not even a minute later, laughter comes from behind, and a shiver of terror crawls up my spine at the familiar sound.

Still running as fast as I can, I glance over my shoulder. My panic rises when I see Lorenzo sitting on the window of a van, heading toward us.

The rifle in his hand goes off, shooting into the air. My heart leaps into my throat, and I force my legs to carry me faster down the yard.

Our haunted screams stab into the air.

Layla struggles to run beside me, so I slow down and wrap my arms around her, encouraging her to keep going.

She looks terrified, and her right hand rests over her bulging belly. My heart tugs at the sight of her tears.

"Come on, Layla. You can do it. Keep running," I plead, and she forces her legs to run faster.

The house Cleo was telling us about comes into our view, but by then, Lorenzo is about a yard away, and he's shooting at us.

The girls enter the house one by one until it's only Layla and me.

They wave for us to hurry. The silence behind me makes my shoulders stiffen.

Layla screams as she's pulled out of my grasp, and my heart falls to my stomach when I see a man lifting her in his arms.

"Layla!"

Her feet kick, and her arms swing around as the man lifts her.

"Fucking bitch!" The man shouts when she bites his hand.

I glance from Layla to the girls, whose mouths are open in horror. Then I look back at a screaming Layla.

I can't let them take her. Not when she's pregnant and has more to lose.

"Come on, Victoria," I mutter, looking around me. "Think!"

My eyes widen when I see a shovel nearby. I grab it right as Lorenzo appears.

The shovel trembles in my grasp.

I see Francisco, Luca, Angelo, and Kaden running toward us.

"Put the shovel down, sexy. I don't want to shoot your hand. You'll be needing it later tonight," Lorenzo says, looking at my legs, and his tongue runs over his bottom lip.

"Fuck you!" I retort, raising the shovel.

"Don't say I didn't warn you." He shrugs and shoots at the ground near my legs.

The bullet misses by a centimeter, and the heat of the bullet whizzes past my ankle. I jolt back with a scream.

Layla screams again, and I see the man getting ready to toss her over his shoulder.

"Let Layla go," I beg Lorenzo, and he scoffs.

I try again, but this time I bargain with him. "Please, I'll go with you. But you have to leave Layla." He screws his face in thought, and he doesn't answer me. "Take me instead, but you have to let her go," I repeat, and Layla screams her complaints.

"No, don't listen to her; es una pendeja!" Layla shouts. "Desgraciado infeliz no me toques!" she curses when her attacker puts his hand over her butt.

Lorenzo thinks over my offer with pursed lips, and his eyes glance toward Leo's capos heading our way. His sinister eyes widen, and I see panic wash over his features, but he masks it with a sneer.

"Leave the bitch Mark. We're taking this one willingly," he says, cocking his head, telling me to hurry and get into the van.

The man drops Layla onto the ground, and she looks at me with a quivering lip. She cries out, trying to reach out for me, but Lorenzo pushes me forward when she's about to grab me.

"Keep walking!" He presses the gun to my back.

I clench my teeth to stop from cursing him and slowly step toward the van.

"Victoria, no! Let me go, goddammit!" Sofia shouts through sobs, and my heart breaks at the sound of her fear. She's struggling to escape Nora and Chloe's arms, and I'm thankful the two are keeping her in place.

"Lorenzo!" Francisco shouts, pointing his gun at him. The rest of Leo's men also arrive with their guns out.

The man with Lorenzo goes to pull out his gun, but Francisco shoots him in the neck.

I cry out when Lorenzo grabs me by the neck and presses his gun against my temple.

"Ah ah ah. One wrong move, and I blow her brains out, killing her right here, right now."

My muscles become heavy with dread, and I peer at Leo's capos, trying not to let my tears fall.

"It's over, Lorenzo. Let her go," Francisco says, his gun not wavering.

From behind Francisco, I see the black SUV with Leo driving toward us. My tears fall from fear of what the next few seconds will bring.

"If I die, so does she." Lorenzo's words are harsh, and he forcefully presses the gun to the side of my head.

"Move!" Leo snarls as he pushes past Angelo and Kaden. His eyes widen at the sight of me at gunpoint, and his lips curl in anger.

"Ah, Leo, nice of you to join us," Lorenzo taunts, and his free hand gropes my right breast. I fight in his arms, trying to get out of his grasp, but Lorenzo grabs my neck and chokes me.

Leo becomes furious and launches himself toward Lorenzo. The safety of the gun goes off, and everyone freezes.

The sound forces Leo to stop, and he casts an agonizing glance at me. His eyes fill with anger, pain, and fear when he can't do anything but watch as I'm assaulted in front of him.

Estephano appears covered in blood and places a hand over Leo's shoulder.

Leo doesn't acknowledge his dad. His attention is on me as he tries to figure out what to do.

"Let her go, you fucker, or else," Leo warns, his voice deadly.

"No, you listen to me! You're all going to put your guns down and move aside. That way, this little thing and I can run off into the sunset," Lorenzo says behind my ear, placing a sloppy kiss on my cheek.

I grimace and pull away, but he drags me back to him, trailing his hand up my thigh. He slips his hand inside my skirt and cups my lower half. The memories I forced myself to forget rush back, and my heart pounds painfully hard in my chest.

I'm trapped with fear until he pushes my underwear aside. My senses kick in, and I force the trauma and fear aside with a determination not to let this asshole hurt me anymore.

"Don't touch me, bastardo!" My voice breaks when I shout at him, and I grab his hand, trying to get him to let me go. He removes his hand and moves it to my neck. His fingers dig into my jugular.

"Shut up, or I'll press the trigger!"

I bite my lip to stop from crying at seeing Leo fighting in Kaden and Estephano's arms. Anger and fear rage through him in powerful pulses.

Kaden and Estephano don't let him go because if they do, they know he'll let his anger get the best of him and put him and me both in danger.

"Drop the guns now!" Lorenzo warns, his finger ready to press the trigger. I cry out when the end of the gun digs into my scalp.

My cry has Leo's hand extending out to me with a need to hold me, but he can't.

"Drop your fucking guns!" Leo orders and shrugs off Kaden and his dad's arms from around him.

"Thank you, now if you—"

Lorenzo never finishes because a loud bang comes from behind us.

The gun around my temple falls onto the grass, and I kick it.

Lorenzo falls to the ground, and Leo runs toward me, clutching me tightly

I can't control the little sobs spilling from my mouth after being assaulted in front of them all.

My chest rises and falls, and I bury my face in Leo's chest.

Right behind Lorenzo's unmoving body stands Sofia, huffing in anger. The shovel I had earlier is now in her hands, and she glares at Lorenzo.

"That's why I love you, piccolo fuoco," Francisco says with pride, as he wraps his arms around my cousin, whose eyes are on me. She releases a breath of relief.

Lorenzo groans, and I see him rising. My eyes turn into a silent, menacing glare, and a venomous calmness consumes me.

I pull from Leo's grasp and run toward Lorenzo, kicking him in the stomach. He bellows in pain, but this isn't enough.

Anger emits from within me, and I want to kill him. I want to make him pay for all the damage he has done to me, Erika, and many other girls.

I'm angry. No, I'm furious because I was finally feeling like myself again, and now it's like I'm back to square one.

I kick him in the face, breaking his nose, and pain shoots up my foot from the impact. I ignore the pain, too consumed by my silent rage.

With trembling hands, I grab the shovel from Sofia, and she gives it to me without hesitation. She and Francisco step back, giving me room.

I plummet the shovel onto him, letting my anger overtake my muscles.

"This is for Erika!" I hit him on the head.

"This is for kidnapping me and calling me your sex toy!" I launch the shovel back onto his bleeding scalp without remorse.

"And this is for touching me and looking at me!" I strike the shovel five times on his head, neck, and back. With each thrust, he laughs, and I grow more furious. I don't stop my assault until Leo pulls me back and presses me into his chest.

The shovel falls to the ground with a thud, and my muscles become numb as I fall victim to a panic attack.

I can still feel Lorenzo's fingers and how he touched me.

My lungs are heaving, my face is burning, and my sight blurs from my tears. I clutch onto Leo, and he cups my face.

"Shhh, I'm here, amore." His touch works to keep me grounded. "Baby, look at me," he murmurs, and my chest tightens. I try to catch my breath, but I can't.

I look at Leo, blinking the tears away, and he's worried as I hyperventilate in his arms.

Leo grabs my trembling hands and places them over his chest. I feel his steady heart, and mine tries to match the soft rhythm of his heartbeat.

"That's it, amore. Take steady breaths." He kisses my temple and lifts me into his arms. "I'm here. You're safe," he mumbles, his voice shaky. I bury my head in his neck, my tears rushing out, and they soak the collar of his dress shirt.

As we pass an unmoving Lorenzo, Leo steps on his fingers, and his jaw clenches.

"Lock him up," comes Leo's order.

Kaden and Luca lift Lorenzo and haul him away.

No one says a word as Leo carries me inside the house. His warmth brings me some comfort, but not enough to ease the pain from my assault.

52

LEO

"Leo, tell Victoria I'm in debt to her after what she did for my wife and child." Alejandro places a hand on my left shoulder, and my face reveals my confusion.

"What are you talking about?" I say, lifting a brow.

"Victoria didn't tell you what she did?"

"No, she didn't. Why what happened?"

"Leo, she was ready to sacrifice herself for Layla. They were going to throw her inside the van when Victoria told Lorenzo to take her instead," he says, and a cold stillness takes over my heart. This information brings me anger, guilt, and pride. But more so guilt.

"Thank you for telling me," I say, and there's a break in my voice. Alejandro gives a tight-lipped smile and takes his leave.

I stare at a sleeping Victoria, and my heart clenches at seeing her cheeks stained from her tears.

Concern overwhelms me after what Alejandro told me. I don't want her to be placed in another situation where she feels the need to sacrifice herself.

I've failed her again, and now she's hurting.

She needs to know how to protect herself in both hand-to-hand combat and weaponry. I need her to carry a gun from now on. I won't be at ease until then.

Victoria tosses in her sleep, and she's crying. My heart leaps, and I feel hopeless.

"I'm here. It's only a dream," I whisper, holding her in my arms and running my fingers through her hair. She holds me tight, and she shakes her head.

"No, it's not," she whispers, and I feel my world crumble from seeing her in pain, and I can't do anything to take it away.

"It's not a dream. It's real." She sounds so broken, and her brown eyes have a hollow sadness in them. She's dissociating herself, and I can't bring her back to me.

From the pain Lorenzo has brought to her, a smouldering rage takes over my body, and there's a quench for violence and a need for the blood of the man who hurt my girl.

"I won't let him hurt you anymore." I hold her teary face between my palms, and she's cold. "I'm going to make him pay for what he's done to you."

Her breathing slows, and her glowing brown skin is ashen. I find myself staring at the fingerprint bruises around her neck.

That piece of shit will pay for hurting her and touching her with his filthy hands.

Victoria presses a hand to her temple, where there's a bump from when the gun barrel pressed into the area.

She drifts away again as she remembers everything he did to her. When her thoughts become too much, she wraps her arms across her chest, and her face morphs into a grimace. Her throat moves as she swallows once, twice, and a third time.

"Alejandro told me what you did for Layla." She looks away, waiting for me to scold her. "I'm not mad; I'm just upset you had to do that," I say, and she looks at me with teary eyes.

"I need you to learn how to use a gun." As soon as the words leave my lips, she takes a sharp breath, which tells me she doesn't like this idea.

"I understand you might not be comfortable with this. But amore you aren't in California anymore. My world is nothing like what you're used to." My voice is gentle yet firm, hoping she understands where I'm coming from. She stares at me for a few seconds and nods.

"Okay," she whispers, taking in a ragged breath.

I kiss the corner of her mouth, glad I was able to get through to her.

Victoria insists I leave her to finish my work, but I refuse, not wanting to abandon her after what happened this morning. She's my number one priority, and she will always come first.

"Leo, please go do what you need to."

"I'm not leaving you." My words are final, and she sighs.

"Do you love me?" she asks, looking at me through her lashes coated in tears.

"So fucking much," I breathe, clinging to her.

"Then go to work and find Adriano. I don't want to keep looking over my shoulder." The fear in her words brings a pinch to my chest, and I swallow the lump in my throat.

"Are you sure?" She nods, and I let out a breath, giving in to her demands. "If you need anything"—I stare at her hard—"anything at all. You come and find me."

A smile stretches across her pink lips, and she nods.

"I love you," I say, kissing her.

"I love you too. Now go find that piece of trash." She pushes my chest, and I laugh at her attempts to get me to go.

The first thing I see when I reach the front of the house are the holes littered across the walls and shattered glass. I kick the bullets scattered across the white granite stone pavement, which is now stained a dark red.

"I'm going to kill him," I grit through my teeth and stare ahead at my men lifting dead bodies into a truck.

Francisco comes to stand beside me. He gives me a tight-lipped smile.

"How's she doing?" he asks, and worry is clear in his voice.

I sigh. "She's doing better than earlier. If it weren't for Sofia, I don't know what would have happened to her."

Francisco's thin lips tug into a grin, and I don't miss the glint in his eyes at the mention of Sofia's heroic move earlier.

"What are we going to do with Lorenzo?" he asks as we make our way toward the basement, where we have the bastard chained to the wall of a cell.

"I'm going to make him pay for hurting what's mine."

We enter the cell where Angelo, Kaden, and Luca are.

Lorenzo has blood dripping down his temple from the gash Victoria gave him earlier. The sight of it brings me pleasure, and it reminds me of the way Victoria's dormant anger revealed itself. She's the perfect combination of rage and serenity.

Bone hitting flesh draws me from my thoughts.

Luca's knuckles continue to ram into Lorenzo's face. His shoulders are tense, and his jaw spasms with anger.

Lorenzo laughs.

"What's so funny, asshole?" Luca's fist crashes into Lorenzo's right eye.

I place a hand on my friend's shoulder, and he tenses. His blue eyes are as dark as the bottom of the ocean.

Luca lets out a hard breath, drops Lorenzo, and steps aside.

I tower over Lorenzo's slumped, beaten figure. My vision grows red, and my shoulders twitch with an uncomfortable itch that will only be relieved after hurting him.

Lorenzo's only good eye stares at me, and he draws back when he sees my deadly glare.

I've been waiting for this moment since I learned he was the one who had bought Victoria.

Lorenzo licks the blood from his teeth, and his fear turns into cockiness.

"How's Victoria? Is the pussy as tight as I know it is?" he mocks, and rage takes over my body from the sound of him saying her name with his shithole mouth.

I wrap my hands around his neck, lifting him from the ground. The chains around his feet clank below him.

"How dare you say her name!" Lorenzo struggles in my grasp, and he stares at me with amusement.

I pull out my pocket knife, place it on his ear, and cut off the top half. His guttural screams vibrate throughout the bottom level.

"I'm going to make sure you feel every ounce of pain known to man. You're going to wish death by the time we're done with you." I press the knife into his cheek, and blood exudes from the cut.

Lorenzo stays silent. Nothing he says will get him out of the ditch he's dug for himself. Adriano is nowhere in sight to get him out of this one.

I drop him and grab the bat from Kaden's hand. With a flick of a finger, I motion for Kaden and Angelo to spread his legs.

"This will teach you not to think with your dick," I sneer, thrusting the end of the bat between his legs, crushing his testicles.

He passes out from the pain after ten strikes, and I let out an unsatisfied breath.

I hand Francisco the bat.

"Tell me when he wakes up," I say, motioning for Luca to follow me.

"Were you able to find anything?" I ask Luca, and he pulls out the phone we found in Lorenzo's pocket.

"A couple of messages from Adriano and..." Luca pauses, and I narrow my eyes at the look of disgust on his face.

"And what, Luca?"

He exhales before going to the pictures on Lorenzo's phone to reveal multiple images of women chained to walls, naked. A black cloth covers their heads to hide their identities.

Bile rises in my mouth, and a chill crawls up my spine when I realize this could have been Victoria if I hadn't rescued her.

Luca shares the same expression of horror as I do.

"Those fucking pigs!" I say through clenched teeth, and I want to go back into the cell and kill Lorenzo on the spot. But no, he wouldn't get a quick death. He's going to suffer for all his crimes and for what he did to Victoria.

"I also found this," Luca says, showing me an image of an electronic invitation, and I can't believe my eyes when I see the information on the screen.

Lorenzo has given us the date, time, and exact location of the masquerade ball Adriano is hosting.

Two words amidst the invitation stand out to me, and my throat grows thick with dread.

Date required

We're all fucked, is what it should say.

Luca gives me a knowing grin, laughing and patting my back.

"This is going to be good," he says, and I glare at him before texting the men that we have a problem.

VICTORIA

There's a knock on the door, and when I open it, the girls all come tumbling into the room.

Layla runs into my arms, and she's a crying mess.

"Victoria!" she says through tears. "Why did you do that?"

"I couldn't let them take you. You have a baby to think about." I look at her stomach, and her bottom lip quivers. "I will always do whatever I can to protect you guys."

The girls run toward me, and we're now all in a tight ball of arms.

When I start to get choked by all their arms, I laugh and try to pull away from them.

"Alright, that's enough," I tease, and they all disperse around me.

I stare at my cousin, and her features soften.

"Thank you for saving my life."

Sofia waves a dismissive hand.

"Consider this my apology for getting us kidnapped in France," she says with a smile.

I laugh, and the mention of France reminds me how our lives would have been different if Adriano hadn't kidnapped us.

Fate has a weird way of working, and I'm grateful things turned out the way they did for us. But I wouldn't wish what happened to Sofia and me on anyone.

Human trafficking isn't a joke. I may have been rescued, but many others, like Erika, are still in captivity. It pains me to think about what she's going through right now.

Lorenzo was the one who trafficked her, and now we have him in our grasp.

The mere thought of him brings a pounding to my ears, and the temperature in my body rises.

I want nothing more than to go to Lorenzo and make him suffer imaginable pain for what he's done to her.

Leo's torturing him, but this isn't satisfying to me. I want to do it myself. I want to hear his screams begging me to stop, but I won't stop. I'll ignore his cries just as he ignored mine when he tried to rape me.

The pent-up anger I've carried inside me for months is suffocating.

"Victoria, what's wrong?" Cleo places a hand on my arm, and her voice is laced with worry.

"I don't know," I say as my pulse elevates, but not from a panic attack. My thoughts are actively thinking about hurting Lorenzo. The outburst I had earlier wasn't enough and has left me unsatisfied.

"Where do they have him?" I say, voice low and rough. My hands tremble at my sides as the tension in my body crackles with the flames of my anger.

The girls stare at one another and remain quiet.

As the seconds pass, my heart pounds angrily in my chest with frustration for the girl's unwillingness to talk to me, as well as a new sense of vicious anger toward those who have hurt me.

"Cleo, please. I need to know where he is. He knows where someone I care about is being kept prisoner." I blink back my tears, and Cleo's features soften.

"Victoria, I'm sure Leo will get him to talk." She places both her hands on my shoulders, but her touch does nothing to ease my trembling body.

"If you could hurt those who hurt you and those you love, would you?" Cleo freezes at my words and lets out a breath.

"There's a guard. If I take you, I can't promise they'll let us in," she says, but I don't care. I'll force them to let me in, even if I have to break down the door.

Cleo takes my hand and leads us downstairs to the basement, where, true to her words, stands a guard.

When he sees us, he raises an eyebrow and clears his throat.

"You ladies shouldn't be down here," he says, voice firm.

"Move." My words hold a frosty edge, and he looks taken aback.

"I'm sorry, regina, but I can't do that."

"Please." The guard shakes his head, and his unwillingness to let me inside has me exploding with anger.

"I said move!" My scream is so loud he flinches, and the girls gasp behind me.

The door behind him opens, and Kaden pops his head out to see what the noise is all about. When he sees me, his eyes widen in shock.

"It's fine. I'll make sure they're safe," Kaden tells him, and the guard steps aside.

I waste no time and enter, but Kaden grabs my shoulder, halting my steps.

"What's wrong?" Worry is evident in his voice as he stares at me.

I turn to him, and my eyes tell him all he needs to know.

"You know I have to tell Leo you're down here, right?" he says, and I nod as my steps take me down the dim, cold hallway with the girls following close behind us.

Kaden leads us into a cell, and my body tingles at the sight of a beaten Lorenzo knocked out on the ground. Blood is gathered between his legs.

Angelo sees me; his eyes widen, and he stands from the wooden chair.

"Kaden, what the fuck?" Kaden responds by motioning a pointed look at me, and Angelo raises an arched brow in question.

"Wake him up," I say, and gone is the softness of my voice.

Angelo blinks a few times at the unfamiliar tone coming from me.

I give him a hard stare when he's unmoving, and he leaves and returns a few moments later with a bucket of water.

Angelo chucks the water onto Lorenzo, who wakes with a gasp, coughing violently.

Lorenzo glares at Angelo, but a grin replaces it when his stare falls on me.

"Well, if it isn't my favorite girl."

"Shut up," I snap, and in my peripheral vision, I notice a table with various tools and weapons. I grab the pliers resting on the metal tray.

Lorenzo cocks an amused brow.

"What are you going to do with those?" He laughs.

I glare at his bruised face, content when I see he's missing the top piece of his ear. I don't answer Lorenzo and instead turn to Angelo and Kaden, who have a look of curiosity on their faces.

"Open his mouth," I instruct, and they glance at one another, not sure what's happening to me. But I know exactly what's happening. I've erupted with fury and reached the end of my patience.

I want Lorenzo and every man who had anything to do with Adriano to die for what they did to the bodies of innocent girls.

"Please," I beg, my voice gentle, and they approach me.

The girls standing behind are on edge, waiting to see what will happen.

"What are you going to do?" Lorenzo repeats, and this time I detect a hint of fear behind his words.

"You're going to tell me where Erika is, or I'm going to pull out every single tooth in your goddamn filthy mouth."

Kaden and Angelo, now on either side of him, grin when they hear my plans.

"Why do you care about what happens to the bitch?" Lorenzo snaps, and darkness swirls in his brown eyes.

"Her name is Erika!" I yell, my right finger pinching the top of his ear where the exposed tissue is, and he yelps in pain.

"Where is she?"

"Do your worst." His eyes carry a challenge, and he glares at me. Angelo and Kaden grip his jaw and open his mouth. I clamp the pliers on his top front tooth, and he trembles under me.

"Oh, I will," I say near his bleeding ear.

I press on the pliers and hear the crunch of his tooth breaking. As I yank my hand back, his blood coats my fists, and his screams and curses fill the room.

As his warm blood drips to my elbows, I'm sucked into an out-of-body experience. I don't acknowledge Leo or the others when they enter the room. My attention is stuck on a bleeding Lorenzo.

"I said, where is she!" I slap him, and the sharp, loud sound reflects off the cement walls.

"Probably with a dick six inches deep inside her," he spits back, and the blood dripping down his chin gleams sinisterly with his smile.

"Pinche puto!" I sneer, positioning the pliers on the center of his tongue.

Lorenzo thrashes in Angelo and Kaden's arms as the blade digs into his tongue, and I cut the tip in half.

"This should teach you to watch your tongue."

Leo's scent filters through the metallic stench of Lorenzo's blood, and my body relaxes.

"Amore…" Leo calls out to me, and his hand on my left shoulder is heavy. The pressure in my chest falters when our eyes lock.

A smug smile takes over Leo's face when he sees the pliers in my bloody hands. A soft laugh comes from his parted lips.

"Come here, my love," he says, grabbing my hands and pressing me to his chest. Lorenzo's blood coats his white dress shirt, staining it a bright red.

I peer behind us to see our friends staring at me in awe.

Luca has a toothy grin, and he sends me a thumbs up while Lei gives me a wink, bobbing his head.

As my breath evens out, I sense myself changing inside.

I'm becoming stronger but also resentful. I can feel myself turning into a monster who wants revenge on those who have hurt me, and I don't have any remorse for feeling this way because any man who doesn't treat a woman as if she has a heart of gold doesn't deserve any of my pity.

Adriano and his men, and those who take part in the darkness of human trafficking, don't deserve any mercy.

They deserve pain, fear, and, above all, *death*.

5 3

VICTORIA

The gun's weight presses heavily against my palms, and no matter how hard I try to keep my wrist upright, my hands tremble.

When the burning sensation in my wrists becomes unbearable, I drop my hands to my sides.

I let out a frustrated sound, and Leo laughs. I turn and send him a warning glare, which makes him more amused.

I exhale heavily and turn around to try again. This time, Leo comes from behind, and he bends to my level. His left hand rests at the base of my hip, and his other hand helps me steady the gun.

"Is it too heavy for you?" His breath kisses the side of my face, and a pleasant chill rises under my skin. "Victoria?" he murmurs when I don't answer him. I push the desire aside and give a slight hum.

Leo lowers our hands and takes the gun from me, placing it behind him in its holster, and he pulls out a small black handgun, giving it to me. My fingers wrap around the handle, and I stare at my name carved into the gun.

I trace the cursive letters, and Leo smiles.

"It's not a normal gift, but I'm not a normal boyfriend." I laugh, looking at him through my lashes, and he runs his thumb over the curve of my jaw. "I want you to carry it with you at all times." His voice takes a firm approach, and he gives me a pointed stare.

I cup his left cheek.

"I'll carry it with me like it's my ID," I tell him, and his shoulders relax. "Now can you teach me how to shoot?" I ask, wanting to get this training over with.

He lets out a small laugh.

"Amore, first prove to me you can hold a gun," he teases, kissing my pouting lips.

I groan but turn around and lift the gun, pointing it straight ahead. This time I don't tremble because the gun weighs almost nothing.

I'm still for two minutes and drop my hands, content with my progress.

"What about now?" I edge, glancing at the other girls who are practicing how to shoot a gun.

"What happened to not wanting to learn how to use a gun?" he says, positioning himself behind me.

"It's like you said; I'm not in California anymore, and you aren't a normal boyfriend." My response comes out breathless when he presses his lower half into my backside.

"You got that right baby," he whispers, kissing behind my ear, and I have to bite my lip to control my desire.

Leo is unsuspecting of my lust as he teaches me how to release the safety of the gun. The entire time he's talking behind my ear, I find it impossible to focus on anything he's saying when all I can think about is him rocking his hips with mine.

"...do you understand?" he says, and I nod even though I don't know what's happening.

My stomach clenches when his bulge digs into my backside. I swallow my groan.

"Alright, go ahead," he says, slapping my ass from behind, and I let out a breathless pant. My eyes widen in horror at the sound, and Leo takes a sharp intake. His hand around my hip tightens, and his head bends to my ear.

"Hurry and practice, so we can go upstairs." His voice is low against the side of my face, and my stomach knots from the sound.

I let out a breath, trying to suppress the excitement inside me, and aim the gun toward the target. When I think I have it in range, I exhale and press the trigger. The bullet misses, and I keep going, each time missing. After the fifteenth missed shot, I let out a frustrated grumble. Leo comes behind me once again and helps guide my aim.

"Shoot," he breathes, and I release the trigger. The bullet hits the little red dot.

"I did it! Well, sort of," I beam, and Leo takes the gun from me.

"That's enough practicing," he says, lifting me in his arms and rushing to our room.

He presses me against the door of our bedroom, and his mouth comes crashing against mine. His erection brushes between my thighs, driving me to grind into him.

Our steps toward the bed are sloppy, and we strip out of our clothes.

Leo's pointer finger traces my backside and twirls my thong. He pulls away from my mouth, looking at me from head to toe.

"Fucking hell, if I had known you were wearing those under your jeans, I would have fucked you the moment you woke up."

I laugh and wrap my arms around his neck. We are silent as we stare into each other's eyes.

His eyes are dark, and his love for me is written all over his face. And to think, I thought he and Cleo were dating.

"What's so funny?" he asks when I stifle my laughter. I shake my head, too embarrassed to tell him. "Tell me," he persists, hovering over me and caging me between his chest and the bed.

"You won't stop asking unless I tell you, huh?"

"Pretty much. Now tell Papi what's wrong?" he says, and I can see the shimmer of mischief in his eyes.

I cringe at his words, and he laughs.

"Don't say that again," I say, and his lips curve into a satisfied smile before he pins me with his stare, wanting to know what's on my mind.

As I trace the crown tattoo on his chest, I find myself telling him what he wants to hear.

"Back in France, I thought Cleo was your girlfriend," I explain, and his laughter fills the silence between us.

"So that's why you got all quiet on me when I was on the phone with her." Heat rushes to my face, and Leo gives another smile.

"Well, I'm happy to say I'm not into incest," he says with humor, and I roll my eyes. "Victoria, you're the only one for me. I tried to push my feelings for you away to protect you. I really tried. But I couldn't do it because I love every single part of you, and if loving you makes me a selfish bastard, then so be it, because I don't want to live without you." He presses our mouths together, and I liquefy into the kiss.

He's left me speechless once again, and my heart has so many things it wants to tell him.

"Leo, when I first saw you after you saved my life, I knew I was in trouble of falling in love with you because of the way you treated me. You gave me a second chance at life, and I can never repay you for that. But I'll gladly spend the rest of my life trying to do so." He breaks out into a wide smile and presses me against his chest.

"*You* gave me a second chance at happiness," he whispers, and I can see the pain flash in his green eyes. It disappears when he looks at me, and his eyes darken when they peer at my lips. "By the way, when you speak like that, you make me want to ravish you."

"Then ravish me." I tug him down, kissing him, and his jaw clenches as he works on removing his briefs.

His erection springs out, and he reaches over the counter for a condom.

"You've taken enough Plan B these past two weeks." His words have me swallowing hard, and my entire body flushes with a heat that drives me to feel weak.

I watch as he slips the condom over his erection, and when it's on, he plunges deep inside me. Every thrust has my toes curling, and I tighten around him. Our bodies grow hot and sweaty, and our breaths are hard.

Leo's thrusts are desperate, and I match his unrelenting tempo. I'm clinging onto him, and my thighs quiver.

"Fuck amore mio!" Leo moans, bucking his hips into me. "You feel so good. Nice and warm." He pants out, his muscles contracting.

I whimper, pressing our naked chests together, and my nails dig into the skin around his shoulder blades.

When the pleasure is too good, I bury my face in his neck and taste his salty sweat and musky cologne when I kiss the skin.

The smell of sex fills the air, and the room becomes hot. An intense heat builds in my abdomen.

Leo pulls out and grabs my legs, placing them over his shoulder, and thrusts deep into me.

I feel myself flutter around him, letting me know a sweet climax is about to rip through me.

Leo and I groan, and it mingles with the sound of two other moans.

My eyes flash open from the sounds, and I glance at the now opened door. My heart stills when I see Sofia pressed against it. Francisco is kissing her, and her hands are inside his pants.

I let out a small scream when I see them, and her eyes widen. We make eye contact, and she pales.

"Oh my god, this isn't our room!" Sofia says, mortified, her eyes closed, and she's covering Francisco's eyes.

"Are you fucking serious?" Leo grumbles, covering us, and my cheeks are blazing hot with deep embarrassment.

Francisco tenses, and the two rush out, closing the door behind them.

"Francisco, why weren't you paying attention?" Sofia slaps Francisco, and his cries filter into the room from behind the door.

"Fucking Francisco." Leo pulls out, his teeth grinding. "Francisco, you are officially kicked out of this fucking house!" Leo shouts, and his voice hints at his frustration at the two.

"You can't kick me out. I'm your underboss. You need me here!" he retorts back.

Leo glares at the closed door.

"Then you're taking your shit to the other side of the house. Far away from this goddamn room."

"You don't have to tell me twice!" Francisco says before he and Sofia leave for their room, one door down.

Leo gets out of bed and lifts me into his arms.

"Let's finish this in the shower." He nips on my earlobe, sending a pleasurable pinch through me.

Leo keeps his promise, and the moment we step into the shower, he presses my back against the wall.

With each thrust, I glide up the shower wall, and my legs tighten around his waist. He grips my ass, squeezing with each plunge.

Small droplets of water land on my parted lips, and strangled moans come from me as I reach ecstasy. This time I find my release without interruption, and he follows suit.

Leo presses our foreheads together, and there's a rapid rise and fall in both our chests as we try to catch our breaths.

We finish our shower and start the trip downstairs, where we'll have to see Francisco and Sofia after our awkward encounter.

I groan in embarrassment, dreading the next few minutes.

LEO

When I enter the dining room with Victoria, I send a menacing glare at Francisco. His mouth sets into a tight line, and his cheeks are red. Sofia avoids our stare.

From beside me, Victoria tenses, and I wrap my arm around her waist, bringing her to my side, where she eases into my touch.

We take our seats at the foot of the table, and as dinner rolls around, I mull over the plans for the masquerade.

We have three months to form a plan and, worse, tell the girls about the date requirement.

They can't come with us, and we know that when they find out that we'll have to take other women, they'll kill us.

Victoria places a hand on my forearm.

"Is everything okay?" she asks, sensing my nervousness.

I clear my throat and nod. She purses her lips, not convinced.

"Leo?" she inquires, and I give a simple hum. "I never asked you, but how did everything with Moises go?"

I stiffen.

Of all the questions she can ask me, she asks me the one I'm not ready to answer.

"Was it a dead end?" she asks when I don't respond.

The guys look at one another in panic, and the girls notice.

"You guys are hiding something," Nora says, narrowing her eyes at Arthuro. He brings his glass of wine to his lips and gives her an innocent smile. She glares at him, and he grimaces.

When I look at Victoria, I see her arms crossed over her chest. Her stare is challenging.

I let out a nervous chuckle, realizing I wouldn't be escaping this one.

From beside me, my father cracks a smile and leans back in his seat.

The back of my neck becomes warm, and my heart races in my chest. Victoria's eyes narrow in on me.

"Amore..."

"Don't amore me. What are you hiding, Bandoni?"

She gives me a calculating look, and I tell her about the masquerade.

"Adriano is hosting a masquerade in Paris in three months."

Victoria raises a perfect brow.

"There's more. What is it?" she says, and Luca's laughter cuts through the tension.

"This should be good," he says, leaning back in his seat like my father. I send him a warning glare, and he flicks his chin in the familiar hand gesture.

"Tell me the entire truth," she says, getting angrier by the second.

"A date is required." As soon as the words are out, I brace myself for her response. When she doesn't shout at me, my shoulders relax.

"That's it? Why didn't you tell me?" she says, and the sound of Layla hitting Alejandro on the back of the head resonates throughout the room.

"Alejandro Martinez, how dare you consider taking another woman to a ball!" Layla's Spanish accent is full of anger.

On cue, the girl's expressions go from confusion to anger.

Alexander yelps when Emma pulls on his ear. Nora glares at Arthuro, and Chloe laughs. Lei's lucky ass sits bemused as the rest of them get knocked on the head by their partner.

I glance at Victoria, and she has an emotionless expression. I become worried when I don't know what she's thinking.

"Amore," I call out gently, and she says nothing. "Don't ask me to bring you to the ball," I plead, and she lifts her chin defiantly. "It's not safe," I remind her, and her eyes are possessive. Her jealousy has my cock going stiff until I remember she's angry with me.

"Neither is this house when you're away, or have you forgotten?" she counters.

"Shit," I curse under my breath because she's right.

"It looks like you guys better come up with another plan on how you guys are going to kill Adriano and protect us." She has a sickly sweet smile that could kill.

I glance at my father for help, but he shakes his head.

"I think you all should return to your conference room and not come out until you have a solid plan. One that doesn't involve taking other women to dances," Emma says, and the girls all nod in agreement.

Sighing in defeat, I motion for the guys to follow me, and we all exit the dining room.

When we make it to the conference room, we all let out a breath.

"Well, shit, that was entertaining! I'm glad I don't have that problem." Lei laughs, and we roll our eyes, knowing he'll be eating his words soon.

"What are we going to do? Victoria has a point. They aren't safe here, and if Adriano finds out we aren't with them, he won't hesitate to take them while we're miles away," Alexander says as we all rack our brains for a plan.

"We can't take them with us, right?" Alejandro asks, rubbing his temple in frustration.

"Either option means the girls are at risk. But, at least by taking them with us, we know we can protect them," Arthuro states.

"Arthuro has a point," Alexander says, shifting his eyes to me. "What do you think, Leo?"

"If we take them with us, we need to make sure we train them so that they can protect themselves if anything goes wrong," I say, and they all agree. "We'll also have to make sure we plan everything out so we can get the girls out before we attack."

"I think we can do that," Arthuro says.

"Then it's settled. They come with us, but only if they prove they can handle the heat of training," I exclaim, and they all agree.

"It's a good thing you guys have three months to get them into shape," Lei pitches in with a grin. We eye him with vexation.

"At least we have dates. Who are you going to take?" Alexander grins, and Lei stiffens. "Your sister?" he mocks, and we all laugh when Lei's cheeks turn red from embarrassment.

"Since the masquerade is still three months away, I think it's a good idea if you all return to your homes and prepare your men. This way, the girls can also focus on their independent training," I say, and they all nod in agreement, knowing they can't be away from their mafia for that long.

"Let's go tell them." Alejandro rises from his seat, and we all return to the dining room, where we're met with the girls' icy stares. The air is charged with tension.

I approach Victoria, who crosses her arms over her chest.

"Would you go to the ball with me?" I ask, giving her a nervous smile when she sends me a glare.

"Yes." Her answer comes quickly, and I go to kiss her, but she turns away.

"Pull a stunt like that again"—she leans into me—"and I'll make sure you don't get to touch me for the rest of the year." She pulls back, and the tie around my neck suddenly chokes me.

54

VICTORIA

The house has felt lonely since the mafia families left about three months ago.

The days dragged on, and the only reason I haven't died of boredom is because Leo made it a point to train me every day.

After training, I was always so exhausted that I could only crawl into bed to sleep. All the exercises Leo made me do were a pain, but I took them all without complaint. I have to show him I can protect myself if I want to go to the masquerade. And there's no way in hell I would let him go with another woman.

Plus, I have a mission of my own, which requires my presence at that ball.

No matter what it takes, I have to find Erika at that dance.

Whenever my bones ached or I became nauseous from running, I sucked it up and kept going.

Luckily, today is mine, Sofia, and Cleo's last day of training.

We are all going to be flying to France tomorrow.

Unfortunately, because this was the last day of training, Leo didn't make it easy for us. Instead of two laps around the house, it was four, and instead of two hours of training, it was three grueling hours. The exhaustion, added to my nervousness about the masquerade, has unsettled and stretched my stomach.

The familiar sick, sweet saliva rises, and I rush to the bathroom.

It's the calm before the hurricane. All I can think about is how we are embarking on a ship and taking to the water where a storm is brewing. The thunder and harsh waves of what Adriano has in store for us makes me fearful for the future.

We are the lesser of the two evils.

Adriano has no human compassion, and, to an extent, Leo doesn't either.

But Leo has something Adriano doesn't. He has love. Love for his family, which he would die for in a heartbeat, and as admirable as this is, I can't bear the thought of losing him.

The familiar warmth of Leo's hand caresses my back, and his soothing voice helps loosen the knots twisting in my stomach.

"Are you okay?" He sounds worried as he holds me while I spill the contents of my lunch into the toilet.

I wipe my mouth with a tissue and give him an assuring smile. His frown deepens, and he places the back of his hand over my forehead to check if I have a fever. He notices nothing unusual about my temperature, and I remove his hand from my temple.

"Leo, I'm fine. I'm just anxious about the masquerade." He sighs and lifts me onto his lap.

"Amore, if you want to back out, that's fine. I can find somewhere we can hide you," he says, hoping I'll agree to this proposition.

My eyes draw close together until I'm glaring at him.

"Leo, I'm not about to back out after training for the past three months!" I snap, and he raises his brows at my outburst. "I need to go. What if Erika is there? You won't be able to find her because you don't know how she looks," I remind him, and the twisting in my stomach returns. I close my eyes, trying to stop myself from throwing up.

"Amore, everyone is going to be wearing masks. How are you going to find her with all the people who are going to be there?" Leo's words are soft as he sugarcoats how my hopes of finding Erika are slim. But I don't care. I'm going to try my best, even if it means tricking every woman in that ball to take off their mask.

"I don't know. I'm hoping fate can lend me a hand one more time."

He gives a simple nod, kissing my forehead.

It's true. All I have to rely on to find Erika is luck and fate. I can't give up on her. Not when I'm all the hope she has of getting out.

If I don't find her at this party, I'll have to spend the rest of my life knowing she's somewhere being enslaved.

She's so close to me, but still so far away.

With the masquerade approaching, my nightmares have resurfaced. Each ends with Erika crying out for me, begging me to help her as Adriano rapes her, and I can never get to her.

I can't hold back the disgust any longer, and I bolt out of Leo's lap. I'm again face down in the toilet.

"Victoria, I don't like this," I hear Leo say from behind me, concern oozing out of him. "Do you want me to get the doctor to make sure it's not something serious?"

"Leo, I'm fine. My body has been under a lot of stress from training, and then the thoughts of the masquerade don't help my nerves."

When he hears that his training has taken a toll on my body, he turns me around and cups my face.

"Why didn't you tell me I was being too hard on you during your training?" he mutters, the pad of his thumb trailing down my cheek in a soft stroke.

"Leo, you had good reason to be tough on me. I want to make sure I can defend myself if anything happens during the masquerade." His eyes soften, and he exhales a soft breath. Then a small smile appears.

"You have improved so much," he boasts, kissing my temple, and my stomach flutters from his words.

I have improved, and I've also never felt stronger, both mentally and physically. I'm not the girl I was six months ago or even three months ago.

The noise level in the plane is loud, giving me a killer headache.

There's laughter—lots of it.

Profanities are being thrown among the men playing poker, and the smell of cigarettes lingers heavily in the air, making my nose wrinkle.

Vegas smells better than this plane.

From beside me, Leo pulls out a cigarette and positions it between his lips.

I didn't know he smoked, and before I can control my anger, I glare at him, and he freezes.

"Give me that!" I pull the cigarette from between his lips and snap it in half. "It'll kill you, and it stinks." He swallows hard and presses his lips together. A soft chuckle comes from him, and he crushes the box of cigarettes.

I'm getting annoyed, and Leo notices.

He gives me an apologetic look before snapping his fingers.

This gesture and one glare from him are all it takes for everyone to go silent.

"Do you still feel sick?" he asks, and I shake my head. He sighs in relief, and I stare ahead once more.

Cleo stares at me in deep thought. She gives a gentle smile when she sees me looking at her, and I give her one of my own.

The plane finally lands in France, and I let out a breath, stretching my spine as I approach the exit.

Leo wraps an arm around my waist, and I peer up at him in all his handsome glory. My mouth waters because he looks ten times hotter while wearing black sunglasses.

In the distance, I see Emma and Alexander descending from their private jet. When she sees me, she waves excitedly and begins running down the steps of the plane.

I squeal and do the same. From behind me comes Leo's panicked shout.

"Amore, slow down. You can fa—"

"Woah!" I gasp, my foot missing a step, and I'm about to tumble down when Leo grabs me and presses me to his chest.

He tilts his head to the right, his brows raised. I give a sheepish smile and kiss his perfectly trimmed, stubbled jaw.

"Sorry," I mutter, and the corner of his mouth lifts.

Leo and I head toward Emma and Alexander, and when we are five feet away, Emma hurls herself toward me. Her slender arms bound around my neck, pressing me to her full chest.

"Victoria!" she says, squeezing the air out of me. "I missed you!"

"I missed you too!" As I say this, I see another jet descending the runway.

"It looks like Nora and Arthuro have landed!" Emma says, looking at the jet.

"Emma!" I hear my cousin shout from behind me.

Sofia escapes Francisco's grasp and runs into Emma's arms.

The two embrace, only pulling away when Cleo arrives to greet Emma.

"Are you guys ready for the masquerade?" Emma asks, her voice giving off a slight tremble. I nod, afraid talking will reveal my nervousness about what's coming.

One by one, the rest of our friends arrive, and my eyes widen at the sight of Layla. Her belly has become rounder over the last few months.

She beams at us, ignoring her husband, who's coddling her.

"Layla, you're glowing!" She flashes me a warm smile and kisses each side of my face.

"Thank you, Victoria," she says before greeting the others.

A rough cough from behind draws our attention to the men, who share looks of amusement.

Leo extends his hand to me, and I take it. We make our way into the cars, which will drive us to the hotel we'll be staying at.

Although most of them have properties in Paris, Leo didn't want to risk going to any of the estates or hotels they owned. He wants to avoid the possibility of Adriano finding out we're in Paris.

After settling down in the suite, we all attend a meeting where the men go over the plan for our escape.

As Leo talks, we girls listen attentively, knowing our lives can be in danger if we don't pay attention.

"When Kaden and Angelo tell you to follow them, we need you guys to listen." Leo gives us girls a pointed look. Then his eyes lock on me. "I don't want any fighting or complaining."

We all mumble our understanding, and Leo dismisses us while he and the men stay in the room to discuss their plan of attack.

Once inside Emma and Alexander's room, we discuss what we've missed in the past few months.

My attention is drawn away from the conversation when Cleo places a hand on my shoulder.

"Can I talk with you for a second?" she asks, and I let her take me to the bathroom for privacy. As we leave, the girls all give us curious looks.

The door closes behind us, and I'm faced with an anxious Cleo.

"What's wrong?" I place a hand on her shoulder.

Cleo looks me over while biting her lip and scrunching her forehead.

"Victoria, when was your last period?" As she asks me this, she looks from my stomach to my face.

My body grows heavy from her question, and that's when I realized the last time I had my period was around the time my parents visited Italy. Almost three months ago.

I'm irregular, so missing a period for a month or two is normal for me, and I never worried, but three months! This is a record for me.

I rarely worry about being late, but before, I wasn't having sex.

Regardless, I still can't help but feel like there's no way I can be pregnant because Leo and I use protection, and if we don't, I take the day after pill.

Cleo senses my distress and places a hand on my forearm.

"Cleo, we use protection."

"Those don't always work," she reminds me, and she's right.

The possibility of being pregnant brings a chill to my bones.

This isn't the right time to find out if I'm pregnant. War is around the corner. *Literally*.

"What do I do?" My voice cracks, and my stomach grows queasy. "I can't be pregnant."

"What?" Sofia shouts, and the door to the bathroom opens. Her mouth and the other girls' mouths are all dropped in shock.

I glance at them, and my body becomes numb when the possibility of being pregnant becomes more real by the second.

"Shut the front door!" Sofia squeals, running to me and touching my stomach, where a curve has formed.

It's not much, and it looks like I'm more bloated than anything. And maybe it is that, or maybe it isn't. All I know is that the odds of it being food or a baby are fifty-fifty.

"Sofia, I don't know if I am. I need to take a test."

"Then we need to get you one, sweetie." Layla's words are gentle, like her touch.

"There's no way the guys will let us go to the pharmacy for a pregnancy test. They're all busy planning their attack," Chloe says.

Cleo pulls out her phone, and her fingers tap on the screen before she places a hand on my shoulder.

"Everything will be okay," she assures me.

The girls lead me back to the room, and I remain dazed. I want to scream at myself for being stupid and irresponsible.

"Victoria, everything will be okay. With a baby or without a baby," Sofia assures me, and I stay silent, unable to form any words.

I stare at the scattered nail polish on the ground, and Leo comes to mind. I panic because now I have to tell him one of two things: I had a pregnancy scare, or I'm pregnant. Both terrifying.

A few minutes pass when there's a knock on the door, and we all freeze.

My blood pressure rises as Cleo opens it, revealing a red-faced Luca fidgeting with a pharmacy bag in his right hand.

"Um, here's your request," he says, handing the bag to Cleo. His blue eyes scan the room, trying to guess who the pregnancy test is for. When his eyes land on me, he frowns, taking in my hunched posture, and his eyes widen in realization.

"Thank you, Luca," Cleo says, about to close the door, and his eyes don't leave mine.

He knows it's me, and before he can leave, I get up and run after him. I wrap my arms around his waist, and he holds me.

"Victoria, are you pregnant?" he asks, and I swallow hard. Luca notices and draws his brows together, his eyes piercing my soul.

"I don't know yet," I tell him, and his eyes soften. "Please don't tell him anything," I beg, and he assures me he won't.

Luca lets me go, giving me a smile, which assures me everything will be okay.

"Good luck," he says, crossing his fingers with a smile, which tells me he's rooting for a baby.

When I'm back inside the room, the girls usher me into the bathroom.

I pull out the pregnancy tests with shaky hands and follow the instructions.

How am I going to face my parents and Leo if I'm pregnant?

My dad will blow a nerve. I can practically hear his anger ringing in my ears.

The timer on my phone goes off, and I jump from the sound. My breathing is quick, and I'm terrified.

I find the courage to go to the tests and look from one to the other.

POSITIVE

POSITIVE

POSITIVE

The test results knock the breath right out of my lungs like a deflated balloon. My cheeks become warm from the silent tears raining from my eyes. I'm now consumed with stress, fear, and shock.

Leo is going to be a dad, and I'm going to be a mom.

There's a soft knock on the door, and the next second, it opens, revealing the girls. They look at me with anticipation.

"Am I going to be an aunt?" Cleo asks, and as I take in her features, I can see she is both concerned and hopeful.

I don't answer right away. Instead, I draw my gaze to Layla's pregnant belly.

Layla notices this gesture, and her eyes squint. Her face glows with realization.

"I'm pregnant," I whisper, and the girls bring me into a warm embrace.

"Oh, Victoria, a baby," Cleo mumbles, tears shining in her eyes.

Layla is next to encase me in her arms.

"How do you feel?" She places a hand on the slight bump on my stomach.

All this time I thought I was bloated, but it's actually been a baby bump. If I had to guess, I'd say I'm about two or even three months pregnant.

Those damn Plan Bs didn't work.

"I'm scared," I confess, and they all nod in understanding. "What if Leo says he doesn't want kids right now? Or what if Adriano gets away?"

"Oh, hush. He loves you; trust me, he's ready. You both are," Cleo says, hugging me to her chest. "And Adriano is dying tomorrow." As she says his name, her jaw clenches.

My cousin embraces me.

"I'm so excited to meet them," she breathes, but then her excitement diminishes, and she grimaces. "Your dad is going to kill you."

I groan, knowing she's right.

There's a knock on the door, and we all scramble to hide the tests at the bottom of the trash bin. We exit the bathroom and find Luca entering the room.

"So?" he asks, and his stare falls to my stomach.

Biting my bottom lip, I release a shaky breath and place my right hand over the spot he's looking at.

His eyes widen.

"No fucking way!" he exclaims, his straight white teeth now on display. "You better name the little booger after me because I bought you the tests."

"As if," I say, and he laughs before saying he has to return to the meeting before Leo yells at him for sneaking out again.

When night hits, I enter mine and Leo's room to find him already inside.

The second he sees me, his shoulders relax, and a faint smile takes over his face. He pulls me into his arms and kisses me.

His lips are gentle against mine, and I can't help but notice his touch is different. There's a rawness to the way he holds me in his arms, and this time, when his lips skim over mine, it doesn't feel like fireworks. This time, it feels more like a powerful explosion. Like a bomb of love.

When he pulls back, he caresses my cheek, staring at me like I'm his entire world. But I'm not. Our world is now our baby, which he isn't aware exists.

I want to tell him and get it over with, but it isn't a good idea for too many reasons. I know he'll make me stay in the hotel if I tell him, and I can't risk him doing that. I have to find Erika. I also can't tell him because if I do, he'll worry about us, and I need him to be alert. He's already worried about me. Adding a baby to his plate will make him restless.

"What's wrong?" Leo asks when he senses my anxiety. My heart skips a beat, and a look of worry twists his handsome face.

"I'm just tired," I say, caressing his cheek. He nods and lifts me in his arms, carrying me to the bed.

My backside nuzzles into his front, and I let out a steady breath, savoring the serenity between us.

"Goodnight, my love," he whispers against my neck, pressing a soft kiss to the side of my jaw.

His right arm is slung over my side, caressing my stomach in a soothing gesture as he drifts off to sleep.

My hand draws lazy circles on his arm, and my breathing becomes steady as I find rest.

I push aside the storm Adriano has brewing for us, and before I lose consciousness, I assure myself everything will be alright because, as long as I'm with Leo, everything will be perfect.

55

VICTORIA

Tomorrow is the masquerade, and tomorrow Adriano dies.

Leo's deep, velvety voice stirs me from my thoughts.

"Amore, I know we've been busy these past few days. But how would you feel about letting me take you out on a date tonight?"

His request sends a wave of warmth through my body. But the thought of tomorrow overshadows it with a chill.

"Leo, what about preparing for the masquerade?"

"Everything is all set," he assures me, trailing a finger down the side of my face. I say nothing, and he sighs. "Amore, our days are never certain in the mafia. Let me take you out to dinner before tomorrow comes."

My chest grows heavy from his words. Leo just told me he could die tomorrow, after he once told me he was confident he could kill Adriano. I can't help but feel like him wanting to take me on a date is like he's saying goodbye.

The fear I'm hiding reveals itself as the tears I harbor spill.

"Amore, if I'd known asking you to dinner would upset you this much, I wouldn't have asked." A look of hurt covers his face, and I let out a breath, feeling overwhelmed with emotions.

"That's not why I'm crying," I say, and his face reveals confusion.

"Then what's wrong?" He wipes away my tears.

"I don't want you to die."

If Leo dies tomorrow, he won't know he's going to be a dad, and our child won't get to meet him.

I'm pregnant! I desperately want to tell him, but the words get caught in my throat, and all I can do is let out another cry.

Leo embraces me. His warmth reminds me of what I can lose tomorrow. I hug him tighter.

"Victoria, everything is going to be okay."

A rugged breath escapes me as I struggle to steady the pulsing fear in my gut.

"Let's go on a date and forget about Adriano for a few hours. What do you say?" Leo asks again, and he's right, our days are never certain in the mafia, and there's no way we can avoid tomorrow. All we can do is enjoy the now.

I mold my palms to his stubbled jaw and nod.

Leo smiles and peppers kisses all over my face. When he pulls back, he lets me go and heads toward the bathroom.

"Where are you going?" I ask, and he turns around, a smile illuminating his face.

"To prepare the best date for the love of my life," he says, disappearing and coming back out a few minutes later, now dressed.

I stare at him in his well-fitted dark gray suit with stripes, and black and white spectator shoes.

He looks like one of those gangsters in the 1920s, and my mouth waters at the sight of his muscular body being hugged by the material of the suit.

Leo makes his way toward me and presses a kiss on my head.

"I'll see you tonight, amore mio." He gives me one more smile, and I watch him go, letting out an excited sigh when it's only me in the room.

"...and done," Emma breathes, her hands out in front of her as she looks at the makeup she put on my face.

"You look stunning!" Cleo compliments me with a beaming smile.

"Thank you," I mumble, and heat floods my cheeks from their compliments.

After I texted them about my date tonight, they all ran to my room to help me get ready. I was grateful for their help because I wouldn't have been able to put myself together as well as they have.

Chloe appears, holding a gorgeous, tight satin red dress with a daring V-shape neckline. Beside her, Sofia has a pair of black Louboutin heels in her hand.

They hand them to me and usher me toward the bathroom to get dressed. When I return, they all stop talking and gape at me.

"Wow...You look gorgeous!" Sofia says, and all the girls agree, gushing at my appearance.

I tuck a strand of my curled hair behind my ear.

"Thank you." As soon as the words leave my mouth, there's a knock on the door.

"That's lover boy." Nora grins, placing a hand on my cheek.

My stomach turns with excitement and nervousness.

Deep breaths, Victoria.

When I step out, I lock eyes with Leo. He's smiling, and both his dimples are on full display. His heated gaze trails the length of my body in admiration.

He sinfully licks his lips and grabs my hand, twirling me around to get a complete overview of me.

Leo pulls me to his chest, and I peer up at him to see multiple emotions displayed in his eyes. My hands become clammy, and I get lost in the green forest hues of his eyes.

"You look..." Leo pauses and takes a moment to look at my face, and it's as if it's the first time he's seeing me. "Beautiful, gorgeous, beyond this universe. Mi amore," he breathes, caressing my bottom lip with the tip of his thumb.

His finger leaves behind electric sparks. The desire to kiss him increases when I see him in a black three-piece suit with a little black bow tie.

"You look handsome yourself," I breathe, clutching onto the sides of his suit jacket.

He laughs at the sight of me dissolving from his presence and gives me the kiss I want. I'm about to let him slip his tongue into the seal of my lips when the door beside us opens.

We pull away when we hear Sofia's voice vibrate throughout the hall. She wears a grin.

"Hey, mister, you better have her back in bed by eleven thirty, and no funny business afterward," she warns in a deep tone, trying to imitate my dad.

Leo wraps his arms around my waist.

"Yes, sir."

Sofia's grin falls, and I laugh. She rolls her eyes and returns to the room, and we head toward the elevator.

We reach the rooftop of the hotel, and my heart flutters when I see a path of red rose petals.

Romantic Italian music plays from down the hall, and I let out a slow breath as he leads me down the path until we reach two double doors.

My stomach does a weightless turnover as I take in the details and effort he put into our date.

"I'll see you in a little." He kisses the side of my mouth before disappearing down the way we came, leaving me confused.

Cold air pinches my exposed skin, and I turn back to face the now opened door. I'm met with the faces of eight familiar men. They stand in two vertical lines parallel to each other, four on either side of me. At the end is a white-clothed table with a candlelit dinner. Little fairy lights hang above us, and the full moon shines high.

The magnificent gold sheen of the Eiffel Tower is as bright as my love for Leo.

I glance nervously at the four mafiosos, Leo's capos, and Francisco. They all smile at me before they pull their hands from behind their backs to reveal a black rose.

My stomach grows restless, but the smiles on their faces encourage me to make my way through the door.

I take small steps down the path, and as I do, they individually give me the rose in their hand.

"Thank you." I take the flowers from them, and my hands shake from nervousness.

"You look beautiful, Shortcake." Luca gives me a kind smile as he hands me the black rose.

"Thank you, Snow White." His eyes soften at the nickname, and I continue down the path.

When I reach the end, I take the final rose from Lei. He's about to say something cheeky when Leo appears and slaps him behind the head.

I ignore Lei's whines and stare at Leo in a trance.

The roses are heavy, and as I try to grip them comfortably in my hands, I prick myself on a thorn and hiss, watching as a drop of blood seeps from the tiny wound.

He grabs my hand, and when our fingers interlock, a zap of electricity courses through us.

"I didn't think you were the romantic type."

Leo's lips curve into a smile, and I glance to the side to see the guys are leaving. Luca and I lock eyes. He sends me a wink as he closes the door.

"I'm not. But I'll do anything to show you how special you are." He draws me close to his front, and our chests are pressed together, allowing me to feel his heartbeat thumping as fast as mine.

I clutch the black roses, and my smile stretches.

"They're beautiful. I've never seen a black rose before," I say as the pad of my finger touches the soft pedals.

My gaze drifts from the roses to Leo, who pulls out a bright white rose and hands it to me. I place it between the others, and the white rose against the black roses glows like a halo.

"Do you know why I gave you the white rose?"

I shake my head, not sure.

"Because you are *my white rose*, and the black roses symbolize everything beautiful but dark in our world." He grabs my face between his palms, and my heart skips a beat, my breathing quickening as I soak in every meaningful word he says.

"Victoria, you glow in the dark as brightly as the white rose. The first time I saw you, darkness surrounded you from all angles. But even though the darkness swallowed you whole, you were like a beam of light."

His eyes turn hard as he remembers how Adriano sold me off like some product on a shelf. I place my free hand on his left cheek, and he relaxes.

"Even though you were afraid, in your eyes, I could see you still had *hope*. Something I hadn't seen in anyone since I lost my mother. Victoria, you're my light, peace, and happiness. The moment I looked into your eyes, it was instant love. From then on, I promised to protect the lightness inside you so that it will always glow, just as you are right now."

Love at first sight? With me?

"But you didn't know me," I whisper, unable to believe he fell in love with me before even talking to me.

"You're right, I didn't. This is why, when I saved you, I made sure I got to know you, even if it was only for a short time. But in doing so, I didn't realize I had set myself up, and I learned fast that I would never want to be away from you." He leans into me, our lips caressing, but we don't close the gap. "My precious white rose. Mi amore *today, tomorrow, and for the rest of eternity*," he says, pressing our lips together.

The tears I'm holding back fall, and I cling to him, afraid of letting go. Everything around me is spinning around and around and around.

I kiss him as if my life depends on it, and I try to tell him how much I love him through our kiss before pulling back to catch my breath.

"If I'm your white rose, then you're my hero in Armani." He lets out a laugh at the name but doesn't decline it.

"The last thing on my mind before closing my eyes when you rescued me was how my knight and shining armor saved me. But it wasn't until later that I realized it wasn't a knight who saved me..." I bite the side of my mouth to stop laughing when Leo frowns at my words. "It was the mafia who saved me."

Leo lets out a breath, his eyes flickering with the utmost warmth and admiration.

"I like the sound of that." He grins, and his right hand slips into his pocket. My heart stops when he gets on one knee.

"Victoria, I love you, and there's no one else I would want to spend the rest of my life with than the woman I fell in love with at first sight." He's smiling at me, and I can only stare at him with my hand covering my mouth. "Will you marry me?"

The Eiffel Tower behind him erupts into hundreds of little sparkles, and his words resonate in my mind.

I lower to his height and bring him into my arms.

"Yes, Leo, yes! Of course I'll marry you." I kiss him, and when we pull apart, he slips the diamond ring onto my finger.

I look from the diamond to him. Everything is perfect until I remember I'm pregnant and haven't told him.

Should I tell him?

"Do you want kids?" I ask instead, deciding I should first see his reaction to this question before telling him he's going to be a dad.

Leo stiffens, and his reaction has my chest twisting. A pain that feels like my heart is being torn in half follows when he doesn't answer my question.

"I do want kids with you," he says, pinching his lips together before sighing. "But not right now. Not when Adriano is still alive and wants to hurt you."

That's all he has to say to stop the words *'I'm pregnant'* from coming out of my mouth.

I put on a fake smile, my fingers tracing along his jaw.

"I agree," I say, trying to sound convincing, hoping I'm making the right decision by not telling him.

56

VICTORIA

"It's gorgeous. Did you pick it out for me?" I run my fingertips down the length of the beautiful, long, one sleeve black dress.

"Yes," Leo breathes from behind me. "I thought you would look ravishing in it." He presses his lips on my neck, and his touch sets the skin on fire. I crane my neck sideways, giving him more room, but he pulls away and grabs the black box beside the dress. He pulls out a beautiful gold mask with small diamond studs aligning the edges.

Leo places the mask over my eyes, and it's smooth against my skin. He turns me around so he can look at me.

"How does it look?" I ask nervously.

Leo takes a breath and smiles.

"Look for yourself."

He leads me toward the mirror in the room, and when I stare at my reflection, I don't recognize myself. My brown skin is glowing like melted caramel, my dark hair has grown to reach below my spine, and my eyes have never shined brighter. Femininity is blooming from within me.

Over the last few months, I have matured. I'm not a little girl anymore.

"Leo, this is a gorgeous mask."

"Not as gorgeous as you." His eyes lash me with his love, and he leans in to kiss me when a loud knock on the door pulls us from our intense stare.

"You two better hurry. We leave in thirty minutes!" Sofia shouts.

"Piccolo fuoco stop being loud."

Francisco's comment earns him nasty curses in Spanish from his girlfriend, and he responds by trying to woo her with his words of affection, but Sofia ignores him and storms off. I hear his rapid footsteps as he goes rushing after her.

Leo pecks my cheek.

"You heard them. Thirty minutes." He ushers me to get dressed, and I pick up the dress from the bed.

Letting out an annoyed breath, I turn to find Leo tucking his white dress shirt into his black suit pants. They're unfastened, and I can see his bulge poking out.

Heat gathers between my thighs, and Leo's eyes fall on my thighs, which I'm clenching together.

His eyes flare, and he's grinning. I exhale hard, trying to ignore the fire igniting in my lower half.

I slip into the dress and can't reach for the zipper. Leo notices my trouble and comes to help. The tip of his thumb and pointer finger graze the skin of my lower back, inciting a shudder. He zips the dress at an agonizingly slow pace, and once the zipper reaches the top, he kisses the back of my neck.

He bends to my ear, his lips grazing the skin.

"I can't wait to get you out of this dress later tonight," he says, sliding a hand up my left leg and through the slit of the dress.

His words are enough to bring moisture between my thighs.

Leo's hand keeps sliding up the dress, and I bite my lip when he pulls my thong aside. His pointer finger lazily strokes my throbbing clit, and when I'm on the edge of pleasure, he draws his hand back, leaving me wanting more.

I glare, unsatisfied, and a grin tugs at the corners of his mouth from seeing me flustered.

Leo makes his way toward our suitcases, and I watch as he

rummages through the bags. He pulls out a rectangular velvet box and stalks back toward me.

"You already sparkle like a thousand stars, but why not make you shine like the moon as well," he says, opening the box and revealing a beautiful diamond choker necklace.

Looking from him to the necklace, I'm filled with disbelief.

"Leo, stop buying me these expensive gifts."

"Never," he says, his tone firm. He then turns me around, moves my hair to the side, and puts the necklace around my neck.

Once secured, he turns me back around to face him.

"You, my love, are the definition of beautiful."

My stomach flutters from his words, and my lips tingle with anticipation.

Kiss me already!

I bite my bottom lip, hoping he does what I can't seem to vocalize.

Leo leans into me, and I close my eyes. He tips my chin and kisses me slowly. I let out a soft whine when he pulls away, leaving me wanting more than a kiss.

"Shall we?" He offers me a hand, and I take it, letting him pull me out of the room and toward the elevators. My lower half is burning for his touch.

The elevator descends, and Leo presses me against the wall.

"Leo, what are—"

His hungry lips fall to my mouth, and I kiss him with as much passion.

The back of my head presses against the wall, and I grab onto the front of his suit jacket to keep from sinking to the ground from how dizzy my love for him makes me.

"Mmm," I breathe, his lips running along the length of my neck.

I groan again when his hand slips inside my dress, and he doesn't hold back this time.

He tugs my thong and slides it down my leg—the lace pools around my black stilettos.

A turning over occurs in my stomach, and I choke from the pleasure.

I want him. I need him. I *crave* him.

He releases my lips and gets on his knees in front of me.

"Leo, what are you doing?" I peer down at him wide-eyed, realizing we're in an elevator that can open any second.

"I'm giving you what you wanted."

This is all he says before disappearing inside my dress, and the next second I jolt as his tongue flicks at my clit. With every stroke of his tongue, my fingers curl around the gold railing, and it helps keep me steady.

The sound of his mouth fucking me and my soft whimpers mingle with the soft classical music in the elevator.

"Fuck!" I groan, glancing at the elevator meter to see how much longer we have until we reach our destination.

Twenty more levels.

From against my folds, Leo hums, and my stomach tightens.

He sinks a finger into me, and a moan erupts from my mouth. There's a ding, and the elevator stops. I tense, my eyes growing wide.

Leo lets out an unsatisfied groan and detaches himself from me. My hand flies to my heaving chest to steady my breath. Leo remains on his knees, licking his lips as he pretends to tie his shoe.

My breath quickens again, and I lose it when he grabs my black thong from the ground and puts it into his pocket.

The door opens, and Emma and Alexander appear. Both have their brows arched as they slowly enter the elevator.

Leo rises and straightens his jacket. When he is upright again, he wraps his arm around me and wipes the corner of his mouth with the pad of his thumb. A satisfied grin brightens his face.

"Are you alright, Victoria?" Emma asks, and she's suppressing her smile.

She knows. They both do.

"I'm good." My response comes out sounding more breathless than I would have liked, and my body grows even more warm when Alexander stifles his laughter with a cough.

The entire elevator ride, I wanted to bury my head in embarrassment, and when my ears ring with the sound of the elevator opening, I let out a breath of relief and rush toward the tinted SUV. Leo's laughter comes from behind me.

The embarrassment from what happened in the elevator disappears and turns to fear when the cars take us toward the masquerade ball.

In a few minutes, I'll be in the same room as my kidnappers. I'm terrified of what the next few hours will bring.

When the bright gold lights of the hotel come into view, my breath gets caught in my lungs. My heart is beating so fast it might shoot out of my chest.

Leo senses my uneasiness and brings me into an embrace. His warmth slows my heart rate.

He places an earpiece in my right ear, pulls out the gun he bought for me, and wraps the holster around my thigh.

"Just in case," he says, kissing my temple. "You stay by my side the whole time, and if anything happens, you press the earpiece, and the rest of us will hear you."

As he talks, I can only stare at him.

The black mask covering the top half of his face can't hide how handsome he is.

"I love you," he whispers, cupping my face and kissing me.

"I love you today, tomorrow, and for eternity," I reply, using the words from his proposal, and as I say them, my eyes dampen.

"Everything will be fine," he assures me, interlocking our fingers. I swallow the lump in my throat, and the door to the car opens to reveal a red satin carpet.

He exits first, his hand never leaving mine.

As I make my way out of the car, my dress slides to the side, exposing the gun. With shaky hands, I pull the material of my dress over the gun.

Leo wraps his arm around my waist and leads us toward the event. The closer we get, the louder the noise becomes, and with every step, my chest tightens.

Although Leo is with me, the memories of what these men can do brings fear to my heart. No matter how strong I have become; it isn't enough to forget the memories of my kidnapping.

I was only kidnapped for a few short hours, but they were the most terrifying hours of my life, and they've been enough to give me months of trauma.

"I'm here, amore. You're okay." Leo's voice eases some of the tension in my body.

I smile at him, assuring him I'm fine despite wanting to throw up from how terrified I am. But I need to push past the fear because Erika needs me.

We approach the entrance, where jokesters skillfully throw red balls into the sky.

Once inside, I catch sight of many burly men. Their eyes are cold and hard.

I shrink back when they glance at me. Their eyes darken as they trail over my body. Leo's arm around my waist tightens, and he clenches his jaw. His posture tells me he wants to kill them, but he can't. He has to remain composed until the right moment arrives.

He sends them a silent warning by raising his chin, setting his lips into a scowl, and straightening his broad shoulders until he grows another inch.

His body bleeds with power, protectiveness, and confidence. They all sense his silent warning and shift their gaze away from us.

I survey the room, noticing some of Leo and the other mafia families' men scattered throughout the party. They are waiting for the signal to attack.

In the corner, I spot Luca and Angelo with their dates. Both have a glass of champagne in their hands and wear a similar styled black suit. The silver with black swirl masks, which the rest of our men also wear, conceal their identities.

Luca notices us and lifts his glass of champagne in greeting. I give him a smile before looking around me again.

Everyone wears expensive gowns and beautiful masks of all shapes, styles, and colors. They all look friendly as they talk and drink with one another.

To an outsider, they look like regular people having a fun night at a masquerade, but they aren't ordinary people. Neither are Leo and I. We are all affiliated with gangs and crime. The law hates us.

The moment I became Leo's, I was now also a part of this corruption. It should have bothered me, but it didn't because, in my eyes, Leo wasn't a criminal. The only thing he's guilty of stealing is my heart. To me, the real criminals are the men and women surrounding me who are trying to hurt my family and friends.

A familiar voice comes from behind me, and I'm struck by how easygoing he is when danger is near.

"Let's crash this party!" Lei boasts, tugging on his white suit jacket. A few eyes glance at us, and Leo tenses beside me.

"Shut the fuck up," Leo says through clenched teeth.

Lei laughs, dismissing Leo's comment.

"See you on the other side," he says, grabbing a glass of champagne from a passing server. He drags an angry Chloe into the ballroom, and she almost trips over her baby blue mermaid-style dress.

Francisco and Sofia appear before us, and I hug my cousin.

The beautiful silver mask on her face makes her olive skin glisten under the lights, and her beautiful long satin silver gown hugs her curves in all the right places.

I lock eyes with Francisco, who's holding onto my cousin.

"Please take care of her," I beg him, and he assures me she won't be leaving his side until we make our escape.

Leo pulls me away from them, and his eyes roam the room, looking for his evil cousin. I do the same, but I'm looking for Erika.

An hour goes by, and we haven't found Adriano or Erika.

It's difficult to find them when everyone's identities blur from the masks they wear. Leo was right. It's impossible to find anyone at this party.

"I'm sure we'll find him," I say squeezing Leo's hand when he makes a frustrated sound.

He presses his earpiece, and his voice comes through my earpiece.

"Has anyone seen Adriano?"

The sound of voices filters into my ear.

"No sign of him," Kaden replies.

"Nada," Alejandro's gruff response comes through.

Similar responses from the others follow.

"Let's take a break, but make sure you all keep an eye out. He's here somewhere," Leo says, leading us toward the table where our friends are heading.

The closer we get to them, I find myself admiring their appearance.

Lei and Chloe wear white masks, which make their fair skin glisten like silk.

Behind them are Layla and Alejandro, who wear black masks with gold designs. Layla's gold gown flows over her like a river, displaying her baby bump. Alejandro, who wears a simple mocha suit, has her close to his side.

Nora notices me and waves us over. Her face is covered with a silver mask like Arthuro's, and she looks like a temptress in the beautiful champagne-red gown.

We reach the table, and Cleo beams at us, patting the seat beside her. Although her eyes are covered in a black lace mask, I can tell her smile reaches her eyes.

"You look beautiful, Cleo." My eyes roam her figure in the cream silk gown, and my stare stops on the firm arm wrapped around her shoulder.

I'm stunned at the sight of Kaden's affection toward Cleo, and I wonder when these two have gotten this close until I remember Kaden was training her for the past few months. There's no doubt in my mind that this is the reason for the new comfort between them.

Cleo sees my attention on the two, and her cheeks flush red.

I bite the inside of my mouth to stifle my laugh when something on the upper level of the ballroom catches my attention.

A chill numbs my body, and the air is kicked out of me at the sight of Adriano hunched over the railing.

In his right hand, he holds his mask, which shares an uncanny similarity to the masks doctors wore during the black plague.

He looks like death itself.

"Amore?" Leo calls out to me when I don't sit.

"Adriano is leaning over the railing on the right." Leo stiffens from my words, and everyone's eyes widen, wanting to see him.

Leo turns and pretends to talk to Lei. His eyes glance to where I have directed, and his fist tightens when he sees him.

"Good work. Now, remember to avoid him at all costs. If he approaches you, walk away like you didn't hear him."

I nod as I take my seat, and he grabs my hand from under the table.

"Alex, let's dance," Emma says, grabbing the tail of her royal-blue dress with one hand and lifting a groaning Alexander with another.

She drags him toward the dance floor, and the two disappear into the crowd within seconds.

Bored out of my mind, I stare at the people dancing and notice the way the women's gowns swirl around their feet. Particles of glitter from their dresses mix with the air like dust.

Loud bickering draws my attention toward the twins, who are fighting.

"Lei, stop being a pain in the ass!" Chloe grits out.

"It's not my fault this shitty mask is irritating my skin," he remarks. The next second his fingers go to the mask, and he gives his sister a grin as he pretends to take it off.

"Lei, knock it off before you blow our cover!" Chloe scolds and pinches him as a warning. He grumbles in annoyance.

"Leave it to Lei to joke around during an important mission," Leo mutters in disbelief. I agree with him and nuzzle into his side.

"Victoria, promise me that once we give the signal, you'll leave without hesitation." I glance at Leo and notice his face has morphed into seriousness. His expression tells me that if I don't find Erika by the time they give the signal, my chances of ever finding her are gone.

"I promise," I tell him, cupping his left cheek. "Leo, please come back to me after." My voice breaks, and he gives me a sad smile.

"I will always come back to you," he says, frowning when he sees the rising tears in my eyes. "I promise to end this once and for all so we can start our life together."

If only he knew our life together was going to include another member in a few months.

"We're going to the dessert table because someone is hungry and cranky," Alejandro says, looking at Layla with accusation. She gasps and slaps the back of his head.

"What are you implying, Alejandro?"

The sight of her anger has Alejandro swallowing.

"Nothing mi Amor. Did I tell you how beautiful you look today?" He gives a nervous laugh and wraps his arm around her waist.

Layla pulls away from him with a huff and walks away.

"Layla, mi amor, I swear I didn't mean anything by it." Alejandro sounds panicked as he runs after his now angry pregnant wife.

We all laugh at him, and he glares at us.

"Fuck off!" He flips us off before he heads after Layla like a lost puppy.

"Old hag in an expensive, puffy gown is coming our way," Nora whispers, eyeing something behind Leo and me.

I turn to see an older-looking lady with long, silky black hair advancing toward us. Her dress is over the top, and her corset is so tight her breasts almost touch her chin. Around her long, thin neck is a big, shiny red ruby that complements her blood-red gown.

Although she's still a few feet away, her perfume, which she dumped over herself, makes me nauseous.

At the sight of her, Leo grinds his teeth.

"Who is she, Leo?" I ask, placing a hand on his forearm.

"That's Emily. Adriano's mother," he says, voice cold.

Right after he says this, I hear her deep, snotty voice from behind me, and it demands attention. Her red lips tip into a fake smile, and we give her one of our own, except for Leo, who's still looking forward.

"Hello, everyone. I hope you're all enjoying the ball." Her dark eyes look around the table, judging us. When she casts her stare on me, her eyes stop on the necklace Leo gave me, and her eyes widen.

She tilts her head, inspecting the diamonds around my neck.

"What a beautiful necklace. Do you mind if I ask what jeweler?" Her curious eyes remain on the diamonds, and I roll my lips, unsure of what to say, until Leo comes to my rescue. His response comes across as harsh.

"It's Bulgari." He doesn't give her his attention, as his eyes remain fixed ahead.

Emily looks at the side of Leo's face with a scowl. She ignores him and looks at me again.

"It's beautiful. Only five necklaces exist. I own one. My late sister-in-law owned the second, and I guess you have one of the other three," she chirps. Her eyes don't stray from the necklace, and it's as if she wants to rip it off my neck.

Leo's hand, which rests on my thigh, stiffens, and he curses under his breath.

Emily looks at Leo, who is now taking a lazy sip of his champagne, and her question has us all going stiff.

"Do I know you?" Emily's tone is accusing.

"No," he says, and his rude tone makes Emily's nose scrunch and her eyes narrow into angry slits.

"If you keep being an asshole, I'll have you escorted out with a gun to the back of your head before you can blink." Her smile is gone, and her voice is laced with fury.

Leo's lips turn into a grin, and he scoffs, turning to glance at her.

"My apologies," he says with fake sincerity, and I laugh under my breath.

"Is something funny, little girl?" she asks, her hazel eyes daring me to disrespect her.

I bite my tongue and shake my head.

This short encounter with her has been enough to explain to me why Leo couldn't tolerate her.

"No, of course not," I say, placing my right hand on my chest and batting my lashes.

She huffs and looks between Leo and me before taking her leave.

"You little minx," Leo whispers into my ear when she's gone.

He kisses my cheek, and I pull away, patting his chest.

"Nice try, but you're still not off the hook." I shoot him a piercing, sharp stare of disapproval, and he rubs the back of his neck.

"Leo, tell me this didn't belong to your mom."

"So, what if it did? This is a family heirloom. How else do you think the hag got one? She's a Bandoni, remember."

I cup his face, and his stubble tickles the skin of my palms.

"Leo, this belongs to your mom. I can't accept it." My hands go behind my neck to unclasp the necklace.

It felt wrong of me to wear it. This necklace should have gone to Cleo, not me.

Leo grabs my hands, stopping me from taking it off.

"Victoria, stop being ridiculous," he says, still holding my hands. "My mom wanted you to have it. She engraved into me that when I find the woman I love, I'm to give her this necklace. Victoria, that's you," he explains, and my heart swells from his words.

"Are you sure?"

"Yes." His firm words leave no room for argument, and I sigh in defeat.

"Thank you," I mumble, kissing him, and we pull away when a loud voice rings throughout the ballroom.

"The masquerade ball has begun." Andrew's voice cuts through the room, and uneasiness courses through my insides from seeing his red mask. It glistens like the blood of his next victim. "All the guests are to report to the dance floor."

"Fuck!" Leo curses and becomes rigid from the unexpected setback in our plan.

"Come on, it'll be fun," I assure him, and he grumbles his disapproval but lets me take him toward the dance floor.

His left arm is around my waist, and his hand grazes the side of my stomach. There's a tickling sensation in my abdomen from his touch.

Leo leads me to stand beside the other girls and kisses the center of my forehead. He reluctantly pulls away and goes to stand across from me next to the other men.

I take in his handsome figure, and when he sees me gawking at him, he winks, a grin lifting his mouth.

I'm not the only one who appreciates his good looks because the women beside me are all drooling over him. When I see their heated gaze, I feel a hole of jealousy burning in my chest, and I have to remind myself they aren't a threat because Leo loves me, not them.

I ignore the drooling women by focusing on the row of men in all-black tuxes and women in blue dresses. They stand on the grand white marble staircase in the ballroom, and they all wear masks that cover their entire faces, making them unrecognizable.

Their presence brings uneasiness, and despite hundreds of eyes staring at them, none of them move in the slightest.

Soft classical music plays as the men and women descend toward the dance floor.

As the last pair makes it to the bottom, Emily and Adriano appear, both now wearing their masks.

Emily's curls bounce as she goes down the staircase, and Adriano looks as serious as I remember him to be.

His lips are in a thin, hard line, as if he disapproves of everything and everyone. His pointed chin is held high, and evil bleeds out of them both.

The music picks up its beat when Adriano and his men all reach the center, and everyone dances.

True to Andrew's warning earlier, everyone is on the dance floor.

It frightens me how easily Adriano can turn something as beautiful as a waltz into something that shows his control over a crowd.

With little choice, the women and I advance three steps. Our partners meet us halfway in a clean, swift movement.

Leo extends his right palm out in front of him, and I place my left palm against his hand, feeling utterly confused as I've never been to a ball until today.

He interlocks his fingers with mine, and we sway.

"This is stupid," he grumbles.

I rest my head on his shoulder.

"It's not that bad," I say when I get the hang of the dance. Leo grunts, pulling me back and twirling me like the other men are doing to their partners.

He draws me back against his chest and kisses my temple. When I stare at him, he looks pained, as if what he's about to do is the hardest thing ever. A sheet of coldness encompasses me with his next words.

"Be safe," he whispers before he pulls me outward, twirling me, and he's forced to hand me over to the man next to him. His eyes don't stray from me.

With him no longer beside me, I feel cold and vulnerable.

Thankfully, I'm in Alexander's arms instead of some random man, a sight that eases my worries. But this only lasts a few seconds before Alexander also passes me to another man.

A few minutes go by of the same routine, and I search around me and I don't see any familiar faces.

Panic rises, and I search for Leo in the crowd of dancing people.

When I find him, I sigh in relief to see he isn't too far away, but he's also not as close as I would have preferred him to be.

He's also looking for me, and his face lights with relief when our eyes lock from across the room. I don't stare at him for long because my partner gets touchy.

I clench my teeth when the man's hand lowers until it rests on my butt.

"Get your hands off me," I grit out, and the man smirks.

"Why? I know you like it," he says, groping my left cheek.

I'm about to shout at him when the man beside him gives an angry cough.

"Let her go. You had your turn. Now hand her over," he says, glaring at the man harassing me.

The man rolls his eyes and pushes me to Luca, who catches me before I can fall.

"Here, take her. She isn't that good anyway," he scoffs, turning away to grab another partner.

"Thank you, Luca," I mutter as we dance.

"Anytime, Shortcake." His mouth curves into a gentle smile, and he twirls me three times before handing me to the next man. The cycle continues for another five minutes.

By now, I'm growing tired and want to sit, but the dance is still not over.

I clench my teeth and push through the exhaustion.

As the man I'm dancing with passes me to the next person, I trip over my heels, and my dress wraps around my legs.

The sound of my soft scream fills my ears, and I close my eyes as I wait to hit the ground, but someone catches me.

"I got you," a rough masculine voice says, pulling me upright. When I see Adriano centimeters away from my face, my blood runs cold, and my heart sinks.

He notices my agitation, and his eyes are calculating.

"Do I know you?" he asks, coming closer to me as he sways us. Despite my attempts to escape, he continues to hold me tight.

I don't look at him. I'm too afraid his eyes will bring back old memories, or worse, he'll recognize me.

I scan the dance floor, looking for Leo, and when I find him, he's too far. I've somehow made it to the center of the dance floor, and Leo is at the right end of the room.

He's also busy arguing with a blond woman.

When I see her rubbing herself against an angry Leo, I feel rage swell in my heart. I'm satisfied when he pushes her away from him.

Adriano calls out to me, his voice dark and angry.

"I said, do I know you?" he asks again, this time sounding impatient.

"No," I snap, and he runs his tongue over his bottom lip, studying my face.

"Those eyes are familiar," Adriano says, his hand going to the back of my head.

"What are you doing?" I jerk back when he tries to pull off my mask.

Amusement flickers in his eyes.

"I've seen this type of outburst before." His hold on me tightens. "Hello, Victoria," he says, giving a hollow, sinister grin.

Shit!

A cold sweat gathers at the base of my neck when he says my name.

"Get off of me!" I thrash in his grip, but he squeezes my arm, piercing his fingernails into the skin.

"Be a good little girl and follow me, or I'll have to carry you out and create a scene," he whispers. "If you disobey, I'll kill everyone you love."

He pulls my arm, and it cracks from the pressure.

I panic as he drags me through the dance floor. Then I remember I trained for three months in case an emergency like this happened.

Right on cue, my fight instincts take effect. I lift my knee, hitting him between the legs.

He lets me go and groans, clutching where I kicked.

"Ah fucking hell!" he curses out loud, and a few eyes are now looking at us. From a distance, I notice Luca and Angelo heading my way. They look panicked.

Angelo's voice chimes through my earpiece.

"Leo! Adriano has Victoria!" he says.

Leo's voice comes through the earpiece.

"Where are you, Victoria?" he asks, and I can hear the panic and fear in his voice.

"I don't know, somewhere in the middle," I say as Adriano rises from his hunched position.

"You fucking *bitch*!" Adriano sneers, and I back away as he advances toward me.

I'm struggling to squeeze through the people dancing, and I find myself thrown around. My heels and long dress make it hard to keep my balance, and I become flustered and filled with panic.

"Leo, where are you?" I ask, knowing he's listening to me.

"I'm coming, amore," he says, panting, but I don't find him anywhere. The only thing I see is Adriano and his men coming after me.

The crowd of people swallows me whole, and the tightness in my chest increases. Everything slows until I'm dizzy.

I try to take slow breaths to calm the rising panic in my chest, but it's useless. I'm freaking out, and my vision becomes clouded with dark spots.

Adriano lifts his head over a man's shoulder, and when he sees me, he smirks and pushes the person out of his way.

My eyes widen in fear, and I push the man in front of me, but he's too heavy. He turns to glare at me, and when he notices Adriano is after me, he goes to grab my arm.

I cry out when an icy hand takes hold of my wrist, pulling me out of his reach. As the unknown person pulls me through the dance floor, I tug on their grip to escape.

My attacker is a woman, and she leads us out of the ballroom and toward the hallway to the side by the hotel entrance.

Her blond hair bounces as we run through the hall of closed doors. After running for a while, she ushers me inside an office with an open door.

She lets me go, and I wrap my arms around my body when she locks the door.

The woman turns to face me, and I stare at her, not sure what she wants from me.

"Who are you?" I ask.

The mysterious girl brings her hands to the back of her head to remove the full face mask like the one Adriano's men are wearing.

When she reveals her identity, I'm met with a grin.

"Forgot me already?"

"Erika!"

57

⸺

VICTORIA

Erika is cold and frail. I'm almost certain she'll break if I add the slightest pressure.

"Please forgive me for not finding you sooner. I wanted to find you, but I couldn't do it myself." My face becomes warm and sticky from my violent tears.

"Shhh, Victoria, it's alright. You're here now." Her blue eyes shimmer with tears.

I let out a breath. Relief runs through every inch of my body because she's really in my arms after many months.

"Victoria, when I heard you and the others were rescued, I knew it was only a matter of time before help arrived for the rest of us. But I expected the police to come, not you! What the hell are you doing here?" Her face is set in a grave countenance, and I let out a soft laugh.

"Erika, I'm not here alone." I place a hand on her thinning collarbone and frown at how skinny she is. "I'm here with my fiancé."

Her eyes bulge, and her mouth drops.

"Your fiancé is a cop?"

I shake my head, and she looks at me quizzically.

"No, he's Adriano's cousin."

Erika gasps, her hands now on my shoulders.

"Victoria! I thought they rescued you. Are you saying Adriano's cousin kidnapped you?" she staggers, her voice going an octave higher.

"No, he didn't kidnap me." Her brows knit in further confusion. "He rescued me, and we kind of fell in love along the way." I press a hand on my stomach with a smile.

Erika notices the gesture and gasps.

"You're pregnant!" I nod, and her face brightens. "Tell me everything!" she demands, popping her right hip and crossing her arms over her chest.

"Later, when we aren't running from Adriano." Her eyes widen as if remembering where we are.

The sound of a gun going off makes us jolt, and my heart drops from the sound of chaos ensuing outside the door.

Leo comes to mind, and terror stabs my chest. I don't know if he's okay or if the girls have been taken to safety.

I ruined our attack plan.

Erika grabs hold of my hand and squeezes it for reassurance.

"We need to get out of here," she says right as Leo calls out to me.

"Victoria, where are you?" His panicked voice fills my ears, and I sigh in relief to know he's okay.

I press the earpiece.

"I'm in an office in the corridor to the left of the—"

There's a loud thud on the door as someone tries to break it down. Erika and I let out a yelp.

I grab my gun as wood splinters fly and the door crumbles.

I bring Erika behind me, glaring at the four large men in jester masks, which are set into permanent grins. The only feature noticeable is their dark eyes, which stare at us in hunger.

A roar of laughter comes from within them when they see the gun in my hands.

I flare my nostrils and shoot the man on the right. The bullet hits him in the collarbone.

I'm not so funny anymore, am I assholes.

I watch as my victim falls to the ground, and I don't even flinch, nor am I given time to process that I killed someone because the next seconds go by in a blur.

The men watch their friend fall dead, and their eyes harden before they launch themselves at us. My shots are messy, but one bullet hits another man on the left shoulder.

He slaps the gun out of my hand and punches me in the jaw. The force is so strong my earpiece falls to the ground.

The man looks at it and crushes my only communication with Leo into tiny pieces.

I slap his hand, but he's too strong, and his long fingers wrap around my forearm. Not going down without a fight, I punch him in the jaw and kick him between the legs. He releases me, and I notice the other two men are trying to drag Erika out of the room. She screams and fights in their arms, but her fighting is futile.

I'm about to jump on the men dragging Erika when my attacker rises from his hunched position and tackles me to the ground.

A sharp pain shoots up the back of my head when I hit the floor. What follows is a burning sensation in my throat as he wraps his hands around my neck.

Gasps come from my lips as I struggle to catch my breath, and the more I struggle, the more he tightens his grip. My lungs are on fire, and my heart races. I can feel the fast beat in my throat.

The pig slides his filthy hand up my thigh, and panic rises in my chest.

Not again.

My mind becomes muddled with fear and panic. But I push away the tears. I won't let him assault me without a fight. I'll scratch, bite, scream, and kick. Whatever I need to do to get him off me.

I cry out, and I can't reach for the gun. I'm so close to it that my fingertips graze the cool metal.

The man jerks back when I headbutt him.

I ignore the dizziness and crawl over to the gun right as he grabs my ankles, dragging me back toward him. I pull the trigger, shooting him in the forehead. His blood spills all over my chest and lips, and his heavy body collapses on me. I grimace, pushing him to the side.

I'm quick to kick my heels off and I launch myself onto the man grabbing Erika. I land on his back and wrap my arms around his neck, choking him.

He lets go of Erika and grabs my arms, throwing me over his shoulder, and I go flying across the hall and into the wall.

A guttural wheeze comes from my lips; the air knocked out of me, and pain shoots all over my body. More pain follows when the man grabs me by the throat, lifting me high against the wall. My legs dangle below me, and I kick fiercely.

"Let her go!" Erika pounds on his back, and he pushes her aside with a force that knocks her to the ground.

The gun shakes in my hand as I go to press the trigger, and he snatches it, hurling it to the side.

I'm gasping for air, and my fingers dig into the skin around his knuckles, trying to get him to release me. But his grip is firm; intending to kill.

My sight grows heavy, and my lungs are ready to burst.

A chill crawls up my spine from the darkness swirling in his eyes, the only feature of his face I can distinguish.

My tears come running down my cheeks because I'm going to die before I ever get to tell Leo about our baby. His words from a few days ago come back to haunt me.

Our days are never certain in the mafia.

He's right, and now both me and our baby will die.

Leo will be too late this time, and when he finds me, I'll be nothing but a cold, lifeless body on the ground.

My eyelids flutter shut when the weight becomes unbearable, and my body grows heavy below me as the breath in my lungs disappears.

The last thing on my mind is Leo and how much I regret not telling him about our baby.

58

LEO

"Leo! Adriano has Victoria!"

Angelo's words freeze my heart, and my breath gets caught in my throat. Panic takes hold of my composure, and my head spins. The noise in the room becomes heightened, and I search for her. She's nowhere in sight. She's all alone and in danger, and I can't find her.

"Where are you, Victoria?"

Her voice comes through the earpiece and eases an inch of the tension in my body.

When she tells me she's in the middle of the dance floor, I push those who get in my way when a pair of hands grip my forearm.

Thinking it's Victoria, I'm quick to turn around, only to sneer at the sight of Rebecca, who I pushed away not that long ago.

"Move." My voice is sharp, and Rebecca doesn't tremble from my warning. Her nails dig into my arm.

"Let me go, or I'll kill you right here, right now," I warn, drawing out my gun, and she still doesn't budge.

"Forget about her. Let me give you what the bitch can't." She clings to my arm, and my nonexistent patience thins. "I can give you a good time."

I grab her wrist and crush it in my hands. She cries as the bone snaps, and her smirk falls.

"I will never choose you over Victoria. You're nothing but a piece of gum stuck under my shoe."

Rebecca's eyes fill with tears.

"That's a lie. I know you love me. We made love, Leo! Stop saying you love her. I know you love me!" she shrieks like a crazy person, and the surrounding people stare.

"Damn, you're fucking stupid. We didn't make love. We fucked, and it was eight years ago. If I wasn't wasted that night, I wouldn't have fucked you. I don't love you, and I never will." I throw her arms off me, and she stumbles back. Fat, angry tears fall from her eyes, and she lets out an ear-ringing scream.

"Your bitch won't last the night. Once Adriano hears about you being here, he will end you. Adriano and I will strip you and that whore of everything!"

My jaw tightens from her threat, and I grab her arm, pressing the gun to her side.

No one threatens my Victoria and gets away with it.

"What are you going to do?" she shrieks, thrashing in my arms.

My grip around her tightens, and she winces.

"Shut the fuck up and walk," I warn, handing her to Kaden. "Take her away," I order, and he does as told.

I press the earpiece and signal the men.

"Get the girls out of here. We need to find Victoria," I say as I push through the crowd of people.

"Leo, where are you?" Victoria's voice comes through my earpiece, and she sounds panicked and breathless.

"I'm coming, amore," I say, my adrenaline spiking from the sound of her calling for me.

After searching for what feels like an eternity, I grow restless, as I still don't see her anywhere. There are too many people, making it difficult.

"Where are you?" I ask, and she doesn't answer me. Her silence brings a raw fear so cold my heart stills.

Her silence prompts me to push aside all the idiots who dare get in my way, and one glare from me forces them to recoil.

I reach the center of the dance floor, where she said she was, when a dumbass pushes into me.

"Fuck off!" I shove him aside, and when I see who the man is, my nostrils flare, and my body becomes rigid.

Adriano's eyes widen when he recognizes me.

"If it isn't my cousin," he taunts. "Look, I can't talk right now. I have to find your bitch before she gets lost," he says coolly, as he tries running to the left, but I grip him from the back of the neck.

Is he being serious right now?

"What did you do to her?!"

Adriano's lips curl into a smirk.

"The question you should ask is, what am I *going* to do with your whore," he sneers, trying to get my hands off him.

I withdraw my gun, pressing it against his temple.

"Don't call her that, you fucker."

He laughs, his eyes averting to something behind me.

I turn to see one of his men drawing his gun, and I shoot him in the head. His brain splatters, and the smoke of my gun going off surrounds the air.

Adriano's men come rushing toward me, and my men appear. All our guns are pointed at one another, and hostility stifles the environment.

"Kill him!" Adriano orders, and I release the idiot so I can leap behind a table to take cover as bullets fly. During my escape, I'm hit with the familiar burning of a bullet piercing me.

"Mother fuckers!" I glance at my bleeding forearm before looking for Adriano while our men continue to shoot at one another.

I kill a few of his men who are shooting at me, and when I hear silence, I rise from my spot behind the table to see bodies littering the floor. Adriano is nowhere in sight.

"Francisco, where are you?" I call into the earpiece, and he answers me in the next second.

"In the back room with the others," he says, and I rush there.

When I arrive, I see the girls are still here.

"I told you guys to get them out of here!" I shout, and they freeze in their spots.

I look around for Victoria, hoping someone has found her, but she's nowhere in sight. From her absence, a sense of panic overwhelms me.

Cleo approaches me and grabs my arm, her face paling from the sight of blood soaking my suit jacket.

I give her an assuring smile, and her frown deepens.

"Cleo, I'm okay," I assure her. "You all need to get out of here now," I say, motioning for Angelo and Kaden to grab the girls.

"Leo, Victoria isn't here," Sofia cries, clutching onto Francisco.

"I know. I'm going to find her. Go with Angelo and Kaden, all of you. It's about to get bloody in here." The girls make their way toward my two capos, worry for Victoria clear on all their faces.

Sofia clutches my forearm, and a familiar expression of fear takes over her features.

"Leo—"

I cut her off, already knowing what she wants to tell me.

"I'm going to find her," I assure Sofia, and she lets out a shaky breath.

Francisco brings her into his arms and kisses her before he hands her to Kaden. The girls all run out of the building with Kaden and Angelo.

"Let's kill these bitches," Lei declares, removing his mask and sighing in relief as he tosses it to the side with a clang.

The others follow suit until all our masks are in a pile in front of us.

"Luca, Alexander, come with me to find Victoria. The rest of you find Adriano. Kill any assholes who get in your way. Not one of these bastards gets to live," I order, and they all nod.

"When you get Adriano, don't kill him. I have special plans for him." Nothing else is said, and we all disperse.

"Let's go!" I tell Luca and Alexander as we head toward the mass of people running like crazy.

"Victoria, where are you?" I ask into the earpiece, and her response comes a second later.

"I'm in an office in the corridor to the left of the—"

Fear surges through my veins at the sound of a door breaking down and then a scream.

"Victoria?"

She doesn't answer, and I let out a ragged breath.

"Did you guys see any corridors?" I ask Luca and Alexander.

Luca nods.

"Yes, this way," he says, leading us there.

"Victoria?" I call out, and I'm once again met with her silence. "Shit!"

We're fast as we push through the mass of people and approach the corridor. Hastily, we check the rooms, trying to find her. I let out a frustrated sound every time the rooms are empty.

My worry leaves me feeling antsy, and I can't control my fast beating heart.

We reach the end of the hall, and it divides into two sides.

"Alexander, take the left side," I say, and he runs in the direction I told him to go.

Luca and I make our way toward the right, only to realize she isn't here. We're quick to turn around and head toward the path Alexander took when his voice comes through the earpiece.

"Leo, I found her, but I need backup!" Alexander says, sounding breathless.

"We're on our way."

When we finally reach Alexander, Luca and I see him fighting two guys. Another man is rising from the ground, blood coming from his side where Alexander shot him.

Luca shoots the man rising from the ground, and I pull one of the two men on top of Alexander. I shoot him in the neck and toss him aside. Alexander kills the other man.

"Thanks," Alexander breathes, wiping the blood from his lip.

The sound of a scream rings from the end of the hall, where two men are dragging a girl from a room. A gun goes off inside the room, and the sound stops my heart.

"Luca, get the girl out of here," I tell him as we run toward them.

Luca shoots at one of the two men holding the girl. He's about to shoot the other, but I push his gun down when Victoria jumps onto the man, and I watch as she's thrown into a wall.

"I'm going to kill this fucker!" I grit my clenched teeth, trying to shoot him, but he's too close to her. If I shoot him, I risk the bullet going into her.

My feet are fast and heavy as I run down the hall.

The blood in my veins is hot and pumping faster than ever as I approach my lifeline.

I grab the man choking Victoria by the neck, and when he turns around, his eyes widen as my fist launches into his face. I press my gun under his chin, killing him on the spot.

"Victoria!" I shout, watching as she lies on the ground, coughing and wheezing, her small hands touching her neck in pain.

I crouch, looking her over. My vision goes red when I see the bruise on her cheek and her busted lip.

"Leo!" Victoria cries.

"I'm here, amore. I'm here." I kiss her temple and caress her head when a warm liquid coats my hand.

I look at my fingers to see them coated in her blood, and my jaw pops from how tight I'm clenching it.

Victoria cups the side of my face, and she's relieved to see me.

"Where does it hurt?"

"My back and my head hurt, and so does my throat." She scrunches her face in pain, and her voice sways.

The sound of men screaming and guns going off lingers in the background, reminding me she's still here when she should have left with the others.

I'm gentle as I lift her from the ground, and she nuzzles into my chest.

"We need to get you out of here," I say as I jog through the hallway. She says nothing. Her face scrunches in pain with every step I take.

"I'm going to go with the others to find Adriano," Alexander says, running back toward the ballroom where the sounds of war are coming from.

Luca follows close beside me, carrying the girl in the blue dress.

We reach the exit, and I place Victoria on her feet.

"Victoria, you and your friend have to go with Luca," I tell her, and she nods.

I kiss her, and she grabs my hand, placing it on her stomach.

"Promise me you'll come back to us," she says, cupping my cheek with her other hand.

My forehead creases from her words, and I stare at my hand on her stomach, and it's as if everything stops.

The sound of guns going off disappears, and all I hear is my heartbeat ringing in my ears.

"Victoria..." I whisper, and she swallows, nervousness washing over her face.

"I'm pregnant," she confirms, and a smile curves onto my face at the news.

I'm going to be a dad.

The sentence I never thought I would say replays in my mind, and I'm filled with a wave of indescribable emotions. All of them are happy.

I press her to my chest, and she sighs in relief.

"You aren't upset?" she asks, and the fear in her voice pinches my chest. Then I remember yesterday when she asked me if I wanted kids and the sadness that took over her when I didn't answer.

My poor baby was trying to tell me, but I didn't let her.

"Of course not; the opposite," I breathe, pressing my hand on her stomach. "There's so much I want to tell you, but I need you to get to safety, both of you," I say, looking at her stomach.

She kisses me one more time and prepares to go when a voice halts our movements.

"Awe, how beautiful," Adriano cackles, clapping his hands slowly as he and five men appear from behind us. "Bummer, I have to ruin the moment."

I grab Victoria and pull her behind me, aiming my gun at Adriano. Her hands clutch the back of my suit jacket, and they tremble under the fabric.

"Adriano," I grit out.

"That's me!" he says with a grin.

A few of my men come rushing out of the ballroom after Luca calls for backup.

The click of my gun sounds in the air, and Adriano lifts a thick brow.

"I wouldn't do that if I were you." He glances behind me with a smirk before directing his gaze at me again. "Especially when your precious Victoria is at gunpoint."

"Leo..." Victoria's broken whisper has my spine tightening, and my world crumbles when I see a little red dot aimed at her stomach. Our stares collide, and her eyes flash with fear and sadness. Two slow tears trickle from her cheeks, and my body becomes numb, frozen with dread.

This can't be happening. Not again.

I glance to where the aim is coming from, and Andrew winks at me. His finger is ready to press the trigger.

Victoria gives me a sad smile and closes her eyes. The bang of the gun slices through the air.

"No!!!" My shout rings loudly in the room, and I go to push her out of the way.

A bone-chilling scream rips out of her, and my heart leaps into my throat. It's as if shards of glass have impaled my body.

Within seconds, blood coats the floor crimson as bullets between my men and Adriano go off.

59

VICTORIA

My body stills with fear, and the blood in my veins runs cold. Adriano and Leo's voices blend with the pounding of my heart.

I grip the back of Leo's suit jacket when I see a little red dot make its way down Leo's back until it lands on the side of my stomach. I freeze.

My clammy hands, which grip Leo, move to my stomach.

I glance to see where the beam is coming from and let out a shaky breath when I lock eyes with Andrew. He's on the top banister, to the side.

Andrew sends me a sinister grin, and I can only wait for death.

A few feet from me, Luca, who's holding a crying Erika, notices the red dot on my stomach. He turns pale and begs his brother not to do it, but Andrew doesn't look at him. Andrew's eyes are on me.

Leo's name is stuck in my mouth, preventing me from telling him about the gun pointed at me.

I'm not sure what to do in this situation. Either I'm going to die, or Leo is going to die trying to save me. Both options are not in our favor.

"I wouldn't do that if I were you. Especially when your precious Victoria is at gunpoint."

Leo stiffens, and the words stuck in my throat emerge.

"Leo..." I whisper, and when he sees the red dot on my stomach, his eyes enlarge with fear.

I give him a sad smile, and the deadly trigger is released. I close my eyes, and the piercing sound of the bullet booms in my ears. Images of my life and the future I won't have, flood my mind.

"No!!!" Leo's voice thunders with a wave of unheard pain. I clench my eyes tighter, waiting for the bullet to cut through me. But it never pierces my flesh. Two hands push me to the side, and I fall to the cold floor.

A loud, piercing scream erupts from within me when I see my savior. Their eyes stare at me with sadness, and my gaze falls on their chest, where a bullet has struck them.

A heavy thump follows when their body falls to the floor. Huge amounts of blood spill around them.

"Luca!" I shout, crawling toward him the best I can as bullets ricochet between Leo and Adriano's men.

"Victoria!" Leo shouts my name amidst the chaos. He tries to get to me, but he can't because of the bullets flying around us.

I press my trembling hands against Luca's chest, trying to stop the flow of blood. It won't stop pouring out because the bullet has torn into his body.

I place Luca's head on my lap, and he spews blood from his mouth.

He smiles at me and wipes my tears with a shaky hand. His touch is cold against my skin.

"Snow White, why did you do that?" I choke out, and his face is blurry because of my tears.

He gives me a sad smile, and his gaze drifts to my stomach.

"You think I would let you and my niece or nephew die?" As he says this, he struggles to find the words. The blood in his throat chokes him, and his words are a haunting gurgle.

"You can't die," I cry.

"Shortcake," Luca whispers, and more blood comes vomiting out of his mouth. The liquid coats his chin, jaw, and neck. I can't do anything to stop the blood from coming out.

The rings of bullets stop flying, and when I don't hear Leo, I'm filled with fear.

I scan the room looking for him, and in the corner, I see the men with Adriano dead, but Adriano is nowhere in sight. Then I see him, my Leo. Our eyes come together, and he's relieved to see me safe, but when he sees Luca bleeding out in my arms, he runs toward us.

"Adriano ran down the corridor to the left. Go after him!" Leo orders, and Francisco takes a group of men to go after the coward. Before Francisco leaves, a look of sadness reveals itself when he sees Luca.

"Leo, he's dying!" I shout when Luca's breathing becomes shallow and his eyes start to flutter.

Erika is on his other side, helping me try to stop the blood from coming out of his chest. She's weeping to herself, looking around at the broken glass, bullet shells, blood, and dead bodies surrounding us.

I run my fingers through Luca's ash-white hair, and I cling to him.

Leo crouches beside me, and when he looks at Luca, he wears an expression I've never seen on his face before.

His expression tells me we can't do anything. Luca is dying, and he will take his last breath any second. I can't accept this. I can't.

"Oh, no-no-no," I whisper, cupping Luca's face. His tears wet the tips of my fingers.

Luca's eyes flutter open, and I remember the first time I met him. The memories bring unbearable pain to my chest, leaving me breathless and gasping for air.

Although he's in pain, Luca smiles at us and places a shaky hand over my stomach. My hand covers his, and I caress his cold cheek with the other.

"Take care of her and tell the baby uncle Luca loves them," he says brokenly, his face morphing into pain.

"I promise, Luca. Thank you for saving my family, *little brother.*" Leo's voice is rough, and a tear slips down his cheek.

When Luca hears Leo call him brother, his eyes fill with relief to hear the words he always wanted to hear from someone.

"Awe, man, don't cry. That's for pussies," Luca says with a tired laugh before trembling.

I press my left cheek against Leo's chest, and my mouth fills with the salty mixture of my tears.

Luca's lips part, and the sound of his words are so faint we can barely hear them.

"Leo," he gargles through the blood choking him.

"Yes, Luca."

"I'm scared."

Leo grabs his hand and swallows hard, not sure what to tell him. I have to bite my cheek to stop myself from crying out loud.

"We're right here with you, brother," Leo says as his men and the mafia bosses gather around us. We all watch as Luca's eyes flutter shut, and there's a little gasp, his last breath, and then nothing. The blue in his eyes disappears forever, and a great tremor overtakes my body. The tears are racing down my cheeks, and my breathing turns erratic when Luca falls limp in my arms.

Leo buries my head into his chest, trying to shield me from the sight, but it's too late. The image of Luca dying will remain carved into my memory for the rest of my life.

My tears erode two trails of grief down my cheeks, which makes the skin warm and sticky.

"Leo, he got away," Francisco huffs, coming out of the corridor. Leo's body shakes, and his breathing becomes heavy.

I tune them out and turn to where Andrew stands motionless in the shadows. His expression is one of regret.

My grief turns to anger, and I surrender to the pain.

I grab Leo's gun from his side, and he staggers when he sees the silent anger taking over my once soft face.

A glass-shattering scream explodes from inside me, and I shoot at Andrew.

"You did this!" I shout through the firing of the gun. My wrist trembles, and Andrew shakily rises from the ground.

"You killed him!!"

"Your brother!!!"

My words are venomous as I reveal the gravity of his actions.

Everyone flinches at the sound of the gun and my screams. I don't care if they all think I'm crazy. I'm not crazy. I'm a woman tired of being hurt.

My screams of rage and pain continue to mix with the clangor of the bullets that fire fast at Andrew. Goosebumps rise from beneath my skin, and although my hands tremble, I keep a steady finger over the trigger until the bullets run out and Andrew stumbles out of the building.

The gun falls to the ground with a loud noise, and my body drops forward, my palms keeping me up. The sobs coming from an unforsaken place inside me shake my body. My tears fall like rain during a hurricane, and the salty tears mix with Luca's blood gathered around me.

Leo lifts me off the ground and cradles me. He whispers sweet nothings into my ear. I pick up on none of them. All I hear is Luca's broken voice calling me Shortcake for the last time. I hold on to the memory of his voice, knowing that with time I will forget the sound of him.

Even though I'm in Leo's arms, I find the tightness in my chest doesn't ease with his warmth. Nothing can console me.

Leo carries me toward the back, where the cars wait for us, and I stare blankly ahead of me.

I know I shouldn't look, but I do. I glance behind Leo's shoulder to see Luca one last time. My heart tugs at the sight of Francisco crouched by his body. He wipes his tears, lifts Luca, and follows our path.

Erika looks at me with sad eyes and follows us outside.

The sounds of police sirens in the distance become louder, forcing Leo to take quick steps to get us out of here.

Three days, twelve hours, and forty minutes
That's how long it's been since Luca died in my arms.

A painful, hollow sadness has risen inside me since his death.

People always say you don't know what you have until you lose it. That's how I feel about Luca.

I miss hearing his laugh and seeing his crazy white hair sparkle in the light like a spider web. It's as if someone has trapped me in a ditch of grief with no way out.

Before I know it, the day I've been dreading arrives. Today is Luca's funeral. I can't find it in me to get ready because when I put on the color black, it means his death is final. To have to say goodbye to him all over again is taking a toll on me.

Losing Luca has brought loneliness. I don't want to go anywhere, do anything, or talk to anyone. I only want to be alone.

Leo's worried about me and my health, even more so after a doctor confirmed I was three months pregnant.

He's on edge because Adriano is still alive, plotting our downfall. We only know he's in the Amazon. Lorenzo, who's on the brink of death, hasn't said a single word about his whereabouts.

The bed dips when Leo sits beside me. His fingers run through my hair, and he places a gentle kiss on my forehead.

"Amore, we need to go to the funeral soon," he whispers, caressing my cheek. He wipes the hot tears trickling from my closed eyes. But it's no use because, one after the other, the tears cascade down my face. They fall like a storm of despair fizzing inside my grieving chest.

Luca's lifeless eyes penetrate my soul, and I bite my lip to stop from crying out loud.

"I miss him." The tears and the twisting in my chest won't stop.

Leo sighs. "I miss him too, Amore, but we need to be strong. Luca wouldn't want you to be upset."

"Why did it have to be him? The bullet was for me, not him," I mumble, and Leo's eyes darken with anger at my words.

But he can't blame me for saying them. He, of all people, should understand the pain I'm feeling.

I now understand why it's hard for him not to blame himself for his mom's death. The guilt of someone sacrificing themselves for you has seeped into me. The pain is unbearable. Even clutching my chest doesn't help.

"Victoria, don't say those things, please," Leo says sharply, but without raising his voice.

The bullet was for me, not him.

I say nothing, and Leo sighs deeply.

"Amore, Luca gave us a second chance. Something my parents didn't have." Leo's voice breaks from the mention of his parents, and my bottom lip quivers.

"I don't know what I would have done if something happened to you or our baby." He lifts the shirt I'm wearing and kisses my stomach.

The bullet was for me, not him.

"Luca protected you two without a second thought. He wanted to save you."

Another stretch of silence passes between us.

"You're my lifeline," Leo confesses, and his eyes flash with pain when he remembers how close he was to losing me.

There's a gentle knock on the door, and it opens to reveal Francisco and Sofia.

Francisco's lively blond hair is flat on his head, and dark circles adorn the area under his eyes. Sofia also looks exhausted, and I can tell she's trying to be strong for Francisco and me. But she's also suffering from her own grief.

"The funeral is in half an hour," Francisco mumbles, a pair of black gladiator sunglasses in his hands.

Leo nods and looks back at me with hopefulness.

Francisco wraps his arms around Sofia. The two are ready to leave when my cousin gets out of his arms and walks toward me.

She caresses my cheek.

"Victoria, Luca wouldn't want you to cry. It's not your fault," she whispers. "The stress is bad for you, so please try to get better for your baby, who Luca died for."

I sigh, knowing she has a point. This grief isn't healthy for me or my baby. Luca's death can't be in vain.

Sofia makes her way toward Francisco, and the door closes behind them. Their footsteps fade with the distance.

"Are you sure you don't want to go?" Leo asks.

I set my lips in a thin line before a soft sigh escapes the small crack.

"I want to say goodbye." A quaver creeps into my voice, and when I say the words, relief takes over Leo's features.

"I'll be right beside you." Leo kisses my temple. "Always."

His lips brush softly against mine, and it's a kiss in which he shows me his relief to have me in his arms. A kiss that seals the promise he has made to me.

He will always be there.

60

—————

ANDREW

Luca was always better than me.

*U*pon his birth, he became the golden apple of the family.

Candidly, he was smarter, funnier, nicer, and better in every aspect than I could ever be.

And it was no surprise my parents favored him the most or that he earned himself a high-ranking spot in the Bandoni famiglia mafia.

At eighteen, he was the youngest capo in the mafia. He received a position before me, his older brother. This rejection from the mafia only fueled my hatred for him.

He became a pain in the ass and a constant reminder of how I was a castoff in my own family.

My hatred toward Leo when he didn't make me his right-hand man has blinded me with rage. I let this anger turn into a war against my brother, and now I have killed him.

The only person in the world who has ever shown me an ounce of love is being carried in a sleek white casket, and I put him there.

From where I stand, I can hear my mother's cries. The sound of the pain I caused her stabs my guilt-ridden heart like a million knives.

The memory of my brother jumping in front of the bullet plays out in my mind. Victoria's screams of anger and grief and my mother's wailing are ringing like loud drums. I have to cover my ears to block out the sounds. But they won't disappear because they are all in my head.

Seeing my father's broken expression, which I once expected would bring me pleasure, doesn't. Instead, my stomach aches with disgust at what I have done. There's a cold emptiness inside me. A feeling that makes me stagger back. I'm not sure what to do.

The moment my brother closed his eyes, mine opened. But it's too late; the damage has been done.

I'm an outcast, now paying for my sins.

I've let Adriano poison my already dark heart. The result has left me hollowed out.

My chest pinches, and my eyes burn as Luca's casket passes like a ghost.

"All my fault!" I mutter, my voice sounding as broken as I am inside.

The tears are uncontrollable, and the guilt of my actions doesn't want to go away. It lays heavy over me like a shadow that follows me wherever I go.

"I'm sorry. So sorry, baby brother."

My phone vibrates in my pocket, and I already know who it is.

The sight of his name infuriates me. I don't want to be his puppet anymore.

The blanket of hatred I have let Adriano put over me has been lifted.

Everyone has a breaking point, and this is mine.

I killed my brother.

The phone stops ringing, but this won't be the last time he calls. He hasn't stopped since the night of the masquerade.

Adriano is panicking because many of his men and potential business partners are dead. No one wants to do business with a man who doesn't know how to keep tight security at his own masquerade.

Everything he planned for years has been lit aflame, and there's nothing he can do but wait for the flames to burn him.

I scoff, content to see the consequences of his actions fast approaching him.

When I glance toward my brother's coffin, which is now resting under the earth, there's a sharp, burning pain through my right leg and then my left one. With the pain comes the sound of a gun going off in the morning air.

I fall to the ground, and blood seeps from my legs.

Crying out into the cloudy sky, I fall to the ground, knowing this is the least of what I deserve.

When Leo's men grab me, I don't fight them. I let them take me because *I killed my brother.*

61

LEO

Victoria trembles, and her knees are bound to fold, taking her to the wet ground. I grab hold of her, pressing her to my chest.

Luca's white casket is as white as fresh snow. It glistens from the sun's rays when it's lifted by Francisco, Angelo, Kaden, and those men who called him capo.

All around is silence, cries, and more silence.

Funerals—I've been to so many that I stopped keeping track. After attending as many as I have, you learn that even the toughest men cry. No one can escape grief.

There's a gust of wind and, with it, a manifestation of sorrow.

Luca's mother is on the ground. Her fingernails dig into the soil beneath her. Her uncontrollable cries and screams are like thunder.

Victoria flinches at the sounds and clutches her chest. Her fingers dig into the lace of the black dress she wears, and her throat bobs with every sob she swallows.

My grip around her tightens, and she dissolves from my touch. Her silent tears become soft sobs, and the sounds make my stomach twist when I can't take away her heartache.

I whisper words of comfort to her, and she clings to me. Even with my touch, she is inconsolable. Her tears drip like a broken faucet, and they rush out when Luca's casket descends into the wet soil.

With slow steps, I guide Victoria to say goodbye.

The white marble tombstone appears. Luca's name, carved into the rock, glistens like the tears streaming down Victoria's ashen cheeks. Her body gives up on her when she sees his name, and she goes limp in my arms.

"I'm right here," I whisper, not daring to let her go. She sniffles, and the white rose in her hand trembles when she outstretches her arm to place it over the stone. A chill rests over my shoulders when the familiar name falls out of her mouth like a broken whisper of pain.

"Sleep well, *Snow White*." She kisses her palm and presses it over his name. I place my hand beside hers as we say our goodbyes.

Her misty eyes peer up at me, and we return to our seats to wait for the others to say their goodbyes.

From the corner of my eye, a shadow slumped by a tree catches my attention. A fresh swell of rage rises inside me at the sight of Andrew.

Victoria senses my anger, and her stare falls to where I'm looking. When she sees him, she tenses, and her lips harden into a tight line. Her thick lashes flutter into a glare, and her body shakes not from her sobs but from her rising anger.

"Kill him." Her eyes move to my gun, and her words carry a coldness I've never heard from her. As I process her words and the anger on her face, she grabs my gun and shoots Andrew, and he falls to the ground.

Luca's parents notice their son, and they say nothing. Grief shines in their eyes, as they know they can't help him because he's a traitor. They turn their gaze back to the tombstone of their youngest son, unable to watch my men haul Andrew into a car.

"Let's get you home," I whisper, and Victoria gives a tired nod.

We make our way back home in silence, and once she's in bed, I'm grateful for the girls who gather around her. They assure me they will stay with her while I deal with Andrew, Lorenzo, and Rebecca.

"I'll be back," I tell Victoria, and she says nothing. Her eyes tell me all she wants to say.

'Make them pay.' It's silent in her gaze, and I know she's reached the end of what she can take. She's angry, and she's hurting.

As I leave, her warmth disappears, and the stiffness in my neck and shoulders returns, sending a thrill of anger through me.

They're all going to pay for what they've done.

Andrew's cries blare in the dense air of the warehouse.

I approach the three traitors tied to the most uncomfortable metal chairs. The closer I get, the clearer I can see the fear etched across Rebecca's face and the louder her begging for mercy becomes.

She will not get mercy.

She threatened not only me but also Victoria and my mafia. I do not take these threats lightly or at all.

I stare at a malnourished Lorenzo. The smell of his reeking body hits me even when I'm fifteen feet away. Dirt and blood cover him; his clothes are now torn into shards, which slip off his thinning body.

Revenge is best served cold, and they sure as hell didn't lie because the sight of him on the brink of death is satisfying.

When he sees me, he glares and hurls curses my way. They don't phase me because I'm too busy trying not to laugh at the sight of his missing front tooth.

Is this Victoria's signature move? I'm not sure, but I fucking loved it. Seeing my pliers in her tiny hands while she radiated with fierceness was a beautiful, powerful force, which also pulsed out of her the night Luca died.

I've seen all forms of anger and experienced them all, but nothing is as powerful as the rage of a woman. The second their silence falters and their eyes narrow into slits, you are in the presence of a force greater than yourself.

Erika's gentle steps come from behind me.

She wanted to be here to face the man who betrayed her. To show him she's free and alive, out of the hell he trapped her in.

Lorenzo sees her, and his eyes widen in shock before his permanent sneer reappears.

I stand in front of all three of them. My arms cross over my chest, and a muscle in my jaw constricts.

My gaze falls on Andrew, sitting with his head slumped in defeat.

Like Adriano and Marquez, Andrew was never meant to hold any position of authority. Which is why I couldn't give him what he wanted when I took over for my father.

Francisco, the mafiosos, and my two capos all stand around the three.

The empty spot beside Kaden and Angelo brings a weight to my gut. Luca's radiating presence is missing, and it's a feeling that won't go away, even with time.

"What are you going to do to us?" Rebecca cries as she struggles with the bonds around her wrist.

I bend to her level. My face twisted into a glare.

"I'm going to give you all what you deserve."

"No, please. I'll tell you whatever you want!" Rebecca shouts in a broken voice.

"Oh, I know you will." She swallows when she sees me grinning at her fear.

To her left, Lorenzo curses her.

"You better not say shit, you whore!" She glares at him, but says nothing.

"So, who's going to be first?" I ask with a bored expression, and my gaze falls on Lorenzo, whose stench of piss and blood is making my nose wrinkle.

There's no point in keeping him alive any longer. He hasn't budged in the past few months that we've tortured him. At first, killing him quickly wasn't enough. I wanted him to experience every ounce of pain imaginable for his crimes, and he's suffered most of them. But now I want him dead because while he's alive, there will always be a threat to Victoria and our child.

I glance over my shoulder and turn to the trembling, petite woman behind me.

"Erika." When she hears me call her, she takes slow steps toward the man who betrayed her.

Lorenzo's cold eyes stare at her, and he's emotionless.

"Stupid whore," he sneers.

"Shut up!" she shouts, slapping him. "I want you to look at me," she says harshly, and we watch as she takes back her power with every syllable she utters. "You may have broken me, but you have not killed me. I'm alive and will live. But you will die, and your body will lie in a ditch for the maggots to tear apart," she says near his ear, and her words elicit a quiver in him.

Her shoulders sag, and she heads toward Angelo, who will take her back to the house.

I point my gun at Lorenzo's forehead. He glares at me, and I pull the trigger right as he goes to curse me. His head slumps back and then forward. Rebecca's scream permeates around us, and she shakes in the chair, trying to free herself.

I turn toward her, and she stills under my gaze.

"What were you saying at the masquerade?" My words are sarcastic, and she stops breathing.

"Please don't kill me. I'm sorry, I didn't mean it!" Her face turns pale when my gun rests over her temple.

"In your next life, watch your tongue."

The loud bang of my gun echoes off the crates surrounding us. Its sharp sound shatters the silence.

I advance toward Andrew and grab his bloodied scalp between my fingers.

"And you." My words are hostile, and I want to tear his eyes out of their sockets.

This bastard would have been the one to take my lifeline away from me. History would have repeated itself for my family if it hadn't been for Luca's sacrifice.

"Leo," he says in a choked whisper.

My fist repeatedly crashes into his face, and he cries out with each bone crushing impact.

Kaden hands me a hammer, and my fingers curl around it.

"Where's Adriano?" Andrew stays silent, and I plummet the head of the hammer into his fingers, breaking them.

Andrew screams, his head rolling back in agony.

"In the Amazon!" he says through his pain.

"The coordinates?"

No answer comes from him, and I smash the hammer into his other hand.

"Give me the coordinates, or I swear I will skin you alive and hang your skin on my front door." I flip open a pocket knife, placing it against his cheek. He trembles and is silent, refusing to speak. I press my blade into his skin, and blood seeps from the cut.

"I am so sorry. Please, kill me," he begs, and I scoff in disbelief.

"I'm going to make you suffer for what you did to Luca and what you wanted to do to my family." I'm trembling with anger and grief, and it takes over my entire being. "When you pulled that trigger, you intended to hurt me. You wanted to kill my family, but you killed yours instead." He winces at my words, and tears flow from his eyes.

Andrew won't say a word, and I'm becoming more infuriated with his resistance.

I dig the blade deeper into his jaw, and his skin curls over the knife.

"The location where Adriano is hiding is on my phone." Andrew's shoulders sag with defeat, and Francisco hands me the phone.

"What's the passcode?" I order, and Andrew gives it to me without hesitation. When I find the coordinates of Adriano's location, I turn to my men.

"Don't kill him yet. We still need to talk to his parents," I instruct Francisco before making my way toward my mafioso friends.

Andrew's screams and cries resound behind me as Francisco and Kaden beat him.

"What's the plan?" Alexander asks as he and the rest of them follow me out of the warehouse.

"We finish this once and for all." I give them a hard look, wiping the blood on my hands with a handkerchief.

When I return to the house, Victoria isn't in our room. Her absence doesn't worry me because I know where she is.

She's in Luca's room.

When I passed the empty room, I heard her cries seeping from behind the door. I wanted to go in and hold her, but she needed the space to grieve alone.

I step back into the room after my shower, and I'm relieved to find Victoria sitting on our bed reading a book. The faraway look on her face tells me she isn't capturing the meaning of the words she reads.

I sit beside her, and she looks up at me before her eyes fall on my hand resting on her thigh. A line appears between her brows when she sees the torn skin of my knuckles.

"Leo, what happened?" she says as she meticulously runs the pad of her finger over the broken skin.

"I must have hit Andrew harder than expected," I say, grabbing her hands in mine and kissing them. "I'm okay," I assure her, and her frown deepens.

"What are you going to do to him?" she whispers, and my body becomes rigid from her question because I don't know what I'm going to do with Andrew.

I want to kill him, but the problem is the guilt that will follow. We all know Luca loved his brother, despite everything Andrew did. He wouldn't want us to kill Andrew, who clearly feels remorse for his actions. It's for this reason that I don't know what the right choice is. It's also a decision I can't make on my own. I have to discuss this with her, Francisco, my capos, and his parents.

"I'm not sure yet," I say with a noisy breath.

"Well, whatever you decide, I'll support it either way." She presses a delicate kiss on the corner of my mouth, and I let out a breath the moment I remember I need to let her know I'm leaving tomorrow.

There's a gripping sensation in my chest at the thought of leaving her behind, but it needs to be done. As long as Adriano is alive and plotting against us, there will always be an inevitable threat to our lives and that of our child. My father's mistakes taught me that pushing these matters aside can become deadly.

"What's wrong?" Victoria grabs my face in her hands.

"We know where Adriano is." A tremble takes over her body from my words, and my eyes soften when fear reveals itself over her features.

"When do you leave?" Her eyes mist with tears, and her gaze falls on the white bandage on my arm where a bullet has sliced the surface of the skin.

"Tomorrow." I bring her onto my lap and hold her tightly. She buries her head into my neck, and her tears are warm against my skin. "Amore, please don't cry."

I wipe her tears. Her sadness brings me grief, and when I can't take her worry away, I feel useless.

"What if something happens to you? Leo, I can't do this without you." She stares at me with fear so raw it brings a chill to my bones. "I can't lose you too."

"You won't lose me." I assure her, and she says nothing, her fingers gripping my shirt tightly.

"Victoria, as long as Adriano is alive, you, me, and our baby can never live in peace. I need to do this for us."

She closes her eyes, and I press my lips onto hers, wanting to feel their softness against my mouth before I leave.

Our lips move in a soft touch, full of our love, worry, and passion. Victoria's fingers intertwine through my hair, and she parts her lips, allowing me to savor the taste of her sweet mouth.

I rest her on the bed and hover above her. My mouth glides down her jaw and neck, and she responds to my touch with soft moans.

She's mine, and I am hers.

Victoria's dark eyes look at me, and I bend to her will.

Every time I look into her eyes, I fall in love with her all over again. My mouth falls back onto hers, and our kiss is slow. We only break apart when we work to remove the articles of clothing from our bodies, and we toss them carelessly around the room.

My gaze lingers on Victoria as she lies beautifully naked under me, and her skin blooms with goosebumps under my eyes.

I trace her full lips, and my finger continues down her body, twirling over one of her swollen nipples. She shivers under my touch, and the chocolate bud hardens.

My finger trails down the rest of her body, circling over the slight curve of her abdomen, and I lower myself to her stomach.

She clenches under me as I press soft kisses over the area before my mouth descends lower, and I press two kisses to her inner thighs.

I'm determined to savor this moment with her before all hell breaks loose tomorrow. Tonight is for us.

"Leo," she breathes out, her dainty fingers clutching the bedsheets. I don't make her wait. My mouth latches onto her clit, giving her long, slow strokes. Her sweetness coats my mouth, and my cock hardens.

Victoria rolls her hips, and my grip around her thighs tightens when she presses my mouth into her pussy. When I nibble on her soft clit, she quivers. With one more flick of my tongue, she finds her release.

I lick my lips and rise from between her legs, and I align our hips. Her eyes flutter when the tip of my cock teases her.

"Tell me you want the mafia to fuck you," I rasp, and her eyes flicker. My words have stunned her, and her perfect mouth drops open, tempting me to plunge my tongue into it.

She doesn't say the words I want to hear, so I press the tip of my cock to her entrance. My wetness grazes her clit, and a nerve in her thigh spasms.

"Say it, amore." My words come out strained, and my cock twitches with a painful ache.

She licks her lips, her eyes penetrating my own.

"I want the mafia to fuck me *hard*," she says breathlessly, and a deep guttural groan rips out of my throat from how dark and lustful the words roll off her tongue.

"Good girl," I whisper, diving deep into her, and she stretches wide for me.

Our bodies move slowly, rhythmically, and sensually.

The tempo between our movements increases as tension builds.

I rut my cock into her mercifully until she's screaming my name. Her fingernails pierce the skin on my sides, and I bury my face into her shoulder, where I lightly bite and suck on the skin.

Victoria pulls my head from her shoulder and presses our mouths together. Her tongue explores every inch of my mouth, and I grunt from deep in my throat as I keep riding in and out of her.

My cock plunges into her, and her tongue plunges into my mouth. We take from one another, and we also provide for one another.

With every thrust, my abdomen tightens, and heat courses through every vessel inside me.

Victoria's long legs wrap around my waist, and she stretches. With her opening for me, my thrusting becomes smoother.

The coiling tension inside me is ready to burst, and I chase the pleasure until the familiar flush of heat travels the length of my spine.

Victoria trembles in my arms, and her walls flutter around my cock, squeezing painfully good.

As my release creeps up, I pull her close, wanting to feel her jerk up on my body as I fill her.

I press our sweaty chests together, smothering her face in my right shoulder, and her breath is hot and labored, her lips kissing my hot skin.

We find our release, and her head rolls back. She opens her mouth with a soft moan, and I steal a kiss from her. My vision turns hazy from ecstasy, and it takes a few seconds until I can see clearly again.

I place her on my chest, and we catch our breath. A peacefulness wraps around me as I run my fingers through her disheveled hair. The uneasiness of what is coming tomorrow is at the back of my mind.

62

VICTORIA

The silence in the room brings a terrifying calmness. Inside me is a fear as thick as smog.

Nothing can prepare me for the pain and worry of knowing the love of my life is about to go on a dangerous mission.

Leo's touch is as light as the rays of the sun as his fingers dance across my skin, tracing circles on the spot where our love grows. I want to stay like this forever, but that's not possible. He has to go to the Amazon, and I will remain in Italy, waiting for him to come home to me.

Like a crashing tide, the fear of losing Leo drowns me with tremendous dread.

Not wanting to part with his warmth, I nuzzle myself into him, and his erection presses into my backside. The pleasure has me biting my bottom lip, and I almost draw blood.

Leo groans and moves to hover above me. He cups my face with one hand, and his mouth lowers to mine.

There's a knock on the door as he's going to kiss me. The look of hunger disappears from his dark eyes, and it's replaced with annoyance.

"Leo, everything is ready for our departure," Francisco says, and we hear his receding footsteps announcing his immediate departure.

"I'm giving him one more chance before I kick him out of this damn house. Underboss or not," Leo grits out, his face marred with irritation.

I laugh, running my fingers through his hair.

Leo carries me out of bed, and when we're both showered and dressed, I stand in front of him, buttoning his shirt.

His black suit and towering height make him a formidable force.

Leo's stare is gentle as he watches me fix the collar of his black dress shirt. Something shiny around his neck catches my attention, and I gasp at the sight of a familiar little diamond heart attached to a chain around his neck.

It's the earring I gave him when we separated in France.

The tips of my fingers graze the necklace, and tears prickle the corners of my eyes.

He still has it.

Leo notices my reaction to the necklace, and his hand clutches mine. He embraces me and kisses my temple, leaving his lips there for a few seconds.

"I love you, Victoria." His voice is strained and lets me know he doesn't want to leave me.

"And I love you, Leo," I whisper, pressing my face into his chest and inhaling his warm, musky scent. "You better come back to me."

"Of course, and when I do, we're getting you two checked out by a doctor again." He caresses my stomach and smiles at the slight curve forming.

Nothing else is said, and we head downstairs, where everyone is waiting.

When I see the girls' pale faces, I know we all share similar feelings of dread.

Neither of us knows what will happen, and the uncertainty creates a cloud of anxiety that heavily dominates us all.

The men give Leo a curt nod before kissing their partners, except for Lei, who groans in annoyance. He punches Chloe on the shoulder as a goodbye.

Chloe rolls her eyes, and with his back to her, she shouts after him.

"Don't get your dumbass killed!"

Lei doesn't turn around. He keeps walking toward the cars and lifts his left hand high in the air, holding his middle finger up at her.

"Unbelievable," Chloe grumbles, and our laughter fills the once tense silence.

Leo lifts my chin and sparks rise in the spot he touches. Our eyes lock, and mine soften when I'm met with the familiar deep green color I've fallen in love with.

He kisses me, and when he draws back, I bite my quivering lip. Leo's forehead creases, becoming etched with the marks of guilt.

"I'll be back before you know it," he assures me, and I can only give a meek nod.

He detaches himself from me and looks at his dad. Estephano nods, assuring Leo that he and the rest of their men staying behind will take care of us while they are away.

"Be careful, Leo!" Cleo says, and her arms wrap around him tightly.

"Always." Leo says, giving her a gentle smile and pressing a kiss on the top of her head.

I watch as she points to herself, and her fingers form a heart before pointing at Leo, who repeats the gesture.

Seeing Leo's toughness blend with his gentleness has my heart running with unconditional love.

Family is everything to him, and this love for his family is taking him away from us.

When they separate, Cleo makes her way toward her father. She wraps one arm around him and another around me.

I watch with a heavy heart as Leo walks toward the car.

Leo glances back, and our eyes connect one last time. He swallows, his shoulders slumping as he takes a breath, and then he gets into the car.

"He'll be okay." Estephano places a hand on my forearm. I sigh, pressing him into my chest in a hug, and his muscular arms wrap around me.

The cars drive away, and I repeat the same sentence to myself.

Please come back to us.

63

LEO

The air is moist, and the humidity sticks to our skin despite being swallowed by the shade of the tall trees.

It's been a long journey through *the green hell*. We haven't reached Adriano's hideaway, but we're close.

The sound of our feet shuffling through the dense terrain mingles with the birds chirping and the creek running nearby. Everyone walks with slumped shoulders and tired expressions. Our determination to kill Adriano and his men is the only thing keeping us going.

"Fucking shit," Lei says, slapping a mosquito that landed on his neck. His flushed cheeks scrunch into a scowl, and Alejandro laughs at his misfortune.

"He had to hide in the Amazon rainforest," Alexander grumbles, sipping his water and spilling some around his stubbled jaw. He wipes his mouth as I pat him on the back.

"We're almost there," I assure him, and he grumbles, pushing forward.

"Kaden," I call my capo, and he turns to me, wiping the sweat from his temple. "How much longer does the GPS say?"

He looks at the device in his hand.

"About half a mile."

I release a breath.

"Keep forward, and keep quiet," I tell the fifty men with us. That's ten men from each mafia family. The combined forces and skills of the five strongest mafias made us a group of the best criminals.

I wipe the sweat that has formed along my brow.

Victoria comes to mind. My worry increases because I'm not sure if she's safe or if something has happened back in Italy. I haven't had any internet connection to call her or my father. All I want is to finish this and return to my family.

Kaden looks at something in the distance. He turns around and motions for us to be quiet.

The closer I get to him, the clearer I can see what he's looking at. A grin stretches on my lips when I see the cement building Adriano is taking shelter in.

It's a distance away, but it's now in sight.

"Let's settle here. We'll send some men to scout the area," I say, and when our men return from scouting the perimeter, we begin planning our attack, and Lei once again recommends a not-so-bright idea.

"I say we go straight at it and ambush them all around," Lei says, and we all stare at him as if he's spoken in a language lost in history. Arthuro hits Lei in the back of the head, and he whines, rubbing his head.

My index finger and thumb massage my stubbled chin as I study the rough layout of the building we sketched.

"We want them to come to us," I tell Lei.

Alexander lifts a brow.

"But how are we going to do that?"

"It's not like Adriano will willingly come out," Arthuro pitches, his voice laced with exhaustion.

"We aren't going to tell them we're here," I reply in annoyance. "We're going to fumigate the roaches out." They all wear a look of confusion, so I continue, "There must be a secret passageway some-where. Adriano's a coward. He wouldn't have built his hideout without having an emergency escape ready."

I turn the blueprint of the building around, trying to find anything. But nothing comes to my attention.

"We need to find where the escape route is." I turn to Francisco. "Did any of the men scouting the area find anything suspicious?"

"Nothing out of the ordinary," he says, but then he stops to think for a second.

"What is it, Francisco?" I ask when I sense his hesitation.

"I saw a weird shed a few yards out from here." He points to the spot on the map and moves his finger a little aside. "And another one here. But they were empty," he assures me, but I'm not convinced by his response and decide to check it out for myself.

"Lei, Francisco, come with me. We're going to take a look."

Francisco leads us toward the empty shack, and after searching the place, I find Francisco is right after all. The place is empty.

"Told you," Francisco says with a grin, and we make our way out of the shed. As he crosses the center of the room, I hear the floorboard creak below him. He ignores it, but I hear it, and the hollow sound alerts me.

"What's wrong?" Lei asks when I get on my knees to press my hand on the ground. I lift the rug over the spot Francisco walked over, and I find a secret door under it.

"Empty, huh?" I mock, and Francisco stares wide-eyed as he exhales a breath of disbelief.

I open the secret door, and spider webs and dust come up from below. I wave my hand to get rid of the dust and try to look into the darkness.

"What's the plan?" Francisco says as he stares down at the hole in the ground.

"We need to see how far this tunnel goes out and to where," I say as I make my way down.

"Wait, what?" Lei says in a panic. "But what if Adriano's men are down there?"

"That's why I have you here to be my backup. Now come on, we don't have all day." Lei purses his lips, dissatisfied with this idea. I give him a warning look, and he follows me.

"Francisco, stay here and guard," I instruct as I descend to the tunnel below. Once at the bottom, Lei and I make our way through the tunnel.

After a few minutes of walking, I lose hope when, from the corner of my eye, I notice Lei has found something on the wall. He has his flashlight pointed at it as he wipes the area with his palm.

"Leo, look!" he whispers excitedly, his eyes wide.

I make my way back toward him, and he flashes the spot he was wiping to reveal a map of the underground tunnel.

Adriano is making this too easy for us.

I snap a photo of the map.

"Lei, good work!" He grins. "Now let's get out of here," I say, and Lei runs out of the tunnel, not having to be told twice.

"So?" Francisco asks as we make our way back up.

"We have the layout of the entire structure." I show him the picture, and he laughs.

"Fucking dumbass. Who makes a secret passageway and puts a map on the wall." Francisco shakes his head in disbelief, and we return to camp.

"How did it go?" Alexander asks.

"We found an underground passageway inside the shed, and the idiot had a map of the entire thing on the wall," Lei says, laughing as he shows them the picture of the map.

I ignore their laughter and work on creating a rough sketch of the tunnel. When I finish, I study it, and I'm left speechless.

"He doesn't have one escape. He has five," I say in disbelief.

"What do you mean?" Alejandro asks, peering over my shoulder to look at the sketch.

Grabbing a sharpie, I put an X over the four corners of the rectangle where the entrances of Adriano's escape routes connect to his hideout. All have a long, narrow tunnel extending out on all four sides, which leads to similar shacks in the forest. I then add one more X right in the center of the building, where a vertical tunnel runs right under the middle of the hideout. One tunnel leads south, and the other leads north. The secret passageway Lei and I were walking through was the tunnel on the south side, leading to the center of the house.

Under the building's base, all four corners of the tunnels connect, making it the perfect escape.

Adriano made sure he had more than one escape route for every corner of the building, including the center. I'm going to make this his downfall.

"So, who's going to tell me what the big, funny-looking X's mean?" Lei huffs, flaring his arms out in exasperation like a toddler.

I wave Angelo over.

"What's up?" he says with furrowed brows.

"Where are the bombs Luca made?" The mention of Luca brings a pinch to my chest, and although he's dead, his work will help us kill Adriano.

"I have one, and a few other men have the other seven," Angelo explains, pulling his bag in front of him and pulling out one of the eight bombs.

"Gather them all," I say, and he leaves to retrieve the explosives.

"No fucking way, a bomb! Are you trying to blow us and the forest up?" Lei says incredulously.

"We need them to come to us," I say, and he's still not convinced bombs are the right way to do it.

I sigh. "Lei, the funny X's are where the bombs need to be put. One by one, they'll explode, and the entire house will crumble. This means they will have no choice but to run out in a panic. This is when we attack the ones still alive."

Angelo returns with a duffel bag, and he places the final bomb inside before handing me the bag.

"That's a great plan," Arthuro says, looking at the sketch and then at the bombs. "But who's stupid enough to place the bombs and start them?"

A pang of defeat washes over me because he's right. This is a deadly mission, and bombs are unpredictable. Whoever goes will need to start five of them.

"Draw sticks?" I say, shrugging, when from the side Lei lets out a shaky breath, stepping forward.

"I can't believe I'm about to say this, but I'll do it," he grumbles, coming toward me, and I give him the duffel bag.

"How long after I activate them do I have?" Lei's hands are trembling, and I draw my brows together in a furrow, starting to rethink my decision to let him place the bombs.

"Lei, if you can't compose yourself, I'll plant the bombs." I place a hand on his shoulder, and his face scrunches.

"No! Leo, I can do this. Let me prove to you all and to my father that I am made for this life. The old man doesn't think I have the mental capacity to run our mafia." Lei frowns at the memory of his father's words. "Sure, I'm nervous, but who wouldn't when faced with death? I might not have a girl to fight for like you all, but I still have determination and people to fight for."

"You aren't incompetent, Lei. You're doing great on your own for your age. Plus, your mafia is still strong without your father running it. That has to count for something." I offer him a smile, and he lets out a breath.

"Thank you, Leo. Now tell me, how long do I have to get out of the tunnels?"

"Fifteen minutes," I say, and his eyes widen.

"Fuck, is that long enough for me to plant all five bombs and still get far enough to avoid the explosion?" His voice goes an octave higher, and a sheet of sweat gathers on his temple.

"Lei, you can do it, but you want to be swift and not get held back."

He lets out a shuddering breath and nods.

"How do I activate them, and where do I set them up?"

I grab one bomb and place it in his right hand. Then I grab the sketch I created and place it in his left hand. "You place one bomb in each X and cut the red wire. Right after you cut the wire, the fifteen-minute timer will count down." As I finish explaining, he lets out another nervous breath, nodding in understanding.

"Red wire...X marks the spot...don't get held up...got it." As he says this, he looks from the bomb to the sketch.

"Start the bomb in the middle of the building first. Then work your way toward the other corners. This will give you enough time to get out before the heat of the first explosion causes the others to erupt." When I tell him the heat of the first bomb will trigger the others, his lips roll into his mouth.

"Okay, I got it." He tips his head back and reviews the instructions again.

I'm a little unsettled by my easy-going friend's nervous behavior, but

I know he'll think he's useless if I don't let him do this. I swallow my concern and assure myself he can do it.

"Alright, let's gather everyone," I direct, and the mafia bosses instruct their men to gather around us.

I survey the crowd of men and notice them standing upright. Determination is written all over their rough faces. Automatic rifles hang by their sides, and they are ready for war.

The sun is setting, but I'm not worried about fighting in the dark. Not when the flames from the explosions will give us more than enough light.

My friends stand beside me, and we all glance at the men standing before us. Our expressions are sure to reveal pride in having strong, loyal men devoted to our family and business.

"We have selected you because of your strength and, above all, your devotion to our mafias," I say, glancing at their leaders, who nod in agreement. I then turn to my two capos and underboss, wishing a particular white-haired friend was standing beside them. Francisco gives me a sad smile.

"Today, we fight for what's ours. Not only for what's mine or your leaders. This family, this mafia, is as much yours as it is ours."

I mean every word I say. These men are not only our employees, but they are also our family. We can't succeed without their hard work. There is no mafia without them.

"We're brothers, and we're the mafia. I ask you not to fight for your leaders or for me, but to fight for your family. For your children, whose lives will be at stake if Adriano and his men accomplish what they want. Help us avenge our fallen brothers, who we already lost to the greed of Adriano."

Our men give stern nods; some murmur their agreements, and others depict grim expressions at the mention of their deceased.

I raise my rifle.

"Viva la Mafia!" I shout in Italian, and my men lift their guns, repeating the phrase with pride.

Following in my footsteps, my mafioso friends repeat the phrase in their mother tongue, and their men follow their lead.

"黑手党万岁!"

"да здравствует мафия!"

"Viva la Mafia!"

"Long live the Mafia!"

They all cry out in unison. The words hang in the air, and our men embrace each other as they prepare for what could be their last mission.

Satisfied, I turn to Lei. He gives me a nervous smile.

"Long live the mafia, right Leo?"

I pat his back, and a mischievous grin tips onto his lips.

"Let's blow these bastards to smithereens," Lei says, and I watch as he runs toward the secret tunnel.

Francisco comes to stand beside me, waiting for my orders.

"Let's set up around the outskirts and wait for them to run out."

Francisco motions for our men to take their positions, and we wait amongst the trees for the first bomb to go off, when something in the corner catches my eye.

I make my way toward Angelo and Kaden to give them one more mission before all hell breaks loose.

Alejandro, Alexander, and Arthuro all stare at me with curious brows.

When Angelo and Kaden hear my mission, they laugh, assuring me they will get it done.

"What was that all about?" Alexander asks.

I pat my friend on the shoulder.

"You'll have to wait and see." That's all I say, and Alexander scowls, not content with my response.

64

LEI

After receiving my cue, I run toward the shack, where the entrance to the secret tunnel is.

The bombs inside the bag slung to my side are heavy with every step I take through the dense rainforest.

Darkness is consuming me, and I'm more worried about the abundant wildlife in the Amazon than the bombs themselves.

I force my feet to run faster, wanting to get this over with so we can leave this green hell.

The trees above rattle as the wind blows the branches from side to side.

There's dread in my stomach from the possibility of not making it out alive. The thought of dying has a cold sweat gathering at the base of my neck, and it runs down the side.

"I still want to marry and have a family. I'm too young to die," I mumble, determined to make sure I succeed.

My feet land at the bottom of the tunnels with a thump. I look at the rough sketch of the map Leo drew, and go north until I reach where Leo drew the first X, and I'm relieved to see the secret door to get to the tunnels.

This is the first X. The one in the center of the hideout.

I set the bomb, and with shaky hands, I prepare myself for when I cut the red wire like Leo instructed.

"Please don't blow up on me." I bring my knife to the wire, my breath gets stuck in my throat, and I close my eyes when I cut it.

When I don't explode into chunks, I touch my chest and sigh in relief.

I peer at the clock, which is counting down. The red digits are daunting. A nervous laugh spills out of me, but then I remember time is precious.

"Shit!"

I still have four more bombs to set up.

I make my way north until I notice I have to choose between four paths.

Going straight south will take me back the way I came, and going north will lead me to the other shack in the forest. I pick right and start walking toward the X Leo drew on the top right of the map.

"Fourteen minutes," I count, tracking how long until the first bomb goes off.

When I reach twelve minutes, I get to the second location. There I find the second escape latch. This time I'm quick to cut the red wire.

I'm fast as I go through the tunnels, setting one bomb after the next until I have run in an entire rectangle formation. I only have one more bomb left.

"Four minutes and ten seconds."

My feet speedily carry me through the tunnels, and I ignore the rats crawling on the floor.

As I round the corner to head toward the spot where the last bomb needs to be placed, I bump into a person. We're both pushed back by our combined forces, and the bomb in my hand falls to the ground with a clatter. The red head looks at me and then at the bomb. His eyes widen, and he pulls out his gun.

Three minutes and fifteen seconds.

I struck the gun out of his hands.

I have to kill him, cut the last bomb, and get the hell out of here, and I have to do it all in under three minutes.

I'm fucked.

The flames from the first bomb will make the other bombs go off, making this entire area a fiery hell. I need to get out before this happens.

"Let's dance, motherfucker," I say through clenched teeth, throwing my fist at the man's jaw. He punches me in the chin, drawing my head to the left.

My right fist does an uppercut, and he shouts, sending punches my way.

I grab his hand, put it behind his back, and push him against the wall. Using all my strength, I smash his forehead into the wall one, two, three, and four times. He groans in pain. The noise mingles with my heart ticking loudly in my ears.

Despite the adrenaline of fighting him, I still make it a point to keep track of the time.

I have two minutes, maybe less.

The man throws his head back, and my vision grows hazy from the headbutt I received.

The burning pain of my broken nose drowns me.

"You fucker," I say as blood pours out of my nose.

He roughly throws me against the wall, and the sharp pain behind my head makes me dizzy. He chokes me, but his grip is loose because he's disoriented from when I smashed his head into the concrete wall.

I reach for my gun, but it's nowhere in sight. Then I see it on the floor behind him.

Still struggling under his grasp, I go for the switchblade in my pocket. I stab the man in the neck, ramming it into his jugular, and his eyes widen with the look of death.

I toss him aside, grab the bomb from the ground, and cut the cord while I run. I place it right under the hatch.

"One minute, come on, Lei!" I force myself to run faster down the tunnel where the opening to the shack is.

BOOM!

"Fuck!"

The loud noise of the first bomb going off resonates throughout the tunnel. Before I can react, I hear the other bombs following.

BOOM!!

BOOM!!!

BOOM!!!!
BOOM!!!!!
The soil trembles under me.

I climb the ladder to exit the inferno and almost fall when I miss a step.

I push open the latch, and I'm hit with the cold air from above and the hot air from below. I let out a gasp as the fiery pain consumes me.

65

LEO

"Leo, relax." Alejandro places a heavy hand on my shoulder to halt my pacing.

It's been over twenty minutes, and there's been no sign of Lei or the sound of an explosion.

"Should someone go check up on him?" Arthuro inquires, and his stone-cold front transforms into concern for our friend.

I'm about to send someone to look for Lei when the ground rumbles below us. The loud sound of an explosion follows, but still no Lei.

"Come on, Lei," I say under my breath, looking in the direction he left. My worry increases, but I know I need to give out orders. Adriano's hideout is now sinking to the ground, and his men are running out in a frenzy.

"Leo, we need to attack now. I'm sure Lei is—"

Alexander is cut off from the sound of our men shouting and pointing at a limping Lei covered in ash and blood.

We all run toward him.

"What the fuck happened to you?" Arthuro asks, tilting Lei's head back and grimacing at the sight of his broken nose.

"Nothing much but a little run-in with one of Adriano's minions, but I took good care of him," says Lei, waving a dismissive hand.

"And the nose?" Alexander asks with an arched brow. He touches Lei's nose, and Lei makes a hissing noise, sending Alexander a glare.

"The bastard broke my perfect nose." Lei's voice is muffled as more blood pours from his nostrils.

As we surround him, he looks at us with raised brows.

"What are you all doing surrounding me like a bunch of cows? Let's kill these fuckers. I didn't almost get my ass blown up for no reason." Lei tries to walk ahead and winces with every step.

I place a hand on his shoulder, stopping him.

"You aren't fighting. You've done enough."

Lei groans, about to fight me on my decision, but one glare from me and he draws back.

"Fine," he huffs, grudgingly sitting against a tree.

I load my gun and turn to the men.

"Alright, everyone ready?"

Francisco has excitement spread across his face.

"I'm right behind you, brother." He places a hand on my shoulder, and my two capos do the same.

"Everyone spread out and kill them all." When I give the order, they all head toward the crumbling building. The sound of our men shooting at those who have escaped fills my ears, and smoke from the flames consumes my lungs. Adriano is nowhere to be found amidst the smoke and crowd.

A bullet whizzes past my head and I barely lean to the side. A frustrated rumble comes from my chest when more bullets come racing toward me. I dodge out of the way, and I find the shooter. I strike his leg, and he falls with a shout. Another one of my bullets to the head, and he's no longer a problem.

From the corner of my eye, I see the man I'm looking for. As expected, Adriano is running toward his getaway car.

I knew what I had to do when I saw the Jeep earlier. Adriano wouldn't be going anywhere.

A laugh comes from inside me at the sight of him trying to start the Jeep, but it doesn't budge.

My gaze falls on Angelo and Kaden, who have their heads thrown back in laughter. The car battery is lying near their feet.

Our eyes lock, and they salute me before killing the men running out of the flames.

Everything is going as planned.

A smile spreads across my face as I watch Adriano pound his fist on the steering wheel.

The adrenaline pumps through my veins as I fire my gun at the car, and he flinches, trying to avoid getting hit. The bullets ricochet against the car. Metal shards and glass explode, impaling anyone within twenty feet.

Adriano turns his head in my direction and gives me a hostile glare. My smirk makes him more furious.

He takes cover, and I lose sight of him until I catch him limping around the passenger side. One of my bullets punctured his left arm. His wound doesn't stop him from aiming his gun at me, and I'm quick to get out of his range.

Adriano motions for his men to kill me, and when their guns fire at me, I jump behind the trees to take cover.

My breathing is heavy, and I press my back against the bark of the tree as they continue to fire rounds at me.

I peer out from the side, kill one of the two men shooting at me, and injure the other.

"Stop being a coward and fight me like a real man." Adriano says nothing. "Hiding behind others, as usual!"

"Fuck you!" he yells, outraged by my words.

When I peer out to see him once more, I find him all alone. I move out from behind the trees and make my way toward him.

"We're ending this today," I say, promising him a painful death. His face is cut from the shards of glass that impelled his skin when I shot at the Jeep. The sight is enough to bring a satisfied grin to my lips.

"Yes, we are, cousin."

"You sound a little too confident you'll win. Look around you." I motion to the dead bodies of his gang members, and his nostrils flare. "You lost."

We circle one another, eyes throwing daggers at each other.

"This may be true, but I plan on making sure neither you nor I leave this place alive."

Adriano shoots at me, and the bullet barely misses. More of his shots come flying my way. He's shooting with rapid speed, letting his rage fuel him. Seeing his irrational anger get the best of him is satisfying. Like his father, Adriano's hot temper will bring him to his death.

I shoot his left leg, and he falls to the ground.

He snarls, looking at me, raising his gun and pressing the trigger.

I avoid the first bullet, but he sends two more of them my way, and the third one punctures my left arm, bringing a familiar, heated sting. I ignore the discomfort, letting my rage and adrenaline mask the pain.

Adriano is on the ground, the dirt below him turning a rich red from the blood seeping out of his leg. I make my way toward him, releasing a bullet with each step. A bullet hits the wrist of the hand in which he holds his gun, and the weapon falls to the floor. Another bullet strikes his right thigh.

I grab his gun from the ground and throw it behind me. Adriano's eyes narrow into angry slits as he watches me toss my automatic rifle to the side.

My chest is light when I wrap my fingers around his throat. His face turns red as I lift him. There's a tingle in my fingers when I pull out the handgun I used when I killed his father.

I press the muzzle to his temple.

"Tell your father about the useless fuck you are when you see him in hell."

Adriano's green eyes are malevolent, and his lips morph into a sneer. He lets out a shout and knees me between the legs.

I grunt. My hold around him releases, and he launches himself at me.

We're both on the ground, and he's on top of me, throwing punches.

Gripping him by the throat, I toss him aside, and my right fist begins its brutal attack on his face.

I lift him by the collar of his shirt, and his jaw breaks under the force of my punch. My veins surge with a primal fury, and all my pent-up anger flows out of me as I bust him into pieces.

I'm impelled by the memory of Marquez pointing a gun at me, and then of my mother's lifeless body in my arms. The grief drives my hands to go around his throat, squeezing.

The memory of Victoria on a stage in nothing but lingerie and the words he said before selling her also comes to mind. It brings a tremble to my body, and I smash the back of his head on the ground four times, receiving a grunt from him.

Then the image of my sister bleeding on her bathroom floor resurfaces. The smell of her blood is as clear to my senses as the memory of her convulsing with foam coming from her mouth.

"This is for my sister!" My fist hammers down on him repeatedly until his face swells and becomes torn. His blood paints my white knuckles red.

He's grinning at the mention of Cleo.

"It was satisfying to hear her crying and begging me to stop fucking her." He chuckles, and I see red. The nerve in my jaw twitches.

"You sick fuck!" I grab my gun and shoot him in the balls. He roars out in pain.

"You are no Bandoni! And you are not my family!"

Adriano gives a biting laugh, revealing his teeth, which are stained red from his blood.

"We will always be family, whether you want to accept it or not."

The smirk plastered across his beaten face brings me uneasiness and anger. But nothing compares to the heavy impact his following words bring.

"My blood runs thick in yours and yours in mine. We're more compatible than you think. Look at yourself. We are the same." He jabs a stiff finger at my chest.

"We are not the same," I say through clenched teeth.

He laughs again.

"You're a monster, like me and my father. You will never be good," he counters, and the smile he gives me chills my blood. "Even after death, the world will never be free of me. I've already tainted it, leaving you to deal with the chaos and pain I created!"

The air leaves my lungs with his words. The sad faces of Cleo, Victoria, Sofia, Erika, and many others who have suffered because of his actions bring a stiffness to my body.

"You are unbelievable," I scoff. "Even when you have already lost, you don't give up. Instead, you keep spewing nonsense."

"Don't be so sure about that. My father got what he wanted for Estephano and your mother." He grins when he notices a wave of concern and confusion washing over me. "Ask Estephano what happened to your mother when *Roberto Mesa* kidnapped her…Oh wait, you can't, because he doesn't even know. Your whore of a mother never told him anything."

When he calls my mother a whore, my fist meets the side of his face.

"What are you talking about?" I grip his neck, and his dark eyes brighten. "Tell me now, or I swear I will tear you limb by limb."

Adriano's smile turns into a smirk, and I realize he won't tell me even if I tear him apart. My agitation at not getting the answers I want will only please him. I won't give him the pleasure of tormenting me any longer. I put the gun to the center of his head, and green eyes like mine stare at me.

"Fuck you, your mafia, and your future children!" Adriano spits out his venom, and I pull the trigger, his emotionless eyes thin, losing life forever.

As I stare at his lifeless body, I'm left unsatisfied. Adriano's last words about an unknown family secret press down on me like a boulder.

The adrenalin subsides, and I'm hit with a wave of pain from the gunshot wound on my arm.

Ahead of me, I see the last of Adriano's men lined up and being taken care of with a bullet to the head.

I walk past them and head toward my friends.

"It's done. Adriano is dead," I say, and my words come out flat as I'm consumed with thoughts about the mystery surrounding my mother and Roberto Mesa. A name I've never heard before.

"Leo, you need to see this," Francisco says in a sharp voice.

"What is it?" I say, and my eyes widen when I see twenty women behind him shaking in fear.

"Please don't hurt us," one of them pleads as she stands in front of the other younger girls.

"We won't hurt you. We're here to help," I assure them, and my words bring tears to their eyes.

"Thank you for saving us," the woman says in a shaky voice, and it's as if she can't believe she's free.

I motion for our men to help them.

"Where did they have the girls?" I ask Francisco when I don't remember seeing them run out of the burning building.

"They were being kept in a containment underground a few yards out. Lei heard them screaming for help during the attack," Francisco says, and I'm relieved we didn't leave without them.

As I look at the dead bodies of Adriano and his men and then at the girls we rescued, I know I have kept my promise to my sister. I saved all the girls from Adriano, as she asked me to do all those months ago.

Francisco lets out a deep exhale and rests an arm over my shoulder.

"I can't believe it's over," he says with a smile.

I let out a ragged breath, overwhelmed with thoughts of what Adriano told me. The name Roberto Mesa brings a weight to my insides, and I can't help but wonder if Francisco might be wrong.

Nothing is over until I talk to my father and we figure out what secret my mother kept from us.

66

VICTORIA

"They're here!" Emma shouts, peering out of the window.

We all drop what we're doing, and my heart flutters with excitement when I see the cars pulling into the roundabout.

They've been gone for five days, and although I spoke to Leo over the phone just yesterday, I'm still not at ease. Especially after noticing he spoke in a detached tone, almost as if something was bothering him. Which didn't make sense since he killed Adriano.

The cars come to a stop, and the girls make their way outside.

I still can't believe that after many months, everything that spiraled out of control after being kidnapped is over.

A few months ago, I was sure that when this day came, I'd be packing to go home, but things have turned out differently. I won't be going home. My life is now in Italy with Leo.

I still haven't told my parents about my sudden engagement or pregnancy, and the time to tell them is coming.

Considering Leo and I's relationship might seem rushed, I know they'll blow a nerve. But I don't care what they say because I love Leo, and he's the only one I'll ever want by my side. Being pregnant so soon into our relationship isn't what I would have wanted for myself, but there's nothing I can do about it now.

I look out of the window and see the door to the black SUV open, and Leo steps out.

When I see him, my feet carry me to the front door.

The moment I step outside, Leo's eyes fall on me, and they simmer with the same glint he always has when he tells me he loves me.

I run into his open arms, and he presses me against his body.

"It's really over?" I ask, my right cheek pressed to his chest. I listen to his steady heartbeat, and there's a moment of silence. When I peer up at him, his forehead is bunched together, and his shoulders are stiff. "Is Adriano really dead?" I say instead, my hand resting on the left side of his cheek.

He sighs. "Yes, he's dead. It's all over."

He sounds unsure, and his response has me pressing my lips together. I want to ask him what's bothering him, but my concern shifts to the fading bruises on his face and the bloodied bandage on his forearm.

"Leo, what happened?"

His gunshot wound reminds me of Luca, and I can't control the tears that resurface from the grief overpowering my body. It's like someone punched me in the stomach and twisted my heart all at once.

"Amore, I'm okay." His thumb and forefinger seize my chin. "I came back to you."

I sigh because he's right. He came back to me, but this still doesn't mean seeing him hurt doesn't bring me any less worry.

My gaze drifts to his injury once more.

"Does it hurt?"

"Amore, I've been through worse." He tries to ease my worries, but his words do the opposite. I'm now more anxious because I realize this won't be the last time he gets hurt. Leo's work puts him in danger daily, and I don't want him coming home injured to become a regular thing. But it's out of our control. Danger and violence are a part of his life, and now they're also a part of mine. If having to worry from time to time is a sacrifice I need to make to be with him, then it's a sacrifice I'm willing to make.

When Leo saved my life in France, he did more than rescue me. He loved, respected, and protected me. He's my savior, and I'm his damsel in distress.

The plane ticket from California to France had set the course for my path to lead me to my hero in Armani.

It's as if my life has somehow become a story from a Grimm Brothers fairy tale. However, not everyone is as fortunate as me and Sofia.

My attention drifts from Leo to Erika.

Although free from her enslavement, her kidnappers dehumanized and broke her body, spirit, and soul. She will now have to mend the broken pieces left behind.

Then I turn to Cleo, who is also on a journey to overcome her past.

The pain of human trafficking and the violence against our bodies has left us with a deep wound we will have to try to heal. In the end, a scar will remain as a memory of what happened to us. But the love of our family will cushion the effects of our assault.

With our freedom, we are given the opportunity to use our collective voices and our strength to help our sisters, who are in the same situation we were once thrown into.

Girls are still being forced into prostitution, and they are not whores on the corners of streets. Many of them are victims forced into submission, too afraid to ask for help.

But I hear them, and I see them.

After my kidnapping and the healing that followed, I regained my strength. I now realize that when they touch one of us, we all need to retaliate.

Change won't happen if we sit in silence. The world has to hear the ringing of our screams. Screams that we've been forced to swallow generation after generation. They have to feel our solid fists banging against their chests, which we've been forced to clench to our sides. And it's time they see the flames of anger in our eyes, which we've been forced to conceal with doe eyes and a sweet smile.

For change to happen, I need to tell my parents what happened to me without being ashamed.

Finally, with all my heart, I understand that what happened to me isn't something I need to be ashamed of. It's something those who hurt me need to be ashamed of doing.

I'm reclaiming my power and using my voice to get past the shame of my assault. If having my body abused taught me anything, it's that there's a point where you become numb, and whether you find light or darkness afterward is up to *you*.

For some, they recline into the darkness, like I had been doing when I returned home from France. But for others, they channel their pain into strength, and I have found my way back into the light.

"What are you thinking about?" Leo asks, curious about my silence.

I rise on my tippy toes, and Leo bends, allowing me to press a quick kiss to his lips.

"How much I love you," I say, knowing revealing the pain Adriano has left behind will only make him restless.

Leo's lips tip up, and he kisses me again. I grab his face, and my stomach flutters when his soft lips caress mine. We pull away, and my attention falls on my engagement ring, shining in the afternoon sunlight. My earlier thoughts come to mind.

"Oh, and also, how we need to tell my parents I'm not going home after all." I look from the ring to my stomach, where a baby bump will sprout in the coming months.

Leo grows pale, and his lips roll into his mouth.

"Merda," he curses, throwing his head back in frustration. His frightful eyes look at me. "Your dad is going to kill me."

"He's going to kill us both," I correct with a grimace. Our friends laugh at our state of panic, and we all return inside.

Leo's hand around my waist caresses the side of my stomach, and his touch brings sparks to my body.

With him beside me, I know I'm home.

67

LEO

It's been two days since returning from killing Adriano, and a decision regarding Andrew's life has finally been made. After much thought and discussion, it was decided that Andrew would live, and it wasn't a decision made on a whim. Victoria and I wanted to kill him, but Luca saved his life. The only thing keeping us satisfied is knowing he's guilt-ridden.

Andrew will now have to live the rest of his life as an outcast. He will live with the weight of knowing he killed his brother because of his greed.

Another reason we chose not to kill him is because his behavior is partially a result of a lack of love from his parents.

Luca and Andrew's parents, who were present when we decided what we were going to do with him, agreed they were also to blame for Andrew's mistakes. They confessed they wronged Andrew and tore their family apart when they chose one son over the other.

Adriano preyed on Andrew's weakness, and I can tell Luca's death has brought him out of his darkness.

Although alive, Andrew will not be free. I still can't trust him, and I'm keeping him in tight confinement where we can watch him. One wrong move, and I will snap his neck with no remorse.

With Adriano gone, it's time for the mafia families to return to their homes. Our reunion has ended.

Parting from one another was always easy for us guys, but for the girls, it's different. They've grown attached, and the separation will weigh on them all. With them leaving, I'm now worried about what their absence will mean for Victoria, who's still grieving the death of Luca.

The girls and Adriano kept us busy and kept her grief at bay. But with the absence of her friends, the real pain will begin. The dragging silence and loneliness of having the one person you want but cannot have is coming for all of us.

Grief is the one constant thing in the mafia. It's always there, and yet you never become immune to it. You can only learn to live with the pain.

Emma's voice brings me out of my thoughts.

"You better call me!" she warns Victoria, pressing her into a tight embrace.

I listen as Victoria assures Emma that she will call her. The two release one another, and Victoria bids her goodbyes to the rest of the girls.

When Victoria and Layla talk, my curiosity piques.

"Tell me when the little one comes, and we're having a play date the first chance we can!" I hear Layla telling Victoria.

To my left is an exhausted Alejandro, who's struggling to keep his sanity. The dark bags under his eyes tell me he doesn't sleep much, and it's probably because he's always worried Layla will hurt herself.

I shudder as I get a glimpse of my near future.

Layla and Victoria laugh and whisper to one another. Alejandro and I watch with raised brows as they press their stomachs together.

To my left, I hear Lei flirting.

"Goodbye, gorgeous," he says to Erika, who rolls her eyes when he presses a flirty kiss to the top of her right hand.

"Get lost Lei," she says in annoyance. From beside her, Angelo's lips curl into a satisfied smile. He sees my watchful gaze, and his cheeks flush bright red.

I laugh at the sight of my capo swooning over Erika.

"What's so funny?" Victoria asks as she waves at our friends who are getting into the cars.

"Angelo has a little crush." I motion toward the two, and when Victoria notices Erika laughing at something Angelo said, she awes. Her left hand presses against her chest, and she's about to make her way toward the two when I stop her.

"Oh no you don't." I grab her from behind.

"Leo, let me go," she huffs, trying to get out of my grasp, but I don't budge. "I only want to chat with him, that's all."

I make a mm-hmm noise, lifting her and carrying her bridal style to our room.

"Let them be. It's only harmless flirting." She groans in defeat and purses her lips. I feel a growing urge to kiss her, and when I can't hold off any longer, I capture her lips as I lead us into our room.

I lay her on our bed, hovering above her, and she sends me a dazzling smile, which leaves me breathless. Her fingers fiddle with the buttons of my black dress shirt, and she looks up at me through her long lashes.

"Leo, did you speak with your dad about what Adriano told you?" Victoria's question has my throat going dry, and I press my lips together.

After I told her what Adriano said, she was also concerned and kept insisting I talk to my father. This is probably the tenth time she's asked me this question.

I groan and fall beside her on the bed.

"Leo, you're tense, and not knowing what Adriano meant bothers you as much, if not more, than the thought of talking to your dad." She hovers over me from the side. "Go talk to him. Maybe he knows what secret your mom kept from you." She kisses my cheek, pushing me to get up.

"Amore, I'll talk to him tomorrow," I assure her, and she glares at me.

"No, go now," she says, and when I don't budge, she shakes her head in disapproval. "Leo, talking to your dad might help, or it might not, but at least by talking to him, you can move on and heal from your past. So stop procrastinating and get it done."

I sigh, knowing she's right. The weight of Adriano's words is suffocating me, and until I talk to my father, I'll continue to feel this way.

"Alright, alright, I'm going," I say, and she smiles, satisfied, as I make my way toward the door.

When I approach my father's bedroom, my stomach coils with nerves. I knock on the door, and he calls for me to come in. When I open the door, I find him in my mother's reading chair.

The smile on his face drops when he sees my uneasiness.

"What's on your mind, son?"

He looks at me, and unpleasant possibilities rise in my mind, making my chest feel tight.

"Papà, who's Roberto Mesa, and what did he do to Mamma?"

His body stiffens, and the color drains from his face.

68

LEO

"Where did you hear that name?" My father's fists clench at his sides, and his brows pull together.

"What are you hiding from me?" I persist, my words carrying caution. He responds with silence, fueling my frustration. "Estephano, who is he?"

He runs his fingers through his hair and looks at me. I stagger when I see the tears in his eyes.

"I wish you never found out about him." His voice is soft, almost a whisper.

"Papà..." I say tentatively, watching as he heads toward the nightstand in the room. He pulls out a familiar brown journal embroidered with a gold design. My mouth goes dry at the sight of it. He clutches my mother's journal as if he's afraid of losing it.

The journal is extended out for me to grab, but I hesitate when I remember how my mother didn't like anyone touching it. It felt wrong to go through her stuff.

My father notices my hesitation and pulls his hand back.

"Your mother only started writing in this journal when she found out she was pregnant with you." There's a hint of sadness in his eyes.

"She clung to it like it was her lifeline, and I never knew why until after she died."

As he talks about her, there's a rising thickness in my throat. The past resurfaces after years of burying the grief. Before, when my past came up, I was quick to push away the pain, but not this time. Victoria's right. I need to face this. I need to acknowledge that the pain is real. Only then can I find peace.

"Why do you have it?" I say, my gaze fixed on the journal I forgot existed.

"I missed her and was desperate, so I read it even though I know she wouldn't have wanted me to. If I didn't, I wouldn't have found out what she kept from us." His tears fall, and a gnawing sense of apprehension spreads. "Leo, inside is a letter she wrote to you."

He hands me the journal again, and this time I grab it.

"You asked me who Roberto Mesa is," he says, looking from the journal to me, and he lets out a deep exhale. "He was your mother's deranged uncle who kidnapped, tortured, and starved her for two weeks."

Rage. It blazes in my blood as he tells me who this man is. A man who I now want to hunt down and inflict unimaginable pain.

"I killed him," my father confirms, sensing my anger.

There's a long silence between us, and I wonder how Adriano's father fits into my mother's kidnapping.

"What does Marquez have to do with this man?" I ask, and my father's jaw twitches at the mention of his brother.

"All the answers you want are in the journal. It's best if she tells you everything herself through her own words." He places a hand on my forearm. "No matter what, remember your mother, and I love you. Nothing will ever change that."

I say nothing, and he leaves the room.

I open the journal with slow, cautious fingers, and I'm met with her handwriting. Grief swallows me whole until my hand is trembling. Her smell still lingers on the pages. The familiar floral scent and the elegantly scribbled words pinch my chest. As I take in her writing, I'm a mixture of rage, sadness, and disgust at the horrific things done to her by Roberto.

In the pages, she details how he tortured her with whips, cut her body, and starved her, making her wish for death. True to my father's words, she wrote a letter to me, and as I read, it's as if she is with me now. A sensation I could only ever dream of experiencing.

Dear Leo,

To my son, who I can never find the courage or the words to say what I want. Holding onto this truth is painful, and I need to get it out of my system before it eats me alive. So here it is...

Her pain is clear, and I wish I can hold her and tell her everything will be okay. But I can't because she's gone.

I reach the middle of the letter and see the familiar name, which brings acid to my mouth. The first line is four words revealing my mother's dark secret. A secret she almost took with her to the grave.

Marquez Bandoni raped me.

He took me from your father the same week we consummated our elopement. Then you came along nine months later. The closeness in consummation with your father and the time Marquez raped me means I don't know who your biological father is. You look like them both.

Regardless of this, Leo, you are Estephano's son, no matter what anyone tells you. You're every bit Estephano's son, not that monster. Estephano raised you, and you care and protect like him. You respect others as he does. You're nothing like Marquez. In my heart, you will always be a product of love.

I hope one day I can find the courage to tell you the truth. But for now, all I can do is write it out.

Sincerely,

Mamma

There's an emptiness inside me, and I'm disgusted by what I've read.

Before I can control my anger, my fist slams into the wall, and I throw anything in my path. The sound of glass shattering, wood splintering, and my heavy breathing fills the silence of the room.

When I look at my reflection, I notice the tears that have fallen during the heat of my anger.

'You look like them both,' she wrote, and the mere thought that she saw her rapist in me makes me sick. I let out an angry shout, and my fist crashes into the mirror. It breaks into a million pieces, exactly as the truth has done to my heart.

When the pain is too much and my body becomes too heavy, I fall to the ground and sit with my hands covering my face.

I don't hear when Victoria comes in, but I know she's beside me when I sense her warmth and smell her signature vanilla fragrance.

I let her hold me, and she cups my tear-stained face. Her gaze is soft, with a sense of worry from seeing my distress.

"Leo, what's wrong?" she asks in a faint voice, and like my mother, I can't say the words.

I hand her the journal. Her forehead creases as she takes it, and I motion for her to read the letter.

Victoria is silent as she reads my mother's words. Her face contorts into a frown, and she looks at me with understanding. She presses me to her chest, and I fall to pieces in her arms.

For a split second, it's as if I'm ten again, all alone while sitting in my mother's blood. But when Victoria whispers into my ear and runs her fingers through my hair, I know I'm not alone anymore because Victoria is here with me this time, filling the void of my loneliness.

"Leo, you're not Marquez's son. Estephano is your dad." Her words are firm, and I stare into her brown eyes, which shimmer from her tears.

Victoria grabs my hand and places it over her heart.

"We don't share the same blood, but you and I are family because of our love for one another. My heart beats for you, and this is enough for you to be my family."

"You share the same blood as Marquez, regardless of this news. But Leo, you need to realize that family doesn't have to mean sharing DNA with someone. Family can be those your heart beats for. Your family are the people who care about you and who you care about. Those people are Estephano, Cleo, your mother, me, your men, and our child."

I close my eyes and press my face against Victoria's chest. Her heartbeat fills my ears, and her words are at the tip of my tongue.

Family is those your heart beats for.

With her words, I allow myself not to dwell on the ambiguity about who my biological father is. My mother didn't see me as Marquez's son, so why should I?

I soak in the sight of Victoria, and the pain in my chest lifts. One glimpse at her is all it takes to bring together the shattered pieces of my past. Everything feels like it will be alright with her beside me.

We rise from the ground, and the door to the room opens to reveal my father. He's avoiding my stare, but I can still see the tears he harbors in the corners of his eyes.

"Papà..." I extend a hand to him and embrace him. The tears he holds back fall. "Marquez is not my father; you are. I'm the man I am today because of you."

The bedroom door creaks open again, and this time I see my sister. She has fresh tears running down her cheeks, letting me know she heard everything.

"Cleo," I say in a broken whisper, afraid she will resent me.

"Brother," she murmurs, wrapping her arms around me, and I let out a sigh of relief.

My father pulls back and looks at me, his eyes red.

"My son," he says, then glances at Victoria and Cleo. He places a hand on each of their cheeks. "My daughters," he says, and the two smile, nodding.

Victoria's words from earlier come to mind, and I realize the people in my arms are my real family. This is enough to lift the tension off my chest. The weight of Adriano's words and the pain he and his father have caused my family vanishes.

For the first time after many years of harboring anger, resentment, and sadness, I can breathe again.

EPILOGUE

VICTORIA

Annoyance and frustration are coursing through my pregnant mind.

Letting out a breath, I close my laptop, giving up on my assignment for school, and instead throw my legs over the bed in search of my slippers.

Leo is taking too long, and I'm hungry and want to cry.

After seconds of searching for my slippers, I give up and lower myself onto the floor, trying to find them from under the bed. When I pull out the slippers, Leo enters the room. He's quick to chastise me.

"Victoria, I told you to stay in bed." He sighs, sweeping me into his arms and placing me back on the bed. "I'm gone for ten minutes, and look at you."

Although it's been five months since he killed Adriano, Leo is still as overprotective as ever.

I shoot an angry gaze at him, and a huff is stuck deep in my throat. He lifts an amused brow when I cross my arms over my chest.

"Leo, you won't let me do anything besides stay in bed, and it's annoying," I say, letting out an exasperated breath. "You took too long, and I wanted my gelato."

He rolls his eyes and goes to kiss my lips, but I steer out of his reach.

"My gelato," I say in a firm voice, and I curl my lips into my mouth to suppress my smile when I notice him pouting.

"Here." There's a hint of a groan in his voice, and I grin, taking the strawberry gelato from him.

The bed dips when Leo sits, and he grabs hold of my hands. He looks at my engagement ring, and his eyes tell me he wants to replace it with a wedding ring, and if it were up to him, we would have been married already.

I've asked to postpone the wedding because it still didn't feel right to get married when Luca died a few months ago.

The pain of his death is still fresh, and some days it's stronger than others. Grief didn't have a time limit. There are days when everything is okay, but then I remember Luca is missing. The moment this happens, I feel guilty for living my life while he's gone.

Leo senses my sadness and squeezes my hand. He presses a sweet kiss to the corner of my mouth, leaving me wanting more.

These days, my cravings are not only for food or sleep. I also crave Leo's touch more and more.

His brows pull together when he sees me staring at his mouth. I don't give him the opportunity to make a teasing remark because I press our mouths together.

Leo smiles into the kiss, and I open my mouth, giving him total access. Our tongues brush, and I let him dominate my mouth as he has dominated my heart.

When the uncomfortable itch becomes unbearable, I crawl onto his lap and let out a breathless pant when his erection strokes my inner thighs. He's getting harder by the second.

I unbutton his shirt with speed, our mouths not once separating. It doesn't take long to strip off most of our clothes, but Leo halts his movements when he's about to take off his briefs.

He hesitates to continue because, as usual, he's afraid of hurting the baby.

"Leo, the doctor said it's safe for us to have sex," I remind him. He grins when he sees how desperate I am for his touch.

"I know, but I'm afraid I'll hurt you both." His hands go to the sides of my stomach, and he caresses the bump.

I place my hands over his.

"You won't hurt us, and if you become too rough, I'll tell you," I assure him, running my hands down his solid chest. My fingers trail the waistband of his briefs, and his breath hitches.

I slip a hand inside, and his eyes flutter shut when I wrap my fingers around him, stroking his length.

Leo's mouth parts with a groan, his head of dark brown hair rolls back, and the sight of him produces a pulsing throb in my clit.

"Fine, but you tell me when to slow down," he says, removing his briefs, and his erection springs out. I stare, mesmerized by his cock. "My eyes are up here, amore."

The back of my neck warms from being caught ogling him, and I watch as he lies on the bed beside me.

"Umm, Leo, what are you doing?" I ask, waiting for him to align our hips. He says nothing and grabs me, positioning me to sit on his thighs.

"You're on top this time," he says, and his eyes, which pin me with lust, make my heart beat wildly. His erection kisses between my thighs, leaving behind the sticky substance of his pre-cum, and a shiver rides through my body.

"If you say so." I smile when he caresses my stomach, and when I don't move, Leo's attention goes from my stomach to me.

"What are you waiting for? Aren't you going to ride me?"

"In a little."

Leo's forehead creases in confusion. It deepens when I turn around, giving him a view of my back. His grip around my waist tightens when my hands wrap around his erection.

My heart flickers with the heat of my desire as I part my lips and take him into my mouth. Leo's stomach tightens under me when my tongue twirls around his shaft, and he grunts when I play with his balls, massaging them as I suck him.

"Victoria," he says with a low groan, and I continue to use my mouth and hands to please him. Leo strokes my belly, and when he lifts it, I groan as the downward strain on my lower back is relieved.

He continues to carry the weight of my pregnant belly, and my heart flutters from the gesture, encouraging me to please him more. I take him faster, and he hits the back of my throat. His cock twitches in my mouth, and he responds with a frustrated moan.

"Fanculo!" he grits through his teeth, and my lower half blazes with desire from his sexy accent. I stop what I'm doing, as I can't wait any longer. I want him deep inside me.

My back is still turned to him when I grab his erection, guiding him to my entrance. The base of his cock strokes my wet folds, and my thighs quiver as I lower myself over him. He slips into me, and my stomach tightens. Every inch deeper he goes into me, a satisfied moan comes from both of us.

I place my palms on his thighs for support as I circle my hips around him. When this isn't enough, I ride him fast, and with each passing second, our movements become sloppier, rougher, and hotter until sweat forms on the surface of our bodies.

"Turn around. I want to see you while you ride me." His voice is rough and lust-filled. I slip him out and do as he says. My heart skips a beat because he's looking at me as if he hasn't eaten in years.

His hands are on either side of my stomach, and he holds me in place as I slip him back inside me where he belongs.

My eyes flutter, and black dots fill my vision as he pumps in and out of me. He takes me to sweet bliss when his hips jerk me up like I weigh nothing.

The hands keeping me up tremble under my weight. Leo notices I'm about to fall from exhaustion and moves me to rest on the bed. We are now side by side, and he grabs my left thigh and rests it over his right leg. In this new position, he continues to pump into me.

He takes me with slow strokes, and I take his mouth into a kiss, sucking on his bottom lip and biting.

"Fucking hell, you taste and feel amazing," Leo murmurs, retaking my lips. His fingers lace through my hair, and his thrusts become faster. The tension in my lower half increases, as do the waves of heat washing over me.

As I find my release, my thighs spasm and my stomach clenches. Leo lets out a deep groan into my neck as he also rides out his orgasm.

His pumping seizes, and we try to regain our breath. Perspiration shines on his temple, and his face is aligned with satisfaction.

Leo gives me a peck on the lips, bringing me to his side. I cuddle into his muscular arms when a soft flutter comes from my stomach. The little kick startles me.

"What's wrong?" Leo says in a frenzy when I sit up and place my hand over my stomach. "Is it the baby?"

"Feel." I grab his hand and rest it over the spot where the baby kicked. Leo's forehead bunches until our baby kicks the palm of his hand. His mouth opens wide, and his eyes fill with tears.

The ear-to-ear smile he gives me makes my stomach flutter, and my heart warms with love when he rests his head near my stomach to speak to our baby.

"It seems like my little Principessa has made herself known."

I can't help but laugh at his confidence in thinking the baby is a girl.

"Leo, you don't know the sex," I say, running my fingers through his tousled hair.

"And whose fault is that?" he mumbles, reminding me of my decision not to find out until the birth.

"Oh, hush." His green eyes flash with a glint, and his handsome face glows with a little smile.

"I love you," he says, lifting my right hand and kissing the crown tattoo on my wrist.

"I love you too, Leo."

The baby kicks again, and Leo and I glance at one another with a smile before our eyes fall onto my stomach.

"Oh, and I love you too, my Principessa." Leo kisses my stomach, and there's another flutter.

One month later
My water broke.

One minute I'm video chatting with the girls, looking at Layla's daughter Catalina making babbling noises, and then a sharp pain shoots through my body. Then water trails down my legs, and now I'm clutching my stomach in pain.

There's another sharp pinch, this one stronger. I hunch over, groaning under my breath.

"Victoria, are you okay?!" Sofia, Cleo, and Erika say in unison through the computer before they announce they are coming to get me.

I close my eyes and take slow breaths, only to groan when another sharp cramp hits. The pain isn't too bad, but it still sucks, and it's making me nauseous.

"Victoria, where's Leo?" Emma asks in a panic, unsure of how she can help while she's in New York.

"In the shower." As I say this, Leo walks out of the bathroom. His smile drops when he sees me hunched in pain, standing over a puddle of what looks like my pee.

He runs to me and holds me in his arms.

"Amore, what's wrong?"

"My water broke," I say calmly, and the color drains from his handsome face.

I blink at him, watching as he freezes at my words. When he comes to his senses, he lifts me in his arms and rushes out of the room. The second we come out of the door, we run into Cleo, Erika, and Sofia. Their chests are heaving as they try to catch their breath.

"She's in labor. Can you all grab the baby bag and her hospital bag? I'm taking her to the hospital," he tells them, not allowing them time to respond as he continues his path down the hall.

Another contraction hits, and I scrunch my face, lips pressed together.

"Breathe in and out, amore," he says as he rushes down the stairs. The few men in the foyer glance at us with wide eyes.

"Someone get the car ready!" Hearing the urgency in Leo's voice, a man rushes out to get the car.

"You're in charge while I'm gone," Leo tells a motionless Francisco, who stares at us with a grimace.

"Francisco, snap out of it! You aren't the one having the baby, for fuck's sake." Francisco rolls his lips into his mouth, and I laugh at the two tough men crumbling at the mere thought of me being in labor.

Leo and Francisco hear my laughter and are taken aback at how calm I am.

"The driver's out front." The man from earlier rushes back inside, and Leo runs out of the house.

He clutches onto me as we head to the hospital, and while he calls my family to tell them I'm having the baby, he doesn't let me go.

"Your family is heading to Italy now," he assures me after ending the call. I sigh in relief, excited to see them again.

It took a few months, but Leo and I fixed any final resentments my dad had after finding out I wasn't only engaged but also three months pregnant. My mom was more upset I wouldn't be coming home than anything else.

When we arrive at the hospital, everything turns into a blur, and I only come out of the haze when the doctor tells me to push.

"Ready to have a baby?" I ask, giving Leo a nervous smile.

"With you, I'm ready for anything," he says, caressing my cheek and giving me a quick kiss.

"I need you to push, honey," comes the doctor's instructions as she settles between my legs.

I take a deep breath and push.

When the tightening pain in my uterus increases, I squeeze Leo's hand.

"That's it. Push when your body tells you to." I ignore the doctor's words and close my eyes, biting my lip to stop from crying out.

"You're doing amazing, amore," Leo mumbles near my ear. His voice tightens as my nails press into the soft skin around his knuckles.

After a few minutes of pushing, my body becomes exhausted, and my eyes burn with sleep.

"No, don't stop pushing! You're almost done!" the doctor says when she notices me giving into fatigue.

I see black spots, and I'm about to give up when I hear the fear in Leo's voice.

"Don't close your eyes, Victoria. You can do this." He moves a damp strand of my hair from my face. Tears have gathered at the corners of my eyes, but I don't let them fall. Instead, I give it my all, and I fight the exhaustion.

"One final push, honey!" the doctor says.

"Push, baby, push," Leo encourages, and I send him a glare, which makes him close his mouth.

"I am!" I snap, giving another hard push, and the baby slips out between my legs.

"It's a boy, a healthy baby boy!" the doctor announces, placing my son in my arms.

My tears fall when their little cries fill the room. The exhaustion from before disappears, and I'm overwhelmed with relief to know that he's here after almost being robbed of this moment.

I glance at Leo, and he has tears in his eyes. He kneels beside the bed, caressing our son's forehead. Our son responds by nuzzling into his touch, and my heart melts, unable to believe how much has happened since Leo saved my life.

LEO

I'm complete when I look from a sleeping Victoria to our son.

It's an unreal experience to hold the product of my and Victoria's love, a love I once feared giving myself to.

They're both mine to love, cherish, and protect forever. I would move mountains for them both.

Looking down at my son, I'm reminded of how he wouldn't be here without the sacrifices of those close to us.

My mother had given her and my brother's lives to save mine, while Luca had given his life to save my son and Victoria.

Having him in my arms is a miracle, and I'm determined to make sure he realizes how loved he is.

There's a soft knock on the door, and it opens to reveal Sofia, Erika, Cleo, Francisco, Angelo, Kaden, and my father.

They're all eager to meet the newest Bandoni.

My sister rushes over to me and smiles when she sees her nephew.

"Are they a boy or a girl?" she asks, unable to take her eyes off him.

"A boy," I say, and my friends all look at one another with a glint in their eyes while their partners give a slight awe.

"What's the baby's name?" Erika asks, her eyes softening at the sight of him. Behind her, Angelo smiles, his eyes sparkling with adoration for his girlfriend.

"Luca Bandoni," I tell them, and when they hear the name, the room grows dense with grief. When the grief subsides, they mumble their appreciation for the name.

Cleo hovers over my shoulder to look at the baby, and her eyes glisten with tears.

"Do you want to hold him?" I ask, and she sniffles, giving a weak nod.

I rise from my chair, allowing her to take the seat. I lay Luca in her arms, and tears stream down her cheeks. My chest grows heavy, but the tension in my shoulders releases when she looks at me with a toothy smile. Her smile assures me she has found happiness again after years of pain.

There's a heavy pat on my back, and I'm met with my father's proud smile. He glances at Cleo and his grandson with warmth.

"Your mother would be proud of you all." His voice is thick with emotion, and his eyes glaze with tears. "I'm proud of you all."

I bring him into an embrace.

"I'm proud of you, Papà," I say, knowing his life didn't turn out how he wanted. But he's making the most of living without the love of his life.

When our family leaves, I lay in bed with Victoria and our son. Her head rests on my chest while Luca rests in her arms. His little hand curls around my pointer finger. A tiny sneeze comes from him when Victoria kisses the tip of his button nose.

I lift Victoria's chin, pressing our mouths together.

As I kiss her, I reflect on the first time I saw her and realize I've always made promises to those close to me. But the night I found her was different because that was the first time I made a promise to myself.

When I saw her fear, I was determined to keep hope shimmering in her eyes. But, within my determination to protect her, I didn't realize what I had also promised was to love her, and a year later, I kept both promises.

Luca opens his eyes, and Victoria's face glows with happiness.

She looks from our son to me, and her stare steals the air from my lungs. In her eyes, I see the *hope* that captivated me the first time I saw her. It burns so bright that I feel it seep into me.

Victoria thinks the mafia saved her, but she's wrong. She saved my family and me from the darkness of our past.

She doesn't know the warmth inside me disappeared when I clutched my mother's lifeless body. A warmth which she has returned, and with it the happiness I thought my life could never have.

Victoria saved the mafia.

BONUS

SOFIA

The faint sound of little feet pattering fills the silence in the room. I stir from my sleep-filled state, but my eyes are unwilling to open.

I only wake up when I hear a loud thump and a little cry. My attention falls to where the noise comes from, and I see my favorite human sitting on the ground. Their bottom lip quivers, and their chestnut brown hair sits tousled from sleep.

Luca's face lights up when he sees me, and an innocent smile replaces his pout.

"Luccy, what are you doing here?" I reach out for the three-year-old. He flashes me a toothy smile.

"Thank you, Auntie Sofia." He kisses my cheek, and I cringe as saliva meets air.

My heart warms when he calls me Auntie, and although I'm not his aunt, I never correct him. After all, Victoria is more like a sister to me than a cousin, and we're Mexican. We call everyone family.

"We told you not to climb any more objects," I remind him, and his forehead scrunches into a frown. His tiny lips form a pout. "What did your Papà say the last time you fell and scraped your knee when you climbed the bookshelf?"

"He say no climb cus I no have monkey pows, and I get owe," he mutters in his cute, squeaky child voice.

"Exactly. Now, look at you on the floor." My fingers ruffle his hair, and his face scrunches in annoyance. "Where's your mom? And how did you come here, of all places?"

Luca's lips contort into a slight frown when I mention Victoria. His little green eyes flash with worry, which lets me know something is wrong. Before I can ask, the spot beside me shuffles, *and a blon*d tuft of hair rises. A groggy Francisco gives us a tired smile before plummeting his face onto the pillow with a groan.

I roll my eyes and glance back at Luca on my lap. He has an arched brow as he peeks at the man he calls Uncle Frisco.

Luca outstretches his tiny hand and pokes Francisco on the side before glancing back at me in worry.

"Frisco dead?" he whispers, lips parted and eyebrows lifted in concern.

"No, he's—"

"Yes, and now I'm a zombie!" Francisco's deep voice cuts through the silence, and he curls his fingers into claws, advancing toward Luca. The toddler screams and squirms in my lap. I try to steady him before he falls off the bed again, but he's going wild.

Francisco lifts the child off my lap with one hand and tickles Luca with the other.

I groan when Luca punches me in the chin, and I send Francisco a glare for having excited the child, who already has uncontrollable energy.

Francisco releases a panting Luca, who has a broad smile and a familiar mischievous glint in his eyes.

"Uncle Frisco, you stink!" Luca exclaims, pinching the bridge of his nose.

I burst into laughter, and Francisco's cheeks turn a bright red.

"He does," I whisper, and Luca nods in agreement. "Remember to brush your teeth when your mom tells you. Unless you want to stink like Uncle Frisco."

"Alright, you too, stop ganging up on me." Francisco groans as he gets out of bed and heads to the bathroom, sending me a teasing glare.

I turn to Luca, who's the spitting image of his dad.

"Auntie Sofia, why is Mamma crying?" Luca's round doe eyes stare at me with worry. "Someone hurt Mamma?" he continues, worry for his mother clear in his voice.

His comment piques my interest.

"I'm not sure, but why don't I go find out?" I caress his cheek and turn to Francisco. "Why don't you show Francisco the toy car collection your Papà Estephano got you, and I'll tell you what she says later."

Luca nods in excitement and comments on how Francisco no longer stinks, making me crack a smile.

"Come, Uncle Frisco!" Luca chirps, jumping off the bed. Francisco kisses my temple before he lets Luca guide him to his room. My chest warms at the sight of Luca mumbling about his toy cars to Francisco, who nods and hums in acknowledgment.

When I reach Victoria and Leo's bedroom, I hear crying from the bathroom.

"Victoria, are you okay?" Her crying seizes.

"Yeah, I'm fine," she replies in a shaky voice.

"No, you're not. I'm coming in."

I open the door and find a frantic Victoria wiping her tears. She places her hands behind her back.

My right brow rises in question, and I notice her foot taps below her, and she bites her bottom lip. The two habits tell me she's nervous.

I sigh. "Why are you crying?"

She lets out a breath, and when she pulls out the two pregnancy tests behind her back, my mouth falls open in shock.

"Victoria," I breathe, and the corners of her mouth lift into a half-nervous smile.

"I'm pregnant."

I approach her with a grin.

"That's exciting! Another baby!" I beam, but my smile falters when I see her brown eyes brimming with fresh tears. "Why are you crying? You don't want another little Luca, or maybe a little girl?"

"I want more kids, but two before I'm twenty-three?" she says, her left hand on her temple as if she has a headache. "Stupid birth control didn't do its job," she mumbles, and I laugh.

Her eyes widen, and she gasps, and my panic rises.

"What if this time we have twins!" she says, her hand on her chest.

"Victoria, relax. You have Leo, me, and everyone else in this house. You guys are more than ready for another baby or babies." She lets out a shaky breath and gives a hesitant nod.

"I guess you're right," she mumbles, letting out a breath and sending me a smile. "Thank you, Sofia." She brings me into her arms in a tight embrace.

"That's what a maid of honor is for."

"I can't believe the wedding is next week!" Her eyes twinkle with excitement, and my heart warms from seeing her get her happy ending after almost being robbed of it twice.

Anytime I remember how we were separated when we were kidnapped, the tears rise. With the memory, my body shakes, and I can faintly see the face of the man who almost raped me. Even though years have passed since that night, the memories still haunt me.

I only ever feel better when I remember how Francisco came into the room to rescue me. It turns out Victoria wasn't the only one saved by the love of her life that night. Although Francisco can be annoying, I know I can't live without him.

There's a loud crash coming from somewhere in the house. We both look at one another, and Victoria groans in aggravation.

"Let's go see what they broke this time," she mumbles in disbelief.

She hides the pregnancy tests, and we head toward the noise of panicked curses. I can see Victoria's anger oozing out of her.

We step into Luca's bedroom, and our eyes widen when we see the giant hole in the wall. My eyes fall on the three culprits.

Francisco and Leo's mouths are in a grimace, while Luca sends Victoria a toothy grin.

She crosses her arms over her chest, and her eyebrows rise as she looks at Leo.

I draw my attention to Francisco, who's covered in grime. He coughs, wiping the dust from his face. The idiot gives me a smile, which falls when I give him a warning look.

The two tall men stare nervously at an angry Victoria. Her left foot is tapping on the floor below her as she waits for them to explain themselves.

"Amore, I can explain…" Leo gives a nervous laugh, heading toward her. Victoria glares at him, and he halts his advances. His hand goes to the back of his neck.

Beside him, a disheveled Francisco sneezes. His movement triggers the particles of debris coating him to fall. I bite my bottom lip to stop laughing.

Luca's little voice in the room has us turning toward him, as he's the only brave one to speak amidst the tension.

"Mamma! Papà threw Uncle Frisco into the—" Lucas starts to explain, but he's cut off when his dad lifts him into his arms and clamps a hand over his mouth.

"What Luca means to say is Francisco hit the wall when he tripped on one of your toy cars, right, buddy?" Leo breaks a sweat when he notices an unimpressed Victoria.

Luca looks at his Papà with a frown, which morphs into a lopsided grin when he realizes the hidden message.

"Oh, right! Mamma, it was SOOO funny." Victoria hums, and I see her struggling to hold back her smile.

"Right," she says skeptically, her gaze moving back to Leo, who gives a hopeful smile and tries to bring her into his arms, but she steps back.

"Nice try, but Papà is on time out for wrestling in the house when I told him not to, more times than necessary," she says with gentle hostility. Victoria takes Luca into her arms.

"Come on, amore. It was an accident. I swear."

She points a finger at Leo and Francisco and motions to the hole in the wall. Their eyes follow the gesture.

"The two of you clean this mess up, and I want the wall fixed by the time I put Luca down for his afternoon nap." She then looks at Luca, who pouts at her next words. "And you, mister, need a bath."

"I'll just pay someone to fix the wall," Leo grumbles, and Victoria turns around with a raised brow.

"Oh no you don't," she warns, and he swallows. "You two are going to fix it yourselves," she exclaims, looking at Luca, who giggles when he sees his dad and Francisco stare at each other in annoyance. "And if Papà doesn't do it himself, he's sleeping on the couch, right baby?" Luca perks and gives a firm nod with a cheeky smile.

"What! amore, please. I have work," Leo grumbles, but Victoria ignores him and walks toward their bedroom with Luca in her arms.

I block the exit when Francisco tries to leave.

"Get cleaning, the two of you." I cross my arms over my chest, and Francisco scoffs with a smirk.

This can't be good.

Leo looks from me to Francisco with amusement. The next second, Francisco tries to lift me, but I stand my ground and slap him on the arm. He doesn't care, and tries to move me again.

I don't hold back, and I stomp on his right foot.

"Every fucking time!" he grits through clenched teeth, glaring at a laughing Leo.

I sigh, looking between both men, unable to believe they run the Italian mafia.

That should tell you something about the other mafiosos.

Today is the wedding, and everyone is on edge, running around trying to beat time.

I sneeze. The smell of hairspray and perfume is thick in the air.

All around me is chaos as women chatter and compliment one another on their makeup and dresses.

The Eiffel Tower is visible from the couch I'm sitting on.

I sigh, my fingers touching my plump lips where Francisco had smothered them with his own ten minutes ago.

His warm breath is like a ghost over my neck, where he peppered kisses. We would have continued if Leo, Kaden, Luca, and Cleo hadn't interrupted us.

A tap on my shoulder has me withdrawing from my memory.

I stare at Erika and a pregnant Nora, who's expecting her second child, another little boy.

The two share worried expressions.

"What's wrong?" I ask when they grab my wrist and take me away.

"Victoria's throwing up and crying," Nora says in a panic.

Sure enough, I hear Victoria weeping and gagging from behind the door.

"I think the pregnancy symptoms are getting to her," Erika whispers as Nora twists the doorknob, exposing Victoria in only her white silk robe.

"You guys go get ready. I'll stay with her," I tell them, when I notice they still have to finish getting dressed. They hesitate but give in when I remind them the wedding starts soon.

I close the door and approach my cousin.

"Are you alright? Do you want water?" I ask, noticing she looks exhausted.

"I hate feeling like this," she says in a tired voice, and she dabs at the tears under her eyes.

"It's only the pregnancy symptoms."

She shakes her head.

"That's not what I meant," she whispers in a broken voice. "Yeah, the throwing up sucks, but not as much as knowing Luca isn't here to celebrate with us."

My chest tightens at the mention of our friend, whose death still affects her. The only time she ever finds relief is when she gets to say his name out loud when she calls out for her son.

I bring her into my arms.

"Victoria, he's with us in our hearts and memories. He would want you to be happy, not crying on the bathroom floor before your wedding."

"I know, but it still hurts." Her voice breaks, and I press her tighter to my chest. There's a knock on the door.

"Victoria, are you alright? Mom's worried." Eloisa asks, sounding concerned. Victoria sighs, giving me a sad smile, before she rises from the floor and helps me up.

"I'm fine. I'll be out in a second." She turns to me. "Thank you for always being there for me, Sofia. You're the best, and sorry about being such a crybaby these days." She laughs, going to the sink to brush her teeth.

"It's fine. It's the baby making you emotional," I assure her. "Now hurry; show time is in one hour, and you need to touch up your makeup and put on your dress."

My mouth falls open, and my eyes tear up when I see Victoria in her fitted white, backless lace dress. She looks beautiful.

She sends me a nervous smile. Her fingers fumble with the family heirloom necklace around her neck.

"Are you ready?" I ask, and she exhales a soft breath.

"For what, getting married or telling Leo and the rest of the family I'm pregnant?"

The corner of my mouth lifts into a half smile.

"Both, but for now, the getting married part. For the baby announcement, I'll ask again tonight at the reception."

"I'm nervous but ready." She lets out a heavy breath, and I grab her clammy hands.

"You'll be fine," I assure her, handing her the bouquet of white roses when her dad enters.

"I'll see you at the altar," I say, going to where Francisco waits by the wooden double doors of the cathedral.

When he's near, I become tempted by lust at seeing his muscular body in a crisp black tux. His hair is gelled back, and he looks handsome.

Francisco sees me and presses me to his chest. His eyes darken as he looks me over.

"I'm ripping this dress off you later tonight." His lips graze my ear, leaving behind a tingling sensation.

I let out a pant when his bulge presses into my stomach. I'm biting my lip so hard the skin breaks. When he notices me crumbling, he pulls away with a grin.

"You're so annoying," I grumble as the soft music begins.

"But you love me." He kisses my cheek and faces the front, where the doors are opening.

"That I do," I say as we walk down the aisle together and separate once we reach the end.

Francisco stands beside a nervous Leo, who is adjusting his white suit jacket. When Francisco sees me staring at them, he sends me a sexy grin, prompting heat to flood my cheeks. I turn to face the crowd to forget about the warmth pooling between my thighs.

I smile when I see the now engaged Cleo and Kaden entering with Luca, who looks dashing in his little black tux.

The doors open again, and Catalina, Layla's daughter, steps into the room. The toddler tosses white rose petals down the white carpet.

When Victoria appears, Leo takes a sharp breath, and his body visibly relaxes when Miguel hands Victoria to him.

As the ceremony takes place, I can't focus because Francisco keeps sending me suggestive looks.

I'm going to make him pay for being a pain in the ass later tonight.

I'm brought from my thoughts when the minister gets to the most awaited part of the day, and the room stills.

Before the minister can say, you may kiss the bride. Leo pulls Victoria close and lifts her veil. He doesn't kiss her right away and instead spends a few seconds looking at her before kissing her forehead and cheeks, and giving her one last kiss to her lips.

After the ceremony, Leo pulls Victoria into a white limo, and the two drive off to who knows where. We don't see them again until they arrive at the reception.

"Well, look who showed up," I tease a two-hour late Victoria and Leo. My cousin's face turns red, while Leo remains unbothered. I hand Luca over to them, excusing myself when Leo's dad and Victoria's parents make their way over to them.

My eyes soften when I see Estephano smiling, but despite the smile, the pain of grief flickers in his eyes.

As the night unfolds, the music grows louder, and the people become crazier with all the alcohol consumed.

I watch Victoria and Leo dance with Luca when a tug on my arm prompts me to rise.

"Let's dance," Francisco says, and I let him guide us toward Victoria and Leo.

My aunt comes toward us and whispers something to Victoria, who nods and hands Luca to a confused Leo.

Victoria looks at me with a nervous glint, and I grow excited about what's coming when she heads toward the DJ.

The music cuts off.

"Can I have everyone's attention, please?" she says in a shaky voice, and everyone goes silent. "First, on behalf of my husband and me." She grips the microphone. "We would like to thank you all for joining us on our special day, and since we're all family, I wanted to let you all know some exciting news." The room becomes tense, and everyone wants to know what's happening.

"Leo, I want to tell you how much I love you, and my love only grows more when you give me gifts, like our son." Her eyes glance at Luca, and they soften at the sight of his eyes fluttering with sleep. "I hope you're ready for baby number two, my love."

Excited gasps cut through the air, and I take a sleepy Luca from Leo, and he rushes to Victoria.

Francisco wraps an arm around my waist.

"Another little one, huh?" He chuckles. "Leo sure doesn't waste time," Francisco says, peering at the tired child in my arms. An unknown emotion passes through his blue eyes, and he cups my face, bringing our lips together. "Let's make it two little ones, yes?"

My stomach flutters, and my heart races in anticipation.

"Soon," I assure him, and he grins. His eyes divert to Victoria and Leo, who are heading our way.

I hand Luca back to Leo, and he walks away to put Luca down for bed.

"So, Leo knocked you up again," Francisco teases Victoria.

"Yup, and it looks like you're still failing in that category," she retorts, and I laugh.

Francisco's cheeks turn bright red, and he grumbles something about condoms doing their job.

"I'm sorry I had to," Victoria apologizes to me.

I wave a dismissive hand. "It's fine. He had it coming."

"You're supposed to be my backup!" Francisco complains.

"What did I miss?" Leo asks, looking at a flustered Francisco with a raised brow.

"We're waiting for you so we can do the garter toss and the bouquet toss," Victoria tells Leo, who responds with excitement for the Mexican wedding tradition.

"Great, let's go now!" He pulls her toward the chair in the center of the dance floor, and Victoria turns to me for help, and I send her a wink.

"I'll be back," Francisco says, kissing my cheek and heading to the dance floor after Leo orders all the unmarried men to go to the front for the garter toss.

"This is hilarious!" Emma laughs. The girls all agree as we watch our partners encourage Leo, who prepares to fetch the elastic band from Victoria's inner thigh with his mouth.

"What are they doing?" Cassidy, Lei's girlfriend, asks, and I explain the wedding tradition. By the end, she's also laughing.

After two minutes of watching a sexually frustrated Victoria grip the chair under her, Leo appears from under her dress with a grin, the lacy white garter between his teeth.

Francisco helps Leo out of the handcuffs Victoria's dad put on him. Once free from the bonds, Leo twirls the lace on his pointer finger.

We all laugh as Leo teases the guys into thinking he's going to throw the garter. After a while, he tosses it, and the material lands in Cristian's hands.

Victoria's brother looks at the lace in disgust and throws it into the crowd of guys. Francisco ends up catching it. He looks at it wide-eyed, unsure of what happened, and everyone laughs again. The men pat his back, and Francisco saunters toward me.

"Your turn," he mumbles as Layla and Erika guide me to the dance floor, where Victoria is about to toss the bouquet of white roses.

Victoria sends me a wink and throws the bouquet my way. My heart stops when everyone spreads out.

I gasp as I catch the roses, and the room grows silent. Everyone is looking at me, and my face turns hot. I can hear my heart ringing in my ears.

My cousin gives me a watery smile and motions for me to turn around. When I do, I'm met with the sight of Francisco on his knee with a ring out in front of him. I gasp, my left hand over my mouth.

"Sofia Hernandez, you can be a pain in my ass. Especially when you yell at me or stomp on my foot."

I glare at him for what he called me, and he ignores it.

"But I love you and wouldn't want my life to be any other way. Will you marry me and be a pain in my ass for the rest of my life?"

His blue eyes freeze me in place, and I let out a small laugh.

"Yes, of course, I'll marry you, Francisco!" I fall into his arms and kiss him.

"I love you," he breathes, as he places the ring on my finger.

"I love you too," I whisper, looking at him with teary eyes.

I'm engaged to a hot European man, and all because of a summer trip I took.

The trip to France gave me and Victoria hardship and pain, but in return, we somehow found love and friendship. Our kidnapping strengthened us. It taught us not to let the pain of what happened to our bodies hinder our lives because we are women, and we are *mighty*.

ABOUT THE AUTHOR

Jasmin Vizcaya Salgado is a Mexican American writer from Southern California. She has a bachelor of Arts degree in English from the University of California, Riverside, and is working on her master's degree in English with a concentration in composition and rhetoric at California State University, San Bernardino. When she's not writing romance novels, she's doing research in critical feminist composition pedagogy. Her debut novel, *The Mafia Saved Me,* aims to bring awareness to human trafficking and violence against women. All while still providing readers with a toe-curling dark mafia romance.

CONNECT WITH JASMIN ON SOCIAL MEDIA

instagram.com/authorjasminvizcayasalgado
tiktok.com/authorjasmin.v.salgado